EVERGREEN

EVERGREEN

A NOVEL BY

BELVA PLAIN

DELACORTE PRESS/NEW YORK

Published by
Delacorte Press
1 Dag Hammarskjold Plaza
New York, New York 10017

Manufactured in the United States of America

15   14   13   12

Designed by Oksana Kushnir

LIBRARY OF CONGRESS CATALOGING IN PUBLICATION DATA
Plain, Belva.
Evergreen.
I. Title.
PZ4.P7EV [PS3566.L254]   813'.5'4   77-20778
ISBN 0-385-28299-0 (previously 0-440-02611-x)

To my husband,
companion of a lifetime

One generation passeth away, and another generation
cometh: but the earth abideth forever.

ECCLESIASTES

CONTENTS

BOOK
1

RUGGED ROADS

1

In the beginning there was a warm room with a table, a black iron stove and old red-flowered wallpaper. The child lay on a cot feeling the good heat while the mother moved peacefully from the table to the stove. When the mother sang her small voice quavered over the lulling nonsense-words; the song was meant to be gay but the child felt sadness in it.

"Don't sing," she commanded and the mother stopped. She was amused.

"Imagine," she told her husband, "Anna doesn't like my voice! She made me stop singing today!"

The father laughed and picked Anna up. He had a sandy beard and dim blue eyes. He was slow and tender, especially when he touched the mother; the child was comforted when he put his arms around the mother.

"Kiss Mama!" she said.

They laughed again and the child understood that they were laughing at her and that they loved her.

For a long time the days and the years were all the same. In the house the mother moved between the stove and the table. The father hammered boots and cut leather for harness in his front-room shop. On the big bed in the room back of the kitchen the mother brought new babies to birth; one year there were twin boys, red-haired like Anna and Papa.

On Friday nights there was a linen cloth on the table; there was

3

sugar in the tea, and white bread. Papa brought beggars home from the synagogue; the beggars were dirty and had a nasty smell. They were given the best food in the house, the plum jam and the breast of chicken. The room was shadowed; the white light of the candles burned through Mama's hands as they moved in blessing and flickered on the pearls in her ears. There was a lovely and lofty mystery in her words and on her face.

It seemed to the child that the world had always been and would always be like this. She could not imagine any other way for people to live. The road through the village was dusty in the summer, muddy and icy in the winter; it stretched to the river where there was a bridge and went on for miles, it was said, to other villages like this one. The houses were strung along the road or clustered around the wooden synagogue, the market and the school. All of the people who lived here knew you and called you by name.

The ones who did not know you—the Others—lived on the far side of the little river where the church steeple rose over the trees. Beyond there cattle grazed, and farther still you could see the wind make tunnels through the growing wheat. The milkman came every day from that direction, two heavy wooden buckets swinging from his yoke. People seldom went there. There was no reason to go unless you were a peddler or a milkman, although sometimes you did go with Mama to buy vegetables or extra eggs.

The days were measured and ordered by the father's morning, afternoon and evening prayers; by the brothers in their black coats and visored caps going to and coming from school. The weeks ran from Friday night to Friday night. The year ran from winter to winter, when silent snow fell and voices rang like chimes in the silence. The snow turned to rain, drenching the lilacs in the yard, strewing petals over the mud. Then before the return of the cold came the short, hot summer.

Anna sits on the step in the breathless night, watching the stars. Of what can they be made? Some say they are fire. Some say the earth is fire like them, and that if you could stand far off and look at the earth it would glitter like the stars. But how can that be?

Papa does not know; he does not care about such things. If it is not in the Bible he is not interested in it. Mama sighs and says that she does not know either. Surely it would be wonderful if a woman could be educated and learn about things like that. A rabbi's wife in a far-off district runs a school for girls. There, very likely one could learn about the stars and how to speak other languages and much else besides. But it would be very expensive to go to such a school. And anyway, what would one do with that kind of knowledge in this village, this life?

"Although, of course," Mama says, "everything need not be *useful*. Some things are beautiful for themselves alone." Her eyes look into the distance and the dark. "Maybe it will be different after a while, who knows?"

Anna does not really care. The stars glow and spark. The air is like silk. Clouds foam up from the horizon and a little chill comes skimming on the wind. Across the road someone closes the shutters for the night with a *clack!* and *click!* She rises and goes back into the house.

Sometimes she listens to scraps of talk, the parents' evening murmur that repeats itself often enough to form a pattern. They talk about America. Anna has seen a map and knows that, if you were to travel for days, after a time you would come to the end of the land called Europe, which is where they live. And then there would be water, an ocean wider than the land over which you have come. You would sail for days across that water in a ship. It is both exciting and disturbing.

Of course, there are many people in the village whose relatives have gone to America. Mama has a second cousin in New York, Cousin Ruth, who has been there since before Anna was born. Tales arrive by mail: in America everyone is alike and it is wonderful because there is no difference between rich and poor. It is a place where there is equality and justice; every man is the same as every other. Also, America is a place where it is possible to become very rich and wear gold bracelets and have silver forks and spoons.

Papa and Mama have been talking for a long time about going, but there has always been some reason they cannot leave. First, there was Grandmother who had suffered a stroke. The people in America would not have let her in, and of course the family could not just have gone away and left her. Then Grandmother died, but Eli and Dan, the twins, were born. After them came Rachel. Then Celia. And Papa had to save more money. They would have to wait another year or two.

So they would never go, Anna knew. America was only something that they talked about in their bed at night, the way they talked about household things and their neighbors, about money and the

5

children. They would stay here always. One day, a long, long time from now, Anna would be grown, a bride like Pretty Leah whose father had the chicken farm just past the bridge, led under the canopy to the dance of violins, with a white gauze veil over her face. Then she would be a mother, lying in the bed like Mama with a new baby. But still it would be the same life; Papa and Mama would be here, looking no different from the way they looked now.

Yes, and the sheltering house would be here, too. And Rachel stirring in the bed. The old dog jingling his chain in the yard. The blown curtain; summer nights of pine and hay and Mama's bush of yellow roses at the gate. Rustle of night-birds, trill of frogs: I am alive, I am here, I am going to sleep.

2

Whenever Anna told or thought about the story of Pretty Leah she fell into the cadence and language of the twelve-year-old child she had been when it happened.

"Mama sent me to the farm to buy some eggs. Pretty Leah and I stood in the courtyard counting the eggs. Then I wanted to go into the barn to look at a newborn calf, and I was there when the men came, three of them on plow horses, cantering into the yard.

"I think Pretty Leah thought they wanted to buy some eggs because I saw her smile and look up at them. They jumped off the horses and one of them took her shoulders. They were laughing, but they were angry, too, I think; I didn't know what they were, really, but Pretty Leah screamed and I ran up the ladder into the loft and hid.

"They dragged her inside and shut the barn door. Her screams, oh, her screams! They were drunk and saying dirty words in Polish; their eyes were all puckered in their flat cheeks. They pulled her skirt up over her face. Oh, they will smother her, I thought; *I mustn't look,* and still I could not look away from the things they did.

"Like the bull and the cow, that time when Mama and I were out walking and Mama said, *Don't look* and I asked, *Why mustn't I?* And she answered, *Because you are too young to understand. It will frighten you.*

"But the bull and the cow had not frightened me at all. It seemed

a simple thing, what they had done. Not like this awful thing. Pretty
Leah twisted and kicked; her screams under the skirt had turned to
weeping and pleading, soft, soft, like a baby animal. Two of the men
pinned her arms and the third lay on top of her. Then they changed
places until all three had lain on her. After a while she stopped moving and crying. I thought, *My God, they have killed her!*

"When the men left they flung the barn door wide. I could hear
the hens clucking in the yard. The light came in and fell on Pretty
Leah with the skirt over her face, her naked legs spread wide, blood
sticky on her thighs. After a long time I came down the ladder. I
was afraid to touch her but I made myself draw her skirt down. She
was breathing; she had only fainted. There was a cut on her chin;
her black hair had come unbraided. When she wakes up she will
wish she were dead, I thought.

"Then I went outside and vomited in the grass. I picked up the
basket of eggs and went home."

That was the way she remembered it, all the years of her life, the
way she would often think of a man with a woman, although she
would not want to think of them like that.

In the evening after the dishes had been put away Mama said,
"Come, Anna, we'll sit outside on the steps and talk awhile."

But it was dark blue dusk. There were shadows and movement of
Things behind the trees, and someone was walking in the distance,
rapping on the road, the fast steps coming closer.

"I don't want to go outside," Anna said.

"Very well, then, I will ask Papa and the children to sit in the
yard and we can talk by ourselves."

The mother lay down on the bed beside the daughter and took
her hand; the mother's hand was hot and rough.

"Listen to me," she said softly. "I would give anything if you
hadn't seen what you saw today. Such an ugly, ugly, evil thing!" She
was trembling. The long quivering shook her body, shook her voice.
"The world can be so frightful and human beings worse than beasts.
Still, you must remember, Anna, that most people are good. You
must try to put this out of your mind as soon as you can."

"Will nobody punish those men?"

"In the first place, nobody could prove who did it. Nobody saw
it."

"I saw it. And I remember the faces. Especially the short thick one. He wears a red shirt and sometimes he goes into Krohn's Inn to get drunk."

The mother sat up. "Listen to me, Anna, do you hear? You are never, never to mention that to anybody, to anybody at all, do you understand? Terrible things would happen to you! To Papa, to me, to all of us! You must never, never—!"

The child was frightened. "I understand. But then, there is nothing that can be done about people like that?"

"Nothing."

"Then how can we know it won't happen again? Even to you, Mama?"

The mother was silent. And Anna pressed, "How can we know?"

"I suppose we can't."

"Then they can always do what they want to do. Kill us, even."

"That, too. You're old enough now to know."

The child began to cry. The mother held her. After a while the father came in. He stood at the door. His face was crumpled and creased.

"I've made up my mind. Year after year we put it off. But this year, by spring, we'll manage it somehow! We'll sell the furniture, your earrings, your mother's silver candlesticks. We have got to get to America!"

"There are seven of us."

"And if there were seventeen we would still have to manage it. This is no place to live! I want to lay my head down once without fear before I die."

So all the time, in this home of theirs, they had been afraid. Mama so calmly and skillfully arranging things, Papa humming and smiling while his strong arms hammered and cut. The child thought wonderingly: I didn't know, I never knew.

The winter of 1906 was strangely warm. Snow fell briefly and lay puddled in soggy gray slush. A damp wind blew; people perspired in their heavy coats, sneezed, shivered, ran fevers. Late in February the rain began, racing in long, even lines down the dark sky. The village street turned to sucking mud; the little river that curved at the bottom of the rise rushed over its banks and flooded all the yards along its length.

The sickness started down there at the river. In the middle of

9

· BELVA PLAIN ·

March a baby and a grandfather died in one house. On the other side of the river, where the peasants lived, a whole family died. Each day brought more sickness and some deaths. Sickness traveled north and south; people on farms five miles away brought their dead to be buried in the churchyard. It was like the black rot that spreads some years in the potato fields, creeping down the rows. And there was no place to go, nothing that anyone knew how to do but wait.

Some said it was because the floods had brought filth into the drinking water. The village priest said it was because people had sinned. Hour after hour the church bells rang for funerals and masses of intercession, making a grave, bronze clamor in the rain. Whenever the rain stopped the processions formed: the priest, the altar boys holding candles, carrying banners and a bone relic in a glass box. Men lifted a statue of the Virgin on a swaying platform; women cried.

In Anna's house the shutters were closed. "If this sickness doesn't stop soon," the father said, "they will start blaming us."

The mother spoke sadly. "I don't know which is worse, fear of the cholera or of them."

"In America," Anna said, "there is no cholera and nobody is afraid of anybody else."

"And by summer we'll be there," Papa said.

Perhaps at last they really would have gone that year. Who knows?

The father and the mother died at the end of March after an illness of just two days. Celia and Rachel died with them. Anna and the twins never fell sick at all.

They lived, the spindly red-haired girl and the ten-year-old boys, followed the four pine coffins to the cemetery, shook in the whipping wind while the prayers were chanted, saw the first clod of earth strike the wood. Hurry, hurry, it is so cold, Anna thought. And then she thought, I shall forget them. Close your eyes: Think of their faces, remember the sound of their voices calling your name.

They stood in the kitchen of what had been their home. Someone had aired and disinfected the house. Someone else had brought soup. The little room was crowded with neighbors in dark wraps and shawls.

"So, what's to be done with these children?"

"No family! People without relatives shouldn't marry each other!"

"That's true."

10

"Well then, the community will have to provide!"

And who is the "community"? Why, the richest man, naturally, from whom all charity is expected and to whom all respect is given. He steps forward now, Meyer Krohn, innkeeper, dry goods merchant, money-lender. He is a tall, pock-marked man in peasant boots and cap. His gray beard is rough, his voice is rough, but it speaks with authority.

"So who'll take them? What about you, Avrom? You, Yossel? You have room enough!"

"Meyer, you know I give what I can. I'll gladly take one of them, but not three."

Meyer Krohn frowns; the furrows in his forehead are deep enough to bury the tip of a fingernail. He roars.

"We don't separate families! Now, who here will take in these three orphans? I ask you, who?"

Nobody speaks. Anna's legs are weak; the bones melt.

"Ah," Meyer says, "I know what you're thinking! You're thinking: *Meyer's rich, let him do it!*" He thrusts his enormous arms out. "What am I, Rothschild, that I have to support half the community? 'Meyer, the school needs a new stove; So-and-so broke his leg and his family is starving'—is there no end to what is expected of me?"

Coughing and shuffling. Eli has been told that he must be a man now. He is trying not to cry.

"All right," says Meyer Krohn. "All right." He sighs. "My children are grown and gone. The house is big enough, God knows. There's a room for the boys and Anna can share a bed with the servant-girl." His voice lowers quietly. "What do you say, Anna? And you, Eli? Which one of you is Eli and what's the other one's name? I always forget." He puts his arms around the little shoulders of the boys. "Come along home," he says.

Oh, he is decent, he is kind! But Anna walks naked; everyone is looking at her growing breasts, the secrets of her body. Her clothes have been stripped off. She has been shamed, she has been outraged. Like Pretty Leah.

The Krohns live prosperously. Their house has two stories and wooden floors. There is carpet in the front room. Aunt Rosa owns a fur cape. A servant does the cleaning while Aunt Rosa measures cloth and waits on customers in the store. Sometimes she helps in the tavern; sometimes Uncle Meyer helps in the store.

11

Anna works wherever she is needed, and she is always needed everywhere. She is often tired out. But she has grown tall like her mother, with bright, healthy hair. The Krohns have fed her well.

"How old are you?" Uncle Meyer asks one day. They are rewinding cloth on the heavy bolts and lifting them back onto the shelves.

"Sixteen."

"How the years fly! You've turned out well in my house. A nice girl, a worker. It's time we found a husband for you."

Anna does not answer, but this does not bother Uncle Meyer. He has a way of talking without noticing whether anyone answers or not.

"I really ought to have done something about you before this. But I never seem to have time. People think: he's a rich man, Meyer Krohn, what has he got to worry about? My God, when I lie down at night I can't sleep, my head spins, a hundred things at once—"

He is always complaining, there is always an undertone of resentment even in the best humors. But Anna knows that is because he's afraid. Growing up in a stranger's house, you learn to watch for moods, to anticipate and analyze, to look at the outside and see what is inside. Yes, Uncle Meyer is afraid, even more than Papa was, because he is important and conspicuous in the village. When a new commissioner of police is sent to the district it is Meyer who goes to him for favors that may possibly buy the safety of the community. Also, he has his personal bribes, gifts to the peasants so the store will not be looted and wrecked during the holiday rampage. The same friendly fellow who comes with his cajoling smile to ask for credit—and who, of course, receives it—can just as easily return to boot you down the stairs or set his wicked dogs upon you.

"Yes, and there are your brothers to think about. What's to become of them? Let's see, how old are they now?"

"Fourteen."

"Hm. Fourteen, already. What's to be done with them? How are they to support themselves?" He thinks aloud. "Rosa has an uncle in Vienna. He went there years ago, perhaps we've mentioned him? He sells furs. As a matter of fact, his son will be coming through here this spring to buy fox skins. It's an idea."

He looks like a fox himself, Anna thought. The young man from Vienna was thin and lively; his reddish eyes snapped; his city suit fitted like skin and he talked so much and so fast that even Uncle Meyer was subdued. Eli and Dan were fascinated.

". . . and the Opera House has marble stairs and gilded carving on the walls. It's so enormous that you could fit thirty houses, one whole side of your village, into it."

"Bah," Uncle Meyer could not resist. "Who hasn't seen big buildings? I've been in Warsaw; I've seen buildings in my time."

"Warsaw? You compare that with Vienna? I'm talking about a cultured country! Where Jews write plays and teach in the university, where they don't have pogroms whenever the drunken peasants feel like having a little fun!"

"You mean," Dan asks, "that Jews in Vienna are exactly like everybody else?"

"Well, naturally they don't attend balls at Franz Josef's palace, but neither do other people. They have grand houses, though, and carriages, and they own big shops with porcelains and Oriental rugs and fashions—you should see where I work, we've just doubled the place. Why, if you work hard and use your brains, you can see your family rising for generations to come and no limit!"

The foxy young man has planted thoughts that sprout like seeds.

"I may go to Paris in the spring," he says carelessly. "Did I tell you that?"

"You didn't tell us," Dan says.

"Yes, well, we sell furs to some concerns there and the boss wants to discuss matters. And naturally, you can get new styles in Paris, new ideas for the retail end. The boss has promised to take me along."

The cat scratches vigorously; the water bubbles for tea and the questions hang in the air.

"I shan't be coming back here again. We're making new contacts for furs. In Lithuania."

"So in other words," Uncle Meyer says, "if you're going to take these boys back with you it will have to be right now."

"That's about it."

Dan turns to Anna and she sees his eagerness, his pleading. She thinks: It's true, here there is nothing. Uncle Meyer can't do anything for them. What will they become? Porters with ropes around their waists dragging bundles through the streets of Lublin? Or learn a fine trade in Vienna and wear the look of prosperity and ease?

Good-by, Eli. Good-by, Dan. Little snub-noses, little dirty faces. I am the only person who can tell you apart. Eli has the mole on the side of his nose; Dan has a chipped front tooth.

"I'll send for you from America," Anna tells them. "I'll get there and I'll earn money enough to send for you. America will be better."

"No, we'll earn it and we'll send for you. There are two of us and we are men. You can come back from America. If you go."

People don't come back from America.

They had been gone a few weeks when Aunt Rosa said, "Anna, I have something to tell you. Uncle Meyer has found a nice young man."

"But I'm going to America."

"Nonsense. All the way across the world alone, at sixteen?"

"I'm not afraid," Anna said untruthfully. Maybe, after all—? At least, the village was home. At least, its threats were familiar ones. And yet—America. For some reason she always saw it lying at the end of the voyage like a tropical island rising out of the sea, a silver-green lure. Of course, she knew it was not like that, but that was the way she saw it.

"I shall miss you," Aunt Rosa said shyly. "You've become like a daughter to me. My own I never see since they married and moved away." And coaxing, "Just look the young man over one time. You may change your mind."

He came to dinner on Friday, a gentle person from another village, earning his way as a peddler of tobacco, thread and sundries to the farms. He had pimples, garlic breath and a kind, mournful smile. He was disgusting. Anna was ashamed of herself for being disgusted by a decent, honest human being.

Her thoughts ran back to Pretty Leah, those men, what they had done. But this young man was no drunkard, no brute; it would not be like that! Disgusting, all the same.

"Really, Anna," Aunt Rosa said, "you have to look at the facts. You're a poor girl without money or family! What do you expect, a scholar? Or a merchant prince? Ah," she sighed, "these foolish unplanned marriages! It's the next generation that suffers and pays! Your father was a good-looking man, he had a trade; and if he had married a girl with some family and substance he could have built up a business and left something for his children!"

14

"My parents loved each other! You don't know how happy they were!"

"Yes, of course, I'm not speaking against them! Your mother was a charming woman, a religious woman; I knew her well. It's only that—well, here you are, you see! However, it could be worse. Thank God you're pretty, otherwise you'd have to marry an old widower and raise his children for him. At least this man is young and he'll be kind to you. You don't think we didn't inquire? We wouldn't turn a girl over to a man who would mistreat her."

"Aunt Rosa, I can't . . ."

Aunt Rosa clasped her hands together. Her face puckered into wrinkles. "Oh, but Uncle Meyer will be angry! After all that he's done for you! Anna, Anna, what do you want?"

What did she want? To see the world beyond this village, to be free, to hear music, to wear a new pink dress. To have her own place and not have to say thank you for everything. Thank you for this corner under your roof which keeps me out of the wet. Thank you for the food; I would like a second portion but I am ashamed to ask for it. Thank you for this thick, warm, ugly, brown shawl which you no longer wear and have given to me. Thank you.

She owned four silver candlesticks, a pair from each grandmother. Keep two, the ones with the feel of Mama's hands upon them. Sell the others for the price of one passage to America. And go.

At the top of the rise the wagon stopped to let the horses rest. Below lay the village, held in the curve of the river. There, the little wooden dome of the synagogue. There, the market: jostling and churning at the stalls; flurry and squawk of crated fowl. Round and round, the busy lives in the order of their days.

"Well, come," the driver said. "We've a long way."

The wagon creaked along the road above the river. There, the last huddle of houses, the board fences and a glimpse of lilacs. In another month Mama's yellow roses would flower like a celebration.

Then the road turned and led downhill across level fields, dark earth steaming and wet new greenery swimming in spring light. The village was gone, erased in the moment of turning. The hill blocked out the past. The road led forward.

Dust, flies and dirty inns. The border: guards, papers, sharp questions. Will they perhaps not let us through? Then Germany: neat railroad stations with candy and fruit for sale. Be careful not to

15

spend too much of the little treasure in the knotted cloth wrapped up with the silver candlesticks.

The immigrant-aid people come to expedite the journey to Hamburg. They are German Jews wearing fine suits, ties and white shirts. They bring food, sign documents, rearrange the boxes, bags and feather beds. They are generous and kindly. They are also impatient to get the strangers onto the ship and out of Germany.

The Atlantic is a ten-day barrier between worlds. It is the lonely mourning of horns in dark gray fog. It is wind and the heaving sea, the creaking and cracking of the ship. It is retching out of an empty stomach, lying in a top berth with all strength drained and hands too weak to hold on. There is a noisy turbulence of voices: laughing, arguing, complaining in Yiddish, German, Polish, Lithuanian, Hungarian. And thefts, the poor stealing from the poor. (A woman lost her gold crucifix. Don't let the bundle with the candlesticks out of sight.) A child is born; the mother wails. An old man dies; the widow wails.

Suddenly it is over. There is a wide, calm river. From the deck one sees houses and trees. The trees draw closer; the wind turns up the silver undersides of the leaves. The air is tart and brisk, like witch hazel. Gulls flow over the ship, circle, climb and slide down the sky.

America.

3

The house on Hester Street was five stories tall. Cousin Ruth lived on the top floor with her husband, Solly Levinson, their four children and six boarders. Anna would be the seventh.

"You don't have room for me," she said in dismay. "You're kind to offer but I'd be crowding you—"

Ruth pushed the hair back from her sweating forehead. "So where do you think you'll find a place where you won't be crowding somebody? Better for you to stay here where at least you're a relative. And to tell you the truth, it's not all kindness on my part, we can use the money. We have to pay twelve dollars a month for this place, not counting gas for the light and coal in the winter for the stove. We'll charge you fifty cents a week. Fair enough?"

The smells! The stench surged from the street door and up the four flights: cooking grease; onions; an overflowing toilet in the hall; the sickening steam of pressing irons; a noxious drenching of tobacco from the front apartment where the cigar-makers lived. Anna's stomach contracted. Yet how could she refuse? And if she refused, where could she go?

Ruth coaxed. Her anxious, pretty eyes lay in two circles of dark blue shadow. "When we're through with the sewing at night Solly and I put up the cot for ourselves in the kitchen. We put the machines in the corner and get out the mattresses. The women have the best room to themselves, the room with the windows. And the men sleep in the rear by the air shaft. It's not so bad, really. Can you sew?"

"Just mending. And I can make a plain skirt. I never had time to learn because I worked in the store."

"Well, it doesn't matter. Solly can take you to the factory tomorrow, he has to bring the finished work back."

In a corner stood a pile of black bags stuffed with coats and pants. Two sallow, curly-haired children lay sleeping on top of the pile.

"You can help Solly carry the bags, you'll meet the boss and they can show you how to stitch pants in no time. A good finisher gets thirty cents a day, you know."

Anna set her bundles down and unfastened her shawl. The dark red braids fell free.

"They didn't tell me how pretty you are! A child, a baby—" Ruth put out her hands. Her arms were black to the elbow with the stain of the pants fabric. "Anna, I'll look out for you, you won't be alone. It's maybe not what you dreamed it would be but it's a start. And you'll get used to it."

The noise was the worst. The smells and the crowding could somehow be endured. But Anna had sensitive hearing and the noise attacked her like brutal fists. On the street below the old-clothes man chanted through his nose: "Coats, fifty cents, coats, fifty cents!" Wagons rumbled. The "L" ground into the station with the squeal of metal on metal. And always until midnight the sewing machines whined. Would they ever sleep, ever slacken the struggle?

Sometimes on breathless nights Anna and Ruth went out to sit on the stoop. It was impossible to sleep indoors and they were afraid to join the others on the fire escape since a woman from across the street had rolled off in her sleep and smashed to the street. The sky was a cloudy pink from the glow of factories that smoked all night; you could scarcely see the stars. At home on summer nights they had been so clear, winking and pulsing above the trees.

"You're so quiet," Ruth said. "Are you worried about anything? About your brothers?"

"I miss them. But they're all right, they're doing well. They have a nice room in their boss's house and Vienna is beautiful, they say."

"It's not beautiful here, God knows."

"That's true."

"But one has a future here. I still believe that."

"I believe it, too. I wouldn't have come if I hadn't believed that."

"You know," Ruth said, "you know, I've been thinking there isn't any reason for you to work as hard as you're doing. At your age you ought to have some life. You ought to be meeting men. It's my fault, I've done nothing for you, after four months. I'll ask Solly to look around for you, for a dancing class. There are lots and lots of good dancing classes."

"If I'm going to take the time off I'd rather go to night school. Working here like this I've had no chance to learn English."

"That's not a bad idea, either. If you could learn enough to be a typist you could find a husband more easily, a better class of man. Typists don't earn much, just three dollars a week, but the work has prestige. Only," Ruth's voice grew doubtful, "I really think you have to be American born. Still, it's worth trying."

"I'm not so interested in finding a husband. I just want to learn something."

"You're like your mother, I remember her well." Ruth sighed. "I, too, would like to learn. But with all the children to feed, and now another—" She sighed again, resting her hand on the swelling beneath her apron.

Only ten years ago Ruth had been the age Anna was now. Was this what marriage made you, so tired, so resigned? But Mama hadn't been like that. Or could she have been? What could Anna when she was twelve years old have really known about her mother?

Ruth said, lowering her voice, "One doesn't want to complain. But it's hard to get ahead. Though some people do, I don't know how they do it. There's a knack to making money. My poor Solly hasn't got it."

A shifting light moved in the window. Someone inside had got up to light the oil lamp and a yellow flare fell over the steps.

"There was a girl who came from home with me—Hannah Vogel, your mother knew her. She married a fellow she met on the boat. He didn't have a cent when he came, but he was smart. Somehow he made a connection and moved to Chicago. Opened a haberdashery there. I hear he owns a chain of stores now—" Ruth's voice brightened. "My Solly's got very friendly with the factory manager. You never know, changes are always being made; he might decide to open his own place and take Solly in with him."

Anna thought of Solly in the corner, bent over his machine. A thin man with the timid pointed face of a mouse. Poor hopeful Ruth. Poor tired Solly. They would never get out of here.

People who had come from Europe twenty years before them

19

still lived on these streets. The old men were thin, with dark, beautiful eyes; they seemed more fragile, somehow, than the old men Anna remembered from home, leading their wagons of secondhand clothes, chickens, hats, fish and eyeglasses. Their old wives were fat, potato-shaped and potato-colored, their hanging white flesh untouched by the sun.

Where were the pink dresses, the freedom and the music?

Still, there were many marvels. The streets were almost as bright at night as by day, not like home where you stumbled down the road holding the lantern high. In a vacant store down the street there was a machine, a nickelodeon, where you could look in and see a picture that moved: Indians attacking a train, a beautiful woman named Irene Castle and a tall man swooping and gliding in a dance.

Anna walked, taking no particular direction, just walking and looking. Under the Second Avenue elevated the women sat at the horseradish machines, weeping their smarting tears. She avoided the tramps who slept over the baker's ovens in the yard. She went past the synagogues in the tenements on Bayard Street. She walked five, ten blocks and more, until the people on the streets looked different and spoke in languages that she did not understand. On Italian streets the children swarmed more thickly than on Hester Street. A man sold pink and yellow sweet ices from a little cart. An organ grinder wearing a bandana and earrings made melancholy music in the bright morning; on his shoulder sat an eager, tiny monkey in a red jacket. She watched; she listened to the melody of Italian speech. It was like singing.

Then the Irish streets. The saloons with harps and shamrocks on the signs above the doors. The beautiful women in their ragged dresses and the curving sweetness on their faces.

And Mott Street, where the strange-eyed peddlers sold watermelon seed and sugar cane. Through half-open cellar doors you saw Chinese men playing fan-tan. Their pigtails came below their knees. You never saw Chinese women or children. Why was that? How could that be?

Worlds. Every few blocks another world. From what strange places had all these different people come? Villages in China, in Ireland—how different could they be from home? Had these people felt fears like ours? Are they perhaps like me after all?

4

Her name was Miss Mary Thorne. Thin and precise in her dark serge skirt and starched shirtwaist, she stood at the front of the classroom with the map of the United States on one side and the portraits of Washington and Lincoln on the other. She looks like them, her face is American, Anna thought. Americans are always tall and slender, with long faces.

Evening school was held in a room that must have housed ten-year-olds by day. One's knees didn't fit under the desks; one had to sit twisted sideways. The ceiling bulb glared harshly and the heat from the sizzling radiators made people yawn. They shifted restlessly. But Anna hardly moved. She watched. She listened. Miss Mary Thorne was pouring knowledge like a good drink out of a pitcher.

Toward the end of the winter she was called to the desk after class. "You've done amazingly well, Anna. It's hard to believe you never studied English before. I'm going to promote you to my intermediate group."

"Thank you, miss," Anna said. Proud and embarrassed, she stood looking at Miss Thorne, not knowing quite how to leave the room with grace.

The teacher looked back at her. People were often intimidated by Miss Thorne: she had a stern face most of the time, but not now. Her eyes, magnified behind the unrimmed glasses that clung to the bridge of her nose, were soft.

21

"Do you think about what you want to do with your life, Anna? I ask because it seems to me you are different from so many others. I see so many. . . . Every so often someone sits in this classroom who is different from the rest."

"I don't know what there is for me to do," Anna said slowly. "I suppose what I really want is just to know things. I feel that I don't know anything, and I want to know everything."

Miss Thorne smiled. "Everything? That's a large order."

"Of course, I didn't mean that. But you see, the way it is, sometimes I feel there is a screen between me and the world. I want to pull it away to see more clearly. I don't know anything about the past, or the way the world is now, except for these few streets and the village that I came from."

"Did you study anything there in the village?"

"There was a woman teacher who came to the houses for the girls. We learned numbers and writing and reading. In Yiddish."

"Not Hebrew? Oh no, that's only for the boys, isn't it? The sacred language."

"Yes, only for the boys."

"Well, it's not like that here, as you know. A girl can study whatever the boys do."

"I know. That's a good thing."

"Yes. Well." Miss Thorne stood up and went briskly to a shelf of books behind the desk. "The secret to it all is reading, Anna. Nothing else. I'll tell you something: if you read and read and read you don't even have to go to school, you can educate yourself! Only don't tell anybody I said so! First, you must read the newspaper every day, the *Times* or the *Herald*. Don't read the *Journal*, it's cheap and sensational. Then I'm going to make up a list of books for you, long enough to take years to get through. You'll be reading it long after I don't see you anymore. Now, tonight I'm going to start you with this, you must learn about your new country from the beginning. It's a book about Indians, a wonderful poem called *Hiawatha*, by one of our best poets, Mr. Henry Wadsworth Longfellow. When you have finished it, bring it back and tell me what you thought about it. And then I will give you another."

Over the fireplace there was a round mirror in a gilded frame. Everything looked queer in it: she could see herself holding the

22

flowered teacup on the embroidered napkin, see the little table with
the teapot and the cake plate and Miss Thorne on the other side of
the table. All of these were squat, condensed and flattened out.
Even Miss Thorne looked wide and flat.

"That's a bull's-eye mirror," Miss Thorne said, following Anna's
gaze. "I don't see much point in having it myself. But then, it's not
my house."

"Not?"

"No, my nephew's. He and his wife have only the one child and
it's a large house, so when I came down from Boston they invited
me to live here with them and it has been very nice for me indeed."

"And were you a teacher when you lived in Boston?" Anna asked
shyly.

"Yes, I've been a teacher ever since I left school myself. I came to
New York to be the assistant headmistress at a private school for
girls. That's what I do all day, you see. Then at night I teach English
to newcomers like you."

"And what do you teach the girls in the daytime, since they already know how to speak English?"

"I teach them Latin and ancient Greek."

"Oh. But why—excuse me, I ask too many questions."

"Not at all. How will you find out if you don't ask? Tell me what
you wanted to know."

"Well, I want to know what Latin is. And ancient Greek."

"A long time ago, two thousand years ago and more, there were
powerful countries in Europe where those languages were spoken.
The languages aren't spoken anymore; we say they're 'dead,' but the
laws, the ideas those people left to us, are very much alive. And it's
also true that the languages are the great-great-grandparents of English. Do you understand what I'm saying?"

Anna nodded. "I understand. Those girls in your school are so fortunate, learning all these things, I think."

"I wish they all thought so. Or had your eagerness, Anna. That's
why I like to teach in your school, at night. Because so many of you
want to learn—I feel I'm doing something really important."

Now that she had been invited here to tea Anna felt bolder. It
was different from the classroom, with the elevated platform where
the teacher sat above everybody else.

"Do people speak differently, is that why you speak differently,
because you're from Boston?"

"What do you mean, differently?"

"I notice that some words are different. The way you say 'park,' for instance? That's not the way some other Americans say it."

"Extraordinary, your ear! Yes, it's true, we have a different accent there. In the South, in the Midwest, there are all sorts of accents."

"I see. And will you answer something else, please?"

"If I can."

"Please, I've never had tea in a cup like this. What must I do with the spoon after I've stirred the tea?"

"You just lay the spoon on the saucer, Anna."

"That was probably a foolish question. I might have figured it out for myself. Except that I should like to do things right, the American way."

"It wasn't a foolish question. Only, let me tell you something. Wherever you go, and I hope you'll go far, don't ever be nervous about manners. Manners are mostly common sense, being tidy about things and considerate of other people. I don't think you'll have the slightest trouble about either of those, Anna."

"Then, may I have another piece of cake, please? It's very good cake."

"Of course. And when you've finished I want to give you the list of reading that I've made out for you. I finally got around to it. That's one of the reasons I asked you to come today, because we can talk better than at school."

The list was pages long, written in a neat script that looked like Miss Thorne herself. Anna scanned it.

Hawthorne: *House of the Seven Gables*
Hardy: *The Return of the Native*
Dickens: *David Copperfield, Bleak House*
Thackeray: *Vanity Fair*
Henry James: *The Bostonians, Washington Square*

"Washington Square? That's where we are now, the same?" Anna cried.

"The very same. Henry James lived not far from here before he went to live in England. My family, my father's people, knew him well. My mother's family came from Boston."

"Really American," Anna murmured.

"No more than you. We just arrived sooner. You can be as American as anyone, never think otherwise. That's what this country is all about, Anna."

24

Anna said, suddenly troubled, "I only wish, I wish I had more time to read all these books. It takes me so long."

"You'll find the time. You can get a lot done just on Sundays alone."

"Sundays I work." And as Miss Thorne looked puzzled, she explained, "I took the afternoon off today because you invited me and I was so honored, I wanted so much to come. But I'm really supposed to be working."

"I see. Sewing, where you live at home."

Anna nodded.

"Tell me, then, is there any place where you can read by yourself? I suppose not."

"Alone? Oh, no! Only on the front stoop when the weather is warm, and it's noisy enough there. But in cold weather, there's no place. It's so hard even to write to my brothers. With everybody talking I can't think of what I want to say."

"A pity, a pity. And so many empty rooms in this house alone. If only one could do what one wants to do. One thing, though: my niece is about your size, and I'm going to ask her whether she has a good warm coat to give away. It would be better—shall we say, more American?—than your shawl. Also, I have duplicate copies of a few of the books on this list and I'm going to give them to you to keep, so you can start to build a library of your own. I'll get the things to you, since it's hard for you to take time to come here."

Anna put the shawl around her shoulders and they went out into the hall. On the other side a door was ajar; a room was filled with books from ceiling to floor; a little boy was practicing at a huge dark piano.

"You don't mind the offer of the coat, Anna?"

"Mind? Oh, no, I'm glad, I want a coat!"

"Someday you'll be one of the people who gives, I'm sure you will."

"I shall be happy to give if that day ever comes, Miss Thorne."

"It will. And when it does I hope we shall still know each other. Then I'll remind you of what I said."

I don't believe we shall know each other, almost surely not. But just as surely, I will remember Miss Mary Thorne. Yes, I will, always.

5

"Y ou must be Anna," the young man said.

He stood above her as she sat reading on the steps: *This is the forest primeval. The murmuring pines and the hemlocks—*

Unwillingly she returned to the street, stilled on the Sabbath afternoon, the old men in their long black coats walking on quiet feet, and now this new voice prodding softly.

"May I?"

"Of course. Sit." She moved over, observing him without seeming to. Medium, he was. Medium height and age; medium brown suit, eyes and hair; medium features in a neatly fashioned face.

"I'm Joseph. Joseph Friedman, Solly's cousin."

The American, so called because he had been born in New York. The house painter from uptown. And of course Ruth had arranged this. The same as Aunt Rosa! They can't rest until they've got a man for you. He can be ugly, stupid, anything, as long as he's a man. Not that this one is ugly, but I wanted to read and I'm not thinking about men right now anyway.

"Ruth asked me to come down here to meet you. To tell you the truth, I almost didn't come. They've tried to hitch me up to every girl who ever got off a boat; I was getting tired of it. But I can tell straight away I'm glad I came this time."

Anna stared at him, weighing his astonishing words. But there was no conceit in his face, only the direct and simple return of her look.

26

"I'm so embarrassed," she said. "I knew nothing about it. Ruth shouldn't have—"

"Please! I know you had nothing to do with it. Shall we take a walk?"

"All right," she said.

He pulled her arm through his. He had clean hands, clean fingernails, a fresh collar. She respected that, at any rate. It is no easy thing to be clean when you are poor, in spite of what people say.

They began to see each other every Saturday. In the afternoon heat they walked the shady side of the street. They could walk for two or three blocks without speaking. Joseph was a quiet man, Anna saw, except when a mood came on him and then one could hardly stop him. Still, he was interesting, he had a vivid way of describing things.

"Here's Ludlow Street, there's the house where I was born. We lived here while my father had the tailor shop. After his sight failed—he couldn't even see the needle anymore—we moved where we are now, my mother and I. Or where my mother is now, I should say. Two rooms behind the grocery store. What a life! Open six days a week until midnight. Bread, pickles, crackers and soda. My mother made salad in back of the store. Such a little woman, such a patient smile. When I remember being a child, I remember that smile. And what the hell was there to smile about? It didn't make any sense."

"Perhaps she was happy about her children, in spite of everything else."

"Child. Just me. They were both over forty when I was born."

"And your father? What was he like?"

"My father had high blood pressure. Everything upset him. He was probably already worn out by the time they got to America. But why don't you stop me? Here I am, chewing your ear off!"

"I like to hear about people. Tell me more."

"There isn't any more to tell. You live here. You know what it's like to live on these streets, just walking around, because there's no place to be comfortable inside. We were poor, and that's the whole story."

"Even poorer than we were in Poland, I should think."

"Well, I don't know how poor you were, but I can remember making supper sometimes out of bread and pickles—before we had

27

our own store, that is. Not all the time, of course, but often enough."

"Still, I think," Anna said thoughtfully, "it hasn't hurt you. I think you're a very optimistic person after all."

"I am. Because I have faith, you see."

"Faith in yourself?"

"Yes, that too. But what I meant was faith in God."

"Are you so religious?"

He nodded seriously. "Yes, yes, I believe. I believe there is a reason for everything that happens, even though we don't see it. And I believe we must accept everything that happens, whether good or bad, on trust. And that we, we as individuals, must do our best, do what God intended. I don't give a damn for all the philosophy you hear them spouting in the coffee houses where the loafers sit around and solve the world's problems. They were all solved years ago on Mt. Sinai. That's what I believe."

"Then why is there still so much trouble in the world?"

"Very simple. Because people don't do what's right. Very simple. You're not an atheist, Anna, I hope?"

"Oh, no, of course I'm not! I just don't know much about religion. I don't really understand it."

"Well, naturally, women don't have to. But I can tell what you are all the same. Honest and kind and good. And very smart. I admire you for educating yourself with all these books."

"You don't read, ever?"

"I don't have time. I'm up before five, and when you've been craning your head back on a scaffold with a paintbrush all day you're too tired at night to improve yourself. Although, to be truthful, I never was a student. Except in arithmetic, I had a good head for figures. At one time I even thought I might become an accountant."

"Why didn't you, then?"

"I had to go to work," he said shortly. "Tell you what, there's a place over on West Broadway that's pretty good, we could have supper there. Soup, stew and pie for thirteen cents. Not bad, with a schooner of beer thrown in. Will you go with me?"

"Yes, but I don't drink beer. You can have mine, too."

Ruth said: "One good thing about this country is you don't have to have money to get married. It's not like the other side. Of course, some people still go to marriage brokers, but modern people don't.

28

You like each other, you get married. You both work." And when
Anna did not answer, she said: "Tell me about you and Joe."

"Joseph. Nobody ever calls him Joe."

"And why not?"

"I don't know. But Joseph seems to fit him. It's more dignified."

"All right, then, Joseph. Tell me about you and him."

"There's nothing to tell."

"Nothing!"

"Well, I like him. But there's no—" Anna looked for a word.
"Fire. There's no fire."

Ruth threw her hands up. Her eyes and brows moved upward.
"So why do you go with him?"

"He's a friend. It's lonesome without a friend."

Ruth looked at her. I might as well have spoken in Chinese, Anna
thought.

"You know how many people around here have never even been
north of Fourteenth Street?" Joseph had asked Anna.

"I'm one of them."

"Wait, then, I'm going to show you something."

The slippery cane seats were cool and the spring breeze ran along
with the trolley car as it gathered speed up Lexington Avenue. The
bell clanged with authority. When the car stopped at the corners
one could see on the side streets row after row of narrow houses, all
brownstone, with high steps and tubbed evergreens at the front
doors. Hester Street was a thousand miles away.

"We'll get out at Murray Hill and go over to Fifth," Joseph said.

They walked through the quiet streets from sun to shade, from
shade to sun. Now and then a carriage passed; the horses had glossy
hair and braided tails.

"Going for a ride in Central Park," Joseph explained. Anna was
surprised that he knew so much about this part of the city.

A motorcar stopped in front of one of the houses. The lady in the
back seat wore a wide hat tied with a veil. The driver, in uniform
and leather boots, walked around and helped her out of the car.
She had two small fawn-colored dogs, one under each arm. Then
the house door was opened from inside and a young woman came
down the steps. Her dress was narrowly striped in blue and white;
her little apron was edged with lace and her cap matched it. She
took the two dogs and followed the lady up the steps.

29

"There! What do you think of that?" Joseph asked.

"Oh, it's nice here!" Anna said. "I never imagined anything like this."

"This is nothing. Wait till you see Fifth Avenue. That's something to see!"

The sunshine glowed. The trees in the park across the avenue at Fifty-ninth Street glowed green and gold.

"That's the Plaza Hotel," Joseph said. "And on this side, this is the famous Hotel Netherland."

A young man wearing a straw hat ("That's called a 'boater,' " Joseph said) came out under the awning. The girl with him wore a bunch of violets on her coat, a beautiful coat, pale as the inside of a peach. They crossed the avenue walking swiftly, going somewhere. Anna and Joseph ambled along behind them, going nowhere in particular. When the policeman's whistle blew, the traffic started up and they were stopped on the concrete island where General Sherman, larger than life, reined in his horse.

"Some statue, hey?" Joseph said.

Anna read the inscription. "That's the Union general who burned all the houses when he marched through Georgia during the Civil War."

Joseph was astonished. "I never heard about him! I know about the Civil War, of course, but how do you know so much?"

"History. I've a book of American history," Anna said with pride.

Joseph shook his head. "You're something, Anna, you really are."

Beyond General Sherman stood a great house of red brick and white stone, with iron gates. "The Vanderbilt mansion, that is. Or one of them, I should say."

"That's not a hotel?"

"It's a house. A family lives in there."

She thought he was joking. "One family? It's not possible! There must be a hundred rooms."

"I'm telling you the truth."

"But how can they be so rich?"

"This particular family made it in railroads. All up and down this avenue I could show you dozens of houses like this. Fortunes made in oil, steel, copper, and some just from owning land. You know where you live downtown? A lot of those tenements are

30

owned by people who live here. When people like us pay rent it goes to these people here."

She thought of the crumbling house on Hester Street. "Do you think that's right?"

"Probably not. Or maybe it is, I don't know. If they're smart enough to get it, maybe they're entitled to it. Anyway, that's how the world is, and until a better world is made I'll adapt to this one."

Anna was silent. And Joseph went on, his voice rising with excitement, "I'm going to live like this someday, Anna. Oh, not in a palace like these, but uptown in one of those nice places on the side streets. I'm going to do it, mark my words."

"You are? But how?"

"Work. Buy land. Land is the key to wealth, you know, as long as you own it free and clear. Its value may go down for a time but it always rises again. This country is growing, and if you can hold on to land you're bound to be rich."

"How do you get the money to start?"

"Ah, that's the question! I'm trying to save enough for a small house of flats, but it's hard." He said stubbornly, "I'll do it, though. I'll live like this one day if I have to break my back."

The fierceness that she saw in him disturbed Anna. He hadn't shown it like that before. All of a sudden he seemed too angry and too large, although he was not a large man at all. His voice was too loud. She thought windows would open and people lean out to look, although no one did.

She said quietly, "You think too much about money."

"You think so? I'll tell you something, Anna. Without money the world spits on you. You're nothing. You die like my father in a dirty little shop. Or rot away like Ruth and Solly. You want to rot away like that?"

"No, of course not." One shuddered to think of it. But still it couldn't all be as he said. "The great writers, the artists, they had no money. And the world honors them. You make everything too cruel, too ugly."

Joseph turned her face up to his. His eyes were suddenly soft. "You look about fifteen years old, Anna," he said gently.

The idea came to her on a stifling night, when the smell of frying hung in the airless rooms. The hair at the back of her neck was wet

31

with sweat; she longed for a bath in cool water. But there was no place, no privacy. Other women walked in while you were meagerly sponging off. Some of these women disgusted her; they weren't clean. And one poor creature cried and whimpered into her pillow all night. Ruth's five-year-old was sick and restless. It was impossible to sleep.

She thought of the maid coming down the steps of the house with the tubbed evergreens. On the ship crossing the Atlantic, some of the peasant girls had talked of the jobs that waited for them in America, jobs in neat, clean houses like the ones uptown. In such a house she would sleep quietly, and have a place to keep a shelf of the books which Miss Thorne had given her, maybe even save money and buy some more for herself at second hand. After all, there would be no rent to pay and no food to buy. One could live decently, one could walk on those fine streets. She lay awake, thinking and thinking, and at last made up her mind.

"Ruth says I'm crazy to go to work as a servant," she told Joseph, a few days later.

"Why so? It's honest work. Please yourself, Anna, not other people," he told her.

6

This, then, was how they looked inside, these houses behind the long windows where the shades, demurely pulled, were like downcast eyelids in a quiet face. Velvet carpets; your footsteps made no sound. Pictures in gilded frames. Fresh roses, cream and pink, although it was September. And stairs, turning up and up again. Anna followed Mrs. Werner.

"We're a small family. My daughter is married and living in Cleveland. So there are just Mr. Werner and I and our son, Mr. Paul. This is his room." She opened a door and Anna saw books on crowded shelves, riding boots in a corner and over the mantel a large blue banner: *For God, for Country and for Yale.*

"They're all Yale men in our family. Mr. Paul won't be home from Europe till next week but I'd like to have the room dusted every day all the same. Now, on the top floor is your room." They mounted the stairs again; more dark railings and no carpet on this flight. "This front room we use for the seamstress. She comes for two or three weeks every spring and fall to do my clothes. Back here is Cook's room and yours is next to it."

The two rooms were identical: a neat bed, a dresser, a straight wooden chair. Cook's room had an enormous wooden crucifix above the bed. Unbelievable. Rooms like this, all for one person. With electric lights. Even a bathtub for the maids, a high white bathtub on claw feet.

"Do you think you would like the position?"

"Oh I would, I would."

"Very well. The wages will be fifteen dollars a month. Ordinarily I pay twenty, but you have no experience, you'll need to be taught. Have you any questions?"

"No."

"Anna, it is proper to say, 'No, Mrs. Werner.' "

"No, Mrs. Werner."

"Do you want to start today?"

"Oh, yes! Yes, Mrs. Werner."

"Then you may go back and get your things. It's eleven o'clock now—let me see—I shan't be needing the car until two. Quinn can drive you down."

"In a machine?"

"Yes. It's a miserable trip in the trolley carrying heavy parcels."

"I haven't got very much. Just my clothes and my candlesticks."

"Oh?"

"They were my mother's. They're very valuable."

"Well, bring them, then, of course." There was a touch of amusement, not unkind, at the corners of the lady's mouth.

The cleanness of it. First the bath, the high tub filled with hot, hot water. Anna almost fell asleep in it. Then the fresh clean bed all to herself; she could turn, she could spread her arms and legs to the very edge.

Her mind went back over the day. The ride in that car, all closed in; it was like a little room, lined in pale sand-colored cloth as smooth as silk. A rug of dark gray fur with a big W sewn on it. Quinn the chauffeur sat outside without a roof. He didn't talk to me. I think he didn't like going down to Hester Street with all those people staring at the car. There was hardly room for it because of the pushcarts. Then the children started climbing on the car and Quinn got angry. But he did help me with my boxes.

I wish Joseph had been there to see that car. Ruth said again that I was crazy to give up my freedom to be a servant, but I can't see what freedom she has. And if I stayed there, I'd only get like her. Still, I shall miss her.

"How is it that you are called Mrs. while I am called by my name?" Anna inquired of the cook in the morning.

"The cook is always called Mrs.," replied Mrs. Monaghan. "You're the first Jewish housemaid we ever had here, you know that? Even though the family's Jewish."

Anna was astonished. "The Werners are Jewish?"

"Of course they are, and grand people, too. I've been here seven years now. My sister-in-law told me I was making a mistake to work for Jews but I've never regretted it. A lady and a gentleman, and no doubt about it."

"I'm glad to hear that," Anna said stiffly.

"And did you sleep well, I hope? Your first night in a place, it's hard to sleep."

The coal fire, which had been banked all night, flared up. Something with a smoky pleasant smell was frying in a pan.

"What's that?" asked Anna.

"That? Why, bacon, of course. What's the matter?"

"But you said these are Jewish people! How can they eat bacon?"

"I'm sure I don't know. Ask them. Mister has bacon and eggs every morning. She only has a cup of tea, toast and marmalade in her room. I'll show you how to fix her tray, and you're to take it up at a quarter past eight. You'll have to step lively, there's no time to waste in the morning."

"I can't eat bacon," Anna said, the acid of nausea in her mouth.

"Well, don't eat it!" Then Mrs. Monaghan's face brightened. "Oh, it's your religion, ain't it? You're not allowed to."

"No," Anna said.

"And why would that be?" Mrs. Monaghan asked, flipping the bacon.

"I don't know. It's not allowed. It's bad."

Mrs. Monaghan nodded sympathetically. "Now, the butcher boy will be ringing in the areaway to take the order for dinner. The family will be having duckling and, seeing that it's Friday, I'll be having fish."

"Why must you have fish because it's Friday?"

"Well, our Lord died on a Friday, you know."

Anna wanted to ask about the connection between fish and the death of the Lord. But the bell sounded in the pantry and Mrs. Monaghan scurried.

"Heavens, she's early this morning! Here, reach me a cup and saucer, the blue and white china. And put the *New York Times* on the tray! Oh, for pity sake, that's the iceman ringing! Answer, will you? Tell him fifty pounds, there's a good girl—"

It wasn't hard to learn the life and ways of the house. Open the door and take the lady's coat, the gentleman's hat and stick. Serve from the left and remove from the right; don't chip the china or the crystal. Water the flowers; don't spill a drop on the tables, it turns the wood white. Bring in the tea things at five o'clock: remember Miss Thorne? Mrs. Werner and her friends come in from shopping; the chill air enters on their furs; their perfume smells like sugar. Learn how to use the telephone; you crank it on the wall, you give the number to central and put your mouth close to it when you talk. Be sure to write all messages accurately on the pad.

And when you are all finished in the evening, you may go up to your room, your own private room, with the row of books standing on the dresser. You can lie in bed and read, finish *The Cloister and the Hearth*—what a wonderful story! . . . and even have an orange or a bunch of grapes.

"Might as well eat them," Mrs. Monaghan says, "before they go bad."

"Yes," Mrs. Monaghan says, resting her elbows on the kitchen table, "rich people is queer, all right. The Mister's folks has got a place in the Adirondack Mountains, a big homely house made out of logs, like those pictures of Lincoln's cabin, only big. You look out the windows and all you can see is the lake and trees, not a living soul for miles. Gives you the positive creeps, I wouldn't pay a penny for it. Takes you all night to get there from here. You go up in a sleeper. Though I must say, that part of it is kind of an adventure.

"They was awfully good to my nephew Jimmy! After he broke his leg they took him and his sister Agnes up there with us for the whole summer. Jimmy and Mr. Paul is the same age, you know. They had a great time. When they was kids, I'm talking about. Jimmy works in a garage now and Mr. Paul's in the family bank. Did you know they own a bank? Big place, Quinn says. On Wall Street or somewheres.

"You'll like Mr. Paul, he's that nice and easy to like. They say he's smart, but he's that plain, you'd never know it. Except he keeps buying books all the time. There'll be no more room in the house for them soon, I'm thinking."

It is a treasury of books. Anna always takes her time doing his room. There are antique books on yellowed paper, in tiny print. There are volumes of vivid art: columned marble archways, palaces; mothers and children; women naked under casual scarves; even pictures of the cross and the hanging man (the peaceful expression

36

while the blood oozes from the hands and feet!). Anna turns those pages quickly.

What kind of man is he who owns all these?

He arrives home early in September, taking the front steps two at a time, followed by Quinn and a pile of cases labeled: Lusitania, First Class.

It comes to Anna, standing in the front hall with the family, that she must, without thinking, have expected him to resemble his parents, to move neatly in small spaces as they do, to measure his speech neatly.

He moves, instead, like someone striding fields, too loose a person for narrow halls. His bright blue eyes (surprising eyes in a dark face!) look as if they have just finished laughing. He has brought presents for everyone and insists now on giving them out immediately.

"Perfume?" says Mrs. Monaghan. "And where would I be wearing perfume, an old woman like me?"

"To church, Mrs. Monaghan," Mr. Paul says firmly. The blue eyes twinkle: *Funny old soul, isn't she?* "There's no sin in bringing the smell of flowers to your prayers. Doesn't the Virgin herself wear flowers?"

"Oh, the glib tongue of him!"

"And a bottle for Agnes; she hasn't entered the convent yet, has she?"

"Not yet, and I don't think she will, although it'll break her father's and mother's heart if she don't."

"Oh, I hope not, Mrs. Monaghan." The laughter leaves his face. He says seriously, "Agnes must do what she must with her own life. That's her right and she oughtn't feel guilty about it."

Anna lies in bed that night unable to sleep. She thinks she hears her heart pounding. Whichever way she lies, on either side or on her back, she feels her heart. It seems to her suddenly that the world is full of sharp and beautiful excitement, that it will pass by. She is missing it all, she will work and die, having missed it all.

"Well, what did you think of Mr. Paul?" Mrs. Monaghan asks.

7

The vine grows imperceptibly during the night. In the morning it looks the same as it did the evening before. And then there comes a morning when one sees that it has grown halfway up the tree; how did that happen? It must have been growing all the while, because here it is, thick and strong, clinging so tenaciously that one can barely tear it away.

It is so ridiculous, so shameful to be thinking about Paul Werner all the time! How did it happen? She doesn't know a thing about him and she has no business knowing! He walks in one day, a stranger who scarcely knows that she exists, and he takes possession of her mind. Absurd!

In the morning, straightening his room after he and his father have gone to the office in their dark suits and hard, round hats, she has to hang his dressing gown in the closet and arrange his brushes on the bureau. Her hands tremble. It troubles her so to touch these things, to smell them (hair tonic, shaving lotion, pipe tobacco?). Often she hears his voice from the floor below. Knocking at the door of the upstairs study, he calls: "Father? Father?" Then afterward in her mind's ear the voice repeats, exact in tone and timbre: "Father? Father?" And all day long she hears it, while she is dusting the porcelains, even while she is talking to Mrs. Monaghan at lunch.

Mrs. Monaghan likes to gossip about the family. They have, after all, been almost her entire world for so long. She tells about the cousins from Paris who came visiting. She tells about the daughter's wedding at the Plaza. "You should have seen the presents! It took a van to carry them out to Cleveland. We gave the bridesmaids' dinner here at home; twelve girls, and every one of them got a gold bracelet from the bride. The ice cream came from Sherry's, molded in wedding bells and hearts, oh, it was lovely!"

Mrs. Monaghan would be only too pleased to talk about Paul Werner. Anna could easily guide the conversation that way, but she is too ashamed, not because of the old woman, but because of herself.

When she looked in the mirror her face went hot with embarrassment. The house was full of mirrors. Ten times a day she met herself in apron and cap: a becoming cap, really, a lace coronet on her dark red hair which was now piled high because of course she could hardly wear braids anymore! Sometimes it seemed to Anna that she was a very pretty girl, and sometimes she thought she looked stupid in the cap and apron. Stupid like the organ grinder's pathetic monkey in his cap. She felt anger inside. Why should he look at anybody like her? Why should he? He hardly ever did look at her, except at breakfast and dinner, and he was often out for dinner. She wondered about the places where he must go and the girls who would be there, girls in taffeta and feathered hats like the occasional daughters who came calling with their mothers in the afternoon. At breakfast he only smiled, "Good morning, Anna," which he would have done if she had been Mrs. Monaghan. *Well, what did you expect, Anna, foolish Anna?* Mr. Werner always had some extra remark, some little pleasantry about the weather, all that cold stagnant winter, gray with snow: "Better put earmuffs on if you go out today, Anna, or you'll freeze your ears off."

But the son never said anything.

Whenever she had to talk to him it seemed he must know her thoughts, that they must be visible in her face. The saying of her few words, the delivery of a message (Mr. So-and-So called and will call again at nine o'clock) were made to seem so much more important than they could really have been. Then his answer would sound in her head: (Mr. So-and-So, you said? He will call back at nine?)

Why should one human being be drawn to another this way? Why?

"You aren't yourself," Joseph observed after some minutes' silence. They were having supper in the kitchen on Mrs. Monaghan's

Sunday out. Mrs. Werner, having met Joseph once in the basement hall, had remarked that he was "a very nice young man," and that Anna was welcome to ask him to stay to dinner. "What's bothering you? Aren't you happy here?"

"To tell the truth, I don't like it so much."

"But you said the work was easy!"

"Oh, it's easy enough."

"What then?"

"I don't know, exactly."

"You're awfully secretive, Anna." Joseph's eyes were troubled.

She felt a wave of guilt because of her thoughts. He couldn't know what she was thinking: dull, he's gray and dull, no color in him.

"You're so good," she said. "You're so good. But don't worry about me, I'm all right."

"I think I know what it is," he said, brightening. "You're worried about your brothers. You miss them. That's it, isn't it?"

"I miss them, of course I do. But they're very well. Dan writes that he and Eli will be going to Paris with their boss the next time he goes."

Joseph shrugged. "Fine. But I can't understand why they would want to stay in Europe when they could come here."

Anna said, "I heard Mr. Paul telling somebody on the telephone that if he could be born again he would either choose France or northern Italy. He says Lake Como is the most beautiful place in the world."

"Bunk! Why doesn't he move there, then? The U.S.A. can get along without him, I'm sure."

"You don't have to be nasty about it!"

"I didn't mean to be. But talk like that makes me angry. People should be proud of this country and appreciate it. Especially a fellow like him, living in a house like this."

"He didn't mean anything, I'm sure." She spoke eagerly; she could almost hear the eagerness in her own voice. "But I suppose when you've always lived like this you take it for granted. You don't see how wonderful it is."

"Yes, after your family's put a fortune into your lap you can afford to take it for granted."

"Joseph, you're envious, that's all."

"Of course I am!" He leaned forward in the chair, all tense and tightly wound. "I'll tell you something. I hope the day will come

40

when my children will be able to take these things for granted. Only I hope they won't do it. I hope they'll have a little feeling for the father and the country that gave it all to them. Other than that, I don't care what they do, raise chickens, for all I care." He sighed. "Ah, when you have money you can do anything. Money is class and class is money, even in America. Because human nature is the same everywhere, and that's the truth."

"I suppose it is," she answered, not caring to hear his philosophy.

"Anna, are you really all right?"

"Yes," she said impatiently, "I told you I was."

"Would you tell me if anything were wrong? If you were sick or anything?"

"I would tell you, I promise." She stood up, went to the stove and took the kettle down for tea.

Last night in her room, while reading, she had come upon a word she did not know. She had looked it up in the dictionary. Obsession: persistent feeling which a person cannot escape. She thought now, pouring Joseph's tea, handing the plate of buns, clearing the table, moving dreamlike across the room, *Obsessed. I am obsessed.*

Anna was still working in his room when Paul Werner came home unexpectedly one Saturday before noon.

"I'm sorry," she said. "I'll hurry, I didn't know."

"That's all right! You didn't know I was coming back early," he said considerately. "Oh! You're interested in paintings?"

She had left one of the enormous books opened on the desk. "Excuse me! I only—"

"No, don't close it! What were you looking at? Monet?"

"This," she faltered. A walled and fruited garden. A woman in a summer dress. Sunlight without heat: cool, fragrant and cool.

"Ah yes, that's a marvel, isn't it? One of my favorites, too. Tell me, do you look at these often?"

Might as well tell the truth, come what may. And he was young, not stern like his mother; he would not be very angry.

"I look at that one especially. Every day."

"You do!" he said. "And why that one?"

"It makes me happy to look at it. To think that there is such a place."

"That's as good a reason as any. Would you like to borrow the

41

book, Anna? Take it to your room for a while? You're welcome to take it, or any book you like."

"Oh, thank you," she said, "oh, thank you very much." Her hands had begun to tremble. She was sure he could see the trembling and she clasped them behind her back.

"Don't thank me. Libraries are meant to be used. Here, take it now."

"I haven't finished sweeping the floor. Do you want me to finish?"

"Go ahead, I don't mind. I've a letter to write."

He sat down at the desk. She ran the carpet sweeper over the floor. Downstairs in the yard next door men were beating carpets hung over clotheslines. *Thwack! thwack!* they went, frightening the sparrows, raising spurts of dust in the chill sunny air.

"How is your young man?"

She looked up, startled.

"I said, how is your young man?"

"My what?"

"Your young man. My mother told me you have one. Is he a secret? Have I said something I shouldn't have said?"

"Oh, no! It's just that—he's only a friend. It would be too lonesome without any friends at all."

"I should think it would." He put the pen down. "Do you see him often?"

"Only on Sundays. On my day off he has to work."

"And which is your day off?"

He hadn't even noticed when she wasn't there. "I go out on Wednesdays."

"And where do you go when you go out?"

"Sometimes I visit my cousin downtown. Sometimes I walk in the park or go to the museum."

"You do! What museum do you go to?"

"The Natural History. Or the art museum. I like that the best."

"What do you like there?"

"It's so big, I haven't seen it all yet. But I liked the Egyptian things. . . . And last week I found Cleopatra's Needle out behind the building. I had missed it before."

He shook his head. "I'm thinking, Anna, how strange it is that here we've been living under the same roof for all these months and we've never talked until today!"

42

"Not so strange, when you think about it."

"You mean, because it's my parents' house and you just work in it."

She nodded.

"Isn't that artificial, though? Isn't that stupid? But thank goodness that sort of thing is changing. People make friends where they find them nowadays, not just in the same little group that their families grew up with. Much better that way, isn't it?"

"Oh, yes, much better!"

"Tell me something about yourself, Anna."

"I don't know what you want to hear."

"What your parents did, what your home was like, what made you leave it."

"But I can't now. I have to go downstairs, I have work."

"Next Saturday morning, then. Or whenever else we can find the time. Will you?"

They found the time, odd minutes of it, on Saturday mornings, or in the hallway after dinner—he standing in the doorway of his room, she standing by the staircase, whenever she happened to be going up or down on some errand or other. She told him about her village. He told her about their Adirondack camp. She told him about her father. He told her about Yale. She thought of their talk as a game, a ball going back and forth over a net. She was as breathless as though it had been a game. She sang as she went about the house, and had to catch herself. She laughed a lot and was aware of it.

One day halfway through spring, he said: "Tell your friend not to come next Sunday. I want to take you to tea."

"But I don't see how we can! I don't think—"

"What don't you think? I want to talk to you, to sit down and have a proper talk!"

She hesitated and felt a creeping fear.

"Nobody needs to know, if that's what you're worried about. Although there's nothing to hide! I'm not asking you to do anything to be ashamed of."

They sat on gilded chairs with a screen of palms at their backs. A waiter brought cakes on a little cart. Violins waltzed.

"You look really beautiful, Anna, especially in that hat."

He had insisted on buying the hat for her. When she had protested he had bought it anyway, a magnificent straw hat crowned with red silk poppies and wheat.

"I can't take it," she had said. "It wouldn't be right."

"Oh, damn the proprieties, how idiotic they are! Here am I, a man with plenty of money to spend, and here are you, a girl who needs a spring hat and hasn't got enough money for a nice one. Why shouldn't I make myself happy by giving it to you?"

"You make it sound so simple," Anna had said.

"It is simple. Take it and wear it to tea."

So here she sat, the greenhorn Anna, in this vast perfumed room, watching the people come and go, all the tall, easy, graceful people who belonged here.

"I've been thinking a lot about you, Anna. You're so young and already you've done so much with your life."

"What have I done? Nothing, it seems to me."

"But you have! You've taken your life into your own hands, coming across the world by yourself, learning a new language to get along in—"

"I've never thought about it like that."

"While I have only been acted upon. You see what I mean? I was born in the house where I live now; I was sent to school, then put into my father's, actually my grandfather's, business. It's all been done for me. I don't really know anything at all about what the world is like."

"That's what I think about myself!" Anna laughed.

"You are absolutely lovely when you laugh. I go all over the city, and do you know, I never see girls as lovely as you?"

"Why, right here this minute there are such beautiful girls! Look over there at that one with the yellow dress, and that one, coming through the door—"

"Not like you. You're different from them all. There's wonder in your face. You're alive. Most of these people wear a mask. They're tired of everything."

Tired of everything? How could that be? You would need to live a hundred years to see everything you wanted to see, and then that wouldn't be enough.

The orchestra struck up a charming, spritely dance. "How I love the sound of violins!" she cried.

"You've never been at the opera, have you, Anna?"

44

"No, never."

"My mother has a ticket for the matinee tomorrow, but we're all going to my Great-aunt Julia's funeral. I'm going to ask her to give it to you."

The music questions and insists. It asks *Where?* and answers *Here!* Asks *When?* and answers *Now!*

She leans forward in her seat. Two large ladies in the row ahead have dared to whisper. She taps one on the shoulder, mighty in her outrage.

"Will you be quiet, madam?"

Ashamed, they stop talking and she leans back again. The music swells and rises. The angelic voice of Isolde soars above it. All grief, all longing, all joy are in that radiant song. Tristram replies: the shimmering voices twine and fuse into one.

It is all here: the girl-child's ignorant dream of love and the passion of the woman. It is all here: flowers, sunlight, stars, rapture and death.

I know, I know, she thinks.

She does not move. Her hands are clasped.

It ends. The storm rests and the tension breaks. The final chords sound quietly and die.

Her eyes are wet; she cannot find her handkerchief. The tears fall on her collar. The great curtain falls and the marvelous beings who have pretended to be Tristram and Isolde come before it, bowing and smiling. Applause clatters, people stand to clap. In the rear young men are calling: "Bravo! Bravo!" People are twisting into their coat sleeves. And Anna sits there, unwilling to return from the Breton coast and the summer sea, from dying Tristram, the clasping arms—

The lady in the next seat is curious. "You liked it?"

"I—pardon?"

"I asked whether you liked it?"

"It was—it was heaven! I never imagined there could be—"

"Yes, it was a very fine performance." The lady agrees, nodding pleasantly, and steps out into the aisle.

In the evening Mr. and Mrs. Werner paid a condolence call and Mrs. Monaghan went to the basement to iron her Sunday shirtwaist. Anna climbed the stairs to her room. When she came to the landing at the floor below it seemed entirely natural that he should be waiting for her there.

She clung to him. The wall at her back, which was all that held up her weak legs, was warm and firm. The man was warm and firm, but soft, too; his mouth, wandering over her neck and face, was soft. Finding her mouth it fitted there with a long, long sigh.

Her eyes shut; things spun in a luminous dark.

He broke away. "You're so lovely, Anna! I can't tell you how beautiful you are."

She was dazed, re-entering the light. Gently, he guided her to the last flight of stairs. She thought, between fright and glory, that he was going upstairs with her.

"We must—you must go upstairs," he said gently, and went to his room.

She stood for a long time looking at herself in the mirror. She raised her nightgown. Statues in the museum had breasts like hers. At Cousin Ruth's she had seen women undressed; some had enormous, shapeless mounds; some sagged into long, flattened tubes; others had almost no breasts at all. She took the pins out of her hair, letting it slant across her forehead and fall over her shoulders. The hair felt warm on her bare shoulders. Music sounded in her head, a lovely flow, Isolde's song. He would not have kissed her like that if he did not love her. Now surely a great change had come into her life. A greater change was coming. Now surely.

From the yards below where the clotheslines ran from fence to fence came a wild, lonely cry, the wail of a lost child. Anna started. But then she thought, *It's only cats* and turning out the light, smiled into the darkness and fell asleep.

8

In the morning Mrs. Monaghan said, "Company tonight, you know. My niece Agnes will be coming to help. Just a family dinner, the madam says, but sounds fancy to me. Turtle soup, lobster mousse, lamb. She wants you to go up with her now to set the table."

The dining room glittered with crystal, lace and silver. Silver platters and candelabra. Silver bowls for the chocolates and the roses.

"Some of these pieces are almost two hundred years old," Mrs. Werner explained. "This coffeepot belonged to my great-great-grandmother Mendoza. See, here's the M."

"They brought all this from Europe?"

"No, this is American silver. My people came here from Portugal a hundred years before this was made."

"So different from me," Anna said.

"Not really, Anna. Just an accidental turn of history, that's all. People are the same everywhere." Mrs. Werner's rare smile softened her cool face.

There's something about her that's like Mama, Anna thought. I never noticed it before. Something dependable and strong. I would like to put my arms around her. It would be good to have a mother again. I wonder whether she knows anything?

Mrs. Werner was handsome in dark red silk. She had wonderful white shoulders for an old woman, over forty. The guests at the

47

table looked like a family: parents, a grandmother and two sisters about Anna's age. They had fair, freckled skin; their prominent, arched noses made their faces proud.

"I'd much rather go to Europe," one of the sisters said. She wore blue lawn and her long pearl earrings moved like little tassels.

"Still, a month in the White Mountains is so lovely, don't you think?" the grandmother remarked. "I always come back utterly exhausted from Europe."

Anna moved around the table, passing and repassing the silver platters, pouring ice water out of the silver pitcher. Be careful not to spill. That's Valenciennes lace on the grandmother's collar. Mrs. Monaghan told me about Valenciennes. I'm glad he's not looking at me. Shall I see him later?

Talk circled the table with Anna. Flashes of it sparked in her ears.

"The Kaiser is a madman, I don't care what they say—"

"I hear they've sold their place in Rumson—"

"This outrageous income tax, Wilson's a radical—"

"—bought the most magnificent brocade at Milgrim's."

"Ask Mrs. Monaghan and Agnes to come in, will you please, Anna?" Mr. Werner whispered.

She was not sure she had understood and he repeated it. "Then bring the champagne," he added.

He poured three extra glasses and handed them to Agnes, Mrs. Monaghan and Anna. Then he raised his own glass, and everyone waited.

"I don't know how to tell you how happy we are. So I'll just ask everyone to drink to the joy of this wonderful day in all our lives. To the future of our son Paul and to Marian, who will soon be our daughter."

The wine goblets touched, making chimes. Mr. Werner got up and kissed the cheeks of the girl in pale blue. The girl said something, very sweetly, very calmly, and made the others laugh. The laughter popped like champagne corks.

Mrs. Werner said, "Now I can confess that this is what we've been hoping for ever since you two were children."

Someone else said, "What a wonderful thing for our two families!"

And Mrs. Monaghan said, "The saints bless us, another wedding in this house!"

Only *he* had said nothing. He must have said something, though, something she hadn't heard. But it was all swimming, blurred and faint and far away—

Back in the pantry, Mrs. Monaghan whispered, "Anna! Go pass the cake for second helpings!"

Anna leaned against the cupboard. "The cake?"

"The walnut cake on the sideboard! What on earth is wrong with you?"

"I don't know. I'm going to be sick."

"Jesus, Mary and Joseph, but you do look green! Don't upchuck in my kitchen! Agnes, here take her apron and go back to the dining room. That's the girl! And you, Anna, get upstairs, I'll look to you later. What have you gone and done to yourself? Of all times!"

"You're feeling better this morning, Anna?" Mrs. Werner was troubled. "Mrs. Monaghan told me you wanted to leave. I couldn't believe it."

Anna struggled up in bed. "I know it isn't right to leave you so suddenly, but I don't feel well."

"You must let us call the doctor!"

"No, no, I can go to my cousin's house downtown. They'll get a doctor."

Mrs. Werner coughed lightly. The cough meant: *This is nonsense because both of us know what's the matter with you.* Or possibly it meant: *I can't imagine what's come over you but I am obligated to find out.*

"Is there anything you want to tell me, Anna?"

"Nothing. I'll be all right. It's nothing." No tears. No tears. *He kissed my mouth. He told me I was beautiful. And so I am, much more than she.*

"Well, then, I don't understand." Mrs. Werner's hands clasped the bed rail. Her diamonds went *prink! twink!* "Won't you talk to me, trust me? After all, I'm old enough to be your mother."

"But you're not my mother," Anna said. *An accidental turn of history, was it? People are the same, are they?*

"Well, I can't stop you if you've made up your mind. So when you're ready I'll have Quinn take you in the car." At the door Mrs. Werner paused. "If you ever want to come back, Anna, you'll be welcome. Or if there's anything we can do for you, call us, won't you?"

"Thank you, Mrs. Werner. But I won't come back."

*   *   *

On a damp night a few weeks later Joseph and Anna sat on the front stoop talking. The sun was down. In the last light boys played a final game of stickball on the street. One by one their mothers called them in with long, shrill cries: Benn-ie, Loo-ey! Peddlers led their tired nags back to the stables on Delancey Street, the shaggy heads sunk, the shaggy hooves trudging. The life of the street ebbed away.

They talked about this and that, fell silent and talked again. After a while Joseph told Anna that he loved her. He asked her whether she would marry him. And she answered that she would.

9

He worshiped her. His eyes and his hands moved over her body and worshiped her. In the new brass double bed which he had bought he raised himself on his elbow and studied her.

"Pink and white," he said. He twisted a length of her hair around his wrist, her slippery, living hair. He laughed and shook his head in wonder. "Perfect. Even your voice and the way you pronounce 'th.' Perfect."

"I'll never speak English without a foreign accent. A greenhorn, I am."

"And you've read more, you're more clever than anybody I know."

"Just a greenhorn, Joseph," she insisted.

"If you'd had a chance at an education, half a chance, you could have been something, a teacher, even a doctor or a lawyer. You could."

Sighing, she stretched out her hand, the one with the wide gold band on which he had had engraved 'J to A, May 16, 1913.' "I'm a wife," she said aloud.

"How do you feel about it?"

She did not answer at once. He followed her gaze through the door to the yellow-painted kitchen and the clean, new linoleum on the parlor floor. Everything was clean in the home he had prepared for her. Unfortunately, the rooms were level with the street so that the shades had to be drawn all day. When you raised the shades you could see feet passing on the street, at eye level. You could crane out to see the Hudson and the Palisades, and feel the fresh river wind. At night the bedroom was a closed private world, the bed a ship on a dark quiet sea.

"How do you feel about it?" he repeated. This time she turned to him and laid her hands lightly over his. "I feel peaceful," she said.

She stretched and yawned, covering her mouth. Ten chimes struck delicately from the clock on Joseph's dresser.

"Pompous, silly thing," Anna cried.

"What, the clock? I don't know what you've got against that beautiful clock. You just don't like the people who gave it to us."

One day, a few months after their marriage, a delivery man had brought a package from Tiffany.

"He looked puzzled," Anna said. "I don't suppose he's ever delivered in this neighborhood before."

It was a gilded French mantel clock. Joseph had placed it carefully on the kitchen table and wound it. Through the glass sides they had watched its exquisite rotating gears and wheels.

"I knew the Werners were going to give us a present," he had said. "I wasn't to tell you, but they sent their chauffeur down to Ruth's to ask about your health and she told him we were married. Aren't you pleased? You don't seem pleased."

"I'm not," she had answered.

"I can't understand," he remarked now, "why you resent those people so. It's not like you, you're always so kind."

"I'm sorry. Yes, it was good of them to do. But it's too rich for this house. We've no place to put it, even."

"True. But we'll have a better place someday. Good enough for this and your silver candlesticks, too."

"Joseph, don't strain so much, don't work so hard. I'm satisfied the way we are now."

"Satisfied with a basement flat on Washington Heights?"

"It's the best place I've ever lived in."

"What about the Werner house?"

"I didn't really *live* there. It wasn't mine."

"Well, it ought to be. That's the way I want you to live. You will live like that, too. You'll see, Anna."

"It's after ten," she chided him softly. "And you have to be up by five."

*   *   *

52

Anna's breathing whispered in the dark. She moved her legs and the sheet rustled. Footsteps hurried, clacking on the sidewalk only a few feet from his head. The little clock went *ting!* eleven times. There was no sleep in him, only a rush of thoughts, sharp and clear, one after the other, clear as etching on glass.

He worried. It seemed to him that as far back as he could recall he had always known worry. His parents worried. All the people in the houses on Ludlow Street, all the way over to the East River, worried. They worried about today and tomorrow. They even worried about yesterday. They were never able to let yesterday die.

Naturally, he had never seen the Old Country, yet he knew it well. It was a landscape of his life as surely as the street and the five-story tenements, the crowds and the pushcarts. He knew the Polish village, his grandfather's horse, the frozen walls of snow, the sliding mud, the bathhouse, the cantor who came from Lublin for the holidays, the herring and potatoes on the table, his mother's baby sister who died in childbirth, his grandmother's cousin who went to Johannesburg and made a fortune in diamonds. He knew all these, as well as the terror of hooves on the road and the whistle of whips, the heavy breathing in the silence behind closed shutters, the rush of flames when a torch is put to a roof and the sigh of ashes settling in the morning breeze.

The burning of Uncle Simon's house had been the act that decided his parents. They were a strange couple, still without children, so without reason for living, no? (What else is there to live for but to have children and push them up, healthy and learned, to a region higher than your own? That's what it's all about, isn't it?) But they had none, and his mother grew old before her time. Not fat and old from birthing and nurturing, but dry-old, pinched-old, empty-old. She had a stall in the market, and was known for her charity. His father was a tailor with round shoulders and red eyelids. He sighed as he worked, unaware that he was sighing. When he put his machine away he went to the synagogue. When he had said his prayers he went home. Tailor shop, synagogue and home, the triangle of his days. Why should such a pair bother to go to America? For what?

Then came the burning and something galvanized the husband.

"Your father came in," his mother said. "The village was quiet. They had burned five houses, not ours, but it was an awful thing to see your neighbors, the women crying and the men just standing there, looking. So your father came in and he said, 'We are going to America, Katie.' Just like that he said it, and no more than that."

"Did you want to come? Were you scared?" Joseph used to ask.

"It was all so fast, I didn't have time to think. We got our tickets, I said good-by to my sisters, and we were at Castle Garden."

"And then what happened, Ma?"

"What happened?" Her eyebrows went up, rising in a semicircle under her stiff and fading wig. "As you see, we opened a tailor shop. We ate, we lived. The only difference was that here everybody was all jumbled up, without grass, without trees." For an instant there was slight regret in her voice. "Also no pogroms, no killing and burning."

"And that was all?" Joseph used to press, waiting for the next part, the important part.

His mother played along. "Of course all! What else should there be?"

"I mean, nothing else happened to you after you came here?"

His mother would frown a moment, pretending to be puzzled. "Oh, yes, of course, one other thing! We were here two years—a little more, actually—when you were born."

Joseph would stifle a smile of pleasure. When he was very young, at seven or eight, he liked to hear this part. Later, whenever the subject of his birth arose, he would frown and wince inside, would change the subject or leave the room. There was something ridiculous in such old people having their first, totally unexpected child. He was the only one of his friends who had parents like his; more like grandparents, they seemed. The other boys had thin agile fathers and mothers, who moved about the streets quickly, yelling and running after their children.

His father, heavy and slow-moving, sat all day behind the sewing machine. When he stood up he was stiff, he moved awkwardly, grunting and shuffling to the back rooms where they ate and slept, and to the toilet in the yard. On Saturday he shuffled to the synagogue, came home and ate, lay down again on the cot in the kitchen and slept the afternoon away.

"Shh!" Ma would admonish when Joseph banged the door,

"Your father's asleep!" And her warning finger would go to her lips.

At night Pa would move from the cot to the bed where he slept with Ma. Where they would—? No, not decent to think about that. You couldn't imagine him doing— He was so quiet. Except now and then when he fell into a terrible rage, always over some trivial thing. His face would flame, the cords stand out on his temples and in his neck. Ma said that someday he would kill himself like that, which was exactly what happened. Much later, of course.

The house smelled of sleep, of dullness and poverty. There was no *life* in it, no future. You felt that what had already been done there was all that ever would be done. Joseph spent as few hours there as he could.

"What, going out again?" Pa would ask, shaking his head. "You're always out."

"A boy needs companions, Max." His mother defended him. "And as long as we know he's in good company— He only goes to play at the Baumgartens' or over to your own cousin Solly."

Solly Levinson was a second or third cousin of Pa's, only five years older than Joseph. Joseph could remember him in that first brief year after his arrival in this country at the age of twelve, that first and only year when he went to school, before he began to work in the garment trade. He had learned English astonishingly quickly; he was bright and timid, or perhaps only gentle and hesitant. Strange how he metamorphosed after five children and fifteen years of working on pants! As different from what he had been as the caterpillar is from the butterfly. Strange and sad and wrong, Joseph thought, remembering Solly teaching him to dive in the East River, Solly playing stickball, wiry and fast. He had come from a very rural place in Europe, had swum in rivers, had known how to move and run. Such a brightness in him! And now all quenched.

Anyway, Joseph had liked to go to Solly's. The rest of the time he lived on the street.

His father complained. The streets were dangerous, full of bad influences. He heard his parents talking, often in his presence, more often from behind the drawn curtain that separated his cot in the kitchen from their bed in the back room.

"Bad influences," his father said again. Gloom and foreboding. Joseph knew he was talking about the boys who had gone socialist and worse, the boys who stood in knots on the sidewalk, lounging on the synagogue steps to taunt the worshipers, even smoking on the Sabbath, while the old men with their derby hats and beards looked the other way.

"Joseph is a good boy," his mother said. "You don't have to worry about him, Max."

"Show me a mother who doesn't say her son is a good boy."

"Max! What does he ever do that's bad? Be sensible!"

"True, true." Silence. And then he would hear, how many times had he not heard? "I wish we could do more for him."

Now Joseph understood, but even then when he was a child he had begun to understand, to pick up truths about his parents and the life around him. He knew that his father, like most of the fathers, was ashamed of doing even worse for his family in America than he had done in Europe. He was ashamed of not speaking the language, so that when the gas man came to ask a question about the meter, an eight-year-old son had to interpret. Ashamed of the meager food on the table toward the end of the month when the money was being scrimped together for the rent. Ashamed of the noise, the jumbled living in the midst of crowds and other people's scandals. The Mandels upstairs, the terrible screaming fights and Mr. Mandel leaving, disappearing 'uptown,' Mrs. Mandel's bitter weeping and scolding. Why should a decent family be subjected to the indecencies of others? Yet there was no escape from it.

The father was ashamed too of the dirt. He hated it. From him Joseph knew he had inherited his extreme love of cleanliness and order. For a man to love those things in a place where there was little cleanliness and no order!

They used to go to the baths together once a week, Pa and Joseph. In a way the child dreaded it, the smell of the steam and the press of naked men. How ugly old bodies were! And yet, in another way, it was the only time they ever talked together, really talked, there in the steam and later on the five blocks' walk home.

Sometimes he was subjected to homilies: "Do right, Joseph. Every man knows what right is and he knows too when he has done something dishonest or unjust. He may tell others and himself that he doesn't know, but he does know. Do right and life will reward you."

"But sometimes wicked people are rewarded too, aren't they, Pa?"

"Not really. It may seem so on the surface, but not really."

"What about the Czar? How cruel he is, and yet he lives in a palace!"

"Ah, but he hasn't lived his life out yet!"

Joseph considered that doubtfully. His father said with firmness, "When you do wrong, you pay. Maybe not right away, but you always pay." And then he said, "Would you like a banana? I've a penny here, and you can buy two at the corner. One for your mother."

"What about you, Pa?"

"I don't like bananas," his father lied.

When Joseph was ten Pa's sight went bad. First he had to hold the paper very far away. Then after a while he wasn't able to read it at all. Joseph's mother had never learned to read. In the Old Country it wasn't essential for a girl to learn, although some did, of course. So Joseph had to read the paper in the evening, because his father wanted to know what was going on in the world. But it was difficult; Joseph didn't read Yiddish very well and he knew his father wasn't satisfied.

For a while Pa had struggled on in the tailoring shop, hunching lower and lower in the yellow flame from the gaslight, for even at noon the daylight was shut out by the fire escapes outside the window. When it was evident that he could work no more they had closed the shop and his mother became the unacknowledged breadwinner.

The store was the square "front room," with the counter running across the back and the large brown icebox standing at one side. In the two rear rooms separated by a dark green cloth curtain, they lived, their arrangements the same as they had been in the tailor shop two blocks away. The kitchen table was covered with oilcloth once blue, now a spoiled gray. Here they ate and here his mother made the potato salad and the coleslaw that went into the brown refrigerator in the store along with the soda bottles and the milk. Bread was stacked on the counter; coffee, sugar and spices stood on the shelves; crackers and candy were in boxes and barrels on the floor, along with the pickles floating in their scummy brine. A bell jangled when the door was opened. In the summer you didn't hear the bell because the screen door's spring was broken. His father never knew how to fix anything, so the door hung open. Curving bands of yellow flypaper hung from the ceiling fixture, and huge black flies collected on it, disgusting flies, black and wet when they were squashed, bred in the horsedroppings on the street. . . . Strange that his father, who was so fastidious, didn't seem to mind them, Joseph thought, until he realized that the old man didn't see them.

From six o'clock in the morning until ten at night his mother stood behind the counter. Not that they were so busy; it was just that one never knew when someone might come in to buy. Sometimes the jangling bell would ring past ten at night.

"Oh, Mrs. Friedman, I saw the light, I hope it's not too late. We're out of coffee."

For the neighborhood it was a convenience, a place where one could go at odd hours to pick up something one had forgotten, after the markets had closed and the pushcarts were covered with tarpaulins and guarded for the night. A small convenience. A small living.

'Max Friedman,' read the sign above the door. It should have read, 'Katie Friedman.' Even at the age of ten Joseph was able to understand the tragedy in that.

He had a snapshot of himself sitting in front of the store, the first picture taken of him since his infant portrait when he lay naked on the photographer's fur rug. He was twelve years old, in knickers and cap, high shoes and long black stockings.

"How solemn you were!" Anna said when she saw it. "You look as though you had the weight of the world on your shoulders."

Not the weight of the world, but a great one, nevertheless. For that was the year when he went from childhood to adult knowledge in one night. Well, make it two or three nights, at the most.

Wolf Harris came into the store one day where Joseph was helping after school. He was some very remote relative of Solly's on the other side of Solly's family. He was eighteen and aptly named. His nose was thin; his large mouth was always drawn back in a scornful smile.

"Want to make some money, kid? Mr. Doyle wants a kid to run messages for him."

"Doyle?" Pa had come from his chair next to the stove. "Why should Mr. Doyle need my son?"

"Because. He needs a boy he can trust to deliver stuff on time, not to lose things. He'll give him a dollar and a half a week to come in after school every day."

A dollar and a half! But Doyle was rich, Doyle was from Tammany Hall. He was Power, Government, Authority. Nobody knew exactly what he did, but they did know you could go to him for anything. He had no prejudice. Astonishing America, where the government didn't care whether you were Chinese, Hungarian or Jewish! If you needed money for a funeral or a ton of coal or somebody in the family was in trouble, you could ask Doyle and he would take care of it. All you had to do in return was to mark the square he told you to mark on election day.

Pa went inside and Joseph heard his parents talking for a minute or two. Then Pa came back.

"Tell Mr. Doyle," he said to Wolf, "that my son will be happy to work for him and we thank him, his mother and I."

Doyle had a dignified office near Tammany Hall on Fourteenth Street. Every day after school Joseph went over through the front room where a row of girls sat at their typing machines and down the corridor to the back where he knocked and was admitted. Doyle was bald and ruddy. He had a stickpin in his tie and a ring on his finger which Wolf said was a real sapphire, "worth a fortune." He liked to joke. He would offer Joseph a cigar or pretend to hand him a coin: "Go down to Tooey's Bar and get yourself a beer." And then he would always give a treat, an apple or a chocolate bar, before sending him on his errands.

Doyle owned a lot of property. He owned two houses on the street where Joseph lived, as a matter of fact. Sometimes Joseph had to deliver papers to plumbers or tinsmiths and others having to do with Doyle's houses. Sometimes he had to take envelopes to saloons, or pick up papers there that felt thick, as though there might be money inside. He learned to go right in at the front door and ask for the proprietor, who was usually behind the bar, behind the bar with the glittering bottles and the painting of a naked lady. The first time he saw a painting like that his eyes almost popped out. The men at the bar saw what he was looking at and thought it was very funny. They told jokes that he didn't understand, and he felt uncomfortable. But it was worth it. A dollar and a half! Just for walking around the city carrying envelopes!

One day Mr. Doyle asked to see his handwriting. He got a sheet of paper and said, "Now, write something, anything, I don't care what."

When Joseph had written very neatly, *Joseph Friedman, Ludlow Street, New York, United States of America, Western Hemisphere, World, Universe,* Doyle took the paper away and said, "Very nice, very nice . . . how are you on arithmetic?"

"It's my best subject."

"Is it, now! Well, what do you know! How would you like to do a bit of writing and arithmetic for me? Would you like that, you think?"

And as Joseph looked puzzled, he said, "Here, I'll show you. See these two ledgers? Brand new, nothing written in them? I'll show you what I want. I want you to copy down in these from the lists that I'll give you. See here, a list like this, with names and doll—numbers, never mind what it's for, you don't need to go into all that. . . . Just copy all the names in this ledger with these numbers, see? And then put the same names in the other ledger with these other numbers, see? Think you can do it?"

"Oh, sure, sir, I can do it. That's easy."

"It's important to be accurate, you understand. Take your time. I don't want any mistakes."

"Oh, no, sir, I won't make any mistakes."

"Good. So that's what you'll be doing from now on. You'll work at the desk all by yourself in that little room next to mine, and nobody'll bother you. When you're finished you'll hand the ledgers back to me. And Joseph, one other thing. You're a good religious boy, aren't you? I mean, you go to synagogue regularly, don't tell lies?"

"No, sir, I mean yes, sir, and I don't tell lies."

"You know God punishes you when you do wrong."

"That's what Pa says."

"Of course. Then I can depend on you to keep your word. Never to talk about what you write in the books. Never to mention the books to anybody at all. It's just between you and me. Government business, you understand."

Doyle was very pleased with him. Wolf told him so. And one

day when Doyle was in the neighborhood he came into the store and talked to his parents.

"Your son's a very smart boy. Dependable, too. A lot of kids, you can't count on them. They say they'll come to work, then they go play ball or loaf around and forget."

"Joseph's a good boy," Pa said.

"What do you plan to do with him? What's he going to be?"

His father shrugged. "I don't know. He's young yet. He should stay in school, maybe go to college. But we have no money."

"He'd make a topnotch accountant. And there's always money around for a smart boy like him. When the time comes, I'll see that he gets a chance. He could go to N.Y.U. Just tell him to stick with me."

"Could be only nice talk," his mother remarked that evening. "To make the parents feel good, telling them what a fine boy they have."

But Wolf said otherwise. "He thinks a lot of you, he means it. He wants you to study accounting. He can do it, too. He can get anything done, lay his hands on money whenever he needs it."

Joseph was curious about what Wolf did for Doyle. There were always so many people around Doyle, you could never figure out what they all did. Some were connected with the police and fire departments, others had to do with building inspections or the courts, with Doyle's real estate or with elections, a maze of businesses and interests. Wolf lived with an older brother; he always wore good clothes and had cash in his pocket. But you would never ask Wolf about anything personal. There was a distance between him and you. It was hard to say why; there was just something that put you at a distance.

Joseph had a best friend, Benjie Baumgarten. They walked to school together and back, went to the synagogue on the Sabbath and sat together and confided everything in one another. Benjie was curious about Wolf and Doyle.

"What do you do for him?" he pressed.

"Run errands. And write records."

"What sort of errands? And what do you write?"

"It's confidential. Business," Joseph said importantly.

"Oh, you dumb ass! Sure, private business with the Governor, I'll bet. Or the President, maybe."

61

"No, really." Benjie was envious, of course. Joseph could afford to be tolerant, lofty. "I'd tell you if I could, but I promised. You wouldn't want me to break a promise to you, would you?"

"No . . ."

They were crouched on the cellar stairs in number eleven, an abandoned building down the street from Joseph's house. The house had been condemned and the tenants had all moved out, except for some tramps, who, everybody knew, slept in the basement to get out of the cold.

Benjie had brought a plug of chewing tobacco which they were trying for the first time. This was a good place to avoid being seen.

"The sign says keep out—penalty of the law," Benjie said. "What'll happen if the owner catches us?"

"Nothing. Mr. Doyle is the owner, if you want to know. Well, a part-owner anyway. He wouldn't mind." Joseph felt important.

So they were hiding under the stairs, feeling faintly nauseated and neither one willing to admit it to the other, when the door in the yard creaked open and a wedge of late afternoon light appeared. Wolf Harris came in, carrying a can.

They drew back, making no sound. The can was filled with some liquid, which Wolf poured out as he moved around among the empty boxes, piled newspapers and broken baby carriages. When he had emptied the can he went softly out and closed the door. The fumes of kerosene rose up the staircase.

"Now why do you suppose he did that?" Benjie whispered. "I'm going out to ask him."

"You shut up!"

"Why should I!"

"Because. Wolf told me never to talk to him unless he talked to me first. Not to speak to him on the street, especially when he was with somebody else."

"That's funny. I wonder why?"

"I never asked him."

"You scared of him?"

"Yeah, a little."

"He's got a fierce temper, Wolf has. Once I saw him beat up a guy and break his nose. The blood came like water out of a pump."

"You never told me!"

"Well, it happened!"

"I believe you."

"Why do you work for Doyle?"

"What's Doyle got to do with what we're talking about?"

"Nothing. I just wondered."

"Because we need the money, stupid!" He wasn't going to mention anything about the accountancy course. Benjie might get the idea and horn in on it. Friend or no friend.

"Wolf scares me," Benjie said irrelevantly.

"Oh, shut up, will you!"

Joseph felt suddenly uneasy. The tobacco juice puckered his mouth. "I'm going home," he said.

The fire sirens woke him during the night, they and the noise of the crowd in the street. He and his parents got up and went outside. Number eleven down the block was blazing. Smoke, blown by the wind from the East River, stretched in ribbons across the sky. Flames exploded like rockets inside the tenement. Their light went surging from the first floor to the second, to the third. On the third floor faces appeared at the windows; arms moved in anguish.

"Tramps!" Ma cried. "My God, the house is full of tramps and they can't get out!"

Of course. In the winter, most people puttied the windows shut to keep out the cold.

"Oh, my God," Pa said.

The fire burned all night. Its flames warmed the night air all down the street. The water from the fire hoses froze on the sidewalks. The fire horses neighed at the flames and stamped their huge feet. Toward morning the fire burned out. The interior of the building had been hollowed; the blackened stone front was a jagged ruin. There were seven known dead. The crowds came silently to stare.

Joseph was very quiet. All day at school he turned things over in his mind: to tell Pa first and then Mr. Doyle? Or to go straight to Doyle? He wanted to talk it over with Benjie but Benjie had not come to school that morning.

On the way home at three o'clock Benjie hailed him. "I went over to see your boss this morning, Joseph."

"You went to see Mr. Doyle?"

"I told him I knew who set the fire. I told him about Wolf and the kerosene."

"Did you tell him I was with you?" Joseph demanded.

"Oh," Benjie said, "I'm sorry. I didn't. I guess I wanted to take all the credit myself."

Well, he had no one to blame but himself. Why hadn't he thought of staying out of school today and running over to Mr. Doyle's? Then Wolf would be arrested and Joseph would have been the hero instead of Benjie. Slow, like Pa. Old-fashioned. Let everybody get ahead of me. I don't think fast.

"I can't understand the whole thing," Benjie puzzled. "I thought Wolf and Mr. Doyle were thick. So why would Wolf want to burn the man's house down? Can you figure it out?"

"Oh, hell," Joseph said, brushing past Benjie.

He was still puzzling things over at breakfast the next morning, sore and silent, angry at Benjie and most of all at himself, when Mrs. Baumgarten appeared at the curtain to their kitchen.

"I'm sorry to bother you but I thought you might know where Benjie is? He didn't come home last night."

"I saw him yesterday after school," Joseph said.

Mrs. Baumgarten began to cry. "What can have happened to him?"

Joseph's mother spoke comfort. "He's probably staying with a friend, that's all, and didn't tell you."

"Where? What friend? Why would he do that?"

"Don't worry, nothing's happened to him, I'm sure."

But something had happened. Benjie's body was pulled out of the river on the following Saturday afternoon. The police came to the synagogue looking for someone to come and identify it. Joseph's father shouted to him not to go but he pretended not to hear and went along with the crowd. Afterward he was sorry he had gone. They had killed Benjie with an ice pick and fish had eaten away a part of his face.

Joseph walked back home. People pulled at him with questions, whispering as people do. But he couldn't talk, just walked on past the burnt-out tenement. It was said that the insurance had already been collected. All of a sudden the boy, just twelve years old that summer, saw and understood the whole thing. He went into his parents' store, pushed open the curtain and sat down on the cot next to the stove. All of a sudden he was old; it seemed to him that he had just learned all there was to know about life. That people will do anything, that people will kill for money.

He began to cry. His father and mother came over and sat one on each side of him. They put their arms around his shoulders and sat there with him, not speaking. They thought he was crying for his friend, and of course he was, but also he was crying for much more, for his father's innocence and his own lost innocence, for everything that was dirtied and ruined in the world . . .

He never spoke to Wolf again, making sure that Wolf would never see him. Wolf wasn't around too much on this street, anyhow. It was said that he owned a fancy suit and went to dinner at Rectors with millionaires and Diamond Jim Brady. Another world.

He never saw Doyle again, either, except once to go and tell him, trembling inwardly, that his mother was in need of help at the store and he couldn't work for him anymore. For a long time he wondered, and in a way still did wonder, how you could reconcile the kindness of Doyle, the undoubted kindness (just for votes? just for power and votes?) with all these other things. . . . That would be what some might call the gray area. Well, he didn't believe it; to him nothing was gray. It was black or it was white. You make it too simple, a man said once years later over beer, a learned Russian man who wrote for a newspaper: things are never that simple. Perhaps not, but Joseph preferred simplicity. He was at ease with it. Black or white. Good or bad. That's why religion was a comfort. It gave you the rules of the game, the signposts on the road. You knew where to go. You couldn't go wrong.

For two years his father kept asking him why he wouldn't go back to work for Mr. Doyle when there was such good opportunity in it for him. But he could not, he would not, explain. Perhaps if his father had had more time he would eventually have got the truth out of him. Perhaps. But he didn't have more time. He dropped dead a few months later after a silly argument with the milkman who had left the milk to sour in the sun. *Worked himself into a rage over a few bottles of milk,* his mother said afterward, shaking her head, mourning. But Joseph knew it had not been the milk that had caused his father to stand there, shaking his helpless fists until the cords stood out on his temples, turning his blind eyes toward the flaring, angry light; knew that it might just as well have been a nail or a penny or a scrap of dust that turned on Pa's bitter rage because the world was not what he wanted it to be, what it could be and what it never had been for him. Joseph understood all that. He was not quite fifteen years old.

*　　*　　*

"Your father wanted you to go to college," Ma said.

They were on the roof where he was helping her hang up the wash. In four directions the tenement roofs stretched like a prairie, a network of clotheslines, chimney pots and iron cornices. Beyond to the east were the river, factory chimneys and the flung arch of the Brooklyn Bridge. Farther north and out of sight were Fifth Avenue, mansions, banks and churches. He had been there once and never forgotten them. They too were New York. The real New York.

"I'm not a scholar, Ma," he said.

She pressed hopefully. She was always pressing him, not too hard but ceaselessly. Join the debating club, make a name. There's a city-wide contest, you might win. Mrs. Siegel's son goes to law school at night. You're a smart boy, what are you going to do, stay in the grocery store? Is that what we came to America for?

He wanted to say, *You certainly didn't come for my benefit, you didn't know you were going to have me.* . . . But instead he said, "Even if I wanted to we haven't got the money. We need what I make."

Right after high school he had got a job with a painting contractor. Now, after two years, he was quite skilled and, through working in the tenements alongside other trades, he had picked up some knowledge of carpentry and plumbing as well.

"You could go at night. And I manage in the store. We could manage."

"Ma, I don't want to be a lawyer."

"But Mrs. Siegel's son—"

"Yes, and the Riesners' two sons are doctors and Moe Myerson teaches high school. . . . But I'm not Siegel, I'm not Myerson or Riesner. I'm Joseph Friedman."

His mother started to pick up the clothes basket. He took it from her. She was so old, so much older since Pa died, as if it was an effort to live. His heart ached and he was sorry that he had spoken sharply.

"So tell me, what does Joseph Friedman want to be?"

"Joseph Friedman wants to make money and take care of his mother so she won't have to keep a grocery store."

She smiled. It was a small smile, faintly sad. "It's not easy to make money without a profession."

"That's where you're wrong." He spoke eagerly. "My boss, Mr. Block, started as an ordinary painter and now look at him! He gets the work from all the banks that own property on the lower East Side. Well, a lot of them anyway. His family lives uptown on Riverside Drive. And he did it all simply by working hard and planning and he's still a pretty young man."

"So that's what you want to do? Be a contractor?"

"Ma, I know you'd be terribly proud for me to be a doctor or a lawyer or something and the fact is I have a lot of respect for men like that. It's just not me, that's all. Tell you what, I'll make money and my sons will be doctors and you can be proud of them."

"I won't live to see your sons."

"Please, Ma!"

"I'm sorry. It's just that there's more to life than money. A man wants to be proud of what he does, to use the mind God gave him. Then, if he makes money, that's wonderful too, of course one needs money, but—"

Round and round. One needs money, one wants to pretend it isn't important, one tries to get it while all the time pretending that one isn't trying to get it. I have no time for that, my children will afford that luxury. I'll see that they can afford it.

"I have a chance to work uptown," he said carefully. He had waited a week before getting up the courage to tell her. "Mr. Block has made connections uptown. On Washington Heights. There's a man named Malone who works for him and they want to start a crew uptown. I'd have to live up there."

She did not look at him. He knew that she had always expected this moment of separation and had prepared herself, no doubt, for a long time past. She said quietly, "You want to go?"

"Yes. Well, I mean, I don't *want* to leave you, but it's a good chance. He's offered me fifteen dollars a week, believe it or not. . . . Well, I give him a day's work and more besides and he knows it."

"I'm sure you do."

"I'd come back down and see you every week and send you half of what I make. I want to see you get out of that store."

"I don't mind that store. What else would I do with my time?"

"You don't mind my going, then?"

"No, no, go and be well. Only one thing . . . Joseph?"

"Yes, Ma?"

"You won't lose your faith, going uptown? Living up there mostly with Gentiles, I suppose?"

"There are plenty of Jews, too, and I'd rent a room with a Jewish family, of course. But a man's faith is inside him, he takes it wherever he goes. You needn't worry about that."

She took his free hand between hers. "No. I know I don't have to worry about that."

She was still in the store. He sent her money every week, brought more whenever he came to see her, but he saw no signs that she used any of it. She wore the cheap cotton dresses sold from the pushcarts and to the synagogue she wore the same black dress she had worn when he was a small boy. He suspected that she saved everything he gave her and would someday, at her death, return it all to him. A vast lonely sadness filled him when he thought about her. She was sixty-three and looked much older. More than once he had urged her to sell the store and move uptown to the Heights. But she would not. She had made one great move in her lifetime, across the ocean, had put down a few tentative roots on Ludlow Street and that was enough.

The only thing she seemed to want was for him to be married. One day a year or so after he had moved uptown he had come back to see her and found a visitor sitting at the table in the kitchen, a bearded middle-aged man in a creased black suit. A briefcase lay on the table.

"My son Joseph," his mother said. "Reb Jeselson."

A matchmaker. A flash of anger went through Joseph. He stood rigidly, without acknowledgment.

"Your mother tells me you want to get married."

"I do?"

"Reb Jeselson came by, we happened to meet and we got talking," his mother interposed. There was alarm in her eyes. "And I happened to mention that I had a son, it just came about quite accidentally and he asked, Well, does he know any nice girls, would he like to meet any? And I said, I suppose he knows some girls, of course he must, but I suppose he might want to meet some more, so if you happen to know any nice girls. . . . After all, a man can never know too many!" she said with gaiety, as if they were joking at a party.

Reb Jeselson removed a folder from the briefcase, spreading half a dozen photos on the table.

"Of course we shall have to talk, you and I. You'll tell me what you have in mind. For instance, do you want an American-born girl or one from the Old Country? I'm sure you want a religious girl, I know something about your background," he murmured. "No, not that one, she's a very fine young woman," removing one of the photographs, "only the problem is she's so tall, taller than most young men. You wouldn't want to look up to a wife, now, would you? Let me see, now here's a girl from a wonderful family—"

"I'm really not interested," Joseph said firmly. And, softening at his mother's look of dismay, "Some other time. I didn't expect you today. I wasn't prepared—"

Reb Jeselson waved him aside. "No obligation. None at all. I only want an idea of what's on your mind. Then we'll make another appointment at your convenience, no hurry—"

"But you see," Joseph said desperately, "you see, I already have a girl. So I'm really not interested at all, thanks just the same."

Reb Jeselson turned reproachfully to Joseph's mother. "You didn't tell me! And I went to all this trouble!"

"I didn't know!" she cried. "Joseph, you didn't tell me. Why didn't you tell me?"

"I didn't know until just now myself," he said.

They both stared at him as though he had gone crazy, as though he were an idiot or a fool.

Anna. Anna, white-and-pink. A flower on a tall stem in a garden. He had never seen a real garden, yet in some way he knew what it would be like. Fragrant and cool and moist. He hadn't thought he was ready to be married yet; actually he had planned to wait until he was older, thirty perhaps, and well on his way before he encumbered himself. But now it seemed that he was ready, after all. Almost from the first time he had seen her sitting on the steps, reading some learned book in English, and she not a year off the boat!

Her voice, her little feet in kid boots, her sweet-smelling hair, her pretty laugh. The funny, serious way she talked about things. A girl from a village in Poland, and she knew about painters in Paris and writers in England and musicians in Germany! How did she keep it all in that proud, bright head! Oh, Pa would have been pleased with her! He smiled. Pa wouldn't have had the faintest idea what she was talking about, he would have known less than I, and that's little enough. But he would have known quality when he saw it.

Again she stirred in the bed beside him and murmured something in her sleep. He wondered what she might be dreaming, and hoped it was no pain or sorrow. He knew so little about her. Lying there in the dark, he thought how separate they were after all: is it always so? Oh, surely not! Surely if she needed him as he did her they would come together. . . . He knew that her need, her love, were not like his. But they had been married so short a time, only a few months. He could be patient. They would have a child and that itself would draw them nearer. Yes, they would have a child: perhaps one was already on the way? In the powerful surge and release when they came together surely there was the creation of a child? Such feelings must result in something; wasn't that what life was all about?

His body began to grow light under the covers. His mind began to blur. He thought: now, now I'm falling asleep. Keen thought lost its edge; his mind began to float in a lustrous mist, a wash of shifting shapes and color, red ovoids, lavender spirals, columns of cream and silver rising like smoke. Then a curtain fell, dark foliage of dreams, and through the dusky green a spray of gilded dots, confetti dots. No, coins they were, golden coins, and when he reached out his hand they fell through his fingers and into his palm: not hard, not metal at all, but soft like rain, a soft, protecting rain to wash over Anna and his mother and his father. No, no, he thought, it is too late for my father and soon will be too late for my mother. But for Anna, over Anna, the warm and lovely golden rain must fall.

By midnight he was asleep.

10

They stood modestly back to back in the women's bathhouse until their bathing suits were on, black taffeta skirts, black stockings, slippers and straw bonnet tied under the chin so the breeze couldn't blow it away. Anna had never worn a bathing suit before; her legs, except for the stockings, were uncovered to the knees and she felt ashamed to go out in public like that. But she would not have admitted it to Ruth, who had been often at the beach and was very sure of herself.

"See, I told you the suit would look fine!" Ruth said. "You don't show at all, and the baby due so soon! As for me, I always look like an elephant when I'm expecting. Come, we'll find a good spot before the crowds arrive, that's the best thing about getting here early," she went on, as they lifted their feet through the heavy sand.

Solly and Joseph had already spread the blankets. Harry and Irving, big boys of nine and ten, knobby like their father in maroon striped suits, were already in the water. The little girls had shovels and pails.

"Ah, there you are!" Joseph cried. His expression, that no one else would have noticed, told Anna that she looked very fine. In these few months they had already got a kind of secret "married" language; she had thought it would take longer for a man and woman to do that.

"Now I can really see the ocean!" she said. "It was different when we crossed over, so dark and angry, it seemed."

71

Here the sea was mild and lovely, the surf breaking in rows of ruffled white and sighing softly out again.

"We'll be going in for a while," Solly announced.

"Let me go too!" Anna cried.

Joseph frowned. "No, no. God forbid that you should fall! Next year I'll bring you, I promise I will."

The blankets had been spread next to a breakwater. Ruth propped herself against a rock and put the lunch basket in its shade. "Wait till you see the fireworks tonight. It's a pity there aren't more holidays! Decoration Day we come but it's usually too cold to go in the water then. Look at those boys of mine, look at them splashing! They'll get water in their ears! Maybe I'll just duck in, too, for a minute."

Anna lay back. The baby moved in her, thumping weakly against her spread palms. Her body was languid from its warm burden and the warm sun. What would he be like, this child? She was so impatient to see his face. What would he be *like?* Would he live with them happily, would he love them? Sometimes, no matter what you did for them, children did not love their parents. Would he be like anyone they had known, or perhaps like someone long dead whose name they had never even heard?

Oh, but this was a wanted baby, as much by the father as the mother! Joseph took such pride in her swelling body, the skin stretched tightly, blue-white as milk. He worried and fretted. "You don't have to be cleaning and cooking all day. A couple of eggs for supper will be enough for me. You don't get enough rest, you're always running and doing something." Then, a moment later, he would admonish, "Be sure to get out and take a long walk tomorrow, it's very important to have exercise. That way you'll have an easier time, Dr. Arndt says." She had been astonished. "You spoke to the doctor?" "Well, I wanted to hear for myself that you were all right, so I stopped in."

Yes, Joseph would always take care of things. She thought of him as a builder and planner, moderate and careful; he had come to their marriage with confidence; he would build it carefully, stone on stone, to rise and last. In him there was no betrayal. He meant what he said and he said what he meant. In him there was only trust. Lying beside him at night, she felt his sturdiness, the safety of sleeping there, the tenderness.

And tenderness was all she wanted. The other, the force that drove him as though he would plunge in and become part of her, she did not need. She knew that he was feeling something very powerful, but she felt nothing of it herself. It was only the loving warmth that mattered. She supposed, anyway, that women never really liked anything more than that; the rest was only to satisfy a husband and to have children. Not, of course, that she had ever discussed the subject with anyone. Perhaps, if she had had a sister? But then the sister wouldn't have known any more about it than she did.

Once, when she had been stitching trousers at Ruth's, Anna had overheard two of the women whispering something about being so tired at night, and how no matter how hard they worked men were never too tired. Still, it was good to know that your husband wanted you. The things he whispered at night—it was embarrassing to remember them. But men were made that way, so it must be a good thing, it must be right.

"You look like your mother, Anna," Ruth said. Anna opened her eyes. Ruth was standing over her, drying herself with a towel.

"Do I?"

"I never saw her very often, but certain things about her come to my mind. She was different from other people."

"How different?"

"She didn't talk about the things women in the villages talked about. I always thought she ought to have lived in Warsaw or maybe Vilna, where the schools are. She would have fitted there. Although she never complained, not that I remember, anyway."

"You don't remember anything more?"

"No, I was only a child myself, after all, when I left home."

And I remember standing in the windy burial ground thinking that I must try to hold on to their faces and voices before they should slip away. And now they have really slipped away. And there isn't a human being on this side of the ocean who knows anything about my life up to four years ago. It is a severance, the major part of my life cut off, except in the privacy of my own mind.

"It's too bad when a family is split like that. You've no one close here for your children to know, except for Joseph's mother, of course."

"She's sixty-four," Anna said.

"Is she? I would have thought even more, she seems so old," Ruth remarked.

73

"She's had a hard life. We wanted to bring her today, she's never been at the beach. In all these years, imagine! But she wouldn't come."

"What will you do when she gets too old or sick to keep the store?" Ruth was curious. "Do you suppose Joseph will want her to live with you?"

"I don't know. We've never talked about it," Anna said, suddenly troubled. That gloomy, sour-smelling old woman in the house! Then came a wave of shame and pity. Poor thing, poor thing! To be old in another woman's house, a strange young woman who didn't want you!

"If that ever happens and Joseph wants her, why, we'll have to do it, that's all," she said quietly.

"You're a kind girl, Anna. I'm glad for both your sakes that I sent Joseph down to talk to you that day."

"I've never thanked you," Anna said, with embarrassment.

"Pshaw! I wasn't looking for thanks! But *he* thanked me, he was quite mad about you from the very first time. He thought you didn't like him, that's why he was afraid for so long to talk about marriage. You know," she explained, "he thought you were in love with some-body else, but I told him you weren't. If it had been anyone but Joseph I would have let him go on thinking so, because generally it's a good idea to keep men guessing. But Joseph is different, he's so—" Ruth sought the word—"honest. Yes, that's it, he's so honest."

"That's true," Anna said. "He is." And she sat quite still while Ruth talked on, only half hearing, feeling, in the pouring sunshine, how good it was to be like this. Down at the water's edge Joseph was throwing a ball to the boys. He looked like a boy himself, fast and happy. She could hear his voice ring. She hadn't known he knew how to play. This was the way a man ought to be, the way he ought to live. Perhaps this was what God intended for man when He put him on the earth, to be free, to run in the bright air with all the other living things.

But no, how was that possible? Who was to pay for it? Always it came back to that. This outing today, the carfare, the food, they had to be paid for. "In the sweat of thy brow shalt thou earn thy bread," Joseph always said. He liked to quote from the Bible. It seemed that he could find an explanation for everything in the Bible.

After a while the men came back and sat down. "Feeling all right, Anna?" Joseph asked.

"Just wonderful!"

"Tell me if you get tired."

"Tired! I'm tired of doing nothing!" She took her crocheting, a long rectangle of white lace, out of her basket.

"Solly, look!" Ruth cried. "It's gorgeous! What are you making?"

Anna felt suddenly shy. "A cover for the baby carriage. It will go over a sateen lining, pink or blue, as soon as we know."

Ruth shook her head admiringly. "You know how to do things, Anna! You're so clever, between baking and handwork—"

"Tell her," Joseph interrupted, "about the carriage," and went on to tell about it himself. "We bought it last week on Broadway. White wicker, with a top that rolls back for sun or shade, whichever you want."

"Oh," Ruth said, "the first baby is wonderful. You've plenty of time for it—Vera and June, stop throwing sand at Cecile! You ought to be ashamed of yourselves!"

"Bet you don't know what sand is," Harry said importantly.

"Sand? Why, it's what's on the beach," his mother answered.

"Hah! It's rocks, ground fine, after millions and millions of years. I knew you didn't know!"

Anna picked up a handful. The fine, dry stuff poured between her fingers, sharp, twinkling particles on her skin. Yes, it was like pieces of rock, the shining splinters in rock.

"So, you are getting an education from my son," Solly observed, and in a lower voice confided to Anna and Joseph, "They tell me he's number one in his class. He wants to know everything and he never forgets. You tell him something once, he never forgets," he repeated with pride. Then, falling sober and silent, "I wish I could get ahead! I mean really get enough together so I could start a little business of my own." He swung around, addressing Joseph alone. "Some people do it, I don't know how. My boss started the way I am, but I never seem to get ahead."

"Five children," Joseph said gently. "That takes some doing."

"Yes, yes, God bless them, it does. And I want to do so much for them all!" And he sat a moment, looking out to sea, as though an answer were waiting for him there. Then he jumped up.

"This air gives you an appetite! How about feeding the hungry army, Ruth?"

"Wait, wait, I'm coming!" Ruth admonished, unwrapping the paper bags, and delving in the basket, withdrew one after the other

75

a corned beef, a salami, pickles, sour tomatoes, coleslaw, hard-boiled eggs and two long loaves of dark bread.

"And watermelon for dessert," she finished. "Leave that in the shade till we're ready for it."

"Cookies," Anna said, producing a neat box tied with ribbon. "I baked yesterday, two kinds."

"And an orange for each of you children," Ruth added. "Here, boys, don't grab. Vera, keep your feet off the blanket, you'll get sand in the food."

Joseph always said Ruth talked too much, Anna remembered with amusement.

"Here, Solly, don't eat so fast! That husband of mine, he'll choke himself someday, God forbid, and the boys are the same. Now Cecile, on the other hand, I have to open her mouth and stick the food in, a bird eats more! Joseph, help yourself, there's plenty. And make your wife eat, she shouldn't forget she's eating for two!"

Anna met Joseph's eyes and suppressed a smile. Again, their private language: "Don't get me wrong, I like Ruth, she's the salt of the earth. But if I had to live with her, I'd go crazy. Her tongue never stops: gabble, gabble, gabble."

Solly rubbed his stomach. "A real feast," he sighed, and remembering his duties as a host, "You're enjoying yourself, Anna?"

"Oh, I am, I am! Think, here we are on the very edge of the continent! If you looked straight ahead across the ocean, all those thousands of miles, you'd see—"

"Poland," Ruth interjected. "And I'd just as soon not see Poland again, if you don't mind."

"Not Poland," Anna corrected. "Portugal. And behind it Spain. I'd like to go there someday. Miss Thorne was in Spain, her father was a United States consul there. She says it's beautiful."

"Not me! I never want to see any part of Europe again." Solly shook his head. "Especially now, with the way things are. They look very bad if you ask me."

"What do you mean?" Joseph asked.

"There'll be war," Solly answered seriously.

"You always think the worst!" Ruth cried. "Why do you have to say such things?"

"Because it's true. As soon as I read last week that a Serb had shot the Archduke Ferdinand in Sarajevo, I said, 'There'll be war, you mark my words.' "

76

"Who was he, this archduke?" Anna asked.

"The Austrian archduke, heir to the throne. So that means Austria will declare war on Serbia, and then Russia will come in with Serbia. Germany will have to help Austria; France will come in with Russia. And there you have it."

Joseph took another slice of watermelon. "Well," he said practically, "all that's across the ocean. It won't bother us here."

Anna sat with her head down, fear running through her like water.

And Ruth said with sudden insight, "Anna is thinking of her brothers. They'd have to fight for Austria."

"What's the point of this gloomy talk of things we don't even know about?" Joseph demanded. "Nobody can tell what's going to happen. I'll wager it will all blow over, anyway. Nobody wants war, and here we are spoiling a beautiful day with worry over something that will probably never happen."

"You're right," Solly apologized. "You're absolutely right, Joseph. Who wants to waste a day like this? Let's go back for a swim."

The sun was low and red in the west. "That means it'll be a hot day tomorrow," Joseph predicted, coming toward the women.

"The days I can stand but it's the nights that are awful," Solly said. "Sleeping on the fire escapes, it's torture."

They gathered up the blanket and their baskets. "The girls will come with me," Ruth directed. "Harry and Irving, you go to the bathhouse with your father and change. We'll all meet at the entrance in front."

Across the boardwalk lay Surf Avenue and the roving crowds, the life of the evening. The sky was darkly streaked, gray against coal gray, smudged with a remnant of rose. The lights of the Scenic Railway arched and soared; the Ferris wheel hung like a spider web; in all the booths, lights winked and twinkled. Far ahead, band music blared and faded with the veering wind; near at hand the merry-go-round jangled. Anna was enthralled.

"I don't know where to go first!" she cried. "Where shall we start? Will there be time to see it all?"

"We'll do our best!" Joseph said. "Want to start with the Streets of Cairo? I went last year and you can walk right through a real Egyptian street, the real thing. They've got donkeys, you can ride on a camel—no, I forgot, you can't do that, but you can watch and next year when we come again you'll ride a camel."

She felt, and knew she was feeling, a child's delight, perhaps even more than the children did, who began to be tired. So much to see and hear all at once! Such bright colors, and all the music was like colors! Spinning and wheeling, like one of those little machines—what did you call it?—a kaleidoscope, where you put in some simple thing, a piece of cloth or a couple of pins, and when you turned it endless, unfurling patterns came, a dazzle in the eyes.

Then it was dark and time for the fireworks to begin. Too bad there wouldn't be time for the side shows! But Anna had seen pictures of a calf with two heads and a dreadful bearded woman; she was glad not to go. Luckily they found seats for the fireworks, which were absolutely splendid: rockets of red, white and blue; stars that rushed into the night sky, each one higher than the one before, showered back upon the earth in a spray of gold. Last, the sound of cannon fire, shuddering and crashing until the final boom that almost shook you out of your seat. And silence. And the band striking up "The Star-Spangled Banner" while everyone rose in his place. Anna was proud that she was one of those who knew all the words: "—and the rockets' red glare, the bombs bursting in air—"

It was over. Ended and over, the wonderful, wonderful day. The crowd shoved slowly toward the trolley, the Coney Island Avenue line. Solly knew the quickest way to get there ahead of the rush. Otherwise they would never have got seats. As it was, the boys had to stand leaning on Joseph and Solly, each of whom held one of the sleeping girls. Ruth held the littlest one, and Anna took the baskets. People were standing all along the aisle, even hanging on the outside of the car. The conductors could hardly pass through the crowds; they were hot and sweaty and you couldn't blame them if they were cross. They'd spent the whole day riding back and forth on the cars while all these others had been on the beach. It grew hotter and hotter as they rode through Brooklyn toward the bridge. The breeze died, and what little there was of it was moist. The babble of talk and laughter died, too. People are tired after the long day, Anna thought. Also, they are thinking about tomorrow. It almost takes the pleasure out of the day, this ride and the surging heat again and thinking about tomorrow. Almost, but not quite.

After they parted with the Levinsons and changed to the Broadway car it was not so crowded, not so bad.

"We're lucky we caught the last car," Joseph said. "It will be midnight before we get home. Did you have a good time?"

"Oh, I loved it!" she said.

"Put your head on my shoulder. I'll wake you when we come to our stop."

She didn't sleep. The bell jangled and the motorman sped up Broadway in the dark, the trolley swaying with the speed. She could feel the heat of Joseph's skin through his shirt. "He'll be burned," she thought. They had forgotten the cocoa butter, left it home on the dresser. Perhaps it would not be too late if she put it on him when they got home. He had such fair skin.

My friend, she thought. My one friend in all the world. Now I really know what it is to be married. Not *fairy tales,* she thought scornfully. No girl should know so little about life as I did: when I have a daughter I will not allow her to be so stupid, so unworldly. *Tristram and Isolde.* Fairy tales.

And yet, yet . . . all that soft sparkle, the soaring and the singing, the longing, the touch, the ache and the sweetness, all of those, not true? I'm nineteen now, I ought to know. Why do I still wonder about it?

Joseph bent down and kissed her hair. "We're home," he whispered.

He helped her down the trolley's high step. The wind came blowing from the Hudson when they turned the corner. Their shoes went slap and click on the sidewalk, the man's heel flat, the woman's needle-high, slap and click through the sleeping street.

11

The boy Maurice was born in his parents' brass bed on July 29, 1914. He weighed seven pounds and had a head of thick, light hair.

"Three hours' labor for a first baby!" Dr. Arndt exclaimed. "Do you know how lucky you are? At this rate, you ought to have six more!"

Outside a newsboy cried alarm. "Extra! Extra!"

"What is it?" Anna asked, and Joseph went outside to see. He came back with the *New York Tribune*.

" 'Austria declares war,' " he read. " 'Rushes vast army into Serbia; Russia masses eighty thousand men on border.' Solly was right. The war has come."

The doctor grumbled, "More crazy slaughter, and for what?"

Anna said, "Eli and Dan will be in it." There came a flash of old, old memory: Mama in her bed, the twin boys lying with her, some woman standing there, a neighbor or midwife. She seized the baby.

"Nothing will happen to this little boy. I'll never let anything happen to this little boy!"

"No, of course not," the doctor said gently.

The years of the war were marked off in Anna's mind by the growth of her son. She would remember that the *Lusitania* had been sunk on the day he took his first step holding on to her two fingers, and he only ten months old! When the Russian army drove the Austrians back to the freezing mountains of Carpathia—she

trembled, shedding tears for Dan and Eli—that also was the time
Maury said his first words. By the time the United States entered
the war—the poster with the bloody hand: *The Hun, his mark. Blot
it out with Liberty Bonds*—by that time he was almost three, genial,
alert, delightful.

She studied the face she had so longed to see, the features emerging from the formless round. The nose was straight. The eyes were
almond-shaped and darkly blue. There was a cleft in the chin.
Whom are you like, my son? Yourself alone, like no one in the
world before you or to come.

She felt profoundly that he had made a great change in her. She
no longer thought of herself as a girl. A long age had passed since
the time before his coming. He had enlarged her, so that she had
new feeling for the blind man passing in the street and the young
men dying in Europe. And yet, in an entirely opposite way, he had
made everything but himself so unimportant that she didn't care
what happened anywhere, as long as he was safe.

During the night she often heard Joseph get out of bed to go in to
the crib, and she knew that he was listening for the baby's breathing. No child had ever been more loved than this one! No child was
ever more carefully fed and bathed, dressed and played with, than
this one.

"Maybe he'll be a doctor," Joseph said.

"A lawyer would be fine, too."

They were able to laugh at their own foolish pride. Yet they
meant what they said.

She read to Maury, long before he could possibly have understood the words. But somewhere she had heard that infants can absorb the sound and feel of words even though they do not understand them. So she read peaceful things, poems of Stevenson and
Eugene Field.

"Sleep, little pigeon, and fold your wings—little blue pigeon with
velvet eyes."

In front of the apartment house the mothers sat with their carriages and strollers, observing, criticizing, counseling each other.

"You need another baby," they told Anna. "You're spoiling this
one. It's not good for him or you."

Of course she wanted more children. And certainly Joseph
wanted a large family. But none came. Yet really there was no great
need to hurry. These years with Maury, only a few hundred days

out of a long life, were too perfect to be wished away. All day long, after Joseph had gone to work before light, until he came home after dark, they had each other, Anna and Maury.

Oh, little Maury, little boy!

Darkness still covered the earth and the street lamps still burned near their bedroom window. It was not quite five o'clock. In another minute Anna would rise and make Joseph's breakfast. It was hard to get out of bed these winter mornings. The water stopped running in the bathroom; he had finished his shower. Now he would hang the towels back on the rack and wipe the tub, leaving it without spot.

His clothes for the morning were ready on the chair. He did everything with such care and method. His books of appointments and bills owed and money due him were all in order, so that he was always prepared, always on time, and no moment was wasted.

He came from the bathroom now and stood at Anna's mirror to brush his hair, making an exact center part. The clean overalls that she had washed were in their paper bag by the door with his painter's cap. He always wore a suit on the way to work. It was not, she knew, that he was ashamed of his work; he took pride in his labor and skill. It was just that he saw this work as a way station on the road to another life. He saw himself, she understood, as a man who went to work wearing a collar and tie.

It seemed to Anna, and had from the beginning, that he was a clear and simple person to understand. Yet lately she had been concerned. He was so quiet. He had always been quiet, true. But now he had almost nothing to say. Often he fell asleep in his chair after supper, and she would have to wake him to get him to bed. Of course, he was on his feet all day. . . .

The silence, of itself, did not bother her, for evening was her only time to read in peace. It was the reason, if any, behind the silence that troubled her.

At breakfast he said, "I read your brothers' letters last night. I woke up around one o'clock; I couldn't sleep, for some reason."

"It's so good to be hearing from them again." Their letters since the end of the war had been cheerful enough. Dan had emerged unhurt from four years of fighting. Eli had shrapnel in his arm and would never bend the elbow again, but he had been given a medal for valor and his firm had promoted him, the three men ahead of him having been killed.

"If you aren't killed you can make a good thing out of a war," Anna said now, "outrageous as it is."

"It would seem so," Joseph answered bitterly. "You have only to look at what the war did for Solly."

Who would have thought that Solly, of all people, would have prospered so? His boss had made a fortune turning out fatigue pants for the army and Solly had gone into the new factory, first as an assistant and then as supervisor. They had moved uptown to five nice rooms on Broadway at Ninety-eighth Street, much nicer rooms than Joseph's and Anna's.

"I'm glad for them," Anna said and meant it. "With all those children, they needed some luck. Ruth told me confidentially that Solly and one of the other men may go in business for themselves. Solly's saved a few thousand dollars, you know."

"All you need is luck."

"You're not envious of Solly?"

"Of course I am! He's a decent fellow—you know what I've always thought of him—but, my God, he's no brain, is he? He's a humdrum plodder and now he's way ahead of me. Haven't I got a right to be envious?"

"We're doing fine, Joseph." Anna tried to coax him.

"Fine!" He slapped the table. "I'm twenty-eight years old, thirty before you know it, and I'm exactly nowhere. Living in a dump!"

"It's not a dump! Nice people live here, good solid people!"

"Sure! Department store clerks, bus drivers, postmen. Poor wage slaves living from hand to mouth. Like me." He stood up and began to pace the kitchen. "And when I get older and can't work ten or twelve hours a day anymore, what then? With prices rising while you're looking at them? We'll have even less than we have now, that's what then."

That part was true. Since the war everything was becoming more and more expensive. True too that they were not advancing.

"Anna, I'm scared. I look into the future and for the first time I'm scared," he said.

There were small veins at his temples. One of them jumped when he talked. She hadn't noticed that before. His hands were spotted with paint. They looked like the spotted hands of an old man. She thought, He looks older than twenty-eight. And she, too, was suddenly afraid.

*　　*　　*

One day Joseph came home and began to talk in a bright, excited voice. "You know what Malone the plumber told me today? He knows an apartment house near here that you can buy for almost nothing. The owner lost a pile in some business and on top of that both his kids have asthma. One of them almost died with it in the winter. So he's got to move west and he wants to sell the house fast." He walked up and down the room, as was his habit when he was tense. "Malone and another guy want me to go in with them. I need two thousand cash. Where can I get two thousand cash?"

He left the food on his plate. He picked up the newspaper and let it fall.

"Your magazine is on the table," Anna said.

He always read the *Saturday Evening Post;* it was all he ever read, except for the evening paper. He had no time for the morning paper.

Now he leafed through the magazine and put it aside. She saw that he was entirely intent on his idea. But nothing will come of it, she thought pityingly, and began to mend Maury's overalls. The silence needed to be broken but she didn't know how to do it.

Presently Joseph said, "Anna, I've thought of something."

"Yes?"

"You know, when you were at the Werners', they were very good to you. Maybe, if you asked, maybe they'd lend us some money."

"Oh, no, I'm sure not!"

"Why? I would pay interest. They might just be willing to do it, rich people like them. I've heard of such things before."

She felt weak with dread. What was he asking of her?

"It can't hurt to try, can it?"

"Joseph, please, I'll do anything for you, only don't ask me to do that."

"But I'm not asking you to do anything wrong! Are you too proud to ask for a loan, is that it?"

"Joseph, you're shouting, you'll scare Maury."

They went to bed. She felt his anger and it frightened her. He was so seldom angry. "Joseph, don't make me," she whispered, and moved to touch him, but he drew away and pretended to be asleep.

In the morning he began again. "Damn it to hell, I could do so much with that money! I know I could! Malone and I could fix that place up, raise the rents, then sell it. Don't you see, this is the start I've been waiting for and it may never happen again!"

He will wear me down, Anna thought.

"I'd go myself, but I don't know the people. They'd listen to you."

And on the third day she gave in. "Enough, for God's sake! I'll call Mrs. Werner on the telephone tomorrow."

She climbed the steps of the Seventy-first Street house on Saturday morning. It was a warm day for March, but not warm enough to cause the sweat on the back of her neck. *That woman,* Anna thought. "How well you look, Anna," she will say. "And so you have a son, how lovely!" She will write out the check (will she, possibly?). And hand it to me with her little smile and all her dignity.

The bell tinkled through the house. A moment later Paul Werner opened the door. He was wearing his topcoat and he had a package in his hand.

"Why, Anna," he said. "Why, Anna."

"I have an appointment with your mother."

"But Mother's in Long Branch for the week. The whole family's there."

"She told me to come at ten o'clock."

"She did? Let's go look on her desk. She might have left a message there." And as Anna waited at the foot of the stairs, "Come up, Anna."

The morning room was the same. The flowered chaise and the embroidery basket were still there. There was a new photograph on the desk, a large professional portrait of a baby. His baby?

He rummaged through papers. "I don't see anything. Wait, here's her calendar. It's next Saturday, Anna; you're a week ahead of time."

My God, she thought, I look like a fool. And Joseph needs the money by Wednesday.

"It's too bad. They're down at Cousin Blanche's farm for the week. There's a big house party and Mrs. Monaghan and Daisy went, too. Daisy has your old place, Anna."

She had forgotten his dark, rich voice. Like the deepest notes of a cello, it was.

"Is there anything I can do, Anna? What were you going to see Mother about?"

"I was going to ask whether she would lend us some money."

"Oh? Are you in trouble? Sit down, tell me about it."

"But I'm keeping you. You have your coat on."

85

"Then I'll take it off. I only stopped in to pick up a package and then I'll catch the afternoon train to the shore."

Her voice murmured, telling Joseph's short story. The house was very still. The house was a fortress, safe and solid against the world's attacks, cushioned with soft things: silk curtains, carpets, pillows.

She did not look at his face. With eyes turned down, she saw only the long legs, one crossed over the other, and the fine, burnished leather of the shoes. These strong, lean legs would ride, play tennis, never grow old. Joseph already had varicose veins. From standing so much, the doctor said.

"I didn't want to ask you," she cried suddenly, almost angrily. "I didn't see any reason why you should lend two thousand dollars to a man you don't even know."

He smiled. How could eyes be so bright? Nobody else had such eyes, deep and vivid. "You're right. There isn't any reason. Except that I want to do it."

"You want to?"

"Yes. You have a lot of spirit and courage. I want to do it for you."

He drew a checkbook out of his pocket and took up a pen. Such easy power, commanding life, your own and other people's!

"What is your husband's name?"

"Joseph. Joseph Friedman."

"Two thousand dollars. When you get home have him sign this. It's an I.O.U. You can mail it to me. No, mail it here in care of my mother. I'm sure she would have done this for you herself."

"I don't know what to say!"

"Don't say anything."

"My husband will be so grateful. I don't think he really expected—it was just a last hope. Because we don't know anybody else, you see."

"I understand."

"He's really such a good man. The most honest, good man, believe me." Why did she chatter like this? "But then that's silly of me to say, isn't it? What woman would tell you that her husband was dishonest?"

He laughed. "Not many, I imagine. But really, I hope this will accomplish what you hope."

Anna had unbuttoned the jacket of her suit. She saw now that his glance had gone to the front of her shirtwaist, to the row of spiral ruffling that lay between her breasts. She ought now to stand up, repeat her thanks, and go to the door. But she did not move.

"Tell me, Anna," he said. "Tell me about your little boy."

"He's four years old."

"Does he look like you?"

"I don't know."

"Red hair?"

"No, blond. But probably it will be darker when he grows up."

"You're even more beautiful than you used to be. Do you know that?"

"Am I?"

Her hands were limp in her lap. When he came to kneel on the floor beside her chair and turned her mouth to his, she had no strength at all.

There were nine pearl buttons on the shirtwaist. Then the petticoats: first the taffeta, then the muslin with the blue insertion. And the corset cover. And the chemise.

His voice came from far away, as if from another room. It echoed, a voice within a voice. Her eyes closed; her arms were too heavy to move. She was lifted to the flowered chaise.

"You're cold, my dear," he said tenderly, and reached for a quilted throw to cover them both. They lay in a bliss of warmth. His lips were pressed into her neck; she felt, and heard, his rising, falling breath. She thought: This is a dream.

She opened her eyes. The room was dim with a pearly northern light so pink and pale that it seemed like evening light, like evening calm.

Soft, soft. She closed her eyes. His fingers were moving through her hair, loosening the combs and pins. When the freed hair slipped over her shoulders he pulled it back from her temples.

"Lovely," she heard him say. "Oh, lovely."

Slowly he moved, not like an eager man in a hurry for his own quick release and then sleep, but slowly, flowing over her skin, beating in her blood, murmuring in her ears.

Never, never before.

A tide came sweeping. It rose and receded a little, then rose again, higher. For an instant something called in Anna's head. She thought she had whispered—perhaps she really had whispered "Please"—but his mouth came down over hers, crushing the word.

87

The tide came swelling, wave after rolling wave. And then nothing, nothing in the world, could have stopped the rushing of that tide.

She was jerked awake. Below in the street a hand organ ground and jangled. "Santa Lucia-a-a," it sobbed, and stopped. Silence followed. Anna's heart began to pound. How long had she been lying here?

She heard footsteps below. He had got up and left her to sleep. Her clothes had been picked from the floor and decently folded on a chair.

Slowly she put them on. The room was freezing cold. She trembled. She picked up the scattered hairpins and the combs. Her hands shook, doing her hair. One side of her face was red, roughened by—

She felt weak and sat down on the edge of the chaise, then jumped up and stood there looking at it. *Not good enough for a marriage bed, only for this,* ran through her mind. It looked so naked there, humiliated, a lady's sofa meant for an afternoon nap, or a book and a box of chocolates. And they had—

But it wasn't his fault. You're always proud of being honest; then be honest and fair. He married another girl? That has nothing to do with today.

Wretched confusion. Oh, wretched.

Paul was at the foot of the stairs when she came down. She passed him and ran to the door.

"Wait!" he cried, seeing her face. "Anna, you're not angry at me?"

"Angry? No." Only terrified.

"Anna, I want to tell you—you are the most enchanting woman I've ever known. And also I want to say, in case you think—well, I want to say that I respect you more than any woman I've ever known."

"Respect me? Now?"

"Yes, yes! Do you think, because of this—? It was marvelous, you know it was, marvelous and natural. Remember that."

"Natural!" she cried. Her voice cracked. "I have a child, a husband—"

He tried to take her hands, but she pulled away. Her mouth quivered; tears, forced down, burned the backs of her eyes.

"But you've done them no harm," Paul said gently.

"Oh, God!" she cried.

"Don't, don't feel like that. It's not a thing to cry over. Anna, listen, I've thought about you ever since you left here. I wanted you so. But when you lived in this house you were a girl, a child, and I wouldn't have touched you then."

This must be unreal. The thing that had happened upstairs only a little while ago could not have happened.

"And you wanted me," Paul said, very low. "I know you did. Is that something to be ashamed of, Anna dear, is it?"

Shame. Me. I. Anna Friedman, wife of Joseph, mother of Maury, I did this. On the fourteenth day of March, at noon, I did this.

Nausea lumped and gagged in her throat. "I have to go! I have to get out!" she cried, fumbling with the latch.

"I can't let you leave this way! Here, sit down a minute, let's talk. Please, I'm sorry, please—"

But she was blind, was deaf with her terror.

"No! No! Let me out!" The latch gave. The door flew open. She pushed him aside and fled down the steps.

The street was an ordinary New York street in the spring. A cluster of boys played marbles at the curb. A wagon approached, the peddler calling out his wares and prices: asparagus, rhubarb, potted tulips. But she had to run; something was at her back, as in the dark hall of an empty house. She had to run, away and away. Or else home.

She ran home.

Joseph was out with Maury. No doubt they had gone to the river to see the warships that were anchored there. Little boats went scurrying back and forth between the ships and the shore. You could see the sailors on the decks.

She went into the bathroom and ripped off all her clothes. She ran the water scalding hot in the chipped old tub. *Shame.* I wanted to be lifted and folded, I wanted to *feel.* It's true that I did. I can't blame him. He wouldn't have done it if he hadn't known that I wouldn't stop him.

Her skin began to sting. *Filthy.* She took a bath brush and scrubbed hard up and down. The soft pale skin on her forearms began to bleed. I could drown in here. I could slide down with my face under the water and they would think I had fainted.

The front door opened and Joseph came in with Maury.

"Anna?" he called outside the bathroom door.

She came out pulling a robe around her. "I got a check. It's on the bureau. You can call Mr. Malone."

"They gave it to you," he said wonderingly, as if he hadn't understood. Then he looked as though he were going to cry and he shouted, "You got it! You really did! Oh, Anna, this will make all the difference in the world! You'll see, you'll see." He began to question her rapidly, excitedly. "How did you ask her? What did she say? Did she want to know anything about me?"

"She wasn't there. It was the son who gave it."

"Anna, was it very hard? Yes, it must have been hard for you to ask. But what kind, what decent people! To trust us! You know, now I can tell you the truth, I really didn't think they would do it! But it was the only way I knew."

"Yes. Kind people."

He looked at her. "Is there something the matter? You don't seem—"

"My stomach. I had a sandwich downtown. The butter tasted bad, I think."

"Poor girl! Then go lie down, I'll feed Maury and keep him away from you."

When he had closed the bedroom door she went back into the bathroom and took another bath. *Filthy, I am filthy.*

Am I going to lose my mind?

At breakfast a few days later Joseph watched Anna closely. He was puzzled. "I thought you would be so pleased now that I've bought the house."

"But I am pleased. Very."

He reached under the table for her hand. "Is it—I've been thinking—this is hard to say, but is it because I haven't come near you at night? I know it is a couple of weeks now, but you see, when a man is worried he doesn't feel like it. I mean to say, it had nothing to do with you."

She grew hot. The palms of her hands were wet. *Oh, my God.*

"Have I embarrassed you? But we shouldn't feel embarrassment with each other. These things are natural, aren't they?"

"You don't seem as happy this time," Dr. Arndt remarked.

"I don't feel as well this time."

"Each pregnancy is different. Carry a sweet cracker with you in your purse and don't wait too long between meals. In another two months it'll be over."

Wise and fatherly Dr. Arndt.

Joseph bought a brand-new Model T Ford for three hundred sixty dollars. "I need to get around," he explained. "Malone and I are going to fix up this house and turn it over fast. We're going in for real estate in a big way, I tell you! I have a lot of confidence in Malone. He's honest and he's smart. The two of us are going places."

"I'm glad."

"Have you noticed how things come in bunches? Bad or good. We got the house and we're having another baby. Things are really looking up!"

"I know."

"I'll be able to start paying back next September. I figure I'll be able to give Mr. Werner a thousand dollars. I really ought to go and thank him personally, don't you think? For a total stranger to do what he did!"

"People like them are too busy," Anna said faintly. "A note would be better."

"You think so? Well, perhaps you're right. Do you still feel sick today, Anna?"

"Yes. The nausea—it's dreadful."

"Maybe we ought to get another doctor."

"No, it will pass soon."

If only I had someone to talk to. If I had my mother. But would I tell such a thing to my mother? God forbid. The rabbi, whose wife goes daily down the street with the rest of the women, pushing the carriages to the dairy and the butcher? Dr. Arndt, who will come to deliver my child while Joseph waits in the other room? Impossible.

Ruth came up to visit one day. They walked over toward the river behind Maury on his little tricycle. Ruth prattled down the list of her children. Harry had skipped a year, still at the top of his class. Irving had a business head; no doubt he'd go in with his father. The girls were such a joy; what a difference it made living and going to school uptown! But Cecile was overweight; she had such an appetite for sweets—

The air was heavy. Anna could hardly breathe.

"Why, you can hardly walk!" Ruth cried, becoming aware.

91

"I'm all right. Ruth, you've seen a lot of things, I want to tell you something terribly sad. There's a girl up here, the women are talking about her, she had—well, she had an affair, you understand. I feel so sorry for her; you see, she's married and she thinks—she knows her husband isn't the father of the child. Can you imagine such a terrible thing?"

"You feel sorry for her? I'd call her a whore!"

"Yes, of course, it's awful! But still, you know, one can feel sorry for such people. . . . The poor girl, she made a mistake, one mistake, and now—I don't know what to tell her."

"What to tell her! My advice is, stay away from her. Friends like that you don't need."

"Of course. But what's to become of her?"

"Why worry your head over such a person? She made her bed, let her lie in it. Right?"

"I guess you're right," Anna said.

The new life grew and fluttered awake. Anna thought, I need to love it, I need to long for the sight of its face. But she did neither. Poor thing, poor thing, this creature feeding in her, not wanted in her. At night she lay awake. Joseph's hand loosened on hers; he liked to hold her hand as they lay together falling asleep. If only she could have turned to him and cried out for help.

If only she could tell the truth! Sometimes the truth came rising to her lips so that she tightened them in fear of its escape. The words had a taste. They had a shape and color: bloody red in the darkness. She could hear their sound as they would fall into the quiet room.

Terror plucked at her skin like something alive, and ran over her body, raising the little hairs on her arms.

Joseph said, "I wonder how Maury's going to take it? Maury, would you like to have a baby brother or sister?"

He planned aloud. "I hear there's going to be a vacancy on the corner, five rooms on the second floor. Time we graduated from this dump! And then in a couple of years," he said, "maybe we'll even move to West End Avenue! Might as well aim high, right?" He threw Maury over his shoulder. "How'd you like to live on West End Avenue, son? Think you'd like that?"

My God, he doesn't see that I am strangling.

She got out a book of poetry. The contents were listed under Consolation: Courage: Suffering. She read from Henley's *Invictus* (what pompous nonsense!) to Kipling and Shakespeare. There was no consolation. You had to find your own courage. She put the book away.

One Saturday afternoon she said, "I'm going to look for a hat. You can take Maury for a while, can't you?"

"Of course. But it's going to rain."

"I'll take an umbrella." She had to get out. Last night she had dreamed about a long, curved, evil knife. Someone was coming toward her raising the knife. But who would want to kill her? She ought to do it herself.

The traffic rolled on Broadway through the rain. If I walked in front of the trolley, just stepped quickly in front as it came down the hill, it would all be over. But then—Maury. My little boy. Oh, my little boy.

She struggled in the wind. Her heart began to pound. The seven-months-old burden pressed down in her enormous belly. No strength. No strength at all. If I fall, I'll scream, scream it all out here on the street and everyone will know. I'm losing my mind.

The wind drove the greasy rain into her face and soaked behind her collar; wet wool clung to her neck. The wind rose and the rain came raging. The day grew dark. People shouted, jostling for shelter in doorways, anywhere. There was a flight of shallow steps: a post office or a school? There were people scurrying up the steps. Anna followed, into a place that was dry and still.

It was a church. For the first time in her life she had entered a church.

On three sides there were statues and pictures. The vivid young man with bright yellow hair, his body twisted on the cross. A pale blue plaster woman: that must be Mary, the one they call God's mother. Anna shut her eyes. I didn't buy a hat and Joseph will wonder why I spent a whole afternoon just walking around in the rain.

Someone began to practice on the organ, starting, stopping and starting again. The music rose like smoke, circling behind the gilded altar into the corners. She sat down and rested her forehead on the back of the seat and cried.

Dear God, listen to me, if the temple were open I would go in there. No, I wouldn't, I'd be afraid someone would see me. Dear

God, I don't even know whether I believe in You. I wish I were
like Joseph because he believes, he really does. But listen to me
anyway, and tell me what I'm to do. I'm twenty-four years old. I
have so many years to live through and how am I to get through
them?

Someone asked, "Are you in trouble, daughter?"

She looked up at the young priest, in his long black robe with
the metal chain around his waist. She had never been this close to
a priest. At home when you saw one coming down the road you
went the other way.

"I'm not a Catholic," she said. "I only came in out of the rain."

"I don't mind. If you want to sit here you're welcome. But
perhaps you wanted to talk?"

A human being, a good face. And she would never see him
again.

"I am in such trouble that I want to die," Anna said.

"Everyone feels that way at some time in his life." The priest sat
down.

How to begin? "My husband trusts me," she whispered. *That's
a stupid way to start.* "He tells me I'm the only person in the
world he can absolutely trust."

The priest waited.

"He says he knows I would never lie to him. Never—"

"And you have lied to him?"

"More than that. Oh, more than that!" She could not look at
him. Not at the statue or the pictures, either. Down at the floor, at
her own hands in her lap. "How can I tell you? You will think that
I am—you will not want to hear, you've never heard—"

"I've heard everything."

Not this. I can't say it, no, I can't. But I can't keep it all alone inside, either. Not any longer.

"Has it to do with the child you're expecting? Is that what you're
trying to say?"

She didn't answer.

"It's not his child? Is that it?"

"No," she whispered. "Oh, my God, I would be better off
dead!"

"That's not for you to say. Only God knows whether you would
be better off and He will decide, you may be sure."

"But do I deserve to live?"

94

"Everything that lives deserves to live. And certainly this child deserves it."

"I would feel better if I could pay, if I were punished."

"And you think you won't be? Every day of your life."

The organ, which had stopped for a time, began again. The quiet music curled like smoke, like mist.

"I've looked for the courage to tell the truth to Joseph. I've prayed for the courage, but it doesn't come."

"Why must you tell him?"

"To be honest, to feel clean again."

"At the price of his peace?"

"Do you think it would be?"

"You think about it for a minute."

But no thoughts came, nothing coherent except the face of her little boy. He was sitting on the kitchen floor eating an apple.

"Is it, perhaps, that you love this other man?"

"No. No, it's my husband I love." An easy answer. True, and yet. . . . Peace and life and goodness; Maury, child of my heart; all these, weighed against that short exaltation, that rapture.

She cried out, "And so I have to go on like this!"

"If you were blind or crippled you would. People do." The priest sighed. "Human beings have so much courage, I marvel at how much."

"I've used up all my courage."

"You'll find it again. And thank God for giving it back to you." His voice was even, without reproach or sympathy.

"I hope so."

"And after a while things will be easier for you."

"I hope so."

Perhaps he does know something. He hears and sees so many things. Surely this must have happened before to somebody else?

The priest stood up. "Do you feel any better?"

"A little," she answered truthfully. Some of the weight had been relieved, as though she had taken it from herself and put it on him.

"Can you go home now?"

"I think I can. I'll try. I want to thank you," she whispered.

He raised his hand. His heavy skirt swept down the aisle.

The birth was hard. A neighbor took Maury and Ruth came to help.

"Odd that this baby took so long," she said. "The second is always easier."

Joseph studied the tiny girl in the bed with Anna. "Poor little thing! She looks worn out, too."

Anna sat up in alarm. "Why, is there anything wrong with her?"

"No, no. Dr. Arndt said she's perfect. I only meant, she's thin and that makes her look frail."

She was not pretty, the way Maury had been. She had sparse black hair and a monkey face. She looked anxious. But that was absurd.

"To think you two haven't got a name ready for her!" Ruth said.

"I left it to Anna," Joseph explained. "Maury was named after my father, so now it's her turn."

"My mother's name was Ida," Anna said.

"Something beginning with an 'I,' then," Ruth mused. "You don't want Ida, do you? It's so old-fashioned."

I'm so tired, Anna thought. What difference does a name make?

"Isabel," Ruth suggested. "Or, I know, Iris! That's a lovely name. There's been a serial in the paper about an English countess, Lady Iris Ashburton."

"Iris," Anna said. "And now if you'll put her in the basket, I think I could go to sleep."

Shortly after the new year she wheeled the carriage homeward from the grocer's. Maury trudged along holding her free hand. Halfway up the street a man in a priest's dark suit came abreast of them and stopped.

"Boy or girl?" he asked.

Heat surged into Anna's face. It had been dark in that place, but he remembered.

"A girl. Iris."

"Well. God bless you, Iris," he said, and walked on quickly.

God bless us all. The infant's lips moved hungrily. "I want lunch," Maury said.

"We're almost home. I'll feed you."

And care for you both with all my strength. Where had it come from, this new strength? Like water in a river that had gone dry. Power flowed into her arms and legs, pushed her up the hill. I'm gritting my teeth; I must stop gritting my teeth. I am getting better, though. God bless us all.

12

The city stretched and spread. Its long legs touched the edges of Brooklyn and Queens, and leaped the bridges past the Bronx to the borders of Westchester. The city raised long arms into the sky. All along Fifth Avenue the wrecker's ball, making way for new towers, crushed the Renaissance mansions of the millionaires. Those that were not crushed were turned into museums or offices for philanthropic agencies.

Hammers rang, steel on steel. Huge cranes, delicate as a dinosaur's head, moved over the street. Ten thousand rivets were driven between morning and night, ten thousand steel woodpeckers in a steel forest. Laborers climbed the great skeletons, forty stories above the ground, sixty stories, eighty. Up and up. Everything was rising, the towers, the stock market and the fortunes of men.

These were the years of Harding and of 'normalcy,' although they were not normal at all: such times had never been seen before and would not be seen again until after the next great war, a quarter of a century away.

Those who in 1918 had counted their assets in hundreds of dollars could in a few years' time, if they were canny, hard working and lucky, count them in tens of thousands or more. The building business exploded like a rocket. Houses were sold before they were finished. Land values doubled and tripled and doubled again. If you were smart enough to keep ahead of the forward movement you could turn a tract of empty acres on Long Island into a tidy community of two-family houses or six-story apartment buildings, into a lasting income or a splendid profit.

Not that it was easy. The telling is a great deal easier than the doing. Starting from nothing, one had to work eighteen hours a day to get a foothold. One had to keep on at eighteen hours a day if one were not to lose the foothold. Because, once it was lost, how would a man ever manage to get another?

A painter and a plumber began together with one small, heavily mortgaged apartment building on Washington Heights. They put themselves into it, all of themselves, their strength and every dollar beyond what they needed to buy the food on their families' tables. They bought new stoves and bathroom fixtures. They scraped the floors; they repaired, they renewed from bottom to top. They painted every apartment and every hallway. They polished the brasswork and puttied the windows. They even bought two potted evergreens to stand beside the door.

There was no building on the block, or for many blocks, that looked like theirs when they were finished.

The tenants were astonished; it was years since the place had been so clean. A sign was put up outside: *No Vacancies*.

And then they raised the rents.

One morning a broker called. He had an investor, interested in well-kept, fully rented property needing no repairs. So they sold the house, having owned it not quite one year. Their profit was twenty percent.

They went to the bank that held their mortgage, to the real estate department. "See what we can do," they said. "Now give us a mortgage on another building and we'll do the same."

By the end of the year 1920 they owned two houses on Washington Heights. Neither of them had had a new pair of shoes or an evening out since they began. They were plowing every penny back into property. They bought three vacant lots in Brooklyn. Then luck, pure luck, came into the picture, because the syndicate that owned the property adjoining needed their lots to put up a hotel. They named their price and the syndicate paid: it had no choice.

Now they met an electrical contractor and a firm of masons, father and sons: could they not pool their trades and do some building of their own? The mason knew a lawyer who had clients with cash to invest. They bought more lots and built a row of two-family houses:

it is wise to start small. They had to rise at four in the morning to get to the job in Brooklyn on time.

The houses were sold before they were completed. A dentist down the block approached them with a proposition: would they be interested in a piece of Long Island land? He would like to go in with them. They could have the land for a song. Well, not quite a song exactly, but the price was right enough. More confident now, they built a whole tract of two-family houses, seventy-five houses and a row of stores.

Cautious, patient, tenacious plan and labor. Brick on brick, stone on stone. Buy, build, sell, hold, pyramid and grow. Very slowly, so very slowly at first. Then faster and bolder. A loft in the garment district. A garage on Second Avenue. Big syndicates, big mortgages. Growing profits and a growing reputation. That is how it was done.

And, of course, the times were right.

The times were right for lawyers or brokers, for textile merchants, manufacturing furriers or wholesale jewelers. Immigrants and the sons of immigrants moved northward from the tenements to the simple, respectable reaches of the Bronx and Washington Heights. Most never went any farther than simple respectability. Others, the more clever and the luckier, kept moving with improving fortunes. As the great fortress apartment houses rose along West End Avenue, with their elevators and doormen in uniform, these families came down from the Bronx and Washington Heights to fill them. They came with brand-new Oriental rugs and silver, the acquisitions of an astounding, quick prosperity; brought, too, their vigor and a driving ambition.

The building on West End Avenue was sixteen stories tall, with two apartments to a floor. Joseph and Anna leased the one with the river view, nine spacious rooms and a large square entrance hall on the eleventh floor. Standing in the center of the hall one could look into the living room where the sky filled the tall windows, into the paneled library where Anna's books in their boxes were still packed, into the splendid dining room with the long table, ten tapestried chairs and a Chinese screen concealing the door to the kitchen.

"Beautiful," Ruth said admiringly. "And to think you put it all together so quickly! How did you do it?"

"I would have liked to take more time," Anna said. "I'm not sure I like everything as much as I should. However, it's done."

"Not like everything! Anna, it's gorgeous."

"Joseph wanted it to be finished right away. You know how neat he is! He can't stand living in a mess. He says he lived in one long enough! So he asked Mrs. Marks—that's his lawyer's wife—to show me where to shop, and here we are."

"Well, it's gorgeous," Ruth repeated firmly. "Even a baby grand!"

"A surprise from Joseph."

"Well, a home should have a piano, even if nobody plays. It looks so nice, don't you think?"

"Iris will learn to play. Maury too, if he wants, but you know how Maury is. He won't do anything unless he wants to. Iris will learn, if only to please her father."

"Little old lady," Ruth said. "Little four-year-old lady."

"Let me show you her room."

Iris' room was pink and white and rose. There were shelves for her books, a little white bed with a canopy, a doll house on a table in one corner.

"Oh, the doll house!" Ruth cried.

"Yes, it was Joseph's present for her birthday. She's really too young for it, but he buys her everything he sees."

"Men are always like that with their daughters. June is getting as fresh as her spoiled friends. I don't allow her to get away with it but Solly can't say no to anything."

"And this is Maury's room. I let him help me fix it up. He's a big boy, after all, and so excited about moving here," Anna said fondly, inspecting again the plaids, the trains spread on the floor, the banner on the wall between the windows: *For God, for Country and for Yale.*

"What's that for?" Ruth asked.

"Oh, I thought it was nice. Besides, I would like him to go to Yale."

"My sons are at N.Y.U. and we find it good enough."

"Of course, of course," Anna said quickly. "What's the difference?" And wondering how to avoid the appearance of parading their success, she said timidly, "Joseph's lawyer, Mr. Marks, suggested a good school for Maury. It's where his own children go."

"A private school?"

"Well, you know, I would never have thought of it, but Joseph meets these men, builders and architects, and he comes home with such ideas! . . . What can you do? It's his money, after all, and he can spend it as he wants."

"Private school," Ruth repeated.

"Yes, and Iris will start kindergarten there in the fall. It's more convenient to have them both at the same place, naturally." Anna heard herself apologizing, and was annoyed with herself. What was there to apologize about? If Ruth was a little green-eyed, well, it was only natural.

"And you have a radio! We haven't got one yet. What do you think of it?"

"I don't get much of a chance at it, between Joseph and Maury. They take turns with the earphones. But it is a miracle, really."

"I read that next year they'll be putting out a model where you don't need earphones, so the whole family can listen at once. You'll have one, I'm sure, Joseph seems to buy everything in sight."

"Ruth, do you ever think of where we lived downtown and ask yourself how this happened? I often think, I don't deserve all this."

"How it happened? We worked like slaves, Solly and I, and we both deserve whatever we've got. Not," Ruth added, "that we have anywhere near what you have, but we're doing all right. Solly's got a clever partner, and there's a future."

"Sometimes it doesn't seem real to me," Anna said slowly.

"It's real enough. You'll find out when you try to keep this big place clean, I can tell you! I should think you'll be needing a cleaning woman once a week at least."

"I already have two girls, Joseph called an agency. They're coming tomorrow."

"Two girls? How many days?"

"Well, there are two rooms on the other side of the kitchen. So they'll be living in. Very nice girls," Anna said hurriedly into Ruth's silence. "Two Irish sisters. Ellen and Margaret."

"And to think you were once a maid yourself!" Ruth said.

If she wants to make me angry, she won't succeed, Anna thought. "Yes, to think," she answered calmly, "that I came to this country with a cloth bundle and two candlesticks! Which reminds me, I'd better unpack them before somebody steps on them."

And reaching into a box, as yet unpacked, by the dining-room

101

door, she took out the candlesticks, heavy ornate silver, very old. She blew the dust off; she set them lovingly on the table.

These, too, had seen so many places before this place! She stood there studying them, then looked around the room at the English china and the French crystal, at all the costly, fragile, glossy things that now were hers. And somewhere, under the excitement, lay a certainty that was grieving, guilty and afraid. A quiet certainty that this could not, would not, last.

13

Her parents don't know she is awake. They think she has finished her homework—she is in the fourth grade and they still don't get very much of it—and has gone to bed. They don't know what a hard time she often has falling asleep. Sometimes she gets out of bed and stands at the window. Her room is on the corner; at oblique angles she can see both westward over the river to the lights on the Palisades, and eastward down West End Avenue where fewer and fewer cars pass as the night grows later. She thinks about nothing in particular, just wishes it were already Friday so there would be no school for two whole days; hopes for rain on Saturday so she can read at home and her mother won't make her go out for fresh air; hopes that on Sunday it will not rain so that she and Papa can have their morning walk around the reservoir.

Their Sunday walk is her special time. Mama sleeps later on Sundays and Maury does too, unless he has plans to go skating or somewhere with his friends. Papa never sleeps late.

"Years of habit," he says, "of getting up at five. Now I stretch it and get up at six."

By half past eight they are in the park. On the other side of the reservoir rises the jagged line of buildings on Fifth Avenue. The wind blows, crimping the water. Joggers pass panting in their gray sweat shirts, passing them sometimes twice in their round, although Papa and Iris walk briskly.

"I love being with my girl," Papa always says.

Iris loves to be with him. Often she thinks how nice it would be if Mama and Maury went away. (Died? Is that what she means?) Then there would only be Papa and herself at the dinner table, Papa and herself to sit and talk in the library in the evening. She is guilty about these thoughts. Bad, bad thoughts, they are.

Across the corridor now the light shines out under Maury's door. He studies late, but he has to; he is learning Latin and algebra, he has to keep up his marks to get into Yale. Iris has good report cards too, but it is not as important for her. A girl—a woman—Papa explains, doesn't have to *do* anything with her education. It's a fine thing, of course, for her to learn and improve her mind, because then she will be a better wife and mother, a better person. But she doesn't actually have to *do* anything, the way boys do. Once Mama said someday it might be different, and women would go to work and do all the things men did. But Papa said that was absolutely ridiculous and he'd like to see any wife of his go to work as long as he was able to support her!

She is wide awake. It's chilly; she puts on her robe, and in bare feet—she likes the rough feel of the carpet on her soles—goes padding down the corridor to stand in the corner where it joins the front hall. From where her parents sit in the library they cannot see her. But she can hear them, and their voices comfort her, especially when she is worried about something. (Often she worries about the math teacher, an impatient angry woman. Math is the only subject in which Iris does not do very well and she is afraid to go to school because of it.)

Sometimes her parents don't talk at all. Mama is always studying something, Shakespeare or a course at the Museum of Art. Papa often works on rolls of blue paper spread on the table between the windows. He makes a short remark about them. Mama tells him she has taken a subscription to the Philharmonic on Friday afternoons with Mrs. Davison. Papa says that's fine, he knows how she enjoys it and he's sorry he doesn't, but he might just as well be truthful about it.

Other times they talk about interesting things. Mrs. Malone has had a miscarriage and Mama says it's too bad but, after all, seven children ought to be enough. She learns that Mama is to have a mink coat; Papa wants her to and they can get a good buy from the furrier on the floor below Solly's place. She learns that Maury will

get a new bicycle for his birthday. Maury is always surprised that
Iris knows everything before he does.

She is a little afraid of being found out, but not much. Papa
wouldn't be angry. He is never angry at her. Mama would not be
exactly angry, either, but she would get up and say quite firmly,
"Little girls belong in bed. And nice people don't listen to other
people's conversations. Come, Iris." And Mama would make her
go back to bed. That is the difference between Papa and Mama.

Tonight she becomes aware that they are talking about her. She
draws in her breath and hears her own heartbeat.

"I wish she would go to camp in Maine. It would do her good,
out in the woods with other children."

"Joseph, she would hate it!"

"Maury seems to get so much out of it. He can't wait to go back
every summer."

"Maury is Maury and everything's easy for him. Iris would be
miserable."

It's true. All that she has ever heard about camp tells her that
she would be. The very thought of living in a cabin at the mercy of
five other girls, so far from home, from her room where she can be
safe, is terrifying.

Last year she had a friend. Amy was a small, quiet girl like herself. They used to 'sleep over' at each other's houses on weekends.
They wrote poetry together. They were best friends. Then in the
summer Amy went away to camp, while Iris went with her parents
to the rented house at Long Beach. The first day of school she was
so glad to see Amy again.

"I wrote some more poems over the summer," she told her.

And Amy answered, scornfully and very loudly so that other
people could hear: "Who cares? I'm too old for that stuff anymore."

And Iris, shocked and wounded, saw that Amy had changed,
had gone over to the 'others.' Now she passed Iris in the halls pretending not to see her. Now she and Marcy were best friends.
Marcy has long braids that the boys pull. When boys are around
Amy and Marcy always laugh very loud so that the boys come up
to them and ask, "What's funny?" The boys are so stupid, they
can't see that these girls are doing this on purpose so they will notice them.

105

"Strange," Papa says, "two children, and so different! The same home, the same parents, and so different!"

Yes, true. Maury is on student council and the lower school basketball team. Next year he will be on the varsity that plays against the city's other big private schools. People are always surprised that Iris is his sister, although grownups are too polite to show it. But kids in school often don't believe it.

"You are *not* Maury Friedman's sister!" they say, and once a girl in her class walked up to Maury after a basketball game and asked, "Are you really her brother? She says you are."

"Sure," Maury said, surprised. "Sure I am."

"Maury is like my brothers," Mama declares. "Especially Eli. He reminds me so much of him."

On her dressing table she keeps enlarged snapshots of her family in Europe. Uncle Dan has a chubby wife surrounded by children. Uncle Eli and his wife stand on skis in front of a mountain house with icicles on the eaves. Their little girl is on skis, too. Her name is Liesel. She is Iris' age and she has long unreal blond hair. Liesel and her parents look like sunshine. Iris' head is full of thoughts like that, comparing people with things. Ellen and Margaret are ears of corn, tall and narrow, with large yellow teeth.

Do other people have such thoughts? she wonders. Is there anybody else in the world like me?

Her parents' voices fall away. She leans forward to hear.

"He's supposed to be a first-class pediatrician. I thought he was very thorough."

"And? What did he say?"

"Nothing, really. There's nothing wrong with her. Peaked looking, but basically healthy, outside of being somewhat nervous. But we've known all that."

"She's so sensitive!" Papa says. "Do you know what she asked me when we took our walk last Sunday? She said, 'Papa, do you ever look at your arm and think about how it was made out of people who died hundreds of years ago and wonder whether they would like you if they could know you?' Imagine, a child of nine saying a thing like that!"

"Yes, she's a thoughtful child. An unusual child."

"You know, I often remember when she was only a few weeks old and I used to go in to look at her in the crib. She touched me, Anna, in a way that Maury never did. He was so strong and hungry and healthy. But she! . . . I used to go to the door and come back to look at her again, and I remember thinking that she isn't going to find life easy."

Her mother doesn't speak, or if she does, Iris doesn't hear her.

Then Papa says, "She's my whole heart, Anna! But how I wish she looked like you! It wouldn't matter that she was timid. People would flock to her anyway."

"Ruth said the other day that Iris is the kind of plain girl who will improve with age, and I think she's right."

"Would you really call her so plain, Anna?"

"It's hard to judge your own child. But I wouldn't say she was pretty."

Not pretty. *Not pretty.* You might as well say: *You have a terrible disease. You'll never walk again.* You might as well say: *You have one month to live, you're going to die.* And so that's the way it is. That's what people think of me.

Now suddenly Papa says, "Anna! Mrs. Werner died! It's here in the paper. Survived by husband Horace, son Paul, daughter Evelyn Jonas in Cleveland."

"I didn't know."

"You really should read the obituaries. She was just sixty. I wonder what she had."

"I've no idea," Mama says.

Werner. Iris never forgets names, rarely forgets anything. Those are the people they met downtown when they went to buy her spring coat last week. And the lady *told* Mama she was sick! Why is Mama telling a lie?

They were coming out of Best's that day when the lady stopped them on the sidewalk. "Excuse me, but you are Anna, aren't you?"

"Yes, I'm Anna," Mama answered. "How are you, Mrs. Werner?"

"Paul, you remember Anna, of course?" the lady said.

The man—he was very tall and looked like the lady, so you could see he was her son—just bowed a little and answered, "Of course." But he didn't say a word to Mama.

The lady was really nice. She told Mama, "You were always pretty, but you've become even more so."

Funny red spots came out on Mama's face. She certainly wasn't very polite to those people. She always tells me to say thank you for a compliment and she didn't say a word.

107

Then Mrs. Werner asked, "Is this your daughter?"

"My daughter, Iris," Mama said.

So Iris had to shake hands and say, "How do you do?" The lady smiled at her, but the man just looked at her very hard and didn't smile.

Then the lady said softly, "I see you've had great good fortune, Anna."

Mama didn't say very much, only, "Yes, I have," which was unusual because Mama always talked so long whenever they met one of her friends.

The lady had beautiful gray hair, almost silver, and a fur coat like Mama's. But her eyes were very dark, and the skin below them was dark. She looked sick.

"We've moved from the house, you know, on account of the stairs. All of a sudden my heart's gone bad. But you, you look marvelous! You haven't got one bit older."

"Oh, yes," Mama said, "years older."

"Well, you don't look it. Do come and see us sometime, Anna. We're at Seventy-eighth and Fifth. And my son lives just two blocks down, which makes it very nice."

When they walked away Mama said, not really talking to Iris, but to herself, "Fifth Avenue! Naturally, the West Side wouldn't be fine enough anymore!"

Iris remembers all of this perfectly.

"The funeral is Wednesday at eleven," Papa says now. "I'll try to go with you if I can make it. Otherwise you'll have to go alone."

"I'm not going at all," Mama says calmly.

Iris hears the newspaper rattle. "Not going? You can't mean it!"

"Certainly I do. I haven't seen the woman in years. I meant nothing to her in life, so why should I go to see her in death?"

"Why do people go to funerals at all? Because it's only decent to pay one's respects! I'm amazed at you!"

Mama makes no answer and Papa says, "Besides, they were very nice to us, in case you've forgotten. There's such a thing as gratitude."

A touch of anger comes into Mama's voice. "Gratitude? You take a loan at a bank, you pay it back with interest, and you're supposed to be grateful to the bank?"

"This wasn't a bank. Anna, I don't understand you!"

"Where is it written that you have to understand everything?"

This is not like Mama, who is always saying things like: The man is the head of the house, remember that when you get married. Or: Marriage isn't fifty-fifty; the woman must go most of the way to keep the peace of the home.

The door of Maury's room bangs open and he plunges down the hall. "You little sneak!" he cries, and thumps Iris on the back with his fist.

Her parents come running. "What is it? What are you doing?"

"This sneaky kid's been standing here eavesdropping! If you ever do that to me, Iris, I'll punch the breath out of you, you damn pest."

"Maury, that's no language," Papa says. "Come in here, Iris. What's going on? Were you really standing there listening to us?"

"I didn't mean to listen. I was going to the kitchen for an apple."

"Like heck she was!" Maury says.

Mama shakes her head at Maury. "Please, Maury, go back to your homework and let us handle this. I want to know what you heard, Iris."

She wants to cry out: "I heard you say that I'm not pretty, and Cousin Ruth said I'll be better when I'm older. It's none of her business and I hate her and I hate you!" But she is too proud to say it.

Her mother's forehead is worried. Meanly, craftily, Iris takes pleasure in what she is about to do. "I heard you tell Papa you didn't see that lady, but you did see her!"

"What are you talking about?" Papa asks.

"Mrs. Werner," Iris tells him. "We saw her last week downtown with her son."

"Is that true, Anna?"

Mama sighs. "Yes, we ran into them on Fifth Avenue. I didn't think it worth mentioning."

"But you thought it worth hiding just now, for what reason I can't imagine."

"Joseph!" Mama says. "This is hardly the place—" And Iris knows she means: *Not in front of the child.*

"Very well, then," Papa says. "Iris, your mother will give you some hot milk in your room and then I want you to go to sleep."

"I want you to give it to me, Papa!" Iris protests.

Her father holds the glass while she sips the milk. "Feeling better now? Something's upset you, so can you tell me what it is?"

Her eyes fill. She whispers, "I haven't any friends. I'm not popular."

He says indignantly, "If all those kids are too stupid to see your worth, that's their loss! You're the smartest one of the lot! You're my little queen and when you grow up you'll run rings around them all, you'll show them!"

"I'm not pretty," she says.

"Who says you're not? I'd like to hear anyone tell me you're not!"

"Marcy has thick braids with ribbons on the ends."

"So what? I don't even like braids! Your kind of hair is much nicer."

"Papa, it isn't!"

"Honey, I think it is. Tell you what," he says, taking the empty glass, "next week's your Thanksgiving vacation. How would you like to go to a movie with me? We can go to my office in the morning, and we'll even have time before the movie to buy you a new dress. Mama's having a dinner party and I'd like to show you off to all the people in a brand-new dress. Then we'll see who's pretty!"

"I'd like to go to your office and the movie. But not to the party."

"All right, we won't talk about it now." He bends to kiss her. "Are you sleepy now? Will you go right to sleep if I turn off the light?"

She nods and he turns out the light. But she isn't sleepy. She lies in the dark and her thoughts rush.

Lots of times during school vacations, Papa takes them to his office. Papa is proud of Maury in his navy blue suit and cap, of Iris in her good coat that has a beaver collar, of the braces on their teeth. He takes them into the private room where he has a great mahogany desk, just like Mr. Malone's across the hall.

Mr. Malone is fat and tells jokes. He keeps a box of chocolates in a drawer. The Malones are like family; when Mama had her appendix out Mrs. Malone came to the hospital every day. They live in an apartment quite nearby, except that theirs has more rooms because they have so many children. These children are all big and healthy looking; Iris feels weak and sallow in their company, as though they could see the shoulder blades under her dress, like the frail wings of birds when you pull the feathers back. The Malones like Maury, as everyone does. He goes all over their apart-

110

ment, looking at stamp collections and baseball cards, eating cake
in the pantry. Iris sits with the grownups until Mrs. Malone calls
the daughter who is nearest Iris' age. "Mavis," she says nicely,
"why don't you take Iris into your room and show her the doll
house?" And Iris goes, knowing that Mavis doesn't want her,
knowing she ought to say something lively and unable to think of
anything to say at all.

Mama goes on talking in the Malones' living room. She can
always talk to people, to Mrs. Malone's sister who is a nun, to
Ellen and Margaret at home, to a cranky saleswoman in a shop.
People always smile at her. Papa says her voice is like a bell; it is
one of the first things he ever noticed about her. "Most women
yap and shrill like busy little dogs," he says.

Yes, he loves Mama, it's plain to see. He's always talking about
how smart she is and what a wonderful cook, much better than
Margaret who gets paid for doing it. He boasts about her beautiful
red hair and was upset for three days after Mama had it cut off.

Yes, he loves Mama; he talks about her too much. "Listen to
your mother, Iris," he says, "your mother knows what's right!"

But tonight he is angry at Mama. They are quarreling inside.
She hears them now, in their bedroom. Good, good. I'm glad he's
angry at her.

"It's mighty queer," Papa says. "I don't know who it is that
you've got it in for, the mother or the son? You get all stiffened up
whenever those people are mentioned."

"I do not!" Mama screams. Iris has never heard her shriek like
that.

"Yes, you do! It makes me wonder sometimes what the devil
went on in that house to make you react like this? Can't even mention a chance meeting, won't go to the woman's funeral. I can't
make head or tail of it—"

The door slams. There is more loud talking that Iris cannot dis-
tinguish; then the door is opened again and she hears Papa say,
"Very well, I suppose it's just false pride. You've risen in the world
and don't like to be reminded—"

"Will you leave me alone!" Mama cries.

Then there is silence.

A long time later the door to Iris' room is opened. A wedge of
light comes in and widens. Her mother walks over and stands by
the bed.

"Iris?"

She does not answer

"Iris, you're awake. I can tell by your breathing."

"What do you want?"

Her mother sits down on the bed and takes Iris' hand, which lies in hers, not moving. "I wanted to come in and hold your hand before you fell asleep."

Her face is partly turned away, but Iris sees that her eyes are funny; they look swollen. "Have you been crying, Mama?"

"No."

"Yes, you have. Was it because I told about that lady and that man?"

"What lady and what man?"

Pretending again! "You know!" Iris says crossly. "The lady who died."

"No," says Mama, looking away.

Then something rises in Iris, something she has never felt before. It is a kind of softness, feeling sorry for Mama.

"I did it on purpose," she says. "I wanted to make Papa angry at you."

"I know."

"Aren't you angry at me?"

"No. We all have feelings sometimes of not liking people, or wanting to hurt them."

She wants to say, I'm sorry I can't love you as much as Papa. She says instead, "Papa wants to buy me a new dress for your party, but I don't want to come in and meet all the people."

He always calls her in when they have company. She has to stand alone in the doorway while all the people, the ladies in their perfume and bracelets, sit in a row around the room, their faces turned to Iris as she stands there being looked at.

"I don't want to," she repeats. "Do I have to?"

"No," Mama says. "You don't."

"Do you promise? No matter what Papa says?"

"I promise."

"Because I hate it! I hate it!"

"I understand," Mama says.

She sighs with relief. "I feel sleepy now," she says.

"Do you? That's good." Her mother goes out and closes the door very softly.

*   *   *

She could not then have known what she knew much later: that her father in his blind love lied to her, maybe not even realizing that he did. He lied when he called her a queen, for she had been no queen then and never would be. He lied when he talked of the great things she would do and the people she would 'show.' She would be embarrassed to remember how foolish his loving words had been.

But Mama gave no false hopes. Mama was often ill at ease with Iris, that was plain to see. For this Iris was often to feel great anger, to feel that she could really hate her mother. And at the same time she knew that they were and always would be as closely attached as the fingers to the hand and the hand to the arm. How could she have understood such things when she was nine years old? It was only after passing through a great deal of life that she would understand.

Yet perhaps in a way, though surely she could not have expressed it when she was just nine, perhaps in a way she did understand it, even then.

14

Nothing was done by any of the family in that house, or outside of it, that his father didn't know about. Maury felt sometimes as though his presence was everywhere, even when he wasn't at home. Some of his friends didn't like their fathers; one or two really hated them. Some of them felt that their fathers weren't interested in them. That was not true of Maury and Pa. He was interested in everything about Maury: his friends or his teeth or his manners. He taught him how to tie a tie. He showed him how to shake hands: "A man gives a firm handshake, as if he means it," he said.

Pa took Maury to his barber because he didn't like the way the old one cut his hair. They played checkers and Pa had promised to teach him to play pinochle, although Ma didn't approve. But Maury knew he would teach him anyway. Sometimes they wrestled on the living-room floor—his mother didn't approve of that either—and although Maury was almost as tall as Pa, Pa always won. His muscles were like iron. "That's from years of labor," he said, and now he kept up with exercises every morning. Once Maury saw him pick up a heavy man who had fallen in the street and carry him to the sidewalk all by himself.

But Maury wished Pa wasn't so interested in him. Sometimes he wished Pa would just let him alone. Iris, that stupid whining kid, could talk him out of anything. Not Maury; Maury had to 'toe the mark.' That was one of his expressions. Another was 'measure up,' an expression that Maury hated.

This morning Maury was angry, mad-angry, because he had to go with Pa to visit his grandmother. She was in an old-age home.

"Aw, gee," he said, "do I have to go ? A bunch of us were going to the rink this morning."

"Of course you have to go," his mother said. "You haven't seen your grandmother in months, and she's asked for you." She handed Maury his tie and jacket and got his good camel-hair coat out of the closet. She was all rushed and anxious. "Hurry, hurry, your father's already got his coat on. You know he can't stand being kept waiting!"

Maury strained into his sleeve. "Washington's Birthday, and I have to waste it! When do I get a whole day off to go skating?"

He knew that, if it were up to her, she'd let him go. She did look sympathetic for a moment, but then she said cheerfully, "Go, go. It won't be so bad," and pushed him to the front door where his father was ready to leave.

She remembered something. "Wait, wait, Joseph," and thrust a flowered tin box into Maury's hands. "I baked cookies for your grandmother. I'm sure they don't get such wonderful food in that place."

She kissed his father. She was tall, her face was on a level with his father's. In the morning she wore loose robes, blue or yellow or pale green like the insides of bonbons. Her clothes smelled sweet like candy. His father was all dark, except for the white shining board of his collar. He wore dark suits, sometimes a blue that was almost black, sometimes a gray that was almost black, a hard round derby hat and black shoes.

It was cold this morning; they felt it even in the elevator shaft as they went down to the street floor, and then the wind blasted and slammed them across the sidewalk to where the chauffeur held the door of the car.

"We're going up to the home, Tim," Pa said.

"Yes sir, Mr. Friedman." Tim always touched his cap and asked whether it was cold enough today. Then he went around to the front of the car and swung into the driver's seat.

The home where Maury's grandmother lived was on the fringes of the Bronx. Once it had been open country but now it was empty lots, with scatterings of new brick row houses and stores. It looked unfinished. Maury didn't know anybody who lived here and he only came here to visit his grandmother, which was not very often. It had

115

been a year since he had seen her last, just before his Bar Mitzvah, when his father was so upset because she wasn't able to come and 'see this day.'

"The car runs like a charm," Pa said. He lit a cigar. He always had half a dozen rich black ones in the inner pocket of his jacket; he and his friends liked to exchange them. They urged their brands on one another, blowing out a blue-gray haze of smoke, not unpleasant, although some women objected to it violently. But Pa seemed proud that his wife liked the fragrance, although Maury knew that even if his mother didn't like it she wouldn't say so.

His father struck another match, fumbling with the soggy end of the cigar, took it from his mouth to study it, replaced it and puffed again.

"Ah," he said and repeated, "the car runs like a charm."

The car was new. They had owned cars as long as Maury could remember, but this was the first car meant to be driven by a chauffeur. It had a sliding glass panel between the back of his neck and where the passengers sat. Maury's father was still not used to it, was perhaps still uncomfortable with the chauffeur. There had been some talk about it at the dinner table.

"I drive a lot," he had explained, but it sounded like an apology. "We've got jobs all over the city now and out on the Island. It's too hard to have to worry about parking. Besides, this way I can go over papers and save time while I'm being driven."

Where he himself was concerned, Pa always had to have a practical reason for anything he spent. He would buy the most expensive things for his family, toys or furniture or fur coats for Maury's mother, but with himself he was frugal.

He unfolded the *New York Times* and handed the first section to Maury. "I already read it at breakfast," he said. "Read it thoroughly; it can be a big help with your school work."

Pa was so concerned with what Maury did at school. He never had time to go to teacher conferences; Maury's mother did that, but in the evening Pa wanted to know everything that had been said. And he read the report cards very carefully when they came twice a year. He was always pleased.

He would slap Maury on the back. "Very good, son, very fine," he would say. "That's as it should be."

Maury wondered what would happen if the reports were not 'as they should be.' He knew his father wouldn't punish or scold too hard, the way some fathers did. But he also knew what his father expected.

The home was an old stone mansion, with wings and additions, lawns and a portico over the door. The inside was a net of corridors and cubicles, the corridors clogged with wheelchairs and tin trays of dirty dishes standing outside the rooms. And such a smell! A smell of disinfectant, frying grease and urine. Maury hated it. All the old, old people pushing walkers, and the young nurses, brisk and rapid, rushing in and out of rooms where through half-open doors you could see more old people lying in the beds, their gray hair mussed on the pillows. Maury hated it.

"Your grandmother is seventy-eight," Pa said now. Her room was at the end of the hall and she lived in it alone. Most of the people lived two in a room.

"Danny has a great-grandmother. She's ninety-two."

"That's very rare. And she had an easy life, that woman, never worked a day or worried a minute. Mama, hello, how are you?"

The grandmother was sitting with four other old men and women in an alcove outside of her room. If his father hadn't spoken to her, Maury would have gone right past without recognizing her. All the old women looked alike in their sweaters and printed dresses, either black or lavender. Those who weren't blobby were shriveled. Maury's grandmother was shriveled.

"Aren't you going to say something to your Grandma?"

Maury said hello to her and kissed her. He knew he was expected to. He didn't want to kiss her. His stomach went queasy at the touch; she had a sort of milky film over her eyes that were turned up to him and the spittle was collected thickly at the corners of her mouth. She disgusted him.

Pa drew up a pair of straight wooden chairs. "Give your Grandma the cookies," he said, and then corrected himself. "No, put them in her room, she can eat later." He leaned toward her. "Well, Mama," he said again.

The old woman stared at him and wrinkled her forehead. Her eyes were empty.

"It's Joseph, Mama," Pa said. "Joseph, your son. And I've brought Maury to see you."

Was she deaf, or what? Didn't she know her own son? Maury stared uncomfortably.

Then suddenly she began to talk. She leaned forward and took

117

Pa's hand. She cried and laughed. Pa answered her in Yiddish, and Maury understood none of it.

The fat old woman on Maury's other side touched his arm and tapped the side of her head. "She don't talk sense," she whispered loudly. "Don't pay attention," she said in English. "Her mind goes sometimes. She talks foolish."

Pa heard and frowned. But the old woman was not to be discouraged. "You're too thin," she told Maury.

The old man in the circle stared at Maury and said, "He ain't too thin!"

"What do you know? You got any children?" the old woman argued. "I got four children, three grandchildren, what do you know?"

"I got nieces and nephews, anyway. You got to have children? You got eyes in your head, that's enough!"

"I say he's too thin."

"Maury, why don't you take a little walk around and see the place?" his father suggested.

"There's nothing to see," Maury told him.

The old man asked, "That's your Grandma?"

Maury nodded.

"Why you don't talk to her, then?"

Maury flushed. "She doesn't speak English."

Now she was talking volubly to his father, laughing or crying or some of both, perhaps. She was telling a long story, making complaints or requests. Did they make any sense or not? Maury couldn't tell; his father just listened. Now and then he would nod or shake his head.

Then the grandmother looked at Maury and said something and his father answered. Maury looked away.

The old man said suddenly, "Your father's an important person. I'm eighty-eight and I know an important person when I see one. You can be anything you want," he told Maury. "A boy like you."

Maury looked down at the floor. The old man was wetting his pants. The stain was spreading on his trousers and sliding down the leg. It was starting to soak the tops of his shoes.

Jesus, let me get out of this loony-bin.

A nurse came hurrying and took the old man by the arm. "Oh, my. Oh, my, we have to go to the bathroom, don't we?"

His grandmother began to cry again.

"Maury," Pa said, very firmly this time, "Maury, wait outside. I won't be long. Or take a walk and look around."

"Why don't you go see the beautiful recreation room your father gave us?" the nurse suggested. "Turn right at the end of the corridor, you'll see it there."

It was boiling hot on account of the old people; he'd heard they were always cold. He took off his overcoat and stood in the doorway of the new room. It was large and light, with a bright blue linoleum floor and imitation leather chairs. Some old people were playing cards. There was a new upright piano in one corner and a woman was playing on it, the same chords over and over: "My Old Kentucky Home." A brown radio stood on a table in another corner next to a machine that gave out cokes and candy bars. There was even a platform with curtains drawn back and fastened to the wall so it could be used as a stage. An old man got up onto it now and shuffled, doing a cakewalk. Maury felt embarrassed for him. Then on the wall beside the double doors he saw the bronze plaque: *This room furnished through the gift of Joseph and Anna Friedman,* it said.

His father gave a lot to charity. The mail was always full of requests from the blind and from hospitals and the Jewish poor. He used to see him writing out checks at his desk. Once Mr. Malone even sent some priests. Maury had opened the door and been surprised to see these two men in their turned-around collars. Pa took them into his den and after a while they came out smiling and saying thank you. "We shall remember you in our masses," they said when they left.

Maury remembered feeling a certain pride in that. People respected his father. Wherever they went people listened to him as if they wanted to please him. Sometimes Maury went with him to the construction sites and followed him through the din and bustle of unloading trucks and cranes, cement mixers and men running wheelbarrows full of bricks. They climbed through all the confusion of boards and pipes and tubing and rolls of wire, through the damp, dank smell that is the smell of new building. His father asked questions and pointed out something that had been done wrong or not done at all. He knew what all these things were for. Then they went outside to the little wooden house at the curb marked Rental Office, and there Pa went over books and talked on the telephone. He unrolled plans, white ink on blue paper, and talked courteously to people who came in to inquire. They went back out on the sidewalk. Men in hard hats came over and his father introduced him: "My son Maury," he said, and the men shook hands and looked at him respectfully as if he weren't just thirteen years old. And he knew that the respect was because of his father.

A nurse came up behind him. "What do you think of the room?" she asked Maury.

"It's very nice."

"Your father's been good to us. He's a very generous, kind man," she said.

Pa beckoned from the end of the hall. Maury was relieved and pretended to be surprised. "Are we leaving already?"

"Yes, your grandmother isn't feeling well. I don't want to tire her."

"Do you want me to go and say good-by to her?" He hoped not, but knew that he ought at least to ask.

"No, thanks, it won't matter," Pa said. "She's gone to her room." They stopped at a desk near the elevator where a nurse sat in front of telephones and charts.

"That matter we talked about," Pa said. "I don't want it to happen again. There's no excuse for allowing her to fall out of bed."

"We'll do our best, Mr. Friedman, of course. But you know, she is failing fast and—"

"That makes no difference," his father said firmly. "I don't want it to happen again."

"Yes, Mr. Friedman, of course." She smiled brightly, artificially. "This is your son, isn't he? What a handsome boy! He looks like an Englishman."

"Yes. He's a good boy," Pa said, still not smiling.

She arched her lips at Maury. "I have the most gorgeous little niece. I'll have to introduce you in a couple of years—"

The elevator door opened and closed on her words. "Idiotic woman!" Pa said.

But Maury was annoyed at something else. Here he had given up his holiday because his grandmother wanted to see him and she hadn't even known him! That ruined, old, old—*thing!* Impossible to think of her as part of himself or of his father or anybody at all.

Back in the car Pa took a sheaf of papers out of a briefcase. "Excuse me, Maury, I want to go over these for a minute. I just thought of something."

Maury knew it was the new apartment-hotel, the largest job his father had undertaken yet. Last week the brick was up to the third floor; above that the red steel framework made a design of squares, forty-two stories of squares against the sky.

"The newest thing in apartment-hotel living," Pa said now, pausing over the papers. "The newest thing in the city. Did you know we're half rented already, with completion date not till next fall?"

He reached into his pocket for a cigar and matches and took a few puffs of enjoyment. "You know, sometimes I don't even believe all this has happened. Sometimes I wake up in the morning and I see the light coming through the curtains and for a second I don't know where I am. Isn't that queer? I'm not sure it's all real. Can you understand that? No, how could you? You've never known anything different, thank God, and I'll see to it that you never do."

He would, too, no doubt of that. He could do anything he wanted to do.

"Only in America," he said now. "Think of it! The sons of immigrants. Malone from the bogs of Ireland. And in ten years we've put our mark on the city. Whenever I see our green and white 'M and F' I think of that. But we give good value, we've rightfully earned whatever we get. I can truthfully say we have never cheated the public, our work is solid as the pyramids and that's more than a great many men in our line can say."

He went back to his papers and Maury started the second section of the *New York Times* for lack of anything else to do. It wasn't very interesting. But then, neither was looking out the window. They passed a clock in front of a bank. It said half past twelve and he thought, There's still plenty of time.

"Pa," he said, "is it all right to drop me off at the rink? I could borrow somebody's skates."

His father looked at him and right away Maury knew the answer would be no. "You've missed religious school for two weeks running because of your cold," he said. "You must be way behind."

A memory like an elephant. You would think that a man who had buildings going up all over the city would have no time for stuff like that. "I can make it up tomorrow. I'll get up early before school."

"You know you won't. No, you'll stay home this afternoon and prepare your work."

If he'd only leave him alone with this religious stuff! Most of the boys at his school didn't have all this religion to fuss about. Their families had given it up as narrow and unmodern. Pa's attitude was so stern, so solemn and boring. Now, with his mother, he didn't mind it as much. She made a pretty ritual out of it, the way she blessed the candles on Friday nights, and her silver candlesticks that she had brought from Europe. It was almost like poetry.

On Saturday mornings he hated to get up and go to the synagogue.

"Let him sleep," Ma would urge. "He studied late last night. I saw the light under the door."

"No," Pa said. "There is a right way and a wrong way, Anna."

"There won't be time for his breakfast. Let him miss it this once, Joseph."

"Then let him go without breakfast."

Pa always talked like that. He was angry when people were late and wouldn't wait more than ten minutes for anyone. He was angry when people broke rules. One of Ma's friends was going to Reno for a divorce and they were talking about it at the dinner table. Pa said, "There's no excuse for her, Anna. People know very well what's right, so let them do it and that's that."

"You sound so hard, Joseph," Ma said. "Isn't there any forgiveness in you?"

"There's a right way and a wrong way, Anna," Pa replied, just as he did on Saturday mornings: "Maury is to get up and go with us. No excuses."

He always went; he knew he had to go and no doubt it would have been easier to get up on time and go without protest. But he never did. Somehow, the battle had to be gone through first. He didn't know why it was like that between his father and himself.

And riding home now in the car, Maury thought: He runs everything and everybody. It seemed to him, in some vague way, that his father would loom over him for the rest of his life. Would there ever be a time when he would be able to say what he wanted to say to his father? And get his own way and be rid of this—this *battle* with someone who was always more powerful than he?

He was sullen the rest of the way home and up into his room. The last thing he heard before closing the door and sitting down to his work was his father's voice, not angry, but very firm and positive: "And, Anna, I don't want the lamb to be underdone the way it was last time. Tell Margaret."

*   *   *

Just before dinner his father called him into his den. On the table before him lay a cardboard box filled with pictures, snapshots and photographs.

"Here, son, I want to show you this. I got these out to put them in order."

Mounted on thick cardboard was an old, old photo of a girl, standing against a wall. Her skirt covered her shoes and her dress had big sleeves that went out from the shoulders like balloons. She had two thick long braids, and even in those queer clothes you could see she was very pretty. In the lower right-hand corner was some foreign name, the photographer's name, and the word 'Lublin.' That was a city in Poland, he knew that much.

"Who is it?" he asked.

"My mother," Pa said. "Your grandmother, before she was married."

Maury looked again. She had one hand on her hip in a pose almost impudent, and she was laughing; perhaps the photographer had just said something funny.

"I was always told she was a beautiful young woman," his father said. "And you can see she was."

That—that they had seen today—*that* had been *this?*

He had a flash of amazed vision, a frozen moment, in which for the first time he seemed to see everything there was to see and know everything there was to know. There was a phrase, a line from a poem or something read in English class, something about "long corridors of time." And he thought: This is what happens.

Suddenly, without intending to, he bent over and kissed his father, something he had been embarrassed to do since he was a little boy.

15

The *Berengaria* sailed for Southampton at noon with pennants snapping and music spangling the river wind. Engines rumbled and shook; the ship backed out into the Hudson, turned and moved out past the Statue of Liberty and past the place where Castle Garden used to be, the place where Anna had touched land in America. She hadn't been as excited then as she was now, and wasn't that strange?

Below in the stateroom the empty champagne bottles from their bon voyage party had not yet been removed. The dressers were crowded with gifts: three pyramids of fruit, enough for ten people; boxes of chocolates and cookies; a pile of novels; flowers; a ribbon-tied package from Solly and Ruth.

Anna opened it and took out a leather-bound, gilt-edged diary. "My Trip to Europe" was embossed on the cover.

Joseph smiled. "Ruth knows you're a scribbler, doesn't she?"

"I shall write in it every day," Anna said firmly. "I don't want to forget a minute of this."

June 4th

To go so far away, to the other side of the world! I still can't believe this is happening.

All of a sudden one evening last March Joseph said, "I want to do something grand for our anniversary this year. I want to go to Europe. We can afford it."

It struck me funny that when we are poor in Europe we think only about getting to America so we can get rich enough to go back to Europe.

"Not Paris," Joseph said. "You didn't come from Paris, you know."

So I shall actually be seeing Paris, the Louvre, the Tuileries, the Cours La Reine where Marie Antoinette came riding in from Versailles! I think of the city as an enormous crystal chandelier, all fountains, lights and sparkle.

But mostly I shall be thankful to see my brothers in Vienna. I wonder whether we will even recognize each other?

A whole crowd came to see us off, friends and business people and of course the Malones. Malone and Mary are going to Ireland for about six weeks after we get home in September. They want to see where their ancestors came from. Joseph said he surely wasn't going to go back to Russia to see where *his* came from!

Malone is so hearty, I think that would be the best description of him. He gives the impression of never being worried. I asked Mary whether that was true and she said she thought it was. It must be very easy and relaxed to live with a man like that. He brings humor into every situation. We were watching people arrive up the gangplank and Malone kept joking: "There's Lord Throttlebottom!" (A long man like a string bean with mustaches that went out of style thirty years ago.) "And there's Lady Luella Pursemouth!" He's not unkind, though, just funny.

After they called "All ashore that's going ashore!" we went up on deck. Maury and Iris looked so small standing with Ruth and Solly far below. I would have taken the children to Europe with us, but Joseph wants a vacation without children. We've never had one, not even one day! I can't get over Joseph's being willing to take a vacation at all, he who has worked six days a week and sometimes even seven for as long as I've known him. But I shall miss the children.

Ruth put her arm around Iris and I knew she was giving me a message not to worry. I do worry some: Iris is only ten, and so shy, so wan. My heart sinks, thinking of her, although I know Ruth will take care of her.

Dear Ruth! You were the first person to greet me when I

came to America. I remember how you got up from the sewing machine in that dreadful little room. How far we have come since then, you and I and all of us!

Our stateroom is at the top of the ship, the Veranda Deck. I walked out just now; there is still daylight in the sky, although the ocean is black. There is no land in sight. We are really at sea. There's nothing, nothing at all, but sky and sea.

June 5th

Joseph was really angry at me this morning. I'm not used to anger from him, except rarely and then over trivial things. We were reading on deck when suddenly he almost shouted at me: "Where's your ring?" (meaning the diamond that he gave me last month for our anniversary). And when I told him it was downstairs in my drawer with my clothes he was furious. He says I am to wear that ring all the time, every minute. I said I didn't think it was appropriate to wear such a large diamond with a sweater and skirt but he said he didn't give a damn, that the ring was very valuable and I should understand that it had to be guarded at all times. He sent me downstairs to get it and on the way I was terrified that perhaps someone had stolen it. It must have cost a fortune! but, thank God, there it was, safe among my stockings.

The thing is, I never really wanted it. Things like that truly don't mean that much to me, although Joseph cannot understand that. He thinks all women are absolutely mad about diamonds. I suppose most of them are. I know all my friends were so impressed when they saw it. I do believe that is the real reason Joseph wants me to wear it all the time, why he wanted me to take it on this trip in the first place.

June 7th

At our table I learn that there is a world of ships, and that this voyage, which is such an adventure for us, is a way of living for others. These people all cross the Atlantic as casually as we take the Fifth Avenue bus. One couple from outside Philadelphia, people about our age, are traveling with three children and a nursemaid who take their meals in their suite. They come to Europe every year, renting a house in England, Switzerland or France. Joseph was surprised, he didn't think they looked all that wealthy, but he doesn't realize that their simplicity is very expensive. They don't talk very much and when they do they have more to say to the old lady than to us. The old lady is the widow of a New York banker; she travels all over the world, it seems, with her daughter. The daughter is in her late twenties. She looks lonely and bored. I feel sorry for her.

I listen to the conversations of this traveling fraternity. They know the names of all the captains and pursers on the great ships. They talk about whom they met on this or that voyage and what cocktail parties they were invited to. One night all these people were asked to the captain's table and Joseph and I had the table to ourselves. The hierarchy of the ship! I suppose we were put here because there were two seats left over; certainly we don't belong here. Joseph is more quiet than ever and I know that he feels out of place. Naturally, I am just as out of place but it doesn't bother me; I find it interesting. I watch the spectacle, the procession descending the stairs to dinner: sagging women in brocade and diamonds, tired-looking men, honeymoon couples. Turning heads, energetic smiles, the chirp of greeting: "How *are* you? I haven't *seen* you in ages!"

I watch the food, the great fish carved in ice, the vegetables like a Dutch still life, the spun-sugar baskets, the little iced cakes arranged like a bouquet. What labor and art to cook like that! I look at the nice, fresh faces of the boys who wait on us. They seem so cheerful and respectful as they pull your chair out: "Good evening, madame, have you had a nice afternoon?" I wonder what they really think about all of us.

After dinner last night we went up to dance, and I was saying all this to Joseph. He was a little annoyed. "Can't you ever just enjoy yourself, without all these serious thoughts?" he asked. I told him I was enjoying myself and I couldn't help my thoughts. "Don't you want me to tell you anything anymore?" I answered. And then he said, "Oh, come on, you can tell me anything you want, you know you can." So then he was very good-humored, and we danced until after midnight. The music was splendid and Joseph dances very well. Really we ought to do it more often! It clears the head. One feels so light and easy, not thinking about anything at all. He's right, I *ponder* too much.

June 8th

It rained today and the wind bends you double as you round the corner of the deck. Everyone is inside. Joseph has found a couple of kindred souls and they are playing cards. Some have gone down to the movie. But I don't want to miss a minute of the sea. I went up alone on deck and stood in the blowing spray. How fierce the North Atlantic is, even in the summer! One has a sense of danger, something elemental, although of course on this great modern liner I am only fooling myself about elemental dangers!

The day after tomorrow, when we wake up, they tell us we shall see Ireland. How will the Malones feel when they see it for the first time?

June 11th

I think I must know all the streets in London. The first morning we went out for a walk. Our hotel is on Park Lane. We had planned to see the changing of the guard at Buckingham Palace, and Joseph wanted to see Hyde Park Corner where the radicals come and rant. When I told him to turn left he looked at me in amazement and said: "Are you sure you haven't been here before?" And I said that I had been, in dozens of books, Dickens and Thackeray and all the books on the list Miss Thorne once gave me. That was eighteen years ago and I only finished the list last year. Of course I did read things in between besides all my courses in art and music history.

I wonder about Miss Mary Thorne. I suppose she must be retired now, back in Boston probably, making tea in a little room with shelves and shelves of books. How could she or I have guessed the things that would happen all these years?

June 13th

Joseph has a business appointment with some British investors who are interested in New York real estate. I was sorry that business had to interfere with sightseeing, but he didn't mind at all. I think he really welcomed the interference. So I took the boat ride to Kew Gardens by myself. *Have you been to Kew in lilac time?*

I sat next to a very nice man on the boat, an American from New Hampshire. He teaches history at some famous school; I've forgotten the name. His wife died six months ago. He said they had been planning this trip abroad for quite a while and she had made him promise to go anyway after her death. She had said it would be good for him, that he mustn't sit at home and mourn. What a wonderful, unselfish, large-minded woman!

He asked me where I came from. He thought, because of my accent, I suppose, that I might be French and seemed surprised when I told him the truth.

We got talking about England. He'd been hiking in the Lake District, Wordsworth country, and I said I was sorry we wouldn't be going there. I think I should love a vacation like that, walking through the villages, seeing how people really live, instead of just staying in large hotels where you only see other tourists. He agreed with me. We had a very nice conversation, and by the time we got to Kew, it was only natural to walk around together. It's a marvelous place! What a pity Joseph missed it! Maybe he would have enjoyed it after all, in spite of his saying he wouldn't.

The man's name was Jeffers. They had no children, which is too bad, since now he has nothing left of his wife at all. I told him about my children when he inquired, mostly about Maury, how he planned to go to Yale and was interested in literature. He mentioned some professors there who are especially fine and famous. All in all, it was a very pleasant time and we found ourselves talking as though we had known each other a long while. I seldom, or perhaps never, meet men who like to talk to women. I was thinking how warm it was, how consoling, although that's really not the right word; perhaps cheerful would be more accurate.

On the way back, when we were almost at the end of the trip, Mr. Jeffers said he'd had an unexpectedly wonderful afternoon.

"I shall be so sorry not to see you again," he said. He looked straight at me when he said it, and I saw something very serious and regretful in his face. He was not being a 'smart aleck'; goodness knows I've seen enough of that to recognize it. He really meant it, and so I said, "I'm sorry too, and I hope you'll be very happy again, someday." And I really meant it. I think we had only begun to talk. There would have been so much more for us to say to each other if—a hundred ifs.

Joseph was waiting on the embankment. He first asked how I had enjoyed the trip and then he wanted to know who the man was.

"You seemed to be having quite a conversation," he said. "I was watching you while the boat drew in."

"Oh, yes," I said, "he's an American, a schoolteacher. He gave me some very good advice about Maury."

"You talked about Maury the whole time?"

"I didn't spend the whole time talking to the man, Joseph!"

"Don't you know that I'm jealous?" he said.

But he has no reason to be and never will. I am absolutely, I am completely, to be trusted. And I will stake my life on that.

June 26th

We are on the train, crossing the border into Austria. In a matter of hours I shall see Dan and Eli! Joseph is almost as excited as I am about it. He feels for me and for our long separation. "Families shouldn't be torn apart like that," he says, and he is right. But what can you do?

The scenery here reminds me of *The Student Prince*, which we saw a couple of years ago. First the fortress on the peak above Salzburg. Then an hour or more of lakes like big blue tears spilled on the earth. And a monastery, gloomy, powerful and secretive; "Melk," it says in the guidebook. Now woods, the Wienerwald no doubt, the Vienna Woods. And in a few minutes more, the station where they will be waiting.

Joseph is watching me. "Don't you ever get tired of scribbling?" he asks, and takes my hand and smiles. He knows I am like jelly inside, and strokes it to calm me. I put this book away.

June 26th, later

My brother Eli is called Eduard now. We were met on the platform by him and Tessa. I confess I would not have known him! Nineteen years, after all! But his hair is still red. We cried, both of us, and Joseph was very moved seeing us, but I think Tessa was embarrassed in front of their chauffeur. How-

130

ever, she was very sweet, kissed me and welcomed us. She is not an especially pretty woman but thin and graceful. One wants to look at her, although Joseph doesn't agree. I think he disliked her at once, which is unusual for Joseph, who rarely says much about people.

Eli-Eduard wanted us to stay at their house and was distressed when we told him we had a reservation at Sacher's Hotel. But Joseph says no, we are staying two weeks and that is too long a time to stay in anyone's house. We can see them every day, without getting in the way of their family. That too is like Joseph, very considerate. Or is it independent?

June 26th, later

We are back at the hotel to dress for dinner. Eduard will send the car for us. But first we went out to his house in the eighth district. It is rather far from the center of the city, almost a suburb, with large houses and grounds. They call them villas but, by American standards, I would call them miniature palaces! Eduard's has gold plaster cherubs on the ceilings. I tried not to crane my head up all the time while Tessa was serving coffee and cake. We sat for a while in the garden, a lovely spot with high trees all around, making a private outdoor room, bright with mauve and scarlet flowers. I really ought to learn the names of flowers. I am completely ignorant of anything except a rose or a daisy! Oh, I forgot to say, all the rooms are heated in winter by huge stoves that look like high boxes made of porcelain tiles, with beautiful designs on them. Joseph was amused. On the way back he said, "To think of heating with a stove in the twentieth century! How far behind us Europe is!"

The children came in to meet us, a handsome little boy and two blond girls. Liesel is just Iris' age. She played the piano very well, I thought, although I am no judge. What lovely manners the children have!

June 27th

Now that I have spent a day with Eduard I can clearly see the outline of the boy who parted from me: the same very charming smile, the prominent jaw, the eyes that crinkle. And

131

yet he looks like an Austrian gentleman. I see that he cares about his clothes, or else it is Tessa who cares for him.

But I am saddened about Dan. He doesn't look like his brother anymore, and they are identical twins! He is quite round-shouldered and his smile is almost apologetic. His wife Dena is rather pretty, although too plump. She doesn't care about her figure; she took two helpings of whipped cream. Anyway, she's nice and I liked her at once. I felt easy with her, as I did not with Tessa.

I can see that Tessa does not think much of Dena or Dan; it is obvious that they live in different worlds. Dena helps Dan in his fur shop, though it must be very hard on her. They have six children, and she whispered to me after dinner that she expects again!

I wish I could have had more children. I could have them still; perhaps it isn't too late? I am only thirty-five. Joseph is terribly disappointed that we have only two, I know, although he never says a word. I suppose he thinks it would be a reproach, or perhaps that there's no use discussing things that can't be helped. He is supremely practical and doesn't waste words, as surely I ought to have learned by now.

It was rather an awkward evening. It is apparent to me that my brothers do not get together very often, although no one said so. But what really amazed me was that there should be a language problem between them! An entirely manufactured one, to be sure. Dan and Dena speak Yiddish at home. Dena is a poor girl with no education and she has lived among people like herself ever since coming to Vienna. Tessa naturally speaks no Yiddish, only German and French, as she took pains to let us know. However, Yiddish and German are really so closely related that, with a little effort, they would all be able to understand each other. Joseph swears that they do, that Tessa only pretends not to. He had very little difficulty understanding Tessa's German, he said. I think she is an *unbending* woman. I wonder whether Eduard can be happy?

July 1st

We have been so busy seeing the sights here that I haven't had time to write. We have seen all the museums and the Hofburg, the great palace where the last Emperor lived up to a few years ago. Also the Spanish Riding School, a most glittering hall. Such courtly ceremony, such marvelous white horses, a true spectacle! Joseph enjoyed it, I'm sure, but he did remark to me later that such stuff is at best childish and at worst wrong, in that it perpetuates a useless way of life, catering to people who do not work. Of course, to Joseph that is the worst damnation of all, not to work. I did not think we would get him in to hear the Boys' Choir in the chapel but to my surprise he went, and had to admit that the chapel is gorgeous in the original sense of the word: it glitters.

Oh, and we saw the Burgtheatre and the lovely Burggarten. Eduard has been so eager to show us everything and, since he has his own business, he can take all the free time he wants. We went to Schönbrunn and I was enthralled to think that this is where Maria Theresa lived, and in France at Versailles we shall see where her daughter lived and died. I want to reread Stefan Zweig's *Marie Antoinette* when I get home. Now that I have seen all this she will seem much more alive to me. I am making so many good resolutions!

July 2d

Eduard has been so wonderful. I told him I am almost sorry to have had this time with him because now it will be so very hard to part. It's funny how different he is when Tessa is not with us. And yet I'm sure he loves her; he looks at her with such pride.

This afternoon we were invited to Dan's house and Eduard said he would take us there. (It is Sunday and all the church bells are ringing, there must be thousands of them. That's another thing I shall remember about Europe, that sweet clamor that makes a vibration up the spine. Joseph doesn't like the noise, he says, but I think it is simply that he doesn't like churches.)

Anyway, we drove to Dan's. He lives on a poor street where the stores are all open, in spite of it being Sunday. It is like the lower East Side. They sell dress goods, men's suiting and other dry goods, wholesale and retail. The men sit in the doorways and coax you to come in and buy. Yes, it is like the lower East

Side except more quiet and orderly, without pushcarts. But the people live upstairs above the shops in the same way.

Dan's flat is dark and crowded. The furniture looks too big for the rooms. It must be a struggle for Dena to keep house there with all those children and her father, who lives with them. He is a little old, old man in a long black coat and side curls. He looks more like her grandfather.

Eduard stayed for more than an hour. Dena brought out coffee and cake. They seem to exist on coffee and cake in Vienna but I must say it is delicious, and so rich . . . (Eduard took us to Demel's for pastry yesterday and it was superb). We got to talking, the three of us, about the things we remembered of home. It was very warm and good, not sad as I might have expected it to be. Joseph and Dena sat listening and seemed so happy for us. Joseph said he liked to enjoy my relationship with my brothers because he was an only child. Dena has three sisters but they all live in Germany and she hasn't seen them in years.

"But it's not far!" I said, and then was sorry I had said such a stupid thing because Dan explained, "It's very expensive to travel, Anna." And Dena added, "It's not easy for us here, but in Germany it's even worse. Many people there are starving."

"Business is booming in America," Joseph said. "Anybody can get ahead there. Have you ever thought of coming, Dan?"

Dan said he hadn't thought of it; he was doing all right and this was home by now. He didn't want to move and wander again. And then he added almost mischievously, "I notice you don't invite my brother."

Joseph looked flustered for a moment, but Eduard said, very simply, "No, I've been lucky."

He was so different in that house, speaking in Yiddish to Dena's father, telling jokes. And finally, when he said that he hated to leave but had to, we knew that he meant it.

Dan was different in his own house, too. We had a good supper, a bowl of rich soup, and chicken with dumplings on a platter in the center of the table.

"You can talk and be yourself without all those wooden statues standing around the way they do in Eduard's house," Dan remarked. There wasn't any envy in the way he said it, but I didn't tell him that we had maids at home too, although our Ellen and Margaret are hardly as stiff and formal as the people at Eduard's.

I asked Dan how Eduard had met his wife.

"Die Gräfin, the Countess?" he replied, and Dena scolded him: "Dan, that's not nice!"

"Well," Dan said, "I call her that, anyway. Oh, she's not really bad, just different. How he met her? He became a hero during the war, you know, and there was a party at someone's house—rich people were always giving parties—and that's how they met. I know her father wasn't so pleased at the beginning, but after a while he came to think the world of Eduard and he took him into the family businesses. They have so many connections, textiles, banking, government. So that's the story."

After supper it was still light and I helped Dena clear away while Dan and Joseph went for a walk. Dan said that since Joseph was in the construction business he wanted to show him something. They were gone more than an hour and were in great good humor when they came in. They had visited a schoolhouse from the seventeenth century with walls three feet thick, still in use.

We get along so well together. It is really a sad thing that we must live as strangers! When we left Dena hugged me and said those very words: "It is a sad thing that we must live apart like strangers."

July 4th

Today is the Fourth of July. It seems queer not to be at the beach, going out on the porch to see the fireworks exploding over the water. Iris will be watching at Ruth's this year. She always gets so excited. I remember the first fireworks I ever saw, that Fourth when we went to Coney Island just before Maury was born. I feel far from America, far from my home.

July 6th

I must say Tessa has been very gracious to me. This afternoon she took me shopping and we must have gone in and out of every shop on the Graben and Kärtnerstrasse. I bought a petit-point bag for myself, some gifts and a wonderful porcelain

135

tea service. I told Tessa that, considering what it cost, I should have to wash it myself. I wouldn't trust anyone with it.

"Ah yes," she said, "I can understand that. Of course, I don't have to worry like that because I have Trudl, who came with me from my parents' house when I got married. She takes care of things as though they were her own."

It must be nice to be as confident as Tessa is. I don't think she means to sound arrogant. I think it is we who misinterpret. Are we perhaps envious of her confidence? Anyway, I'm glad I brought the good clothes Joseph wanted me to bring. The women here are really elegant.

I bought a gold wristwatch for Joseph. It cost much less than it would at home, but still it was plenty. I've saved a good bit out of the household money; it is the only way I could get something really fine for Joseph, since he will never buy anything for himself. I shall not show it to him until we are on the ship, or he will make me take it back.

Tessa came in with me for coffee at Sacher's. Joseph was waiting when we walked in with the packages. He looked pleased that I had bought things.

"Wait till she gets to Paris," he told Tessa.

Tessa said that since we hadn't been there before we would undoubtedly enjoy it, but as for herself, it bored her. Her parents used to take her every year for shopping and every year her mother had said it was the last time, because the workmanship in Vienna was far superior.

Joseph was amused, I saw, but he made no comment, for which I was thankful.

July 9th

Eduard and Tessa gave a big party for us tonight. It was splendid and I understood why Dena and Dan had declined to come. I'm sure Dena would not have had anything to wear. There were all sorts of people there, musicians and government people and even a couple whose name began with 'von,' which meant, Joseph said, that they didn't work because somebody else worked for them, or stole for them, a few hundred years ago! Nevertheless, it was very exciting for me. When have I ever, when will I ever, see such an evening again?

After dinner we went into one of the drawing rooms where rows of gilded chairs had been set up. There was a string quartet and a piano. Most of the pieces they played were Mozart. I don't know much about it but I've tried to learn. It's funny, when you first hear Mozart it seems rather dry and twangy. One has to grow used to it. After a while it becomes very beautiful, clear and sprightly. I could tell that Joseph didn't like it, though. The only music he likes even a little bit is Tchaikovsky's, which one of the teachers in my music course likened to an emotional bath. But what's the matter with taking an emotional bath if it makes you feel good?

After the concert everyone went out into the garden and Eduard—how much he reminds me of Maury!—introduced a man who bent over and kissed my hand. When Eduard left us the man, a very good-looking man who spoke beautiful English, asked me what I had seen of Vienna. So I told him we had driven through the Vienna Woods that afternoon.

"Ah, then you know the story of Marie Vetsera and the Crown Prince?"

I knew vaguely that they had had a love affair, but I hadn't known that he was married, she was pregnant, and he had shot them both to death.

"Well, what do you think of the romantic story?" he asked, when he had finished.

I told him it was not as romantic as I had thought, that it was rather more sordid.

"You Americans are so innocent, so moralistic!" he said. "It would be fun to take an innocent woman like you and teach her a few things."

Well, I have met with that sort of thing before! The words and the accent may be different but the question in the eyes is the same: "Do you—? Will you—?" And I know just how to turn blank eyes which say, "I don't and I won't." Thank God that I know how.

I don't know whether to be flattered or insulted at such times. Perhaps a little of both.

July 12th

Tonight was our last night. We invited everyone to dinner at the hotel. Joseph ordered a grand dinner with the famous

Sacher torte for dessert. He told the wine steward to bring the best wines, using his own judgment since, "I'm an American and I don't know the first thing about wines." That is something I always admire about Joseph, his utter honesty and absence of sham.

The dinner was gay, and sorrowful too. My heart was very full. We are leaving early in the morning for Paris and we told them not to take us to the train, but to say good-by right here. It would be easier for us all. So we left with many promises to visit back and forth, which I doubt will be kept. Little Dan . . . little Eli . . . when they had left and we went upstairs, I lay down on the bed. Joseph came over and lay beside me, and took my hand. After a while he told me that he had asked Dan whether there was anything he could do for him and Dan had said that there wasn't. But Joseph had put some money in a bank account for him anyway and he wouldn't get the notice of it until after we had left. I cried with gratitude for this kindness to my brother, this kindness of my husband's.

July 22d

We have been in Paris almost a week and I have been too tired, too busy, too exhilarated to write a word until today. We have seen the great sights of this city, my "crystal chandelier." Today we went up the Eiffel Tower, having saved it to the last.

From the top you can see blocks of white stone buildings, squares and streets thick with summer trees. The awnings are all of a dark burnt orange. I told Joseph that I wanted to stand and look so I would remember it forever.

"We have an appointment at three o'clock," he said, and was so mysterious about it. But when I pressed it turned out not to be an appointment; it was just that he had made up his mind to take me to a couturier for some clothes. I told him they were far too expensive and really I didn't need any. Nobody we know wears Paris clothes. But he insisted, and so we went. I think he learned about the place from a fashion magazine which someone had left in the lobby.

Anyway, I now own a fine navy blue suit which I shall get a lot of wear out of and a pale pink evening dress which is the most beautiful thing I have ever owned. When I move it floats, and when I stand still it stands in folds like the stone folds on a statue.

Joseph said he thought that red-haired women should never wear pink. The vendeuse, a rather haughty person in black, said, "On the contrary, red is very subtle for her. Madame is very striking. But, *vous permettez,* madame? Not so many bracelets. And never, never costume jewelry with real." I knew it, Joseph always insists that I wear too much jewelry.

"It is like a room with too much furniture, too much jewelry," she said.

Speaking of furniture, I should so much like to get rid of all that fancy stuff when we get home. Now that I have seen real French furniture I realize that ours is an overblown, expensive imitation. I wonder whether Joseph would let me get rid of it.

On the way back to the hotel I thanked him for the clothes, which really cost far too much, and he said, "You can wear the pink when Solly's boy gets married next winter. You'll stand out from all the others in their fringe and beads!"

The wedding is to be at a hall in Brooklyn. She's a sweet girl, I met her one afternoon at Ruth's. The dress will be quite out of place there, but I know Joseph wants to show it off.

July 23d

I stand and listen to people speaking French in the stores and on the street. It's such a pert, crisp language, elegant as rustling taffeta. I wish I could speak it. Another one of my many wishes!

August 4th

We are back from our tour of the château country. I have no time to describe it, and no words, except to say that it is a dream of enchantment. They have rushed my dresses through these past two weeks, and Joseph has made an appointment for a portrait of me. He got the name of the artist from an American man whom we met at one of the hotels. It seems that 'everyone' is having his portrait done by this particular artist. I am to wear the pink dress. I feel silly but Joseph is so enthusiastic about the idea that I can't say no. The picture is to be framed and completed after our departure and will be sent to us.

August 11th

The artist has finished the preliminaries of the portrait. The face is finished, the rest just outlined, but enough so that I can see what it will be like. Anyone can tell it's me; it's a good likeness. But the very idea of myself being painted for posterity in that dress seems so ridiculous! My mind goes back to Me stitching pants at Ruth's, Me rolling cloth and dusting the counters at Uncle Meyer's, Me going for eggs across the river to Pretty Leah's—although I don't want to think about *that.*

August 12th

Tomorrow we take the boat train. Europe, good-by!

August 14th

The voyage home is different. There is a touch of sadness in it. I know it will be a long time before we can come back, if we ever do. And still I am in a hurry to get home. Maury has been growing so fast this past year; I wonder whether he is much taller? And even though Ruth has written that Iris is fine, I wonder whether she really has been. Ruth might have wanted not to worry us or spoil our vacation. Or else Iris might appear to be fine and happy; she has that way of concealing things, while inside she may be miserable. I feel sometimes that I know my daughter so well, and then at other times that I don't know her at all. Maury is easy to understand, I think. Or do I delude myself? Joseph says I worry about them both too much.

August 15th

We have better people at our table going back, or should I say people who are more like ourselves, easier to get along with? One of the women, a Mrs. Quinn, reminds me of Mary Malone. She has the same fine white skin and those lovely round Irish eyes. Her husband is in the auto supply business.

140

He and Joseph were talking about a piece of property for him. Later and as always I said to Joseph: "Don't you ever leave business behind? You'll be home soon enough."

August 16th

At the table next to ours there is the strangest couple. The women at our table keep watching them. He is an old, old man, finely dressed and slender, with white, well-groomed hair. But his skin is dry as paper; he must be eighty. And with him is a young girl, who looks like nineteen, although she is probably older. She has the light bones of a swallow. One would think she might be the granddaughter, traveling with him. But no, they are married!

After dinner we saw them again at the entertainment. They were listening to the singer, a young man who sang a romantic song in Spanish or perhaps Italian. It was quite beautiful, passionate music, probably filched from Schubert. I kept looking at that young girl and wondering what she might be feeling while the young man sang.

I mentioned it to Joseph and he said, "She's a whore, what do you think! Some women will do anything for money."

But I think there must be more to it than that. One needs to know the circumstances that make people do what they do. Joseph says I am too soft and always make excuses for people. I think he makes things too simple.

August 18th

One more day and we shall be in New York. I am standing at the prow facing into the wind. It is cold and so clean on the skin. Then I go to the stern and watch the wake fanning in a 'V,' flat silver ripples in the green. Tomorrow I know, as we draw near land, the gulls will come to follow the ship as they did on the way over. I am told they are waiting for the garbage to be thrown out. I had preferred the poetic idea that they came to welcome us in. Oh, well, an incurable romantic, I!

I woke this morning to the thought that we are only one day away from our children. I can't wait. I could get out and push the ship. Then something else came flooding. I realized that

141

all the time we were away I had forgotten, or not thought of—is it possible?—the thing that otherwise is with me every day. Even when I am not consciously aware of it, I know that it is there. Like someone standing behind a curtain, waiting. Now it has come back again, behind the curtain. The presence, waiting.

On the Day of Atonement you ask God to forgive you for sins against Him. Sins against man can be forgiven only by the person who has been sinned against. But here is my dilemma: how can a person forgive another for a sin against him that he doesn't even know about? Yet to tell him would be another sin because it would bring such useless suffering. And anyway, if this particular person did know, this particular person would never forgive. Never, never, never.

My head aches. That man, the priest of another religion, was right when he said: "Do you think you will not pay, every day of your life?"

August 19th

We have just come through the Narrows. Our luggage is on Main Deck and I have run down to check the stateroom to make sure we have left nothing behind. Joseph is standing at the rail because he doesn't want to miss the Statue of Liberty. When I was up there with him just now he put his arm around me and asked me whether I was glad to be home and whether it had been as good a time as I had hoped for. The answer to both is yes, and I said so. "Life has been very good to us," he said, and it is true. I don't deserve the goodness it has given me.

16

In the first week of September, 1929, New York roused from its summer siesta. The balmy, gilded streets were crammed with back-to-school and back-to-the-city shoppers. Fifth Avenue windows drew crowds of ladies to see the latest news from Paris: waistlines had risen from the hip and skirts were definitely dropping to the middle of the calf. The color of the year was *bois-de-rose* and brocade would be favored for theatregoing. Theatre-ticket brokers were rushed, the musical spectaculars being sold out months ahead. The rattle of riveting was heard on the avenues and the towers rose in set-backs and terraces, glittering with glass in the new style of Le Corbusier. The stock market, which was the cause and also the effect of these things, stood at its all-time peak.

On the third of September a single share of Montgomery Ward, bought for one hundred thirty-two dollars in the previous year, was worth four hundred sixty-six dollars. Radio Corporation of America, bought at ninety-four and a half, sold at five hundred five. Many individuals owned thousands of shares like these. One could buy them, after all, for only ten percent down and owe the broker for the rest.

On the fourth of September a little dip occurred, not worth noticing. On September fifth the *New York Times* index reported a drop of ten points, still not worth noticing, although Roger Babson, the financial writer, said that the ride was over and a depression was on the way. But he was some sort of nutty alarmist; everybody knew that nothing went straight up without a break; there were bound to be small, inconsequential dips from time to time before the rise resumed.

But early in the week of October twenty-first the slide had gone too far and brokers began to send out margin calls. When the money was not forthcoming—and how could it be?—the dumping began. And on Thursday, October twenty-fourth, the structure of the market cracked like a rotten nut. Millions of shares were pitched into a screaming chaos on the floor of the exchange, while outside on this Black Thursday, at the corner of Broad and Wall, the crowds stood stunned and curious, talking in quiet voices. They couldn't believe it. Surely something would happen to retrieve it? Something?

For five days it went like that until full panic struck on the twenty-ninth of the month and the slide hit bottom, like a stone crashing to the pit of a well. On one of those days alone General Electric, one of the soundest stocks in the country, lost forty-eight points. There was a still lower level to be reached, although people didn't know that then. They didn't know that by 1932 United States Steel would be down to twenty-one and General Motors to seven.

But if they had known it wouldn't have made any difference. They were already ruined.

Within the next few months the towers stopped rising, and it became apparent that their stone had rested on the foundation of Wall Street's paper. The riveting was stilled, that confident *rat-tat-tat*, that proclamation to the future. Children born in the city that year would finish high school without once hearing the sound.

Everything seemed to be standing still, waiting for Joseph. In his nightly dreams and waking visions he saw a cluster of white faces all turned up to him, questioning and waiting.

It began with poor Malone, the week of October twenty-first. He hadn't known that Malone had put everything into stocks. He himself had never owned many; he believed in land. What he had owned he had sold before leaving for Europe, on the theory that nobody can look after a man's affairs as well as he can himself.

When the broker telephoned, Malone was still spending the fall in Ireland. He needed at least a hundred thousand dollars, or he would have to sell him out.

"Give me until the day after tomorrow," Joseph pleaded. "I'll reach him somehow." And he wondered where Malone would find cash like that.

He tried the transatlantic telephone and after hours got a tinny voice, fading in and out, from a hotel in Wexford: Mr. and Mrs. Malone had rented a car to go visiting relatives out in the country.

No, they had left no address and no, they wouldn't be coming back. The ship wasn't due to sail for another week and by the time he could reach them there it would be too late.

He went to bed haunted by his friend's disaster.

In the morning he was awakened by the telephone. Solly excused himself for calling so early, but he hadn't slept all night and he was calling Joseph only as a very last resort: would Joseph get him forty-five thousand dollars today?

Well, that was an awful lot of money.

Yes, he knew it was, but the bottom had dropped out of his stocks and he'd had a margin call for eleven this morning.

My God, what a terrible thing.

Yes, it was terrible. That was all he had in the world except for his life insurance.

Joseph had thought by the way they lived that Solly would have had more than that, which just went to show, you never could tell.

But this was only temporary, Solly assured him; he had a hunch the market would rebound in a month or two. So if Joseph could just tide him over, as soon as the stocks went up again Solly would sell and pay him back.

That was a lot of money, Joseph said again, not knowing what else to say, not knowing how else to tell him that he wouldn't risk money like that on Solly's hunch, or that if he had been going to take any risk it would have been for Malone.

Solly would gladly pay interest, if that's what Joseph wanted.

No, that wasn't what he wanted; he certainly didn't want to make money out of someone he knew and loved as much as Solly. It was just that he couldn't afford to endanger his own family. He hoped Solly could understand that. He really wished so much that he could come to his rescue. Was Solly sure he had tried everything: the banks, the professional money lenders? . . . Joseph's voice trailed weakly.

Yes, Solly had tried everything and Joseph was his last hope. Was this really his final word?

Yes it was, and he was so sorry. Solly would never know how sorry.

That was the last time they spoke together. By five o'clock that afternoon Solly was dead.

On the way home from the office Tim happened to pass through the street where Solly lived and found it blocked by police cars and crowds. He leaned out and asked a bystander what was wrong.

"A man jumped out of the window," she reported, and Joseph knew, he simply knew, that it was Solly.

When he got home he went to the telephone. A strange voice answered at Solly's house, a neighbor perhaps.

"Has anything—is everything all right?" he asked, the question not seeming odd at all.

"No," the woman said, muffled and crying. "Oh, my God, Solly has killed himself! . . ."

He put the receiver softly back, and sat for a while alone, and summoned Anna. For the next few days they were occupied with Ruth. She was so calm it was as if she had died too. People kept coming in, hesitating, with shock in their faces. What should they say to her? They didn't know what to say. So they put their arms around her, pressing their cheeks to her face, and then went into the dining room where neighbors had put out a coffee urn and platters of food, fruit and cold cuts and cakes, because the living must go on eating and living.

Every few minutes someone said, "I don't think she even realizes it yet," and another answered, "Next week, next month, she will really know what's happened."

In the meantime Ruth sat in the living room on Solly's chair. The fat white mourning candle burned in its holder on the piano which was newly draped with the Spanish shawl that Joseph and Anna had brought from Europe only a few weeks before. It was black silk with flowers and fringe, a gaudy thing that Ruth had wanted so badly. Now she stretched out her hand, thin and transparent against the candle flame.

"Empty, empty," she said, and was silent.

He kept starting awake. He knew he had been dreaming but in the instant of waking the dream fled, and he could only remember that he had been standing or climbing or kneeling on the fourteenth floor and down, straight down, were the tops of cars, crawling like beetles. There was a wind in his face. No, it was not his face, it was Solly's. Was it Solly or Joseph hanging there and in the ultimate instant, frantic with terror, pulling back? Too late, too late, all hold was loosed. Was it Solly or Joseph? The street rushed up, tilting, screaming— Who, Solly or Joseph? Then a hand on his shoulder, Anna's hand.

"Hush, hush. You were dreaming. Joseph, Joseph, it's all right."

And he worried about Malone. The man was whipped. He sat in his office with his telephone turned off. He must have lost twenty-five pounds of jolly fat; the skin hung on his neck in folds.

Once Joseph came in and found him staring out of the window. When he turned, Joseph saw that he had been crying and would have left the room, but Malone said, "Why didn't I know that what goes up has to come down? Tell me, why didn't I know?"

"You've plenty of company," was all Joseph could think of to say.

He worried about the building that was near completion, but Malone was in no condition to talk about it. So he called his lawyer and learned that their bank might not be able to make the final payment on the construction loan. Three large banks had already failed and the way people were lining up to withdraw their deposits, even a bank in sound shape could be made to fail. What if this one failed; how would they finish the job?

He decided to have a talk with his man at the bank tomorrow morning. Do it in person, not on the telephone, and handle it carefully; you didn't just walk in and tell people there were rumors they might be going under.

When he arrived at the bank at ten o'clock the next day there was a crowd on the sidewalk. Old women, men in business suits, men in overalls were shuffling and bustling at the doors. The doors were shut.

What was to be done? Nine stories and penthouse on the stylish upper East Side, a gem of a little job, half of it rented. A hundred thousand dollars would finish it. There was nothing else to do but to use his own funds. After all, it was only lending it to himself, he reasoned. But in doing so he had almost depleted his capital.

He came home, somber and thoughtful, to hear another tale of woe.

"It's Ruth," Anna said. "We thought she had Solly's insurance, at least. But it seems she signed some papers, signed it over when he

147

borrowed money for the stocks. And now they tell her it isn't hers! And Joseph, she hasn't a cent, she's over in that apartment without a cent!"

He thought, he thought with pounding head, "I wish people would leave me alone!"—and remembered Solly teaching him to play ball, and Ruth coming to Anna when their children had been born and there had been no one else to help, and the summer just past when Iris had stayed with them and been so warmly cared for.

"Find out what she needs," he said. "They were good to us, Anna. I don't forget."

That winter there were heavy snows. The city advertised for men to shovel and long lines formed before morning light. Some of the men who came were middle-aged; they wore hand-tailored suits and velvet-collared overcoats. All over the city there were lines: bread lines, soup lines. Joseph passed them while riding in his car; once he saw the face of a man he knew and looked quickly away so that the man would not know he had been seen.

The speed with which disaster had spread was unbelievable. Sitting in his good, solid car behind Tim, on his way home to where it was still warm and there was plenty of food, he could reassure himself that he was not like those poor devils in the lines. And yet, and still, speaking of devils, the small devil fear was there all right, perched inside his head and waiting. Waiting for what?

The new building, the little gem, was not renting. The penthouse had finally been leased for half what they had expected to get. The chain store which had taken a ninety-nine-year lease on Madison Avenue had gone bankrupt. The lofts in the fur district were partly vacant; the swinging racks heavy with furs were gone. The two prime apartment houses on Central Park West were emptying out, but the interest and taxes and maintenance went on. He had been using up his personal funds to keep them going. Malone had nothing to contribute. How long could this last, this slump or whatever it was? How long could he go on?

Advertisements were appearing, offering a five-year lease on an apartment for one year's rent in advance, offering free decoration, free remodeling, anything. Only come in and sign up.

And no new work in sight.

At night he lay awake and held a dialogue with himself.

Air, he said indignantly. They say it was all bubbles and air. But I go past the houses, fifteen stories high, with the doormen in maroon uniforms standing under the awnings, and I know the insides of those houses the way a doctor knows a body. I know the miles of brass pipe, the hardwood floors, the imported tile in the lobby. And you tell me that's all air?

Built on promises, that's what they mean.

Promises? Oh, you mean mortgages, promises to pay. But these buildings cost millions; what man, or group of men, would be able to construct them without borrowing?

That's true.

We always pay back, don't we? And have enough left to live very well, besides.

You pay back as long as somebody else pays you.

The rents, you mean?

Of course.

Of course.

But what when people no longer pay the rent?

They'll pay the rent. They can't find better places to live.

But when they lose their jobs, what will they do?

I don't know. You think it will be that bad?

It is that bad already.

Silence.

There are ten million unemployed.

Silence.

You'll have to dispossess a lot of them.

You mean, put them and their furniture out on the street?

That's what it means to dispossess.

I can't do that. I wouldn't sleep if I had to do that to people.

Well, then, you'll lose your properties, you'll lose everything.

And if I put them out, what then?

You'll lose everything anyway.

Yet he didn't panic. Month after month he trimmed and cut back and managed. Malone and he moved from their lavish office and gave up most of the staff. He sold the car, but kept Tim on as an office boy in spite of not needing one, for Tim had two babies to bring up. The maids were dismissed and Iris changed to public school. She hadn't been very happy anyway with that bunch of snobs, Joseph told himself, knowing it for a rationalization. And he pawned Anna's diamond ring to meet a mortgage payment on a building

149

which he later lost. It was one of the bitterest moments of his life when she drew it from her finger and handed it to him. She urged him to sell it but he fiercely refused. He would get that ring back for her one day if he had to burst his heart to do it.

In the end he saved one building, a small apartment house on Washington Heights, where they had begun, and it was that which fed them during the famine years.

17

"A man called on the telephone for you today," Iris informed Anna at the supper table. "I forgot to tell you."

"Well, who was he?"

"He didn't leave his name. I thought it was the dry cleaner, you said you expected him to call about Papa's suit. But it wasn't."

"Iris!" Anna said. "Do please get to the point."

"I am! It was Mr. Werner and he said he was calling about the picture he'd sent."

"I thought you said he didn't leave his name," Maury scoffed.

"That was the first time he called. The second time he told who he was!"

"Cheer up, folks! This kid will learn how to take a message one of these years," Maury said.

Anna laid down her fork, then picked it up again and took a mouthful of carrots.

"Werner? Picture?" Joseph repeated.

"Yes, he said he'd sent Mama a picture and he hadn't heard from her, so he wondered whether it had got lost or something."

"Oh," Anna said, "I meant to answer. I just haven't got around to it. He did send a picture when his father died. He wrote that they broke up the apartment, and he—Paul Werner—and his sister were going over the things and he—they—came upon this picture and they thought it looked like me, but it doesn't at all, it's a silly-look-ing thing, but they—he—sent it and I really forgot all about it, that's

151

why I didn't even think to mention it—" She got up and began clearing the plates away. "Coffee or tea tonight, Joseph?"

"Let's see the picture, Ma," Maury called into the kitchen.

"Yes, let's see it, Anna," Joseph said when she came back.

"You really want to? I've stuck it somewhere, I'll have to go rummaging all around—"

"I'd like to see it," Joseph repeated.

She is acting very queer about it, Iris thought.

Anna propped the picture on a table in the living room. It was a crayon drawing of a woman. There was a small gold label on the carved gold frame. Iris bent to read it. *Woman with Red Hair*, it said, with the name of the artist below it.

The woman was seated. Her body was a sweeping curve: the bent head with its washerwoman's knot of dusky red hair, the long, slender neck, the naked shoulders, the suggestion of breast, the arm lying on the lap, the hand fading into shadow. Iris bent closer. There was a piece of knitting on the lap; the ball of yarn had fallen to the floor.

It gave Iris a fine, pleased feeling. She looked back at the artist's name. "Mallard. I've seen his work. It was in the museum when our class went with the art teacher. He must be famous!"

"Don't get excited," Anna said coldly. "It's only a crayon sketch. Not worth any fortune, you can be sure."

What a crass thing for Mama to say! Not like her at all. And that sharp tone!

Joseph tilted his head to the side. He looked doubtful. "It must be valuable. They wouldn't put such an expensive frame on it otherwise, would they?"

Anna's mouth twitched. Iris saw it.

"I'm trying to see the resemblance," Joseph said. "It certainly isn't at all like the one we had done of you in Paris."

"It certainly isn't. This one is art," Maury said.

That annoyed Joseph. "Ahhh—what do you know about art?"

Iris was amused. She put her arm around her father's shoulder. "Papa dear, it's you who don't know about art."

"Maybe not," Joseph grumbled, "but I know what I like. This doesn't look like your mother. I can't see how those people can think it does."

"A picture isn't a photograph," Iris explained earnestly. "A good

152

picture suggests. That's what the art teacher said. It shows character, makes you *feel* the person."

"Poppycock!" Joseph snorted. "It either looks like a person or it
doesn't."

"As a matter of fact," Maury declared, "this does look a good deal
like Ma."

"What!" Anna cried suddenly. "With that pointed nose and a long
neck like a goose?"

"It has your spirit," Maury argued. "I'm surprised at you, Ma.
You're the one who knows all about art in this family and you can't
understand what we mean?"

"Oh, don't bother me with the thing!" Anna cried in an unnatural
voice.

Iris felt sudden pity for her mother. She didn't know why, and
she hoped Maury wouldn't answer back.

Her father remonstrated, "I don't know why you're getting so
worked up, Anna. I know you hate to be reminded of the Werners,
but—"

Anna stared at him. "Nothing of the sort. Are you still harping on
the fact that I worked for them and I'm supposed to be ashamed of
it? Don't talk like a fool. I've never been ashamed of working with
my two hands."

Joseph looked at her steadily.

"What is it, then? Why are you so angry?"

"I'm not angry. I don't like it. Do I have to like it? I didn't ask for
it, but here it is, causing dissension in the house. It's ridiculous. It's
absurd!"

Joseph threw up his hands. "All right! Nobody's asking you to like
it. I'll take it to the office. It's not as bad as all that. You won't have
to look at it, then."

"It will look really handsome hanging between the map of Man-
hattan and your certificate from the Board of Realtors. Just what you
need!"

Now that's odd, Iris thought. Papa switching sides like that. First
he doesn't like it, next he offers to hang it in his office.

Joseph sighed. "All right. Do what you want with the thing. It's
really not important, is it?"

"That's just what I meant all along," Anna said. "It's not important."

153

Iris was brushing her teeth that night when her mother came into the bathroom.

"Iris, tell me, what did Mr. Werner say?"

"I did tell you."

"Was that all he said?"

"Well, after I said you weren't home, he asked me whether I was the girl with the big eyes. He said he remembered meeting me with you on Fifth Avenue."

"Anything else?"

"I guess not. Oh, he said something more about my eyes. He said he hadn't forgotten me. That my face was half eyes. I thought that was kind of a silly thing to say, wasn't it?"

"Very silly," Anna agreed.

Something different has happened, Iris thought when she was alone. But I'm glad they're not quarreling. She lay awake, listening for sounds of anger from her parents' room, but there were none. Not like that night which she could still remember, although it had been four to five years ago, after they had met Mr. Werner and his mother and Papa had been so terribly upset.

So much had changed since then. They'd been rich and now they were poor. She knew; she heard the whispering about bills and knew they didn't want to talk in front of her and Maury. She'd heard them say it was a shame to worry the children.

Yes, there was trouble enough now, and so she was glad things were quiet tonight. Not that her parents quarreled very often. Some of the girls at school talked about their fathers and mothers fighting all the time. One of the girl's parents were even getting divorced, which must be awful. It scared you to think about a thing like that.

She had a fleeting thought before falling asleep: she wished that Mr. Werner would stay away, wouldn't call up again.

The picture disappeared. Iris saw a flat parcel, wrapped in brown paper, at the back of the top shelf in the hall closet, and guessed that was probably it.

A few days later a letter lay on the desk in the living room with an envelope beside it, a letter left open as if Mama had wanted it to be read. So Iris did. It was very short.

"Dear Mr. Werner," she read. "My husband and I thank you for the picture. We were sorry to learn that your father died. Sincerely, Anna Friedman."

What a queer, curt note! Written on cheap white paper in a sloppy scrawl, with a blot on the page! Not at all like the pretty notes Mama wrote to her friends with black ink on crocus-yellow paper, in her pointed European script like the marks of birds' feet.

Queer!

It had taken almost a week for her to feel normal again. My God, Anna thought, he must have gone out of his mind to call our house. And to talk to Iris! That night at the dinner table when the child had told of the call, it was a wonder she hadn't gone faint with the shock.

A wonder, too, that Joseph had taken it so easily. That argument over Mrs. Werner's funeral—she would never forget his jealous rage. For that was what it had been, although he would never have admitted it was. This time he had merely asked a few questions and then accepted, or seemed to accept, her explanation that the gift was a gracious gesture from Paul Werner *and his sister*.

But Joseph was changed from what he had been five years ago. He had lost the firmness with which he had ruled the house when things were going so well. Sad to see. He reminded her in a way of the wistful, poor young man she had first known.

She was thinking all this one afternoon on her way home from neighborhood errands, thinking too that the apartment was growing shabby, and how it didn't take long for misfortune to make itself visible when, half a block away from home, someone called her name. Turning, she saw Paul Werner standing there, tipping his hat.

"I got your note," he said.

She could hardly speak. For an instant her heart seemed to pause and then it began to shake in her chest. "Why are you doing this?" she cried. "Why did you send that picture? And now you've come here and if anyone sees you—"

"Don't be frightened, Anna! I telephoned openly and left my name. There's no subterfuge, no reason for anyone to be suspicious."

As she walked he kept pace with her. She had turned down the side street toward the river, away from the apartment house. Iris would be coming home from school any minute and Iris had watched her so warily the other night—

"Please go!" she pleaded. "Please go, Paul!"

But he persisted. "Your letter was so unlike you, Anna! I surely didn't mean to offend when I sent the Mallard. It was simply that I hadn't seen it in years—Father had stuck it away somewhere—and when I came upon it I was thunderstruck by the resemblance. And I wanted you to have it."

They reached Riverside Drive. Cars streamed by, glittering in the lemon-colored light. The air wavered, its radiance trembling before Anna's dizzy eyes. She stood there beside the river of cars, clutching a bag of groceries, frozen as if the curb were a precipice and the avenue an abyss.

Paul took a strong hold of her arm. "We have to talk. Cross over. We'll find a bench under the trees."

Her legs moved. This could not possibly be happening! One minute walking home from the market on a bright, windy afternoon of early spring; the next minute sitting on a bench with this man whom she had thought never to see again! How could it be happening?

"Anna, I had to come," he said. "You've never been out of my mind. Never. Can you understand that?"

She was afraid to look at him. "I can," she whispered.

"I think of you sometimes in the middle of a conference, or when I'm driving the car or reading a newspaper—suddenly, there you are. I wake up and remember you, even when I had been dreaming of something entirely apart from you. But—there you are. And when I saw that painting, the memory of you became so vivid that I had to do something about it."

Her breath had begun to calm. She turned her face to his. "It's a beautiful thing and I felt so—so *stirred*. But it's crazy of you to be here, all the same. Don't you know it is, Paul?"

"Anna, I had to. That's all there is to be said."

He took her hand, his fingers twining in hers. In spite of the thickness of glove leather she could feel the force, the heat, the life of his flesh.

"Don't," she murmured.

But neither of them withdrew and the entwined hands lay on the bench between them. The world went by: children rolling on their skates and bicycles; dogs pulling at their leashes; young women pushing baby carriages. All of these were oblivious to the man and woman on the bench.

After a while Paul said, "Tell me how you are."

She felt a great weight, she felt entranced. "No, I find it hard to talk. You tell me."

"Well," he began obediently, "I've just come back from Europe for the firm. From Germany. Things are going bad there and they're going to get worse with this Hitler fellow. I've been trying to rescue some investments for our clients before it's too late."

There were chords in his voice that Anna would have recognized if she had heard them among strangers on the other side of the world. From her room at the top of that house the music of his voice had carried up the stair well while she had lain in her bed, listening for it—

Now, because he saw that she was unable to speak, he tried to find something more to say. "Other than that—well, I've been collecting art and I go to a sculpture class. I'm not very good at it, but it's a challenge. And I've kept up with Father's charities. He was a great benefactor, an efficient manager, and it's hard to fill his shoes. But I'm trying."

She heard a smile in his voice and turned back from where she had been gazing at the river. Those large, hooded eyes under heavy, rounded lids—brilliant eyes, like dark jewels—his mother had had the same, as well as the high arched nose. And Iris had them.

"You're staring at me, Anna!"

"Am I? I didn't mean to."

"I don't mind if you do. Look at me some more."

Flushing, she looked back at the river. Her heart began to race again; she could hardly breathe.

"Perhaps you want to know more about me? I—we have no children. Never will have. Marian had an operation a couple of years ago."

"I'm sorry," Anna responded automatically.

"So am I. So is she. But we shan't adopt. And she keeps busy with her charities, too. She's very generous with her strength and time, not just with money." He stopped again, then said, "So that's my life. Now will you tell me about yours?"

She drew a deep breath and began. "An ordinary life. Like women everywhere. Keeping the house and children. Coping with bad times."

"Have they hit you very badly?"

"We've lost almost everything," Anna said simply.

"Do you need money? Can I help you?"

She shook her head. "No, no, we manage. And anyway, you don't think I could take it from you, do you?"

157

And, suddenly overcome by a wave of chill reality, she withdrew her hand, clasping her own two hands together in her lap.

"I suppose you couldn't," Paul said bleakly. There was a long silence. Then he cried out, "I should have married you, Anna! Would you have married me?"

"Oh," she said, "you know I would have, the way I felt then! But what's the use of talking about it now?"

A little boat sped down the river. A cloud darkened the spring green on the Palisades. Anna saw them through a curtain of tears. How different everything might have been! You take one path and it leads you here and you become this kind of woman; another path leads you there, and you become another kind of woman. The same body but another life, and therefore another woman. She thought she had forgotten—well, almost forgotten—how it might have been. Goodness knew she had tried to forget.

She turned on him almost fiercely. "Why didn't you marry me? You see, I'm not proud anymore. I don't want to be proud. So I ask you, why didn't you?"

Paul's eyes looked straight into hers and through them. "I was a boy then," he said at last, "not yet a man. While you already had the spirit of a woman. I didn't have courage enough to marry someone I—wouldn't be expected to marry." His voice grew rough. "Can you understand that and not despise me for it? Can you?"

Something sprang alive in Anna, a singing, a flowering, a tenderness of joy and vindication. "Oh," she said, "I was so terribly hurt that I wanted to die! And after that, so angry. So bitter and angry. . . . But I could never 'despise' you, never."

And she thought, Perhaps, after all, I should tell him now? Hasn't he a right and a duty to know that my daughter belongs to him?

Paul said abruptly, "I haven't told you everything. There's something else."

"What is it?"

"Do you remember the time we met on Fifth Avenue a few years ago? I keep thinking of the way you stood with your hand on your little girl's shoulder. I don't know why that moved me so, but it did. And the child's face haunts me. You'll think I've gone mad, but I had—and have had—a revelation that she was mine. My child. And I haven't been able to get it out of my head."

It did not surprise Anna that he had come upon the truth. That rare, discerning mind, those far-seeing, through-seeing eyes—not much eluded them! No, it did not surprise her. Her lips parted to speak, but he interrupted.

"It's true, then, isn't it?"

"It's true."

"I'm not stunned. I'm not shocked. It's as though I'd always known it." He lit a cigarette with an effort at calm control; but she saw that his hands were shaking. "And Joseph?" he asked after a moment.

Anna shook her head. "Only I know."

There was a long, long silence, while the pungent smoke drifted. Paul's eyes closed and he did not move. After a while he opened his eyes and spoke again. "How you must have suffered, Anna!"

"I was so guilty, I thought I wasn't fit to live," she replied, very low. "But then my strength came back, thank God. I suppose human beings can endure much more than they think they can."

"You've had to endure too much! Losing your parents, poverty in a strange country and then this! Why didn't you tell me, Anna?"

She looked at him ruefully.

"All right, I shouldn't have asked that. I know you couldn't have. But will you let me do something for her, at least? I could open a trust account so that she would never be in want."

"No, no! That's not possible! You know it's not! The best thing you can do is to stay away from her. Can't you see that?"

Paul sighed. "Tell me, please, what she's like."

Anna considered how best to sum up a complex, aloof and sensitive little girl.

"Iris is very intelligent, very perceptive. She knows music and books; she has your feeling for art, I think."

He smiled faintly. "Go on, please."

It became easier to speak. Her words, hesitant at first, began to flow. She was, after all, a mother talking about her child. And this listener wanted to hear. So she told about food and school and amusing remarks, searching her own mind for words that might make Iris live in Paul's mind.

"And does she love you very much? I hope so. It's not every child who has a mother like you."

"We have no great problems, she and I. But she's more attached to Joseph. He adores her, she's the heart of his heart. But then, that's the way it is between fathers and daughters," Anna concluded, immediately sorry to have been so tactless.

But Paul quietly agreed. "That's true."

"I'm not really good with her!" Anna cried suddenly. "Not what I ought to be, Paul! I'm good *to* her; I love her just as much as I love Maury. It's just that I'm not at ease with her. It's—different," she faltered.

"Of course. It would be."

"When I look at her I try to think of her as having been born—" she was about to say, "as Joseph's and mine," but said instead, "differently. And most of the time I can do it. I've put you away at the back of the past, you see. And now today the past is here, and whenever I look at Iris I shall think—" She was unable to finish.

Paul took her hand back, stroking it gently.

Then Anna said, "I wonder how much she feels of all this, poor Iris. She *must* feel something!"

Neither of them knew what to add to that.

Presently he said, "I've not been fair. I've not asked you to tell about Maury."

"You're only being kind. You can't really be interested in Maury."

"Yes, I can. He belongs to you, he's a part of you. Tell me."

"Maury is the son everyone wants, the son you think of when you imagine having a boy. Everyone loves him, he—" Anna stopped. "I can't, Paul. I'm brimming over. There's been—too much—this afternoon."

"I know. I feel that way myself, Anna dearest."

And taking the hand between both of his he removed her glove, raised the hand and kissed it, the palm, the fingers, the pulse that fluttered and jumped in her wrist.

They became aware of stir and movement in the park. Mothers began calling to their children and gathering scattered toys. The afternoon was coming to its end.

Paul put Anna's hand down and stood up, startling her. He walked a few paces away with his back to her, facing the river. He seemed so solitary there in his velvet-collared coat, a stranger among the pigeons and the children playing hopscotch on the walk. This tall, powerful man who could command almost anything he might want, this man was also vulnerable through her. He was separate from her and yet bound to her for as long as either of them might live, or as long as Iris lived or whatever children Iris might have, or—

He came back and sat down. "Listen to me, Anna. Life is short.

Just yesterday we were twenty, and where's the time gone? Let's take what we can, you and I."

"What do you mean?"

"I want to marry you now. I want to take our little girl and give you both what you ought to have. I want to stop waking up at night wondering how you are. I want to wake up and have you next to me."

"As simply as that?" There was faint bitterness in her tone; she could hear it. "And what about Maury? And Joseph? What about the small fact that you already have a wife?"

"It wouldn't destroy Marian if I were to ask for a divorce. Trust me, Anna. I am not a destroyer. I don't hurt people if I can help it."

"Hurt? Do you realize what it would do to Joseph if he knew I was sitting here with you now? He's a devout, believing, strait-laced man. A puritan, Paul! This would be past his forgiveness. Divorce? He would be ruined!" Anna's voice rose. "I sit with him in the evening, I look across the room at this man who married me when— when you wouldn't have me, who takes care of me, who gave me every material thing when he had it, and gives me loving kindness now when he has nothing else to give. Sometimes I can't bear the thought of what I've already done to him."

"Everything has to be paid for," Paul said gently. "I understand what you're saying and I understand that it would be very, very hard in many ways. Still, you have to weigh all that against your own life, what you want to do with your own life. And I know— *know*, Anna!—that you want to come to me."

The blood poured into her cheeks. "Yes, yes I do! I can't deny that I do!"

"Well, then, you see?"

"But also, we've been through so much, Joseph and I!" She seemed to be musing, recollecting, almost as if she were alone, letting her thoughts run. "Struggling uphill, then sliding almost all the way back down again. And he works so hard! I think sometimes it will kill him. And he never wants anything, never takes anything for himself. It was all for us, for me and the children."

"For my child," Paul said.

Anna sighed, a long quivering breath like a sob. "So how can I, Paul? Can I put a knife into a man like him, can I? And besides, I love him! Do you know what I mean when I say that I love him?"

He didn't answer.

161

"But you do see, Paul, you do see the way it is?"

He cried out, "I'm so sorry for us all! Oh, my God, how sorry I am!"

Anna began to cry.

"Ah, don't," he whispered then, and took out a handkerchief. "Here, you mustn't go home with red eyes. Then you'd really have some explanations to make!" He began gently to dry her eyes. "Anna, Anna, what are we to do?"

"I don't know. I only know I can't marry you."

"You think so now. But things change. I'll wait. It will look different to you after a while."

Anna shook her head. "We shouldn't see each other anymore. You know that."

"And you know that's impossible. Neither of us could stand it."

"I told you before, people can stand a whole lot more than they think they can."

"Perhaps so. But why should we torture ourselves to prove we can? I want to see you again, Anna, and I'm going to. Surely I have a right at least to hear about Iris now and then?"

"All right," she said softly. "I'll figure out some way. I can't think right now. But I will."

She took a mirror from her purse, anxiously examining her face.

"You look fine. Can't tell a thing. Except that you're still an entrancing woman, even in that coat." He flushed. "I didn't mean there was anything wrong with your coat. I only meant—well, it doesn't do for you what black velvet and a pair of diamond earrings would do."

She laughed and he said, "That's better. I love to hear you laugh. It's a long time since I first heard that laugh."

"I'd better go back, Paul. It's awfully late."

"Go ahead, Anna darling. But I'll telephone in the morning around ten. Will that be all right?"

"Yes. At ten."

"You'll have had time by then to decide how we can meet again."

"You stored the picture away," Joseph said that night when they were in bed.

"Yes. Since neither of us liked it."

"I wonder why that fellow sent it to you?"

162

"Rich people like to give things, that's all. It makes them feel powerful."

"But he hardly knows you. It's not as if you were someone in his circle."

She didn't answer and he did not press her. Poor Joseph! He was skirting the subject, wanting to ask more and yet afraid to. These past years had been too much for him, had beaten down some of that first strong assurance. He had been ladling out the ocean with a cup since the Depression began and he was tired. Soft pity moved Anna and she spoke lightly, wanting to soothe and ease his mind.

"What it comes down to is simply that I was a pretty little maid in that house and people are kind to pretty little maids. You're surely not jealous?"

"Well, I could be, but since you explain it that way, I won't be."

"Please. Let's not have any repetition of that business when I met them on the street that time."

"I was awfully angry, wasn't I?"

"You were. And without reason."

He was silent.

"Joseph? Please. No tempers now. I just—can't take it."

"Why? Am I so fierce?"

"You can be."

"I won't be. Anna, dear, forget it. Forget the damned picture. It's not worth talking about. Let's go to sleep." He sighed and, drawing her to him, lay his head in the curve of her shoulder.

He sighed again. "Ah, what peace! No matter how cold and tough it is outside I have this refuge! For a few hours here at night I can forget debts and new business and the office rent. Just think of basic things, of you and me. That's what it's all about, Anna, the way it all began. Just you and me and the beautiful little boy and girl we've made together."

She swallowed hard. There was such a lump in her throat, such a lump of pain.

"And I have to fight for all of you, my people. Ah, well, maybe with this new man, this Roosevelt coming in, things will be better. I hope so," Joseph murmured.

When he had fallen asleep Anna turned over. Such trust, such loyalty and trust! It was an armor that he wore without knowing

163

that he had it on. You couldn't wound a man who wore such
armor. A line of poetry trailed through her head, something Maury
had memorized for his Latin class, something like "virtue defends
him." Tears trailed down her temples toward her ears. *Alone I am,
entirely alone. For who else can get inside my head, my heart, and
feel what I feel? All my confusion, tension, terror? I stand before
the great dark future and I can't know what is waiting there for
me.*

It grew cold. Fear chilled. She crept toward the solid bulwark of
Joseph's back, feeling for comfort in its warmth. Then came a fleeting recall of Paul's words: "I want to wake up and find you next to
me." A feverish wave of heat dispelled the chill; she trembled with
desire, shame, fear, and then grew cold again.

The clock's hands glimmered on the night table. With wide-
open eyes Anna lay, watching the hands move steadily forward
through the night.

The telephone rang at ten o'clock. It rang once only; she had
been waiting beside it.

"I didn't sleep all night, Paul," she told him.

"Neither did I. Have you decided when and where?"

"Paul, I can't see you now. I don't say never, only not now."

"I was afraid of this."

"It's I who am afraid. Guilty and afraid. I haven't got the
strength to cope. Please understand, and don't be angry."

"I don't think I could ever be really angry at you. But I am
miserably disappointed."

"It's so hard! So very, very hard!"

"You're sure it's not you who're making it harder?"

"I don't think so. I did try to explain to you yesterday how it is."

"Yes, you did. And I understood. But I'm not going to let you
cut the cord between us, Anna. Not ever."

"I'm not asking you to. If you let me know where you are I'll
send you a postcard every now and then, a harmless postcard that
anyone might read. Only you will know that it is about Iris and
me."

"Tell me again: I think you said a moment ago that you didn't
mean 'never'; you only meant 'not right now.' Isn't that what you
said?"

"Yes, yes."

"Then I'll be patient. And I'll always let you know where I am. With a postcard, too. Do you have women friends who travel?"

"Oh, yes. Pick any name. It won't matter."

"I'll do that."

"Paul? Will you hang up now?"

"In a moment. Just remember this: when you have changed your mind about meeting again or about marriage, or if you ever need me for anything, send me three or four words and I'll come to you. And you will change your mind, you know."

"I'm going to hang up now," she said softly.

"All right. Hang up. But don't say the word 'good-by.' "

BOOK
2

RANDOM WINDS

18

Maury was the only one of the family who made no changes; they had kept him in the school because it would help him, they believed, to get into Yale. Besides, it was more important for a boy. Joseph knew Maury would get as good an education at City College; some of the best brains in the nation had come from there. But somehow it had always been taken for granted, he didn't remember how or why, but just as far back as he could think it had been assumed that Maury would go to Yale. It had been a kind of promise and he couldn't diminish himself in the eyes of his family by breaking it. However much they might deny the diminution, and they would, Joseph would feel that it was.

And so the acceptance had come from Yale and the family was gathered around the table to celebrate. The Malones, who had 'known Maury before he was born,' were invited, too. Besides, Joseph had some other news for them.

Anna removed her apron before sitting down and hung it on the doorknob. The only elegance that remained from the past came from her silver candlesticks and the flowers she had put out, a handful of inexpensive daffodils from the market. She had cooked all the things the family loved best. There were stuffed fish in its own silky, quivering jelly, a pot roast in dark gravy, potato pancakes crisp as celery, baked carrots sweet with prunes, hot, puffy rolls, a tart, cool salad and apple strudel running with cinnamon juice, crunched with nuts, wrapped in its rich brittle crust.

Joseph leaned back and sighed with repletion. He looked around the room at the people he loved and it came to him that things could have been a great deal worse.

After the young people had left the table, the others lingered. "Now," Joseph said, "I have something to tell you. I went to see the president of the bank last week. I'd been thinking and thinking of something for us to do. We can't just coast along until prosperity appears around that corner they sing about. So I told him, I said, 'Listen, Mr. Fairbanks, you owe us something. We only got back fifty cents on the dollar from our accounts and I'm not complaining—not too much, anyway. But I think you owe us a chance to make a living. We're going into the management business—' "

"We are?" Malone interrupted.

Joseph put up his hand. "Let me finish. I said, 'I want your properties to manage. We know how to take care of buildings, my partner and I. Goodness knows, we've built enough of them.' And he said he'd think it over."

"He won't do it," Malone said glumly. "They've been using the same people for years. Why should they give the business to us?"

Joseph smiled. "I don't know why they should, but they did. He called me this afternoon, and we're to go in on Monday morning for instructions."

Malone stared. He opened his mouth and shut it and opened it again with a whoop. "Well, I'll be damned! If this isn't a smart man, a real man, my idea of a man, if you want to know! And the best friend I ever had in the world, or hope to have. I want to propose a toast to him, and then to us!" He stood up and flourished his empty glass.

Joseph pushed the bottle in front of him, ignoring the signal of Anna's small frown: *he's had enough.* If the man wanted to drink this was surely no time to stop him; it was the first time in a couple of years that he had laughed.

"I want to tell you a story about our trip abroad," Malone said. "Our one and only trip abroad, cursed be the day! For if I'd been home—ah, well, that's another story. Anyway, we went to visit the family in Wexford. So here we were, pulled into this hick burg; God, the toilet all the way down the hall, and cold, cold, I've never felt such cold! So I said to my cousin, little old wiry guy with a wool hat, 'Fitz,' I said, 'look here, the wife and I want to invite the family to dinner tonight. I'll order up a big feast and you go out now and do the invitin', ask all the relatives, okay?' So he says sure he will, and Mary and I go in and order steaks and pies and all the liquor you can drink. Then we go to dress up, the relatives from America showin' off, you know, and we go downstairs and there they are waiting for us. Would you believe it, I guess you wouldn't, but I'll swear to you there were fifty-four of them there. Fifty-four! It's a good thing I had plenty of traveler's checks because they ate enough for a hundred and fifty-four."

He sat back laughing at the memory of it, then suddenly sobered, the tears of laughter turning to real tears, and he wiped his eyes.

"Oh, what a fool I was, what a fool! On top of the world, and look at me now; look what I've done."

"Well," Joseph said, "consider it this way. If you had sold a month before the bust you'd be a millionaire now and everybody would be saying how smart you are."

"Yes, and if my aunt had balls she'd be my uncle."

"Malone!" cried his wife, shocked and mortified.

"Let him be," Joseph said. "There are no children here and I'm sure we've all heard the word before."

Anna was laughing. She looks so young, he thought. With all the troubles she looks so bright and young. What would I ever do without her? She had put the apron back on to clear the table and at that moment stood beside her portrait, which hung in its carved and gilded frame between the windows. He had an instant's vision of their years together, all the way back to the stoop on Hester Street where he had proposed, and his real life had begun.

She had been painted like royalty, seated for all time in a high-backed chair, with one hand, the one with the diamond, resting on the arm; the other was curled, fingers up, in her lap. Her skirt, a fountain of pink silk pale as the inside of a shell, spread to the floor. And on her face, Anna thought long afterward, although she had not seen it at first, on the slight upward curve of her smiling mouth, the artist had placed a look of surprise.

171

19

The Bar Harbor Express made a nice click and clatter rolling through the night. They were an hour and a half out of New York; the berths were made up and the observation car where Maury sat was emptying. The man across from him, a neat man in a summer suit, about his father's age, finished the newspaper and smiled over at Maury.

"Going up to your family's place for the vacation?"

"No, visiting friends about fifteen miles down the coast."

"Well, as one Yale man to another, have a good stay."

"Thanks. How did you know?"

"The emblem on your racket cover. I saw you get on at Grand Central. I was a tennis player, too."

"It's a great game," Maury said politely.

"That it is. I still play every morning I can." He stood up, nodding a pleasant good night. "Enjoy yourself, son. These are the best years of your life."

"Yes, sir," Maury said.

He sat on awhile, watching the speckle of small-town lights as Connecticut went by. The best years of your life. The language was full of clichés like that, and middle-aged people were especially apt to use them. But still there was a good deal of truth in some of them.

He had gone up to Yale with a mix of feelings. (He supposed this was the meaning of adulthood, the discovery that nothing is simple.)

First, there had been satisfaction. His parents, his mother primarily, had in their innocence taken for granted that their bright boy would be accepted. His headmaster had assured him that if any boy in the school was going to make it, Maury would. So he had been really pleased about not having disappointed anyone. But also he'd had a very small feeling of guilt because it was a financial strain upon the family, and hence a strong sense of pressure to do very, very well.

"You're one lucky boy, Maury," his father's friends would tell him when the men were talking in his parents' house. "Yale, in times like these! You've got a good father."

And they would sigh, these tense, worried men, and look at him. He knew they were seeing him in his fortunate youth, as though he had gone to inhabit another world.

And it was another world. The seasons moved in neat progression, from golden fall to commencement—stately music under ancient trees—and back to fall. Four whole years of that, a gift of time. Oh, if he could stay there, stay there! . . . Wouldn't that be something? Sometimes, late at night when he had put his books away, he would sit at the window and just let himself feel the peace. How old it was, how tranquil in the white winter nights! Solid and rooted. Trees like these, buildings like these, had nothing to worry about. No one would ever tear them down or burrow underneath them for a subway.

It crossed his mind that lately his thoughts didn't fit the image people had of him, or that he had of himself. The image was of a boy to whom everything was easy, sports, learning, life. Well, learning was easy enough; not, he saw honestly, because he had any tremendous thirst for it, but only because his memory was superb. His memory served just as well for the store of jokes that gathered laughter in the center of a group, the laughter which made him a "great guy" or a "sunny personality," expressions which depended upon the age of the person who was talking about him. This new quietness of his which was almost, but not quite, melancholy—this he didn't like to think about. He guessed that it too was merely a part of growing older.

Anyway, there was no melancholy in him tonight. He got up and made his way back to the sleeping car. By morning light he'd be in Maine. He could almost smell tart pines and briny water, remembered from the years at camp; he could feel the cheer of being with Chris again.

It was the most unlikely friendship, one would have thought. Chris was a "preppie," whose great-great-grandfather had grafted the pride of Yale into the family's bones. His mother's family, he explained, always went to Harvard; his grandfather had been a trustee there. It made for an odd situation, he would say with mock gravity, at the Harvard-Yale game every year.

He belonged to all the good clubs. His family had a summer home. His father sailed in the Bermuda races. Yes, it was an unlikely friendship indeed. And it never would have come about if Chris hadn't torn a ligament one icy night, crossing the quadrangle on his way home from a date, and if Maury hadn't happened to be stargazing at the window.

"There wasn't a soul out that night; I'd have frozen to death on the ground if Maury hadn't seen me." Chris liked to tell it that way, and it was probably quite true.

They talked frankly about their different backgrounds. Chris wanted to know about Maury's family and asked questions about his religion. He had never really known a Jew before.

"Of course there've been Jewish fellows in all my classes," he said. "But you know how it is, you just don't mix. Funny, you and I would have gone all the way through without knowing each other if it hadn't been for my accident. I wonder what the *real* reason is, why we don't mix?"

Maury didn't know, either. These artificial differences! Who the hell cared who your grandparents were or where they had come from? They got along so well; he and Chris laughed at the same things, wrestled and punched in the locker room after swimming and were perfectly matched at tennis, which they discovered as soon as the courts were ready in the spring. Tennis was what they both liked almost more than anything. "A couple of tennis bums," they called themselves. They liked to bicycle into the country on Sunday afternoons, with a stop for beer, now that repeal had come. Sometimes they studied together, although Chris and his friends weren't so great at that. A solid B would do them, or even an occasional C. Why break your head? Such easy optimism was calming to Maury, although he never was able to bring himself to apply it to himself.

His roommate, Eddy Holtz, was puzzled. He frowned, shaking his head, and his heavy black curly hair wobbled like a cap.

"What are you doing with that crowd, Maury? You don't fit. Why are you doing it?"

"What do you mean, I don't fit? They like me, we're friends."

"They don't like you well enough to take you into their clubs."

"That's not Chris's fault. He thinks that sort of thing is stupid. But prejudices die hard, although they all do eventually. And meanwhile, we've a lot in common."

"Something disturbs me. It's as if to them you were an exotic pet, a new kind of dog that nobody else in the neighborhood has."

"Thanks, thanks a lot!"

"I'm sorry, maybe that was a bad way to put it. What I mean is, there's a barrier. There's bound to be, and you know it, Maury. You can't ever be sure you won't say something they'll disapprove of and then—"

Eddy reminded him of his father, the part of his father that had always disturbed him. He was so apprehensive, plodding and somber, poring over his books to get into med school. There wasn't a laugh in him. And he told him so.

"You sound just like my father."

"Maybe your father and I know something you don't know."

That sort of talk from a person his own age infuriated Maury. "You people are paranoid!" he cried.

And Eddy had sighed. Always that sigh of weary, knowing gloom. There wasn't a trace of that around Chris, none of that tension. Chris was vigorous, cheerful, healthy.

"I'm sick of being constricted," Maury had burst out. "Shut into your fears, your narrow choices. There's a whole free wide world out there, Eddy! I'll leave you to the burdens of being Jewish, since you're afraid to get rid of them."

"Shit," Eddy said. "You're burdened and you're constricted as much as I am. And you've no way out. My advice is: get used to it."

As soon as they were able to change rooms they did so. They had been best friends, he and Eddy Holtz, and they never exactly became enemies. They still waved a greeting in passing, but neither would go so far as to cross the street for anything more than that.

Maury settled the suitcase and stowed the five-pound box of candy for Chris's mother in a safe place. Ma had bought the candy and laid out his clothes, whitened his shoes, sent his white flannel trousers to the tailor for pressing and even bought him a couple of new ties.

He smiled now, remembering his mother. "You're not taking those old slacks? They're faded, Maury!"

"I know. We're going fishing. And anyway, these people don't dress up."

"Better listen to your mother," his father had warned. "Rich people with a summer house like that are bound to dress. You don't want to look like a beggar."

Maury had tried to explain, feeling as he spoke a surge of enthusiasm. "They're not rich, Pa, not in the way you think of it. Chris doesn't care what he wears. His sweaters have holes in them. He and all his friends are simple. They don't struggle. You'd be surprised."

"Maybe I wouldn't be surprised," his father said. His eyebrows rippled. "They don't struggle, you tell me. They can afford to be simple. If I go downtown with a hole in my overcoat, they'll say Friedman's broke and they'll have nothing to do with me. People like us have to dress right."

From the moment he was met the next morning at the station he was glad he had used his own judgment. Chris, his brothers and their friend Donald were in an old station wagon loaded with sacks of dog food. Their clothes were as old as the car and their sneakers were tattered.

At dinner, though, they dressed, and then he was glad his mother had taken care of his white flannels, he thought with amusement.

The house was low, with brown-weathered ells and wings. From the row of wicker chairs on the front veranda one looked out over lawns and water to the pine hills on the other side of the cove. After dinner they all went out to watch the stars come up.

"As you can see, we're not famous for our night life here," Chris remarked.

"No apologies in paradise," Maury answered.

"This is my fifty-seventh summer in this house," old Mr. Guthrie remarked abruptly.

"Sir?" Chris asked.

That was something Maury had never heard. At home you asked: What did you say? when you hadn't understood.

"I said, 'This is my fifty-seventh summer in this house,' " the grandfather repeated.

"I thought that's what you said."

The old man, erect in the fan-backed wicker chair, tapped Maury's knee with his cane. "Young man, would you like me to tell you about how this house came to be built?"

"Yes, sir, I would."

"It was in 1875 and I was twenty-five years old, just out of law school. I had been married a year and my wife was expecting our first child. Her people had been seafaring folk here on the coast and, although she was contented enough in Boston during the winter months, she hankered after her home place in the summer. So when I came into a little unexpected legacy from my grandmother I decided to build a house near my wife's family village. We had to travel by boat then, you know, from Boston to Bar Harbor; then overland by buckboard for the luggage and buggy for ourselves. It took five hours on a single-track dirt road all the way. I'm eighty-two years old next Thursday."

"Do you like being eighty-two, Gramp?" asked Tommy. He was eleven, the youngest of Chris's brothers.

Everybody laughed and the old man answered, "Can't say that I'm delighted with it. But since the alternative is to have died young I'll say, yes, I like it well enough."

In the gauzy light Maury's eyes moved around the semicircle. What an agreeable, variegated family! First the grandfather's baby brother Ray, a lively tennis player at the age of seventy-one. Then Uncle Ray's daughter with her husband and two vigorous children, who had come in their camper from a nature tour of the national parks. And Chris's Uncle Wendell with his wife; both close to sixty, he estimated, but, like all the rest of the family, thin and flat of stomach and taut of skin.

"Uncle Wendell's a departure from the family pattern," Chris had explained. "Didn't give a damn for banking or law or business. Teaches classics at St. Bart's, when he's not on a dig in Greece or someplace."

"I wonder how James is doing," Chris's mother remarked now.

Someone answered, "As usual. He insisted that Polly and Agatha come for the Fourth, which is like his usual considerate self."

Chris explained to Maury, "My Uncle James is crippled from

177

polio and he doesn't always feel like traveling, though he comes sometimes. But it's a long trip. They live over in New York State. Brewerstown."

"How horrible!"

"Yes, it is. He was a prominent lawyer, representing American banks in France, when this happened to him about twelve years ago. So he came back home and runs a small practice to keep busy. But the whole thing just turned their lives upside down, as you can imagine."

"Aggie's great, you'll like her," Tommy said now. "She goes to Wellesley. Last year when she came for Gramp's birthday we went to the fair and we rode on the Ferris wheel. She plays a great game of tennis, too."

Mr. Guthrie laughed. "Tommy's enthusiastic about girls because he's never had a sister. A girl is a real novelty around our house, I can tell you." He stood up. "Well, I don't know about all of you, but I'm turning in. Who's for tennis early in the morning, and I mean early?"

"Maury?" Chris asked. "I thought we could pack a lunch and sail down the coast tomorrow. But we could get a set of doubles in first, if you're willing."

"Any time you say."

"Six o'clock. Game?"

"Game!"

He was so pleasantly tired, yet he didn't fall asleep for quite a while. He lay in bed listening to the night, to low thunder from a little storm passing in the hills and to rising wind. He was enchanted. This graceful, peaceful family, this simple ease. Oh, this is where I want to be, where I fit, where I belong. . . .

He supposed you wouldn't call her beautiful, and yet he didn't want to look away from her. She was small and moved lightly. He thought of birds and fawns, of quick, alert, soft things. She was tan; her skin, her hair, even her eyes were golden brown. Cat's eyes. If there had been such a name for a girl, he would have thought she ought to be called September.

They lay on the float together on her second day. Everyone had gone sailing, but Agatha had not wanted to go. "Don't go sailing," she had said to Maury, "keep me company for a swim. No, of course I don't mean that. Do whatever you want," she'd said.

178

And he had answered, "I want to keep you company."

So they lay, while the sun burned and the wind cooled. And Agatha spoke into a drowsy silence.

"Maury, do you mind if I ask you something?"

"Ask away."

"Are you poor?"

He sat up on one elbow. "What a question! What makes you ask that, of all things?"

"I'm sorry if it sounded horrible. But most of Chris's friends are so awfully rich, and I wondered whether, well, whether the reason you seemed kind of quiet was that maybe you were poor. Because we're the poor ones in our family, so I sort of know how it feels."

Poor, Maury thought, remembering the tenements from which his parents had come, where people still lived and eked out their days . . . poor, he thought grimly.

"No," he said quietly, "not really. My father manages all right, considering the times."

"Well, then, I suppose it must be because you're Jewish."

He was astounded. He didn't know what to say to this girl.

"Chris told me you were."

"Is that such an interesting subject?"

"I think it is. I don't know many Jews, just one or two girls in my dorm. But Dad talks about them so much that it's made me curious."

"There's nothing to be curious about. They're only people like everyone else. Some saints and some sinners."

"My father hates them. He blames them for all the troubles since the world began. It's a kind of hobby with him, like Uncle Wendell's digs in Greece."

A kind of hobby! He swallowed and changed the subject. "That must be an interesting life, your uncle's."

"Oh, yes, you ought to get him talking sometime. He's got more stories to tell! He's from the bookish branch of the family. Not like this house."

Maury had observed that the house was filled with plants and needlework, all the cozy comforts, but no books. Nothing to read except an old set of the *Britannica* and the *National Geographic* magazine.

"I'll bet Chris seldom gets over a C, does he?" Agatha remarked.

179

"Well, now, I really can't—"

She laughed. "Don't worry about being disloyal! It's no secret and his parents don't care."

"Don't care? I can't imagine that."

"Why? Do your parents care so much?"

"I should think they do." He thought of the last semester in high school, when he had got his first grade below an A minus. It had been a B minus in chemistry; he hated science. And his father had said mildly enough, "Maury, I saw your report card. What's the B minus doing on it?"

"They never pushed me," he said now, "not the way some parents do. It's a kind of silent pressure. You know they want you to do well. They expect you to take advantage of all the good opportunities and somehow, if you don't do well, you feel as though you had hurt them."

"I've always heard that Jews set so much store by education."

There it was again. You could hardly touch on any subject without having that creep in. The Difference.

"Have I said something to upset you?"

He turned to her quickly. "I want to know, are you like your father?"

"I? How do you mean?"

"About Jews, I mean?"

She laughed. "Of course I'm not! How can you ask? I don't believe in that stuff! Nobody else in the family does. Why, Uncle Wendell is the most liberal, broad-minded man—"

"And your mother?"

Aggie waited a moment. She said slowly, "Mother is—well, it's hard to know what Mother would be if it weren't for my father. But she's been especially influenced by him since he's been home all the time. I really think a lot of his thinking is because of his sickness. When you don't move around in the world, you narrow down, you don't see any new people, and you get—well, fanatic. Goodness," she said ruefully, "he doesn't even like Catholics, especially the Irish! And maybe Mother has got a touch of that. Yes, I would say she had."

"She doesn't know about me?"

"I'm sure it hasn't been mentioned." Agatha frowned. "Maury?"

"Yes?"

"Perhaps it would be better not to mention it to Mother."

Ah, the hell with them all! The hell with her frosty, pinch-faced mother and the whole damned lot!

"Maury?"

"Yes?"

"I don't want you to think, I mean, it's a dirty bird that soils its own nest and all that sort of thing. . . . My father is really a very wonderful, kind man in spite of that. He's suffered horribly and I really love him very much. I wouldn't want you to think I came from some sort of abnormal, awful family where the people all hate each other."

Why should she care what he thought about her and her family?

She looked into his face. She had the most appealing, sweet, sweet smile. He smiled back. Her smile broke into a laugh, not the silly artificial laugh of a girl who wants to show how gay she can be, but a bright laugh, honest and true.

"Hey, you know you people have been stewing in the sun for two hours?" Chris called over the water.

They scrambled up and dove in, racing to the shore.

She had put an idea into his head. Maybe Chris hadn't told his parents, had only mentioned it to Agatha? He didn't want to ask, to seem to be making a big thing out of it. In a way he hoped that Chris had told his family, because if he had not and it were later to come out that Maury *was,* why, then it would appear that he had come under false pretenses.

At dinner that evening something had been said that made Maury think they did know. In talking about a banker whom he had met in London, Chris's father mentioned that the man possessed a famous collection of paintings and that he was a man of great culture, as so many Jews were. So Maury thought probably they knew, or else why would he have said that? Or maybe it was the other way around?

Very distressing, a nuisance really. Of course, the name ought to tell them something. Still, it sounded German. Or did it? What a nuisance! Not that there was anything to be ashamed of. Surely he was not ashamed of his people who had given the world so much, and been so unjustly treated by the world. Certainly he was not ashamed. But what, then? Well, he was ill at ease, wondering what they might be thinking, since undoubtedly so many of them

181

did think. Or perhaps didn't think, merely just felt something? Funny, he hadn't been this way, really hadn't been this way on the campus with Chris and the other fellows. He'd felt equal, genuinely comfortable and good.

But in the presence of these polished elders it was, for some reason, different. For the first time since his arrival he felt that it was. The dinners here were so different from home. He looked at the cool table, sparsely set, the thin-sliced roast beef on the platter. No wonder they were all so lean! He could have eaten more, but Mrs. Guthrie paid no attention to anyone's plate. At home Ma would have been urging, insisting that everyone take more, and sometimes when they refused she would put it on their plates herself. Here there were formal manners. At home there were discussions, often emotional ones about business, about politics, about Iris' math teacher who seemed to torment the poor child.

Yes, it was different. He felt angry that it should be. Angry at whom? At himself? Or at life that had made him what he was?

By the Fourth of July, for some reason, his mood had lifted and floated away. When he woke in the morning to the sound of firecrackers booming in the hills, he felt good again and normal. They had played two sets of tennis, had a big breakfast, then gone swimming; and now at noon they stood on the main street, really the only street, of the village watching the parade go by under the elms.

People had come in farm trucks and on foot; there were even a couple of wagons drawn up in front of the post office. There were groups of summer people like the Guthrie group, scouts in uniform and volunteer firemen with equipment. Some of the farm families had brought lunch and sat now on the grass near the bandstand, with their dogs and children running loose. Maury was delighted. It was an old engraving, a print by Currier and Ives. It was real America.

One band after the other came swinging down the road: the firemen, the high-school band, the American Legion and a grade-school group with their teacher, singing "Yankee Doodle." And at the last, in an open car, driven slowly so that everyone might see, came three old men bowing and waving their blue caps, the last veterans of the Civil War.

"The one in the middle," old Mr. Guthrie said, "that's Frank

182

Burroughs, some sort of relative by marriage of my late wife's, I never did figure out the relationship."

"He must be awfully old," Maury whispered.

"Not much older than I am," Mr. Guthrie replied.

The flag went past; hats that were not already off were swept off. A band played "The Battle Hymn of the Republic" and, hesitantly, somebody began to sing. Then others joined and Maury's heart was stirred here among these people in their home, on this old street under the leaves, with the thump of the brasses, the triumphant drums, the regimental flags and the voices. He heard his own voice, firm and joyous and proud: "Mine eyes have seen the glory—" and stopped, struck with embarrassment as Chris turned and smiled.

"Go on, sing!" the grandfather said. "Sing out! I like to see a young man with enthusiasm. And you've a nice voice, too."

So he sang out with the rest until the parade had passed and vanished to disband in back of the school, and people started home.

"Who wants to walk back with me?" Agatha asked.

There was a general groan. "It's two miles, for Pete's sake."

"I know. But it's a beautiful walk, by the short cut, not the road. Who'll come?" she waited.

"I will," Maury said.

They entered a lane, a dirt track that led off the road through pasture and brush. It was early afternoon and very still. Even the cattle had lain down, chewing with solemn faces in the shade.

Presently Agatha asked him, "Why did you have tears in your eyes at the parade?"

He was so humiliated that he was furious. How could she be so candid? And he answered stupidly, "Did I?"

"Why are you ashamed?"

"You make me feel foolish."

"Why? I was touched myself. And I was curious to know why you were."

"Well, I suppose because for a while there I felt so much a part of it. I felt what it must be to have roots in a place like this, to say, 'this is my place.' And when an old man marches with the Civil War veterans he's someone of your own blood. I was just very much moved by all that, and wondering what it must be like."

"What it must be like? You don't know?"

183

He opened his mouth to explain and closed it. How could she possibly understand the whole complex, forlorn, confusing business?

Then he began, "You see, we—my people—we're all fragmented. Not whole, not of a piece, like you. My mother, for instance, came from Poland. Her brothers live in Austria; they fought on the other side in the war. Now they don't even speak the same language to each other. One of them has a wife whose father's people live in France, and my father has relatives in Johannesburg; I don't even know what language they speak!" And he repeated, "We're all fragmented, don't you see? All scattered."

"But I should think that would be very interesting! Old American families like mine, who've been in one place for centuries, they're like a little enclave into which nothing fresh or new ever enters. I sometimes think, especially since I've gone away to college, that we're even rather boring, we're so predictable."

"No," Maury said, patiently, "you're basic, you're strong." And he was suddenly compelled to go on. "Sometimes I think: What are we, where do we belong? What country is ours, really ours, where we have always been and will always be? I feel so light, so without grounding, that it seems as if I—all of us—my family and our friends, all the people I know, could be blown away like leaves and it wouldn't matter. Nobody would even notice."

"That sounds so sad!"

"I'm sorry, I didn't mean to be depressing."

"It's my fault, I asked you. Here, here's our short cut, up the hill. Let's run! There's the most gorgeous view at the top, you've never seen anything like it."

He never had. The hill fell away beneath them in loops and folds, and rose again all silvery-gold in the sun and green-black in the running shadows of the clouds. The land was cut by the bay and its crooked coves. Islands lay scattered in the water and beyond rose other hills, as far as they could see.

Agatha spoke deliberately in a warm and lovely tone,

> "All I could see from where I stood
> Was three long mountains and a wood."

Maury smiled and answered,

184

"I turned and looked another way,
And saw three islands in a bay."

They stood still, looking at one another. Agatha said, "I thought when I first saw you that you were like Chris and most of his friends, with nothing on your mind, sort of."

"I don't know what I'm like, really."

Something so moved him that he turned away. There were some tall plants in a clump, taller than he. "What are those things, with the little white flowers?"

"Oh, those? Just meadow rue. It's a weed."

"And this stuff, that's so fragrant?"

"Another common plant. It's yarrow."

He looked up. She was still standing there, with such an expression on her face— He said, "I don't really care what they're called, you know."

"I didn't believe you did."

And then they were standing together, their flesh joined from mouth to knee, with a hundred pulses beating, beating through layers of cotton cloth.

"When do you have to leave, Agatha?"

"Tomorrow morning. And you?"

"The day after. You know that we'll have to see each other again."

"I know."

"When? How?"

"In September. You'll come to Boston, or I could go to New Haven. Either way."

"Something's happened that's crazy. I'm in love."

"It is crazy, isn't it? Because I am, too."

He was certain he must look different, that people must surely notice it. But nobody did and it was better so. Even Chris had no suspicion and Maury, with a certain premonitory caution, was glad to keep it that way.

He heard her voice in his head. Sometimes, driving the car, her face rose up in front of the windshield, to dazzle him. He thought about her naked body, tried to imagine it, and grew weak.

They met in Boston in September. Once she came to New Haven and he rode the train back with her. They walked and

185

walked and lingered over drawn-out meals in restaurants. Their feet ached in the museums. On the sidewalks, as the weeks moved toward winter, it was clammy cold and the wind seeped through their clothes. There was never any place to go.

One time she produced a key. "This is for my friend Daisy's apartment. They're away skiing in Vermont."

"No," he said, "no, we can't."

"Why? I trust Daisy. And we've never been alone. I should just like to sit someplace together, quiet and alone."

He was trembling. "I couldn't just sit alone in a room with you, don't you know that?"

"Well, then. I'd do anything you want to make you happy. I want so much to make you happy."

"But it wouldn't make us happy afterward. Aggie darling, I want to start right, to do everything right. We've so much against us, I don't want to add more."

She dropped the key into her purse and snapped it shut.

"You're not—you don't think I don't *want* to, Aggie?" he cried.

"It's just," she said bitterly, "that I wonder whether we ever will be alone in a room together."

"Of course we will. You mustn't have thoughts like that."

"You haven't mentioned anything about me at home?" she asked.

"No. Have you?"

"My God, no! I've told you about my father. Oh," she said, "we even got in a fight last time I was home. He was talking about how the Jews are in back of Roosevelt; of course he thinks Roosevelt is the arch villain of all time and our descendants are going to have to pay for what he's doing to the country.

"And I said what you told me your father had said about Roosevelt, that people are starting to get a few dollars in their pockets and that probably he is really saving the American system . . . I thought my father would have a stroke! He asked me what kind of crazy, radical professors we had at college, and then Mother signaled to me not to say any more, because he gets so excited. So that's the way things are in my house."

"We'll think of something, some way," Maury said confidently. A man was supposed to have confidence in his powers. But he didn't feel very much.

*   *   *

186

The telephone was a life line and a misery at the same time. Agatha took his calls in a cubicle at the end of a corridor in her dormitory. For all the clattering, slamming and talking she was barely able to hear him. He had to repeat in a shouting whisper: "*I love you, I miss you so,*" feeling foolish, frustrated and sad. And then silence while time raced, with nothing to say, or rather, so much to say and no way to begin. Then the three minutes were up.

Thanksgiving vacation had to be endured. He went with his father to the apartments on Washington Heights to collect the rents and check repairs. He stood on the sidewalk and watched the lift vans being unloaded as the refugees began to arrive from Germany; stood while heavy ornate furniture from some villa in Berlin-Charlottenburg was lifted out, furniture too big and dark for the flat over the delicatessen or the laundry. His father stood there too, talking to the new arrivals in a mixture of German and Yiddish. His face was grave and he sighed. Always that sigh: What's to happen? What's to become of us? It was depressing.

Then home to Iris at the dinner table, giving her earnest daily rehash of the *New York Times,* pushing the untidy hair behind her ears. "You can't oversimplify, Pa. This thing that is happening in Germany has its roots in the Versailles Treaty and the economic collapse—"

Poor Iris! Would any man ever rejoice in her as I rejoice in Agatha?

He recalled the dinner table at Chris's house. Everything was so *emotional* here. But perhaps that was unfair? Perhaps the emotion was in him, too?

At Thanksgiving dinner there were some new faces.

"Mr. and Mrs. Nathanson," Pa said. "He's our new accountant and a very bright guy. His daughter's coming too," he added casually.

Just as casually, the daughter was seated next to Maury. But he had to give them credit. They had too much respect to foist just anyone upon him. She was a nice, a really nice girl. She went to Radcliffe and she was very smart, but she didn't try to impress him with it. He liked her pale gray wool dress and her shiny thick black hair. He even liked her nails, dark red ovals, perfectly manicured. Aggie had short nails like a little boy's; he suspected that she bit them. But he could have been locked in a room with

187

this girl, or any other girl, and it wouldn't have meant a thing.

"What are you planning to do after Yale?" the girl asked.

Everyone at the table had caught her question. He hadn't planned to answer as he did, hadn't even been sure of what he wanted. It was just an idea that had been growing, perhaps because of Chris's own plans or Chris's fine old grandfather.

"I want to go to law school," Maury said.

His father's mouth fell open. He almost chuckled. "Maury! You never said a word!"

"Well, I wasn't certain."

"By golly, this is great news! You know," he confided to the table, "when he was a baby his mother and I used to talk, we'd talk about him being a doctor or a lawyer. Well, you know how it is."

The Nathansons smiled. They knew how it was.

"So what's it to be? Harvard or Yale?"

Maury answered modestly, "I'll have to see who'll take me."

"Well, well, I'll have to do some hustling, but I'll do it. For Maury I'll move the earth if I have to," his father said.

"When the building business comes back," Mr. Nathanson observed, "it'll be a good thing to have your own son handle the legal end. You'll have it made. And you too, Maury. It'll be a good thing for you, too."

That was not at all what he had in mind, but he didn't say so. What he had in mind, as the idea took form and grew, was a good American life in some old town, or some small city. He saw himself sitting behind a roll-top desk with maple trees outside the window. He felt an atmosphere clean and quiet and austere. Like Lincoln in Springfield. Yes, that's how it would be. Like Lincoln in Springfield.

A few days later his mother remarked, "A nice girl, that Natalie, don't you think so?"

"Oh, very," he agreed. His mother was waiting for more but he did not give it.

Then a few weeks later while they were talking on the telephone, his mother said, "I spoke to Mrs. Nathanson today. She happened to remark, I don't know how it came about, you never called Natalie."

"No."

A pause. "You didn't like her?"

"I liked her."

"I don't want to interfere. A young man wants his privacy, I've never interfered, have I, Maury?"

"No, you haven't." And that was true.

"So forgive me this once. . . . Have you got another girl, is that it?"

"Well, it's too early to say. I'll tell you, Ma, I promise, whenever there's anything to tell."

"I'm sure you will. Whatever you do will be fine with us, Maury, you know that. As long as she's a Jewish girl. Not that it's necessary to say that to you. We trust you, Maury."

Christmas vacation was no better. Agatha came to New York for a Christmas party. He met her in the lobby of the Hotel Commodore. Feeling fiercely jealous, ineffectual and stricken of manhood, he listened to her assurances that Peter So-and-So, and Douglas So-and-So meant nothing to her at all, that they were only party escorts, that nobody meant anything to her at all (Oh, God, Maury, do I have to tell you?). And he knew that was the sacred truth and died of his jealousy anyway: hands that would touch her while they danced; ears that would listen to her voice; eyes that would look at her freely, publicly, with no apology. . . .

By March and spring recess he was close to desperation. "Pa, I'd like to have a car for a day or two," he said. "I'd like to run up and visit a fellow near Albany."

He drove north on the Albany Post Road, then crossed the river at West Point. It grew colder. The little villages were still shut into the silence of winter and there was snow on the slopes. He stopped for lunch in a place that smelled of hot grease. When the door opened cold air came in with the noisy men who pushed to the counter, bantering mock-sexy innuendoes with the middle-aged waitress. He had a desolate, hopeless feeling. He thought of turning around and going back, but he did not. Instead he filled the tank at the next gas station and drove. The farms grew larger and farther apart. There were miles of woods; of old, unpainted houses and shaggy cattle penned in barnyards. Toward evening he drove into Brewerstown.

He thought he had driven into the eighteenth century. He felt an absolute surge of delight and recognition. My time, my place! But of course that was absurd; it was only in pictures that Maury

189

could have known this place. Yet he knew it perfectly. He knew the wide, wide streets and the elms that would form a dark green aisle in leaf. He knew the white church with the graveyard on one side, the parish house on the other. And all the white fences, the brick walks, the fanlights, the driveways lined with rhododendrons. It took half a century to grow rhododendrons that size.

The town was shut down for the night, except for a drugstore on the main street. Maury went to the telephone book and marked down the address and the telephone number. The store was empty except for the man behind the counter.

"Is Lake Road far from here?" Maury asked.

"Depends where you want to go on Lake Road. It goes five, six miles around the lake, then joins up with the highway. Who you lookin' for?"

Maury shook his head. "Oh, I don't plan to visit tonight. I'll call first."

He dropped a nickel into the slot and gave the number to the operator.

"The line is busy," she said.

He wondered whether he would have the courage to try again. The man behind the counter looked at him curiously while he waited.

"You're not from these parts?"

"New York City."

"Ayeh. Been in New York once. Didn't like it."

"Well. Can't blame you. This is a beautiful town."

"Ayeh. My folks came here when they was just Indians around."

Maury put the nickel in again. This time someone answered. "Is Agatha at home, please?"

"Miss Agatha?" He was relieved to know it was a maid. "Who shall I say is calling?"

"Just a friend. A friend from New York."

When she came to the phone he whispered, "Aggie, I'm here in town."

"Oh, my God, why?"

"Because I was going out of my mind without seeing you."

"But what am I going to say? What am I going to do?"

Suddenly he was decisive. "Say you need something at the drugstore. Anything. I'll be waiting down the block in a tan Maxwell. How long will you be?"

"Fifteen minutes."

"That's just about as long as I can hold out," he said.

They drove about two miles out of town and stopped the car. When they put their arms around each other it was like the healing of a wound.

"I have to know," Maury said, "what's going to become of us."

She began to cry. "Don't, don't," he murmured. "Ever since that Christmas dance in the city I've been thinking the world is full of enemies, people who want to take you away from me . . ."

"Nobody can do that," she said fiercely.

"Then will you marry me? In June, after I graduate? Will you, Agatha?"

"Yes, yes, I will."

"No matter what?"

"No matter what."

At least he knew now where they were going. He hadn't the faintest idea how they were going to get there, how he would manage law school and this marriage, but he had her promise. It sustained him, through the spring session, through the finals, through commencement.

His mother had a habit of drinking a late cup of coffee in the kitchen before going to bed. He sat there with her on the night after commencement. He had known all day that there was something she wanted to say, he knew her so well.

"Maury," she began now, "you have a girl, haven't you? And she isn't Jewish."

He felt a giggle, an absurd shocked giggle and quelled it. "How did you guess?"

"What other reason could there be for you to be so secretive?"

He didn't answer.

"That's where you went when you borrowed Pa's car last spring, isn't it?"

He nodded.

"What are you going to do?"

"Marry her, Ma."

"You know, of course, what trouble this is going to make?"

"I know. And I'm sorry."

His mother stirred her coffee. The spoon made a pleasant, comforting sound against the cup. She began to speak softly. "My mind

191

is so often divided. I can see two sides of everything, as though I were holding a ball between my hands. I think: Maury, you're right. If you really love another human being—if it's real, and God knows there is so little real love and it's made up of so many things that even at my age I don't understand it, so I suppose I should use the word 'want' rather than 'love' . . . if you really want to be with a person, why shouldn't you be? Life is short enough; why suffer and sacrifice? One is born with a label, one could just as easily have been born something else. You see what I mean, Maury?"

"I see. But what is the other side?"

"The other side," she said quietly, "is that you *were* born what you are, nothing can change it and your father is right. So that side says to me: Tell Maury to listen to his father."

"You know what he's going to say? You've discussed it with him?"

"Of course I haven't! And of course I know what he's going to say, just as you know it." She swallowed her coffee.

What a beautiful face! he thought. She has a lovely, serious, gentle face, my mother . . .

"He'll say," she went on, "and he'll be right—he'll say that you come from a proud, ancient people. You may not always think so when you look around at the children of the eastern ghettos. We're not educated; we're often noisy; we don't have the finest manners; where could we learn them? But we're only one very small part of the history of our people."

"I know. I understand."

"Sometimes I've wondered," she said, "I've wondered whether perhaps, since you've been in a different world at college, whether you might have been ashamed of me, only a little? A foreign-born mother with an accent. Has that bothered you?"

"No, Ma, no," he said, and felt a touch like pain. She was so assured, with her tall carriage, and good clothes or what remained of them, her books and her courses. He thought: Has this been inside her all the time? We don't know anything about anybody, after all.

And it seemed to him as he sat in the cold, white kitchen among the looming white boxes, the tall rectangular bulk of the refrigerator and the lower bulk of the stove, with the chilling glare of the ceiling light in his eyes, that it was an operating room and he was helpless, pinned down, fastened and exposed like a patient on the table.

"Ma, I can't, I can't."

"Can't leave her?"

He could hardly speak. For a grown man to weep! The thing in his throat was a lump of tears. "Can't leave her," he repeated thickly, and closed his eyes.

She was silent. He did not look at her, but he felt a stir of warmth in the air behind him and knew that she was standing very close, not touching. Then she did touch him, her hand stroking his hair.

"Maury, Maury, I'm sorry. Living can be so terribly hard."

"Now, you wanted to talk to me, Maury?" Pa asked.

They were in his den among his familiar things: cigar smoke, the mahogany humidor and all the photographs of Ma and his children and his own parents, the father in a derby hat with the tiny wife next to him, wearing a plumed hat and an 1880s dress. The globe stood in front of the window. It was Iris' present. She always gave presents like that, a globe or books or antique maps.

"I suppose Ma has mentioned what I want to talk about," Maury said.

"She has. But you must know there is really nothing to talk about," his father said gently. "Not that I refuse to talk. I'm willing to listen."

Maury began. "What else is there to say but that I love Agatha? I love her so—"

"I'm sorry. Sorry to see your pain."

"It needn't be pain. It could be so simple."

"It's never simple."

"It was for you and Ma, wasn't it?"

"It's never simple, I tell you. And your mother was a Jewish girl."

"Pa, tell me, you're a practical, rational man. Is it so strange for me to be in love with Agatha? She's such a lovely person. You would really like her. She's so intelligent and happy and kindhearted."

"I believe you. I don't think you would care about anyone who wasn't all of those things. Still, to marry her—it's impossible."

193

"How can you feel that way and still be such friends with Mr. Malone?"

"Why not? Malone and I understand each other, that's why we're friends. He's a good Catholic and he expects his children to marry Catholics. And I respect him for it."

"But why? Really why? You still haven't explained. I'll grant that it's easier not to marry out, but—"

Joseph stood up. "Come," he said, spinning the globe. "There, that's Palestine. That's where it started. We came from there. There we gave the world the Ten Commandments, and if everybody would obey them there would be no trouble. There we gave the Christian world its God. And from there we were burned out and dispossessed and driven here—" his finger made a long sweep across Africa, up into Spain. "And here—" a sweep of the palm across Europe, eastward into Poland and Russia. "And then here, across the Atlantic, and everywhere else you can think of. Africa, Australia—"

"Yes, yes," Maury said impatiently, "I've had a bit of education. I know our history."

"You know, but you only read the words, you didn't feel them. Maury, all this history, this wandering, has been written in *blood*. And it is still being written today, right now, while you and I stand here. Tonight in Germany our people are being tortured for no reason at all and the world does nothing, it doesn't care. Oh," he said passionately, "how we have suffered, this People of the Book, this proud, strong people who have enriched the world! My son, we need every soul we can hold on to. There are so few of us and we need each other. How can you turn your back on your people? How can you?"

He was moved, and angered that he was moved. His father had never been so eloquent. It was not like him, silent man that he was, not gifted with words. Tears had even come into his eyes as he spoke. He has no right to do this to me, Maury thought, and he knew he was losing the battle, knew he had already lost it.

He made one more try. "Pa, I wouldn't turn my back. I wouldn't change. Did you think I would convert? I'll stay what I am and Agatha will stay what she is."

"And your children? What will they be? I'll tell you: nothing! And you ask me, you come in casually and ask me to accept, as if it were only a small thing, that I should live to see my grandson, son of my son, a nothing? Why don't you come in and ask for my right arm? Why don't you?"

"Pa, will you at least meet Agatha? Let me bring her here. Then you can talk to her and—"

"No, no, I tell you. There's no sense in it!"

"Then you're no different from her people. You're just as much of a bigot."

"What? No difference between the murderers and the murdered? You must be crazy! So her people are against it too, are they?"

"Of course! What did you think?"

"So you see, you see how impossible it is? Oh, Maury, listen to me, I want to reach your heart and your mind. Believe me, there is nothing a human being can't get over. You don't think so now, but take it on faith, please do. Parents lose children, husbands and wives die and hearts break, but they go on living. And eventually the break heals.

"Believe me now, you'll suffer for a couple of months, I know you will. But then it'll be over and you'll meet a fine girl of your own kind, and she'll meet another man, this Agatha. It'll be better for her, too."

Something burst in Maury. "I don't want to hear that! Don't dare tell me that!"

"Maurice, don't raise your voice to me. I'm trying to help you, but this sort of thing won't do any good."

He went to the door. He wanted to break something, throw the lamp to the floor, smash things. God damn world! God damn life! "What will you do if we get married anyway?" he asked.

His father's face looked sick. It looked green. "Maurice," he said very low, "I hope you won't do that. I hope for your mother's sake, for mine and for us all that you won't do that. I beg you, I warn you, don't bring the unthinkable to pass."

Agatha was tearful on the telephone. "I talked to my parents, Maury. Or at least I tried to. They were absolutely horrified, I thought my father had lost his mind, he went into such a tirade. He said he thought I must be insane! I can't begin to tell you the things he said!"

"I can imagine," Maury said grimly.

"He went on about our family, our ancestors, and what they

stood for and what America stands for, and the church, and all our friends. And he said that if—if I did this I'd be no daughter of his. First my mother cried and then she got furious at me because Daddy turned absolutely white and she thought he was going to have a heart attack. She made me get out of the room. Oh, Maury, how terrible to be married this way, to walk out of your home like this!"

He thought for a moment. "Do you suppose if I spoke to Chris he could talk to them?"

"Oh, Maury, I don't know. Try it!"

"He's coming to New York for the weekend. I'll go see him at his hotel."

"Oh, yes," Chris said, "my parents spoke very well of you. 'A very attractive young man,' my mother said. I remember her words."

"Well, then, if they thought well of me, maybe they or you would talk to Aggie's parents? It would help a lot, I think."

"I don't really think it would," Chris said gently.

"You don't? Aggie thought it would."

"Aggie knows better. She's grasping at straws."

Maury put his head in his hands. He thought he had spoken so persuasively.

Chris went to the window and looked out for a minute, as if he were making up his mind about something. Then he turned back to the room. "Listen, I have a proposition. Your nerves are pretty bad, one can see that with half an eye. Why don't you just chuck everything and sail to England with me next week? If money's a problem I can lend you some. We'll go tramping through England and you'll be born again. What do you say?"

"You don't understand. You say you want to help me. Then why don't you give me the help I want? Tell me, Chris. Be honest with me."

"You mean that?"

"I mean it."

"Because I don't approve of the marriage. If I had known about you and Aggie I wouldn't have let things get this far."

"Why, Chris, why?"

"Come on, Maury, you're not that naive. Because you are what you are, that's why."

"And in what way am I so different from you?"

"I don't think you are, but the world thinks so. And you'd be asking Aggie to be the world's victim along with you."

"She doesn't care."

"She thinks she doesn't care. Clubs and friends, many of her friends—she'd have to give them all up. Her children would be rejected by people and in places where she's been welcomed."

"She doesn't give a damn, I tell you!"

"She gives more than a damn about her parents! Aggie is very close to them, especially her father. Ever since he had polio she's been his right hand. I remember when she was a little kid, no more than eight or nine, and she used to help him learn to walk again. It would have broken your heart."

"And this doesn't break your heart?"

Chris looked at him, not speaking. Maury opened the door. "*My friend. My good friend,* Chris. Well, you can go to hell!"

They were married at city hall on a blazing day in July. "You could fry an egg on the sidewalk today," the clerk said as he stamped their certificate.

In their stifling room at the hotel a fan stirred the air at ten-second intervals. Through the open window came the sound of a record playing "Pagliacci" over and over. They sent downstairs for a meal of overcooked steak and soggy potatoes. It was the most beautiful room, the most sumptuous dinner, the most marvelous music they had ever known.

Aggie took a bottle of wine from her suitcase. "I brought some wine for our wedding toast. Look at the label. Nothing but the best!"

"I don't know a thing about wines. We never had any in our house."

"I got used to it, living in France. You drink it there instead of water."

"Don't people get drunk?"

"Just a pleasant haze. Your health!" she said.

"And yours, Mrs. Friedman."

So they drank to each other, pulled the shade and went back to bed, although it was only three in the afternoon.

In the morning, after he was sure that his father had left for work, he telephoned his mother.

"Maury," she said, "oh, how I want to see you! But I can't. Your father has forbidden me." And she cried, "Dear heaven, if only you hadn't done this! It's like a morgue here since yesterday. Iris and I, we can scarcely breathe. And your father looks ten years older."

He was not angry at her. "Good-by, Ma," he said softly, and hung the receiver up.

Between them they had a little more than four hundred dollars.

"If we're very careful," Maury said, "we can make this last a couple of months. But I'll have a job long before then." He felt very strong, very confident.

"I'll get something too. I can always teach French as a substitute until there's a permanent opening."

"Meanwhile, we'll find the cheapest decent apartment we can until we decide where we want to go permanently."

Cheerfully, purposefully, they bought newspapers, took subways, and finally found a furnished apartment on the top floor of a two-family house in Queens. The owner was Mr. George Andreapoulis, a polite young Greek-American who had just graduated from law school into the Depression. On a trip to Greece he had gotten a bride, Elena, a strong girl with a white smile and hairy arms.

The apartment was newly furnished in yellow maple. There were clean curtains and an ugly imitation Oriental rug.

"I should get fifty a month for it," said Mr. Andreapoulis, "but the times are so bad that, frankly, I'll be willing to take forty."

Maury stood looking out of the kitchen window to the small concrete-and-cinder yard, the endless lots without trees, just dry waving grass as far as the distant billboards on the highway. Bleak, even in the glittering sunlight. If the world were flat this would be the place where you dropped off into the void. Still, it was immaculate, the landlord was respectable and friendly and they wouldn't be here long anyway.

"My wife speaks no English," said Mr. Andreapoulis. "We're newlyweds, too. Maybe you will help her to learn English, Mrs. Friedman? And she will teach you to cook, she's a wonderful cook." He looked suddenly flustered. "Excuse me, how stupid, I only meant that so many American young ladies don't learn cooking—although probably you're a fine cook already."

Agatha laughed. "No, I can't boil water as the saying goes. I'm ready to be taught. Until I get a job, that is."

So it was settled. They made two trips on the subway with their suitcases, a heavy box of books, and their one purchase, a superheterodyne radio which Maury bought for thirty-five dollars. They placed it on the table in the living room next to the lamp.

There was a certain amount of guilt over its purchase, but in the end it turned out to have been a good investment. People needed some recreation, and the movies cost seventy cents for the two of them. For nothing at all, the radio brought the Philharmonic on Sunday afternoons, and a good dance band almost any time. They could dance on the kitchen floor to Glen Gray's Casa Loma Orchestra or to. Paul Whiteman at the Biltmore. They could Begin the Beguine, Fly Down to Rio, or turn off the lights and Dance in the Dark, alone together in their private world. Dazed and entranced, they moved like one body across the room to where, still not separating from her, he switched off the sound, and then in the sudden fall of silence they moved again like one body to the bed.

20

They walked up Riverside Drive and turned toward West End Avenue at Iris' street. It was a warm evening for April and people were out, fathers of families walking their dogs and young people singing "When a Broadway Baby Says Goodnight," shoving at one another and laughing boisterously. They were on their way to a party. Iris and Fred were coming back from one.

"Sorry to break it up so early," Fred said when they reached the building where Iris lived. "I shouldn't have left so much homework for Sunday night. My fault," he said apologetically.

"That's all right," she told him. "I've got work too," which was not the case.

They stood a moment. It was awkward; should she ask him upstairs for a few minutes, after all? She didn't really want to and she knew he didn't want to come.

"Thanks for inviting me," he said. "It was a great party. I didn't know you and Enid were friends."

"We're not. It's just that our mothers work on the same charity committee and it happened through them." It occurred to her as she said the word 'charity' that it really was odd for her mother to be doing charity when there was never an extra dollar at home. But then, Ma always said, we must be very thankful, there are so many people far worse off than we are.

"Well, it was a great party," Fred said again. He started to move away. "Don't forget, newspaper meeting after school tomorrow."

"I won't forget," she answered. She went inside and took the elevator upstairs.

Her mother was reading in the living room. She had a look of surprise. "So soon? And where's Fred?"

"It broke up early. And he had homework."

"My goodness, it's only nine-thirty. He could have had something to eat. I put the cocoa pot out and some cake."

"We had too much to eat, we were stuffed."

"So you had a good time, then," her mother said. "Don't bother your father, he's doing the income tax. I guess I'll go read in bed, it's more comfortable."

Iris went to her room and took her dress off. It was emerald green, the color of wet leaves. Her mother bought it when Fred first took an interest in her. That was when they started to work on the school paper together. Her mother said she ought to pay more attention to her clothes now that she was fifteen.

Fred was a serious boy. When he filled out he would be a fine-looking man in spite of his glasses. Right now he was very tall and skinny, but he had a nice face. And he was one of the smartest boys in school.

They had been having such good discussions all winter, working in the editorial room, and sometimes walking home in the late afternoons. He was interested in politics and they had great arguments, although mostly they agreed on things.

"I respect your mind," he told her. "You reason things out. You think for yourself."

They felt, although they did not say so, rather superior to most of the other kids. They filled their lives, they didn't waste time. Fred did a lot of reading too, and they talked about what they read.

She knew he liked her, and this was one of the happiest things that had ever happened to her. It was like having something new to look forward to every day.

A week ago he had invited her to a wedding. One of his cousins was getting married and he had been told to bring a girl. It was to be a big formal wedding, and everyone would wear evening clothes. Iris had never been at any wedding at all, and she was excited about that and about having been asked by Fred.

Her mother said, "Well, we shall have to get you something very nice to wear." She had an idea. She went to a box on the top shelf of her closet and took out a dress. It was pink silk and Iris recognized the dress in the portrait of her mother, her Paris dress.

"We can take it to a dressmaker and have it altered for you," her mother said. "Look," and she pulled the skirt out into a fan, "ten yards of material, and such material! We can make a magnificent dress for you. And shoes dyed to match. What do you think?"

It was truly beautiful. Iris wondered, though, what the other girls would be wearing and wondered how she could find out.

Now she hung up the green wool dress. At this party tonight there was a girl who kept looking at Iris' dress. She was one of those girls who look good with an old sweater tied around their shoulders, the sort of girl who is born that way and cannot be made. This girl gave Iris' dress a long, slow look, so that she sank lower into her chair and knew that her dress must be awful, must be all wrong. (Years later she was to meet this same girl at someone's house and the girl was to tell her: You had a dress once, emerald green, the most beautiful color; I never forgot it. But of course Iris could not know that now.)

It had really been a dreadful, miserable party. She was sorry she had invited Fred, but Enid had told her to bring a boy. All those friends of Enid's were the kind of people Fred didn't like: shallow and showoffy, speaking in wisecracks which you were supposed to answer with more wisecracks. It had been very tiring. Fred and Iris had exchanged looks and she had known he was thinking the same. She telegraphed her regret, and Fred brought her a plate of food. "The food's good anyway," he said, and went back for more. He had an enormous appetite.

Iris had watched the girls. It had been almost like a show, to see them giggling and giving the boys that arch look, the sideward and upward sliding of the eyes. Boys were so stupid they didn't see how affected it was. Except for Fred, who would see and understand. It was remarkable how his mind and Iris' worked on the same track.

"My goodness," Enid had said, "you look as if you'd lost your best friend! Aren't you having a good time?" She had smiled, but it was a cold smile.

Iris had been mortified in front of Fred. "Of course, I'm having a very good time," she had answered stiffly.

Perhaps she really ought to smile more. Cousin Ruth had told her once that she had an unusually nice smile. In fact, what Cousin Ruth had really said was: "A light seems to turn on in your face when you smile." After that Iris had gone home and practiced in front of the bathroom mirror. It was true. Her lips did draw back sweetly and her teeth were very bright. When the smile withdrew her face fell back into severity, although she didn't feel severe. She must remember to smile, but not too much, or she'd look like a nut.

Enid and some of the boys had taken up the rugs in the hall and put the phonograph on. Everyone got up to dance. Fred held his arm out. Iris loved to dance. She must have got that from her mother; her father danced well but he didn't love it all that much. She remembered the day she came home and found her mother all alone, dancing in the living room. Mama hadn't heard Iris come in and there she had been, whirling around in a waltz, with "The Blue Danube" playing on the phonograph. It was an Edison, with thick records; you had to wind it up when the record was only half over. Iris had been so embarrassed for her mother, but Mama hadn't been at all. She had only stopped and said, "Do you know, if I could be reincarnated for a few days, I would like to be a countess or a princess in Vienna and go whirling in a marvelous white lace dress, waltzing under the crystal chandeliers. But only for a day or two. It must have been a very silly, useless life."

"I wish they would put on a waltz," Iris had said to Fred.

"They won't," he had answered, and laughed and put his cheek on hers. She had felt very excited, being that close to him. It had started to be a good time, Iris thought now.

She went to the bathroom and ran the water for a bath, although she had taken one before getting dressed this evening and was certainly quite clean. But she wanted to lie in the warm water and think. There was great comfort in warm water.

If that girl hadn't arrived it might have been lovely, after all. The minute she walked in everything had changed. She was one of those lively girls who make everyone look at them. They don't even have to be pretty.

"This is Alice," Enid had said. "She's just moved here from Altoona. We went to camp together."

"Alice from Altoona," Alice had said and everybody laughed, although it wasn't funny. Right away everybody was interested in her. They all wanted to know: When did you move? Where are you going to school? This your first time in New York?

She had taken all the attention as though she expected it. No doubt she had always had it. Iris had watched her, thinking again: It is like a play, only now the leading lady has come in; the others were just bit players up to now. Iris had observed what she did, what was different about her. She saw that Alice didn't talk too much. When she did say something, it counted; usually it was something to make people laugh. Or else it was a compliment, not too thick, just a comment almost casual, something to make the other person feel important. It looked so easy, the way she did it, never overdoing it, but Iris knew it really wasn't.

She had told Enid's mother that the apartment was just beautiful and she'd love to have her own mother see it. (Her mother would be invited.) She had let everyone know that her brother was a sophomore at Columbia. (The girls would ask her to all their parties.) She had told every boy there that he was a simply marvelous dancer. "I couldn't help noticing," she'd said. (Immediately, they all wanted to dance with her.)

"You're so *tall!*" she had said to Fred, as though, Iris thought disgustedly, he were some sort of giant that she had never seen before.

But Fred had been pleased and asked her to dance. They did the Peabody; Alice knew some variations. "We know a thing or two in Altoona," she said and did a whirl. Her skirt swirled high till it showed the lace on her panties. Fred picked her up the way they do at the ballet and everybody stepped back into a circle to watch the performance of Fred and Alice. Fred was delighted and exhilarated.

Iris had tried to look as if it were really fun to stand there and admire. When Enid had changed the record, Fred had gone right on dancing with Alice. Soon everyone was back on the floor except Iris. Then a boy came and invited her; she was so relieved until she found out that he was Enid's little brother. He was almost thirteen. His hand was sweaty on the back of her dress and he didn't really dance, just walked around the floor. He kept on and on as the record changed; perhaps he would have liked to get rid of her and didn't know how? She would have liked to get rid of him and didn't know how. After a while she told him she wanted to sit down.

Fred had seen her sitting and had come over. No doubt he remembered his duty as her escort. Besides, someone had cut in and taken Alice away from him.

"You know," Iris reminded him then, "it's Sunday and don't you think we ought to get going home soon?"

She had been surprised when he agreed. He said he still had

homework to do. She had thought that now probably he would want to stay to the very last. But he had agreed.

Now she ran more hot water. Her mother always warned her not to fall asleep in the tub, but it was such a soothing place to think. Perhaps Maury would know what I do wrong? Everything Fred always said he didn't like is what that girl did. Perhaps Maury would know. So often she wished she could ask him about what she always thought of as his golden charm, but he would be so embarrassed. Once, when she was perhaps eleven, she had peeked through the crack of his door and seen him sitting at the window for minutes and minutes. And finally she had gone in and asked him, "Are you unhappy about something?" And he had been so cross. "Damn pesky little kid!" he had yelled at her. But then later that night, she remembered, he had come to her room and said he was sorry, and asked her whether she had wanted anything. He could be so tender, Maury could, but he didn't like to show that side to people.

I feel so sorry he has left us this way. I suppose he couldn't help falling in love with Agatha. Anyway, religion never meant very much to him. I used to see on his face that he wasn't feeling anything when we went to services. Not the way Pa or I do. (I never could tell about my mother; I know she loves the music.) But I truly love it, I love the old, old words and the ancient people. I think of a long caravan of people, trailing back in time, I think of all the people in all the rows as if they are a part of me and I them. Afterward, when they get up and go out, they will be strangers again, not caring an instant's worth about Iris Friedman, but while we are there and the mournful, plaintive music sweeps over us it draws us all together and we are one. When I was very little, I used to think that God was like Pa, or Pa was like God and could do anything, could make anything happen. Now I know he can't. . . . He couldn't do anything about Maury. He is so sad about Maury; I know he is, because he doesn't talk about him anymore. When Pa isn't home my mother talks about Maury. She talks so much about when he was a baby. She never says: When you were a baby, Iris.

The water began to grow cool. She climbed out of the tub and put her nightgown on. The telephone rang in the hall. Her mother answered and called her.

"For you," she said.

Iris looked at the clock. It was almost eleven. She picked up the phone and Fred said, "Iris? I'm awfully sorry to call this late, but I just found out something and I wanted to tell you—"

"Yes?" She waited.

"It's about the wedding," he said. "I'm so embarrassed. But it seems that I or somebody made a mistake and I'm not supposed to bring a girl, after all. I feel lousy about it, but—well, I know you'll understand."

"Sure." She spoke brightly. "Sure, I understand."

He talked a minute or two longer, something about the paper, but she wasn't really listening. She was thinking: Why don't I tell him not to bother to lie? I know perfectly well he intends to take Alice. He probably went back to the party after he left me. Why don't I?

When she hung up her mother came out of her bedroom. "My goodness," she said, smiling, "couldn't he even wait until he sees you tomorrow in school?"

"It was about the wedding. He made a mistake. He's not supposed to bring a girl, after all."

"Oh," her mother said slowly, "I see." She looked troubled for a minute, and searched Iris' face, which was guarded and proud. Then she said, "Oh well, there'll be other weddings. You'll make the best of it."

Mama didn't mean to be indifferent, not at all. That was the way she treated herself. "Short of a catastrophe, you will never admit when anything has gone wrong," Pa always complained, and yet he was really grateful for his wife's placid optimism, which Iris often found so exasperating. Didn't anything ever upset her? When Iris asked her that one time she didn't answer at once, and then she said, "If it does, I keep it to myself. Your father has enough to worry him already."

She went back to her room, brushed her teeth and got into bed. It was funny, but she didn't feel as bad about this as she would have expected. Perhaps, in a way, it was a relief not to have to go. Not to have to think about what impression you were making, or to worry about girls like Alice. Anyway, Fred was only a boy. Someday there would be a man, a real man, who would have eyes only for her.

I'm sure my mother thinks now that I'm crushed because of this—for she knows as well as I do that Fred lied. She used to think I was unhappy when we were at the beach years ago and there was a crowd of kids out on the lawn, while I was in the hammock reading. I remember the summer I read *Ivanhoe* and *The Last Days of Pompeii,* all those fat, wonderful books, the stories and tragedies that are so sad but never real enough to break your heart, just enough to make the sweet tears rise. I used to lay the book down and let them rise and I was very happy.

When I get to college I want to major in English literature. I've been in love with the sound and cadence, the charm and fragrance of words, as long as I can remember, probably ever since Mama first read stories aloud when I was three years old. Maybe younger than that. You can feel words, the way fingers feel velvet. Once I made a list of words that are especially beautiful. Sapphire. Tintinnabulation. Grass. Angelica. I wish my name was Angelica. I must make it a duty to learn five new words every day.

She wanted so much to write. The problem was that she had nothing to write about. Once she had written a piece about a lonely girl away at camp, and the teacher had said it was lyrical, but that was the only time. She guessed she didn't have any special talent, although perhaps after she had really lived she might find something to say.

At school there was a girl, only Iris' own age, who left to study at a conservatory; she had already played with an orchestra. How marvelous it must be to have such a way of expressing what is in you! It seemed to Iris that something was alive inside of her that wanted to get out and couldn't. There was a rising in her chest, so beautiful and dazzling that people would stop and look with surprised faces if they could know about it.

It's true, Iris thought, the person who lives inside me and the person that other people see are not at all the same.

21

In the autumn of 1935 there seemed to be no place for a well-spoken, fine-appearing graduate of Yale who had majored in philosophy and was willing to do anything at all. Nor was there a place for an attractive Wellesley girl of excellent family who had studied fine arts in Europe and spoke French better than many of the natives of France. She couldn't even fill a job as a lunch-room waitress because there were fifty applicants for every such job and they had all had experience. He couldn't get a job as a porter because in the first place he didn't look like a porter and in the second place everyone was laying off, not hiring. There was no sense in it.

Every night at midnight Maury went out for the early-morning editions of the papers, read the help-wanted pages, then took the subway at five o'clock, walked from store to loft to factory, rode from the Bronx to Brooklyn and back and came home with nothing.

By October they had to believe that there were no jobs. They had seventy dollars left. And one day Maury didn't bother to buy the newspaper; it would be wasting a nickel. That was the day when, for the first time, they knew panic.

Agatha asked timidly, "Don't you know anybody? I mean, you've always lived in New York—"

How to explain? He had lost touch with all his childhood friends. He couldn't call up now and beg a favor. Besides, most of their fathers were doctors or lawyers who couldn't do anything for him, or else they were in business and had their own troubles.

The only possibility was Eddy Holtz. To be sure, they had drifted coolly apart. Yet there was something about Eddy that would make it possible for Maury to swallow his pride, and he recognized what a tribute that was to some quality in Eddy. Eddy was at Columbia Physicians and Surgeons. His painful grind had paid off and Maury thought wistfully that he would always hang on and get where he wanted to go. His father owned three or four shoe stores, a small chain, in Brooklyn. Perhaps he just might—

"I'll ask my father," Eddy said. "I'll see what I can do. You're happy, Maury?"

"Yes, yes, except for the job situation. You'd heard I was married?"

"Chris Guthrie's cousin, isn't she?"

"Yes, and our families don't—we don't have anything to do with them. That's why I thought of you. I may not always have agreed with you, Eddy, but I knew you wouldn't forget the time when we were friends."

"I haven't helped you yet. But I will try."

The store was two blocks from the subway station, which was good. He didn't have far to walk. It was a long, narrow store wedged between a Woolworth's and a Kiddy Klothes shop. One entire window was a display of children's shoes. There were two other salesmen, Resnick and Santorello, men who had been there fifteen years. They earned forty dollars a week. Maury was to get twenty, taking the place of an older man who had dropped dead the week before.

"Boss saves money with Binder gone," the other men told him. "He was here longer than we were; he got forty-five dollars."

What worried Maury was that there really wasn't enough work for three men. Sometimes no more than half a dozen people came in during the hours before three o'clock: mothers with toddlers, a man buying work shoes, young girls buying cheap patent-leather pumps for dancing, an old woman with shoes cracked and split, who counted out her money for the new pair in dollar bills, the last dollar in coins from her change purse. After three, when school was out, there was a flurry and scurry of children crying and fighting over the hobbyhorse. He learned to handle them with dispatch and patience so that, coming with the rest of the family on another day, the mothers often asked for and waited for him. It saddened him that

209

these shabby people could clothe and shoe their children only by neglecting themselves.

During the long mornings he stood at the windows and found that he had acquired Resnick's and Santorello's irritating habit of jingling the change in their pockets out of restless boredom. He watched the dull, ambling traffic, the bus discharging at the corner and two or three people coming out of the subway in midmorning: going where? An ambulance came for someone in a store across the street; that was an event of note. He would have liked to bring a book from the library. He could at least have used the time to take himself away from that dreary street, away from 1935 to a brighter place and a more vital time of man. But to do so would be to turn his back upon the other two men, and he knew it would not only be unwise to incur their dislike by seeming different, but in some way unkind. He didn't participate fully in their conversations, except when they talked baseball, which they often did. Mostly they talked about money and family and these came down to the same thing, making one word, money-family. How to pay for the wife's hysterectomy, what to do about the father-in-law who was unemployed. They would probably have to take him and his wife in with them, which meant that their oldest boy would then have to sleep on the sofa, and then where would the daughter entertain her boy friend? She was keeping company with a nice fellow who had a good job with Consolidated Edison, and it would be a helluva thing if she lost her boy friend because of that old bastard, who had never done a thing for them when he had it! But after all, Santorello said, he's my wife's father and she cries her eyes out, it's hell to go home at night and listen to her. And Resnick nodded, understanding and wise; his dark hooded eyes, somber, cynical and resigned, reminded Maury so much of Pa that he sometimes couldn't look into Resnick's face. Resnick nodded and sighed: Family, family, my brother owes me a hundred and fifty dollars, I know I ought to make him pay, he could take a loan someplace, he keeps promising, we've always been like *that*—with two fingers raised, pressed side by side—I hate to make trouble between us, but, gee, a hundred and fifty dollars.

At least, Maury thought, feeling such pity for them, for me this is temporary. These times can't go on much longer. For me at least, there's something else. But for these two who are, after all, not really any different from me except that I've read some books that

they haven't read, is this all there is? Bending over feet and tying
string on a shoe box until the end?

Too much time to think. Melancholy. Must stop. Be thankful I
have Aggie at home, not their nagging, miserable women. And we
are getting along. Two weeks' wages go for rent. That leaves forty
dollars or thereabouts for the rest of the month. Eight a week for
food, that's thirty-two, with eight over for carfare, gas and electric.
Can manage, as long as the clothes hold out and we have no medical
bills. Anyway, George Andreapoulis said something about needing
some typing done. He can't afford a secretary in that two-bit office.
Aggie could do it for him; she knows how to type pretty well. Only,
George would have to provide the typewriter because I gave mine
to Iris and Aggie left hers at home, which means it's lost to us.
Unless—his head whirled and it occurred to him that he'd never
spent so much energy on so many details—unless Iris could prevail
upon their parents to buy another for her and return his to
him? . . .

He had come home one afternoon a month or so ago and found
his sister sitting at the table with Aggie. She'd come directly from
school, wearing a plaid skirt and sweater and the string of pearls,
probably the good ones that she'd had since she was a baby, and the
saddle shoes that all the girls wore. She had her books in a heap on
the floor next to her chair. She'd risen to kiss him.

"I've surprised you, Maury?"

"And how! Gee, I'm glad! You girls introduced yourselves to each
other?"

"I just got here a few minutes ago," Iris had said. "I got lost. I've
never been in Queens before."

"How'd you know where to find us?"

"From the post office. I figured you must have arranged to have
your mail forwarded."

"I ought to have remembered how smart you are."

She had flushed; the pink had made her austere face look tender.

"Did you—did you tell anyone you were coming?"

"I told Ma, and she cried a little. She didn't say anything but I
knew she was glad."

"But that's all you told." He couldn't, wouldn't say the words: Pa,
father.

"Well, I didn't want to be sneaky, so I said this morning that I'd

211

be late because I was coming here. I said it loud enough so Pa could hear it from the hall. I wouldn't do anything sneaky," she had repeated with pride.

Something had welled up in Maury. She was a *person.* Either she had changed or he had. He'd never really looked at her before, just known she was there like a sofa or chair that has been standing in a room as long as you can recall, and that sometimes gets in the way when you stumble over it in the dark. But she was a *person.*

"I love you, Iris," he said then, simply.

Aggie, with the tact that was part of her charm, had made a bustle with the tea, saying cheerfully, "Iris is right where we were five years ago. Puzzling over college catalogues."

"Not really," Iris had said, "there's no choice for me. I'm going to Hunter. Not that I mind. I'm looking forward to it."

"What's Hunter?" Aggie had wanted to know.

Maury had explained, feeling a wave of guilt, though it wasn't his fault that they'd kept him in private school and sent him to Yale, "Hunter's a free college of the city of New York. You have to be very bright to go there, have to have top grades."

"Oh. And after that, Iris? Have you thought what you wanted to do? I hope you have, then you won't be in the position I'm in."

"I'm going to teach," Iris had said. "That is, I will if I can find work. At least I'll be prepared."

She'd stirred the tea. There'd been something quite calm and collected in the way she sat. She's come out of childhood, Maury had thought, and as he was looking at the top of her dark, bent head, suddenly she had raised it and asked, "Don't you want to know how things are at home? Is it that you just don't want to ask me?"

He had been astonished at her perception. "Well, then, tell me," he'd said.

So he learned that Pa and Malone were building up more management work. They were making ends meet, although just barely. Ma was busy in the same ways. Ruth and two of the girls had been staying with them for a few weeks in between moves. June was married and the others had part-time jobs working for June's father-in-law.

"But most of their support comes from Pa," she had finished, and Maury could supply what she had left unsaid: Try to remember how good Pa is, try to understand him, don't hate him too much.

But Iris was always the one who loved Pa the most.

And then Maury had walked with her to the subway entrance because it was growing dark and had seen her descend the stairs and, turning, call back to him: "I'll come again," and take a few steps and then, turning once more, call, "I like your wife, Maury. I like her very much," and hurry down the steps, her books piled in one elbow. He had stood there until she was out of sight with a hurt in his throat, such a softness of pity or loss or goodness knew what. A whole mush of feeling, he'd thought angrily, blinking his eyes, and turned back home.

Well, that's how it is, and while you can't expect life to be entirely clear and uncomplicated, surely for some people, somewhere in the world, it must be so sometimes. But not for us in this damned place, this damned time. I want so much for Agatha, he thought; she ought to be surrounded by flowers. He counted the buses at the corner; that made two within the last five minutes and sometimes you had to wait half an hour for the next one. Ridiculous, he thought, and was thinking that when the door opened and three skirmishing boys came in with a weary mother.

"Mister! We need three pair of sneakers."

One day a few months later they received an invitation to the wedding of a girl who had been at college with Aggie. Maury saw it lying open on her bureau: Fifth Avenue Presbyterian Church, reception immediately following at the River Club.

"Hey," he said, "this ought to be fun! You'll see all your friends."

She was slicing bread, and didn't look up.

"Is anything the matter?"

"No. But we're not going to the wedding."

He thought instantly: She has no dress. That's why. "Aggie, we'll get a dress," he said gently.

"We can't afford one."

"You could get a nice dress for fifteen dollars, maybe even twelve."

"No, I said."

Lately he had noticed a sharp protest in her voice. Nerves, and why not? he thought, and said no more.

The next day he said gaily, "I saw a dress in Siegel's window that looks like you. It's white with blue flowers and sort of a cape thing. Go on down tomorrow and look at it."

"I don't want to go to the wedding," she said.

"But why don't you want to?"

"I don't know." She was knitting. The needles twisted in and out and she did not raise her eyes.

He felt rejection and anger. "Don't shut me out! What's this mystery? Are you ashamed of me?"

She raised her eyes. "What a disgusting thing to say! You owe me an apology for that!"

"All right, I apologize. But talk to me, give me the reason."

"You won't understand. It's just that it would be so artificial. One afternoon and all over. We'll never get together, we're in different worlds. Why start something you can't continue?"

"So I have taken you away from everything, after all."

"Oh," she cried. She jumped up and put her arms around him. "Maury, I didn't mean it that way. Do you think I really *care* about Louise and Foster? It's just all so complicated. Sometime when we're settled in a permanent place I'll be more in the mood and we'll have lots of friends."

Holding her there in the center of the little room, he was for the first time not close to her at all.

On the day of the wedding he came home feeling especially tender; he thought she must be thinking of her friend, coming down the aisle in the lace and flowers that Aggie hadn't had. He opened the door—and saw at once, to his utter disbelief, that she was drunk.

"I'm celebrating Louise's wedding," she announced, "all by myself."

He was completely bewildered, angry and scared. He had had very little experience with this sort of thing but, remembering black coffee, went into the kitchen to prepare some for her and made her drink it.

He saw, through her attempts to make a joke of it, that she was ashamed. "I'm really sorry," she said. "I took a bit too much on an empty stomach, I should have known better."

He said carefully, "What puzzles me is why you took any at all, sitting here by yourself."

"But that's just it," she said. "That's why I did. It's so depressing here. The stillness rings in my ears. Stuck all day in this dreary hole—"

214

"Can't you read, go for a walk, find something else to do?"

"Maury, be reasonable, I can't read till I go blind, can I? Do you ever stop to think what my life is like? I do a little typing for George, run the dust cloth over these few sticks and that's my day."

"I'm sorry, Aggie, I didn't realize it was that bad."

"Well, think about it! I take a walk, I don't know a soul, they're all pushing baby carriages and we've nothing in common, anyway. Oh, I forgot, I do know one soul. Elena. I can always take her to the market for her English lesson. This is a radish, say rad-ish, cucumber—"

"How is it that Elena gets along? She's thousands of miles away from home and can't even speak the language."

"Come on, Maury! Elena's got a whole loving family here, real family plus dozens of friends in the Greek church. Her parents adore George. She's as loved and sheltered as anyone can be. . . ."

He understood what she meant and was silent. Somehow they would have to find a fuller life than this. But he didn't have any idea how. Tense and restless in bed he twisted from side to side, until suddenly he felt her turning to him, felt her arms and her mouth, and everything, all tension, fear and worry ebbed and drowned.

He was drifting into the softest sleep when suddenly he heard her whisper: "Maury, Maury, I forgot to put the thing in. Do you suppose—"

"Oh, for God's sake," he said, awakened and alarmed. "Oh, for God's sake, that's all we need."

"I'm sorry, it was stupid of me. I won't let it happen again."

But he was cautious now. On the next night he suddenly drew back. "Have you got the thing in?"

She sat up. "What kind of a way is that to talk? My, you're romantic, what I would call an ardent lover!"

"What the devil do you mean? Haven't I got a right to ask?"

She began to cry. He switched on the light.

"Turn the light off! Why do you always have to have that glare on?"

"Don't I do anything right? I'm not a lover, I turn the light on—I ought to just shoot myself and be done with it. Hell, I'm going into the kitchen and read the paper."

"Maury, don't! Come back to bed. I'm sorry, I'm awfully touchy, I know."

215

He was instantly softened. She was a child sitting there in bed, with her wavy cap of hair, the ruffled white cotton nightdress, the wet eyes.

"Oh, Aggie, I'm touchy too. It's not your fault, I only meant we can't afford to have a baby. And I'm scared. Maybe I shouldn't tell you that. A woman ought to be able to lean on her husband."

"Tell me, tell me, darling."

"I'm afraid I'm going to lose the job. Santorello said today he heard they may close this store. There's not enough business."

"Maybe Eddy's father will give you a job in another store."

"No, I wouldn't even ask. He's got men who've been with him ten years and more. He couldn't fire one of them and take me."

Toward dawn he woke with the sensation of being alone in the bed, and he got up. There was a light in the kitchen. Agatha was sitting there, just sitting at the kitchen table looking at nothing, her face sunk in sadness. There were a bottle of wine and a glass on the table.

"Aggie, it's five o'clock in the morning! What the hell are you doing?"

"I couldn't sleep, I was afraid my twisting and turning would wake you, so I got up."

"I'm talking about the wine."

"I've told you, it relaxes me. I thought it would make me sleep. Don't act as though I were drunk or something."

"It's a bad habit, Aggie. I don't like it. You shouldn't depend on it to solve your problems. Anyway, it's expensive."

"I used the fifteen dollars that you wanted me to spend on a dress and I bought a couple of bottles. Don't be angry, Maury."

The job lasted another month. On the Friday when he got his final pay he dragged home. He went quietly up the stairs hoping that George Andreapoulis wouldn't hear him and come out with an evening greeting. On this night he was in no mood for old-world courtesy.

He opened the door. Tell her now, get it over with and then sit down and puzzle out what we can do. Pray heaven that Andreapoulis has a lot of typing these next few weeks.

Agatha was sitting on the sofa, with her hands clasped in her lap. She looked like a little girl in dancing class, waiting to be asked to dance. "Maury, I'm pregnant," she said.

*   *   *

216

Everything happened to them against a background of heat. When I am old, Maury thought, and I remember New York and all our troubles, I'll remember the subway grinding and the sour smell of hot metal. I'll remember the signs that read *No Jobs* and damp sheets and Agatha lying on top of them with her belly swelling. And the public library where I spent the days after noon rather than go home: if you didn't find a job early in the day there was no use looking any further that day; you might as well go to the library.

"Summer is the worst time to be looking for a job," said George Andreapoulis sympathetically.

"The winter will be worse. I'll need an overcoat this year and new galoshes. My luck, the snow will be knee-high this year."

"Maybe," George said doubtfully, "one of my clients will have a job . . . I'll keep an eye open. I drew up a will for the man who has the delicatessen over on the avenue. He's doing pretty well and maybe he'll take on a man in the fall."

One morning in September, Agatha said, hesitating, "I don't know how you would feel about this; promise you won't be angry?"

"I won't be angry."

"Well, then, I was thinking; you know my father has a cousin, I've mentioned him, I always called him Uncle Jed. He's really just the husband of my father's cousin, and she's dead now, but I'm sure he hasn't forgotten me. He never had children and he was so fond of me. I remember he always sent the most beautiful dolls for Christmas and when I was sixteen he gave me my first pearls."

"Yes, yes." He stifled his impatience with her prattling. They ought to be so happy now. No worries. Damn world to spoil what should be so beautiful. His child and Agatha's child, his child growing in her, its little fingernails and eyelashes. So beautiful.

". . . vice-president in charge of trusts at the Barlow-Manhattan Bank. I didn't want to involve him because I didn't want Daddy to hear about it, but that's false pride and now I don't care. Would you go to see him?"

He was silent. Crawl before those people? Beg?

"I'd call him first, of course. Maury?"

For her. For the baby, the soft thing growing in her. When it comes out it will be pink, naked and soft; I'll have to warm it, feed it, fight for it.

"Call him in the morning. I'll go," he said. "Did you get polish for my black shoes?"

217

*   *   *

The door swung inward from Madison Avenue to a lobby with
murals of Peter Stuyvesant, of Indians on the trail, the Treasury,
George Washington taking the oath of office, hansom cabs on Fifth
Avenue, children rolling hoops in Central Park. No pushcarts, no
tenements.

He walked tall and easily across the moss-green carpet. A Yale
graduate, as well educated, as presentable and worthy as anyone;
what was he afraid of?

Jedediah Spencer, it said on the door. Funny! That old Hebrew
name had dignity when you saw it in brass on a mahogany door.
Nobody he knew would ever think of giving a child a name like
that nowadays.

Everything was dark brown, the wood, the leather and Mr.
Spencer's suit.

"So you are Agatha's husband. . . . How do you do?"

"How do you do, sir?"

"Agatha telephoned to say that you were on your way. I'm sorry
she didn't call sooner. She could have saved you the trip."

"Sir?"

"We have no openings in the bank."

"Sir, we weren't thinking of that. We thought—Agatha
thought—that in your position, knowing so many people in so
many businesses, perhaps you could recommend me somewhere."

"I make it a policy never to ask personal favors of our clients."

Mr. Spencer opened a drawer and took out a pen. His hand was
hidden by a large photograph in a silver frame, and Maury did not
see what he was writing until a paper was handed to him. It was a
check for a thousand dollars.

"You can cash it at a window in the lobby," Mr. Spencer said.
He looked at his watch. "Naturally I don't want Agatha to be in
want. Perhaps it will tide you over until you can straighten yourself out."

Maury looked up. In the cool, correct face he read intense dislike. "Straighten yourself out." It's not I who need straightening
out, he thought. It's the world. And he laid the check back on the
desk. "Thank you very much. I don't want it," he said, turned on
his heel and walked out.

His hands were sweating and his heart pounded. He felt a terrible shame. It was like one of those dreams in which you are walk-

ing on a grand avenue when suddenly you look down and find that you have gone out in your underwear. After the shame came nausea.

There was a drugstore on the corner. He had had only coffee for breakfast, and he knew the nausea was from hunger. He wondered whether he could afford a sandwich and an ice cream soda, a thick, rich soda, with cream on top.

He sat down at a table, too weak to sit at the counter stool, even though a table meant another dime for a tip. The cool bastard, he thought. He didn't even have the kindness or decency to say he would try to help, even if he didn't mean it. He had so much contempt for me that he didn't even bother to pretend. . . .

A man came in and took the other seat. Maury became aware that the man was looking at him steadily. Then the man said, "I think I know you. Saw you at a wedding in Brooklyn a couple of years ago."

"Yes?" Maury was cautious.

"Yeah. Solly Levinson—may he rest in peace—his boy Harry got married. You're Joe Friedman's boy, aren't you?"

"Yes. I don't—"

"Name's Wolf Harris. I knew your old man when he was a kid. I wouldn't be high-class enough for him now, though."

Maury was silent. A strange encounter. And since the man had so frankly been staring at him, he returned the stare, seeing a keen, immaculate face perhaps fifty years old, a face like thousands of others on the streets of the city except for the fierce, intelligent eyes. His clothes were dark and expensive; his watch and cuff links were gold; the shoe that was exposed in the aisle was handmade.

"I wouldn't have made that crack about your old man if I didn't happen to know he kicked you out."

At another time, when Maury was younger and not as battered, when he had more pride—or more false pride, if you wanted to call it that—he would not have allowed such an intrusion. But as it was, he said only, "I know two things about you. You have a remarkable memory and a good information service."

The man laughed. "Information, no. Just an accident. I met Solly's daughter on the street, you know the fat kid who talks too much?"

"I know. Cecile."

219

"So she told me about you. Not that I give a damn or wanted to hear. But my memory, that's something else again. A memory I've got, never forget a fact. Never. That you can't take away from me. What's funny?"

"I was thinking, I don't believe anybody could take anything away from you."

Wolf stared a second and laughed. "You're damn right! You're okay. You're not so dumb yourself!"

"Thanks."

The waitress came with pad and pencil to take the orders.

"Gimme a double cheeseburger, French fries, onions on the side, a malted and a couple of Danish."

Maury said, "I'll have a tuna sandwich on toast."

"To drink?" The girl was impatient.

"Nothing. Just the sandwich."

"Come on! That'd feed a canary. Give him the same as me, miss. That's right. On me."

Maury flushed. Was it so visible, then, the hunger? No, it was the suit. The collar of his shirt was worn, and perhaps he had seen Maury's shoes when he walked in.

"Place is a dump. But it's quick and I've got to see a man at Forty-fifth and Madison at one."

There was a silence. Maury had nothing to say. Then Mr. Harris leaned forward. "Well? What's new? What are you doing these days?"

He felt—he felt like such a child, timid and obedient. Why couldn't he just say, I don't want to talk about my business. I'm not in the mood to talk at all. Why? Because he had nothing and was nobody. And that's what happened to you when you had nothing and were nobody.

"The news is that my wife is expecting a baby. And what I'm doing, unfortunately, is nothing."

"Unemployed, eh?"

"I had a job in a shoe store but they closed the store."

"What can you do besides sell shoes?"

Bitterness rose in Maury. He could taste its heat. "To tell you the truth, nothing. Four years at Yale and the result—nothing."

"I quit school at the seventh grade," the man said, with slight amusement.

220

"And?" Maury raised his eyes to meet the other's sharp, bright regard.

"And I'm in a position to offer you a job, if you want to take it."

"I'll take it," Maury said.

"You don't know what it is."

"Whether I can do it, you mean? If I don't know how, I'll learn."

"Can you drive a car?"

"Of course. But I haven't got a car."

"No problem. I'll buy you one."

"And what do I do with it?"

"You drive around, Flatbush section, drive around to some addresses I'll give you, pick up some papers every morning and take them to an apartment."

"That's all?"

"That's all. You haven't asked me about the pay."

"Whatever it is, it's more than I'm earning now."

"You're really beat, kid, aren't you?" The tone was surprisingly gentle. "Well, put your head up. I'm offering you seventy-five dollars a week."

"Just for driving around and delivering papers?"

"And for keeping your mouth shut. You understand?"

"I think I do. I'll ask you the rest when we're out on the sidewalk."

"You've got the idea. Eat. And if you're still hungry after all that, speak up. I like people who speak up. At the right time, that is."

He had been starved, not just because of this morning, but hungry for weeks. He never ate quite enough of real food, just crackers and canned soup, saving the milk, the oranges and the lamb chops for Aggie. He felt the good warmth deep inside now: the meat, the cheese, the rich malted milk. *Policy.* That's what it must be, of course. *Numbers.* Well, it didn't hurt anybody, did it? Nobody suffered or died because of it. The rich gamble for thousands in casinos and that's all right; why can't the poor try their luck with pennies? So I'm rationalizing, and I know I am. But the refrigerator will be filled; we'll buy things for the baby and some winter clothes for Aggie. I won't have to avoid Andreapoulis when the rent is due.

They went out to the sidewalk. Madison Avenue was friendly.

221

Two vivid young office girls went by laughing and glanced at Maury. A man went into a haberdashery store. The window was full of good shirts and nice foulard ties. The world was friendly.

"What a piece of luck that I happened to sit down at your table, Mr. Harris," Maury said.

"The name's Wolf. And here, this is my number, where you'll call me tomorrow morning. Come in and I'll lay it all out for you. No use talking more now. You know what it's all about."

"I know," Maury said. "And you can rely on me absolutely. I want you to know that."

"If I didn't know that I wouldn't talk to you in the first place. I size men up in two seconds flat. What are you going to tell your wife?"

"That I collect rents. She wouldn't understand."

"I figured as much. High-class, is she?"

"Sort of."

"Yeah, well. Call me tomorrow then. At ten-thirty. No earlier. No later. And here's a twenty for expenses in the meantime. Wait, here's another. Buy yourself a pair of shoes."

"I don't need twenty for shoes. I can get a pair for six dollars."

"Twenty. I don't like cheap shoes."

There was an autumn chill in the air and Maury brought the baby in. He pulled the perambulator up the steps and parked it in the hall by the stairs; the Andreapoulises were nice about things like that. Anyway it was a kind of ornament, that carriage. It was the finest English pram, navy blue leather and chrome, the kind you saw on Park Avenue pushed by a nursemaid in a dark blue coat and veil. They'd sent it from the office when Eric was born. No doubt that meant Wolf Harris had ordered it, the way he did everything, so lavishly, so meticulously: funeral flowers and a basket of fruit when Scorzio's mother died; presents for weddings and First Communions and Bar Mitzvahs. He had an astounding memory.

Maury lifted the sleeping baby. The warm, fragrant head flopped on his shoulder. He carried him upstairs and laid him, still asleep, in his crib. He looked at his watch. A half hour before the next bottle. He slipped a finger under the diaper. Wet. Well, better not to disturb his sleep for that; he'd only be wet again in another fifteen minutes. He smiled, feeling expert and competent.

On afternoons when he came home early, and they were frequent because his hours were so easy, he was glad to let Aggie go out. This whole summer in the months since Eric's birth he'd sat with a book on the front step while Eric slept. Some of the women in the neighborhood, especially the foreign-born, nudged each other as they passed. They thought it was funny for a man to be doing that. To hell with them.

Aggie would be home soon. He'd given her a nice check with which to go out and buy clothes. She had already bought a suit the color of cranberries, and looked delightful in it, as slender as she had been before the baby. There was nothing like it, the feeling a man had when he commanded: Go out and buy yourself something, buy what you want. A man felt like, he felt like—a man!

They'd given him a raise. He was making ninety dollars now plus the expenses of the car.

"Get a black coupe," Wolf Harris had instructed him that first morning. "Keep it inconspicuous. Be careful not to get a ticket, no parking tickets, nothing. And when you're out, watch through the rear-view mirror. Keep your eyes on it all the time. If you have any idea you're being followed, drive slowly, don't arouse any suspicion. Stop at the first bar you see, and get out slowly; go into the men's room and empty your pockets into the toilet. Then when you come out, slowly, you understand, go on up to the bar and have a beer, like any guy minding his own business, and then out to the car again, clean. Everything clear?"

Quite clear. He'd bought a black Graham-Paige and had no trouble so far. It was nice; they'd even taken the baby out to Jones Beach in the car. He didn't feel like a conspirator. He didn't even feel he was doing anything *really* wrong even though it was against the law; that part he hated. But as for the actual *thing* itself, it didn't seem so terrible. They weren't hurting anybody. It was the law that made it evil.

They had the 'offices' in various apartment houses, which were changed every few months; they were now on the second one since he had started working. They kept their books and took their calls in the kitchen of a very modest apartment. The woman looked even younger than Aggie, if possible. She had two babies. It all seemed so innocent, sitting there tallying the books, while the little girls had their lunch!

And the men he worked with were no more criminal types than

Maury was. Scorzio, with his 'dese' and 'dose,' and Feldman, too, were just like the men who had worked in the shoe store, family men like them except that these weren't worried sick about money. These sent their children to summer camp and talked about their piano lessons. Windy, called that for somewhat indelicate reasons, although tough in manner, was so decent, so generous. The day Maury had had the flu he'd driven him home and couldn't have been more considerate. Bruchman the accountant, there was a brain! Quick as an adding machine; if it hadn't been for the Depression he wouldn't be doing what he was doing, that's sure. Tom Spalding, the detective who stopped by every week for his hundred—there was a nice open face, looked like Thomas Jefferson. No harm in him, except the need of money. He had four children, one in dental school; how could he have managed otherwise?

Talk about money! The amount that went through their hands was staggering. And this was only one small group. Total it all up and you had a few million dollars a week! And this was only one of Harris' enterprises, not even the main one. They said he was gradually relinquishing this to other hands; he didn't need it anymore. Since repeal he'd gone legitimate. He owned distilleries in Canada, a network of liquor-importing firms here and with all that cash had branched out into choice real estate all over the country. Fascinating, a study in itself, the ramifications, both financial and human, of all this. The man behind it, a bigger boss than Harris, Scorzio confided one day in whispered awe, was actually Jim Lanahan, father of the Senator. He and Harris had made theirs during Prohibition, and now Lanahan was worth tens of millions. Harris was nothing by comparison; he only counted his in millions, Scorzio said, grinning.

"But Harris is a prince, never forget that. He likes you, he does for you. Nothing is too much."

Maury wanted to know whether they ever saw Harris. He himself hadn't seen him since the day he was hired.

"Only about once a year. Around Christmas, he gives a party. Has a place way out on the Island, big place with a stone wall around it like Central Park. You'll be invited next time."

Naturally Aggie wanted to know whom he worked for and what he did. Collect rents for a big real estate outfit, he said, and then, not wanting to lie entirely, feeling somehow cleaner if there were some truth in his story, gave the name of Wolf Harris, which meant nothing to her, of course. From time to time he mentioned the names of some of the men in the office, names which also could mean nothing to her.

She pressed him to make some friends for them where he worked. "I don't see why you can't invite some of the men and their wives one evening," she insisted. "We don't see a soul except George and Elena, and there's no way of making friends in this neighborhood. We've no other contacts possible except your office."

"They're not your type," he said lamely.

"Can't I meet them and judge for myself? At least I could talk to the women about their babies, couldn't I?"

Of course she was dissatisfied. It was unrealistic of him to think that the baby could be enough. A woman needed more than that, especially a woman with all the life that was in Aggie, the life that had drawn him to her the first time he had seen her. What they needed, he knew, was to belong somewhere, to be a part of something, to have roots. He hadn't used that word for a long time, not since he had seen the rootedness of Aggie's home town and envied it. A place where you walked down the street and people knew your name! Friends telephoning and coming to the door! Well, someday, surely: it was what he aimed for. He grieved over the pain she must feel at her loss of it. Her mother's letter hadn't helped, either. Son of a bitch!

Apparently Aggie had written to her parents when Eric was born, although she hadn't told him. But, going through bills on the desk, he had seen the answering letter and read it through. "You and your little boy are welcome"—or something like that. "But your father will not receive your husband. I myself would reconsider, but I can't press the issue with Dad in his state of health. His heart is absolutely broken, he looks like a sick man. Everything he stood for is gone, his only child is gone." And then something about how nothing was forever and if a mistake had been made it was better to correct it than to live with it, so if Aggie should ever change her mind about what she had done— And then the conclusion: "Be assured again that we love you still, and you may come home with the baby and be so welcome."

225

He was outraged. "Be assured—!"

"Excuse me," he'd told Agatha, "for reading the letter. It wasn't honorable, but I couldn't help it."

"I don't mind," she'd said. "I would have told you anyway," and had begun to cry. If he had had her stupid mother and bastard father there in the room he would have killed them in cold blood.

The baby stirred and broke into a cry, a bleat like a lamb's. Little soul! Round mouth open, hits himself in the face with his own fist, slams his heels against the sheet. Furious, aren't you, because you're hungry? Swiftly, pleased with his own swiftness, Maury unpinned the diaper. Wonderful little body, the firm thighs not seven inches long, joined by the marvelous tiny convoluted rose of maleness! Little man. Homunculus. He fastened the diaper firmly, settled the boy in the crook of his left arm, inserted the bottle, not too warm, just right.

The baby sucked and bubbled. He doesn't know anything but warmth of hands, warmth of voices. May he never know anything else! No, that's impossible. The gray eyes, light as opals, studied his father. One hand went up and curled around the father's finger with surprising strength. My son. I promise myself to remember this, no matter what else happens, how far he goes away from me, and he will, I promise to remember this day in October, with the sun on the floor and his hand around my finger.

He heard Agatha at the door and didn't move, wanting her to see them like that.

"I want to talk to you," she said, and at her harsh tone he turned. She was standing in the doorway, wearing the cranberry suit, holding a hat box, a shoe box and a newspaper.

"You lied to me," she said. "You don't collect rents. You're a racketeer. You collect policy slips. Here, it's in the paper."

"What's in the paper? What are you talking about?"

She held the front page for him to see. The police had raided an apartment rented by Mrs. Marie Schuetz and arrested a man named Peter Scorzio. A large operation had been uncovered, he read, with an estimated take of one hundred fifty thousand dollars a week.

"I doubt there can be two men named Peter Scorzio," Aggie said.

The baby had finished. Maury moved him over his shoulder to burp him. He didn't say anything.

"So the food we eat, the clothes I have on, everything that touches Eric, comes from this *dirt!*" Her anger was cold and controlled. "Why did you lie to me, Maury? Why did you do such a thing?"

He began to tremble, not only because of her, but also because if he had stayed late today, they would have caught him too. Somebody must have slipped up, perhaps a new cop in the district.

"I was ashamed. I knew what you would think. So I took the easy way of lying and I shouldn't have."

"What are you going to do now?"

"What can I do?"

"You can march over there in the morning and tell them you aren't coming back. Or no, you can call him up now, whoever runs the gang," she said scornfully, "and tell him you're not coming back. That's what you can do!"

"Then what? You think I haven't tried to see whether there was anything else? Yes, I found a job, one job, at the A & P for twenty-two dollars a week!"

"Well, take it!"

"Can we live on that? Milk for the baby, the pediatrician—can we? And now we've become used to more—"

"Do you think it was worth it? Oh, I should have guessed there was something odd! A boss sending gifts like that when Eric was born, and a wristwatch for me at Christmas. How naïve I am! Do you know what? I feel dirty in these clothes, I could take this watch and throw it into the garbage pail!"

He let her talk; he couldn't think of anything to say. She began to cry. "But most of all, most of all, Maury, what might have happened to you! Suppose it had been you instead of that Scorzio! To spend years of your life in jail, a man like you, people like us, ruined, ruined—"

"He won't spend years of his life, not even a night. He'll be out on bail, he probably is already. And in a few weeks the charge will be dropped for lack of evidence."

She stared. "You mean, somebody will be paid off—a judge, or somebody."

"Exactly. That's the way it works."

"You think that's right?"

"Of course I don't think it's right. If I could change it I would,

227

and as soon as I can get away from it I will. But in the meantime—"

"You're going back?"

"In the meantime I'm going back."

The telephone rang. He handed her the baby. "That'll be for
me, telling me the new address for tomorrow."

He never knew what he would find when he got home. Agatha
might be on the floor with Eric and a pile of blocks. Now that Eric
was walking, the floor was always strewn with his toys, making a
disorder which pleased Maury, a natural, cheerful disorder. The
sound of their two voices, the child's and the mother's, would ring
into the hall before he got the door open. And there would be the
fragrance of cooking, something spicy and foreign; he thought with
amusement, Aggie has turned out to be a pretty good Greek cook.
He might open the door on all that.

Or else he might open it on a dark kitchen, a dim living room
and Eric crying in the playpen with his diapers soaked. Agatha
would be asleep on top of the bedspread. He never knew.

He bought a book on alcoholism. It took him four days to muster
courage enough to buy it. When he had unwrapped the book and
placed it on the seat of his car he knew he had made the final admission to himself.

Above all, the book advised, don't lose your temper; it will accomplish nothing. More easily said than done! Yet he was being
quite patient, he thought. Not that she was ever offensive, maud-
lin or nasty; she just merely began to feel hazy and fell asleep. But
it was sick; he knew so little about it but he knew that much, and
that people used alcohol to relieve their anxieties. Apparently his
wife's anxieties were too much for her.

"Elena asked me today what kind of job you had," she reported
once."I'm sure they suspect something. Even if there were women
around here for me to make friends with I'd be afraid and
ashamed."

Such heavy guilt he had, remembering the place where she had
been born, the white houses, the old, old calm and dignity. And
now this. And all his fault.

While the key was still in the lock one evening he heard the
delightful sound of crowing, and knew that the boy was in his high
chair, spraying a mush of pureed carrots or spinach on his bib. He

threw his coat on a chair and hurried into the kitchen. His sister Iris was feeding Eric.

He stared. "Where's Aggie?"

"Nothing's wrong! She was lying down when I got here. Had a little headache, that's all. So I told her to stay there and I'd feed Eric."

"Don't lie to me, Iris! Don't cover up for her! She's been drinking again and you know it."

"There," Iris said, "all through! Let Auntie Iris wipe your mouth, and we'll have some peaches."

"Damn it," Maury said. He beat his fists on his thighs. "Damn it to hell and back again."

"Don't do that now. Get it out of your system later, Maury. You're scaring Eric."

The child had turned his head away from the spoon to stare at Maury. He walked out of the room. He went to the bathroom. He walked to the living room window and looked out at nothing. He opened the bedroom door; it was dusk and he could not see Aggie's face. She was huddled on the bed asleep, her knees drawn almost to her chin. Fetal position, he thought disgustedly, and walked closer. Her hand with the wedding ring lay open on the pillow. Something made him touch it to see whether she would stir, but she did not. He was furious, pitying and grieving. He wished he could make sense of all the things he was feeling.

He went back into the kitchen. Iris had put the baby into the playpen, where, now that his stomach was full, he would be content for half an hour, at least.

"There's nothing in the refrigerator except a roasting chicken. I guess Aggie intended it for supper. But it's already half past five."

"Make some scrambled eggs. I'm not hungry. I hope you aren't." He sounded gruff. He hadn't meant to.

"I'll make a jelly omelet," Iris said.

"Anything."

They ate silently. Suddenly Maury realized how ungracious, how self-absorbed he was being. "You've just finished mid-terms, haven't you? How did you do?" he inquired.

"I did well," she answered quietly. "And you don't have to be sociable, Maury. I know you have a lot of trouble."

He didn't answer.

"Aggie told me what you do for a living."

229

"She had no right to!"

"Don't be angry with her. She told me months ago. A person has to talk to somebody, you know."

"Well, am I doing anything so terrible?" he burst out.

"She's not used to things like that."

"And I am used to them?"

"Of course not. Except that you seem able to stand it. You feel you have to. But she's made differently and she can't face it. That's why she takes a drink, don't you see?"

"She doesn't help herself that way. She doesn't help us."

"I'm sure she knows that, and it makes her feel worse."

"Do you always understand so much about people?"

She looked up quickly. "Are you being sarcastic?"

"Iris! For God's sake! I meant you understand so much, and you're only seventeen."

"That's funny. Most of the time I think I don't understand very much at all."

He put his head in his hands. "I wish I could find a decent job but there isn't anything. I've tried, believe me I have."

"I believe you."

"Tell me, do they know at home what I do?"

"They found out. Not through me! Through Cousin Ruth. You know she has relatives who keep up with Wolf Harris. It seems all some people do is talk about other people."

"Did they have anything to say about it? The truth."

"Ma didn't. She waited for Pa the way she always does. And he said it was a disgrace, a scandal."

"Then can he get me anything better?"

"You never asked him to."

"Would you, if you were in my place?"

"Don't make me take sides."

"Why doesn't he call me? Answer that!"

"He's older, Maury. He is the father, after all," Iris said quietly.

Agatha was still asleep when Iris left. He ran the water for Eric's bath and wondered how she was with the child while he was away. She could be so delightful! She loved to sing, and often he had heard her singing while taking her own bath or working in the kitchen. He hoped she wasn't silent all day. Since Eric had been born he'd been reading the child-care articles in the newspaper and learned that babies can sense moods and read expressions. He hoped the boy was getting a good start.

Eric was sleepy after the bath and Maury lifted him up and held him. The child was a comfort to him; wasn't that odd? This tiny sleepy thing to comfort him? His mind darted, darted. He laid Eric down and went to their closed bedroom door. Seven o'clock. She ought to have something to eat. His hand was still on the knob, half unwilling to turn it. He had an odd flash of recall: long before they were married they'd had a conversation, about being behind a closed door together, and he thought how strange it was that once they would have almost died as a price for one hour alone together, behind a closed door.

She was just waking up. "What time is it?" She sat up, startled, frightened, apologetic. He sat down on the edge of the bed and took her hand.

"Aggie, I am, I really am going to try to find some other job," he said.

They gave him a new stop. Timmy's place, they said: be there around eleven for the pick-up. It was a summer day, one of those days when the sky is lofty blue as porcelain, and anywhere else but here the air would smell of grass.

He drove out New Lots Avenue and turned left. The landscape was familiar: the ragged, unkempt edge of the city, with a few rows of attached houses among empty lots and some one-storied buildings with small stores. Taxpayers, they were called, which meant that they just about paid for themselves and no more; you kept them until times were better, then tore them down and built something that would show a real profit. Until times were better.

He stopped in front of Timmy's. It was a candy store on a neglected street. You couldn't do much business here unless there was a school somewhere in the neighborhood, he thought idly. Then it would be busy after three o'clock and on warm nights when the kids would congregate. He went inside. A couple of fellows, a short one and a tall one, were at the magazine stand. They didn't look like cops but he glanced at them to be sure, raising his eyebrows at Timmy for a signal.

"Come in," Timmy said and they went in back, so the men must be all right, not cops. Timmy had expected him, of course.

"I'm Maury, expect you'll be seeing more of me," he said by

way of affability and took what Timmy handed him and put it in his pockets. On the way out, just to be sure, but also out of friendliness, he bought a pack of Luckies, then went outside and started down the block to where he had prudently parked his car.

A car had drawn up behind his. If it's cops, he thought, I'll just keep walking steadily. He heard running steps behind him and, turning, saw the two men from the candy store. He stepped aside but they slammed into him where he stood and knocked him to the ground. Somebody in the car opened the door and he was dragged in yelling and kicking. There was nobody on the street, which was empty as a cemetery. Not cops, he thought, but who—? And then he was on his back on the floor and the men were holding him down. The car roared away.

"What are you doing to me? For Christ's sake, lemme go, what do you want, I'll give it to you—"

"He'll give it to you, Shorty, you hear that?" the big one said.

The car filled with laughter and he couldn't tell whether there were one or two in the front seat. Shorty brought his fist down on Maury's nose. The pain was dazzling.

"Who are you?" he cried. "What do you want? Just tell me. Please. I'll do what you want, only don't—" The tall one had slid half off the seat, digging his knee under Maury's ribs.

"You tell us," the big one said. His knee ground deeper. "You tell us what you were doing in Timmy's place. We know what you were doing, we just wanna hear you tell it."

"If you know, then you know I was picking up for Scorzio . . . Jesus Christ!" Maury screamed. Shorty brought his fist down and when Maury twisted away in time to save his eye, it caught the cheekbone and the side of his bleeding nose. "Ask Scorzio. Call him. He'll tell you—"

"You're a friend of Scorzio's? Ain't that nice?"

"Call him, ask him!"

Someone in the front seat called back, "Christ, is this fruit for real? Where the hell do they pick up a fruit like this?"

"Bull, you tell him," Shorty said, mincing his words. "This is my friend Bull, this gentleman. His real name's Bullshit but we call him Bull. He'll tell you all about it."

Bull's knee dug deeper. I'm fainting, Maury thought, fainting or dying.

"Look dearie," Bull said, "you got yourself into a helluva lot of trouble just now and Scorzio can't help you out of it. You and Scorzio just happened to cross over the line into our territory. Now, Scorzio may think it's his, but he's thinking all wrong because it ain't his, it's ours, and you goddamn son of a bitch better keep the hell out of it." He caught Maury's ears, and pounded his head against the floor of the car.

"I didn't know—" Maury was crying, weeping, screaming. "So help me God, I didn't know, so help me, I wouldn't have—"

"Shut the friggin' bastard up," someone said. "Toss him the hell out, we're through with him."

The car lurched and swung and slowed. They were opening the door; it fell wide; they were shoving him, lifting him, kicking him; he heard his own screeching terror, and grabbed crazily, blindly at the door beyond his reach, then at the running board, then at the air.

It was dark and there was a distant humming as of bees or traffic on a highway. He struggled to discern it, raised his head and felt a pain so sharp that he thought a knife had been thrust into his ear. He screamed and suddenly everything flashed light; he was in a room; there was a fluorescent bulb on the ceiling and someone was standing over him; there were low voices. Then one by one things floated into reality. These were nurses and he was on a bed. It had been their voices, humming and buzzing.

"Mr. Friedman," one said, "you're feeling better."

The other voice inquired: "Do you know where you are?"

He frowned, not comprehending, and then came a white rush of clarity and he understood that they were trying to see whether his mind had been affected. He would have laughed, only his mouth hurt, and he said, mumbling, "Ospil? Ospil?"

"Yes, you're in St. Mary's Hospital. You've been here two days. You fell out of a car. You remember that?"

"Yesh." Remember. Panic, crimson blinding before the eyes. They're killing me. Wet his trousers. Pinned down. Pinned. Screaming, witch voices. Witch screams. Theirs? His? And the opening door, rush of speed, air. Remember.

He shook, gasping.

"There," the nurse said. "There. You'll sleep. Don't talk. I know you understand me. I just want to tell you before you sleep that you're going to be all right. You've had a bad concussion and a cut on the forehead that will heal nicely. Your collarbone is broken, and two fingers. You're lucky to've come out like that. Your wife's been here with your neighbors. We sent her home, and she's all right, too. So don't worry about anything."

Flat calm voice of authority. A mother's voice. He went to sleep.

Later on, a man's voice. Smooth, cool, also authority. "I'm Detective Collier. The doctor says I can have five minutes with you. Can you tell me what happened?"

Alert now, thinking clearly. The fuzz of drugs mostly gone, so the pain is sharp. Face all sore, wonder what it looks like? Careful how you answer.

"They pushed me out of the car." Feign sluggishness. He won't know the fuzziness is gone.

"We know that. Who were they?"

"Two men. Grabbed. Pulled me in. Then pushed me out."

"Yes." Very patient. "Do you know the men, ever see them before?"

"Never."

"Think, now. Is there anything you remember about them, the way they looked or a foreign accent, or anything? Did you hear them call each other by any names? Think carefully."

Anything I remember? Never forget. Ugly gnarled fellow, left eye wandering toward the shoulder, tall muscular guy like a Western movie, green tie, tie staring at me, he leaning over, pounding my face. Bull, name of Bull. Short for Bullshit, Shorty said, laughing.

"Take your time. I know it's hard for you."

Oh, I'd like to see them hang, I'd stand there laughing. But they know who I am, Agatha alone in the house. He shuddered. "Can't think. Sorry, I want to, but—"

"Did you happen to hear the name Bull? Have you heard that before?"

"Bull? Bull? Nope, nope."

The voice, not as patient now. "I hope you're not trying to conceal anything, Mr. Friedman. It's hard to believe you don't remember anything, not one word, that was said from the time you got into that car. What were you doing when they pulled you into the car?"

"I was on the sidewalk."

234

"Yes, yes, of course. What were you doing in the neighborhood, what was your business there?"

"Bought a newspaper in the candy store."

"Yes. Well, what do you do for a living? You weren't working that time of the morning?"

"I don't have a steady job. Laid off."

"Unemployed?"

"Yes, unemployed."

"We were at your house to see your wife. You live quite well. Drive a nice car."

What would Agatha have said? He felt strings winding, netting him, and wasn't able to think strongly.

Then another voice, "Sorry, Officer, it's more than five minutes. This man's been badly hurt and you can see he's not fit to answer any more questions."

"I could get at the heart of this in less than a minute, Doc, if only he'd cooperate."

"Cooperate? Officer, take a look at him! He doesn't even understand what's going on! You'll have to go, I'm sorry." Firm. Firm. "You can try again tomorrow. There ought to be improvement by then, I hope."

"Look, I'll go easy. Just another minute."

"No, now. You'll have to go now."

Much later, the doctor's voice, tough Brooklyn snarl. "I don't like cops."

"That why you helped me this morning? You knew I understood everything."

"Yeah. I knew. Lie back, I'm supposed to look under this bandage."

Light fingers, almost fluttering. "Am I hurting you? I'll try not to. We don't want any infection under here. Spoil your handsome mug."

Small thrill of pain, tingles down to the belly.

"Sorry, had to be done."

"It's all right." Wincing, looked into narrowed eyes, black brows like caterpillars, intern, about my age, no, has to be three years older. "Why'd you help me this morning?"

"I'm always for the underdog . . . and today you were it. In my experience cops are always against the underdog."

235

He's all mixed up. Sometimes the cops *are* the underdog. He's mixed up, but no matter, this isn't the place for philosophy or sociology. "Tell me the truth, Doctor, am I going to be all right?"

"It'll take a couple of weeks. Take it easy, let the collarbone heal and get over the shock."

"Just a couple of weeks, you're sure? I've a family to support, I've gotta get working." All panicky again thinking about it. Feeling the responsibility. Like lifting a ton.

"How many children?"

"One boy. God, I couldn't afford any more, not now."

The doctor stood back from the bed, far enough for Maury to see the whole of him. The stethoscope hung from the pocket of his long white coat. Interns were proud, liked to display that first stethoscope. You could see the pride in him. Also fatigue. Also intelligence, very, very much intelligence.

"And your wife? How is she?"

"She's all right. The nurse said she was coming back today."

"A very lovely girl. And frail."

"Is there something wrong? What did you see?"

"Don't be alarmed, I shouldn't have said that. I only meant I could see she's delicate, can't stand up under too much. So I know what you mean by responsibility. Am I right?"

Maury sighed. "You're very perceptive, Doctor."

"That's what they tell me."

His head throbbed with every step. He had been home for three days and the doctor had said he ought to walk a little. He went to the end of the block. There was a grassy space between the houses and he sat down on a stone. His forehead had begun to itch under the bandage, and that meant it was healing. A big gash, they had said, but it will heal fast because you're young. Thank goodness, he'd saved his eyes from those vicious animals. Animals? Animals didn't do things like that to each other. It was a warm day, but he still felt cold. He had even worn a thin sweater. Nervous shock. It would take time to get over it. He was surprised Agatha was doing as well as she was. She had been so scared about him that she hadn't even asked what he was going to do.

When Bruchman had come to the house she had gone into the bedroom with Eric, but she had overheard their conversation. Bruchman had begun by explaining that somebody—he didn't say who—had made an awful mistake, hadn't clarified the new districts, and so Maury had mistakenly been sent into an area that wasn't theirs. But that had been corrected now. Also, the detective who had questioned Maury in the hospital had been taken care of and nobody would be asking him any more questions. By the way, Maury had handled that very nicely. As a matter of fact, as soon as he got on his feet, they would be wanting him in the office, and no more running around the way he had been doing.

"No, thanks," Maury had said.

If it was a matter of money, surely he knew that money was never a problem. He could earn double what he'd been getting. Hadn't they paid for his private room in the hospital and come right out here to make sure his wife had money while he was gone? No, it wasn't a matter of money, and indeed Maury appreciated everything, but quite simply he wanted to be through. No hard feelings, he just wanted to be through. He lied to make it easier. He might even be moving away from New York.

Bruchman had tried some more, had even been quite insistent, but then finally, seeing that it was no use, had gone out after shaking hands and wishing Maury good luck.

Agatha had opened the bedroom door and come out crying. The tears were running down her face, but her face was shining and she had clung to him. "Oh, if anything had happened to you, I don't know what I would have done, how I would have borne it!"

"I'll take care of you," Maury had said, "I swear I will." And she had replied, "I know you will, Maury, I know."

But how he would, he had no idea. How? Where? He got up and walked slowly back to the house, remembering the want ads and the patient lines at five in the morning, a hundred men for every job, the lines and lines from the Bronx to Brooklyn and Queens and back again.

How? Where?

He turned the corner, his head still throbbing, and climbed the stairs. Agatha heard him and opened the door. Then behind her in the living room he saw his mother, and sitting on the sofa, holding the little boy, his father.

"Ma?" he said wonderingly.

"Who else?" Her voice was bright and trembling. "And you don't have to talk. We know it all. Thank God, thank God, you're alive."

237

22

He stood in the dusty office waiting for the girl to make out his paycheck. The room had a linoleum floor and there was a zigzag tear in one of the window shades. He thought of the big office on Broadway: three floors, rows of desks, mahogany, rugs, like a bank.

Pa hung up the telephone. "I read your mind, Maury. It used to be different."

"At least, you're in business."

"True, true. We're keeping our heads above water." His father lit a cigar, not a Havana of old, but black and pungent nevertheless.

"The cheap ones smell better to me than the ones you used to get from Dunhill's."

"That's because you don't know anything about cigars. I've still got the humidor and the day will come, mark my words, when I fill it with Dunhill's again."

"I hope so, Pa."

"I know so. I have confidence in this country. We'll pull out of this. In the meantime, I'm sorry I can't do more. Fifty dollars a week isn't much to pay. But it's the best I can do."

"I'm lucky to have a job at all."

"Ah, but it's a disgrace that you, with all your education, should be walking around tenement houses collecting rents. I could get sick thinking about it."

"Don't think about it, then. As you say, we're keeping our heads above water. That's more than a lot of people are doing. Well, I'll start home. Don't forget, we expect you at seven."

"You could wait and ride in our car. Why take the subway?"

"Thanks, but I want to get back to see Eric and give Aggie a hand."

"I hope she's not going to too much trouble over dinner. We're not company, after all."

"Aggie likes to cook. Don't worry about that."

"Your mother's bringing her strudel, enough for an army. You know your mother."

"Aggie'll be pleased. Well, I'll see you."

"Maury, wait. Are things all right at home? You're happy?"

He could actually feel his face closing up, the muscles growing stiff. "Why, yes, of course. Why not?"

Now his father's face closed. "Good, good. I only asked."

The subway lurched and roared. Games. Playing games with each other. Pa knew he knew they were aware. Iris was loyal, but surely it had been discussed anyway. Well, he was not going to talk about it. Not now, not yet. Maybe sometime it might spill out of him. He couldn't swear that it wouldn't, but he wasn't ready yet to expose the secret places.

Maybe after they moved, his mind said, and the other half said: That won't make any difference and you know it won't. They still had almost a year to go on their lease. His father had mentioned an apartment in one of the buildings he managed; you could get three good-sized rooms, really four counting the kitchen, for forty-five dollars a month. It was on the Heights, though, which these days was jokingly—some joke—called the Fourth Reich because it had filled up with refugees from Germany. You hardly heard English on the streets.

He couldn't imagine Agatha up there. It occurred to him now that whenever he was somber or serious he thought of her as Agatha, but when everything was going along happily he thought of her as Aggie. Well, he couldn't imagine Agatha sitting in the park and wheeling the stroller up there on Washington Heights. She would be a total outsider as she was where they lived now. Come to think of it, she would be an outsider almost anyplace in New York City except on Park or Fifth or the streets in between. He thought wryly, We are hardly ready for that.

The subway swung around a curve, his body sagging with it. He was tired. His work didn't warrant such tiredness. This was a tiredness of the spirit, of frustration. She wouldn't admit that she drank. He could come in and see it in her eyes, smell it on her breath, and she would only insist stubbornly that he was imagining things. She would go over to the attack, leaving him on the defensive. He begrudged her an afternoon nap, she said; he was suspicious, a monomaniac. For a while he had measured the bottles and sought out the places where she hid the cheap wine she bought a bottle at a time, a small one so that it could be quickly consumed and spirited away in the garbage. He had done all that, but had got nowhere and finally stopped because it was a futile proceeding, without point.

He reasoned with her . . . "You said your nerves were bad because of the work I was doing and I could understand that. But now I'm working respectably for my father, and you've nothing to be afraid of. Why are your nerves bad now?" To which she countered with entire reasonableness, "If a person could tell you why his nerves were bad they wouldn't be bad, would they?" So there they were, round and round. Nowhere.

But he knew what it was. He was sure he knew. She was sorry she had married him. She might not know it herself, but she was. She loved me when she married me, oh, God, she loved me! And she loves me still, but it's wrong for her, all the same. Of course she won't leave me, and I won't leave her. I couldn't leave her. Not I, son of my parents and all their parents before them. A man doesn't leave his wife and child. But I couldn't do it, anyway. I wouldn't want to live without you, Aggie. Only, why aren't you the way you were? Why?

Round and round.

The subway doors were jammed. All the gray-faced city people in their dark clothes were carrying packages in red and green wrappings. He had forgotten it was Christmas on the day after tomorrow. Now Santa Claus came in and hung on the strap, across from two little boys with scared, awed faces.

"What's he doing on the subway?" one whispered, and Santa turned, clearing his throat.

"Just giving the reindeer a bit of a rest," he said, and people smiled approvingly and winked and patted the boys' caps.

Most people don't want much, Maury thought. When you come

down to it they just want a place where they don't have to be afraid
of what's coming, and they want somebody to love them.

So much for philosophy, he thought, and was glad to get out into
the damp night air, and walked the few blocks to his house looking
forward to Eric, who was always so totally, so unreservedly overjoyed to see him, thinking of Eric's row of teeth and his thickening
hair, his feet in red galoshes, his pealing laugh.

The first thing that he saw when he opened the door was the tree.
It was a bushy one, sharply fragrant and as tall as Aggie. She had a
carton of glass ornaments and tinsel and had begun to decorate the
tree. She hadn't told him a word about it.

"You haven't forgotten that my parents are coming?"

"Of course I haven't! Can't you smell the turkey? It's almost
done."

"But the tree," he said. "The tree."

"What about it?"

"Perhaps it's my fault," he said. "I didn't know you were going to
get one. I ought to have told you . . . we don't have Christmas
trees."

"We don't? Who's we?"

"Why, my father and mother, I mean. They don't have a
Christmas tree."

"Well, of course I know that! But what has that got to do with
us?"

This was not a question of too much wine. She hadn't had any, he
saw at once. This was another question.

"I should think," he said carefully, "that it had something to do
with us."

"I don't see how."

"Well, it's not that I personally have any objection. You can have
all the trees you want as far as I'm concerned. But it would be an
awful shock to my father, Aggie, and after all the grief we've had in
this family I just don't want any more."

"Your father can do what he wants in his own house. But I don't
see why Eric should be deprived, do you?"

"Eric hasn't the least idea what this is about," Maury said patiently.

"All right, but what about me? A tree is one of my loveliest memories of home."

241

"I shouldn't think you'd have too many lovely memories of home." He regretted the words as soon as he had said them. Hitting below the belt, that was.

"If you're referring to my parents' prejudice, I can only answer that yours get A in that department, too."

"Okay. I don't want to argue about it. But please, Agatha, I beg you, take the tree down. Don't slap my father in the face with that the minute he opens the door. We've come this far, must we spoil it? Please."

She answered him gently and stubbornly, "Maury, I truly don't want to make things harder, but this is our home and if your father really wants to accept me—us—isn't it better not to sham?"

"Aggie, the man is going on fifty and he's had a tough struggle. Do we need to upset him?"

"That sounds like a Jewish mother, having a heart attack every time one of her children displeases her."

"I don't care for that kind of remark, Agatha," he said stiffly.

"Oh, come on, don't get all huffy about it, as if I were an anti-Semite! Jokes about Jewish mothers are part of the language, for heaven's sake! Besides, they *are* possessive! And you always say Gentiles drink too much, don't you?"

"No, I don't say Gentiles do. I say *you* do."

She ignored him and, reaching up, tied a red satin ball on a branch.

"What the hell am I going to say to him when he comes in? You don't know what this means to Pa. Listen, Agatha, in the towns where his parents grew up, where my mother grew up, Christmas was the time that the Cossacks and all the local rowdies used to come riding in with dogs and whips to rape and burn and—"

"There are no Cossacks here and it's time you people stopped living in the past. This is America. Besides, you yourself said your father lives in the past. Behind medieval walls, I think you said."

Maury flushed. "Probably I did. But then your parents are so modern, so broad, so kindly! And at least my father is here!"

"What did it take to bring him here? You had to be almost killed before anything could penetrate that heart of his!"

"At least he's here," Maury repeated.

"Maybe mine would be here too if I had let him know the truth! Perhaps I should have told him my husband is running numbers and some thugs have beaten him up, so please come, I need you!"

242

The chiming clock on the radio struck half past six.

"Agatha, they'll be here any minute. Take it down now, and I promise I'll help you put it up again tonight after they've left. I swear I will," he said, unfastening a silver ball.

"Don't touch that! Listen, is this our house or isn't it? You resent any suggestion that you should hide your heritage; why should I hide mine? How would you like it if we went to visit my parents and I asked you to—"

"That's an academic question. You know damn well they don't want to see me in their house. And do you know something? I don't want to see those bastards either."

"Do you have to be so vulgar?"

"Sure, I'm a kike. Kikes are vulgar, don't you know that?"

From the room across the hall came Eric's sudden wail.

"See what you've done? He'll remember this, Maury. Children remember these things." She began to cry. "It was going to be so lovely and you've ruined it! I hate your voice when you yell like that! You look mean! You ought to see yourself."

"All right, all right. Stop crying, will you? Keep the blasted tree and I'll explain it—"

"I don't want the tree. Take it away." A glass ball fell to the floor and broke into chips of glitter. "All the joy's gone out of it. I'm going in to Eric."

She rested her head on his shoulder. "Was it awful, Maury? Was the evening all spoiled?"

"No, no, they had a good time. They were just glad to be here."

"Because I wouldn't want your parents to hate me."

"They don't hate you, Aggie. They like you, honestly." He stroked her trembling back, feeling the great sadness in her. How gay she had been—

"Such a hard world," she said. "How is one to bear such a hard world, tell me?"

"It's not hard all the time. And it's the only world we have."

"Do you think I've been drinking, Maury?"

"I know you haven't."

"Then give me a brandy now. I'm awfully cold."

"Hot tea will warm you. I'll make some."

"It's not the same. It won't relax me. Please, I *need* it tonight."

"No. Let go, I'll make tea for both of us."

243

"Then never mind. Just stay here."

"Aggie, darling, everything's all right. You are. We are."

"But I'm afraid, I'm so afraid. Oh, my God, Maury, what's happening to us?"

23

The evening that they would remember began in the kitchen, now the heart of the house. When Joseph came home from work he went straight there; this night he had brought Maury. Iris had gone downtown shopping with Agatha because winter coats were on sale, and later they were all to have dinner.

Anna stirred a pudding on the stove. How many years it had been since Maury and Joseph had consulted together! Report cards, camp, religious school, all those things that had been of topmost importance then, were nothing compared to this.

"When did you really know?" Joseph asked.

"There's no date to put a finger on," Maury answered. "I can't say: On such and such a date I was sure of it. For a long time I knew she liked to take a little something to help her over a bad spot—"

"Bad spot!" Anna cried out. "A lot she knows about bad spots! What troubles has she ever seen in her life?"

"Very few, until she married me, Ma. But she's had plenty since then."

"No one forced her to marry you!"

Joseph stood up. "You're talking wildly, Anna. Anger won't solve this. You hear me?" he asked, taking hold of her arm.

His fingers hurt her flesh. He was right, of course. But his calm tolerance amazed her and had, throughout all the secret discussions between Iris and themselves, up till the time that Maury—she wasn't sure just how—had brought everything into the open.

"How often does it happen?" Anna wanted to know. "Iris said—"

245

Joseph put his hand up. "Leave him alone, Anna. We don't need to go over the details again. I know them already."

"You and Maury have talked?"

"We've talked," Joseph said shortly.

How invariably, when there was a crisis, people began to snap at each other! "I see," she replied. "And what did you say when you talked; do you mind telling me?"

Neither of them answered. The pudding foamed over on the stove with the smell of burning sugar and Anna dabbed at it angrily. "Oh, what is the matter with that girl? The shame of it, the shame!"

"Not shame," Joseph corrected. "Sickness. Don't you understand she can't help it?"

"A rotten sickness!"

"All sickness is rotten, Anna."

"Well, if it's such a sickness, let her go to a doctor!"

"She won't go."

"Send one to her, for God's sake. What are you waiting for?"

"That's already been done."

"Already been done! And what happened?"

"She ran down the back stairs. She wouldn't see the doctor."

Maury got up. His chair scraped abruptly and Anna turned from the stained mess on the stove. A line of sickly flesh stretched across his forehead. It would probably remain, a permanent reminder. He looked so much older than twenty-four! Why should just he have all this pain, why should just his life be so hard? He had been so bright and quick, always busy coming and going, carrying his books and tennis racket; the house had been noisy with his friends; they had struggled so to see him through college. Even Ruth's children, in spite of what they had been through, even they were enjoying some youth, while my son, only my son, is burdened like this— The anger swelled in Anna's throat.

Joseph sighed. "You took her away from her people, Maury, she went with you willingly. For better or worse. So now it's worse and we'll have to find a way to make it better."

Maury looked up. "How?"

"Yes, how?" Anna repeated.

"I don't know." Joseph frowned. "But I've been thinking, Maury, why not take Agatha and the baby to Florida for a few weeks? I'll pay, I can swing it. A few weeks on the beach, just getting away, can work wonders. Sunshine heals, you know."

246

"Sunshine heals alcoholism?" Maury asked gently.

"Well, but the time away together in a beautiful place—it helps the spirit. Who knows?"

"It's awfully good of you, Pa. I want you to know I appreciate it. I really appreciate it."

"Then you'll go?"

"I'll talk about it with Aggie."

Anna thought of something. "When you speak to her about the drinking, what does she say?"

"She doesn't admit it. But it's well known that people seldom do."

The swinging door from the dining room whirled open. "You're talking about *me?*" Agatha cried. "Maury, you're talking to them about *me?*"

"We were only—" he began.

"Don't lie! I heard every word. You didn't know we had come home—" She beat with her fists on his chest. "Apologize! Admit that you lied about me?"

Maury caught her hands. "I'm sorry, perhaps I shouldn't have discussed this even with my parents. But I won't say it's not true, because both of us know that it is."

"I don't understand—" Agatha turned to Joseph and Anna. "He's got this—this puritan obsession about having a drink! Just because he doesn't like it, he thinks that every time a person has one or two he's drunk. Or if I lie down for a few minutes it can't be because I'm tired. Oh, no! It must be because I've been drinking!"

Joseph and Anna were silent. Such a child, Anna thought with pity and dislike, a child standing there in her jumper and blouse, with her tear-smudged, angry face. She wasn't even pretty; what had he seen in her? When I think of the girls he could have married, such beautiful girls! And then, pity again. The man-woman thing! How helpless we are, like netted birds, when we are caught by desire! I, surely I, know all about that—

"We'll never get anywhere, Aggie, if we're not honest with each other," Maury said. "If you would only admit you have a problem, we could help you."

"A problem? I? Or maybe I do have one and you're it!"

"Why? Because I find where you hide the bottle behind the stove?"

"What's happening?" Iris interrupted. "I was on the phone when I heard such a racket! I had to hang up!"

247

"Iris," Joseph said, "we're having a discussion here. Will you leave us for a few minutes?"

"I want her to stay!" Agatha cried. "She's the only one here I can talk to. Did you know they're accusing me of being a drunkard? Tell them, Iris, have you ever seen me drunk? Tell them!"

"Leave Iris out of this," Joseph said sternly. "Now listen, Agatha, listen calmly. I want you to come into my den and we'll sit down together and talk."

"Why don't we have dinner first?" As though she were standing outside herself, Anna heard her own words, offering food again. So often it seemed to be the only thing she knew how to do. "I've a beautiful roast and it's all ready."

"No," Agatha said. "I'm going home! I can't stay here, can't sit down at your table!"

Iris blocked the front door. "Aggie, I don't know what started all this, but listen to me, stay a little. Anyway, it's pouring, you can't even see to drive the car, wait a little."

But Agatha's coat was flung on, she was out of the door, and Maury was in the outer hall arguing at the elevator door, "I'm not going to let you drive. If you insist on leaving at least I'll do the driving."

"If I want to drive that car I will," they heard her say, and then the elevator door opened, and closed, and they heard its smooth sigh as it descended to the street.

Anna put the food on the table and the three of them sat hardly touching it, hardly speaking, except that once Anna said, "Never once, in all the years in this house—" but did not finish. Iris helped her clear the kitchen and Joseph sat in the living room with the evening paper, not reading it. The wind from the river rattled the windows. Down on the deserted street the rain blew whirlpools in the puddled light of the street lamp on the corner.

Later, when after a long, long time they were able to speak or to recall the particular sound and feel and texture of that February night, they saw it as a play in two parts, a prelude and an ending, with no middle.

It was almost half past eight when the doorbell rang. When she saw the two policemen in their wet, black rubber capes, Iris was sure she knew.

"Mr. Friedman?" one said.

Joseph rose from his chair and came toward them, walking

so slowly, Iris thought impatiently: Hurry up, do hurry up!

"Come in," Joseph said.

"There's been—I have to tell you," one began. He stopped. The other one, older, so he must have done this sort of thing before, took over. "There's been an accident," he said softly.

"Yes?" Joseph waited. The question waited, repeating itself in the dull light of the foyer. "Yes?"

"Your son. On the boulevard in Queens. Can we sit down somewhere?"

Quarreling, Iris thought, fighting in the tight little car.

The policeman had such an odd expression. He swallowed as if there were a knob in the back of his throat. "They were—a witness said—the car was speeding very fast. It passed them, too fast in the rain, and it missed a curve."

"You're telling me that he's dead," Joseph said, making a statement or asking a question. And this, too, hung in the air repeating itself: that he's dead, he's dead.

The policeman didn't answer right away. He took Joseph's arm and sat him like a doll in the stiff carved chair in the foyer.

"They didn't feel anything," he said, very softly. "Neither one of them. It was over so quick."

The younger man stood there, turning his wet cap between his hands. "No, no one felt anything," he said again, as if this confirmation, this assurance, were a gift and a mercy.

"They couldn't tell who was driving," the first one said. He turned to Iris. "Young lady, is there any whiskey in the house? And may we call someone? Someone in the family, or a doctor?"

In the background near the door to the inner rooms, and yet sounding far away, came a stabbing scream. Again and again it ripped the air, over and over. It was Anna.

"They were such a nice quiet couple," said Mr. Andreapoulis. He sat with Joseph and Anna in his little parlor. Through the open door to the kitchen they could see his wife rolling some dough on a table. "They never said anything, but we knew from the start there was something sad about them. No one ever came to see them. They used to go for long walks together. We felt sorry for them, my wife and I."

Neither of them had ever mentioned their families, not until after

249

the little boy was born. Then one evening they had come downstairs looking very serious and said that they supposed now they ought to have a will, and would he draw it up for them? Not that they had anything much to leave, but there ought to be some plan for the care of the child in case something were to happen to them both. Mr. Andreapoulis had concurred in that. They had been uncertain and uneasy, but finally they had decided that, in the event of their deaths, the little boy should go to live with his mother's parents as guardians. He had asked them whether they had discussed this with her parents, and they said that they hadn't, but that it would be all right; her parents lived in the country and had plenty of room. Then they had begun to laugh, out of a kind of embarrassment which Andreapoulis had understood. A will is such a formal and pompous document for young people to be writing. People their age don't die and leave a baby behind. It was all academic and therefore foolish, in their thinking.

So that was how it had come about. They had left the will with him and he supposed that, given their attitude, they had forgotten about it. As a matter of fact, he had forgotten about it himself until the night of the accident.

"And so," Joseph said, "there's nothing that can be done to change it."

"Well, as I've told you, anyone has a right to contest a will. But you certainly couldn't show undue influence in this case, could you? These people didn't even know about it." Mr. Andreapoulis' hooded eyes were mournful. "And they really want the child, you see. Although any court would give you visitation rights, of course."

"In their house?"

"It would have to be, wouldn't it?"

"Like visiting in a jail," Joseph muttered.

"Well, do you want to fight it? I don't hold out much hope, but you never know."

"Courts and lawyers. A dirty business. Excuse me, nothing personal, only—"

"I know what you meant. It's all right."

"A dirty business," Joseph said again. His eyes filled.

The young man looked away. He waited.

Joseph stood up. "We'll think it over," he said, "and let you know. Come, Anna."

*　　*　　*

On the wall behind the doctor's desk hung an arrangement of diplomas, forming an impressive frame for his head. The bookshelves on the side nearest Joseph and Anna were filled with texts, the doctor's own and many more. *The Psychology of the Adolescent,* Anna read, and *The Psychology of the Pre-School Child.*

"Yes, I would say this baby has suffered trauma enough," the doctor said. "Of course I know what I've told you is not what you were hoping to hear."

Anna wiped her eyes. "No, I believe it's right. I can see that it makes sense. Splitting the time would be no good for him even if the court were to allow it, which the lawyer says they very likely wouldn't, anyway."

"That's mature thinking. Courageous, too, Mrs. Friedman."

"And yet I don't know!" she cried out bitterly. "If the will had read the other way I wouldn't have treated those people the way they're treating us!"

"But I would," Joseph said. "I would have done exactly what they're doing. And that's the truth."

"Which proves," Dr. Briggs remarked, "why the child ought to be spared exposure to such hostility. He's had enough confusion and shock in his little life already. The kindest thing, if you really love him, and I see that you do, would be to bow out and leave him alone. Let these other grandparents rear him and give him stability. He's not a prize to be fought over."

"Not even to visit," Anna said.

"I wouldn't, if I were you, in these circumstances that you've described. How would he cope with so much hatred? And why should he be forced to take sides? When the boy is older he'll want to see you. Teen-agers are very concerned with identity. Then that will be another situation entirely."

"Teen-agers!" Anna cried.

"It's a long time to wait, I know," the doctor said.

At home Anna mourned, "If we hadn't known him, it wouldn't hurt like this. He was starting to call my name, did you know that? He called me Nana the last time I saw him."

I never knew I loved Maury so much when he was alive, Iris thought. But when I remember Eric, his little face, his little hands, I know how I loved my brother. And now that they have taken Eric away, it's like losing my brother twice over.

24

After the first blinding pain of loss came long, desolate nights and days. Why? Why? And no answer. Nothing anymore. Never. It was too much effort to eat, too exhausting to dress or go down to the market, a burden to answer the telephone.

Then one morning there came to Anna a stirring of desire to feel again. And she took out a sheaf of letters, tied together, that had arrived from Europe during the terrible time when Maury had been struck down. Voices called out of the dark: her brothers' (Eli and Dan, snub-nosed, freckled boys in their mother's kitchen and suddenly, in Vienna, as old as their father had been when he died); Liesel's (Eli's fair, silvery little girl); the unknown voice of Theo, the little girl's husband.

1.

Vienna, March 7, 1938

Dearest Uncle Joseph and Aunt Anna,

Now that I am actually sitting down to write you a letter I feel ashamed and must begin by apologizing for not having written before, except for the note in which I thanked you for the beautiful wedding gift that you sent to Theo and me. I suppose my only excuse for not having written in all these years, and not a very good one, is that Papa writes to you, and it seemed that he was really writing for all of us. Anyway, here I am, your lazy niece Liesel, sitting in the library, looking out at the melting snow and the little garden room where we had afternoon coffee when you were here. Was it really nine years ago? I was such a baby then, staring at the relatives from America! And here I am, married; our boy Friedrich, Fritzl, we call him, is thirteen months old, just starting to take a few steps, and now *we* are going to America! I can't believe it.

For that is what I want to write to you about. Theo left for Paris by train this very morning. He will take a ship from Le Havre, arriving in New York on the nineteenth. He has your telephone number, so don't be surprised when you get a call! He spent three years at Cambridge and speaks English beautifully, not like me. (That's why I'm writing this in German; because I remember that you were able to understand it very well.) I know you will like each other so much.

The reason Theo is making the trip is to make plans for our immigration. As you know, he is a doctor, and has almost finished his work at the clinic here, studying plastic surgery. I saw the work he did on a child with a burned arm; he is so talented and loves his work! He needs to find out how you go about getting a license to practice in the U.S. and perhaps he might find a doctor who needs a young assistant. . . . It is all quite unsettled, as you can imagine. So I thought that maybe among your many friends you might know a doctor who could advise him. Also, we shall be needing an apartment. Theo wants to sign for one and have everything ready; then he will come back and get Fritzl and me, and arrange to have all our furniture shipped. Perhaps you could tell him where to look for an apartment.

I have such very mixed feelings about all this, I must admit. Theo is absolutely certain that the Nazis are going to occupy Austria within the next year or so. He has been saying it since before we were married, even when we first met. He is very interested in politics and sounds too convincing; he is determined to save us by emigrating. My parents and all Mama's relatives and Theo's own parents, too, think his ideas are pure nonsense. They refuse to leave and they are heartbroken that we are going. For a while Papa was really angry at Theo because he is taking the first grandchild and their daughter away, but now that the actual time is drawing near, he is too crushed to be angry.

As for me, I shall miss my parents, my young brother and sister, most terribly. And Vienna. Theo's father and Papa had arranged to buy a lovely small villa for us near Grinzing. Up to now we have been living in a very nice apartment only a short walk from the Ringstrasse. I shall miss it all so much. . . . And I forgot to mention I was invited to start next season playing with a small orchestra here. At last I felt I was really getting somewhere with the piano. It will be hard to start all over in New York.

But I realize, if it should turn out that Theo is right about the Nazis, our lives here would be in danger because of being Jewish. It's strange, because I have never felt Jewish. I have always felt Austrian—Viennese, to be exact. Forgive me if I offend you, since I remember Papa said you are still quite religious. But then, I am sure you will understand; to be religious or not is entirely personal, is it not? And one does whatever makes one happy.

Speaking of religious people, you may not know that Uncle Dan has already left. He and his whole family went last month to Mexico. He tried to go to the United States but it was impossible because of having been born in Poland; the quota is filled for years ahead. Of course Papa thinks Uncle Dan is quite stupid—they never seemed to get along very well, did they? Anyway, I hope they will succeed there, better than they did here.

This has turned out to be a very long letter, longer than I intended. Now I hear Fritzl up from his nap. We all thought he was going to have red hair like Papa and you, Aunt Anna, but his hair has turned quite blond, almost white.

I hope you are all very well, and I thank you so much for whatever help you can give to Theo. He doesn't need any money, only advice.

> With hearty greetings,
> your loving niece,
> Liesel Stern

2.

Vienna, March 9th, 1938

Dear Sister and Brother-in-law,

You letter came here this morning, and I am sick with sorrow. To lose your son, your dear son! Destroyed in a pointless accident! Not even in a war, fighting for his country! That would be painful enough, but at least there is some reason in it, and hence some consolation. But this! I am sick for you, heartsick, and so is Tessa, so are we all. (I understand that Liesel wrote to you only a day or two ago, not knowing.) If only I could do something for you, dear Anna, dear Joseph.

It seems that all of a sudden the world has gone mad with sorrow. Not that I compare my burden with yours, of course not, but we here are bent down with the grief of parting. . . . As you have learned by now, my son-in-law, a fine young man of excellent family, has got a wild idea into his head about going to America. Please do not think I am prejudiced against America. When you went, Anna, from where we lived, it was understandable. But to leave Austria, because some fanatic across the border makes threats—it's absurd. Even if the Germans were to take Austria, and believe me, it would not be so easy, even then it would not mean the end of the world! Possibly some of the extremists here would deprive some Jews of their jobs; there's nothing new about that. We've always had that sort of thing in Europe, sometimes a little more, then again, a little less. It's nothing that one can't live through. And anyway, I tried to tell Theo, his own parents tried to tell him, with our family connections we are the last people to be bothered.

Tessa's people have lived in Austria for so many centuries that nobody knows when they first came. Her father is a top-level official in the Finance Ministry. Her grandfather's sister married a Catholic and converted; one of their grandsons just became a bishop! So much for Tessa. I can't boast of any such connections of my own, unfortunately, but I have made my modest success. Also, as you know, I fought in the war and wear the Emperor's Medal of Valor. Really, I can't see any reason for this hysterical behavior. Ah, well, the young are often unreasonable, and so it is.

Forgive me for talking about all this when your hearts are so full. Please, take care of yourselves and your daughter Iris and the surviving grandchild. Know that we are thinking of you. We are with you, praying that you will find the strength to endure this terrible thing, and go on.

Ever your brother,
Eduard

3.

Paris, March 15, 1938

Dear Aunt and Uncle,

I write in haste to explain my failure to arrive in New York. By now you must be wondering why I wasn't on the ship, or perhaps you have understood from the news why I wasn't.

The day before I was to sail Austria was occupied. I have been trying to get through by telephone to my house, to Liesel's parents or to mine. But the lines are dead. I must assume that they have all left Vienna for the country. Perhaps they have gone to Tessa's people's mountain house near Graz. At any rate, I am taking a train tomorrow for Vienna, where they must have left some message. I will write as soon as I know something.

Respectfully,
Theodor Stern

4.

Paris, March 20, 1938

Dear Aunt and Uncle,

I write again in great haste because I can imagine how anxious you are. I am almost out of my mind. I can't find out anything. It has been a nightmare. I tried to get back to Austria, but they told me in France here that if I tried I would be arrested on the train. I didn't want to believe it, but then the papers here in Paris began to print names and incidents involving people who had tried to rush back to their families just as I was trying to do. And it's true, they were all seized

and imprisoned. So, obviously, that would not have done anyone any good. But I have some contacts here that will surely
be of help. I shall keep you informed.

Respectfully,
Theodor Stern

5.

Paris, March 26, 1938

Dear Aunt and Uncle,

Still nothing. The earth has opened up and swallowed all
the people I love. But that's not possible. I can't believe it. I
won't. I am working day and night. I shall write immediately
whenever I learn anything.

Respectfully,
Theodor Stern

6.

Paris, April 3, 1938

Dear Aunt and Uncle,

Thank God! They are alive! They are in the detention camp
Dachau where prominent people in government, journalism
and so forth have been taken for interrogation. I am told that
the purpose is to weed out subversives . . . so then we have
nothing to fear; certainly our families have hardly been sub-
versive! So it should be over for them very soon. I have people working in the highest circles and shall be getting them
out to France to join me here.

The way I found out all this you can't imagine. I mentioned
my father's business contacts here in Paris. But I recalled also
that one of my friends from Cambridge, a German fellow, was
now attached to their embassy here. So I got in touch with
him, and through him, plus the International Red Cross, I
managed to get some important telephone calls through.

Oh, if they had only listened to me! True, I did not know it
was coming so soon. I thought we had another year's leeway,

257

or I would have made Liesel and the baby go with me right now. But there is no use in such thoughts.

My German friend assures me that they will be released in a short time. I have put a large sum of money at his disposal and that can't help but hasten things, the world being what it is. Meanwhile, I am making arrangements with the Cuban visa office to have Liesel's parents go to Cuba, where they can wait in peace and comfort for my father-in-law's turn to be reached on the Polish quota for the United States.

I shall write to you again, probably by next week, as soon as I hear more.

Respectfully,
Theodor Stern

7.

Marigny-sur-Oise, August 14, 1938

Dear Monsieur and Madame Friedman,

You don't know me, but I am a friend of the family of Dr. Theodor Stern, and so I believe indirectly of your family's, too. Dr. Stern has been living with my wife and me for the last three months. We had been acquainted with his father many years ago. Last April we met him again in Paris, where we tried to be of some service to him with regard to his wife, child and parents . . . but, tragically, we were able to do nothing.

I understand that when you last heard about your relatives they were in the concentration camp Dachau. Dr. Stern had moved heaven and earth to obtain their release, but it is heartbreaking to say that he was unsuccessful. All of them, the entire family, has gone to its death, some there and some in other camps to which they, and many thousands with them, had been transferred. The only detail we know is that the baby died of pneumonia a few days after their arrest. As for the others, one doesn't want the details.

Dr. Stern was taken very ill at the news. I personally had been concerned about him even earlier, as he had had no rest, hardly slept, was unable to eat, ran around Paris like a madman calling upon every source of possible help. When the news came he collapsed, quite understandably. It was then that we took him to our country house, a quiet place, where we obtained an excellent doctor, and have tried to do the best for him.

He seems somewhat recovered now. He eats a little and is calm, but very quiet. He asked me to write this letter for him, and I thought it was a good suggestion, rather than have him put all this into writing, freshening it all in his mind again, as it were.

Yesterday he told us that he had decided to go to England where he spent such happy years at the university. He plans to offer his services to the British army and be ready for the war which he is certain will come soon. I am to tell you that he will write to you again, since he feels you are a link with the wife he lost.

> Be assured of my very kind
> regards,
> Jacques-Louis Villaret

8.

Mexico City, August 23, 1938

Dear Joseph and Anna,

It is a long time since I have written to you, and you must be wondering what happened to us. So I write to tell you, and hope that you will let our brother Eduard and his family know where we are. Give them our address and please send me theirs. I suppose they must have left Vienna, but as Eduard has always had so much influence in high places I am sure they are all right, and thank God for that.

As for us, well, it has been quite a change, as you can imagine. We would have preferred coming to the United States, not only for the sake of the country itself, but because it would have been good to live near you. Family is everything; what else can you count on in this world? I would so like to be with you, to break bread together every Friday night, but it can't be helped.

Still, we are doing all right for a beginning and we can't complain, especially when we read about what is happening in Europe. It doesn't bear thinking about, and I could wet this page with my tears if I were to go on thinking about it.

Mexico City is very grand. The mansions along the avenues are more grand than anything in Vienna! We arrived last February having left in great haste and it was very odd to be in such a springlike place at that time of the year! We have rented a quite decent little house, built around a small court-yard, the way they build houses here. Dena has planted flowers. Everything grows in this sunshine. And the old man—I forgot to tell you the old man is with us, ninety-three years old, and still keen in the head—the old man sits outside moving from the sun to the shade, and he actually enjoys it here, I think. At first he didn't want to come, you know, but of course we wouldn't leave him behind, so we forced him and he stood the voyage very well. You would be surprised.

I have got a job as a furrier with a fine firm. The fur business is good, in spite of the mild climate. There are many rich people here and they are very fashionable. Tillie, our younger daughter-in-law, is a first-class seamstress and has also got a good position with a dressmaking establishment, copying Paris models. Saul is a watchmaker and he has a job too, while Leo is still looking, but I am sure he will find something. Our younger ones, all five of them, have started school and have learned Spanish so well in these few months that we take them with us for shopping or business. For Dena and me it is much harder to learn a new language. After all, we are over forty, and this is the second time in our lives that we have come as immigrants and strangers to a new country and a new language. But we shall manage. Even the old man has learned a few words. You would laugh to hear him!

Our plans are to save as much as we can and then in a few years my sons-in-law—and by that time my sons will also be old enough—we shall open some sort of import-export business together. I think it will be much easier to get ahead here than it was in Vienna. There seems to be room for newcomers here as there wasn't over there. Anyway, thanks be to God, we are at peace here. We rest easily at night, all of us together, and what else matters when you come down to it?

We hope you are all well, and now that you know where we are let us hear from you often.

Your loving brother,
Daniel

P.S. I had no idea North America was so big. I was about to say come and visit us, when I looked at a map and saw that New York is thousands of miles from Mexico City. Still, perhaps you will come anyway?

25

On a blowy, bleak morning early in November the telephone rang. When Anna answered it, she heard an unmistakable voice.

"Anna? I'm here. I got off the ship last night."

"Paul?" she questioned in disbelief.

"Right after your card arrived I caught the *Queen Mary* over. I don't know what I can do for you, or whether anyone can do anything. But I had to come."

Ah, yes! A month or more ago, on a very hard day and in one of those hours that come long after a great grief, and are worse to live through than the first hour was, in such an hour, driven after long silence by some unexplained impulse, she had sent a card to Paul. "Maury is dead," she had written, and nothing more: no signature, no date, only a cry from the heart. She had mailed it to London and afterward been sorry that she had.

"Anna? Are you there?"

"I'm here. I can't believe you've come all this way—"

"Well, I have. And I'm taking no chances this time with broken appointments. I'm downstairs across the avenue with a car. So put your coat on and come."

Trembling and agitated, she ran a comb through her hair, found a purse and hat and gloves. All these years! Three or four times a year their brief messages had gone back and forth: "Iris graduated third in the class"; "Leaving for Zurich on business, back in six weeks." She had grown used to thinking that this was all the contact they would ever have. Now here he was.

He was waiting beside the car. When he took her cold hands in his, it was without greeting, without a word. How thin he had grown! Thin and grave, Anna thought as she stood there, letting him search her with his eyes. When they were in the little car together she repeated, "I can't believe you've come all this way."

"Can you tell me what happened, Anna? Do you want to talk about it?"

Very simply, she told him. "It was an accident in a car. His wife was killed, too. Last March."

"Last March? Why have you waited so long to tell me?"

She made a little gesture of resignation.

Paul mourned, "I know what Maury meant to you."

"He left a little boy, two years old. But we don't see him."

"Why not?"

"There's been a sort of feud. His other grandparents have him."

Paul said softly, "It's a good thing you're very, very strong."

"I? I feel so weak, you can't imagine."

"You're one of the strongest people I've ever known!"

He put the car into gear and it began to roll down the avenue.

"Let's ride around a little. Do you want to tell me any more? Or would you rather not?"

"There isn't any more to tell. That's it, the whole of it."

"Yes, it speaks for itself."

"But it is good to see you, Paul. It's been six years since that day in Riverside Park."

"Seven in the spring," he corrected. "It was the third of April."

The car turned eastward through Central Park, emerging on Fifth Avenue where General Sherman still rode his proud horse to victory. The first time she had seen that statue she had been a greenhorn, fresh from Miss Mary Thorne's class. The city had sparkled like diamond dust, city of a million secrets: secrets between the covers of books and behind the doors of great stone houses. A rich city it had been, rich with music and flowers; the world itself had opened before young eyes like a great curled, closed flower.

"We went to the Plaza for tea," Anna said, thinking aloud.

"Yes, and you didn't want to accept the hat I had bought for you." He smiled.

"I wonder whether it's a good thing or not that we can't look ahead to see what's going to happen."

263

"A bad thing," Paul answered promptly. "If we could see we'd do a lot differently."

"Not if what is to be is ordained anyway."

"Ah, metaphysics! You know, it seems forever since I've been in New York! London is a magnificent old lady, but New York is a young girl preparing for a dance. Look there, Anna! To ride down Fifth Avenue! Isn't it splendid?"

She knew he was trying to coax her into a lighter mood, but she answered anyway, "Only when you've got nothing on your mind and something in your pocket, I think."

"How are things in that area?"

"Better, although we're being terribly frugal. Joseph is putting every cent he can find into land. When the Depression ends prices will soar, he says."

"He's right. They will. Tell me, do you have to be home at any special time today?"

"I have the whole day. Joseph's not coming home to dinner and Iris is going to study at a friend's house."

"Then you can spend the day with me. I want to hear about Iris. I want to talk about everything. Do you like the seashore in the winter?"

"I've never seen it then."

"Ah, it's beautiful! Just gulls and silence! Even the noise of the ocean is another kind of silence, I always think."

He turned the car toward the tunnel. "We'll drive to the Island. I've a little place there, which has been rented out the last few years. But it's vacant this time of year, of course. We'll walk on the beach and it will do you good."

The highway was almost empty. They sped easily through villages and past sere fields.

"You wanted to hear about Iris. She's a fine student, doing very well at Hunter."

"What about boys? Is she enjoying life?"

"Not really. She's so timid, so self-conscious. She thinks she isn't pretty."

"And isn't she?"

"I've a picture here in my wallet. You can decide for yourself."

Paul drew to the side of the road. For a few minutes he studied the photograph. While he was doing that Anna studied him, his keen profile, his somber eyes. What feelings must be stirring in him now at sight of this young woman who belonged to him and whom he did not know?

At last he spoke. "No, she isn't pretty, is she? But she has a distinctive face. I've seen the same face on young Roman noblewomen whom people call beautiful only because they're aristocrats and haughty."

"Iris is far from haughty. It would be better for her if she could be, just a trifle." Aristocrats. Joseph used to call her his queen when she was a child. Anna sighed.

"She looks more like my mother than anyone," Paul continued.

"Yes, but your mother had style and confidence. I haven't given them to Iris."

"Maybe confidence is something that can't be given, Anna."

"I think it can. But—I've never been at ease with her. I told you that once."

"What does—he think?"

"Ah, Joseph thinks the sun rises and sets in Iris! He can't see that there's anything lacking at all. If ever a man adored a daughter—" She stopped abruptly.

Paul started the car again and they drove on through wider fields and more scattered villages into a calm countryside.

"I wish I could see her," he said. "A part of myself is alive, walking through the world with thoughts and feelings perhaps like my own—and I don't know her." And when Anna made no comment he went on, "When you walked away, that day I learned the truth about her, I sat there on the bench until dark. I had no strength at all. I remember trying to sort my feelings out, what I was supposed to feel and what I actually did feel."

"And have you sorted them out?"

"No, not even now. What can a man feel about a—a biological accident? Can I love her, when I've only seen her once for five minutes?" he asked bitterly. "And still, when I think what a miracle it is that she is made out of you and me, I do love her. . . . Oh, Anna! I've dreamed so of a message from you! 'I've changed my mind,' it will say. But it never comes."

"Please," Anna whispered.

He glanced at her. "All right, no more. You've had enough to think about. I want this to be a day without problems for you, and no pressure."

They stopped on the single street of a tidy village: salt-box houses under maples, a white board church and belfry, bow-front shop windows displaying books, tweeds and imported foods.

"Pleasant, isn't it?" Paul remarked. "An artificial enclave in a sooty world, very privileged, very unreal. And, to be honest, I enjoy it. At least, for a couple of months in the summer, I do."

There were few cars or people on the street. Obviously the village was three-quarters asleep and would not wake up again until Memorial Day.

"Come, we'll get ourselves something to eat before we go out to the place."

The food shop shone like a jeweler's. Paul took a wicker hamper, filled it with quick decisiveness and carried it to the counter.

"You've enough there for six people!" Anna protested, for he had bought cold meats and cheese, crackers, cake, fruit, tinned artichokes, a little jar of caviar, a bottle of wine and a long French bread.

"You'll eat. My guess is that you haven't been eating very well."

"That's true," she admitted. "I haven't been hungry."

"This air will make you hungry, I promise."

From the end of the street a blacktop road led past comfortable houses and, between clumps of woods, quick glimpses of the slate-colored sea. Then came a dirt lane; brittle, brown mulleins and milkweed stalks stood tall on either side of it. The car bumped along for a quarter of a mile before Paul stopped.

"Here we are," he said.

A little house of weathered boards shone silver in the vast light from the ocean that crashed only a few yards from its front door. A low fence, to which still clung dead sticks of last summer's roses, kept the wild marsh grass from intruding on the yard.

"How lovely!" Anna cried. "It must be very, very old!"

"No, although this part of the island was settled in the seventeenth century and there are some genuine survivors left. But this is just a skillful copy."

"Oh, lovely," Anna repeated.

It was spare and simple, with rag rugs on a polished floor, a cavernous, blackened fireplace, country furniture and not too much of it. Dried flowers stood in a brass bucket on the mantel.

Paul ran a finger over the mantel. "Clean," he announced. "I've a tiptop caretaker. Wait, I'll get more heat up in a minute." He flipped the thermostat switch and a low rumble rose immediately from the cellar.

"We're well equipped. It can be chilly out here in late August. Come, let's go walking till the house warms up. You'll want to wrap the scarf around your head because the wind's fierce on the beach."

The tide was coming in. It raced up the hard sand to its appointed mark and raced out again. It boomed and thundered at the breakwater, where clouds and mists of spray obscured the view that elsewhere lay clear to the gray horizon. Every few minutes a listless sun slid behind the clouds and as quickly slid back. The wind tore savagely at Anna's scarf. It drowned their voices so that they had to shout at one another to be heard, and so they walked together without speaking. A tern plummeted into the sea for a fish, its forked tail tipping toward the sky as its head went under water. Herring gulls cried their wild cries. In the marsh at the end of the beach, wood ducks, black ducks and pintails quacked and scuttled as Anna and Paul drew near.

There was no one in sight. At the far end of the marsh Paul stretched his arm toward the point where, past acres of sedge, a rambling wooden structure faced the sea.

"The inn," he shouted. "Great seafood! One of the best vacation hotels in the world!"

Joseph would scorn a place like that—old, ramshackle and remote. Why did she always think of what Joseph would think? Even now?

Back at the cottage they rubbed their hands in the welcome warmth. "But we need a fire for extra," Paul said.

In a few minutes he had got one started. From newspaper to kindling wood to a great cedar log the flame spread, fluttering, swaying, stretching its filaments of orange, of scarlet and white-gold. Anna watched while Paul fanned and poked.

"I'm entranced," she said slowly. "I feel as if I'd traveled a thousand miles since this morning!"

Paul rose from his knees and straightened up. "This place suits you, Anna. Or, better yet, I see you in some Elizabethan country house, coming down the steps to the garden." He made a sweeping, intentionally romantic gesture. "Or else in a white Spanish villa with a red-tiled floor and a fountain in the courtyard. I don't see you in an apartment house on New York's West Side."

267

"Nevertheless," she said quietly, "that's where I live."

"Well, you oughtn't to! When I first knew you I used to think, 'There's a woman for whom beautiful things were meant to be, diamonds and—' "

"I had a diamond, a huge one. I never wanted it. Joseph had to pawn it. I told him to sell it but he wouldn't; he plans to get it back with the first money he can spare, he says. I don't know why it should matter so much to him that I wear a diamond," she mused.

"But I do know," Paul said harshly. He frowned. Then his voice turned gentle. "Let's move the little table nearer the fire and have some lunch."

"You see," he exclaimed a while later, when Anna had emptied her plate, "the air did give you an appetite!" She admitted that it had and he added, "You've lost a lot of weight, haven't you?"

"I guess so. I haven't really been paying attention. But you're thinner, too."

"I'm working very hard," he answered briefly.

He lit a cigarette, making much of the small ritual and prolonging it. Anna sensed that his thoughts had for the moment left the room where they were. Then he shook his head, as though he were trying to rid himself of some troubling reflection, and spoke again.

"About Iris—you must see that she learns something practical, not just the humanities, some Latin, some madrigals and a course in nineteenth-century drama."

"You sound almost scornful!"

"Not at all. Those are all fascinating subjects. But one must also be prepared to earn a livelihood in the world."

"Joseph will take care of her," Anna replied defensively.

"That's not what I mean. There's also the question of self-respect. It's bad to have to take from others all your life, especially if you think as little of yourself to begin with as you say Iris does."

Anna hadn't thought of it that way. One expected a girl to get married; every girl, any girl. Moreover, it struck her that she hadn't given very much thought to Iris anyway during these past few years of Maury's troubles and death.

"I do see," she said now. "Yes, you're right. Well, she's taking some education courses, so she will be able to teach."

"Ah, well, that's all right, then."

She was not accustomed to having a man take charge like this, analyzing and planning. Joseph had never—yes, yes, she corrected herself, for Maury he had! Maury's homework, Maury's religious school—she recalled the battles over the latter—and Maury's law school which he hadn't entered, all had been part of his father's ambition for him. But for Iris there had been nothing of the sort, nothing but a cherishing, blind, protective love.

Paul had risen to clear the things away. When Anna moved to help, he waved her back. "No, today you're my guest. Sit there."

But she stood up to walk restlessly about the room, and stopped before a dusky antique mirror between the windows. Something in her own posture now reminded her of the woman in that painting which Paul had sent: the same thin face; the head top-heavy with dark red hair, its wind-blown wisps loose on the long neck; the quietude which could be read either as tranquillity or melancholy, as one chose.

When Paul was ready they sat down on the rug before the fire. They glanced at each other and then quickly looked away, as strangers do who have just been introduced and are then left alone together.

Anna searched for a way to break the sudden silence between them.

"And are you going to stay, now that you're home?"

"No, I shall be in London until the war comes, and it's going to come soon, you can count on that. Then I'll have to get out."

She was puzzled. "But your business, your bank is here."

"I'm not on bank business there."

She understood that she was to ask no more and waited. He poked at the fire, unnecessarily, for a fountain of sparks gushed up. Some fell on the rug. He beat them out, then looked at Anna.

"Oh, why shouldn't I tell you? It's this: I have been making trips into Germany to rescue some of our people from the concentration camps and prisons. First we raise funds, and then we make contacts. For money, you see, these Nazi thugs will do anything. The trouble is, there isn't enough money to save more than a very few here and there, the lucky ones whom we happen to hear about."

"That's what you meant when you said you were working hard?"

"Yes. I'll tell you something: it tears the heart out of you. When you know that what you're doing is only a drop in the bucket, and when you see some of the survivors—I met a man at the French

border who had been released. One eye was gone and every tooth
in his mouth had been knocked out. A professor of bacteriology he
was, or had been. What's left of him will never be fit to do his
work again."

Anna considered. "You yourself go into Germany? But that's
dreadfully dangerous, isn't it?"

"I won't say it isn't. I'm an American citizen and that's a great
protection, but also I'm a Jew, so one never knows. People can disappear there swiftly and secretly. The American embassy wouldn't
be able to prove a thing."

"Where will it all end, in heaven's name?"

"Perhaps heaven knows. I surely don't. But we have to try.
We're also working in Palestine. The British are trying to keep us
out but it will be the only haven for many and so there's a giant's
work to be done there, too. Only that—I'm sorry—that I cannot
talk about."

"I have a very general idea of what may be going on. I know that
Joseph sent a check last week, money he couldn't spare, but he
sent it anyway. . . . Paul, don't get killed there."

He smiled. "I shall certainly try not to. But someone has to do
the dangerous jobs, and a man like myself who has no family to
care for, has plenty of money and is young enough to have the
energy—such a man has an obligation," he concluded simply.

Anna's eyes filled with tears and she turned her head away. But
he had seen.

"Anna, what is it?"

"You'll think, you'll think I have nothing but troubles! It's almost
unreal, the things that have happened in my family . . ."

"Tell me, what is it?"

"My brother in Vienna. He and his wife and children, all of
them died in Dachau." She put her head in her hands.

Paul stroked her hair. "You've had too much. My God, it isn't
fair."

The hollow of his shoulder was so firm, the wool rough on her
cheek as she murmured, "Like sleepwalkers we are, walking the
edge of a cliff. I've been so frightened since we lost Maury. I keep
thinking, although I try so much to be reasonable, still I keep
thinking: What terrible thing is going to happen next?"

"It's all thrown dice, my darling Anna. The odds are that you've
had everything thrown at once, and after this there'll be no more."

Turning her face, he kissed away a few tears on her lashes, kissed her wet cheeks, found her mouth and held to it.

It was warmth and balm; his strength was comfort and ease. With a little cry, she clasped him closer and the grieving soreness ebbed from her chest. After a while she lay back in the firelight as, with quick and gentle purpose, he drew off her dress. For a moment she was aware of her own hand stretched toward the blaze, its fingers curled, translucent in the brightness. She saw his luminous eyes before closing her own. Then she was not aware of anything at all but hunger and demanding need, a clamor for pure assuagement and a wish to prolong the marvel forever. . . .

A long, sweet time later came a fine calm while his arms still held her and, finally, the soft flow of sleep.

Paul sat on the floor beside her, anxiously scanning her face. "I was afraid you would be conscience-stricken again."

She blinked. "No, strangely enough."

"Then what were you thinking of before you opened your eyes?"

"I just woke up."

"You've been awake for a minute or two. Your eyelids were moving."

So sharp he was! You could never hide anything from this man. "All right. I was remembering how I used to think of that other time, and wonder whether it had really been like that or whether I had only been imagining it."

"And had you?"

"No. It really was—is—like that."

He laughed. "Good! Good!"

The sight of his triumphant pleasure brought a smile to Anna's lips, and then a laugh. It was the first time she had laughed in months. Yet the sorrow was still there, she knew, and it would surge again when this hour was past and gone.

As if he were able to read her mind, Paul said, "I want to tell you a story I once heard. There was a woman whose child had died, in some especially tragic way. When they came home from the hospital, or maybe it was the funeral, the husband wanted to make love to her. And she was outraged, so he felt terribly guilty and they couldn't understand each other at all. What do you think about that?"

"Oh," Anna said, "he wanted comfort, he needed love! And she

271

didn't see that? Because when you're all alone, when you're dying inside, loving like this brings you back from the grave. It is the most alive thing you can do. Yes, yes, I do understand."

"I think you understand everything," Paul told her.

When they were dressed they came back to the fire. The log was burning down, and the afternoon outside was darkening. Paul turned the radio on.

"Tell me," he began, "if you can be like this when you and I are together, how can you be happy with anyone but me? I'm not speaking of these last tragic months. I'm excluding those."

Anna considered and answered slowly. "What is being 'happy'? I have peace, warmth and order. I am busy, I am loved."

"I know I said in the car that I wanted no grave talk today and that I wouldn't press you for anything but—marry me, Anna."

She shook her head. "I'm tied, Paul. Don't you see? I think of Maury and one day, perhaps, his little boy—"

He interrupted. "You can't live for what is gone or for a hope that may never come true! And don't you owe yourself anything *now?*"

"I do owe myself something, that's just it. I couldn't cut myself away from my family and live."

"But how can you weigh anything—anything at all—against this afternoon? You don't think I'm *fond* of Marian? But I am! She's a fine person and I would do anything to keep her from harm. Yet we could part as friends, with decent feelings. Knowing that she was well and would never lack care, I could put her out of my mind. And she would do the same with me."

"But I—I should be thinking of Joseph every day of my life!"

Paul sighed. It was a grieving sound from deep inside. "I hope he knows what he has."

"He does. He loves me. He believes in me."

The fire crackled as it burned out; music sang tenderly from the radio. And Anna cried out in pain. "Paul, tell me, how is it possible to care so much for two different men in such different ways? Is there something wrong with me?"

"You've just said it yourself. 'In such different ways,' you said. Here, put your head back on my shoulder."

So they sat until the light left the sky. The fire was a sprinkling of sparks in ash. The music, having risen to a passionate finale, came to a stop.

"I'm going back tomorrow," Paul said quietly.

She sat up straight. "Not tomorrow? But why?"

"The *Mary* returns at midnight. I only came to see you, Anna. I have to get back."

"All this way to see me? That was the only reason?"

"Reason? It wasn't a thing I reasoned out. It was something I had to do." And, standing up, he gave her his hands to pull her to her feet. "Come Anna, my Anna. It's time to go."

Today was mine, she thought, alone in the silent apartment, for neither Joseph nor Iris had yet come home. It was for me. I know I am rationalizing, finding a pardon for what I have been taught is wrong. And inasmuch as deceit is always wrong, it was wrong. But we are flesh, and it was inevitable. We are acted upon far more than we act.

The door will close with a hollow thud when Joseph comes in. He is coughing again. Very likely he will have the flu for the third time this year; he strains himself; he works far too hard; I tell him to stop it and I don't want him to strive; it was good to have things but there's nothing I want at the price that he is willing to pay. Yet I can't stop him.

Iris is earnest, prolix and troubled. There's nothing I can do to make her what young girls are supposed to be: genial and rosy with dreams. Yes, I was such a young girl, rosy with dreams, but perhaps I was foolish. Anyway, I can't change Iris.

Things happen. Things are. I am I, torn in two directions. Shall I ever see Paul again? I believe that I shall, but I can't really know. Tomorrow night he will set out across the ocean, into a thousand dangers. He will wait, he says, for the message that I have changed my mind. It will not come, Paul. It will not come.

But I shall not forget today. The other time I scrubbed myself in the bathtub; now I cherish the feel of your flesh on mine. I was young that other time and the world was either black to me or it was white: a simple view, with nothing in between. Now I know it is not like that, although Joseph always says it is. Perhaps Joseph is right? But if he is, I can't help that either. Today was mine.

I have hurt no one. I shall hurt no one.

"Oh Maury! Iris, Joseph—" she said aloud.

The front door opened with a key and Iris let herself in. "You're still reading? Is Papa home yet?"

273

As always, she asked for Papa.

"No, he'll be late tonight." Anna got up and crossed the room. "Iris," she said, pushing the girl's hair back and kissing her forehead.

"Mama, what is it? Is anything wrong?"

"No, no. It's only that you mean so very much to me, my darling."

Iris was startled, perhaps embarrassed. "Well, but I'm all right, Mama."

"Nothing must ever happen to you. Nothing, do you hear?"

"But nothing will! Go to bed, Mama! Take a book and you'll fall asleep reading. Go on, do."

Sleep. Yes, sleep, if it comes, if it wants to come. One cannot command that, either. Sleep comes and peace comes with it, if it wants to. The thoughts roll in, pour in: Iris, Joseph, Maury. And Eric. And Paul. They surge, they beat, they crowd like waves of the vast ocean and peace doesn't want to come.

26

One day the mood stirred again—her 'cleaning fits,' Joseph called them—and ever since the mood had come over her Anna began to work on closets and shelves, rooting in drawers that had been untouched for the last few years.

The lower drawer of the desk in the hall was stuffed with papers: postcards from friends in Florida, receipted bills, letters, wedding invitations. One was from a name she didn't even recognize, out of the years when people gave lavish entertainment to other people whom they hardly knew. Throw those out. Here was a pile of letters from Dan in Mexico: most of the people were Indians, he wrote; their monuments were marvelous, they still spoke their ancient languages. It would be a wonderful thing to see all that, to see Dan again, but they couldn't possibly afford it. Here were letters from Iris, the summer they had gone to Europe: "Dear Daddy and Mommy, When are you coming home?" Here was the wedding announcement from Eli in Vienna: "Elisabeth Theresa to Dr. Theodor Stern"; the pointed Gothic letters were like the peaked and medieval roofs of middle Europe. And these letters, this paper on which their hands had rested, was all that remained, the only trace of people swallowed up? She ran her fingers over the engraving—and put the card back into the drawer. Here next was a letter from Maury at Yale; shall she open it, shall she read it? No, some other day perhaps, and she put it too back into the drawer, knowing that there would never be another day when it would be easier to sift through any of these things.

After Maury had died, in that long wet spring of dirty snow when it seemed the sun would never come to comfort, that spring when the letters from Vienna had arrived—she remembered them lying white on the dining-room table where they were first opened, a summons to doom, a cry of horror, an accusation so terrible that it seemed the pages must burn the hand—all that spring she had walked and walked, back and forth, and ended always in what had been Maury's room. There she had gone into every corner looking for something that would tell her why. She had found one sneaker, a high school text of *Julius Caesar* with Maury's name in a flourish of bright green ink and a doodle of a fat man smoking a pipe, his teacher perhaps. The crumpled banner, *For God, for Country and for Yale*, had been there too, along with a Red Cross swimming card award for one hundred yards' back crawl or trudgen crawl; what was a trudgen crawl? She had found all these, but no answer, and had longed for work, hard work, carrying bricks or stones, something to break her nails, to tear her skin and to exhaust her.

They didn't talk about Maury anymore. On his birthday Joseph didn't say a word. Perhaps he didn't remember; he wasn't very good at remembering dates, but perhaps he did; with Joseph you could never tell. For a long time after Maury died it had seemed that Joseph was strengthened by his faith and Anna had wished she might feel whatever it was that made him able to say, and actually appear to mean, that we must praise God even in our suffering. "That's what the Kaddish is," he said, "a prayer of praise to God, and that's why we use it in time of death." And he tried to explain, seriously and at length, how we must pray that someday it will be given us to know why we suffer. "Surely there is a reason for it, as there is for everything," he said, and if she had not known him to be a man without hypocrisy and a totally honest person she would have scoffed.

Joseph believed in sin and retribution. But what was Maury's sin to deserve such punishment? Or the sin of the child who had lost his parents? Yes, she thought, if I believed in retribution I would have lost my mind by now. Because then all of it would be my punishment, for what I did.

She had read too much about primitive religion, too much Freud and his search for the father figure—or, to be exact, too many articles about them—not to have diluted her earliest faith. So now she could not truthfully say of herself: *I am a believing person*, nor yet, *I don't believe at all.* She was, rather, a person who wanted to believe and often did, but that was a very different thing from what Joseph was.

Yet how much had he hidden, did he perhaps still hide, from her? She remembered a night, weeks or months after it happened, when, lying in bed, she had stared at the white oblong of sky through the window; they were so high up there was not even the comfort of trees, and she remembered the trees of her childhood in the attic room where you looked out upon warm, dusty leaves, and in the windy seasons twigs scratched on the windowpanes. Here in this city you were in limbo, hung between earth and the cold enormous sky. Strange how she noticed such things after Maury's death; she had not thought of them before, but when you had sleepless hours the tags and remnants that slipped in and out of your head were astonishing. Lying there like that, she had felt something in the wide bed, then knew that what she had felt was a shaking cry and, putting out her hand, touched Joseph's face wet with tears. She had said nothing and only held him, and made no sound. Nor had he.

They never spoke of it afterward. Nor did Anna tell of her recurrent dream, always the same dream. She was walking into a room, known or unknown; there was a window, with a large wing chair at an angle so that she could see the crossed legs of a man sitting in it, but not his face. She came nearer, and when the man turned she could see he was very young. He began to rise in greeting and she saw that he was Maury. "Hello, Mother," he said. The same dream over and over.

The gilded clock chimed in the bedroom; it still stood on Joseph's dresser. How perverse that, of all the gifts and gadgets which had come to them in their prosperous years, it should be just that clock which appealed to him the most! Not that its presence bothered Anna anymore; with or without it, she knew what she knew and felt the weight which had been placed upon her. She felt a stinging behind her eyes, and watched in the mirror as a swollen tear, slick as glycerine, filled one eye and slid over. How ugly we are when we weep! The grimace of sorrow, the spotted red skin stretched over the animal skull! And when we see how ugly we are the tears come faster.

The house was so still. Iris would be home soon; she must have been delayed after school. She had gone to work two years ago at her first job, teaching fourth grade. Jobs were easy to find because all the young men were in the army. Iris was a fine teacher; she would do anything well, for she had Joseph's commitment to hard work. It was good for her to be earning her own money and to clothe herself, not that she cared very much about clothes. Too bad that in just these years of her youth the men were all gone! If only she were a little older or even a few years younger, for surely the war would be over soon. But she was just in the middle years, twenty-three, and there were so few men left at home. There was one odd small fellow who taught in her school, a reject of the army and, not to be unkind, of much else besides. He was the only man who had ever called Iris more than two or three times. Friends gave names of men stationed in the area; Ruth's daughters invited her to meet men, but they rarely called back. Ruth's daughters! With all they had gone through, none of them as bright as Iris, and not all that much better looking, either, all of them were married. Often Anna met them at their mother's, wearing the harried look of over-worked motherhood, which is a mask for their satisfaction and their pride. But whatever it was that they had and Iris lacked, she wasn't suddenly going to acquire it now.

Who will care for her? Who will love her? She's not all that lov-able. Sometimes I want to put my hand out to her but she will only shrink from my touch. She always does. There is no enmity between us, never a word, now that she is a woman; still, I know, as one knows such things, that she doesn't want me to touch her. Ruth says she is jealous of me; I wish Ruth hadn't said it. Sometimes Ruth says things that are too intimate and I am not prepared for them. Yet perhaps it is true; can it be true?

Jealous of me. And Anna put her hands to her heated face.

Days go by sometimes when I don't think of it and then suddenly it strikes me. Like the times when Joseph says, so lovingly, "I think she looks like me, don't you think so, Anna? She certainly isn't like you." No, and not like Joseph, either. Those eyes, the nose, the long chin— He and his mother, all over again. Only without their poise and pride, poor little soul! Almost as if she knew she was born wrong. My fault. My fault.

If I had these thoughts every day I think I'd go mad. But time, as they always say, is merciful and so it has been. One finds a way to favor a wound, to spare a crippled leg. Just once in a while comes a misstep and a cruel thrust.

278

Last week at the picture gallery (Joseph doesn't really like exhibits, but he goes to please me, and besides, they're one of the few recreations that don't cost anything), I said, unthinkingly, "Goodness! I've seen that one lots of times before!" And Joseph said, "You couldn't have. It says this is the first time it's ever been on loan." And then I knew. The walled and fruited garden, trees spread flat against the wall, a woman in a white dress, reading. ("Take it to your room, Anna, books are meant to be used.") A book on a table, in a room in a house that I can't forget.

Four years it is since I saw him. There's been no word; no more cards go between us, since the only one he wants is one that will offer him what I can't give. So it is better this way.

The key turned in the front door. "Ma?" Iris called.

"In here, in my room," Anna called back cheerfully. It wasn't good for the girl to see that she was in a 'mood.' And she took an armful of clothes on hangers and laid them on the bed.

"What are you doing?" Iris stood tall and anxious in the doorway. The dark brown dress with the white collar made her neck look elongated. The dress was stern and clerical.

"Cleaning out closets. Look at these, they must be fourteen years old, above the knees! And here they are back again. If you keep things long enough they'll be new again," Anna said, prattling, feeling a need in Iris to be met with unemotional, trivial words. The world is good, it's not all that frightening and everything is manageable, such prattle said.

"Where's Pa?"

"He'll be late. He and Malone went to Long Island to look at some more property. Their potato farms."

"He works too hard. He's not that young anymore," Iris said darkly.

"It's what he wants to do."

"I won't be having dinner. Carol's invited me to her house."

"Oh, nice. Is it a party?"

"No. We're just going to the movies together."

"Oh, nice." That was the second time she had said that and it sounded stupid. "Are you going to change?"

"No. What's wrong with this dress?"

"Nothing. I just asked."

"Then I'll be going. I think I'll walk, I want some air. What are you smiling at?"

279

"Was I? I was just thinking, you do have a lovely voice. It's a pleasure to hear you talk."

"You're funny," Iris said. "Your daughter's twenty-three years old and you're just noticing her voice." But she was pleased.

Really, her face was attractive when she was pleased about something. It was a fine, intelligent, gentle face. Yet something to which other human beings are drawn was missing. There are children in the kindergarten who stand aside while the others fight and play. Why? What is missing? Whatever it is, one learns early that it isn't there. Wanting it, trying and wanting so much, one develops a timid posture, smiles too eagerly, talks too much out of a fear that silence is boring and dull. It *is* boring and dull.

Oh, my children, my fairy-tale children who were never born, grouped around me, their mother, smiling in some eternal sunshine! I can't do anything for you, Iris; I couldn't for Maury, or for Eric, either.

A gust of wind struck like a stone against the window and Anna got up to draw the curtains shut. The pane was cold as ice. You could almost feel the cold upon the river and the streets below. She thought: It's colder where Eric is. I should hate it; I like to be warm. But perhaps he will grow up loving it. In a flash she saw him in sweaters and knitted caps, on a sled or on skis. She saw all of that, but not his face, which she did not know.

"Please don't send any more gifts," they had written. "It will soon be too hard to explain."

"I don't give a damn," Joseph said.

He wouldn't know now what love went with the yellow wagon and the stuffed cat, but later, when he was grown, he would remember these things for the joy they had given and, by then, he would know who had sent them. When he was old enough to read they would send books and the giving of books would tell him something about them, what sort of people they were.

"I have to stop this," Anna said aloud. "It's been going on all day, a wasted, useless day. I have no right to waste a day. There is nothing I can change."

She went into the bathroom and brushed her hair. Thank goodness it was still dark red. People said she looked years younger than her age. Anyway, the forties weren't old these days. Her hair made an oval frame about her face. She wondered how different her life might have been without her beautiful hair; perhaps no one would have noticed her! The speculation made her smile, appealing to some fortunate dash of irony or humor which was, she knew, the only thing that saved her from her own romanticism.

Then she went into the kitchen and made a cup of tea and some toast with jelly. She sat there stirring the sugar in the cup; the click of the spoon was a homely, reassuring sound in the silence. Tomorrow was Red Cross day again. Perhaps a troopship would be sailing. They never knew until the last minute, when they were summoned to the docks to stand while the young men filed past toward the gangplank, pausing for their cup of coffee and their doughnut. The last time it had been the *Queen Mary* going out, stripped and darkened for her race across the Atlantic. She remembered that young man on the dock; when Anna handed the cups she rarely looked at their faces, and this was partly out of haste but also because she didn't want to look at them, knowing where they were going. This time, though, she had looked up and been so startled to see Maury's face, even the separation between the two front teeth, and the eyebrows rising in an inverted 'V' to give the face a faintly wistful gaze. She had held the cup an instant in the air between them, and then he had taken it. "Thank you, ma'am," he'd said in flat Texas speech, and turned away.

Enough! She got up and emptied the rest of the tea into the sink, took an apple and a book, went into the living room and turned on all the lamps. She was sitting there with the apple core and the book in hand when Joseph came home with Malone.

"Let me fix you a drink," Joseph said to Malone.

"Just a quick one. Mary's waiting up for me." He sat down heavily and as quickly jumped up. "I've got Joseph's chair."

"Goodness, no. Sit wherever you want."

A good man. Going quite gray, looking much older than Joseph, although he wasn't that much older.

"You seem especially thoughtful, Anna."

"Do I? I was remembering the first time I saw you, up on the Heights. Joseph brought you in, carrying your plumber's tools. You were going into business together."

"I remember the day."

"And the war was just ended. It felt more like a war then, I was

281

thinking, with all the songs and parades. This time it seems like just suffering and getting it over with. We've learned more, I guess."

Malone said, "My boys are in places I never heard of. I looked some up on the map, took me ten minutes to find them."

I know that my son is dead and I've learned to live with the knowledge; I've had to. But Malone is tortured every day: Are my sons still alive this morning and will they be alive by tonight? "How's Mary?"

Malone shrugged. "Worried, as everyone is. One thing's good, though: Mavis is taking her vows in June. That's something Mary prayed for, and thank God it's one thing that's come true."

"I'm happy for her," Anna said truthfully. Mary Malone had been praying that one of her daughters would enter a convent and at least one son become a priest. So half of her prayer had been answered, and for that Anna was glad, although for the life of her she would never understand it.

Joseph came back with the drink. "You know what I was thinking on the ride home? I was reminded of when we started out together, Malone. We had nothing but energy and hope, and it's not a hell of a lot different now."

Malone sighed. "Except we've learned a few things in between." He raised the glass. "This drink's to us! If we don't make it this time—"

Anna asked, "What do you mean?"

"Didn't he tell you? We bought the land, three hundred acres of potato farms."

"I always thought you were joking about the potato farms."

"No joke," Joseph explained. "There's no building going on now, but after the war there'll be ten years or more to make up for. You remember, when the Bronx River Parkway opened in 1925, how they started building houses, how the towns spread out? It'll be the same after the war, only more so, because the population's bigger. And the prices will soar. That's why we're taking every penny—and I mean penny—we can lay our hands on. . . . After this I've got my eye on a farm in Westchester. I want you to go out with me on Friday, Malone." His words snapped briskly, his alert eyes snapped and he looked six feet tall. "Listen to me," he went on, "there's going to be a whole new way of life. People are going to move out of the cities. There'll be a big demand for low apartment buildings with green space between them. There'll be a need for shops. People won't want to go into the city to the stores, so we'll bring the stores to them. I predict that every one of the major New York department stores will have suburban branches within ten years after the war."

"You talk as if the war were going to be over tomorrow," Anna said. "We've got a long way to go yet, it seems to me."

"True. But I want to be ready. We'll have something for your boys to do when they come home," Joseph said, turning to Malone with a smile.

The men stood up and went to the door. "Give my love to Mary. I'll let you know what time Friday."

Anna put out the lights and they went to the bedroom. "The salt of the earth," Joseph said.

"There's something sad about him, I always think."

"Sad? I don't know. Of course he's got a lot on his mind and always has. It's no cinch to raise seven children."

"I suppose not."

"Still," Joseph said, drawing off his shoes, "still, I wouldn't have minded having that many. I think I could have managed."

"You would have. Sometimes I believe you could manage anything."

"You mean that? That's the nicest thing you could have told me. A man likes to think his wife has faith in him. And I'll confess, Anna. Lately I feel young again! I feel I'm going to accomplish big things, to put us on top of the world."

She had a vague, floating sensation, hard to define. It was almost a fear, a fear of challenge, of conflict and tension. She thought of the breathless rush of their first ascent, how hard he had worked, and all of it come to nothing. She wanted to say, We've had enough of that; let us live quietly in a small way, with no more large undertakings, no more feelers put out into a cutthroat world. And she said, not knowing how else to express all of that, "Joseph, we don't need to be on top of the world. There's nothing the matter with the way we are right now."

"Come on! Nothing the matter? We've lived this meager existence for almost thirteen years! We haven't been any farther than Asbury Park! I want to move out and up. Some day, not too far off, I want to own a house with ground around it. I've got a head full of plans for us."

283

"A house? Now, at our age? It's not as if we had a family to rear. What would we do with a house?"

"Live in it! And what do you mean by 'our age'? Look at yourself! You're a young woman still."

"Are you really serious about the house?"

"Not now, not yet, but as soon as I can."

"Iris wouldn't want to leave the city."

"Iris will come, and if she doesn't, she has her own life to live. Anyway, she'll probably be married in a few years."

"I don't think so. I worry about her so much; I don't always tell you."

"I know how you worry. But you can't be all mother forever."

"You're a fine one to talk! You don't worry?"

He laughed ruefully. "You're right. We're a pair of worriers. I suppose we're no different from other parents. No, I'll correct that. Everybody isn't like us and maybe they're right, and we're wrong. People owe something to themselves, not just to their children."

From her dressing table she could see him in the mirror. He had laid the newspaper down and was sitting up in bed, watching her.

"I like your new hair style," he said.

Since the war began people had started to wear their hair high over the forehead in a pompadour, then flowing softly over the ears. Her mother had worn it that way. More and more Anna saw her mother in herself, or, at least, what she thought she remembered of her mother.

"I didn't think you'd notice," she said.

"Do I neglect you so much, Anna? I don't mean to."

She laid the brush down, a monogrammed silver brush from a long-ago birthday. "You don't neglect me."

"I don't want to," Joseph said seriously. "You're the heart of my life, though I don't say it well."

She looked away, down at the pattern of the carpet: three whorls of rose against beige, a spiral, a moss-green leaf, three whorls of rose.

"I'm very glad," she answered, "since you are the heart of mine."

"Am I? I hope so. Because I know I wasn't when we were married."

"You shouldn't say that!"

"Why not? It's true," he said gently. "It doesn't matter now, but don't deny it. Everything must be open and honest between us, always."

"I was a very young, very ignorant girl who didn't know a thing about life! Nothing at all, don't you understand?" Tears prickled and she wiped them roughly away. "Don't you understand?" she repeated.

"Now that we're talking about it, I'm not sure I do understand everything. I've felt—I feel—there are things I still don't know about you."

Fear that was almost panic washed through Anna. "Why? What can you possibly not know?"

He hesitated. "Well, as long as we're talking, I'll tell you. Do you know when I was really beside myself?"

"I can't imagine," she lied.

"It was the time when Paul Werner sent you that picture, the one that was supposed to look like you. I tried not to let you see it but I was pretty frantic inside."

"But that was—that was years ago! And I thought we had talked it all out and settled it then!"

"I know we did, and I suppose it's foolish of me to let it stay in my head. But I can't seem to help it."

"It's a pity to make yourself miserable for nothing," Anna said softly.

"You're absolutely right. But tell me just once again, and don't be angry: did you love him? I won't ask whether he was in love with you, because it's obvious that he was, and besides, I don't mind that. I only want to know whether you loved him. Did you? Anna?"

She took a deep breath. "I never loved him." (I went through agonies of longing, and often I still do. But that's not the same, is it? *Is it?*)

I wonder what it would be like for me now if I were married to Paul. Would I feel that he needed me the way Joseph does? Does perfection—and it was perfection—would it, can it, last?

Joseph was smiling. "I believe what you tell me, Anna."

"You won't bring it up again? It's really finished and over?"

"Finished and over."

She thought, if only I could feel sure of that, Joseph! What I

285

would give not to have hurt you! You've become so dear to me, you couldn't know. And it's strange, because we are such different people. We don't even like or want the same things most of the time. Yet if it were necessary, I would die for you.

So, is that love? Love is only a word, after all, like any other word. If you repeat it a few times you take the life out of it. Tree. Table. Stone. Love.

"Anna, darling, put out the light and come to bed."

Her bathrobe dropped to the chair with a swish of silk. The wind struck again, shivering the windowpane. Feeling her way in the dark across the room, her thoughts flew as they had been flying all that day.

We are driven by random winds, blown and crushed under passing wheels, or lifted to a garden in the sun. And for no reason at all, that anyone can see.

BOOK
3

MEADOWS

27

Gramp had a blue Chrysler with a top that could be rolled down in fine weather, and usually was, even on such a cold, bright April day as this. He was a believer in fresh air as a medicament for everything. The car had been specially fitted for his almost power-less legs; the clutch worked by hand when the gears were shifted. They kept the car back of the house in what for past generations had been the barn and stables. When Gramp went out on his crutches, he reminded Eric of a crab, the way his legs jerked, the way he veered to swing himself up onto the front seat. When he was seated there with his cap on and his pipe in his mouth he looked like any-body else; you couldn't tell he was crippled. Maybe that's why he liked to go driving so much.

"Okay, young fella," he said, "be sure the door's closed; put the button down." He reached to fit the key into the ignition and sud-denly stopped. From the clump of trees between the barn and the lake came a sweet whistle: *"Pee-wee! Pee-wee!"*

Gramp put his finger to his lips. "Shsshsh . . . know what that is? That's a wood pee-wee. Close cousin to the eastern phoebe."

"What does it look like?"

"Gray, like the phoebe, except for two white bars on the wings." *"Pee-wee! Pee-wee!"*

"Could I see it if I got out now?"

"You probably could if you went in under the trees there verrr-y quietly and sat down and didn't move, not even a finger. I

289

wonder whether you could learn to use my binoculars? I don't know why not. Maybe tomorrow I'll show you how. They're on the second shelf of my cabinet in the library, next to my bird books."

The car slid into gear and down the driveway, turned through the gate posts and on down the road past his friend Teddy's. Next came Dr. Shane's big yellow house, then the Timminses' and the Whitelys' who kept saddle horses on their long fields. The car slid into the main street of Brewerstown.

"We need gas," Gramp said. "Reach me the ration book in the glove compartment, Eric, please."

The gas station man was stooping under a car. When he saw them he straightened up, wiping black, oily hands on a rag.

"Afternoon, Mr. Martin. Fill her up?"

"If you please, Jerry. I'm being extravagant today. It's Eric's birthday and we're going for a ride."

"Is that a fact? Happy birthday! You must be nine, or is it ten?"

"Seven," Eric said, very pleased.

"Seven! You're mighty big for seven!"

"Tell me, what do you hear from Jerry junior?" Gramp inquired.

"He'll be finished with basic training at Fort Jackson next week. I guess he'll be going over soon after that."

Gramp didn't answer. There was no sound but the whir of the pump; then it shut off, and they waited while Gramp handed over the ration book and some bills. Jerry tore out the stamps and handed the book back soberly.

"Well, good luck," Gramp said softly. "Remember me to Jerry junior. Tell him I expect him back. We all do, soon."

"Thanks. I will."

Gramp started the car again and they rolled down Main Street to the lake road.

"Where we going, Gramp?"

"I'm doing a will for Oscar Thorgerson. You know the big farm on the other side of Peconic? I thought I'd run over with some notes to see how he likes them. Then I can draw it up officially. It'll save him a trip in ploughing time and it gives you and me an excuse for an outing." He smiled down sidewise at Eric.

The road ran beside a strip of groves and summer cottages, still boarded up. There were glimpses of the lake between the trees. Then the road curved away from the lake, mounted a ridge of hills and straightened, dividing a wide valley with farms and fields on either side. The wind made a rushing noise like a waterfall in Eric's ears. A man was ploughing an enormous field; ahead of him it was dry tan with stubble of last year's corn; behind him it was dark and wet like melting chocolate. The great horses trudged steadily uphill.

"It's been years since I've seen horses pulling a plough," Gramp said.

"Why? How else can you do it?"

"With tractors. But now there's a war on and no gas, so the horses are out again. Say, look at that!"

A flock of birds soared and slid and whirled across the sky.

"Swallows," Gramp said. "Oh, birding has been one of the great pleasures of my life! I've sighted birds that people wait years to see. And when we lived in France I had to learn a whole new vocabulary, not just the names, but new kinds of birds that we don't have here. I remember the first time I heard and then saw a nightingale. It was a delight, a pure delight."

"Say something in French, please, Gramp."

"Je te souhaite une bonne anniversaire."

"What does that mean?"

"I wish you a happy birthday."

"It sounds pretty."

"French is a beautiful language. It's like music."

"Can you say anything you want to say in French?"

"Oh, yes. Although I'm not as proficient as I was when we lived there. You need to use a language or it slips away from you."

"I'd like to go to France. Are the trees and houses and everything the same as they are here?"

"Well, yes, and then again, no. I mean, trees are trees and houses are houses, aren't they? But there are differences. Someday you'll go and see."

"Will you go with me?"

"I'm afraid not, Eric. It would be too hard for me to travel with these crutches."

"Then I won't go either. I'll stay with you."

His grandfather took one hand off the wheel and covered Eric's hand with it. "You'll go and see things. I want you to. And I'll wait for you to come back. I'll be here waiting." He withdrew his hand. "I was going to surprise you, but I can't keep a secret. Gran and I have a surprise for your birthday. It's a present that you can't have

291

until the middle of the summer. Around the Fourth of July, I should think. Oh, don't look disappointed! We've got other things for you that you'll get at your birthday dinner tonight. But this big present that you have to wait for—can you guess what it is?"

Eric frowned. "No, I can't. What is it?"

"Something you've been wanting very much. Something you've been asking for."

A smile started somewhere in the back of Eric's throat and then bubbled up to his eyes and lips. "A dog? A puppy? Is it, Gramp, a dog? Really?"

"Yes siree, a dog. And I mean a dog of dogs. A prince. A great big Labrador retriever like Dr. Shane's."

Eric bounced on the seat. "Oh, where is it? Where are you going to buy it? Can I see it now?"

"That's one of the reasons I took you along. Mr. Thorgerson's lady dog is going to have puppies any day now. The reason you have to wait is that it'll be too tiny and young to take away from its mother for a while. But as soon as it can eat by itself out of a dish we'll come and get it."

"Oh, Gramp, oh, Gramp, I want a boy dog! I want to name him George."

"That's settled then. George."

A long lane led off the road between fences. The house was attached to the barn, making an 'L' with the barns and sheds. Chickens scratched under the wet and scattered straw. Gramp stopped the car. A moment later Mr. Thorgerson, in rubber boots up to his hips, came around the corner.

"Seen you coming up the lane. Been fixing my pump and got myself soaked," he said. "How you, Mr. Martin? How you, young man?"

"Fine, thank you, Mr. Thorgerson."

"I've brought these papers for you to look over," Gramp said. "You and your wife can think about them for a few days, and then if you're sure this is what you want, then give me a call. I'll have it drawn up properly and you can sign."

"Good enough. Let me go into the house and wipe my hands 'fore I dirty them up." He leaned over and whispered something in Gramp's ear.

"Is that so?" Gramp looked pleased. "Well, I'll tell you, I wasn't able to keep the secret. I told Eric on the way over so he knows all

292

about it. What do you think, Eric! Lady had her puppies this morning, and if you'll be very quiet and not disturb her Mr. Thorgerson will take you in and let you look."

The mother lay with her puppies on a soft pile of blankets in a corner of the kitchen. Stretched in a panel of sunshine they made a black fur tangle like a rug. The puppies, not much larger than mice, Eric thought, mewed and wriggled one over the other.

"They're just starting to get hungry," Mrs. Thorgerson whispered. She stood looking over Eric's shoulder. "She's going to be a good mother, she's so gentle. I've been working here in the kitchen all morning and she never minds a bit when I step near."

"She knows you won't hurt her puppies," Eric said wisely.

"Which one do you want?" Mr. Thorgerson asked.

"I can't tell. They all look alike."

"He's right, Oscar. You'll have to come back in a couple of weeks when they're a little older and then you'll pick the one you want."

I'll put out my hand, Eric thought, that's what I'll do. And the one that crawls toward it, if he's a boy, is the one I'll take because I'll know he likes me. And I'll bring him home and he'll sleep in a basket in my room, maybe even on my bed. And we'll be friends and I'll be so good to him. Maybe that one?

They all laughed. One of the puppies, all tiny, wet, blind things, but this one a bit stronger than the rest perhaps, rolled over and, with a piping squeal, shouldered another one out of its place at the mother's nipple.

"Would you like a jelly doughnut?" Mrs. Thorgerson asked.

"Yes, please, I mean thank you, I would."

"They're still warm. . . . Does your grandmother allow you to?"

"Oh, yes! Sometimes I go to Tom's Bakery in town after school. But Gran says they're greasy. She doesn't like me to have them, only if they're homemade."

"Well, these are certainly homemade," Mrs. Thorgerson said. "Here, sit down and have a glass of milk while Mr. Thorgerson goes outside and talks to your grandfather."

The kitchen smelled pleasantly of sugar and hot baking. There were plants on the windowsill next to the table where he was given his milk and two doughnuts on a white plate. It was nice to eat in the kitchen, handy to the icebox and the stove, more comfortable than their dining room at home, where you had to be careful not to spill anything on the carpet or on the shiny wood table. You had to keep everything on the place mat with its lace border and the mat was so small. But at home only Mrs. Mather, the housekeeper, ate in the kitchen.

Mrs. Thorgerson stood looking down at him. "Was that good?"

"Very good, thank you." It was good, but still he liked the ones at Tom's Bakery better, to tell the truth. Only he didn't tell the truth, of course.

"It's a long time since my boys were home to eat at this table," Mrs. Thorgerson said, sighing a little.

They went out to the car. Mr. Thorgerson was leaning against the fence talking to Gramp. "He'll ruin the country. Something for nothing, these loafers want. Mark my words, this young fellow here will pay for it. All the generations that come after us will be left with the bills."

"Roosevelt again!" his wife said. "You raise your blood pressure, harping on that man. I swear you do, every time."

"Me too, then, Mrs. Thorgerson," Gramp said. "Any man who's worked hard and knows the value of a dollar can't help but feel disgusted with things. Time he got out anyway, war or no war, before he ruins the country. We've had ten years of him and that's ten years too many. Let me see, is that jelly on your face? Here's a handkerchief." He took a white handkerchief from his breast pocket. He was so clean, Gramp was, even a little jelly bothered him.

"He had jelly doughnuts," Mrs. Thorgerson said.

"Well, that was nice, wasn't it, Eric? Doughnuts and a new puppy. What a day!"

"Gramp," Eric asked, when they were out on the road, "what did you mean when you said Roosevelt was going to sroon the country?"

"Sroon?" Gramp looked puzzled. "You mean ruin! That means to spoil."

"Oh. Why is he going to?"

"Well, that's a bit hard for you to understand. It's just that we don't agree with the way he manages things. We think another man would do a better job."

"What other man?"

"Almost any other man, I should say."

"Do you hate him? I think Mr. Thorgerson hates him. He was awfully angry."

"Not hate. We have to respect him because he is the President.

But we think he desecrates the office. Do you understand? Desecrating is like—well, it's like having no respect, wearing your hat or laughing out loud in church. Something like that. Do you see what I mean?"

Eric nodded, and thought of the familiar face in the newspaper, with the cigarette tilted upward out of the side of the mouth.

Gramp said seriously, "It's a wonderful thing to be an American, Eric. It's a kind of sacred trust, do you know what I am trying to say? It's having something you love very much that was given to you by your family and you must take the best care of it so that you can hand it over to your children unspoiled.

"Ours is a very old family, Eric. Our people came here when the English king still owned this land, when Indians camped here. This road that we're on was one of their trails to what now is called Canada. They came here when it was all forest, hundreds and hundreds of miles of trees." He swept an arm out. "All you could see here was dark trees. And they cut the trees and cleared fields, built cabins, planted crops. It was hard, hard work, much harder and more dangerous than anything you can think of that anybody does today."

"Did the Indians kill any of them? With tomahawks?"

"I'm sure they did. There's plenty in the history books about that. There were forts all through this state. Fort Stanwyx, Fort Niagara. Forts are where the people went for safety when the Indians attacked."

"But there aren't any Indians now."

"No, that was a long time ago. After a while everything was calm here and people made beautiful big farms like Mr. Thorgerson's. Our own family were all farming people, except here and there a son went into some profession. I had an ancestor, let me see now, he would be your great-great—no, your great-great-granduncle, he was one of the engineers who worked on the Erie Canal. I remember hearing from my grandfather about that uncle. He was present on the day, November 4, 1825, when Governor De Witt Clinton poured a keg of Lake Erie water into the Atlantic Ocean. The canal joined the waters of the lake with the ocean, you see. A great piece of work, that was. And we had soldiers, of course; we've had men in all the country's wars. And schoolteachers and lawyers."

295

"That's what you are! A lawyer!" Eric cried triumphantly.

"Yes, I'm a lawyer and I've always been proud of my profession. But I never forget that my origins were in the soil, on the land, the basis of everything. My origins and your grandmother's too. Her family is as old as mine."

Eric remembered something. "Is that her father in the picture? The one over the mantel in her room?"

"No, no, child, that's her grandfather. Your great-great-grandfather. He fought in the Civil War." Abruptly, Gramp swung the car around. "We're only a couple of miles from Cyprus. I want to show you something there."

The car rode lightly along a level stretch of road between apple orchards, faintly white. "Cyprus is the county seat. That's where the courthouse is and the Civil War monument. They've a statue there put up to honor the men from this area who fought in the Civil War. And they've written on it the names of the ones who were killed in the war. You'll see that man's name there."

"Whose name?"

"The man in the picture in your grandmother's room," Gramp said patiently.

The courthouse stood back on a stretch of lawn. A walk with rows of stiff red flowers, tulips, Eric knew, ran to the front where a kind of porch was held up by plump white wooden columns. On one side of the lawn stood a tall flagpole. The flag made a snapping noise in the wind. On the other side, in the center of a concrete circle, was a statue of a crouching soldier wearing a kind of square cap; he was pointing a gun, and the pedestal on which he was placed had names cut in the stone on all four sides.

"Walk over there," Gramp said. "The names go by the alphabet. You can find the 'Bs', can't you? Then look for a long name, it's almost at the top of the 'Bs'. Bellingham. Go look. It's too hard for me to get out of the car."

Eric walked over, found the 'Bs' without any trouble and was proud that he could read the names. The first one was Banks. Then came Bean. That was funny, because you could also spell it without the 'A.' Some of the kids in his class got mixed up by things like that, but letters never bothered him. They were easy. Here it was: Bellingham. He stood there a minute looking at it, and at the way the shadow of the soldier's stone arm fell right in the middle of the Belling—. Then came a comma, and another name: Luke. He knew that it was like his prayer that Gran said: "Matthew, Mark, Luke and John, bless the bed that I lie on."

He ran back to the car. "I found it! I found it! It says Luke Bellingham, right near the top."

"Good. I knew you could. Be sure to put the lock down, that's it. Yes, that was your Gran's grandfather," he said, as they turned around the square back to the road they had come on. "He was at the second Battle of Bull Run, Antietam and many more. That's when Abraham Lincoln was the president."

"Did he deserate like Roosevelt? Lincoln, I mean?"

Gramp laughed. "Desecrate? I should say not! He was one of the greatest men in the world, Eric. When you are a little older I shall tell you about him, and give you some books about him. Anyway, now you've seen the name of your ancestor cut in stone. Gran's name was Bellingham, you know, before she married me."

"And your name is Martin."

"That's right."

Eric considered a minute. There was a question he had on his tongue. Then he asked it. "Why isn't my name Martin, too? Why is my name Freeman?"

"Because. Because people take their father's names."

"Why do they?"

"Because that's the law. That's the way it is."

"Who makes the laws?"

"A lot of men are chosen to think up the laws for us. They sit and talk about things and then vote to decide. They're called the legislature."

But he didn't really want to know about that. "Did the legislature decide what my name had to be?" he persisted. Something nagged at him. He didn't know exactly why he felt that something was a secret.

"Not just your name. Everybody's."

Eric thought there was a change in Gramp's voice. Was he cross about anything? But no, he looked at Eric and smiled and said with his teeth locked around the stem of his pipe, "I'm going to put some music on the radio. There's a program that goes on at four."

Piano music was plucked out of the air. They were riding along on the smooth road and above their heads the leaves were starting to come out, unraveling small sheaves of yellowish-green. Piano music tinkled through the leaves.

Freeman. His father's name was Maurice Freeman. He had asked Gran once, "Was my father French, Gran?"

"No, he wasn't French." And her mouth closed in the straight line it made whenever he asked for something he knew he wasn't going to get, like permission to sleep overnight in the woods, or a third piece of pie. *No, you may not.* Her mouth would shut in a straight line like a dresser drawer closing tightly into its frame. *Snap. Click.*

"I thought the name sounded French. Because of Gramp's friend in France that he always tells about. His name was Maurice, too."

"He wasn't French."

"What was he, then?"

"Why, American, of course. American."

"Oh. Can I see a picture of him?"

"You could if I had one."

"Why haven't you got one?"

"I don't know why I haven't. I just haven't, that's all. Oh, Eric, now I have to go back and count my stitches again, you've got me so mixed up." She was always knitting sweaters for him like the navy blue one he was wearing today. He didn't like her sweaters. They itched. The back of his neck itched now, thinking of it.

He had been very stubborn that day. "If you haven't got a picture, tell me what he looked like."

"I don't remember what he looked like. I only saw him once."

He had been about to ask, "Why?" But he opened his mouth and closed it again. In some way he knew that she would not have an answer for him. There was a blankness there, an end, like being closed in someplace and trying to get out, or being shut out and trying to get in. You might try and try but there was no way. He felt that with no particular emotion, only a kind of puzzlement.

Now his mother was different. Pictures of her were everywhere, photographs in silver frames on desks and dressers, and a painting over the piano, wearing a short white dress and a ribbon bow on her head. She was in leather albums, snapped on the deck of an ocean liner with a life preserver in back: *S. S. Leviathan*, it said. "That was the year we went to live in France," his grandparents told him, bending over into the lamp light on the library table, turning the pages, going too slowly and boring him with things he didn't care about. "That's the place we took in Provence one summer. See, those are olive trees, and there in the background, see those terraces? That's how they grow grapes. Your mother acquired a Provençal accent that summer; she already spoke French like a native, anyway."

He liked the picture of her as a baby, maybe two years old, sitting on the front step with a big white collie. There above her head was the brass knocker with the head of a lion. He went outside and, when nobody was looking, sat down in the same spot under the knocker and rubbed his palms over the stone step, this very step where she had sat, his mother; and felt that maybe some of her was still there on the stone; and felt not sad, not regretful, but only curious.

He could barely remember when he had first known that his position and his life were not like the other children's whom he knew. Somebody, Gran? Gramp? Mrs. Mather, the housekeeper? Somebody had told him his parents were dead. He was an Orphan. That was wrong, though. In fairy tales like *The Little Match Girl* and *Cinderella* an Orphan was a sad person. An Orphan was hungry and had to sleep in doorways. How did you sleep in doorways? Where did you stretch your legs and wouldn't people trip over you, going in and out?

But he, Eric, had a house and a big room in it with a fireplace and a bed with a quilt that had animals printed on it, and a shelf of books, and a cupboard where he kept his Erector set and Lincoln Logs and his big dump truck and hook-and-ladder. And he had plenty to eat. They were always making him eat when he wasn't hungry. *You must finish that good hot cereal before you go to school.* So how could he be an Orphan?

Because of the Accident, that was why. Something had happened in a car far away, in New York City. The car got smashed and after that he didn't have any father and mother. He had come here to live with Gran and Gramp. After the Accident. He saw it like that, in big letters. Like the letters on the monument: Luke Bellingham.

"Well, here we are," Gramp said, switching off the radio. "Hand me my crutches from the back seat, will you please, Eric?"

His grandmother came out of the house to help Gramp in.

299

"Why, I was worried about you, it's almost five o'clock and Teddy's here waiting for you."

"Oh, we had a fine time. Eric saw his new puppy that got born this morning, and we had a beautiful drive. I see you're all dressed up."

She had on a white silk blouse and her gold-and-pearl brooch. "Of course, it's Eric's birthday."

"Look what you've got!" Teddy shouted as soon as they came into the hall. "Look what you've got!"

An enormous carton lay on its side and half in, half out, was a bright red perfect car. It was big enough to sit in and pedal. It had headlights and a brass horn and bucket seats like a racing car.

Eric's heart stopped. "For me. You bought this for me."

"I didn't, silly!" Teddy said. "My present's still wrapped up in the dining room with your others."

"It's from Macy's in New York," Gran said. She turned to Gramp. "I thought it was those folding chairs you ordered, so I opened it."

"Couldn't you have—?"

"Teddy was with me. We opened it together and then it was too late."

"I see," Gramp said. "Well, you'll enjoy the car, I'm sure. Better go up and wash your hands and change. We'll be having dinner soon."

"I'll go home and put on my suit," Teddy said. "My mother says I have to wear my good suit because it's Eric's birthday."

"Yes, of course. Be back at six, Teddy," Gran said.

Eric shook his head. "I can't believe it."

"What can't you believe?" his grandmother asked.

"The puppy George and this car, all in one day."

"Ah, but you haven't seen everything yet!" Gran said gaily. "Go on up, dear, will you?"

His suit and clean underwear had been laid out on the bed. His Sunday shoes stood under the bed. He was so happy, so excited! The dog, the red car with the headlights from Macy in New York! He didn't know Macy but it surely was nice of him to send a present like that. "*Wheeeeeee,*" he said and turned a somersault on the rug near the bathroom, and then another and another, four of them before he reached the farther wall with a thump. He won-

300

dered where he would keep the car. In the garage, perhaps? He wanted to find out right now.

His grandparents' adjoining rooms were at the end of the hall. He could barely hear them talking. It was a very quiet house. "Don't ever call from one room to another," his grandmother always said. "If it's important enough to tell me, it's important enough for you to walk where I am."

He went down the hall. They were talking quietly in Gramp's room. Suddenly his grandmother's voice grew louder and he heard her say, "But I couldn't secrete it! How could I when Teddy was there? He would have told Eric. I'm sorry, James. It couldn't be helped."

"I thought they had agreed that it was for the child's own good that there be no contact. It's too confusing, too unsettling! They agreed, didn't they? So why don't they keep their agreement?"

"Well, they have kept it, really. I suppose they feel that a gift isn't—oh, I don't know, they must feel some need to give something."

"Awfully ostentatious! It must have cost a hundred dollars."

"I'm sure it must. Well, I'll write an acknowledgment and let it go at that. But I do feel a little sorry for them, James."

"I have one concern, and that's for Eric," his grandfather said firmly.

"Well, of course."

There was a rustling, as of someone rising from a chair. Eric scurried back to his room.

Why were they annoyed with Macy for sending the car? That was funny. Such a beautiful car! Better than anything Teddy had. And that was good, because sometimes Teddy made him angry. "Don't you feel awful not having any father and mother?" he would say. Well, he didn't feel awful at all. He had everything he wanted, Gramp and Gran gave him everything he wanted and they loved him. And he didn't feel awful at all! He stuck out his tongue at an imaginary Teddy. You haven't got a car like this, Teddy! And you haven't got a dog like George, either!

But it was a funny thing about Macy. He remembered last winter he'd got a pair of skates from him and it wasn't even Christmas. Gramp had said something to Gran. He'd thought then that they weren't pleased about the skates, but afterward he'd forgotten

301

about it. Anyway, he had the skates and now he had the car and it didn't matter really. Only, it was funny.

There were steak, fried onions and biscuits and all his favorite things. Teddy had given him a kite. Gran and Gramp had bought a sailboat that came up to his waist; he could sail it on the lake. Mrs. Mather had made a chocolate cake with white icing and seven candles. No, eight, because there had to be one to grow on. First she turned off the lights in the dining room. Then she brought it in with the candles flaring and everyone singing "Happy Birthday." Eric blew out the candles and cut the first slice.

"What did you wish?" Teddy wanted to know, but Gran said, "If you tell it won't come true," so he wouldn't tell. He really didn't know what he wished; there was nothing he wanted except that he knew he wanted it always to be now. Just the way everything was now.

"You must thank Mrs. Mather for the beautiful cake," Gran said. "Go into the kitchen after dinner and thank her."

So he went in to thank her and she bent down and kissed him. "Bless your heart," she said.

Then he and Teddy rode the red car. They took turns up and down the hall, while Gran and Gramp went to listen to Gabriel Heatter with the war news on the radio, the way they did every night. Every time Eric passed the door they looked up and smiled at him, his grandmother from the chair by the window where she sat with her shawl around her, for the house was chilly and they were saving heat. "A good citizen should," his grandfather said. He himself sat upright, intent on the news, in his own wing chair that smelled of leather-dressing, a clean sharp smell that was like Gramp's shaving lotion; his own smell that he always used, in the chair where he always sat.

Presently it was time for bed. Teddy's father came for him from across the road. And Eric went up to bed. Gran kissed him and folded the sheet around his shoulders.

"It was a lovely birthday, wasn't it?" she said, and turned out the light.

He lay there all warm and sort of floating away. It wasn't entirely dark yet. He could partly see the late spring evening past the window, and partly imagine the familiar landscape: the yard and the lawn, the hemlock grove, the thickets where you could be an Indian and the lake beyond. Peepers set up a sharp, sweet call, one note over and over. A bird, thinking perhaps that it was morning, whistled once and was still. Tomorrow he would find the phoebe and ride in the car, and sail the boat. He would have to get string, a terribly long, long string for the boat. Then he would eat up what was left of the birthday cake. Seven. Today I was seven. Sev—

The peepers throbbed.

28

J oseph and his reflection traveled down Madison Avenue together, going back to the office. Whenever he looked away from the afternoon press of taxis and buses, whenever a glass door swung open or a flame of opalescent sunlight struck a window, he saw a vigorous man in a gray suit walking fast, swinging his arms. He hadn't realized how high his arms swung.

He was in good shape. Didn't look his age. In the morning, after waking automatically at six, he did his calisthenics. He watched his diet, although not stringently: he didn't run to fat. Anna was envious; she would go for days on cottage cheese and salads to keep thin. A little weight wouldn't hurt her, he always said, and was told that his tastes were old-fashioned. Well, at fifty-five, why shouldn't they be?

Still, that wasn't old these days. It was hard to think that his father had been only two years older when he died, worn away, shuffling and bereft of will. That was the main thing, will. You got old when you lost it.

He ought to be, and he was, thankful down to the marrow that he hadn't lost his. He'd been able to build again from the ruins, or at least to make a promising start. It wasn't given to everyone to have a second chance. Poor Solly. Ruth was living now in three rooms that Joseph had let her have in that very first apartment house on the Heights, the one for which Anna had borrowed the money. That

304

house, he admitted with amusement, was a foolish kind of talisman to him. He didn't suppose he'd ever sell it. Anyway, Ruth was living there. She paid a small rent. He would have given it to her for nothing, but she wouldn't accept that and he admired her refusal. He would have done the same if the circumstances had been reversed. God forbid.

Waiting at Fifty-sixth Street for the light to change, he was shocked into a reminder of sadness by a window that still displayed the black-bordered photograph of Roosevelt, dead two weeks. It was a personal grief, the death of this president. A solemn grief: the funeral train from Georgia, the slow march down Pennsylvania Avenue, the horse with stirrups reversed. Symbolism of the fallen warrior. A brave man. He felt he would miss that man, his fine confident voice on the radio.

Yet there were people who had hated him . . . and not the very rich alone, those who thought of him as a traitor to his class! Joseph knew a workman who had lost twin sons in the war; he blamed Roosevelt, said we should never have gotten into the war. But that was nonsense; frantic, bitter, ranting. Understandable, but ranting all the same. Malone had lost a son-in-law, Irene's husband, killed at Iwo Jima, and now Irene had come back home with her two babies . . . not an easy thing for the Malones, what with teen-agers of their own still at home, but they never complained.

Irene's boy looked like Eric, or what they could remember of Eric when he was two. Joseph felt his mouth twist. Always that small involuntary twisting when certain things came to mind.

Don't think of them, then. Don't think of what can't be helped.

The light changed and the crowd poured across the street. Crowds looked different today from the ones you used to see in midtown New York. For one thing, they were larger. The city was so crowded that you couldn't get into a restaurant, couldn't get a hotel room. He'd had an architect come in from Pittsburgh last week and they'd had to put him up at home. People were jamming the shops; people who'd never had anything before the war were coming in to the fancy stores with cash to buy furs and pianos and diamond watches, never even asking the price of anything!

For me too, Joseph thought, and in a very limited way, it's been like the twenties all over. The land they had scrimped for during the late thirties—when Anna said they were crazy to go into real estate again—had doubled and tripled. They'd built three hundred houses for the workers at the Great Gulf Aviation plant on Long Island, just rolled them out in rows on the old potato fields and sold every one in eight weeks' time.

Then they had moved on and done it again.

Yes, like the twenties, except for a steadier caution. He'd never again feel as confident—and ignorant—as he had back then. He knew now what can happen.

Knew also what a terrible thing it is that there is so much wealth to be made out of human blood.

Still, that was the way of things. Now his desk and his head were full of plans again for undertakings they would start as soon as the war was over. They said it was only a matter of months. . . . Suburban shopping centers, he reflected; he ought to get to some of the big stores before anybody else did.

They had a good office now. Maroon carpet. Nice prints. Dignified, but not lavish. Anna would see to that. He smiled. She was always restraining him, Anna was, and she was probably right. Not that they could have afforded anything too rich anyway, the rent was so high. They were in a very good building, a prestigious address near Grand Central. Convenient for commuting, too, now that they'd got the house.

Let's see. Three months to the closing and a couple more to fix it up. They ought to be in by the end of September.

Anna hadn't wanted a house, but then, Anna never wanted very much of anything. She had her friends and her Friday afternoon concerts again, now that they had a few dollars to spare for things like that. She had her women's committees for half a dozen charities. And when she wasn't doing any of these, she read.

But he had been wanting a house for a long time. When the Malones bought a place in Larchmont a year ago he'd made up his mind. They had spent every fall and winter Sunday driving around Westchester. He reflected how perverse it is that when you haven't got a cent all you see are things you wish you could have; now that he had a good down payment and could afford something decent, they couldn't seem to find it. Maybe because they didn't really know what they were looking for? And then two weeks ago on one of those warm, windy days of April, they'd come upon this house and Anna had gone crazy over it.

He couldn't understand her. It was a big old place, probably in its eightieth year, with twelve—he'd counted in dismay and disbelief—

twelve gables and three chimneys. It had a spiral staircase, a turret, six carved marble fireplaces, even in the bedrooms, and a porch fringed with wooden lace. Name of heaven! Even the young man from the real estate agency had looked doubtful. Not a very good salesman. Brand-new and inexperienced, to wear his doubts on his face!

"What style do you call this?" Joseph had demanded of him.

"Well, sir, they tell me it's an authentic type, Gothic Victorian. I'd have called it gingerbread, myself. This was the Lovejoy family home," he had explained. "One of the oldest families in the area." And, irrelevantly, "I'm not from here, I'm from Buffalo. But I'm told they once owned a couple of hundred acres. The last one of the Lovejoys has a house over there, over the rise; you can't see it unless you go upstairs and look out over the trees. He wants to sell this old place off with two acres."

Anna spoke for the first time as they climbed the stairs. "It's like something in a book. Feel the banister," she said.

The dark old wood was worn as sleek as silk; they'd had the best materials in those days. But all these angles, nooks and crannies!

"Look here!" Anna cried. "This round room in the turret! This could be the most wonderful office for you, Joseph. You could spread your maps and—come, look at the view!"

On the lawn below, the hyacinths—or so Anna said they were— had come into bloom, rising out of a bed of last year's wet leaves. "A south terrace! It would catch the sun way into the winter, Joseph. You could wrap up in a steamer rug, the way we did on the ship, remember, and read—"

He noted that the cement was crumbling and the bricks were rotted away.

". . . up there on the hillside, those are apple trees. When they bloom it will be all white. Imagine opening your eyes and seeing that, the very first thing in the morning!"

He followed her downstairs. The agent and Iris, who had come along this day, followed him. The kitchen was in sorry shape. There was an old black monster of a stove. The icebox was in the entry, an enormous brown, scarred relic. The cabinets were so high that a woman would need a ladder to reach them. But the cabinets would all have to be ripped out, anyway. Hell, the whole kitchen would have to be ripped out.

"See," Anna cried. "They've a separate room with its own sink: I do believe it's meant for a place to arrange flowers! Yes, it is! Here are some old vases left on the shelf. Imagine having a separate room for flowers!"

She was talking like a not-too-bright child instead of a woman fifty years old. He'd never seen her like this before.

"Any house can have a separate sink for flowers, Anna," he said irritably.

"Any house can, but none of them do," she answered.

"It's got a thousand things wrong with it," he burst out. Ordinarily he would have had more tact in front of the agent; he'd been harassed often enough himself in this business to know how it felt. And, wanting some support, some confirmation, he turned to Iris. "What do you think?" Certainly Iris would be more practical, more cool in judgment than her mother was.

"You know," Iris said, "it does have a lot of charm, in spite of its faults."

"Charm, charm. What kind of talk is that? You're not talking about a woman!"

"All right, if you want another word, it has *character*."

"Character! Oh, for God's sake! Now can you possibly tell me what you mean by that?"

Iris had been patient. "It's original. As if the people who built it had done a good deal of thinking about what they wanted, so that it pleased *them*. It had meaning for *them*. It wasn't just a house stamped out by the hundreds to sell in a particular price range but to please nobody in particular."

"Hmpp," Joseph said. He had never been able to win an argument with his daughter. Never wanted to, was more the truth.

Anna cried, "Oh, Joseph, I love it!"

The young man waited without comment. Inexperienced as he might be, he was clever enough to know when he was winning and not to spoil it.

Joseph walked off by himself. He walked around examining the outside, the shaggy shrubbery, and the garage where horses had been stabled. He went down into the cellar. The coal furnace hovered in the corner like a gorilla. The vastness and the darkness reminded him of a dungeon in one of those castles through which Anna had dragged him when they were in France. He climbed back upstairs into the light with relief.

The bathrooms would all have to be torn out and replaced. With

308

these high ceilings it would take a lot of oil to heat the place. You could bet it wasn't insulated either. Heaven only knew what condition the plumbing was in! Probably corroded, and every time you ran the bath water or flushed a toilet the pipes would groan and shudder through the house.

But she loved it.

She never asked for things, he thought for the hundredth time. Never spent any real money except on books; her few extra dollars went to Brentano's. Sometimes on Fifty-seventh Street she would bring him to a halt in front of a gallery window and say, not complaining, just musing, "Now, if I were rich that's what I'd have," and she'd point to some picture of a child or a meadow. "If it costs anything within reason I'll get it for you," he'd tell her. And she'd smile and say, "That's a Boudin," or some such foreign name, French probably, since she loved anything French—"It's at least twenty-five thousand," she'd say.

She loved this house.

The roof was slate and in good condition. That at least would last forever. The house was probably cool in the summer too; the walls were a foot thick. They didn't build that way anymore, that was certain! Nice piece of land for the money too. Someday you could even sell that stretch up the hill where the orchard was and turn a fine profit. Land here was bound to soar, it was so near New York. Actually, it was worth the price for the land alone.

"Well, I'll think it over," he told the agent. "I'll call you in a couple of days."

"Very good," the young man said, adding predictably, "There's another couple very much interested. I think I really ought to tell you, not that I'm rushing you into a decision or anything. But they'll be making up their minds this week."

Naturally. Anna shouldn't have let him see her enthusiasm. A very poor way to do business.

"Well, I'll let you know," he'd repeated, and gone home and lain long awake thinking.

It did have a kind of elegance, something solid and real that belonged to another age. In a very small yet undeniable way it reminded him of those great stone houses on Fifth Avenue where he'd used to walk and gape and marvel at the beginning of the century. It would, he thought, it would make a setting for Iris. It was the kind of place that you saw in magazines, where old, distinguished families gave their daughters' weddings. Inherited wealth likes to be a little dowdy, out of fashion. He laughed at himself. Distinguished families! Inherited wealth! Still, perhaps it would do something for Iris, enhance her, put an aura about her that a West End Avenue apartment couldn't give?

His thoughts embarrassed him. They hurt him, too. As if his daughter were an item on sale! Yet, a girl needed to be married; who would take care of her through life, and when her father was gone?

There was something about Iris, his lovely, lovely girl. He'd tried to talk about her to Anna, but for some reason, Anna was never able to talk about Iris without such visible pain that he would drop the subject. She could talk more easily about Maury! He wished sometimes that he himself could speak openly to Iris but he couldn't do that, either. He couldn't ask: "What are you like when you're out with fellows? Do you smile, do you laugh a little?" Hah! Out with fellows! There was less and less of that every year. She was getting older: twenty-six. And the men were mostly away. He tried. That young widower he'd brought to dinner last winter. His wife had died of pneumonia. Might he not be looking for a fine, steady wife to mother his baby? But nothing had come of it.

So, maybe the house would make a difference.

He'd gone back three times to look at it that week, wavering toward the thought that he had really wanted something newer and more impressive, and back again to the fact that Anna loved it. In the end he had signed the contract of sale. It was like putting his name to a written blessing. Words like 'dear home' and 'peace' floated through his unashamedly sentimental head while he wrote his name.

He turned into his building and, waiting for the elevator, sought his name on the directory: Friedman-Malone, Real Estate and Construction. He put his shoulders back. Look forward.

"There've been a couple of calls," Miss Donnelly said. "I've put the messages on your desk. None of them urgent except one. A Mr. Lovejoy wants to see you this afternoon."

"I'm seeing the accountant at four. What Lovejoy? The man who owns the house? What does he want?"

"I've no idea. I told him you had a four o'clock appointment, but he said he'd come over at half past. He'd wait for you to see him at your convenience."

A gray-haired, quiet-voiced, Brooks Brothers type. "I don't want to waste your time or my own, Mr. Friedman. We're both busy men. So I'll get to the point. I've come to ask you to withdraw your offer for the house."

"I don't understand."

"The agent made an unpardonable error. He was supposed to have given preference to another couple, very dear old friends of ours, as a matter of fact. . . . He actually sold it right out from under them."

"I still don't understand. I gave my check and your agent signed the contract of sale."

"I've been in Caracas, just docked this noon and went home, but as soon as I learned what had happened I came right back to the city. I'd given the agent a power of attorney to sell the house, with the understanding that if my friends should decide they wanted it, it was to go to them, you see."

"Apparently they didn't want it, or he wouldn't have sold it to me, would he?"

"He was an inexperienced young fellow, substituting for his uncle who was in the hospital. I'm afraid he's been severely reprimanded for the mistake. I'm truly sorry."

Maybe this was an omen, a sign that the house was wrong for them. They could go out looking again, now that the weather was fine, and come up with something much more to his liking.

"I'm prepared to return your check with two thousand dollars' profit to you," Mr. Lovejoy said.

Joseph picked up his pen and tapped it on the blotter. Why should the man be so eager? There was something odd here. It was like feeling a presence in a dark room: you can't see it or hear it but you know something is there.

He fenced. "My wife likes the house."

"Ah, yes. These other people—the wife went to boarding school with my wife and it would mean a very great deal to them both if they could be neighbors."

Mr. Lovejoy leaned forward a little. There was a certain *pressure* in his voice and his eyes were anxious. His forehead was

311

gathered into a small lump over each eye. For a moment Joseph
had some fleeting thought of a criminal conspiracy: Mafia, perhaps,
who needed the house? But that was absurd. This man was of a
definite class, in banking, brokerage or shipping. Something like
that. His dress, his face, his accent all belonged in that category.

"You know how women are . . . old family friendship, going
back for three or four generations . . . it would mean a very great
deal to us, I assure you, if you'd withdraw. And I'm certain this
very same agent could find you another house which you'd like as
well or better. After all," he smiled deprecatingly, "the house is
awfully old and quite run-down too, as you no doubt saw."

"Oh, I saw," Joseph said. "It's run-down, all right. But as I told
you, my wife loves it." The man was pushing him, ever so delicately, but pushing all the same, and he didn't like it.

Mr. Lovejoy sighed. "Perhaps there are a few things you haven't
considered. I mean, you don't really know the area very well . . .
you're strangers to the town, aren't you?"

"We're strangers."

"Ah, yes. Well, then, you see, we're a very old community, very
close knit. We even have an association on our side of town: the
Stone Spring Association, you may have heard of it? It's a kind of
improvement group and social club of people with mutual concerns: our gardens and tennis courts, maintenance of the roadside
shade trees, protection of our general interests in the town. Things
of that sort."

"Go on," Joseph said.

"You know how it is, when people have lived together most of
their lives, their attachments are formed. It's very difficult for a
newcomer to move in. Difficult for them and for the newcomer.
. . . Just human nature, after all, isn't it?"

A flash bulb flared and went out in Joseph's head, illuminating
everything.

"I see," he said. "I see what you've been trying to tell me. No
Jews!"

A flush spread up from Mr. Lovejoy's collar; it was the pink of
rare roast beef. "I wouldn't put it that way exactly, Mr. Friedman.
We're not bigoted people. We don't hate anyone. But people *are*
always more comfortable with their own kind."

It was a statement, but it had been presented like a question, as
if the man expected Joseph to answer. He didn't answer.

"A good many people of your faith are buying over toward the Sound. They're even building a handsome new synagogue, I'm told. Actually, it's better over there, much breezier in the summer . . ."

"Usurping the better part of town, are they?"

Mr. Lovejoy ignored that. "The agent should have told you all this, as a service to you. He really did a very poor job."

"I wouldn't say so. I didn't ask him to do anything but show me the house, which he did, and take my money, which he did. As simple as that."

Mr. Lovejoy shook his head. "Not simple. There's a great deal more to buying a home than four walls. There's a whole neighborhood to be taken into consideration. All kinds of social events. People give parties—I should think you wouldn't want to live someplace and be left out."

The man is absolutely right. But to retreat now? It's unthinkable. For myself I don't give a damn. Whether he wants me there or he doesn't, it's all the same to me. I could do a lot better than that old heap of a house. In fact, some people will think I'm out of my mind to buy it, and me in the building business. . . . That stuff about people wanting to stay with their own kind: fine, I'm the first to say so myself. Except that it should be by choice, not by being told you must.

He said, "We don't expect you to invite us to your parties and we don't expect to invite you. We only want to live in the house. And that's what we intend to do."

"That's all you have to say?"

"All."

"I could take this to court, you know. It would be a long, complicated legal tangle and would cost us both a good deal of money and time."

He was thinking: She's never had anything except for those first few hectic years before the crash. A trip to Europe. A diamond ring which I had to pawn and only got back now. (I knew she didn't even want the ring, but I want her to have it; it's for me.) And a fur coat which she wore for fifteen years. He could see her creamy face above the rusty old fur which she had kept on wearing because they couldn't afford a new cloth coat. If she knew about this business today she wouldn't want the house. She'd make me back down. So she'll never know. I'll never let her know.

313

"Mr. Friedman, I don't want to wrangle this out in court. I'm too busy, and I'm sure you are too."

Yes, and it's too ugly to be brought out in the open, Joseph thought, still not speaking. He was very, very tired and angry with himself for being hurt. What, after all, was new or surprising about this conversation? He ought to have known better.

Mr. Lovejoy, too, was struggling with anger. His voice rose ever so slightly. "If you're not satisfied with two thousand we can talk it over."

Joseph looked up from his vision of faces: first Anna's, then Iris', even Maury's and lastly, strangely, Eric's: a face he could only imagine, which had been taken from him by just such a man, very likely, as this one: this thin man, gaunt almost, wearing the ascetic expression of some figure in an engraved historical tableau, wearing that and a blue silk foulard tie.

"I'm not to be bought off," he said softly. "I want the house."

Mr. Lovejoy rose and loomed above the desk. Joseph looked up at him. He was the tallest man he had ever seen.

"Is that your final word, then, Mr. Friedman?"

"It is."

Mr. Lovejoy walked to the door and turned back. "You ought to know," he said, "that in all my dealings with your people, all my life, I have found them baffling, difficult and stubborn. You're no exception."

"And for two thousand years in our dealings with your people we have found you the same, and worse." *I shall go home and tell Anna that the tension between us could have been cut with a knife. No, of course not; I shan't tell Anna anything at all.*

Mr. Lovejoy's hand was on the doorknob. Such cold eyes he had, gray as the North Atlantic in the winter: deep, deep, cold and gray. He bowed slightly, then turned and went out, shutting the door without sound behind him, as a gentleman should.

Joseph was still at his desk when Miss Donnelly came in with her hat on.

"Is it all right for me to go home, Mr. Friedman? It's after five."

"Yes, yes, go ahead."

"Is there anything the matter? I thought perhaps—"

He waved his hand. "Nothing. Nothing at all. I was just thinking."

Anna's eyes. When she didn't know he was watching her, he

could catch a look in them, as if she were seeing things other people didn't see. Mourning eyes, and wondering; eyes that could lighten so quickly into laughter. Quality, his father used to say. You can always tell quality. And this man says he doesn't want her living on his street. His fury mounted.

I'm going to have that house if it's the last thing I do.

Painters and masons were still working when, in early September, they moved in so that Iris could start the school year. She had been fortunate to get a position as a fourth-grade teacher in what they later learned was the best school in the area. It was not what she had wanted. She wanted, she said, to teach poorer children whose need was greater. If she could have had her way she would have liked to teach on the lower East Side, or even Harlem.

Joseph groaned. "It's taken most of my life to get away to a place where there was no chance of being pulled back down there. I could take all the bathrooms out of this house so you'd get the feel of Ludlow Street, if you want."

He was the first to admit that his humor wasn't humorous, although Anna laughed. But Iris looked exasperated, and Anna's laugh turned to a sigh.

Oh, Iris was so earnest! She had no real joy in anything, just seemed to stand apart, watching and making her skeptical, acerbic comments. She thought the neighborhood too polished, too self-consciously expensive, and the children she taught reflected the houses they lived in. She disapproved of the things Anna was having done to the house.

"I liked it the way it was," she said, as the kitchen took new form with stainless steel, white porcelain and dark red tile.

"You can't mean that!"

"Naturally I don't mean the dirt. But what you're making is like something in a magazine."

"That's what I'm taking it from. A magazine," Anna said firmly.

It was the first time in her life that she could really have what she wanted. The costly pseudo-French furniture which they had been living with all these years had been Joseph's choice. The odd thing was that when at last she had gotten rid of it and the second-hand men had carried it out of sight with its gilded curlicues, painted flowers and bulbous legs (as if it had rheumatoid arthritis, Anna had used to think) she had felt a pang. They had gone through so much living with these tables and chairs! And when they took the sideboard which Maury had once gouged with his toy hammer she had turned away. (Only the little white bed from Iris' childhood room had gone with them and was wrapped now in the attic of this house, although Iris didn't know it. She would have understood what Anna was still hoping for.)

Joseph had told her to buy what she wanted, and she was doing so, spending far less than he would have spent. She'd furnished the dining room at an estate auction in the neighborhood, with a long, plain pine table and an enormous Welsh dresser. . . . These high rooms needed massive pieces and massive pieces were old; they didn't make them anymore for the cramped spaces of this century. There were flowers all over this house: clustered on the carpet in the library, scattered in blue and white bouquets on the walls of an airy bedroom. Geraniums in wooden tubs stood at the front door.

It was beginning to take on the look she had striven for, the look of a family which had lived long in one place and slowly collected its possessions through the years. (Hadn't she lived once in a house like that? *This silver has been in my family since before the Revolution,* Paul's mother said.) A false impression? Of course! But so much of life is bound to be false. . . . And middle-class? Oh-so-genteel, so understated, so English-countryside! Such a house for Joseph and Anna, once of Ludlow Street! And why not? If they liked it, and were comfortable with it? And she had done it well. If it didn't look like this when the original owners lived in it, then it ought to have.

The one concession to Joseph, who was far too busy these days to care about anything else, was the hanging of her portrait over the mantel in the living room. No, two concessions: the other was the gilded clock, which was to go under the portrait.

"I just don't like meeting myself every time I walk into that room," Anna objected, to no avail. About the clock she said nothing.

She unpacked the silver candlesticks, clutching them in her fists for a moment, feeling them before putting them on the dining-room table. The places they had seen before this one! The shelf on Washington Heights, because there had been no dining room table there, wrapped in a blanket for the ocean crossing. She could remember her mother saying the blessing over them, but where were they kept during the week? She thought and thought, straining herself to remember, and could not. And before that they had stood in the houses of a grandmother and an unknown great-grandmother. Her own mother had died before Anna had thought to ask about those other women, or had even cared about knowing. So now she would never know.

When everything else was in place, Anna unpacked her books. She took long afternoons arranging them on the shelves in sections according to the subject: art, biography, poetry, fiction. Under those headings, she arranged them again in alphabetical order according to author.

Here Iris gave approval. "You really have the makings of a library. I'd no idea we had so many."

"Half of them have been stacked away in barrels and boxes all these years."

Iris looked at her, Anna thought, with curiosity. "You're really happy, aren't you, Ma?"

"Yes, very." (It's a thing you learn and cultivate, this 'happiness.' You count what you have and are grateful for it. And if that sounds pompous, I can't help it.) And, not wanting to ask, yet not able to refrain from asking, "I hope you are too, a little, Iris?" The question came out almost like a plea.

"I'm all right. I'm better off than nine-tenths of the rest of the world."

Quite true. But it was not the answer Anna had wanted.

If only she would make more friends! There had been two or three young women who taught at her school in New York whom she saw regularly. They used to go to theatre and lunch together on weekends. But now even these few were lost to her unless she wanted to go into the city every week. Mostly now she stayed at home playing the piano, reading or correcting papers. No life for a person of twenty-seven.

She didn't stop and talk to people. She'd nod and go walking on; Anna had seen her do it often enough. But you needed to make an effort; people didn't just drop down the chimney and seek you out! On the Broadway block where Anna had done her shopping for all those years she had known everybody; generations of roller-skating kids, the shoe repair man, the butcher. Hadn't the butcher had a

317

nephew just out of Columbia Law School, and asked for Iris' telephone number to give to him? But when Anna had mentioned it Iris had been furious.

She had tried, since moving here, to get her out to some of her own activities. There was a very active group of women at the temple sisterhood, some of them even younger than Iris. But, naturally, they were all married. There were the League of Women Voters and the Hospital Guild, which was right now raising funds for a new wing. Anna liked that sort of thing, had done it often enough in the city. People said she had a talent for making these fund raisers a success, for getting the people to come and finding speakers who could hold their attention. It wasn't hard; you just put a smile on your face, let people know you were available to work and you could be busy every day. It was almost a challenge to move into a new community and see how quickly you could make a place for yourself!

"You must have won the popularity contest," Iris remarked one afternoon when, on arriving home from school, she found a ladies' meeting just breaking up. The way she said it, and she had said it before, was odd: in part it was an accusation, in part a question.

Anna had tried the simple answer often enough: *When you're friendly to people they're friendly to you.* But it had produced no results, except perhaps irritation on Iris' part. And anyway, it sounded like some scout maxim or else one of those pious declarations that used to be embroidered on samplers or printed and hung over the boss's desk in an office. So she fell back on lame humor.

"My red hair, no doubt." And kept it at that.

If it hadn't been for all these friends or acquaintances, whatever you wanted to call them, the house would have been unbearably empty. Empty rooms were the hazard of middle age. After the birds have flown the nest, et cetera. And if there had never been a nestful at all?

Mary Malone was distressed about her son Mickey, who'd been in Hawaii during the war and had gone back there to live. But she still had the rest of them nearby, not to speak of the grandchildren already born and yet to come! While I, while we—

More than once Anna had thought of getting into the car with Joseph, driving up to that town and knocking at the door: "We've come to see our grandson," they'd say. And then what? No, it couldn't be done in the face of those people's refusal. The child would be the one to suffer. It couldn't be done. Someday, when he is older, people said, someday he'll want to see you. Yes, after all the lovely years of his childhood were past, he might, perhaps, come to them. A stranger, come out of curiosity or God knows why else.

On days like that Anna would need to be active, to work with her hands. She would go down into the kitchen and help Celeste with the cooking. Celeste had represented herself as a 'good plain cook,' but had turned out to be more plain than good. Anna was just as glad that the cooking hadn't been taken out of her own hands. . . .

She hadn't wanted anyone living in the house in the first place. With three adults, two of them gone all day, they could have done very well with a woman to come in once or twice a week to clean.

But Joseph had been firm about it. "This enormous house? No, you're to get someone and without delay. I insist," he'd said.

And so Celeste had come to them. She was a large, dark brown woman whose presence was marked by a loud voice that laughed whenever it wasn't singing sorrowful hymns. She had come north from Georgia for no reason that she ever disclosed, leaving behind her a vague family: children? Husband? She never told them and, after one unsuccessful attempt, they never asked her.

She was to live in their house as long as they did and know them perhaps better than they knew themselves.

During their second autumn, before full dark, Joseph came driving home from the railroad station and was startled by something at the side of the road not far from his house. He backed the car up to look again.

It was a small dog, lying in tall grass. He leaned out of the car. The dog raised its head an inch or two and fell back. Its chest and one of its legs were soaked in blood.

He'd never been very useful around blood or pain and he knew it. Maybe he ought to leave the dog and telephone the police when he got home. But in the meantime some other car might come along and kill it or just mangle it some more. He shuddered and looked again. It was a little white dog with a sheep's face, the Lovejoys' dog. He knew nothing about dogs and really didn't like them. But he remembered this one because when they had seen it

319

on the Lovejoys' lawn Anna had exclaimed over the sheep. Then Iris had looked in a book—leave it to Iris to look things up—and told them it was a dog, a Bedlington terrier.

Would it bite if he were to pick it up? He couldn't leave it there like that. It raised its head again, or tried to, and he heard its whimper. No, he couldn't leave it there like that. He got out of the car. There was no cloth, nothing to lay it on. He took his coat off. If the spots didn't come out it couldn't be helped. The dog whimpered again when he picked it up, feeling clumsy and sick with pity for it.

He drove up the hill and turned into the double driveway of the Lovejoy house. A maid answered the bell, and in the hallway behind her he heard a woman's voice.

"Who is it, Carrie?"

"It's Tippy, Mrs. Lovejoy. He's been hurt."

"I found him on the side of the road," Joseph said. "I'm Friedman, your neighbor."

Mrs. Lovejoy gave a little scream. "Oh, my God!"

Joseph held out his arms and she took the little bundle of dog and coat. "Carrie, tell Bob to get the car and call Dr. Chase, tell him we're on our way." She whirled back to Joseph. "How did this happen?"

"I don't know," he said, and, suddenly understanding, added, "I didn't do it. I found him on the road."

She turned away. He saw that she didn't believe him. "My coat, please. May I have my coat?"

And when it was dropped upon the floor he picked up his bloodied coat and let himself out the door.

At dinner, having said nothing about the incident to Anna, he heard himself asking her quite suddenly, "Tell me, do you ever think this house is too far from your friends?"

She looked surprised. "Well, everyone does seem to live twenty minutes or so away, but I don't really mind. What makes you ask?"

"Just wondering. We've been here awhile and I wondered whether you liked it as much as you thought you would. We can always sell and get another place."

"Oh, but I love it here! You must know I do."

Yes, true. The way she stands in the doorway after we've been out, and walks around touching things. At night when it's warm she sits on the steps, watching the stars. She used to do that when she was a child in Poland, she says.

The doorbell rang and after a moment Celeste came in. "There's a gentleman to see you in the hall."

Just inside the door was Mr. Lovejoy. He stood somewhat uncertainly.

"I came over to thank you. My wife was terribly upset about the dog. She realized afterward that she hadn't thanked you."

"No, she hadn't. But that's all right."

"He had cut himself on a broken bottle. The vet said he would have bled to death in a short while if you hadn't picked him up."

"I don't like to see anything suffer. Not animals or human beings, either."

Anna had come into the hall. "What's this all about, Joseph? You didn't tell me!"

"There was nothing to tell," he answered shortly.

"Your husband was very kind. The dog means a lot to us, like one of the family."

"Then I'm glad he could help," Anna said. "Won't you come in for a minute?"

"Thank you, I'd better be getting back. You've made some changes in the house," he added, addressing Anna. "I'd hardly recognize it."

"Anytime you want to see it you're welcome."

"Thank you again." Mr. Lovejoy bowed and the door closed behind him.

"Well! You weren't very gracious to that man, Joseph. I've never seen you so rude."

"What did you want me to do? Kiss him?"

"Joseph! I don't know what's got into you! Such a nice man, too."

"What was nice about him? What could you tell in half a minute? Sometimes, Anna, you talk like a child!"

"And you talk like a nasty, insulting crank! I don't mind, but I should think you'd want to be nice to the neighbors. We might get to be friends, for all you know."

"Sure! They're waiting for us!"

"Well, we're friends with the Wilmots down the street, aren't we?"

"Okay, okay, have it your way." He patted her on the back.

Friends? Hardly. But something human had come through, all the same. He stood a moment looking through the door down the length of the living room where the fire sparked under the mantel and Anna's portrait hung above it. No, he wouldn't sell, wouldn't leave this house. It was his house. It was—home.

29

At the last minute her parents remembered that they had been invited out to dinner and Iris would have to be hostess alone to Theo Stern. It was a clumsy trick. They might have thought of something more clever.

As if it would make any difference! It was just one more humiliation and this one worse than most, because Theo was so un-ordinary and would see right through it. They were always praising his brilliance, so how could they think he would be stupid enough not to know what they were doing?

She was afraid. What to say to him during the long meal and the longer evening, knowing he would be wishing himself away and back in New York? He came to their house to see Joseph and Anna, not her. She had really never been alone with him, unless one could count four or five polite invitations to theatre by way of repaying her parents' hospitality. And one time at the beach with two of the Malone sons and their wives.

Celeste was coming upstairs, humming. Did she know she was constantly singing, or was it by now an unconscious habit? Iris came out of her room.

"Celeste, there'll only be two at dinner."

"Your ma told me. What I wanted to know was, shall I make a pie? There's time enough."

"Good heavens, anything. I don't care. This dinner tonight is the last thing I wanted."

Celeste looked sly. Sly and merry. "You shouldn't oughta say that. He's a real nice man, Dr. Stern. I taken a liking to him the first time I opened the door and him standing there asking if this was the Friedman house. I knowed right away I liked him."

"I like him, too. That's no reason why I have to entertain him, is it?"

"He likes you, I see that."

"Of course he does! He likes all of us. You, too."

"Then I'm going to make the pie. And biscuits with the chicken. He ate four biscuits last time we had them."

Even Celeste was captivated by his Viennese charm! But it wasn't fair to be sardonic about that: there was so much else beneath the courtesy and wit, including one's awareness of what the world—the Nazi fury—had done to Theo Stern.

He had traced them down last year upon arriving in New York. The last they had heard before then was a letter written from England just after the United States had entered the war. Mama's eyes had run with fresh tears, reading all over again about the Uncle Eli family, all destroyed: the old people and the young, Theo Stern's wife Liesel and their baby—all annihilated. Horrible, horrible! Like one of those ghoulish fairy tales in which ogres devour children and people are thrown into furnaces. But this had really happened. You looked at Theo and, remembering, were so *moved*—you wanted to put your hand on his, you wanted to say I know, I know. Except that you didn't know: how could you, unless you had been there?

He never spoke of himself directly. His story had been drawn out of him in short sentences, answers to questions tactfully and obliquely put.

He'd had friends in England, made in the years he'd spent at Cambridge, and these had taken him in, had given him a base from which to reconstruct himself. When he enlisted in the British army it was not as a doctor. He had wanted to fight, to be used in a less passive way than healing wounds. He had wanted, he said, to work 'vengefully,' and that's how they had put him to use. As a child Theo had lived four years in France while his father opened a branch of his business there. Because of that he spoke colloquial French, slang and all. So he had been enlisted to work with the underground, and had been parachuted into France, complete with a French identity. He was supposed to have been born in a provincial town, son of a teacher; to have gone to school and church there and prepared for

324

the university; all this was in case of capture by the Nazi occupying forces. He had seen, Iris reflected, seen in the flesh all the things that made you shudder and turn away when you saw mere bits of them in the newsreels. Theo had lived through them.

Once her father had risen and put his arm around Theo. He had been deeply affected, and Theo had been too. For that instant, standing there, they had seemed to the others in the room like a father and a son. As if, Iris thought, as if my brother Maury had come home.

She moved quickly, choosing her dress and shoes, then ran the water in the bathtub. She had never gotten over the need to ease herself in hot water and her mother had never ceased to warn her that she might one day fall asleep in it and drown.

She sank into the burning heat and lay her head back. She would have liked to stay in this deep comfort, then get into bed and read the evening away.

Papa was making a—a project out of Theo! He'd talked him into opening an office here in the suburbs rather than New York, had even helped him find office space.

"If you really want the Grosvenor Avenue building I can help you, I know the owner. I might be able to get a good deal for you on the rent," he'd suggested.

And if Theo was short of money for equipment, which came high, why, Joseph would be glad to advance him some. No, Theo wasn't short. Money was no problem. But he would never forget the offer; they were being as good to him as family. Well, they *were* family! He felt that way toward them. They were all he had.

Iris' flesh prickled with embarrassment. Papa came on so *strong!* Yet, if Theo minded, he didn't show it.

He was a good-looking man, too thin now and older looking than his age. His features were what is called 'strong.' He had attentive eyes that searched you when you spoke to him: Iris had had to turn her own away sometimes. Women would be attracted to him. Probably he would get anyone he wanted badly enough. He would want, she guessed, someone like the one he'd had before. "A beauty," her mother said. "She had a brightness like my brother Eli." And like Maury, because Maury was like Eli.

Men. What do men want? Beauty like that, naturally, if they can get it. But not only that, and not always. The mothers of the children she taught came in all shapes and sorts, with every kind and degree of tenderness, intelligence and manner. Yet must they not all have had something in common to have been chosen? What? What?

If you talk too much, that's not good. If you're too quiet, that's not good. You lie in bed at night thinking about it and trying not to. You are surrounded by sex, the man-woman thing. The movies, the embraces that will end in bed, even though they don't show it. But you know that's what it's all about. Always. Even the women's magazines with their preachy articles and stories. Educated women should have more children, they tell you. Motherhood and wifehood are the most rewarding careers. Decorate the house, drive the station wagon, work on the school board, campaign in community politics and make your town a better place for your children to live in. Charities are obligatory (making the world a better place for other people's children to live in). But it all starts with the bed. Man-woman. Sex.

I feel sometimes—I feel so *cheap*. As if, when people look at me, they must know what I want and can't have, will probably never have. My mother tries to be so tactful. She talks to her friends and sometimes even to me, so seriously, so respectfully, about my 'career,' as if she wasn't at the same time putting out her feelers for every stray man who passes. Papa brings a widower to dinner, thinking he must be needing a mother for his children. Not me, Iris, for what I am. No, a mother for his children.

Why don't I give up? Give up in my mind, I mean. One more birthday after the next, and I'll be thirty. It's time to settle for what I have. A job with tenure in another year, so if I want to I can plan to go on teaching for the next forty years in the pleasant brick school with the old trees and the nice lady teachers. Papa says I'll never have to worry about money. I'll have a nice home full of good books. I'll listen to good music in the evenings and maybe take a trip to Europe now and then with a group of teachers.

That's living?

"What's that plant I smell?" Theo asked. "It's a little like perfume and a little like burnt sugar."

"It's phlox. My mother planted a bed of it under this window."

She turned on the outdoor light, picking the phlox out of darkness. The cream and lavender domes were bent with the weight of the rain. The trees dripped in a forest stillness.

"My mother's become a country woman. Those are raspberries by the hedge. We had them for breakfast."

Theo said quietly, "It seems centuries since I knew people who were able to plant something and wait peacefully for it to grow."

No answer seemed to be called for. He went on, "Do you really know how wonderful this home of yours is?"

"Oh, yes. Most of the years of my growing up were depression years. We've only been living like this a very short time."

"I didn't mean the house. I meant the family. You have wonderful parents. Warm people. Gentle people. I have a feeling they seldom argue with each other. Am I right?"

"I think because my mother anticipates whatever my father wants. Not only that, of course. But that's part of it."

"A European woman!"

"She was born in Europe. I don't know how European she still is."

"But American women are different, aren't they?"

"It's a land of variety here . . . who can say what 'American' is?"

"Tell me, are you like your mother or your father?"

Those attentive eyes! As if her answer were really important. As if it were even possible.

I don't really know, she thought, what my parents are 'like,' let alone myself. No, that's wrong. Papa is relatively simple. But my mother has hidden places. I think Papa knows she has, too, and can't puzzle them out. He teases her about being mysterious, yet he means it, it's more than teasing. It's true that they love one another; one *feels* their devotion; also, though, one feels a tension. Sometimes I have odd thoughts: Could Mama really be keeping some great secret from us both? I remember that man, Paul Werner, as if in some way, I don't know how, he were involved with us. With her. Then I'm so ashamed of my thought. Mama, so *moral* and honorable and—how can I think such things? Yet I do think them.

She blinked herself back into the present. Theo was waiting for a reply, and so she said lightly, "It's hard to see yourself, isn't it? But—well, I like books; that's the main way I'm like my mother. And I'm sort of, more than sort of, religious. Like my father."

"Religious! You must know, that's something quite new to me. We never thought about it at home. Nor in the house of my father-in-law, Eduard. Oh, you called him Eli, didn't you? I forgot for the moment. Your Uncle Eli."

327

"You think it's ridiculous?"

"No, no, of course not!"

"Tell the truth. I won't mind."

"All right then, I'll tell you. I find it rather charming, rather picturesque. Perhaps I'm even a little sorry that I have no feeling for it myself."

"But you must have. Not the form, perhaps. And forms change, anyway. Like Papa being Orthodox and now he goes to Reform; at first he was shocked by the thought, but now he likes it tremendously. So what I mean is," she said earnestly, "it's not the form but what you feel that counts. And I'm sure you must feel the truth of all the things we believe in!"

"Such as?"

"Well, you've seen better than I have what a nation without religion, that's to say without morals, can do."

"Yes, I suppose that's true. I just never thought to connect religion with those events."

"I guess when you're in the midst of—what you were in, you can't do much thinking. You just want to live through it," she said gently.

"You don't even care much about living through it. One of the feelings I had, as a matter of fact, was guilt that I *was* alive."

"I understand."

"And then when it's over and the world begins moving again, you start to feel angry. All that ugliness and waste of years! When you might have been—growing raspberries!"

"I hope you don't still feel it was a waste . . . what you did, I mean."

"No, I have a better perspective on it since I've been in America. All war is criminal waste, but in a purely personal sense I didn't waste the years. I spent myself with profit. I fought back."

He got up and walked to the end of the room, pulled a book from a shelf and replaced it. "So now, so now I just want to live. I want to work and listen to music, and to the devil with politics and getting ahead! I just want *real* things. Like looking at a woman with marvelous eyes and a lovely blue dress. That is a lovely dress, Iris. It's the color of your name."

"The New Look," she said shyly. "My mother bought it."

"Your mother buys your clothes?"

"Oh, no! This was a present. She knew I wouldn't buy it, I only shop when I have to. I'm not that interested in clothes."

"So? What are you interested in?"

What she had to say was so stilted, formal and dreary. Yet she knew nothing else to say. "I always thought I'd like to write. I tried short stories, but I got too many rejections and I've given up. I play piano too, but not well enough to do anything much with it. So I'll say I'm interested in teaching, because it's what I do best."

"And you're happy."

"Oh, I like it. They tell me I'm good at it and I feel that I am. Except that these children don't really *need* me. They're so well cared for already; they have everything, and what I do for them is—" She was talking too much, and she finished abruptly, "I guess I really want to do something more important, only I don't know what."

"I am imagining you as a child," Theo said irrelevantly, "a very solemn little girl."

"I'm sure I was." Still am. Solemn.

"Tell me about your childhood."

"There's nothing much to tell. It was very quiet. I read a lot. It was almost a Victorian life in the twentieth century."

Why was she talking so much? This man drew the words from her.

"I sometimes think I should have been a Victorian. In the early part of the century, before the factories and billboards, when the world was still green and lovely."

"It's the factories that have made this beautiful house possible, you know. A hundred and twenty-five years ago you would have been living in a hovel, or a Polish ghetto more than likely."

"That's what my father says. And of course you're right. I'm just given to silly talk, sometimes."

"It's not silly to reveal yourself. Goodness knows I've just been doing it."

Theo lay his head against the back of the chair. She shouldn't have reminded him of Europe and the war. The rain began again, splashing on the heavy leafage at the window, and the room was quiet.

Presently he stood up and went to the piano. "I'll play something jolly. Have you ever heard this?"

He played a teasing little waltz, played it with a sparkle, and

329

swung around on the bench. "I'll bet you can't guess the title of that."

"I'll bet I can. It's Satie. He wrote three of them, called 'His Waist,' 'His Pince Nez,' 'His Legs.'"

They burst out laughing, and then Theo's laugh broke off. He stared at her.

"You're the most extraordinary girl!"

"I'm not. I happen to have a crazy kind of memory, that's all."

He stood up and came to where she was sitting. He took her hands and pulled her lightly to her feet. "Iris, I'm going to say it right out while I have the courage. Why shouldn't we be married? Can you think of a good reason why we shouldn't be?"

She wasn't certain she had heard. She stared at him.

"Because I think we go so well together. I don't know about you, but I haven't been happy like this for so long."

Was it, could it be, some sort of cruel wit, some kind of mockery that passed for a game in sophisticated circles? Still she didn't answer.

"I'm clumsy. I should have done something before this to prepare you. I'm sorry."

He was looking into her face, forcing her eyes to his, which were troubled and soft. She saw it was not a game. It was true.

She began to cry.

He put her cheek to his and kissed her forehead. "I don't know what that means," he said. "Does it mean yes or no?"

"I think—I think it means yes," she whispered and felt her tears wet on his cheek.

"Iris, my dear, I want you to be sure. Tell me you are."

"I am sure. Yes, yes, I am."

He pulled out his handkerchief and dried her eyes. "We'll be very, very happy, I promise we will."

She nodded, laughed, and her tears kept pouring.

Theo, understand why I am crying: because I so hoped this might happen and knew it couldn't; because of being almost thirty years old; because of the narrow bed in which I sleep alone. And now you are here.

Iris has done something wonderful. There is a murmur of flattering laughter all through the house. Celeste carries in the packages of gifts, the silver and the crystal in their tissue paper wraps. Her mother works at her desk and on the telephone over the menus, the invitations, the bridal veil. (It is an embarrassment to be dressed like a teen-age bride at an age when other women are taking their children to kindergarten.) At least, her mother will keep things fairly simple, although not as simple as Iris wants. Papa would have her come riding in on a white elephant, its howdah embroidered in brilliants. He is so happy, engrossed with his plans for Theo's new office. The blueprints are spread on the big desk in the round room; Theo and Papa confer over them after dinner. Papa is ecstatic because she is marrying a doctor. A doctor from Vienna! And now there will be a son in the house again, vigorous and bright and full of hope, as Maury was once. Our Maury, so long ago. Poor Papa! Poor good Papa!

It is almost as if Theo were a trophy she has won. She is ashamed of the joy in the house. She is ashamed of herself for begrudging them their joy. Her heart beats faster almost all the time now.

Sometimes she thinks she is dreaming the whole thing.

They lay on the sand. It was a perfect, silken Florida afternoon.

She had thought, when they were alone in that first room together, that she would fail. She had read so much, had bought and hidden marriage manuals and Havelock Ellis. It seemed there was so much to know about what, after all, had been done long before books were written!

Her mother had asked, while looking at the floor, "Is there anything you want to know?" And had been relieved when Iris had told her there wasn't.

It had seemed from the reading that there were so many ways in which you could please or displease, succeed or not; and if she failed, if she did not satisfy, what then?

But she had not failed. It was the marvelous delight, the most total merging of spirit and flesh that could have been imagined, and she had certainly imagined it enough! To have waited so long! That was the only pity, to have waited so long!

Theo said lazily, "You look pleased."

"I am. Pleased and proud. Smug and proud."

"Proud?"

"To be your wife."

"You're a darling, Iris. And puzzling, in a very nice way."

"What way?"

"I'd thought, you see, you gave the impression that you might be hesitant or timid in bed."

"And I'm not?"

He laughed. "You know very well you're not! I'm a very, very lucky man!"

He took her hand and they turned over to burn their backs.

"This day is too perfect to know what to do with it," Iris said.

"It seems to me you know quite well what to do with it. And with the nights too," he answered.

"When I was a little girl," she began.

"You still are a little girl."

"No, but really, listen, I want to tell you. I was about seven and there was a doll that I had been wanting. It had a pink velvet coat with white fur, and long, dark curls. I remember it exactly; it was the incarnation of doll. Do you know what I mean? And I had been wanting it so long. Then on the morning of my birthday, when I found it sitting on my chair, I had such a queer feeling, not disappointment, but a kind of ebbing away. . . . It was so perfect! I didn't want a speck of dirt to touch it, and still I knew that it would, that with each second some of its perfection was passing away."

"Such sorrowful thoughts on a day like this!" Theo protested.

But she persisted. She wanted him to understand. "I'm not sorrowful. It's so wonderful that I want to keep it, remember it always. Theo, someday years from now we'll look out on a soggy winter street and we'll talk about how we lay here in the sun predicting how we'll be looking out on a soggy winter street—"

"You're thinking about years from now and I'm thinking about tonight. I'm hoping they serve that fish soup again. It's the best I ever ate."

"Theo, darling, tell me again, tell me you love me."

"I love you, Iris. I do love you."

She raised her arm toward the sky. Her skin was turning reddish gold.

"What are you looking at? Your ring? I wish you hadn't insisted on a plain band. Let me at least buy a diamond one for evening."

"No."

"Is it because you think I can't afford it? I can."

"It's not that. It's just that I'm never going to take this one off."

"Never?"

"Never. I know it sounds superstitious or something, but this is the one I wore when we were married and now it's like another part of myself."

"That's primitive."

"Maybe. All I know is, something happened to me when you put that ring on my finger. And I know that if the ring ever comes off all of my life will come loose and I shall be left floating, without an anchor."

"All right, then, no diamonds."

The clouds moved slowly; the sun poured on their joined hands.

"I'm falling asleep," Theo said.

Iris closed her eyes. Sparks whirled through her lids, a catherine wheel of ruby, mauve and peacock blue. So beautiful! Life, and the vibrating earth! I want to have it all, see it all, be everywhere at once. I want to hear all the music ever written and never die. Let Theo never die, just stay like this in the sunlight, forever and forever and forever.

30

Cousin Chris stowed the oars, letting the boat dance of its own will. There was something different about him today and it disturbed Eric. Usually when Chris came it was so jolly. He didn't visit very often; he had a wife and children and a job, although you wouldn't think it to look at him. He seemed too athletic and quick, just too young for all that sort of thing. Still, he had been Eric's mother's favorite cousin, so he couldn't really be that young. They'd used to have great adventures at Chris's house in Maine when she was a girl. Like the time they'd got caught in a fog on the bay—

But Chris had no stories for Eric now. He bent forward, his sober face looming large, while behind his head, far at the end of the lake, the hotel buildings and the golf course lay spread like a toy village on green felt.

"So I told your grandmother. We had a long talk last night—"

"I heard you downstairs," Eric said.

"You heard what we said?"

"No, just your voices. But I knew it was something serious. I thought probably you were talking about me."

"Yes. Well." Chris had anxious, troubled eyes. He began speaking fast, as if he wanted to get all this over with. "You're thirteen, almost grown-up. I told your grandmother you're old enough to handle the truth. Women never think you are, but—"

"The truth about Gran?"

"To begin with, yes."

334

"You don't have to tell me. I know it's cancer." This was the first time he'd said the word out loud. People always whispered it or said C.A. or else just *looked*. He didn't know why he didn't feel more, saying this awful thing. Was there something wrong with him, that he didn't feel more?

"How long have you known?"

"Since last winter. That time she was in the hospital, people stopped talking when I came in the room. So I guessed that's what it must be."

"I see," Chris said.

"Is she afraid, Gran?"

"She hasn't said she was. But I should think so, wouldn't you?"

Chris waited a moment. "What she's really worried about is you. And that's why I want to talk to you. She asked me to. She thought it would be easier for both of you if I did the talking."

"She needn't worry. I'll take care of her. I was very good with Gramp, and you know how crippled he was."

"I know you were. But this is different."

"How different?"

Cousin Chris didn't answer right away. Instead, he took the oars and the boat sprang ahead. They had to bend their shoulders under a fall of willow leafage, and in this hidden cove at water's edge he put the oars down again. The boat lay still.

"How is it different?" Eric repeated.

Chris took his wristwatch off. It was an extraordinary watch. He'd bought it overseas when he was in the air force during the war, and he'd shown it to Eric yesterday. It could tell the date and it had an alarm. You could read the dial in the dark; it was a wonderful watch. Now Chris examined it, shook it a little, held it to his ear, frowned and slowly strapped it on again.

"Something wrong with your watch?"

"No, I just wanted to check it." Suddenly the words came rushing out. "Eric, the difference is, your Gran is going to die. I didn't know any other way to tell you but like this."

"But Jerry—he's a boy in my class—his father had cancer a long time ago when we were in third grade, and he's fine!"

"It doesn't always work that way."

"I'm going to ask Dr. Shane!"

"Do, if it'll help you any. But he'll tell you the same thing, Eric."

Had he been asking himself a minute ago why he felt nothing inside? Now, suddenly, there was a tightening, a pounding in his chest and his head. He thought he tasted something hot under his tongue, hot like blood.

"I don't believe it! It isn't true!" he shouted.

"I know how you feel. It was the same for me when my grandfather Guthrie died."

Beyond the screen of leaves a motorboat shot by, rocking the quiet water. Billy Noyes and his father in their Chris-Craft, probably. They were always racketing around together in that boat, Billy and his father.

"I know how you feel," Chris said again.

Neither of them spoke for a minute or two. Then another bleak thought formed itself into words.

"I'm thinking of how empty the house will be with just George and Mrs. Mather and me in it."

"Well, that's just what I was coming to next," Chris said. He felt for the pack of cigarettes which was sticking out of his shirt pocket in plain sight, but he seemed to have trouble getting hold of it. Then he had to fumble in another pocket for a match, and after that had more trouble lighting it.

"The thing is," he said at last, "the thing is, you won't be able to stay here. I mean, Mrs. Mather isn't family, so she couldn't be responsible for you, could she? You need to live with someone in your own family, you see."

"Would I go to live with you?"

"Well, no. Not that I wouldn't like it a lot, but as it works out—" He paused. Oh, if he would just say it all quickly! "As it is, well, Gran has had this on her mind for a long time, and she's talked about it with me and my parents and Uncle Wendell, even with Dr. Shane and Father Duncan. And they all think, they really all think that the only right home for you in the circumstances is with your father's people."

Chris's voice made a final descent to a period, as at the end of a speech or a piece of music. Eric saw that he was watching him closely. He had a kind of narrow expression that said: "Well, now, that part's done with and what's to come next?" Eric himself had a habit of observing faces closely: the masters at school to see whether they were only satisfied with your answer or really liked it, all grownups to see whether they were telling you the whole truth or keeping something back. He saw now that Chris was telling him the whole truth.

"I didn't know my father had anyone!"

"Oh, yes," Chris said carefully. "He had parents and a younger sister."

"Alive?" Eric's voice rose, and squeaked, as it often did recently.

"Yes. Living in New York City. Or, I should say, nearby."

"But why, but why? Why has everybody lied to me up till now?"

"I wouldn't say it was lying, exactly. They never told you that your father's parents were dead, did they?"

"No, but they were always saying: 'You're all we have, Eric, and we're all you have.' So I thought—"

"Well, that was a way of putting it. Not a lie, just not talking about it. There's a difference, isn't there?"

He was so shocked, so absolutely stunned. He had no feeling as to whether this was a good thing or bad.

Chris went on, "They planned to explain it all when you were older, probably would have done so before now if your grandfather had lived. Then you could have met these other grandparents." He went on confidently, more rapidly, "Yes, that was definitely their intention."

"But why was it a secret for so long?"

Chris paused. "You know how it is, Eric. People don't always agree about things. To put it quite simply, they didn't like each other. There was a lot of hard feeling when you were taken to live with your mother's parents instead of your father's."

"You mean, they wanted me, too?"

"Oh, yes, they did, very much. After all, they loved their son and you're their son's child."

"But what was everybody angry at everybody about?"

"I hate to say this, Eric, although I'm sure you've learned a few things about this imperfect world by now . . . it was a matter of religion."

"Were they—were they Catholic, then? Was that it?"

"Not Catholic. Jewish."

Jewish! But that was—that was the *craziest* thing! How could that be?

Jewish! Like David Lewin at school. He couldn't think of anyone else he knew who was. He remembered when David had first come to the Academy in fifth grade. Everybody liked him except one boy, Bryce Henderson. No, two boys. Phil Sharp also. They'd said nasty things to David about being Jewish and David had punched Bryce and made his nose bleed. Then the headmaster had called David in and asked him why he'd done it and David wouldn't tell, because everybody knew the headmaster was always talking about bigotry and prejudice. "That's something we tried to wipe out in this war we've just finished," he would say. So David didn't tell on them and took his demerit, which was really swell of him and afterward most of the guys said it was.

Yes, he was a nice enough guy, David. Once he and Jack Mackenzie had been invited to David's house, near where his parents had the clothing store in Cyprus. It was some kind of holiday with a big dinner and wine. The father drank his out of a silver cup and everybody sang. It was neat, yet queer and foreign, too. Eric had invited David back to his house once, but that was all. There hadn't been any reason why they should become special friends, although probably David would have liked to.

And my father was like David! Hard to *believe!* His heart was really drumming now. He didn't *like* it. It was too odd, too strange. Different. Like David.

"I suppose they really should have told you before." Chris was almost talking to himself, thinking out loud. "At least, I always thought they should. We all thought so. . . . But they did what they believed best, goodness knows, they did."

"Did you know my father?"

"I certainly did. He was a very great person. He was one of my best friends at Yale."

"He was?" Eric felt a smile break out on his lips, a silly smile close to laughter; and close to crying, too. And he felt excitement, the way you do at a mystery movie when you're so scared of what may be coming next, and you laugh because you're scared. . . . "Have you—I never even knew what he looked like."

"Have I got a picture? I'm sure I've got snapshots of us playing tennis. I'll look when I get home and send them to you. I'll do it the minute I get home."

"Tell me in the meantime what he looked like."

"Well, something like you, as a matter of fact. I think you're going to be tall like him. He had light hair, too, and thick eyebrows like yours." Cousin Chris leaned forward with his chin in his hands and the boat rocked. "Funny, we were both going to be lawyers . . . we were both so certain of the future. And he's not here, and I'm in the oil business. Life is changes and surprises, Eric, as you're finding out right this minute. We never know what's around the next corner."

He had a sudden awareness of the planet whirling in empty space around the sun, with nothing to hold it up but its own speed. What if it were to slacken and fall? Fall where? A terror came over him. There was nothing to hold to, nothing firm, not even the ground under your feet.

"When am I supposed to go?" he cried in panic.

"When the semester's over at the end of this month."

"I don't want to go to live with them! I don't even know them! How can I go live in their house?"

Chris swallowed. He had a huge Adam's apple and it moved under the skin of his neck as if it would pop out. Eric had watched it at dinner last night. "Listen, Eric," he said, "I know it's a helluva hard thing, I wouldn't want to be in your shoes, and I'm going to level with you about that. You know I wouldn't fool you, would I?"

"I guess you wouldn't."

"You know I wouldn't. So listen to me. These have got to be good people. They couldn't have had a son as kind and good as your father if they weren't. They're going to love you; they love you already! It isn't their fault that you don't know them. And they're as close to you really as Gran and Gramp, don't forget."

I don't want to go, I don't want to go. . . .

He thought of something. "What about George? I can't go without George!"

"I'm sure you can take him."

The dog, hearing his name, pricked his ears and looked from one face to the other as if asking a question. Then he laid his enormous paw on Eric's knee.

"Why can't I live with you, Chris? I wouldn't be any trouble, I really wouldn't."

"I know you wouldn't. But you see Eric, Fran and I are going to Venezuela for the company, it might be for four or five years. And we have three children already."

"I could help with the children."

Something rippled across Chris's face. Eric thought he looked as if something hurt. "Eric, I wish I could. But Fran is expecting another baby, and she can't—she doesn't feel she can take on any more responsibility. You see what I mean? Do you, Eric?"

He didn't see, and he didn't, wouldn't, answer.

"I know it's hard for you to understand. My brothers are bachelors, my parents travel all the time now that Dad's retired, Uncle Wendell's past eighty. But you do have another place where you'll have a home and an education and—Eric, you'll see, you'll be happy there! I'll write to you, all the time, and you'll answer and tell me what you're doing and how happy you are, you'll see you will. Eric? You do understand, don't you, that it's not because we don't *want* you? Eric?"

He knew that if he were to answer his voice would come out in that high silly squeak again. There was a pain in his throat, and he didn't want to bawl like a little kid. He hadn't cried in years.

Suddenly he was bawling like a little kid, sobbing, his breath in gasps. He couldn't believe the sounds he was making. He was so frightened and ashamed of himself, and alone, cold and alone. And, hiding, he put his hands over his face.

For a while Chris didn't say anything. Then he began to talk in that way he had which was so quiet, as if he were almost talking to himself again and didn't care whether you were listening or not.

"I cried when my friend was shot down over Germany. Yes, I remember how I cried. I saw the plane go down, a long flame like a red pencil across the sky. . . . For a long time I had nightmares and woke up crying. I saw a lot of grown men cry in those years. Yes, yes."

The boat bobbed. George left his seat and went to lie down on the bottom, his nose resting on Eric's shoe. After a few minutes Eric felt a handkerchief being thrust into his hand. He wiped his nose and eyes and looked up. Chris was turned away from him, still not looking at him. Then Chris bent to the oars and began to row, parting the lime-colored curtain. They came out into sun and water so bright that it made you blink. They moved slowly toward home.

"Cousin Chris? Do I have to go right away? Couldn't I just stay here till the end of the summer, and then leave in time for school in the fall?"

Chris looked at him for a moment. Then he said gently, "That wouldn't be a very good plan," and Eric understood that he was saying, *Gran may not live until the end of the summer.*

"So then," Eric began, "are you going to tell them?" He didn't know what he was supposed to call them. He couldn't say 'Mr.' and 'Mrs.,' could he? But he certainly couldn't say 'Gran' or 'Gramp', either. "Are you going to call them up and tell them that—" He couldn't finish.

"That's already been done. As a matter of fact, they're on their way here now to see you."

"Today? This afternoon?"

"Yes, it's much too sudden for you, I know. I was supposed to get here last week to talk to you, but I had to go to Galveston instead and that's why it's all being done at the last minute. I'm sorry."

"I just wish I'd had more time to think about it before they came."

"Maybe in a way this is easier. Not to have so much time to think about it, I mean."

George climbed back up on the seat, his great head almost on a level with Eric's. The dog leaned heavily, closer, as if he knew. Eric was sure George knew when to give comfort. He thought of the time he had been scolded, his worst and only real, furious scolding, the time when he was ten and he had started the car up and taken it out the driveway. And then there was the time, not long after that, when Gramp had had his heart attack and died out on the porch after dinner. He remembered going up to his room, and sitting there all that evening with his arm around George just like this. There was something between himself and George that he'd never felt with anybody else.

The boat drew up at the dock with a soft bump and Chris tied the rope.

"Gran will be wanting to talk to you, Eric." They walked up through the hemlock grove toward the house. "You know, she's been far more worried about you than about her sickness. You'll make it easier for her to go back to the hospital and—you'll make everything easier for her if she knows you're all right. Remember it's hard for her, too. Not only for you."

He knew he would find her at her desk in the upstairs sitting room. She was mostly there lately, paying bills and going over papers, those stiff long crackly sheets that come from lawyers' offices. Trusts and wills and deeds, he heard her say, when she talked on the telephone.

He waited in the doorway. "Gran?" he called. Sometimes she didn't hear people coming up the stairs. "Gran?"

She swung round in the chair and he saw at once that she had been crying. It was the first time in his life that he had seen her tears. Even when Gramp died, she had said very quietly with a still, sad face, "He went without suffering, in his own home, at the end of a happy day. We must remember that and not cry."

But now she was crying. She stood up and put her head on his shoulder. He was as tall as she. And he was consoling her the way Chris had been trying to console him in the boat only a few minutes ago.

"I'll be all right, Gran, I promise I will." *Remember, it's hard for her too,* Chris had said. "Just take care of yourself, Gran. Don't be afraid for me."

She straightened up. "Oh, my dear, how wrong of me! As if there were anything for you to be afraid of! You'll have a good home, you'll be cared for! I'm not crying about that, it's just that—"

And he understood that they were being uprooted, torn away and apart. It was all without warning, like the night that the storm had destroyed the great elm in front of the house, the tree that had soared above their roof for almost seventy-five years, Gramp had said. In a few minutes of rage the storm had torn it out of the earth and it had fallen, with its great roots ripped, the clotted wet earth dripping from them. He remembered wondering whether trees could possibly feel pain.

"Sit down," Gran said. She wiped her eyes and wiped her glasses, straightening her face into the one he knew. Her face never changed very much. Even when she was happy it was kind of firm and plain. When she was cross—and she could get quite cross sometimes—he'd even hated her face. But not now. All he could think of now was that this face was soon going to disappear.

"Surely there must be a lot of questions you want to ask me? Things Cousin Chris didn't explain?"

"He explained, but I still don't understand it."

"No, of course not. How could you absorb all these changes in just a few minutes? I wish so much that there were more time."

342

"Tell me, why didn't they come to see me before? Why was everything such a secret?"

"We agreed, we all agreed, it would have been too confusing for a young child. You were only a baby. . . . This way, you had no doubts about where you belonged. It was really healthier for you. Yes, it must have been right, because you've always been so happy. . . . Still," she said thoughtfully, "still, I always did feel sorry in many ways. Mr. and Mrs. Friedman—by the way, Eric, we've been spelling your name differently, because we wanted to make it easier, more English. But they say 'Friedman. I, E, D.' That's the German way." When Eric didn't comment, she added, "I know it must be awful for you to find out that even your name isn't spelled the way you thought it was." He was silent.

"You'll make a new life, Eric. You'll see so many things in the city! You remember what a fine time we had that weekend last year when we went to the theatre and the planetarium and—"

He didn't want to talk about things like that. "Why did everybody hate everybody else so much? Why did it matter so terribly that they had another religion?"

But while he asked the questions he knew the reason, really. It was because—because Jews were odd people, not like the ordinary, everyday people you knew. They were different. He didn't know why, but they were. And he was one of them! Was he, or wasn't he? Yet, if he was, he didn't feel any change in himself.

Gran sighed. "The hatred, if you want to call it that, well, whatever it was, it wasn't all on our side. Believe me. Of course, Gramp did have very definite ideas, I can't say I agreed with them all. Sometimes they were extreme, but he was a very proud American and in a sense I can see what he meant by keeping your own ways, among your own people. . . . 'Let them go their way and I'll go mine,' he always said."

"But if he—disliked them so—how is it he never talked about them to me?"

"I suppose he felt he'd be talking about you, or a part of you, wouldn't he? And he loved you so!" She stopped. Her eyes had a remembering look, as though she were seeing things that had happened long ago, and hearing voices. "Yet I always felt," she went on, "that I would have done it differently, if it had been left to me. Not that I'm finding fault with your grandfather. He did what he thought was best for you. Perhaps he was right; dividing a child between two worlds is wicked and harmful. . . ."

Eric thought of something. "Did you ever see them? My father's parents?"

"Only once, when your own parents died. Oh," Gran said, "they're nice people, Eric! Gentle people, I thought. They'll talk to you about all this, I'm sure, when you get to know them. I've been speaking to them on the telephone these past few weeks and—"

Chris knocked at the door. "May I join you, or is this private?"

"Not private. Eric and I were only finishing what you began. I think—I hope he understands things a little."

"Aunt Polly? Perhaps you ought to go and lie down for a bit," Chris urged.

"Yes, I think I might. For fifteen minutes or so." She stood up and Eric saw that she tottered and had to take hold of the back of the chair. Her face was an awful yellowed gray; there were sweat stains under her arms. She was so fastidious. He'd never seen her sweat before.

He looked past her to the window. When the wind moved the leaves you could see the flat silver shimmer of the lake. He would be leaving that, too. It was like shedding one skin and growing another. This house, these trees, these faces would all be here, except for Gran's face! They would be here, and he not here. He would be someplace else, where he had never been before.

"Gran! Have you asked them—I mean, I have to take George. I can't go without George, you know."

"I'm sure that will be all right," Gran said. She looked at Chris and smiled. At the door she remembered something. "Eric, don't forget who you are. We've tried to teach you and I know you've learned good ways. You won't forget them?"

"I won't forget," he said. "And now I think I want to go out." And, seeing the question on their faces, added, "Not far. I won't be long."

He had a vaguely formed idea of talking to Dr. Shane, but when he passed the yellow house and saw that there were no cars in the garage he was in a way relieved. As Chris had told him, the doctor would only repeat what he now knew. He retraced his steps to his friend Teddy's, but Teddy had gone to the dentist and again he was relieved. He felt that he had to talk to somebody, had to tell somebody, like Chicken Little in the ridiculous childhood tale, running out to report that the sky had fallen. And yet he didn't really want to talk to anybody at all.

The Whitelys' horses were grazing near the road. He went over and stood by the rail fence, waiting until they saw him. He wondered whether they really knew him, or were only smelling the sugar in his pockets. Their soft noses snuffled into his palm. The brown and white pony, Lafayette, had a habit of shoving into the hollow of Eric's shoulder. He thought, I'd like to get on him and ride through empty woods; I'd just like to shed everything, feel empty of everything but motion, not think about Gran or school or whether I'll make senior basketball (I never will now, not in that school, anyway: somewhere else, perhaps; but where?). Not to think of anything at all. Animals understand. Dogs and horses. I'd rather be with them than with people sometimes. Gramp had promised him a horse of his own when he got to be twelve, but Gramp was dead by that time and Gran said that, what with tuition at the Academy and all, she just couldn't afford to maintain a horse. But the Whitelys were really nice; they let him ride Lafayette anytime.

"No more sugar," he said aloud, giving the last, and then walked on down the road, not knowing where he was going, with George plodding slowly behind. Now and then their feet cracked last year's fallen twigs.

At the top of a small rise the road branched off. Half a mile beyond you could see where one branch ran into the state highway. This was as far as he had been allowed to walk when he was a little boy. He remembered how, when he was so young that he had hardly been out of Brewerstown, he had stood there looking at the blacktop road with the white dividing line, wondering where it went after it rounded the curve and fell out of sight, who lived there, what *happened* there, where he couldn't see. He smiled to himself. Such a *child!* He hadn't known anything at all, still didn't, for that matter. He hadn't been anywhere except to Maine, to Niagara Falls with Teddy's family and last year to New York City with Gran. He wondered whether any of that curiosity, that surging excitement, would come back again, that feeling that there must be 'something down the road.' It didn't come back. There was only a great, looming dark. School and Teddy and all his friends, the scout troop, his boat and his room and Lafayette, all to

345

be wiped out, to disappear, as when you wipe the eraser over the blackboard.

He turned around and started back. He was ashamed; he oughtn't to be thinking about himself, when Gran was going to lose everything. He oughtn't to be thinking about what would be coming next for him when for Gran there would be nothing coming next. Or probably there wouldn't. He hoped he was wrong about that, hoped she would really meet Gramp again, as she was certain she would. (Was she really, truly certain? Or did she only say so for his sake, and perhaps for her own as well?) Anyway, one thing he could hope for her, that she wouldn't have too much pain.

Ahead of him he recognized Father Duncan's car turning into the Busbys' driveway. He would be making his weekly visit to the old lady, who had broken her hip. He started to cross over, not wanting to be caught up in greeting or conversation, but Father Duncan hailed him and he was caught after all.

"So everything has been straightened out, has it, Eric? I talked to your grandmother on the telephone awhile ago."

It seemed that everyone except himself had known about what was to happen to him. His future had been disposed of the way you sell a horse or a dog, except that he would never sell a horse or a dog, never send it away from its home.

"Yes, Father. All settled," he said.

Father Duncan had a keen gaze, a way of putting his head on one side as if he were estimating your size and weight. "If there are things that puzzle you, that trouble you, Eric, come and talk to me. Tomorrow or anytime. Will you?"

"There isn't anything," Eric said. Or rather so much that he didn't want to talk about it. It was like looking for the needle in the haystack; you'd never find it, so why even try?

"Let me just say one thing quickly, Eric. Your other grandparents—they're of a different faith. You must respect it. I know I don't have to tell you that. Respect it, but hold on to your own. You can. It's perfectly possible for you to live there happily and love them as I know they love you, and still keep your faith. You understand?"

"Yes, Father."

"You remember Christ said to his disciples, 'And lo, I am with you always, even unto the end of the world.' If you remember that

He is with you, times when you may feel lonely, missing people, it will help enormously."

"I know," Eric answered, feeling nothing.

"Well, I'll be going in to Mrs. Busby," Father Duncan said.

Dr. Shane's car was still out. Lafayette was still grazing near the fence. Nearing home, Eric saw the car in the driveway. It was a long dark car. Even from here he could tell it was a Cadillac.

He slowed his walk. Jeepers, he thought, and hoped they wouldn't get all sloppy, maybe cry and hug him and kiss him and all that crap. He went sweaty with embarrassment and fear.

Gran was standing with some other people on the front steps. She was looking up and down the road, looking for him. Then she saw him.

"Eric!" she called.

His heart began to knock, actually knock inside him. He was so scared he hoped he wouldn't do something awful like crying again or throwing up. He had a crazy flash of memory, something about Gramp and Indians and battles and brave ancestors. He knew it was ludicrous, that it had nothing to do with the present situation. Still, Gramp would have expected him to put his head up.

They were all turned now, looking toward him. There was a man in a dark city suit. There was a tall lady in a bright dress, looking too young to be a grandmother. *His* grandmother. He had a crazy sense of unreality: maybe I am dreaming all this? The lady had red hair, and that surprised him. He hadn't expected red hair, although he didn't know just what he had expected.

They were coming down the steps. He straightened, and with one hand resting on George's collar, walked toward them slowly across the grass.

31

Anna lifted the warm dough from the bowl as carefully as if it were alive and placed it on the porcelain table, then floured it and took up the rolling pin. A fine, soothing, calm washed over her, as always when she had the kitchen to herself. She moved without haste, handling the familiar pans and spoons.

Eric came in from the yard. "What are you making?" he asked.

"Strudel. Do you know what that is?"

He shook his head.

"It's a kind of pie, only much better, I think. I've already made one batch this morning for your Aunt Iris' house. It's in the pantry. Go take a piece and tell me how you like it."

When the dough had been rolled flat she brushed it with salted butter and began to pull it carefully, so as not to tear it, stretching it as thin as tissue paper until it hung over the edge of the table. Eric watched silently. He had cut a small piece and stood there, eating.

"Is that all you took? Don't you like it?"

He nodded.

"Well, then, take more! Go take a big piece. A tall boy like you, you've two hollow legs to fill up." She smiled and he smiled back, returning measure for measure. She wondered whether her own smile had been as urgent. Probably it had been.

"Don't you want milk? Something to wash it down with?"

He went to the refrigerator and poured a glass. She saw that he had been thirsty. Cutting the strudel dough, mixing the filling, she watched him without letting it seem that she was doing so.

After four months of living together she was not yet accustomed to the sight of this stranger who was of her flesh. She kept noticing new features: a mole on the cheek, a scar on the elbow. He would have distinction when he was grown, she thought. His hair, now sun-streaked, was exceptionally thick and rich. The aquiline nose, found usually on darker, Mediterranean faces, gave his a kind of elegance. His eyes were guarded by the arc of heavy lids; when he lifted them abruptly you were surprised by a gaze of charming candor.

She wondered whether, in that other life, he had ever been talkative. When boys came over after school now, pushing noisily into the house on these bright fall afternoons, she saw that Eric always stood a little apart, a little quietly. It was not that he was rejected or ignored; it was just that he seemed to be not quite *of* them. She suspected that it was his height and good looks which were passing him successfully through the cruel gamut of adolescence. Thoughtfulness at that time of life, she reflected, remembering Iris, was not a social asset, especially when it was accompanied by private school manners. Eric's homeroom teacher here in the public school had told him not to address teachers as 'sir,' an instruction which had confounded Eric; he still forgot sometimes and used the form when speaking to adults.

But he had brought assets with him, too. He was a top basketball player and the years of living at the lake had made him a sturdy swimmer. Iris, concerned as always with 'psychology,' had gone to the school before it opened and spoken to his adviser about Eric. She had followed up again only last week and been told how well he had adjusted. Extraordinarily well, Iris reported, considering the bewilderment anyone would feel after such an upheaval.

The courage it must have taken! On the ride back, that first ride from Brewerstown, if that man Chris, the cousin, hadn't come along—and stayed for two days to help 'settle in'—it would have been unthinkable for them all. As it was, the boy had spoken hardly a word on the entire ride. What was there to say? Joseph had been so tense that he hadn't talked, either. So Anna and Chris had spent a couple of hours making conversation about Mexico, where he had just spent six months. He had described Mexico City from one end to the other. He knew the area where her brother Dan lived; the houses there were very fine, he said. Then he had talked about Maury. She had forgotten that Chris was the young man whom

Maury had so admired and visited in Maine. He'd talked of how
bright Maury had been and of how they had met when Chris had
had an accident. And Anna had thought: A stranger falls on the ice
on a winter's night, and half a dozen lives are changed. A new life
exists because of it. How does one begin to understand it all?

But Eric was doing well. Thank God, he was doing remarkably
well. Everyone said he was.

She opened her mouth to say something, wanting to make a connection, such as: Eric, I love you; I'm still not over the marvel of
your being here; Eric, it's like having your father back again—

But she had done that once. It had been during his first month,
when suddenly she had been moved to tears, tears so jubilant and
so painful that she had not been able to hold them back. She had
seized his hands and kissed him. And he had pulled away with such
an expression (of alarm? distaste? embarrassment?) that she hadn't
done anything like it again.

She said calmly, talking half to herself and half to him, "Now we
put in the apples, some raisins, some almonds, and I always like to
add currants. Most people don't, but it gives a nice tart flavor, don't
you think?" she went on, turning the long, fat roll over and over on
the table before cutting it into three sections and putting it in the
oven.

Eric nodded again.

This time she had to say what was on her mind. "You never call
me anything, or your grandfather, either. Of course you can't call us
'Gran' or 'Gramp.' But I do think we need to have names. Won't
you decide on something?"

"I don't know what to choose," Eric said.

"When you were a tiny boy, just starting to talk, you called me
'Nana.' "

"I did? I don't remember."

"Naturally you don't. But would you like to call me that? And
your grandfather could just be 'Grandpa,' couldn't he?"

"All right. I'll start now, Nana."

"Eric? Is it very hard for you here? What I mean is—oh, I've put
it clumsily, of course it's all been hard for you—but what I meant
was, because it's *here*. Is it too different? That's what I meant."

"No, no. It's very nice here. I like the school and my room and
everything. Honestly."

"I realize that we're probably very different in ways that we mightn't even be aware of. It's not simple. But if you'll just remember that we love you it will be simpler. Can you understand me?"

"I do understand."

"Well, then, enough of that! What are you planning to do with this nice Saturday?"

"I've got a pile of math to get out of the way. I thought I'd go sit outside to do it."

Every chance he got he went outdoors. Perhaps he felt confined in the house? This town, this house and yard, must seem so small after all that free space.

"I told you Cousin Ruth is coming to spend a few days, didn't I? Grandpa's gone into the city to call for her. Maybe if you're finished with your work by the time they get here he'll take you out to buy the football helmet and things you need."

"That'd be neat."

She watched him spread out his books and then started upstairs to change out of her work clothes, thinking with a pleasant thankfulness of him and Joseph going out in the afternoon. Joseph had taken charge of fitting Eric out for school and that was good; the boy needed a man; he'd been too long with an old woman, and a sick one, at that. Joseph and he had had lunch and gone to a couple of baseball games during the summer; it seemed as if they were really coming together. A pity that Joseph couldn't spend more time with him! But he was always so busy.

They had joined a small beach club for Eric's benefit. People here sent their children to camp and, except for the two Wilmot boys down the street whose parents couldn't afford to send them, there had been no one around all summer. But Iris, because Anna had never learned to drive, had dropped off the Wilmots and Eric at the beach every day, which was generous of her, busy as she was with her two babies.

Such darling little boys! Just eleven months apart and Stevie was walking now. Their coming had made such a difference in Iris. But not only their coming: first Theo's coming, and the house, and the perquisites that go with the title 'Mrs.'! If she were a Sicilian peasant, Anna reflected, Iris would have a dozen children gladly. She was at her best when she was pregnant. All the tension went out of her face. Even her voice was pitched more softly, more confidently. She had grown enormous each time, but she hadn't made the usual attempts to minimize her size. In fact, she had flaunted it, especially in front of childless women or women with only one child who weren't able to have any more.

She'll not stop at two. It isn't kind of me, but I envy her fruitfulness.

Not kind of me, either, that I feel such pride in showing Iris off to Ruth. Not that Joseph won't have been doing it before they reach here, if only to save himself from her babble. "That woman talks my ear off," he'd grumbled again before leaving this morning.

But I do feel pride! All those years of having people feel sorry for Iris! Especially Ruth, with her three daughters married young. Now Iris has what she wanted; she's had so little. (The innocents, born into trouble, Iris—and Eric, too.)

Ruth will be amazed at Iris' new house. Joseph had built it for them; it was nothing that either he or Anna would have wanted, but it was what Iris wanted and Theo apparently had no objections to it. A kind of glass box it was, glass and dark, stained wood, standing in a grove. A startling house, airy and light, but quite plain, almost severe. Still, it had been written about in an architects' magazine, and people did slow their cars down to stare at it when they went by.

One thing, surely: Iris would never, nor would her children, have to stand in shame in front of an Uncle Meyer waiting for somebody to offer kind charity and a roof. Nor would Eric.

She glanced outside. He had moved to the top of the wall. His books were open beside him and he was sitting quietly, looking toward the orchard, with his arm around the dog George. Curious, she watched. What was he thinking? Certainly he was not demonstrative or revealing, as Maury had been. Maury had worn his heart on his sleeve. He must be like his mother.

He had been remarkable at his grandmother's funeral, hadn't cried at all. Of course, her death had been expected, but it had been shocking, all the same. Death always is. It had been in Eric's second month with them that the call had come and a dry, old voice (Uncle Wendell, he'd said) had told them that Mrs. Martin had passed away. So Joseph and Anna had driven back to Brewerstown with Eric, purposely avoiding the street where he had lived, but he had been asleep on the back seat anyway.

352

"Such calm!" Joseph remarked later. "That part of him certainly isn't like our family." Anna had acknowledged that he was referring especially to her, who cried so quickly and easily.

But Eric had sat quietly through the funeral service, shaken hands with the minister and dozens of townspeople, then got back in the car with them and fallen asleep again all the way back, a good six hours' drive.

"He's got courage, that kid has!" Joseph said. "He can take what comes. That's what you call grit."

But it was a hard time, all the same.

Hard for me too, Anna thought with abrupt irritation. I didn't realize I could get so tired. I thought I was younger than I am. People assume I can do everything: help Iris with the babies, rear a teen-age boy and start to worry about college and all the other complications— With equal abruptness came the prickle of hot shame. Self-pity! Of all the disgusting qualities a human being can have!

She heard the car come up the drive and, a moment later, Ruth's and Joseph's voices in the hall.

"Where's Eric?" Joseph inquired of Celeste.

"He and the dog walked down the road a few minutes ago, Mr. Friedman. Went down toward the Wilmot house."

"Oh, well, you'll see him later," Joseph told Ruth. He carried her suitcase upstairs to the guest room and set it down. "Well, I'll leave you girls to yourselves and look at the paper till Eric gets back." Beneath the courtesy Anna could read his impatience and knew that he had been drowned on the ride by torrents and floods of words.

"So how are you?" Ruth asked, and went on without waiting for an answer, "Country life agrees with you!" (She called this coming to the country!) "You look better every time I see you, Anna, in spite of your troubles."

"I have no troubles!" Anna objected. As if, she thought wryly, by denying them they will cease to be.

"Good, then, good, that's more than I can say. I don't know what I'd do if Joseph didn't let me have the apartment so cheap. He's a prince, Anna. You know the old saying, a mother can provide for five children and five children can't provide for one mother. Not that I'm complaining. After all, they have their own children, things aren't so hot for any of them, and you can't take blood from a stone, right? So what's this room? This isn't Eric's room?"

"Yes, it's Eric's room. We bought all new furniture, light and cheerful, as soon as we knew he was coming."

They had had to return the desk because he had brought his own. It was a completely incongruous drawing room piece, ponderous in its dark Chippendale dignity. But they hadn't dared tell him so. Apparently it meant a great deal to him. On it he had placed photographs of his mother and grandparents. Hanging above it was a portrait in oil, very old, of a man with mutton-chop whiskers and a string tie.

"That's my great-grandfather Bellingham," Eric had told them when they inquired. "No, my great-great-grandfather. He was a sort of hero in the Civil War. Have you any portraits on your side?" he'd asked Joseph, who seemed to have thought for an instant that the boy might be joking. But of course he had not been.

"They didn't have portrait painters where I came from," Joseph had answered gently.

Beside the desk Eric had hung a shelf of books, all about birds, Anna saw, the identification and classification of birds. But when she had made comment he had said no, he wasn't especially interested in birds. She had wondered, but asked no more. Celeste reported that Eric wanted the desk because his grandmother had always worked at it. Probably there was some similar memory attached to the bird books.

"I felt so sorry for him when you brought him here last June," Ruth remarked now.

"I know."

Nevertheless, he had been cared for most lovingly. That was plain to see, Anna thought with some jealousy. And then: how sad it all was! How hard for that woman, after so many aloof, proud years, to have to appeal at the end to Joseph and Anna, after all!

"What courage it must take to face one's own death like that," she had told Joseph.

"We all face our own death, don't we?"

"Not like that. Not to have to say, 'By August I shan't be here; now what shall I do about this, that and the other?' As if you were preparing to move to a new house."

Ruth interrupted her thoughts. "As usual, Joseph hasn't spared anything, has he?"

Anna smiled. No, he hadn't. He had filled the shelves and closets with books and clothes, cameras, ice skates and tennis rackets.

There were a radio and a record player. He had even wanted to buy a television for Eric, although they already had one downstairs and most people didn't own any yet. But Anna had said a firm no to that. Too much was too much and besides, a boy ought to do his homework in his room and read, not watch television. Iris agreed and the subject was dropped. Often it annoyed Anna that Joseph would take advice so readily from Iris, but when *she* said the same thing he might choose not to hear it.

Eric's photograph album was open on the bed.

"This is where he lived?" Ruth never bothered to hide her curiosity.

"Yes. Look through it. Eric won't mind."

It was a record of his years in Brewerstown, the pictures carefully dated.

"You had a good time with that car we sent, didn't you?" Anna had remarked of a picture that showed Eric, aged seven or eight, sitting in a huge toy car.

"You sent it?"

"You didn't know? We sent you many, many things. Your rocking horse and roller skates and your two-wheeler." Then she had stopped, hearing herself boastful and bragging. But she hadn't meant to sound that way.

Joseph joined the two women briefly at lunch.

"My son Irving tells me he sees your signs all over Long Island," Ruth told him. "They tell me you're one of the biggest builders in the East. Well, I knew you when! That's right, isn't it, Joseph?"

"You knew me when," he agreed quietly, and Anna knew he was amused.

Ah, the sin of pride again! I'm full of it, she thought. But she was proud, proud of Joseph in the dignity of his achievement. She was aware that a rivalry existed between herself and Ruth, different from the ordinary rivalries that existed among all women, whether they are willing to admit it or not. Theirs came because they had known each other so long; they had started out at the same place and edged on parallel tracks through life.

Ruth was discussing the refugees in her neighborhood. "So hoity toity, talking German! They only came here ten or fifteen years ago. I've been in this country almost fifty years."

The Daughters of the American Revolution versus the Society of Mayflower Descendants, Anna thought, amused again.

355

Lunch over, they went out on the terrace. It was mild for October, the sun just hot enough to be a comfort on the flesh. A flock of crows flew clattering above the trees, and pointed south.

"This brick needs doing again," Joseph observed. "He did a lousy job. Where the dickens did Eric go, anyway? We were going to buy his football stuff."

Anna saw that he was bored and restless. "He'll be back soon. In the meantime, I've made strudel for Iris and Theo. Why don't you run it over and see the babies?"

"Good idea," Joseph said, sounding relieved, and disappeared into the house.

"So Iris is doing well? Joseph drove me past her house on the way up. I can't say I like the style but it must have cost a fortune."

Ruth's tart remarks had no more power to wound, poor thing. Anna responded calmly, "Yes, everything has turned out very well for Iris."

"She certainly wasted no time in starting a family! Of course, at her age, one can't afford to wait too long. Still, I must say, I was right, Anna. I'm the one who always told you she was going to improve in middle age and you must admit I was right."

She wanted to say, "Iris is thirty-one, which is hardly middle-aged," but caught herself and said instead, "I made pot roast for tonight with the recipe you gave me when I was first married. It's still the best way."

"Why do you work so hard over cooking when you have Celeste?"

"I just enjoy it. I send a lot of things over to Iris. Theo likes my cooking."

"You cook when you're worried," Ruth said sagely. "I know you a long time, don't forget. You cook, and I sew. I make dresses for my granddaughters, which they probably never wear."

Anna was silent, and Ruth went on, "Why don't you take a trip? You never do any traveling. If I had your money, believe me, you wouldn't see me for dust. Why don't you visit your brother in Mexico City? You haven't seen him in years."

"Twenty years. But we couldn't go now and leave Eric."

"I suppose not. Tell me, how are you going to bring him up? His religion, I mean. What's he to be?"

Anna sighed. "To tell you the truth, I don't know. Joseph and I hadn't thought of it, I'll admit, but it was Iris who said he might want to go to church. So Joseph said, all right, he would take him.

And Iris said, 'You'll go in with him, of course.' Well, we had thought of bringing him there and calling for him. But going inside? No. Iris said, 'How can you let a child that age walk in alone?' So we took him to that big Episcopal church in town. It was so strange, wondering what any of our friends would think if they should see us, and wondering what the people in the church must be thinking, those who might know us." Anna paused to recollect. A splendid organ, singing, and Eric's clear voice. Great decorum, a *high* atmosphere.

"And so?" Ruth prodded.

"It was a very pretty service, Joseph said. I almost laughed. If it hadn't all been so serious and so confusing, I would have. Can you imagine, *Joseph* in a church? 'Will it kill us?' he asked me. 'As long as the boy believes in something,' he said. But after the first five or six times Eric wouldn't go anymore. And do you know, Joseph was upset about it?"

"Why didn't he want to go?"

"He said he didn't believe in it anymore. We tried to talk to him, but he wouldn't go back."

"Maybe he wants to go to temple, do you think?"

"We took him there once. And Joseph asked him if he might like to learn something about our faith, but he said no, he didn't care about that either. So that's where it stands."

Ruth sighed. "Well, you've got plenty of problems, Anna. I don't envy you."

Joseph was just coming in. "Problems? What problems? We haven't any. Eric's a great kid, if you're talking about him. He's got guts and he's one of the brightest boys I've ever—"

"Was he at Iris'?" Anna interrupted.

"No, they haven't seen him today."

"I wonder where he went? It's almost dinner time."

An hour and a half later Celeste came to the door. "Shall I wait dinner? Eric's not home yet, is he?"

"No. I mean, no, he's not home yet. Do you want to wait dinner, Joseph?"

"Might as well eat. I'm going to have a talk with him when he does come in. Funny, he's so well-mannered, so considerate. He never did this before."

"There's always a first time. And he's only thirteen." Her voice pleaded, but pleading was entirely unnecessary, she knew. For if

357

anyone were ever going to 'have a talk' with Eric about anything, it would not be Joseph. He was that soft with the boy.

Celeste served the dinner. Ruth was the only one who ate. Anna began her usual struggle against the sense of doom, the dark half of herself which she had been trying all her life to submerge. Why am I so distressed because a boy is late for dinner? It must happen in thousands of households every night of the year.

"He's been gone since morning," Joseph interrupted one of Ruth's monologues.

"Then why don't you call some of his friends, if you're so worried?"

"Who's worried? Why, are you?"

"No," Anna lied. "But go call the Arnold boy, he's the captain of the basketball team. Maybe Eric's visiting there."

From across the hall they could hear the murmur of Joseph's voice at the telephone. Apparently, he was making one call after the other. Celeste brought in the dessert, which Anna didn't touch. She strained to hear Joseph and couldn't. Even Ruth fell silent.

Joseph came back. "Well, nobody's seen him. But there are seventy-five boys in his class. I can't very well call all of them," he said brightly.

And a minute or two later, "I wonder whether he could be avoiding dinner with me? I hurt his feelings about the dog, I think."

"No, no, of course not! And he got his way about it, didn't he? Joseph didn't want to let the dog into the living room," she explained to Ruth, "on account of the light carpet."

"I should think not," Ruth agreed. "Carpet like that costs a fortune."

"Joseph is neater than I am," Anna admitted. "Besides, I feel sorry for the dog. He hates being left alone."

"My wife and her animals! I'm liable to find a stray horse in the house some night, too," Joseph said. He got up and went out again, adding, "I just thought of another call I could make."

"The real reason," Anna whispered, "why he gave in about the dog was that Eric said his other grandmother never even minded that he slept on the bed with him."

"On the bed! Is that quite clean?" Ruth asked doubtfully.

Anna shrugged. "What's the difference? So now George is allowed everywhere, as long as Eric promises to wipe his paws first before he comes in from outside."

Joseph came back. "That kid!" he said, and turning to Ruth, "You know, he's so well liked, there's no telling what friend's house he might be at. Probably playing chess, forgetting the time. He's quite a chess player for his age; it's a scientific game, you know that, of course. An intellectual game. We've got a very brilliant boy on our hands," he concluded.

"Of course, of course, Joseph. I told Anna, anyone can see that."

"So," Joseph said, "I'm going upstairs to look over some papers I brought home, and you girls can entertain each other. Let me know when he comes in. I'm going to give him a piece of my mind. But not too big a piece." He winked at Ruth. "Sure you girls can get along without me?"

The joviality was entirely unlike him, and it worried Anna. "You go on up and do your work," she said, "and don't be upset, Joseph."

"Will you stop talking about being upset? For heaven's sake, it's eight o'clock, and a thirteen-year-old boy is a little late. Honestly, Anna, sometimes you—" He shook his head, took his briefcase and trudged up the stairs.

"Shall I turn the television on?" Anna asked.

"No, it hurts my eyes. The children got me one for my birthday and would you believe it, I hardly ever look at it? I've got a magazine here, the last installment of my serial."

Anna took *The Conquest of Mexico* from the shelf. Joseph had promised a visit to Mexico time and time again. When Eric had been with them a little longer, she was determined to visit Dan. Perhaps during this winter's vacation; they might even take Eric with them! It would be a fine experience for the boy.

The book was hard going. She forced herself to concentrate, almost to memorize, as if she were going to take an examination on it. Her chair was turned deliberately away from the clock. It struck nine. Or had she counted wrong? Had it actually struck ten? She refused to turn around and look. Her mouth was dry. She was unexpectedly frightened.

"It's getting cold outside," Ruth remarked. "Listen."

"Those branches need to be cut," Anna answered, forcing a level tone. "They always knock against the window in the least wind."

She got up and went to the front door. A gust of chilling damp rushed into the hall. On the front lawn the tops of the trees tossed violently against a white sky. At eye level the darkness was absolute. There were no street lights in this section of town; that was one of

its rural charms. But tonight the darkness was grim. The wind
rushed like ocean tides. She closed the door.

Joseph was just coming down the stairs. "It's ten-thirty," he said.

"Perhaps you ought to call the police," Ruth suggested.

Joseph flashed her a furious look. "What? The police? Why? Ridiculous! What was he wearing, Anna?"

She frowned, trying to recall the morning, which seemed to have
been ages ago. "A plaid shirt, I think. It's hard to remember."

"The radio said the temperature has fallen twenty degrees since
six o'clock," Joseph said.

Anna was silent. She went back to her book, read one sentence
four times without understanding it and laid the book down. In the
kitchen, she could tell by the sounds, Joseph was making tea. She
heard the kettle whistle, heard the cabinet door click as he took out
a cup and saucer. Ruth sat quietly, she who could never sit more
than two minutes without chattering.

It began to rain. There were no preliminaries, no first patterings.
The squall simply came raging out of the sky and beat at the windows.

Joseph walked in, carrying his tea. "It's raining," he said, raising
his voice above the drumming.

"I know." They looked at each other.

"This time I'll really let that kid have it!" Joseph shouted. "You
know, it's not being fair to a child to let him get away with things. A
child needs to know limits," he said, as if he were imparting some
discovery or lecturing a class. "Yes, a child is happier when he
knows what's permitted and what isn't. No doubt he's sitting somewhere with one of his friends, having a good time, not giving a
thought to us, how we're—"

The doorbell rang. Their hearts lurched in their chests. It kept on
ringing as if someone were leaning against it.

"My God!" Joseph cried, running to answer.

He ripped the door open to the vicious weather, to the bobbing
arcs of a pair of flashlights in the hands of two state troopers who
stood behind Eric and the huge, wet dog.

They stepped inside. "Is this your boy?"

Ruth screeched, "God above, where have you been? You've
frightened your Grandpa and Nana to death, you ought to be—"

"Not now, lady." The trooper turned to Joseph. "You're the
grandfather? We found the boy on the highway, trying to hitch a

360

ride. He was heading for Boston, but he thought he was going northwest. Someplace in upstate New York . . . where was it, kid?"

"Brewerstown," Eric said. "It's where I live. I wanted to go back."

He stood there shivering and suddenly very small. The borrowed windbreaker enfolded him like a cape and hung almost to his knees.

"I don't understand," Joseph said. "You were running away?"

Eric kept his eyes on the floor.

"Seems so," the trooper said. "It's a good thing we came along. He got a lift, he and the dog, with some guy who was—you understand," he said, glancing at Anna and Ruth, "excuse me—some sort of queer. Luckily he was able to get out of the car when it stopped at a light. I guess maybe the dog protected him, too."

The veins pulsed on Joseph's forehead. "Why did you do it, Eric? You've got to answer me. We've been good to you, haven't we, Eric? Why did you do this to us?"

Eric raised his eyes. "Because I hate it here," he said.

Joseph and Anna looked from one to the other, then at Eric, and back to each other.

"Kids!" the trooper said. "Don't pay too much attention, Mr. Friedman. He needs a good old-fashioned hiding and he'll shape up. They usually do. Only not tonight, I wouldn't. He's tired out and scared to death." He turned to Eric with rough kindness. "You're some lucky boy, living in a house like this. I wish I could have grown up in it! And you had a narrow escape. You could be in plenty of trouble by now, and don't you forget it."

He replaced his cap. There was a flurry of thanks, then offers of repayment and refusal.

"A drink? A cup of coffee, at least?"

"No, thank you, Mrs. Just take care of the boy here. And you, mind your grandfather from now on, hear?"

The door closed, thudding into silence. Where Eric stood, in cotton trousers and thin shirt, a smudge of wet spread on the floor.

"Eric, tell me," Anna whispered, "tell me what's wrong?"

"I hate it here! It's a mean, ugly place. I hate this house! You had no right to take me away from my home, and I'm going back. I'm not going to stay. I'll run away again. You can't keep me—"

"What kind of crazy talk is this?" Joseph cried. "*This* is your home. You know there's no place else, no one but us to take care of you. You ought to be glad that—"

361

"Joseph! Hush!" Anna commanded. "Eric, listen to me. We can talk about all that tomorrow. But tonight it's late and you can't go anywhere in weather like this. There's nobody out tonight."

He swayed and grasped the back of a chair. "Come, come upstairs and then in the morning we can decide what to do," Anna coaxed, urging him toward the stairs.

He was so weary that he had to pull himself up by the banister.

"I'll heat a can of soup," Ruth whispered.

Joseph followed them and started into Eric's room.

"No," Eric said, "I don't want anybody. Leave me alone, all of you. I hate you all."

The door slammed in their faces. They stood in the hall.

"I don't understand it," Joseph said again. He twisted his hands together. "He's been so cheerful, so agreeable. We were going to buy football gear today. I don't understand—"

Last week Anna had noticed that Eric trembled, or so she thought, but when she had mentioned it, Joseph had said it was nonsense. She didn't remind him now.

Ruth came up with a cup of soup and joined them in the hall at the closed, defiant door.

"I don't know what to do," Anna whispered.

"This is ridiculous," Joseph said. "Three adults intimidated by a naughty boy. I'm going in."

He pushed the door open. Eric lay on the bed in his underwear, his face half hidden. His wet shirt and pants were on the floor. In the weak smudged light from the desk lamp they could see that he was weeping.

Joseph laid a hand on his shoulder. "Now, why should you be crying? A big boy like you, basketball champ, football player?"

"Joseph, get out," Anna said fiercely. Talking to the boy as if he were a backsliding three-year-old who had soiled his pants! He forgets how *he* cried, how we held each other when this child's father—

"What did you say?"

" 'Get out' is what I said."

"What are you talking about? Here's Ruth with hot soup, we only want to help—"

"You'll help by leaving him alone. Yes, there's one thing you can do. Hand me a quilt from the linen closet; there's a heavy blue one on the top shelf. And then go," she said, turning upon him a look which seemed to amaze him.

When she had covered Eric and shut the door she came and sat down on the bed.

"Now cry," she commanded. "God knows you've had reason enough. Cry it out. As loud as you want."

She had a glimpse of an anguished face; then the head went down to hide in the quilt, the body thrashed, shaking the bed. The sound of grief, deadened at first by the muffling quiet, rose into gasping cries, tearing the air, tearing the heart.

What can he think of a world in which his family always dies? Twice now, his home has been destroyed. Is he afraid that we too will die, Joseph and I? And then where will he go? Ought we to talk to him about that? Some other time, of course, not now?

A baby, Anna thought. Because he's tall and smart and speaks well we think he can cope with anything. It's hard enough for us to cope, old as we are. One foot stuck out of the muddle of quilt, one arm thrust over the head. Thin childish arm, large dangling hand of a man. Voice that veered from a squeal to a growl. And the first fuzz on the cheeks, so cherished, so anxiously examined in the mirror every morning. Maury used to take a hand mirror to the light at the window.

"Yes, cry," she repeated. "You've had enough to cry about."

On the opposite wall the haughty, elegant face of Bellingham looked at them from above the desk, surrounded by the books and photographs, the relics of the shrine that Eric had made. Yes, a shrine, built for the same reasons men have always made shrines.

Long minutes later (how many? Five? Fifteen?), the heap of quilting moved and struggled. A wet face emerged and was laid upon Anna's shoulder. Her arms went out and she raised the cheek to her own. And they sat there, rocking slightly, while the weeping died away into a long, shaking sigh. Then a quick sob, another sigh, long sighs and quivers and, finally, ease.

"Ah, yes, ah, yes," she said.

"I'm not asleep," Eric whispered. "Did you think I was?"

"No."

"Where is Grandpa? I want to tell him something."

"Grandpa, if I know him, is walking up and down the hall outside this room with his hands behind his back, the way he always does when he's terribly upset. Shall I call him?"

"Yes."

"Joseph?" she called.

The door opened instantly. "You want me?"

"Eric wants you."

Eric's head went back under the protection of the quilt. "I only wanted to tell you I don't hate you," he whispered, without looking up. "I don't hate it here."

"We know you don't," Joseph said. "We know." He cleared his throat. He coughed.

"George is hungry," Eric said.

Joseph cleared his throat again. "I fed him. He was very hungry. And thirsty, too. He's asleep now in the living room."

"I feel sleepy too, I think."

"Yes, yes," Anna said. "Lie down, I'll cover you properly."

"Doesn't he need something to eat?" Joseph asked.

"No, better for him to sleep now. In the morning he can have a big breakfast."

"Here, let me fix the quilt," Joseph said.

She stood a moment, watching his clumsy arrangement of it, feeling his need to do something, some little thing, anything.

Oh, for Joseph's sake, for mine, oh, not to lose this boy, too! Was it our fault? Can one ever say, "If this hadn't been, then that wouldn't have been?" But if it was our fault, let us hope not to repeat it—

So much to learn about this child, so little time left before he would be a man. And always, always, the secret places never to be entered. On those ancient maps that Iris collected there was a lonely boundary with a legend: *Terra incognita.* Unexplored land.

West of Gibraltar, Anna thought, where the world ended. They went out softly and as softly closed the door.

32

Vision blurred in the shimmering light; the sky, the sea and the sand merged in a white glare; figures were seen as red or blue dots in a painting by a Pointillist. But sound was distinct. It carried from far down the beach; swimmers' voices were heard on shore; they had the clarity of voices heard across snow.

The little boys were laughing in shallow water. Or rather, Jimmy was laughing while Eric held him, teaching him to swim, although he was only two and a half. Steve screamed and resisted.

Anna said, "It's strange that it's the older one who's scared."

"Jimmy's a tough little guy." Joseph chuckled. He admired toughness.

Iris was silent. She laid her book face down on her enormous belly, which formed a shelf; she was pregnant again, only five months, but she looked almost ready to deliver. She was thoughtful. People were beginning to think Jimmy was the elder boy. He was almost as tall as Steve and when they were seated Jimmy looked bigger and sturdier. Only this morning, when they had all arrived at the beach, Mrs. Malone had walked over to greet them and made the mistake. Iris read so much about the psychology of children but the books didn't really tell you what to do. In each special situation you had to use your own judgment.

Steve screamed again and Eric released him. He sat down in two inches of water.

"Don't you think—?" Iris began, but Theo, who had been walking on the beach with a colleague, came up behind her.

"You don't have to worry with Eric there. He knows what to do."

Theo had great regard for Eric. They all had. He was so dependable for his years, Eric was.

Now Eric carried Steve to the semicircle where they were all sitting. Jimmy trudged alongside. His walk was still a baby waddle.

"You don't have to," Eric soothed. "We won't swim anymore if you don't want to!"

"What's the matter? Why is he scared?" Joseph wanted to know. "Shouldn't you make him go back and learn that there's nothing to be scared of?"

"He can't learn all stiffened up like that, Grandpa. You'd just make him hate it. He's only three and a half, anyway."

"Yes, only three and a half," Anna repeated. "We forget because he's so smart."

Steve had astounded them this past week by picking out some words in the newspaper. He had remembered the 'c' for 'cat' in a picture book, the 'a' for 'apple' and the 't' for 'tree.' He had recognized the word 'cat,' and after that two or three more words, amazing the family.

Steve dove for his mother's lap. He burrowed, but there was no place to sit, so he butted his head hard against her.

"No, no," Iris said, holding him away. "You'll hurt Mommy, you'll hurt the baby in her tummy."

Joseph shook his head disapprovingly and muttered, "What next? You think he understands that? Much easier to tell him it's the stork and be done with it."

Privately Anna agreed, but, after all, it was Theo's and Iris' business. "Come here, come to Nana," she said. "Look what I have for you."

She was sheltered under a beach umbrella to keep her thin skin from peeling. She had a beach chair and a bag. The supplies that came out of this bag were seemingly endless: tissues, sun lotion, handkerchiefs, Band-Aids, a bag of homemade spice cookies, a novel for herself and picture books for the children. People always laughed affectionately at Anna's organization and took advantage of it.

"Here, sit down, Nana will read you a story," she told Steve.

He crawled on her lap, dripping wet sand. If he couldn't have his mother's lap, Nana's would be a good substitute. He was still shaking from his fright in the water, although he trusted Eric, knew Eric wouldn't hurt him. But he was scared anyway. And Jimmy was splashing water in his eyes. Jimmy hurt. Mommy was always saying, "Don't be so rough with Jimmy, he's still a baby." But Jimmy *hit*. He threw his pail at me.

He leaned his head against Nana's softness. She read *The Little Engine That Could*. Every day, somebody read it to him. It was his favorite book and he knew where all the words were supposed to come, beneath every picture.

Nana pulled two cookies out of the bag. "One for you," she said. "And one for Jimmy. Come and get yours, Jimmy."

Jimmy took his and walked to some people sitting near them on the sand. He stood and stared, holding his cookie.

"Oh, isn't he darling!" a woman cried. "Look, Bill, isn't that the cutest ever? What's your name, sonny?"

"Not sonny. Jimmy," he said.

"Well, hello, Jimmy. Bill, look at those eyes!"

Theo scrambled up to fetch Jimmy and apologized.

"He isn't bothering us . . . he's just a very sociable fellow."

"That he is." Theo smiled proudly, agreeing.

Jimmy came over and stood listening to Nana. He never listened very long. Nana said it was because he was too little to understand very much of the story. He still hadn't eaten his cookie, although Steve had finished his. He always walked around carrying his food as if he didn't want it and sometimes he would even drop it on the floor, but if Steve should pick it up and eat it he would howl. Seeing him standing with that uneaten cookie made Steve want another one.

"I want another cookie," he said, but his mother heard and said no, he wouldn't eat any dinner and one is enough. At Nana's house, he knew, he would have gotten another, but now Nana said, "Your mommy said no."

Jimmy's cookie was almost touching Steve's arm. He couldn't take his eyes away from it.

"Why don't you eat the cookie, Jimmy?" Nana asked.

Jimmy didn't answer. He laid it on the sand and picked up his shovel. Steve reached out and took the cookie. Jimmy howled and hit Steve with the shovel.

"No, no!" Nana cried.

Steve slid out of Nana's lap and shoved Jimmy. He fell and hit his head on the umbrella pole. He screamed.

His father jumped up and grabbed Jimmy to examine his head.

There was nothing wrong with it, but Jimmy kept crying. His father yelled at Steve, "If you hit Jimmy again you're going to be sorry!"

"He hit me with the shovel!"

"That's true," Nana said.

"I don't care, he's the older one and he's got to learn."

"I want my cookie," Jimmy sobbed.

"Did Steve take his cookie?" Mommy wanted to know.

"I think," Nana said, "I think he thought Jimmy didn't want it anymore."

Joseph groaned in mock despair. "Good God! You need King Solomon to settle this."

"Sibling rivalry," Iris explained. "A pain in the neck and perfectly normal."

Eric had just swum in from the float. "Come on, I'll build you a sand castle," he told the boys and drew them to the water's edge. "I'll build you a great big one, big as you are. I'll show you a shell I found. I'll put it to your ear and you can listen to it."

"Have you seen his shell collection?" Joseph asked. "Tell him to show it to you when you come next Friday, Theo. He's got a cabinet full in his room, all classified and labeled. Very methodical."

"He built the cabinet himself," Anna interposed. "You know, he's got golden hands. He can fix anything. Last week I wanted to call the plumber for the kitchen sink but Eric figured out what was wrong with it for me."

"You think he's content here, Theo?" Joseph asked anxiously.

"Yes, yes, he's come a long way in two years. You can see it for yourself, can't you?"

Joseph nodded happily. "Sure, but I wanted to hear somebody else tell me."

The beach was given over to the young. They dove off the dock and raced to the floats where they could be seen, when you shaded your eyes and squinted in the lowering sun, prone and spread-eagled, rocking and tilting on the water. They paraded along the strip of sand at the water's edge and gathered at the shed where ice cream was sold. The group of boys and girls formed and reformed in a ritual of watchful laughter and calculated ease, a ritual as carefully rehearsed and learned as fencing or ballet.

Three girls with new breasts and not one blemish sauntered casually toward Eric. Their perfect skin reminded Anna of a fresh white dress, just lifted out of tissue paper and not yet worn; it would never look quite like that again.

Eric said something to the girls and they saw him turn in their direction. Iris called to him and he walked over.

"Go along with your friends," she said. "You didn't come to baby-sit. And thanks for amusing the boys. ."

"Good!" she exclaimed when Eric had gone down the beach with the girls.

"What's good?" asked Joseph, who had roused from a half nap.

"That he didn't ask permission. He just went and didn't say where he was going." And when no one answered, Iris declared, "He's fifteen, you know. It's time."

"Yes, you're right," Anna said. Iris had the true gift of understanding. She had established something easy and trustful between herself and Eric. He dropped in often after school to visit; he was at home with Iris and Theo. That was as it should be. All the adults in his life had been too old, like Joseph and herself.

"Eric's so patient with the boys," Iris remarked. "He really loves them, you know?"

Anna observed, "Because he's been an only child, I suppose."

No, Theo thought, not so. Because, like me, he's been an orphan of the storm and he's grateful for the warmth. Grateful, that's what we are, he and I.

The sun struck with a penetrating sweetness; at the same time a breeze moved over his flesh. It was so good drowsing here, good to do nothing, to think of nothing. He lay back on the blanket. Theo liked beach life. Having grown up in Austria, he had never had any, yet now that it was available he didn't have much time for it.

But that was all right; he surely wasn't about to complain that his practice had grown so large! Sometimes he couldn't believe the changes in his life during these few years since he had emerged from disguise and taken part in the liberation of Paris. A friendless stranger only a few years ago, and now so—so established! A fine, gentle wife. Two and a half children. A beautiful house. He smiled inwardly. He really didn't admire the house; it was too modern, too austere with its abstract paintings and bare floors. So Spartan. The food was Spartan too, for Iris was no cook and didn't even know how to train a maid to cook. But all of that was unimportant, and plain

food was better for you anyway. Besides, Anna kept sending things
over to them, or inviting them. At her house one dined richly on
sauces, wines and whipped-cream cakes. Afterward one relaxed on
flowered chairs; Anna would bring out fruit and chocolates; Joseph
would pour brandy. They were lavish givers and enjoyers of good
things, his parents-in-law. They reminded him of Vienna. He closed
his eyes . . .

And started up, his heart drumming, bruising itself against his
ribs. Had he cried out in the agony of the dream? But no, no one
was looking toward him. He shut his eyes again. It had been a few
years now since this terror had last come over him, half waking, half
sleeping. An explosion in slow motion, it was, like a movie montage:
fragments of peaked Nazi caps and smart boots; his own garden wall;
a tiled corner of his roof; the rose-carved bed where he slept with
Liesel; the fuzzy head of their newborn baby; his father's hands,
pleading and chained; Liesel's eyes, screaming; all rose roaring into
the fiery air, splintered and crackled and broke, then settled into
ash.

It is said that time is merciful and that is true. The first mad
anguish fades to heavy sorrow and, after a long while, into a soft
weakness of tears that can be blinked away before anyone sees. But
not always.

In an old gesture he reached to twist the wedding band on his
fourth finger, a habit of his when he was agitated. Then he remembered that in this marriage he wore no ring.

This marriage, this new life. He had been thinking before he
drowsed that Anna and Joseph reminded him in some ways of
Vienna. Of course they were not at all like Vienna in many other
ways, or at least not like the Vienna he had known. He remembered
his parents' somewhat formal, somewhat rigid bearing, the modu-
lated voices at the table, with never any argumentation, no bicker-
ing, friendly or otherwise. *That* part was surely not like the Fried-
mans', where everybody talked at once, with such eagerness to be
heard! When they had more than a few guests the confusion was
dizzying. He smiled to himself. His heart had slowed to its normal
beat. Calm and reality returned. This was *now* and he was *here*.
These were his people. Such good people, such *home* people!

On Sunday mornings Joseph got up as early as on every other day
and brought fresh lox and bagels to their door. On Friday nights
when Iris and Theo arrived for dinner there was a package with two

toys for them to take home to Steve and Jimmy. No use protesting that the old man was spoiling the boys. It was his pleasure, and he wouldn't have listened to the protest anyway.

Usually Theo went home after the dinner while Iris went with her parents to the synagogue. But now and then of late he had gone with them too, surprising himself by doing so, for he had hardly been half a dozen times in a synagogue during his entire life. He found it boring and meaningless, but it pleased Iris so much that he went, and pleased his in-laws too. Joseph especially was so proud, so bursting-proud, to be seen walking in with his son-in-law, the doctor.

He felt a true fondness for Joseph. You would have to be callous to return nothing to a man who so evidently loved you, even though you knew you were in part a substitute for his dead son. No matter. A kind, kind man, Joseph was. He liked to call himself a simple man; it was a favorite expression of his. And actually he was. His pleasures were simple, not counting his work, which was probably his greatest pleasure. Other than that, he liked to eat the food his wife prepared, to be honored among the prominent for his charities and to play pinochle with old friends who were simple, too. One of them still drove a taxi; he always arrived at the house in his yellow taxi.

Theo liked to think of his children growing up in this un-complicated family. A warmth spread in his chest, thinking of it. The security, the safety! This broad peaceful country, this orderly town where his children slept in their clean beds. It was a miracle and there could be no other word for it. Out of the dregs and chaos of his own life, all this. This house, this family, these people. His.

A ripple of rising wind fell chill upon his shoulders. The sun was low in the sky. In small reluctant groups of threes and fours people were gathering their towels and bags and walking toward the parking lot.

He got up and helped his wife to her feet. She plodded heavily through the sand, holding Steve and Jimmy by the hand. The little boys were sleepy; they curled up on the front seat between Theo and Iris, their legs interlaced with one another's, for once not squirming or fighting. The grandparents sat in the back.

"A lovely day," Anna sighed.

Quiet settled over the beach. Even the gulls were gone (where had they gone?) except for one who stood at the end of the dock, a

371

dark, still shape against the light. The sun blazed its last fire, balanced on the rim of the sea, bleeding pink into the clouds.

"It'll be a hot one tomorrow," Joseph predicted, shaking his head.

Tomorrow and tomorrow and tomorrow. Separate from the other unnamed billions who walk the earth, each of these little groups of three or five or twelve, brought together by the shuffle of chance, then welded by blood, sees in itself the whole of earth, or all that matters of it. What happens to one of the three or five or twelve will happen to them all. Whatever grief or triumph may touch *any* one will touch *every* one, as they are carried forward into the unknowable under the brilliant, terrifying sun which nourishes all.

33

In the beginning it was primeval forest, ash and hemlock, maple, elm and oak. Then came the settlers to level the woods, plant corn and graze cattle. Trees were planted again for summer shade. During long years, two hundred or more, the farms were given by father to son and the land flourished.

Toward the end of the last century came men of wealth from the cities, gentlemen farmers assembling their estates among the working farms, building their country mansions behind walls and wrought-iron gates. Still the trees flourished, for these men liked to play at rural living. On their terraces they sat and watched their fine blue-ribbon herds; their burnished horses hung their heads over the post-and-rail fences that kept them away from the gardens and the specimen shrubs.

After the Second World War the developers arrived, answering the pressure of population from the cities. Now, for a second time, the trees came down, not selectively, a few here where needed, a few there, but drastically and ruthlessly, in a total leveling. An oak stood tall against the sky, its leaves at the crest still tossing in the summer wind, while the saw screeched at its base. It stood, leaned very slightly for an instant, then plunged in a wide arc to the ground and lay there shuddering, prone on the earth out of which its first soft, timid finger had emerged a century and a half before.

So the trees came down; the meadows were divided and subdivided and the bulldozers ripped the earth. Acre after acre, row

373

after row of identical houses like checkers on a board lay flat in the glare of the sun. The streets were given the aristocratic English names of poets and admirals. The houses were sold as 'manors' or 'estates,' in spite of the fact that very often one could reach out of a window and shake the hand of a neighbor leaning out of his.

Like a stain on a tablecloth the tracts spread over the countryside, covering the land. Then came the shopping malls, the crisscross highways; great transit systems in which roads looped and turned back upon themselves to handle the enormous flow of cars, so that the traveler who wanted to go west had first to turn east, find an overpass and swing back in the opposite direction.

Growing, growing, spreading, with no end in sight.

34

E ric sat on the steps of the sales bungalow, waiting for his grandfather. To the left stretched long rows of completed houses, all alike under the gray March sky. To the right, frames were going up; hammers racketed; dust rose in spurts of reddish cloud when a truck dumped a load of bricks; cement mixers rumbled. Enormous pipes, wide enough for two men to crawl through, lay among coils of glittery copper wire. A truck ground up a small incline. Another dropped a load of sheetrock. Confusion out of which, to be fair about it, would come order.

Soon he would be starting the fourth year in his 'new family,' so he had been on these visits to the building sites many times by now. He didn't really mind, as long as he wasn't asked to go too often. Today they had combined the trip with shopping for shoes and a raincoat. Grandpa said that was a man's business, not a grandmother's.

He didn't really need a new raincoat. Gran would have looked at his old one and said, "It'll do for another year," just as Gran used to say, "You already have enough sweaters, you don't need another one." Or, "You've really had enough to eat, Eric," a statement that would be unthinkable in the Friedman house.

Here, food was urged upon you, more than you could swallow sometimes. Here, something was always being bought for you. "You like the sweater? It's nice, I'll get it for you." Giving was a way of loving, not as a substitute for time or caring but only because, Eric

375

realized, they never seemed to find enough ways. If Chris and the family had had any worries about how he would be loved—and he had no reason to think so—they needn't have had them. He was bathed, surrounded and enveloped with it.

Chris wrote to him regularly. The other Guthries wrote from wherever they happened to be. Cards were mailed on 'round-the-world cruises. Greetings and small presents came from the house that the elder Guthries had rented in the south of Portugal. Chris wrote really long letters with descriptions of Venezuela and snap-shots of the children sent, Eric knew, to stave off any loneliness Chris thought he might be feeling. Eric tried to respond in kind. I've made the basketball team, playing forward. I got a new bike for my birthday. Everybody is good to me. I've got lots of friends. I'm in a new scout troop.

The truth was more complex than these flat facts. It was so very different, this household. For one thing, it was so busy. The sense of a busyness almost hectic came from his grandfather. Take today: it was supposed to be his free day. But as always there was some emergency which he absolutely had to attend to, even today, with Passover starting at sundown. He was always rushing somewhere. Eric had been surprised to learn that his grandparents had only lived seven years in town; they were as involved as if they had been there all their lives. His grandmother was on the hospital board and so many other charitable boards that he couldn't remember them all. Grandpa had built a chapel for the new temple and turned over his half of the profits as a gift. (Grandpa wouldn't have told him, but Aunt Iris had; she was so proud of him.) Last week a policeman had been run over chasing a suspect and the town had taken up a collec-tion for his widow and children; Grandpa was the head of the com-mittee. There was talk of his being appointed to a state commission to study public housing. No, he was not the kind of man with whom a boy could spend long afternoons in the woods with book and bin-oculars, hunting for birds. He wouldn't have been interested, even if he had had the time.

Perhaps, though, that wasn't fair? When you thought of his life and where he had come from? Once in New York they had driven past the house on Ludlow Street where he had grown up and past the house on Hester Street where Nana had come as an immigrant. He'd been shocked at the narrow, crowded streets and the mean houses. He'd never seen such places except vaguely in pictures.

376

. . . What could you learn of forests and birds living in places like those?

Last fall before school opened Grandpa had had to go to Boston on business, and Nana had suggested they travel north through New England for a few days. It was surprising, but Grandpa had agreed. They had gone all the way up to Mt. Monadnock in New Hampshire, staying in old wooden hotels with sunflowers in the yard and stacks of pancakes to start the chilly mornings. They'd walked around the white little towns and Nana had gone into antique shops and bought knickknacks of old glass.

"Keeps a woman happy, buying toys," Grandpa had said, and winked at Eric.

They had walked down a road, Grandpa and Eric, and stopped on a bridge over a stream where a couple of boys were fishing.

"Know anything about fishing?" Grandpa had asked and when Eric said yes, he'd often used to fish for trout outside of Brewerstown, he'd looked out over the sloping fields where the corn stubble was dry, and then to the hills, to the far blue ranges overlapping one another; he had looked and looked and finally said, "There's so much I've never seen, Eric."

So perhaps it wasn't right to say he wouldn't be interested.

On the way south it was Nana who had made a suggestion, as if she had been reading Eric's mind. "Maybe we could go back through New York State and Eric could see Brewerstown again."

It wasn't that he'd been afraid to ask. By this time he knew he could ask them for anything and they would give it or do it. The reason was that he hadn't wanted them to think he was homesick or not happy with them. They were so dreadfully sensitive about him! Once he had overheard his grandmother talking to that old lady Ruth who came to visit.

"Eric has grown even closer to our hearts than Maury was at that age," she had said. "Joseph used to be strict with Maury, remember? But Eric can do anything he wants." And she had sighed. "I don't suppose he can have any idea of what he means to us."

They would have been surprised to learn that he did have, that he observed far more than they knew. He saw, for instance, that when Grandpa was working especially hard and long he could be quite cross with Nana. Small things irritated him, a purse or a pair of gloves left lying on a chair, or being kept waiting for five minutes. And Nana didn't answer him back. But he was never cross with

377

Eric, never once, although Nana sometimes was, but not very often, either.

They were soft with him because they were afraid he wouldn't love them, he knew that clearly. There had been times when he'd been so sorry for himself, especially during the first year; no kid he'd ever known had been in his position. In a way he still sometimes felt a little sorry for himself. But most times he was more sorry for the two old people, he didn't know just why.

So they had stopped in Brewerstown. Driving down the main street toward the house he'd had a sick feeling and slumped in the car, hoping nobody he knew would see him. He'd remembered the day he left the house almost three years before. Gran had gone back to the hospital where she was to die. They had carried her out, all shrunken and dark yellow, with a strange unpleasant odor not like Gran, who had always smelled of lemon soap. When he had gone down the front walk for the last time he had been thinking that the house would be lonesome for them. On the way out he had stopped to stake an enormous peony head that otherwise would have drooped in the dust along the front walk; Gran was so particular about her peonies. He'd tried in those last minutes to memorize everything: the hawthorne tree, a real hawthorne from England, with wicked needles; the mulberry bush where he used to make a shady cave for himself and George when they were both very young. It had seemed to him that all of these were aware that he was going away. He'd gone down the path between Grandpa and Nana, strangers then, had got into their car and all the way down the road, until the house was out of sight, had not allowed himself to look back, had just stared straight ahead.

So now they had come up before the house again and, astonishingly, it looked the same. There was a doll carriage on the front walk. A baby carriage with a mosquito netting stood on the porch. They had sat in the car observing a croquet set on the side lawn and wash blowing on the line near the garage. The house was alive, as if Eric had never lived in it and left it. . . .

"Would you like to go in?" Nana had asked. "I'm sure the people wouldn't mind—"

"No," he'd said firmly. "No." They had understood and started the car and driven away.

Wanting to say something, Eric had pointed out the horses in the

Whitelys' field. "That's Lafayette, the brown and white one. I used to ride him almost every day."

"You never said you could ride! Why didn't you tell us? I'll buy you a horse," Grandpa had exclaimed. "There's a good stable not fifteen minutes away from our house!"

"No," he'd refused. "No, thanks. I don't have the time now, with school and basketball practice and everything."

But that wasn't the truth. The joy of riding, the free wind, the horse-companion—all that belonged to the other life. He mustn't mix them up. It had been confusing enough. He must keep the lives separate. That other was finished and closed. Forget it.

The door swung open now and Mr. Malone came out. He sat down with Eric on the step.

"Your grandfather will be through in a couple of minutes." He wiped his forehead. "This is some big job, let me tell you. Think you'd like to run this business?"

"I don't know, sir," Eric answered politely.

"Silly question, wasn't it? How could you know? But you will! My boys have taken over magnificently. And your grandfather will be in seventh heaven the day you hang your hat in our office." He lowered his voice. "You know, Eric, he's a different man since you came. Not that there was anything wrong before, but now it's as if he'd shed years. I can tell. I've known him long enough. You know how long I've known him?"

"No, sir."

"It was in 1912. Let's see, that's thirty-nine years. We've seen a lot of life together. Did he ever tell you how I was wiped out in the stock market in '29 and how he took care of me?"

"No, sir."

"Well, of course, he wouldn't. But *I'll* never forget! He fed me and my whole family until I was able to pull myself together again. Yes," Mr. Malone said, "old times. Old times. Seeing you here reminds me of when your father used to come to visit the job in the city. He was younger than you are. You don't mind my mentioning your father?"

"No, sir."

" 'Sir.' I like the way you say 'sir,' although I wouldn't object if you didn't. But it shows you've been well brought up. Kids these days don't say it. Except the parochial school kids. *They* have manners. They have to, or Sister would rap their knuckles for them."

Strange how many different kinds of people there were around here, Eric reflected. Mr. Malone was so Catholic! And one of the engineers was Chinese; after you got used to his odd face you could see it was really handsome.

"Your grandfather had better put a move on." Mr. Malone looked at his watch. "If he wants to be home in time for the Seder."

Imagine Mr. Malone reminding his grandfather of the Seder!

Grandpa came out and they got into the car. "Some project, hah?" he said, as they bumped their way around bulldozers and cranes. "Three million dollars' worth! Don't get me wrong, we don't make that out of it." He laughed. "Not by a couple of long shots, we don't. What I meant was, we have to get that much together from the banks and syndicates to get the thing started. A thousand hours of headache, I can tell you that. But it's a great challenge, Eric, a thrill to drive past when it's all finished, and see the cars in the driveways, curtains in the windows, kids playing on the sidewalks. To think that you—we—conceived it in our heads and saw it through. Think you'd like it?" he asked, as Mr. Malone had done.

"There's an awful lot you have to know," Eric said.

"Ah, but you'd take to it like a duck to water, you would. We sold nineteen houses last weekend alone. What do you think of that?"

"Gosh," Eric said.

"Say, it's your birthday next week, isn't it? I don't suppose you'll tell me what you want. You never do."

Actually it seemed to him that he already had everything. But then, as the car turned a curve and they passed a pair of gates set in stone pillars, he suddenly did think of something he would like.

"You know what I would like, Grandpa? If it isn't too expensive, I think it would be great if you'd join the Lochmuir Club. Then I'd have a place for tennis anytime I wanted. Even in the winter."

"The Lochmuir Club? What do you know about that?"

"It's really nice. I was there, remember, last year when those friends of Chris's were visiting relatives in town? And Chris asked them to look me up? They took me out to dinner there."

"I didn't know that's where you had gone."

"Some of the kids at school belong. They've got squash courts and an indoor pool. The swimming pro there trained for the Olympics, too."

"Sounds very fine," Grandpa said slowly.

"So you think we could join, do you?"

"No," Grandpa said, "we couldn't."

"Is it too expensive? Is that why?" Although, if that was the reason, it would be the first time his grandfather had ever denied anything because of it.

His grandfather took his eyes off the road for a moment. "That isn't the reason. Don't you know what the reason is?"

"No."

"Think, Eric."

It dawned upon him, and a warm flush prickled his neck. "Is it because you're—"

"Don't be afraid to say it. Because we're Jewish and we are not admitted to that club. Not as members. Not as guests in the dining room. You never knew about that?"

"Well, I've read things here and there, but I guess I've never thought about it very much."

"No, you haven't had to, have you?" His grandfather's mouth looked grim.

They rode for a few minutes in silence. Then Eric said, "Those people said they were coming back east this summer and they'd call me again. I'll tell them I can't go."

"You don't have to do that. You can go."

"I don't think I want to."

"Well, it's up to you." Another silence. Then his grandfather turned with a smile, a manufactured smile? Eric wondered. "Well, here we are, in plenty of time to change for your grandmother's big dinner. You remember, of course, that we dress for Seder, Eric."

"I remember," Eric said.

The table was set with a lace cloth and the silver candlesticks which always flanked the bowl of flowers in the center. Tonight were added the holiday objects which Eric would be seeing for the third time, not counting the dinner, long ago, at the house of that boy David, the dinner which then had seemed so queer and foreign, but which now seemed very natural. It was a festival of freedom, as Grandpa had thoroughly explained. He recognized the matzoh under its embroidered cover, the plate of horseradish, symbol of the bitterness of slavery, and the green parsley that celebrated the first fresh growth of spring. He knew that the silver goblet, already filled with wine, had been prepared for the prophet Elijah who was to announce the coming of the Messiah, and it was there "just in case he might be coming tonight," Grandpa would say with a wink.

There were twelve places at the table this year, places for friends who had no family to go to, and a place for a young man at Grandpa's office who had just tragically lost his wife. Two of the places were for Steve and Jimmy, old enough this year to be present for the first time.

Everyone was dressed up; the clothes looked new and the women had just come from the beauty parlor. Everyone babbled. Aunt Iris was worried about the baby, Laura, who had been left at home. She was worried that the little boys wouldn't behave. "So what's the difference?" someone said, "it's family!" Grandpa picked the boys up and squeezed them. It was Jimmy who would ask the four questions, Eric knew, because he was the youngest male at the table. Yes, by this time Eric knew exactly what would happen, the order of the evening. " 'Seder' means 'order,' " Grandpa had told him. He knew that the food would be delicious. Nana had been working in the kitchen over soup, fish, and chicken; there would be cake and strawberries and macaroons for dessert. But it would be a long time until dessert, a long time even before they had the first mouthful of food, and Eric was prepared to be restless.

Grandpa took his place in the armchair and waited for Nana to bless the candles. His eyes were shining. This was one of the greatest hours of the year for him. His eyes rested in turn on everybody up and down the table. Then he turned back to the illustrated Haggadah which lay open beside his plate. He lifted his cup and said the blessing over the wine. The men at the table—except for Eric and Uncle Theo—joined him in the old words that they must first have heard when they were the ages of Steve and Jimmy, who were sitting surprisingly still, with big, round eyes.

"Now, what does Passover mean? It commemorates the night when the Angel of Death spared the homes of our forefathers in Egypt and we were led out of slavery."

Eric watched and listened. It was all bright and beautiful, like poetry. But it would be artificial for him to learn this ritual. It was not his. Aunt Iris told him once (they had had many talks together; she was frank and honest to talk to) that his father hadn't really liked being Jewish.

"He wanted to be more American," she had said. "But I never saw any conflict. We have a four-thousand-year-old tradition and it's a part of the American tradition, woven into it. The Puritans were Old Testament people, you know."

"It's strange," Eric had observed, "that he and you lived in the same house and this means so much to you. Why do you sup-pose—"

"I don't know," she had answered.

And Eric had told her, "I don't especially want to be Jewish ei-ther. I don't *not* want to be; it's just that I don't care one way or the other. Can you understand?"

And she had said, "You don't have to be. You have a choice either way. Or no way, although I don't think that's so good."

Then he had cautioned, "Aunt Iris, don't tell Grandpa or Nana, please."

"No, I certainly won't," she had promised.

He had added, "I feel guilty about it, do you know? To have thoughts like those and keep them hidden?"

And she had told him not to feel guilty, that guilt was a crippling thing, that you could get sick because of it. "All young people keep things hidden from their elders. It's quite normal, Eric."

He always found it so easy to talk to her. "And you? Did you keep anything hidden?"

She had looked at him steadily. "For years I suffered because I knew they thought I was a homely girl whom nobody would ever want."

"I don't think you're homely," he had told her. "You don't look like most other people. I think you're even sort of pretty. Doesn't Uncle Theo think you are?"

And she had laughed and said, "I guess he must. If he doesn't he's cheated himself."

When she laughed, which wasn't often, Aunt Iris really did look pretty, Eric thought. And she was smart. Sometimes when he had to do a history project or something and didn't know how to go about it, she'd give him ideas. She could make things so direct and clear.

They were both smart, she and Uncle Theo; their kids would learn a lot from them. Uncle Theo's name had been in the paper last month in an article about some doctors in New York who were reconstructing the faces of Japanese war victims. 'An international gesture,' the paper said. He had a plastic surgery service at the hos-pital here where they'd built a new wing—Grandpa had made a big

donation for the wing; there'd been a dinner and speeches and
Grandpa's name had been in the paper too.

Now Eric was starved. They were still going through the ritual,
eating the matzoh, "symbol of the bread of affliction," Grandpa said.

Jimmy was prompted. He had been rehearsed by his mother all
week, and he spoke up in a pure chirp, asking the first of the four
questions: "Why is this night different from all other nights?"

Aunt Iris reached around Jimmy's chair and took Uncle Theo's
hand. She was really crazy about Uncle Theo. Once, when Eric had
been at their house and they hadn't known he was coming through
the door, he'd seen her run up to Uncle Theo and throw her arms
around him and kiss him so—so *violently*. It had made Eric feel all
strange, embarrassed and strange.

Now everyone started to sing. The song was in Hebrew. Naturally
Eric had no idea what it was about, but it sounded merry. Nana had
a thin, sweet voice, not loud, but you could hear it clearly alongside
all the other voices.

She liked to sing. Often when she worked in the kitchen he heard
her singing as far away as his room upstairs.

"My mother used to sing in the kitchen," she'd say, and he'd try
to imagine what it must be like to remember your mother singing.

Once he asked her, "What was my mother like?" and waited, almost holding his breath. What would she answer? He had an idea,
although no one ever told him so, that she hadn't liked his mother.

She hesitated, as if she were trying to recollect, and then she told
him, "Your mother was a gentle girl. She was quite small and graceful. She was intelligent and quick-witted. She loved you and your father very, very much."

Nana had been making buns that day, pouring the yellow batter
into the pans, and she said, "These were your father's favorites. He
could eat a half a dozen at a time."

She spoke almost shyly. Eric had already learned that she never
mentioned his father in Grandpa's presence. He had felt bold
enough to ask her why that was so.

"Gran used to talk about my mother. Why doesn't Grandpa like
to talk about my father?"

"Because it hurts him too much," Nana answered.

"Doesn't it hurt you?"

"Yes, but people are different," she said quietly.

He still sensed something heavy and unsolved in the air, and

384

thought he knew it was because his grandfather was sorry about something he must have said or done. He was grateful for the little things that Nana told him at unexpected times.

"Your father used to say your eyes were like opals," she had told him once, and he had felt a smile creep about his mouth. She had a way, with these remarks, of making his parents, especially his father, seem real. Up to now they had been cut-outs, silhouettes; even his mother, who was talked about so much in the Brewerstown time, always seemed like a doll to him, too sweet to be true. His first knowledge of his father, coming to him through Chris, had been no knowledge at all. What is it to say, Your father was a great guy, a great student? He got much better grades than I ever did? He played a great game of tennis, too?

That was only a caricature of the manly man at Yale. *Who was he?* It helped more to learn from Nana that he liked buns.

Still, it wasn't enough. Eric began to understand that it never would be enough, that his quest for knowledge of his father and mother would be a journey without end, a passage through rooms and doors, each one leading, after he opened it, to another room with another door. Doors going nowhere. Or else not opening at all.

Grandpa spoke now in a grave, impressive tone. *"Ani ma' amin:* I believe. I believe in the coming of the Messiah, and though he tarry, yet will I believe."

(Christ said, "Lo, I am with you always, even unto the end of the world." The Egyptians put food and clothing in their tombs to be ready for the next life. They, too, were sure they were right.)

For the moment the ceremony came to a halt. The fish was being served. With enormous appetite and relief Eric took up his fork.

That ache in the throat and behind the eyes was what Iris called her 'brimming' feeling. It was not so much that the cup of joy would overflow; it was rather that the cup would break from the pressure. How could life sustain so much?

The little boys in their twin suits were staring at Papa in his carved armchair. To a child, Iris thought, remembering how it had been when she was the age of her sons, that tall, dark chair stands like a throne on another level. The voice that issues from the throne is transformed, not Papa's everyday voice at all. It is kind but serious and, if anyone dares to interrupt while that voice is speaking, he is immediately, sternly silenced.

385

She smiled now at her boys, shaping silently with her lips, 'Good boys.' They looked awestruck; they looked almost as if they understood what their grandfather had said, although that was impossible. Yet it was true that they would never forget all this.

Eric looked remote except when he was eating. Even then he was only concentrating on the food. She doubted that he even heard what was being said. Suddenly Iris remembered sitting in the kitchen with Maury and Aggie when Eric was born. They were talking about him and one of them said, "Let him be free, he can choose what he wants to be when he grows up." Iris had made no comment. She had been a schoolgirl; what could she have known? But when they asked her, "What do you think?" she had told them: "A child should know who he is." And Maury had answered, "A good and decent human being, that's who. Isn't that enough? Does a person need a label, like a can of soup?"

They had seen it so simply but she remembered having thought even then that they were wrong. It wasn't that simple.

Papa was laughing with Mr. Brenner at the other end of the table. Probably it was a joke that he considered risqué. Yes, they were saying something behind their hands and Papa was glancing at the women to make sure they didn't hear. Papa's idea of a risqué joke was something that would bore the average boy in junior high today. Papa must be the last of the Victorians. Not the hypocritical Victorians (Iris had read enough about the period to know the subtleties of it), but one of that high-minded breed who lived what they believed and believed what they lived.

That steady optimism, that certainty that anything can be straightened out; what would we all do without it? Only once did it fail him, when Maury died. And even so he managed. I don't know what we shall do when Papa is gone. Sometimes I feel that he holds us all in his strong hands.

"Iris, Mrs. Brenner is talking to you," Mama chided.

"What? Excuse me. I'm daydreaming. It's all that wine," she apologized.

"That's all right," Mrs. Brenner said. "I only said something about your mother's new crystal bowl. I love Lalique, don't you? And your mother says she's bought one just like it for you."

"You didn't tell me," Iris protested. She didn't want the bowl. It didn't fit in their house. Mama persisted in bringing presents of her own taste, which was too fussy and flowery for Iris.

386

"I forgot to tell you," Mama said. "I meant to give it to you today."

Iris caught Theo's look and his message. He sometimes told her she was sharp with Mama. She supposed she might be when Mama annoyed her, yet she knew she had no right to be. Why was it often so difficult for her and her mother to say the simplest things to each other?

"Thank you, Mama, it's handsome," Theo said now. "You're always too good to us."

"Yes, thank you, Mama," Iris said. "It's beautiful."

Mama smiled as if it were she who had been given the present.

The wine stirred in Anna's head, too, along with the rising heat of the room and the spice of carnations. Her thoughts rushed from the strawberries, which weren't as good as they should have been, to what Joseph was saying about how free we were here in this glorious America, and how we mustn't forget those places in the world where men were still in chains.

He spoke well. His ideas were organized and clear. A man like him, unread, with so little education! He had been called upon to talk fairly often of late, at the county real estate board, at the Community Chest dinner last month. She was always so proud to see him on the platform, honored and tall. He really wasn't tall, but he looked it, and she always felt herself sitting taller as she watched him.

Hard to think he was the man who went to work carrying his painter's brushes and overalls! Yet he hadn't changed. He was still plain and direct. He had no airs like some who pretended they'd never been down on the East Side, that they'd never heard of Ludlow Street and couldn't understand Yiddish.

Of course, he did have a quicker temper than he used to have. He got irritable over trivial things. Yet he was so quick to say he was sorry; one mustn't forget that. He worked too hard and too long, but try and stop him.

"I have a tiger by the tail," he said. "I can't stop."

Anna wanted him to have his portrait painted. He insisted that was too highfalutin for him. She reminded him that he hadn't thought it was highfalutin for her to be painted years ago in Paris.

"Women are different," he told her.

But Anna wanted it. She knew just where she wanted to hang it,

387

over the mantel in the dining room, a fine portrait of him wearing a dark suit like a nineteenth-century diplomat. She'd have to talk to Eric. If Eric asked Joseph to do it, he'd do it. He'd do anything for Eric. So would we all.

She glanced down the table. Iris was leaning over to talk to Eric. She knew that Eric and Iris often had long talks, especially about Agatha and Maury. It had worried her one day that Iris might let slip some things about his parents that Eric shouldn't know.

"I haven't said a thing," Iris had assured her. "But now that you bring it up, why shouldn't he, at least someday, know the whole truth? Isn't that what growing up is about, to face the truth?"

And Anna had answered, "Only when it will make a difference, when you need to know. Some truths can destroy, and then it's kinder to lie." Secrets. So many secrets around this table. And still everything holds together. Please God that it always will.

She remembered now that Iris had looked at her with surprise.

"Delicious, Anna," Joseph said. And he proclaimed to the guests with pride, "No prepared or ready-made food in our house. My wife makes everything herself."

At the far end of the table Anna was serving the little boys. The ring sparkled on her busy hands. Her sleeves fell back from her white wrists. He thought: We should have had a big family like Malone's; she was meant to have one.

This was not the evening for regrets, yet emotions ran in currents and cross-currents. Under the joy he regretted. If only his achievements of the seven years since the war had come sooner! So many years of their lives had been drably wasted in keeping alive. (As with most of mankind.) Well, he had put away enough in tax exempts now so that none of them would ever have to be afraid, especially if anything should happen to him. He had seen to that. God forbid that there should be a repetition of the thirties. The economists all said there wouldn't be; too many safeguards had been built into the system. But who knew?

If only Eric had come earlier, he thought, watching the boy accept a second helping. Nothing shy about his appetite! He wondered what Eric really felt about this ceremony, whether it moved him at all with any sense of family, if nothing more. Even a sense of history? Probably not. It was all too recent and too sudden. He had been thirteen already when he came to them. It had been hard enough to make Maury see it as he should. And Maury had been nurtured in their house.

No matter. Just let the boy be healthy. Let him be happy and never mind anything else. I never thought I'd hear myself saying that. He seems happy. He's smart in school, talks like a professor sometimes! And the boys like him. He's an athlete and that opens doors, always did, even in my day when they admired the guy who was fast at stickball, dodging the pushcarts. He's good with his hands, too. Anna mentioned something in his hearing about a bird house and didn't he go and build one for her? With a front porch and a chimney?

Yes, Joseph thought, there's so much to be glad about. He felt a surge, a bursting in his throat. He was afraid his eyes would tear in another minute. They often did when he was moved and it was embarrassing. He filled the cup of wine again.

"Let us say the third grace," he said, and suddenly thought he heard his father's voice issuing from his own mouth. "Praised be He of whose plenty we have partaken and through whose goodness we have lived."

BOOK
4

THUNDER

35

The new Home for Convalescents opened with fanfare, flourish and publicity in the papers. The architects, so it was said, had been inspired; they were young men with radical ideas about "the human dimension," the use of light, curved space and greenery. The builders had done an admirable work of carrying out the design without cost overruns; quality had been adhered to; in short, there was a panegyric of compliments.

Joseph and Malone were photographed and interviewed. Joseph was shown bending over a spread of blueprints. He was asked about his personal history. "This modest man," one reporter wrote, "spoke with gratitude of the good fortune that has come his way. It was learned that he began his rise with the purchase of a small apartment building on Washington Heights in 1919. He had to borrow two thousand dollars to do it." He went on to say that the building's official opening was to be celebrated with a dinner, at which the architects and builders would be honored along with the many benefactors of the Home.

Anna had always been of the opinion that clairvoyance, ESP and all that sort of thing were absolute nonsense. And yet she knew, she had a feeling—absurd!—that Paul Werner would be at the dinner.

So, shortly after they had finished the main course, when she saw him walking across the enormous dining room to the table where Malone was sitting with his family, she was actually not surprised. She watched as Malone rose to shake hands, observed the introduc-

tions and Paul's easy little bow, heard in her mind's ear the throb of
his voice, although he was too far away to be heard, and knew that
in a few moments he would come to their table.

What shall I say? What will he say? Will my face flush? It gets so
hot and red, and people will see. Surely too, they'll hear my
drumming heart.

Paul came directly to Joseph and held out his hand.

"Paul Werner," he said. "I came to congratulate you and Mr.
Malone on this magnificent building. I've just had the tour."

For an instant Joseph was startled. Then he stood and answered
with dignity, "Thank you. You're very kind." He turned to the
others. "This is the man who first gave me my start. He—"

"Please," Paul interrupted. "That's not important. What you've
done, you've done by your own efforts."

"You know my wife, Anna," Joseph said. "And this is our daughter, Iris. And our son-in-law, Theo Stern. Doctor Theodore Stern."

He hadn't looked at Anna; what should she do when he did turn
to her?

Joseph drew up a chair. "Come join us, Mr. Werner."

Paul sat down. Anna felt a lightness in her head. She mustn't be
sick here, she mustn't.

"Are you alone?" Joseph inquired. "Perhaps your—"

"My wife wasn't able to come. Actually," Paul explained, "this
evening is in the line of business for me. I'm on the board of the
Parsons Trust, you see, and since we contribute to the Home it's my
duty to see how some of our money's being spent." He smiled.
"And I shall be happy to report that it seems to be spent very well.
What I like, you know, is that here you've got the functionalism of
the Bauhaus style but you've eliminated the bareness."

One of the other men at the table addressed him. "As an architect
I must say I'm gratified; that was our purpose exactly: the surface
decoration to take away that spare factory look. Are you an architect,
Mr. Werner?"

"No, only a banker. But I dabble. Perhaps I'm a frustrated architect."

How carefully he manages to turn in the other direction, Anna
thought. How could he have done such a daring thing as this? She
met Iris' gaze and smiled back weakly. Why was Iris staring at her?
But perhaps she wasn't really. Suddenly conscious of playing ner-
vously with her pearls, Anna put her hands in her lap. Then she was

conscious of the pearls themselves, three fine, matched strands. Paul would see that Joseph treated her well. Vulgar thought! She flushed.

Paul saw her distress and felt contrition. This was a rotten thing to do to her. (I knew she would be here and I wanted to see her. And everyone has a right to be selfish once in a while. Lord, she's beautiful! There was a time when a woman in her fifties was old. But Anna looks as if she'd never had a day's worry or done a day's work.)

"My wife is quite a fund raiser herself," Joseph was saying. "She's head of the hospital drive in our town, and head of their opera benefit in the spring too. Why, those women raised a small fortune this year! I wish I could get paid help in the office to work as hard as they do for nothing."

Paul addressed Iris. "And are you one of those hard-working ladies, too?"

"I'm afraid not. We have three children and they don't leave me much time for anything else," Iris said, thinking, Mama is acting funny. She has two red spots on her cheeks. What's the matter with her?

"But my wife used to teach school," Theo put in with pride. "She has an outstanding talent for it. They keep calling her to come back."

"Perhaps when the children grow older—" Iris began.

"Nonsense!" Joseph interrupted. "You've enough to do raising your family."

"What did you teach?" Paul asked.

He is sounding her out, Anna thought. He wants to know her, poor Paul. Surely people must see how alike they are! Fear dried her mouth and her palms were wet.

"I taught sixth grade, a gifted class. I would rather have taught at a slum school in the city, but Papa didn't approve." She smiled to Joseph.

"Listen," Joseph said, "I've come up from the slums too recently to want to be reminded. Maybe that's selfish. But a person who doesn't come from there can't know how a man feels when he's reminded. I wouldn't allow it, not while she was under my roof. Have a cigar?" And he offered a handful around the table, stopping at Paul.

"No, thank you. Cigarettes are my vice." Paul's long fingers unclasped the cigarette case.

I'm not ashamed to say where I come from, Joseph thought defensively. Not like some these days. Anyway, this man knows. And he sees where I am now, too. Hell, I know it's small potatoes to be proud. But I'm only human, and he'd feel the same in my position. Anybody would.

"Did my partner happen to tell you what we've got on the fire in Florida?" he inquired of Paul.

"He mentioned something very briefly."

"Well, it's a huge thing, the biggest we've done yet. Condominiums, and single-family homes, all tied in with a first-class shopping center, a golf course, a marina—you name it. There's our architect, right there across the table."

The young architect, eager to be heard, said to Paul, "As a frustrated architect, Mr. Werner, you must be familiar with the Scandinavian new towns. We're trying to reproduce some of their self-sufficiency; streets without automobile traffic, that sort of thing."

"Now that's really innovative," Paul said.

And they launched into a conversation illustrated by drawings on the backs of the menus and little structures built of forks.

Anna watched Paul's hands. She tried not to look at them but she was drawn back, under the pretense of interest in the subject, to his hands. They were strong and supple. Joseph had strong hands, too, but they were blunt and different. Different.

Joseph wasn't interested in the conversation. Theories were not for him. Give him the design and he would carry it out. Instead he observed Anna, who was listening so carefully. Anna knew and cared about things like that. She was so lovely in that dress, all iridescent gray and rose. Changeable taffeta, she'd said it was, tonight while they were dressing. "Do you like the rustle?" she'd asked, and flounced across the room, making the skirt swish. Wonder what that fellow thinks of her now? The scared girl going up the steps of their fine house. And now this. Only in America.

". . . the refreshing simplicity of Danish design," someone concluded.

Anna saw that Paul was trying to extricate himself from the conversation. "And have you ever been in Denmark?" he inquired of Iris.

"I've never been in Europe," she replied.

"Ah, haven't you? You must try to go soon. There's nothing like seeing it with young eyes. And young legs," he added.

"Theo isn't happy about seeing Europe again," Iris said quietly.

"I keep promising Anna a trip," Joseph interjected. "She's dying to go back. Only, I get so darned busy, I keep putting it off."

Paul returned to Iris and Anna understood that he was trying to draw her out. He simply wanted to hear her talk. He wasn't aware that one had to know Iris a long time before she would talk. She wondered what had gone through his mind at first sight of Iris, grown-up. She wondered whether Joseph was puzzled over Paul's staying so long at their table.

"No, I never want to see Europe again," Theo said. "I lost my family there."

"I understand," Paul answered. He paused for a moment. "Then perhaps you ought to see Israel. It is, after all, the remedy for the sickness that attacked in Europe."

"Have you been there yet?" Theo asked.

Words took shape in Anna's mouth: *Why, he was one of the movers who created Israel!* Startled, she thought: What if I had blurted that out loud?

"Many, many times," Paul told Theo. "Both before the state was founded and since then too." He smiled. "I recommend a visit, especially to you."

"When the children are older," Iris said, "perhaps we'll go then. My father has done a lot too, not on the scene, but raising funds. We all feel very involved."

"I'm glad to hear that," Paul responded.

He said to himself, She's prettier than I expected. It must be the marriage that's turned the trick. She's certainly poised, and speaks so well! And those enormous, brilliant eyes! Anna hasn't said a word. I shouldn't have shocked her like this. She's a good actress, though; you wouldn't think there was a thing going on. Come to think of it, I'm a pretty fine actor myself; my heart's in my mouth, but nobody knows it. Except Anna. She knows it.

"Why aren't you young people dancing?" Joseph asked. "Go ahead, don't mind us!"

Iris stood up with Theo. That man and Mama, she was thinking. That man. Doesn't Papa see anything?

A moment later Malone came over. "Mr. Hicks would like to see us both," he told Joseph. "He's in the office."

When Joseph had excused himself and all the others at the table had got up to dance, Anna and Paul were left alone.

397

Then for the first time he looked at her. "Fifteen years, Anna," he said at last.

"Oh, Paul, you should at least have warned me—"

"I know. It was thoughtless. But forgive me. A man's entitled to one lapse."

She didn't reply. The heat in her neck was suffocating.

"When I read about this in the paper I knew you would be here. I hoped she might be here, too."

"What do you think of her?"

"She's lovely, and different. Complicated, also, with a lot held back. And I have a feeling she's curious about me."

"What do you mean?" Anna asked quickly.

Paul hesitated. "Nothing precise. It's just a feeling I have about her feeling."

"She's made a fine marriage. It's been good for her."

"I knew. I saw the announcement."

"It's a marriage your mother would have approved. Socially, I mean."

"That's hitting below the belt, isn't it, Anna?"

"Perhaps it is." Yes, it was. But she couldn't resist. "Theo comes from a very distinguished family in Vienna—or they were, before they were wiped out. Distinguished and rich. He was educated at Cambridge and—"

"Fine. I'm sufficiently impressed. What kind of a man is he?"

"A wonderful, good man. And they're happy together."

"So you're not worried anymore."

"Well, I do feel that Iris is on her feet, and that's probably added a few years to my life!"

"And there are three children."

"Yes, two boys, very bright, especially the elder one, Steve. He's a bit of a problem, he's so advanced. The girl, Laura, is an angel, a healthy, good-hearted child." Anna stopped. Paul's face had simply closed, that subtle, tense, patrician face. And she knew that her recital, although he had asked for it, had touched a deep, wounded place.

"Go on," he said.

"Go on?"

"Yes. Tell me everything that has happened. Fill in the fifteen years."

She could have wept for him. "Well," she resumed, "well, one

398

beautiful thing did happen. Eric came back to us five years ago. He's going on eighteen now."

"Eric?"

"Maury's son."

"I'm glad for you, Anna. And for Joseph. You know," Paul said ruefully, "one has to like Joseph. I have very jumbled feelings tonight."

"Mine are pretty mixed up, too." Anna's lips quivered suddenly.

Paul looked away. "Anna, dearest, I'm upsetting you. It isn't fair to do this to you here."

"No."

He looked out over the dancers, changing the subject. "Who's that Iris is dancing with?" For Iris and Theo had switched partners.

"One of the Malone sons."

"He's a handsome specimen."

"All the Malones are 'specimens.' One more healthy and handsome than the next."

"You'd have liked a lot of children, wouldn't you?"

"Oh," she said softly.

"You deserved to have them. It doesn't seem like too much for a woman to ask."

"Who is to say what's too much, Paul?"

He made no answer. For just an instant she had the strangest sensation of unreality: it was impossible that they should be sitting here together! She knew nothing about him, after all these intervening years, and yet he was Paul; she knew him well and dearly. Now suddenly she needed to know everything, to fill in, as he had said, the fifteen years.

"What are you seeing in the air, Anna? You're a thousand miles away."

"No, I'm right here, thinking about you. I'm trying to imagine your life and I can't see beyond offices, ships and airplanes: you rushing here, going there. That's all I see and I want more."

"Well, but that's pretty much the way it is. I go wherever I want. Last year I needed a vacation, so I went to Morocco and through the Atlas Mountains. It was fascinating."

"That's still not telling me anything about *you*."

"Oh," he said somberly, "I've just been dodging, haven't I? All right, then. Here it is." Roughly he stabbed the fresh cigarette into the ashtray. "My wife and I . . . there's nothing particularly wrong between us and nothing particularly right, either. Her family's in Palm Beach. She spends most of her time there. I hate the place, so I'm rarely there. I work and I like my work. I have women wherever I go and whenever I need them. But they don't mean anything." He looked up. "I can't get you out of my mind, Anna."

"It hurts. It hurts me that you're unhappy," she said softly.

He lit another cigarette, cleared his throat as if it were tight, and went on, "I suppose I could be philosophical and ask you back, as you've often asked me, What is 'happiness' anyway? And whatever it is, why do we think we're entitled to it? All that sort of talk, in which, incidentally, there's a good deal of sense. The fact is, Anna, I really don't know. I'm confused. I'm guilty and I'm angry, although I don't know at whom. At the fates, perhaps? Or at myself? I should think that after all these years I could forget you—"

"I know," she murmured.

"Do you remember our last time? At the beach house?"

"I remember. We were still young and—"

"But you're young now. You always will be." He leaned forward. "Do you know a crazy thing? I still have hopes that someday, in some way, you and I—"

"Please," Anna interrupted with alarm. "Don't look at me like that. Iris is watching."

Paul leaned back and Anna poured another cup of coffee, which she did not want. But it was something to do with her trembling hands.

"I wish," she began to say, when the music stopped short.

Theo and Iris came back to the table. Then Joseph returned with Malone. There were a few pleasantries. Paul walked away. It was over.

"My goodness, Mama," Iris remarked curiously, while they were riding home, "you looked so serious, you and Mr. Werner! I couldn't help seeing you. What on earth were you talking about?"

The partial truth came easily. "I'm sorry to say I was telling him about Maury and Eric. And I'm afraid I may have gotten somewhat emotional."

"That's understandable, God knows," Joseph said. He sighed heavily, then brightened. "He seems to be a nice enough chap, that Werner. To tell the truth, I always pictured him as kind of a snob, but he isn't, is he?"

"I don't think so," Anna said.

"Funny how he and I met, after all these years."

"Yes, very."

It was late when they reached home. Joseph went to the refrigerator. "I'm going to make myself a sandwich. Food's always lousy at those affairs. Want one, Anna?"

"No, thanks." She went outside to the terrace. The night was cool and fresh. It smelled of wet earth. There were millions and millions of stars in a clear, limpid sky. Beautiful, so beautiful! And such a sadness at the heart of it! That marvelous order which held the stars where they were and moved them so predictably, while human life was just—just confusion!

All chance. Where you were born, when, and to whom. Whom you met and married. All chance.

"What are you doing, standing out there?" Joseph called. "You'll catch a cold!"

"Just looking at the sky," Anna said, coming indoors.

"You and your stars! You should have been an astronomer. Come up to bed."

"So," he said, sitting on the edge of the bed while he took off his shoes, "so I met the great financier."

She ought really to show a normal interest. "Is he truly a great financier?"

"Well, it's a small private banking house, no Morgan, but a power, all the same. Very well run. And what do you think? He told Malone they'd be glad to consider an application from us to underwrite our Florida project. Eight million dollars' worth!"

"That much?"

"Of course! What did you think? It's one of the biggest projects on the East Coast!"

Anna looked up. His eyes were shining. "You know, Anna, I couldn't help thinking of that first loan, with us coming, hat in hand, for two thousand dollars. And today that same man is eager to do business with me in the millions! It's kind of unbelievable, isn't it?"

"Yes. Yes, it is."

"Werner must have been thinking of it, too. But of course he wouldn't mention it. He's a gentleman, no question."

"And are you going to deal with Werner's bank?"

"No, Malone told him we're practically signed up elsewhere. But I got kind of a kick out of it, all the same."

The shoes dropped to the floor with a bang. "Imagine, three, maybe four generations in the business! Boy, that's the way to do it! Pick the right grandfather, that's all you need, hey? We didn't do it right, did we, Anna? Still," Joseph went on gaily, "I'm steaming ahead under my own power! Yes, I believe our grandchildren will be able to say they picked the right grandfather."

In sudden panic, Anna ran to him. She put her arms out, held to him tightly. Ah, love me! Don't let me do anything crazy that will ruin us all! Even if I should ever want to, don't let me!

He kissed her. "You looked beautiful tonight, Anna. I was so proud of you, you can't know how proud! Why, what's the matter? You're not crying?"

"Not really. Only a few tears. Because everything is just the way I want it to be, with Eric here and Iris' babies only ten minutes away. And I'm so afraid it won't stay like this."

"But you've always been an optimist! What's got into you?" And Joseph laughed. He shrugged and spread his hands out to the universe, in a gesture left over from childhood. "Everything is so good, and she worries, she cries! No wonder a man can never understand a woman!"

Anna went to the lobby during the last intermission. The opera house was filled with women, for the ladies' hospital guild had taken a huge block of seats and sold them all. Pleased with success, she walked down the corridor to the water fountain.

"Anna," someone said.

Even before she looked around, she knew who it was. He was standing against the wall as if he had been afraid to startle her by coming forward. "Don't be angry with me, will you?"

"I'm not angry! But I am scared. Paul, you shouldn't have."

"It's the only possible way I could think of to see you. We couldn't really talk at that dinner."

"We can't really talk here."

"Afterward, then. Let's go somewhere afterward."

"I can't. I have to go home, Paul."

"Well, when?"

"I'm afraid," Anna said. "If I see you again, something will happen."

"Maybe. I don't think so."

She stared at him. His gravity reminded her of Iris in that lonely time before Theo came. She put her hand on his arm and they stood there, barely touching, just looking, looking—

"If I believed in reincarnation, Anna, I would say that in some past century I had had you and lost you, and that I've been searching for you ever since."

A woman, coming from the fountain, gave them a frank stare, having perhaps caught their last words or sensed, as it is possible to do, the dense emotion that lay between them.

If I had had to see him every day all this time, Anna was thinking, who knows what might have happened? For all my strong belief in permanence and stable trust? Twenty times one would refuse to go away with a man, yet perhaps the twenty-first time, one wouldn't refuse. And in sudden terror she thought: Can any human being be that sure of his will? Chemistry! Only a modern term for the enchantment, the pull between the sexes, the lure against all prudence, all—

Chemistry!

Paul's expression was very tender. "You still glow. That brightness you had when you were a young girl—it's never been put out, has it? In spite of everything."

She felt a small, cutting pain. "I've been so torn, for so long. I wish I could feel whole!"

The bell sounded for the last act. People began moving back inside, brushing against them as they stood by the wall.

Paul grasped her arm. "I understand what you mean. I won't tear your family's life apart. Nor hurt Joseph. Or my daughter. Do you think I would hurt Iris? Trust me. But we must see each other again."

"I'll have lunch with you."

"Tell me what time and—"

Two large ladies in 'afternoon' dresses and droopy furs bore down on Anna, one of them shrilling gaily, "We've been hunting for you everywhere! Hurry, the curtain's going up in a minute!" And she was led back between them into a chattering group of friends, without a chance for another word.

Paul stood an instant looking wildly after her, as if he would pursue her. Then, with a small despairing shrug, he gave up and walked rapidly away.

* * *

403

The departing crowd pushed Anna outward through the main door. As had been arranged, Joseph was waiting.

"Come. The car's around the corner. How was it?"

"Marvelous. I always love *Aïda*, anyway."

The car turned northward, heading out of the city. In the west the somber winter sky had been torn open, and in the empty space between the clouds lay a lake of lavender, pearl and green.

"A beautiful sunset," Anna said. "The days are getting longer."

"So they are."

Joseph was very quiet. This must have been one of his difficult days. It was just as well; she wouldn't have to make conversation. If only sleeping dogs were allowed to lie! She had been feeling, for the last year or two, a welcome lightening of care—the natural result of Iris' good fortune—and in consequence she had been able to go for more than a week sometimes without even thinking of certain things. And now the sleeping dogs had been awakened.

Her body was drawn into a tangle of hot, trembling nerves. She pushed her coat back over her shoulders.

"What's the matter? Heat wave in February?"

"It's this dress. It's meant for a winter in Lapland, not New York," Anna complained.

He said no more, except to ask, a short while later when she lay her head back on the seat, whether she was not feeling well.

"I have a headache," she answered. "I think I'll just close my eyes."

They were almost home when Joseph spoke again. "You had a big crowd, did you? All women, I suppose?"

"Almost all. Just a couple of older men, like Hazel Berber's husband. But then, he's practically retired."

"I suppose you saw a lot of people you hadn't seen in a long time."

"Well, naturally, at an event like this." Something in Joseph's voice alarmed her. She sat up, pretending to fuss with her coat, and glanced at him. But he was looking straight ahead with a quite ordinary expression.

In their room she began to change into a cooler dress. The heat was still overwhelming. Then she heard Joseph coming up the stairs, striking each step with force, warning her of confrontation. He entered the room and firmly shut the door.

404

"Well, Anna! I waited all the way home. I gave you every chance to tell me and you didn't."

Best face it armed with innocence. "What can you be talking about?"

"You're a very good actress, but it won't work. Because, you see, I was there. I got there early, before the final act, and I saw the whole thing!"

"Would you mind telling me what you're talking about? What whole thing?"

"Come on, Anna, come on! I wasn't born yesterday. You were talking to that man for fifteen minutes."

"Oh!" she cried in a high, clear voice. "You mean Paul Werner! Yes, I ran into him at the water fountain. What's wrong with that?"

"You didn't just 'run into' him, you had fifteen minutes of very serious conversation, so don't try to tell me—"

Go over now, go over to the attack. It's the best defense. "What did you do? Carry a stop watch? And why didn't you come up and talk, the way any husband would instead of standing there spying?"

"Any husband in my place would be damned curious to know what his wife was doing! He came on purpose to see you, Anna! He knew you were going to be there because—I recall it now—I said you would be."

"Did you mention it on purpose to trap me?"

"Damn you, Anna, for a dirty thought like that!"

"And what about your dirty thoughts?"

"Don't try to put me on the defensive, because you can't do it. He came to see you and you lied to me. Those are the bare facts. You can't make anything else out of them."

"I did not lie to you! I just didn't think of mentioning it."

"Why didn't you?"

"Because I—" She heard herself stammering and began again. "Because it was of no importance to me. It was trivial. Do I give you a list every night of the people I happened to run into during the day?"

"Happened to run into!" Joseph mocked. "It's so usual for you to run into Paul Werner, isn't it? Like the milkman or the mailman! Do you think I'm an ass? But on second thought," he said slowly, "on second thought, maybe you do see him. Maybe it isn't so unusual."

405

"What a monstrous thing to say! Have you gone completely out of your mind?"

"No, I'm not out of my mind. I'm thinking very clearly. And I want to know why he came and what you were talking about. I'm waiting," Joseph said.

She had seen tempers often enough, explosions over the children when they were little or over household trivia, but never a cold fury like this. She drew her thoughts together. Everything was at stake, everything. "We talked about—let's see, the opera, of course, and the new tenor. Then he asked the usual polite questions about the family, things like that. Nothing, really, when you come down to it."

Joseph whipped the evening paper through the air and snapped it against the back of a chair. "No, that won't do! He grasped your arm. You pulled away. I saw your face when you went inside and I saw his. You can't tell me you were talking about the new tenor! What did he want, Anna? You will have to tell: what did he want?"

She bent her head. It whirled, as though she were going to faint. "I feel ill," she murmured.

"Then sit down. Lie down. But you can't get out of it that way."

She sat down, holding her head. Celeste had turned up the radio in the kitchen; a blare of revival music sounded up the stairs before it was cut off. A horn blew in the yard across the road. The stillness inside the room rang in her ears. He was still standing there waiting. She didn't know whether one minute had passed or five. She raised her head.

"Well?" Joseph said.

She wanted to cry out: Mercy! Leave me alone, I can't stand any more. But she was silent.

"Well?" he repeated.

And then she saw it was no use. She wet her lips, and sighed, and spoke.

"He asked me to have lunch with him. The reason I didn't tell you was that I knew you would be very angry. And I knew you had business dealings with him. I thought it could end in dreadful unpleasantness, so I thought it better to handle it myself." She stopped, trembling.

"And how did you handle it?"

"How do you suppose? I refused. I told him never to ask me again."

She looked directly into Joseph's eyes, and he into hers for a minute or more. Then he turned away.

"The bastard," he said quietly. "The fine gentlemanly bastard. Goes behind a man's back to make—arrangements—with his wife."

He walked the length of the room. He raised the window shades to look out into darkness and, after a little while, turned back to Anna.

"He's in love with you, isn't he?"

"Why? Because he asked me to go to lunch?"

"You can't be that stupid! Or shall I be tactful and call it naïveté? A woman of your age! What in the name of heaven do you think he wanted?"

"The fact is he asked me to lunch and that's all."

"The city's full of women, a lot younger than you, for a man to take to lunch and for whatever comes afterward. There's got to be more to this story."

"Perhaps it's just—one of the things some men do. I mean, he saw me at that dinner and I suppose he—liked me. Don't men do things like that?"

"A cheap philanderer! Another man's wife! You haven't seen him since that time?"

"No."

Joseph passed his hand over his forehead; he was sweating. "It's funny, you know, I never mentioned it, but at that dinner, I thought I saw him looking at you. I thought I felt something. But then I told myself not to act the fool. I put it out of my mind. I told myself it was nothing."

"But you see," Anna said softly, "it really was nothing very much. Another man on the make. I suppose he found me—interesting. Because of having known me so long ago."

How ugly this cajolery, this deceit! Even the slander of Paul was so ugly. But there was no choice. She had to defend herself, and not herself alone. They were all bound up in what was being said and believed, here in this room.

Below, in the kitchen wing, a door slammed and there were voices. Eric would be coming in from basketball practice, too

407

hungry to wait for dinner. What disaster for him if this couldn't be straightened out!

We are all so interwoven. There is no way ever to isolate the evil, the sickness. Everyone is touched by its cold coils: Joseph and I and Eric and Iris, with her children. And Paul. Yes, Paul. We cause each other so much suffering without wanting to.

"Anna, tell me. I have to know. I've asked you this before and you've always denied it, but I'm going to ask it again: Were you in love with each other, years ago?"

"Never. No, never."

"And there was never anything between you?"

Her fists were clenched at her sides. She relaxed them and breathed deeply. "No, never."

"Will you swear it?"

"Joseph, isn't it enough that I've answered you?"

"Maybe it's foolish of me, but I would feel great relief if you would swear it. By the health of Eric, and Iris and her children. Then I would know it was true."

She was in a corner. She had actually retreated to the corner of the room and it seemed now that the corners were narrowing their angle, curving to trap her between the walls.

"No, I won't do that. I won't swear by their lives."

"Why won't you? If I ask you to?"

"It's insulting to ask me to do that, as if you didn't take my word."

"I don't mean to insult you. It's just that—"

"And for another, I feel superstitious about it."

"Why? Afraid that something would happen to them? It wouldn't as long as you were telling the truth."

"No, Joseph."

"Swear without that, then. Say, I *swear* I never had anything to do with Paul Werner that my husband couldn't know about."

Now, from some corner of Anna's soul, fierce strength emerged, born out of terror. She went over again to the attack.

"Now it's I who'll be angry, Joseph! Why do you want to humiliate me? What kind of a marriage is it in which people don't trust one another?"

"I want to believe you," Joseph said, retreating before her anger.

"Then believe me!"

There were tears in his eyes. "Anna, I couldn't bear it if—The world is a shifting place; you never know where you stand in it. There has to be one person who never changes. If I lost that, I tell you—you know the things I've been through, and I've kept on going—but if I thought that you—" He swallowed. "I wouldn't care to open my eyes on another day. So help me God."

"You haven't lost it. You won't lose it," she said, gently now.

"I know I'm lucky to have you. A woman like you could have had any man she wanted."

Pity. Pity. The tension broke in her and she began to cry.

"Anna, don't. It's all right. I'm over it. I understand what happened now."

He never could bear to see anyone cry. Iris had known that when she was a little girl. *Papa will give you anything if you just stop crying.*

"That damned bastard," Joseph muttered. "To put you in a position like that! He'd better not come around here."

"He won't."

Someone knocked at the door. "It's me, Eric. Celeste says dinner's ready."

"We'll be right down," Joseph called back.

"I'm not hungry," Anna said. "You go eat with Eric."

"No, no! I don't want the boy to think there's been anything wrong. Wash your eyes. Nobody'll notice."

Faces are for concealment, Anna thought, powdering her pink eyelids. They speak of 'frank' faces; who looks more candid than I do? She bent to the mirror; yes, an innocent face, still young. A lovely face: a fraction of an inch here, another there, and the combination could hold such power over men! Because Paul loved her, he pursued her. Because Joseph adored her, he believed her. And also because, she reflected with pity and tenderness, Joseph was a very simple man. He believed the best of almost everyone, in spite of his bluster. Paul would never have let her get away that easily if the situation had been reversed. That subtle mind would have seen behind and through her.

Tomorrow she would have to tell Paul how things were. And the long silence between them would have to begin again. It would have to be that way.

Then, if she could but speak to Joseph, loose the whole load of lies and be free of them forever! Yes, and she would be free of everything else besides, free in the ruins of all and everyone she loved! Never. No, never. Live and carry the load alone. So help me God, as Joseph had just said.

So help me God.

36

Iris runs among enormous, ancient trees. She turns, seeks, walks back and turns again. There is no end to these woods. No one has ever seen such trees before. The trunks rise like cathedral towers, yet their dark, soft tops sway like plumes against the rim of the sky. She knows where she is: these are the Muir Woods, north of San Francisco. She has never been there, but she knows; knows, too, that she is dreaming.

She runs faster. She mustn't stop. Race, hurry, for Steve is lost. He is somewhere among these endless trees. How did it happen? How can it be that nobody had seen him? Can a child, can anyone just disappear like this? She tries to strangle her tears; when panic stuns one can't think, and she must be calm, be sharp, to get back her little boy. Have you seen him? she implores, for these are not tree trunks, after all; these are people, tall, silent people who won't answer. Surely somebody must have seen him? she pleads. A little boy like him?

Mama! she cries, to a woman with a face like her mother's; but the mouth is stern and no answer comes from it.

Papa! she cries, help me, oh, help me, Papa! He bends to her, he puts out his arms. But his face is Paul Werner's face, sorrowful, pitying. He speaks; she cannot understand what he is saying. She strains to hear, but he melts away into fog. She cries: Papa! Father! She thinks, I am losing my mind.

She is frantic. There is a pain in her chest, it runs up into her throat, the pain is colored bright red. Is it possible to suffer like this and live? Somewhere her child is looking for her, crying for her; he can't be far. But she has looked everywhere, running, running through shadow and striped shafts of light, and he isn't here. Such loss she feels, such anguish. How will she live with such loss and anguish?

There are shadows on the ceiling and the beam of the hall light cuts across them, falling on her eyes as she turns her head toward Theo's shoulder. She wonders whether she may have cried out during her dream, her nightmare. But no; Theo sleeps lightly and he hasn't stirred. Whatever can have caused this? Safe here in her bed with her children asleep down the hall: what reason can there be for such internal strife?

It's so cold; the winter air seeps into the house on nights like this. She doesn't want to get up, but she has to. She creeps down the hall to Steve's room, careful not to bump into anything in the dark, for he, too, sleeps lightly. She steps on his stuffed cat. He always goes to bed embracing it, but sometime before he falls asleep he throws it out of bed. He is a rounded hump under the blankets, lying on his stomach with his head pushed against the headboard. So soft, so small. Even the sound of his breathing, the breath of his life is so small.

On silent feet she goes back to her room. Theo has turned and in his sleep reaches out, his arm flung over her as she lies back into the warmth. She remembers that she didn't go to look at Jimmy or Laura just now. But she knows that they are all right. Her cheeks are cold and sticky with the tears of her dream.

37

They came out of Carnegie Hall into a crushing wind and fought it toward the parking lot. Theo turned his face up into the cold. It felt bright as light, as clear and soaring as the Verdi Requiem which they had just heard, and which now and forever after would sing to him of a particular death.

A cluster of people waited at the corner to hail taxis or to cross. Thrusting through them, he glanced at a face; it vanished and then it turned and reappeared. He saw it clearly, hesitated for a second and was sure—

"Franz! Franz Brenner!"

"Theo! *Mein Gott!* I heard you lived in New York, I couldn't find you—"

"What are you doing here?" And remembering Iris, "This is Franz Brenner, one of the finest lawyers in Vienna! We grew up together. Iris, my wife."

Franz laughed. "Theo is too generous. And I'm too old to have grown up with him."

"But we can't stand here! Come, we'll get something to eat."

In the light of the Russian Tea Room they searched each other's faces.

"Theo, you look well! You must be happy, you haven't changed."

"And you—"

"Don't tell me I haven't."

Franz had gone almost completely white. There was a deep

413

crease on one cheek, a fold of flesh like a wound, which twitched when he spoke.

"What are you doing here?" Theo asked again.

"I'm here on business. Knit goods. But I live in Israel."

"No law?"

Franz shrugged. "Israel is crammed with German and Austrian law degrees. They don't mean much there. But tell me—"

"Order something, order a supper," Theo interrupted. "We need time to talk! Or, listen, I have a better idea!" He felt the rise of his own excitement. "You'll drive home with us. We live only an hour away. You can spend a day or two."

"*Ich kann nicht, ich fahre morgen ab.* Excuse me, Mrs. Stern, I'm not used to English yet. I studied years ago at the university, but I forget and start to speak German. What I mean is, I have to fly back tomorrow morning." He leaned across the table. "So tell me what you do, Theo! You have children?"

"Two boys and a girl. And you?"

"No children. I lost Marianna. . . . But I married again, a widow with grown daughters. I have a pretty good job. The living is hard there; still, it's home to us now. But you know, I heard—a grapevine, do you say? I heard you were in New York. But there was nothing in the New York telephone book. Did you know it was worth a fortune in Europe in those days, a New York phone book? You might find the name of a relative in it—a third cousin of your grandfather, maybe—or any name of any stranger who would send you, out of human pity, the papers that would save you from the fire in Europe."

"I only lived in the city a year. I had a room here when I first came, in '46."

"Ach, so! Well, Liesel learned that you—"

"What did you say?"

"I said that Liesel had learned—"

Theo sat up. "God almighty, what did you say? What Liesel are you talking about?"

Franz was astonished. "Why, Liesel your wife, of course," he murmured.

"Franz, Liesel is dead."

"I know, I know that."

"She died in Dachau with all our family. It's not decent to speak of her! Don't you know any better? We never mention her name!"

Franz's face was still. His steady eyes didn't blink. He said: "She didn't die in Dachau. I thought you knew. I thought the committee, the people in Tel Aviv had informed you."

"Damn you, Franz! Damn you! Will you talk, or shall I shake it out of you?"

"Theo! Theo!" Iris laid her hand on his arm. A man at the next table turned quickly and looked as quickly away.

"I don't know now where to begin," Franz pleaded. "Dear heaven, I—"

Something went wild in Theo. "Begin at the beginning. Or you'll never get on that plane tomorrow. What do you know?" And as Franz glanced toward Iris, "She can hear it! Damn you, I want to *know!*"

Franz looked down at the saltcellar. "I met Liesel in the winter of '46 in Italy. I had tried to get to Palestine but the British had turned us back. So I was preparing to try again, waiting for an old tub willing to run the blockade. There were a few hundred of us, some who'd lived through the camps, some who'd hidden out with false papers."

"She—had false papers?" He was charged electrically. He thought his head would explode; he thought he was dreaming; he thought he was going to be sick.

"No, no false papers."

"What then?"

Franz raised his eyes. "Theo, she's dead. That I know, I was there. What's the use of all this? Let it rest as it is."

Theo trembled. "I have to know. Or you won't get on that plane, I tell you!"

Franz sighed. He took a deep breath, like a child beginning a recitation before the class.

"Well, then. They came. It was the very first week after the *Anschluss*. The Germans came to the house for the family. It was strange, they thought their influence would help them, but it was just the opposite. Other people, those who were not so important, many of them had time to get away.

"So they came. It was early in the morning, cold and raining. The baby was sick with a fever. She begged them not to take him out into the weather. And they told her she could leave the baby behind if she wished: 'You can take him or leave him here alone in the house. It's your choice,' they said.

415

"As they were leaving, one of the soldiers knocked a painting off the wall. His superior was angry: 'Don't wreck things! It's a first-class house and we'll be needing it!' So they knew they wouldn't be coming back.

"They rode with two men in S.S. uniform. The baby screamed all the way. He had not yet had his bottle that morning."

Iris caught her breath. She began to cry.

"Stop it!" Theo said furiously.

"After a few days the baby developed pneumonia and died. Then for a while the others were together in the camp, before they were separated, sent to Poland. Ah, Theo, you know all this! You know how it happened! The whole world knows, even the ones who don't want to know."

"Go on!" Theo said.

Franz's gaze went back to the saltcellar. "The old people, they went quickly to the ovens. The young and strong were put to work. So she—there was a workshop where they made belts and gloves, leather things for the army. She worked there a long time . . ." He swallowed, resumed in an even drone, "Then, some long time after, I don't know how long, it might have been a year or perhaps two, yes, it could even have been longer—I don't remember exactly—"

"Never mind *when*. Just say *what*. Go on!"

"Well, then, you see, one day some officers, some higher-ups from the Gestapo, came in. They were looking for, you know how it is, they were looking for girls. Pretty girls, blondes who looked Aryan. For the headquarters farther front." Franz was silent a moment. Then he looked up, afraid. "They took them away and stamped their arms: 'For Officers Only.' "

Theo started fiercely, scraping his chair. A glass of water overturned and spilled across the table.

"Please, Theo, you don't have to listen anymore," Iris whispered. "Mr. Brenner, Franz, there's no sense in this, it's enough."

Theo sat down. "Franz, don't make me pull it out of you. I want all of it, every word you can remember. And Iris, shut up."

"She told me, she said that the person who saved her sanity had been a prostitute, and this girl—she came from Berlin—this girl said to the others, 'Listen, they're not touching *you*, not *you*, you understand? It's only flesh, skin. If you were made to clean filth with your bare hands, you wouldn't despise your hands afterward,

416

would you? You wouldn't cut them off. So this is the same, these are filth, swine, shit.' Excuse me," Franz said to Iris.

So she closed off her mind and lived waiting, waiting for the Germans to lose the war. . . .

"The doctors came regularly to examine them for diseases. Cold, hard men they were. She—Liesel—was astonished that doctors could be such. She had thought always of doctors as different. She had been, so she said, so ignorant of the world, had known so little about human beings.

"One day a man came in who recognized her, a lawyer, Dietrich, from Vienna."

"I knew him, he was a bastard. One of the first to jump on the bandwagon."

"He recognized her because he used to play in a string quartet that met in somebody's house. Her parents', I believe."

"My parents'. It was my father's Tuesday night music group and she—came in sometimes to play the piano."

"Well, he remembered her. And shortly afterward she was put back in the factory. Because of him, of course. She thought it was an act of mercy. She was still innocent, even after all that. Of course it was because the war was ending and a lot of these torturers were suddenly becoming 'humane.' They hoped that some wretched survivor might put in a good word for them when the judgments were handed down.

"Anyway, we met in Italy. She didn't know me at first; I had lost sixty pounds. . . . For a minute I didn't know her either . . . she had got old. One would have thought she was well over thirty—but somehow she was still—still lovely. Even those monsters couldn't destroy all of that. . . .

"We waited for weeks in Genoa. They kept coming, the walking corpses with skin sores and shaven heads who had crawled across Europe, out of hiding, out of the camps, and now were fleeing from the Russians. . . . All they wanted was to get out of Europe and never see it again. The group with which I spent my days was waiting like me to get to Palestine. We spent the few pennies which we got from the Joint in cheap cafés. You could sit forever, as one did—does still, I suppose, in Europe?—over a glass of wine or a cup of coffee. We sat in the sun and tasted the feeling of not being terrified, the feeling of being alive. And we talked about the future.

417

"Some of us persuaded Liesel to go with us. We thought you were dead, you see. There were so many rumors in those days. At all the places where people like ourselves were gathered, whenever a newcomer arrived there would be questions and comparing of notes. People carried lists, with dates, names and addresses: have you seen, or heard, of So-and-so? A man came who had heard from someone who had been in one of the camps where French Jews were sent that you had been rounded up in Paris, and that you were dead. Later somebody else confirmed it; he was certain he had seen you among the contingent that went right after the fall of France.

"There was no reason not to believe it. After all, everyone else was dead, her parents, brothers, child; why not her husband also?

"God above, the bravery I've seen! The patience, the will!" Franz stopped. He stared at the wall. And began again:

"Then, I remember, a terrible thing happened. . . . There was a doctor in the group that was waiting for the ship, an older man who had suffered like the rest of us and, like the rest of us, was overwhelmed at the absolute miracle of having survived. He was very steady, very firm and kind, talking to people who weren't doing so well emotionally, encouraging them with so much hope and wisdom—he was a rod and a staff. And suddenly one day while we were sitting there—I remember I was eating a pasta; I couldn't ever get enough to eat at that time—all of a sudden this strong man jumped up from the chair and ran across the square. There were some *carabinieri* standing, chatting with a shopkeeper, and the doctor grabbed one of their guns and started screaming, simply went berserk there in the sunshine on the square. They wrestled for the gun, and the doctor was shot, shot and killed. Lying there on the ground, our kind, wise doctor.

"After that, there was a change in Liesel, as if—I think she actually did put it into these words—as if it was a delusion to think you could ever straighten out such lives as ours, to go back again to normal living; that it was simply too difficult, too hard to believe in hope.

"Anyway, the boat came. It was a miserable old tub, scarcely seaworthy, but that was the least of our worries. The real one was the British blockade. We had to sail at night without lights. On deck we whispered.

"So we crept across the Mediterranean toward Palestine. The ship was crowded and filthy. People were seasick. Children were bored and crying and so many of the adults hadn't strength enough to be patient. Still they tried. And everyone was so afraid, so tense. We watched and strained for the sight of ships, the nearer we got.

"One day during one of our interminable talks, a man mentioned an encounter he'd had with a German-Jewish refugee, a soldier in the American army. This man had a letter with a list of names from a certain Dr. Weissinger who had gone to America from Vienna in 1934. The list was of others from Vienna who were in New York, and Theodor Stern was on it. You see, in those times, it was important to write everything down, to bring people together, to know who might still be alive. You must know Dr. Weissinger, Theo?"

"He died a few years ago. Yes, he was one of the smart ones. He came here at the beginning when nobody believed how it would turn out." Theo's voice was unfamiliar to his own ears. It was a false, artificial voice. The true one would have howled and cursed and beaten the air.

"This man had copied the soldier's list. And we saw your name, with the address where you had lived in Vienna, although none for New York. Still there could be no doubt.

"I told Liesel that as soon as we got to Haifa we could write, that it would be simple to find you. I myself could have traced you after she died. I don't know why I didn't. Perhaps because someone told me the authorities had informed you. Yet a lethargy comes over a person when there's so much confusion and uprooting. One doesn't know where to begin. And then one has to start making some kind of a living.

"We talked a great deal together, she and I. We sat on the deck until late at night. It was so hot and noisy below."

"Tell me everything she said." He thought he couldn't bear to hear any more. Yet he knew that if he didn't hear it all, afterward he would not be able to bear that, either.

"It's hard to remember. One speaks of so many things in the course of days. And still, one doesn't really say very much, does one? She did say several times, she said: 'I hardly remember Theo. I remember things we did: the day we walked down *Mariahilfer-strasse* and bought the wedding rings. Theo wanted to buy them right away and I asked whether he wasn't going to speak to Papa. He said of course, he was, but since we knew Papa was going to say yes, we might as well buy them now. I remember that,' and she laughed. 'But I can't remember his face,' she said.

419

"Oh, and she talked sometimes about skiing. She said she remembered especially a day in the Dolomites, how you skied all day and then played duets for everyone in the evening after dinner at the hotel. Things like that she remembered. And she said, 'We were so young; how could we ever have been so young?'

"That's how she talked. Often she would be silent for a long time. And I was too; I had my thoughts. We all did. It was a ship burdened with thoughts. Strange, all those heavy thoughts, on those marvelous, mild nights with the air like warm water on the skin.

"Except that last night. It began to rain, and the ship wallowed through a slow, heavy swell. A lot of people were sick, more than usual. We went up on the covered deck, she and I. The rain blew on us in a mist.

" 'It's so clean up here.' she said. 'And I'm so filthy, Franz.'

"I remember protesting, saying the things one would say, and her arguing, 'Why would anyone want to touch me again?' and I arguing back as one would.

"And she said, 'I wonder how many people have just slipped over the side of a moving ship at night?'

" 'What a morbid thing to wonder about!' I told her. I was alarmed.

"She said that it wasn't really, that it would be a pure way to die, going down into clean water . . . she used the word 'clean' so often . . . she said it would be like coming into a room waiting for your comfort, the covers turned down on the bed and the lamps low.

"I wasn't sure what to think. After what we had endured such talk was common enough. We were all given to it at times. It was a pattern from which, as our hopes rose, we gradually emerged. Still, I wanted to be cautious. I urged her to come below because it was late. 'No,' she said, 'it's stifling and dirty down there. At least up here in the air it's clean and free.' I said I would stay with her, then, and she protested, but I stayed."

Franz raised his eyes. "Only, I fell asleep. Theo, I fell asleep. And when I woke up, she was gone. And that's all there is."

Beneath the shirts in the middle drawer he had laid the double photographs of his parents, still in the leather traveling folder that he had taken to Paris so long ago on his way to America. What impulse had, at the final moment, caused him to put them in the suitcase? If he had not done so, there would now be no record of their faces, except in the minds of those who had known them, and for as long as those minds survived.

Iris was still downstairs. They had driven home in silence; she had not even tried any words of comfort, and he was grateful for that, because there could be none. . . . He supposed, as he opened the folder, that she must have seen these when putting his clothes away. But she had never remarked on them and for that, too, he was grateful.

The photos of his parents had been taken in that time when youth turns gracefully into the pride of early middle age. His father wore the officer's elegant uniform of the First World War, and with it the appropriately stern expression. His mother was dressed in the limp silk of the era, her overskirt edged with lace, her pearls waist-length. She was slender and stood tall. Young girls of her time were taught to stand that way, she always said. Had she walked straight and slender to the freight car, the van, or whatever vehicle had taken her to her death?

He studied them. For some time now he had been able to look at them. Then he slid his mother's picture out of the case, removed what he had hidden beneath it, what he had not been able to look at, all these years.

She gazed up at him: smiling or not smiling? It was hard to tell about the mouth, which turned up naturally at the corners. But the eyes smiled. They seemed, unless he imagined it, unless it was just the way the flesh happened to be molded, they seemed to hold mirth even when she had been quite serious or even angry. They were hazel eyes: cat-colored, he had used to tell her. The little boy was on her lap, holding a felt polka-dotted ball. He remembered the ball. He had bought it one afternoon on the Graben. Fritzl had rolled it under the sofa and they'd had to move the sofa to get at it. One leg was tucked out of sight; the other dangled from his mother's lap. There was—Theo bent closer—yes, you could see a dimple in the round knee.

Liesel, darling Liesel, what did you ever do to anyone? And I thought you had died quickly. My God, how did you manage to live so long?

The bedroom door opened and the light from the hall filled the opening. Iris' steps had made no sound. She came beside him and

421

for a long minute examined the photograph. He saw fear in her face, as if she knew that something had changed and would change. He was sorry for her: wasn't that crazy? To be sorry for Iris, who was alive?

"I swore at poor Franz," he said.

"It's all right. He understood," she answered quietly.

Then he began to weep. She put his head on her shoulder and stood there holding him, and was very gentle, and did not speak.

38

T heo had been mourning for more than half a year. It was too much for Iris to endure. He was distorted and crippled with grief and she felt all the pain of his crippling.

That first night when they had left Franz Brenner on the sidewalk at Fifty-seventh Street she had offered to drive the car home, but Theo had walked to the driver's side. She could still see his mouth, set like a gash or a scar upon his face; she could remember her own awful fear, not so much that they would have an accident, the way he drove, but that this night had done something to him that was irrevocable. And why shouldn't it have done so?

The family gathered, encircling Theo. Papa had come to their house the next day and silently put his arms around him. Mama had cried—of course, she never restrained her tears—cried all over again for her brother and his family.

"Oh, that lovely child!" she said when they were alone. "I can see her now in the garden of Eli's house. She had a velvet band around her hair, like Alice in Wonderland." And she whispered in recollected horror, "I saw a girl raped in Poland."

"You never told me!" Papa exclaimed.

"One wants to bury a memory like that," she answered.

Eric was stunned. Of course he had known about the atrocities of the Nazis, but somehow, he admitted, they had always sounded a little exaggerated. Somehow.

Theo went back to the office on the second day. All that first day

423

or two Iris feared for him. She couldn't have said specifically what she was afraid of, but she feared. She kept telephoning his office on pretexts, not asking to speak to him, but just to find out from the secretary in some oblique way whether everything was normal there.

At night she felt him lying awake. She heard him swallow a sob. But after that first night he wanted no comfort.

"I have a cough," he said clumsily, and this foolish deception touched her almost more than anything.

With the children he became exceptionally gentle. His voice was tender even when he said the most ordinary things at table. "Steve, are you sure you washed your hands? Jimmy, you have to finish your milk before you may have dessert."

Once she found him sitting with Laura on his lap and his arms around the two boys as if he were guarding them all. There was such an expression on his face! Something so resolute, fierce and sad! When she spoke to him he started; she had to repeat her words and she saw him blink, shaking his head to bring himself back to the room from wherever he had been.

Every evening now, although not in Iris' presence, but when she was having her bath, she heard the drawer being opened and after long minutes shut again; she knew he had been looking at the photograph of Liesel and their child. Sometimes, coming down the hall and entering their bedroom unexpectedly, she could tell by his swift movement that he had just taken it out again. One day, for some reason, the action evoked in her not shock and pity, but irritation: "He'll wear out the paper, handling it so much." Immediately she was ashamed of herself and wished with utmost penitence, truly wished, that it were possible for her physically to lift his anguish and take it on herself.

She was deeply alarmed. How long could a human being carry such a heavy load? With all that he had to do at the office and the hospital? With a wife and three children, and now this other thing clouding his mind?

And she raged against the rotten world that had savaged such good and gentle people.

At what actual moment her sorrow began to turn toward resentment Iris could not have said. Was it in the third or fourth month, or the fifth, that she knew she could no longer stifle or deny the resentment? Perhaps it was the morning when one of Theo's secretaries telephoned. Somehow, Iris had no idea how, the people at the office had learned the story.

"We've just heard what happened to the doctor's wife," the woman said. "It's not believable in the twentieth century! We're all so terribly sorry, and we want you to know that we're trying to make things as easy as possible at the office for the doctor."

Iris had thanked her with proper gratitude and hung up. *What happened to his wife.* Horrible, horrible and true. But now I'm his wife and I'm here. How long will this grieving go on? Everybody tiptoeing around Theo—my parents, Eric, those few of our friends who have been told. An atmosphere of mourning, a house of mourning.

He had developed the habit of staying up late. Very well, she could understand his sleeplessness. She had tried staying up with him but her eyes had fallen shut and he had told her to go to bed, that he'd come up soon.

One night she had peered downstairs to see what he was doing. He was sitting in a chair staring at nothing, just sitting. Then she saw him get up and go to the piano. He began to play, very softly, so as not to awaken anyone.

Night after night she heard him playing. The sound of it drifted up the stairwell; mostly Chopin nocturnes, nostalgic music of summer gardens, of love and stars.

One night she raised herself on her elbow and looked at the radium dial of the clock: one-thirty. For two hours she had been lying there alone while her husband was lost in the music of another time and place, with another woman.

When he came upstairs and found her still awake, he moved toward her. She felt that he expected from her as always an eager, quick response. But her desire struggled with humiliation. All the times of their lives when she had been so absolutely uninhibited, so free in expression of her passion for him, had he perhaps not been thinking of *her*, not wanting *her* at all? Had he been thinking of—

She did not want him to touch her. Don't come to me with this face of mourning, she wanted to scream at him; she screamed it silently, even while she put her arms around him. You've shut me out. *Me, me,* don't you understand? Keep away until you can be what you were again. But can you ever be?

She knew this sort of emotion was dangerous. If she didn't bring

425

it to a stop soon, it would go out of control. But how to stop it? In
the eye of the hurricane lies a lonely hollow where nothing moves,
where panic lies still. The darkness rustles and morning is an eternity away. After such nights, there were hollows under her eyes.
Her face was sallow at best; the hollows gave her a look of tragedy.
People ought to look pink and cheerful in the morning, and the
awareness that she did not depressed her. That, and Theo's haunted
face. There was a tired silence now at the breakfast table, filled by
the crackle of the newspaper.

Little by little, inch by inch, a wall is built.

Then one afternoon he came in and told her they had joined the
country club. She was astonished. They had both agreed that club
life wasn't something they would enjoy enough to warrant the expense. It's true that Theo was a good tennis player, but he had been
satisfied with the public courts in town. Iris was clumsy at sports
and wouldn't have used any of the facilities at the club. Some of
their friends belonged, but most of them did not. Many of their
closest friends were Europeans, random doctors and others in the
musical groups who played in quartets at each other's houses. So
she was astonished.

"I want to get out among people who aren't so serious," Theo
said. "People who like to dance and laugh."

Well, she loved to dance! What did he mean? For a moment she
felt that he was accusing her. She felt a rush of quick anger which
subsided as quickly. He was only trying to escape his thoughts by
changing his routine! She who prided herself on her 'understanding'
ought to understand that much, oughtn't she? Poor man! Rightly or
wrongly he thought that crowds, new faces and 'jollity' would bring
forgetfulness and ease.

Yet there was something else behind his jollity: Anger? Bitterness?
Defiance? Something has eluded us, Iris thought; slid out of our
hands.

She remembered thinking, a long time ago when she had first
known Theo, that he was a man who could have any women he set
his mind to wanting. At the club, all through this past summer, he
had gathered women to him without effort: young girls and women
much older than Iris. He would stand at the bar holding a long
drink—he drank very little, one tall glass sufficing for an hour or
more—and the women would be drawn to his knowing eyes, his

barely promised admiration. Then, of course, there was his accent, the faintly foreign, faintly British accent. He really did nothing she could blame him for. She felt sometimes like slapping him, all the same.

Once at home again his sadness came surging back. It was never expressed in words—for Theo had caused the subject to be closed—but in tone and gesture and above all in silence. The sadness was a presence, like a tiny draft from a forgotten window that has been left open a crack: just enough to chill the air. His friends at the club would not have recognized him if they had seen him in his home.

He had become two people.

If she could have talked to somebody about what was happening in their house! But it was too intimate; she had never been able to be intimate. Iris knew herself and knew she had too much pride—false pride?—to disclose anything as close to the bone as this. Perhaps in absolute extremity she could talk to Papa. He was the only one. Yet she couldn't talk to him about this, wouldn't let him know that his daughter's life was troubled or less than perfect. He needed to believe that it was perfect. Papa wore blinders. He had a picture in his head of the ideal family of tradition. That's the way it's supposed to be; therefore it must be. There's no other possibility.

She stood in the center of the bedroom trying to make up her mind what to do with the morning. It was Saturday and Theo had gone to the club for tennis. Downstairs on the lawn she heard the creak of the swings; Nellie was outside with the children. Really she ought to go downstairs and be with them, letting Nellie do her work indoors. She ought to take Laura shopping, for all her clothes were too short. And Steve was a worry: surely he was much too solitary? Thrusting up the hill alone after school, with his shoulders hunched and head down, whereas Jimmy tore along with a crowd of friends? But she had no energy to deal with these things; she felt so great a lassitude. It was hard to make a decision to move.

The telephone rang.

"Why don't you and Theo come over for lunch? I just thought of it," Mama asked.

"Theo's having lunch at the club. Besides, you just got back from Mexico! Do you have to start entertaining already?"

"Having you at lunch isn't entertaining. And Eric's coming down from Dartmouth. He phoned last night that he'll be here by noon.

So come, and Theo can drop in after lunch. Bring the children, too."

"No, they're playing nicely. Nellie can watch them. I'll come alone."

She had so little patience with the children lately. She seemed to have lost her strength for nurturing and comforting; she wanted those things for herself. Thought of the luncheon table in her parents' house brought now a total recall of childhood when, after a bad day at school, she had fled to the warmth of home. She needed her parents—her father—and was terribly ashamed of having the need.

There was an autumn melancholy in the burning sun as she drove through the town. It felt hotter than summer, yet yellow leaves were falling, floating down in windless air. The main street was crowded with station wagons. These were loaded with dogs and children, and adorned with the stickers of prestigious colleges: Harvard, Smith, Bryn Mawr. On the sidewalk in front of the bank women sat behind rickety tables selling raffle tickets for cerebral palsy, mental health, Our Lady of Sorrows and B'nai Brith. All these things were now unimportant.

She passed the school where next year she would move up to the presidency of the P.T.A.; then the temple, and Papa's handsome wing outlined in autumn flowers, marigolds and zinnias, burnt yellow and dark red. Unimportant.

"I can't go to temple anymore," Theo had said last week.

Iris had stopped in the center of the room. She didn't mind so much that he didn't want to go. He hadn't come with them in the last few months anyway. If only he had said it differently! There had been argument in his tone, a throwing down of the gauntlet. And she had picked it up.

"No? Why can't you?"

"I wonder that you need to ask me. Can you really expect me to sit there listening to all that talk about God? God, who allowed Dachau to exist?"

"It's not for us to judge what God allows. There are reasons for things that are beyond our understanding."

"Bosh! Rubbish! I only see that your God destroys. I'm more merciful than he is: I spend my days rebuilding."

"One might say it's God's work that makes you want to rebuild."

"Come, come, you're too educated to believe that! Your parents I can understand, but not you! Mt. Sinai and the Torah given to Moses, carved on stone! You know better than that. You don't really believe those legends!"

"Don't I? Then why do you think I go to services every week?"

"You go because it's a lifelong habit. Nice people are supposed to go. And besides, the music is beautiful. You take an emotional bath in it."

"I could be furious but I won't be. Theo, more to the point, when are you going to get over all this? I don't mean to be unfeeling, heaven knows, but after all, Liesel isn't the only human being who died cruelly. Look at my brother, don't you think that my parents—"

"I don't want to talk about Liesel," he'd said coldly.

"I was only trying to help you."

"There is no help. 'We are born, we suffer and we die.' I forget who said that, but it's the truest thing that anybody ever said."

"I don't know about that. It sounds more profound than it really is, once you think about it. And it's awfully, awfully bitter."

"Iris, there's no point in this conversation. I'm sorry I started it. Go to your temple, if it makes you happy. It isn't even kind of me to take it away from you when it makes you so happy."

"You couldn't take it away from me. But thank you anyway."

At what point, Iris thought now, reliving that particular conversation, at what point, on what day, had they begun to talk to each other like that? With irony and coldness, like debaters sparring cautiously? Whence this distance, this semi-courteous enmity?

Her heart beat heavily all the time. Driving the car through the quiet streets, turning into the driveway of her parents' house, she was aware of its slow, steady thudding and of the chill in her flesh. It was a sensation she remembered from school when you entered the room where finals were being held: the same chill and thudding as the unknown loomed.

At the front door she arranged her face into a standard welcoming smile. "Hello, hello, Papa! Mama, you look marvelous! Eric, how are you?"

The house smelled of furniture polish and fresh air; the table in the dining room was set with pink linen mats; Mama's hair was perfect. She was aware of her own hair, which she hadn't bothered with in a week, and tucked the untidy strands behind her ears.

"Too bad you didn't bring the children," Papa said. "We'll have to run over later this afternoon, after Laura's nap. Has she grown any, my doll?"

"I can't tell, Papa, I see her every day." Papa's doll, red-haired, lucky Laura who had skipped a generation and looked like Mama.

"So," Mama sighed, when they were at the table. "So I got my wish, I saw Dan and I'm satisfied. It's a fascinating country. They took us all over."

"Did you see the Pyramid of the Sun at Teotihuacán?"

"Of course, of course! I'm glad I had read *The Conquest of Mexico.* Otherwise it would have been a heap of stones, an engineering feat and nothing more. But this way it really meant something. I could see it all in my mind, the way it had been when Cortez came. Such brutes!" Mama exclaimed.

Iris half heard. Dan. Dena. Their children and grandchildren. Stone house with a wrought-iron fence. Shop in the Zona Rosa. Wholesale operation with seventy employees.

"And Dan said your mother looked beautiful, she had hardly aged at all," Papa finished. "Yes," he said, "I made a good choice, I did. You do as well as I did, Eric, and you'll have it made. Oh, I had plenty of girls, but none of them ever worth more than ten minutes of my time until I met this one."

Iris drank the coffee with downcast eyes. *Her* husband couldn't say that about *her.*

"Theo in better spirits?" Papa inquired. He shook his head. "What he's been through!"

"I imagine," Mama said, "the club does him good. Tennis and all the exercise. It's therapeutic."

"I must say," Papa observed, "it was a surprise to me when you joined a country club." He shook his head again. "There's a very fast crowd up there. Do a lot of drinking."

"Oh, nonsense," Anna contradicted. "You pick and choose wherever you go! We've loads of friends who belong and they're hardly what you'd call fast."

"All the same," Papa insisted, "there's a lot of hanky-panky going on. I shouldn't have thought the atmosphere would appeal to Theo."

"He plays tennis, takes a swim and comes home," Iris said briefly.

"You don't enjoy the club, do you?" Papa asked now. For some reason he seemed determined to pursue the subject.

"I don't mind it one way or the other," she replied.

"A whorehouse. Pardon me for the expression. Morals like alley cats."

Eric laughed and Mama raised her eyebrows. "My goodness, Joseph! Those are strong words!"

"Maybe they are. I had lunch a while ago with a crowd of men who belong. Some of them my age, one even older. I think I and two others were the only ones there who were living with their first wives. I got dizzy listening to them: three sets of children; stepchildren; one guy married to a girl younger than his own daughter; another shacked up with some other man's wife. Crazy! Crazy!"

"So, Grandpa? What can be done about it?" Eric asked.

"I don't know. Tell you one thing, though, we're too easy on that sort of thing. There won't be any whole families left, at this rate. You know what the Bible says you do with an adulteress? Take her out and stone her, that's what!"

"Surely, Joseph," Mama said very quietly, "you don't believe in that?"

"Of course not. That was speaking figuratively. But I'll tell you one thing you don't do; you don't invite her to your house to sit at your table and meet your wife. People like that should be dead to the community! All these divorces and shenanigans," he grumbled.

"You sound like Mary Malone!" Mama said. "Like a good, old-fashioned Catholic!"

"The Malones and I are very close together on most things. You ought to know that by now. Hi, here's Theo!"

Theo stood in the door of the dining room carrying his racket, with his tennis sweater tied around his shoulders. He had such easy grace as he stood there; Iris wondered how many other women saw it too. He took a seat at the table.

"We were talking about the club," Papa told him.

"I know. I heard you as I was coming in."

"Yes. Well, our people are becoming assimilated, aren't they? All the dirt of modern civilization clinging to their skirts as they pass through."

Theo laughed. "They seem to be enjoying it."

"Oh, they enjoy it well enough! But they'll pay for it, you can be sure. Some fellow wrote an article in the magazine section last week about Rome, all the filth masquerading as pleasure. They paid too, in the end."

431

Theo stirred uncomfortably. He always said that his father-in-law had just one flaw: he moralized like an Old Testament prophet. He turned to his mother-in-law.

"How was your trip? What did you think of Mexico City?"

Anna began to go into raptures over the Reforma as compared with Fifth Avenue, the Champs-Elysées and the Graben. Then Theo joined in with word-pictures of Vienna, which for years he hadn't mentioned or wanted anyone else to mention, Iris thought angrily. Why, Vienna had been wiped off the map, as far as he was concerned! And now he was talking to Mama about the Prater and Grinzing; Mama was joining in as though she were an expert on the city, after having spent two weeks there a quarter of a century ago . . . Theo was laughing. It was almost like flirting, what he was doing, and he was doing it, she knew, only to irritate her.

He rose abruptly. "I'm going to go home and shower. By the way," he said, addressing Iris directly for the first time since he had come in, "I made a reservation for dinner with some people at the club tonight. Seven-thirty."

"All right," she said and became aware of her mother's eyes, examining her. She dropped her own eyes, feeling a blush prickle on her neck. Mama was too sharp; she saw too much.

She stood with the cold glass in her hand. There seemed to be no place to set it down. She was squeezed into a corner talking to an elderly lady, a Mrs. Reiss, who knew her mother. Always she seemed to end up talking to old people! Yet, she had to admit, it was more comfortable and easier to talk to them. But now her mouth ached from having smiled for the last hour, and she wished they would serve dinner so she could sit down and stop talking.

Gusts of perfume, smoke and whiskey poured on her as people squeezed by. She couldn't move, couldn't wriggle out of the corner where she was pinned against a topply vase of roses on a table at the small of her back.

"—seven hundreds in the Boards, he's always been an outstanding student, but the competition is murderous, you never—"

"—offered them a hundred twenty-five thousand for the house without the adjoining lot and really I would consider it a mediocre neighborhood. Ray says—"

"—everybody admits the course at Shadyvale is far superior, if you want to put up with the class of people they're taking in. We're quite comfortable here at Rolling Hill."

"I see they've got those little water chestnut things," Mrs. Reiss remarked, raising her voice above the noise. "Shall we get some?"

"No, thanks," Iris said.

"Well, I think I'll just go try to find some. Will you excuse me?"

Even an old lady like that is bored with me. I've the personality of a clam. No poise. When Theo married me I began to have it. I know I did, because I never thought about it anymore and when you don't think about it, that means you have it. I just *knew* I was somebody when we were married, and now I don't know, I've lost it again.

She found Theo in the middle of a jovial group, almost all of them new to her. She had hoped they might be sitting with Jack and Lee, their neighbors, or with Dr. and Mrs. Jasper, good, solid people with whom there would be things to talk about. These were all new people, his tennis friends probably, and she saw at once that they had sized her up and found her wanting.

They went in to dinner. She felt a frenetic activity in the room. Everyone seemed—she sought a word—feverish; yes, that was it; their alert eyes looked past and beyond to the next table; the people at the next table are always more important. *How can I get myself invited to sit with them next time?* That's what they're thinking. *How can I get to meet the So-and-So's?* Not that there's anything wrong about wanting to know people and be liked. But they're so *intent* on it, using all their energies, like a runner sweating to the finish line. And then, the crafty cruelties that go with this sort of climbing! The flattery and snubs!

Only Theo doesn't need to climb; he's already there. He lures and captivates without even trying. He ought not to have a dull wife like me. He ought to have an equal.

He ought to have a wife like Liesel.

Theo leaned toward her. "You're a thousand miles away," he said.

"I? I'm just watching everyone, enjoying the scene." Her lips were dry. Why can't I say I'm uncomfortable and I want to go home? "Who's that, that woman in red? I seem to know, but I can't place her."

"Oh, that's Billie Stark. She's a great tennis player. We played doubles today and I really had a workout."

Oh, Lord, another of those vivacious types! The agitated red bird comes swooping in our direction. One heard her approach from the far end of the dining room, her little animated squeals and whoops and shrieking mirth. Her mouth stretches from an ellipse for a smile to a circle for astonishment. *"No, you can't mean it!"* Eyes blinking, popping, batting, scrunched in a nest of fine dry wrinkles, or stretched in ingénue affectation. Tossing hair, flung arms, pelvic twists. Never quiet, never still for more than a second or two. Exhausting to watch her gyrations. No peace where such people are.

Lady in red, Billie Stark, why the hell don't you shut up or go away?

"Of course I remember you, you're Billie Stark. How are you?" Iris said, holding out her hand.

Why don't I like anybody; why do I feel they don't like me? I used to have compassion, used to try to understand people. Maury always said I understood so well. At least, I used to try. I know I've helped Eric.

Somebody asked Billie Stark to dance. Then everyone got up to dance.

"Aren't you having a good time?" Theo asked, as they circled the room. "You're so quiet."

"All right," she said. It was on the tip of her tongue; she tried to hold the question back but could not. "You like that woman, Billie Stark?"

"Well, she's lively. She certainly knows how to enjoy herself."

Was that meant for me, I wonder? I could enjoy life too, if you were—

"Don't you feel well, Iris? Are you coming down with something?"

He knew perfectly well she wasn't. "I'm well. But I feel like a stranger here. I don't belong with the Billie Starks. And I'm trying to figure out what makes you think you do. *Do* you belong? Which is you, Theo who plays in Ben's quartet on Thursdays, or this one?" There was pleading in her voice. She could hear it.

"Which am I? Must I be either one or the other? Can't I go wherever I choose whenever I want to?"

"But one has to fit somewhere, to *be* something."

The music beat and stabbed. It was absurd to be jiggling there in the middle of the floor, feeling the way she did.

"You read too much junk popular psychology," Theo said with annoyance.

She allowed herself to be annoyed in return. "Do you know what I really think of your new friends? They're full of crap. Racing around outsmarting and outdoing each other. They have to see your Dun & Bradstreet report before they decide whether it's worth their while to say hello to you."

Theo didn't answer. She knew he didn't entirely disagree with her. He had made similar comments often enough himself. But they drove home without speaking. He turned the radio on and they listened to the news as if it were the most important thing in their lives.

She knew that, while she was having her bath, he would go to the drawer in his dresser and take out the picture. Tonight she got quietly out of the bathtub and put on her robe. By opening the door very quickly, she was able to catch him holding the photograph up to the light. She caught a familiar glimpse of the Madonna pose, the long hair curving, the child on the lap, before he put it back in the drawer.

They stood there looking at each other. "You should never have married me, Theo," Iris said at last.

"What are you saying?"

"You don't love me. You never have. You're still in love with her."

"She's dead."

"Yes, and if she had lived you'd have been happier than you are with me."

"At least she wouldn't have nagged me!"

"There, you see? Well, it's too bad, isn't it? Perhaps I should accommodate you by dying. Except that that still wouldn't bring *her* back, would it?"

He slapped his fist into the palm of his hand, making a loud crack in the room. "Of all the stupid, childish—Iris, how long is this going to go on? I shouldn't have said that about nagging, I really didn't mean it. But I don't know why you're so insecure. You value yourself so little! It's pathetic."

"Maybe I am insecure. If you think I am, why don't you help me?"

"Tell me how. If I can, I will."

She knew she was burning bridges and yet she couldn't refrain.

435

"Tell me that if you had known she was alive you would still have chosen me. Tell me you love me more than you ever loved her."

"I can't say that. Don't you know that every love is different? She was a person, you're a different person. That's not to say that either one was better or worse than the other."

"That's an evasion, Theo."

"It's the best I can do," he said gently enough.

"All right, then. Answer the other half of my question. If you had known she was alive would you have left me and gone to her? Surely you can answer that."

"Oh, my God," Theo cried. "Why do you want to torture me?"

She knew she was beating him like a helpless dog on a leash. Once on the street she had seen a man doing just that and had been sickened by it. But she couldn't stop.

"I ask you, Theo, because I have to know. Don't you see it's a matter of how I am to live, to exist?"

"But this is brutal! I simply cannot, I cannot answer these pointless questions."

"So we get back to what I said in the beginning. You never wanted to marry me, really."

"Why did I do it, then?"

"Because you knew my father half expected you to—"

"Iris, if I hadn't wanted to, ten fathers couldn't have made me."

"—and because you were lonely and worn out and came to rest in my family. And yes, because, after all, I'm intelligent enough for you, and have your tastes, or had. Your cultured European friends can come to our house and I know how to talk to them. But that's not love."

Theo considered a moment. Then he asked, "What do you mean by love? Can you define it?"

"Semantics! Of course I can't. Nobody can, but everybody knows what he means when he uses the word."

"Exactly. Everyone knows what 'he' means. So it's a different thing for everyone."

"Oh, this calm, philosophical trickery! Putting me on the defensive! When all the time you know what I'm talking about."

"Very well, let's define it then, let's try. Would you say that being unselfish, thinking of the other person's welfare and good, is a part of love?"

"Yes, and one could do that for one's aged grandfather."

"Iris, you're twisting my meaning. You're making unnecessary grief for yourself. If I only knew what you want!"

Her lips began to quiver. She put her hand to her mouth to hide it. "I want . . . I want . . . something like Romeo and Juliet. I want to be loved exclusively. Do you understand?"

"Iris. Again I have to say—that's childish, my dear."

"Childish? All the world is enthralled with it! It's the most intense, deep, marvelous thing that can happen to a human being. It's what the world's art and music and poetry are all about. And you call it childish!"

Theo sighed. "Maybe I used the wrong word again. Not childish. *Unreal.* You're talking about emotional peaks, high moments. How long do you think they can last? That's why I say *unreal.*"

"I'm not stupid. I know life isn't a poem or an operatic drama. But still I would just like to experience some of those 'high moments,' as you call them."

"And you don't think you have?"

"No. I've been sharing you with a dead woman. And now with a lot of cold and silly featherheads as well."

"Iris, I'm sorry for you. Sorry for us both. Did the photograph bring all this on tonight? All right, I won't look at it anymore. Time would have brought that to a stop anyway," he said bitterly. "But if that won't satisfy you— It seems there's something in you that doesn't want to be satisfied, that wants to suffer."

"Ah, so now we are going in for psychoanalysis!"

"You don't have to be an analyst to see things. You *want* to be hurt, otherwise you would listen to my reasoning."

"Reason has nothing to do with it. This is something I feel. And you can't reason yourself out of something you feel. Or else you would reason yourself out of remembering Liesel, wouldn't you?"

Theo passed his hand over his forehead. "Can we continue this in the morning? It's past midnight and I'm exhausted."

"As you wish," she answered.

They lay down in the wide bed. Her heart began to pound. Her hands were clenched and her arms held straight at her sides. She wondered whether sleep would come to relieve her. And she knew by the sound of Theo's breathing that he was not sleeping, either.

After a while she felt his hand upon her, sliding over her shoulder, touching it softly in a gesture meant to comfort. Then his hand went to her breast.

"No," she said. "I can't. I don't feel anything. It's gone."

"What do you mean, gone? Gone for always?"

"Yes. It's dead. It died in me." She began to weep. Cold tears slid down her temples into her hair. She made no sound, but she knew he was aware. He put his hand out again, trying to reach her hand, but she drew away. Then she heard him turn, heard the swishing of the sheets, and knew that he had turned his back to move as far apart as he could.

Early in the morning, after a night with only an hour or two of sleep, Theo got up and went downstairs. He had no trouble finding the number he wanted in the New York City telephone book. He paused a moment.

A week or two ago, coming out of his dentist's office—he went to a dentist in the city—he'd had to wait at the threshold for the slackening of a sudden downpour. And this girl, a dental technician in the next office, had come out and stood there waiting with him. She was about thirty-two, he guessed, a Scandinavian with all the frank, healthy grace of her kind. They had stayed there talking until the rain stopped, talking about skiing and New York and where she'd come from in Norway.

Then he'd told her how he had enjoyed talking to her and she'd said, "Call me up if you ever want to talk some more. I'm in the book."

So here he was. His finger moved the dial.

"Hello, Ingrid?" he said softly, when he heard her voice. "It's Theo Stern. Remember me?"

39

The car hummed northward through the glittering cold that Theo loved. Winter had always been his time. He loved sifting snow in gray air; the spare design of branches, so Japanese; the expectation of fires, thick soup and quilts. Crossing the line between Massachusetts and Vermont, he thought that it was not very different from Austria.

He leaned forward, trying to adjust the radio, but the farther he got from the city the more it faded and Mahler's Ninth was scratched out by static. When he switched it off there were no sounds but the click of the windshield wiper and the clack of the tires.

It would be good to have Ingrid riding along. Her presence was pure ease and had been so for almost a year. Neither her laughter nor her silences demanded anything of him. Once every week he went to the city to teach and, taking the rest of the day and evening off, spent the hours with her. He was so absolutely free there in those two small rooms! She'd have good music playing and bread baking in the oven. The bed was next to the windows where hanging plants, which were the only curtains, dropped their green shade and moist fragrance onto the bed. Sometimes they lay all afternoon listening to music, while Ingrid smoked the sweet cigarettes that he had come to associate with her. When he left he was enlivened for the rest of the week.

But it would have been foolhardy for them to travel and arrive together. You never knew whom you might meet, although he had chosen this little ski resort because it was out of the way and he had never met anyone who had even heard of it, much less been there.

He had mentioned to Iris, knowing that she would refuse to go with him, that it would be nice to take a few days off for skiing. "There are pleasant things for you to do while I'm on the slopes," he'd said. "You could take walks around the village and look for antiques." But she had declined.

"You go, it will do you good," she had said, with the polite concern one has for one's friends.

Things were like that between them.

But he could think of no way to change them. Iris' mood had gradually dimmed. (Clouds drift one by one across a sunny sky; you look up after only an hour or two and are surprised to find that the sky has grown completely dark.) She hadn't moved out of their room because all the others were occupied; but had instead removed their bed and bought twin ones. She had waited for him to make comment but he had made none. If that was the way she wanted it, Theo had thought angrily, that was the way she would have it. Everything that could be said about what stood between them had already been said, anyway. He remembered having heard stories about couples a generation or two ago, who lived out their lives beneath one roof without speaking to each other. He had never believed it was possible to live that way, but he saw now that it might be. Not that they lived without speaking, Iris and he; they were both far too concerned as parents to inflict anything like that on their children. No, they made decent conversation at the table and went to P.T.A. meetings and local dinner parties with unsuspecting friends. (He almost never went to the club anymore. Iris had been right about that; it wasn't the atmosphere he really wanted, and his weekly day with Ingrid more than made up for its loss, he thought now, smiling to himself.)

So that's the way things were. He hadn't been able to change Iris' thinking, nor had she changed—but she *had* changed his a little, he reflected. Yes, in an odd way some of her convictions had begun to influence him. Things she had said, dredged out of what tortuous channels, chambers and coves of her mind, had begun to seem true. Or to have some truth in them, at least.

Perhaps she is right and I didn't really want to be married? Sometimes I think—and I'm sad and ashamed of thinking it—that I really didn't want to be. I was so tired, I remember. I just wanted rest. Maybe all I wanted was some sunny rooms, a piano in a bay window, birds in the trees outside the window, and there wasn't any simple, efficient way of having these things without being married. Could that be?

Yet I did want children, another little boy—as if anything could bring back that first one! But these were beautiful children: Jimmy, a bright rascal; sensitive, thoughtful and sometimes difficult Steve; Laura, pink and curly—but how does a man begin to describe his ·darling, only little girl?

I wish it was enough for Iris that we have all this, and that life is—was—good together. Because it *was* good together! But that's not enough . . . she wants something I don't seem able to give her. I feel—I have felt—sometimes as if I had given coins to a beggar who needs more than I have to give. She wants me to *adore* her. I don't *adore* her.

Before they were married Iris had trembled in his presence; he had seen that she was in love with him and been very moved. He remembered having thought that he would be so good to her (then perhaps, after all, he had really *wanted* to marry her?), and, in turn, enjoy her quiet ways, the refinement of her face. A lovely lady, she was. Stuffy concept in America, but still valued in Europe, or at least it had been when he had lived there. Reason enough in Europe, the best reason, in fact, for choosing a wife.

But he hadn't expected the intensity of her love. Those trusting, worshiping eyes! A man could feel guilty without having done anything. Her soul was in her eyes. All that grave emotion! It was almost frightening. To be responsible for the survival of another soul!

He frowned. His thoughts had made his head ache, or perhaps it was only the woolen cap that was tight. He pulled it off. If he had met Iris away from the vitality and welcome of her home—the first home he had been in for so many years—if he had met her in an office, say, sitting with pad on knee, her dark, pensive eyes looking past him to the corners of the room—would he have been as easily drawn to her? The truth was: no. Yet, once having known her subtle and resilient mind, her shy pleasure in being with him, he had quite simply wanted to be with *her.* They had slipped into a pattern of understanding, and a common language. It wasn't that often that two people were able to walk so easily in the same rhythm through the world, including the rhythm of sex.

441

They had had all that, and yet he was unable to talk to her about this obstinate, fixed idea that he must feel for her and toward her in just such and such a way, just so and so and in no other way nor for anyone else, either present or past.

Women! But not all women.

That first time with Ingrid she had told him, "You have the body of a dancer or a skier. V-shaped, tapering from the shoulder to the hips. Especially marvelous for skiing."

Theo had been amused. "I happen to be fairly good at skiing."

"You see? I could tell. So different from a boxer's body, for instance."

"You're an expert on male bodies?"

She'd laughed. "I've seen enough of them!" And when he didn't answer, "You're not shocked?"

"Of course not. Just surprised. You don't seem to be—"

"A tart? But how provincial of you! Does one have to be vulgar to take pleasure in what was made for pleasure? Must sex be either sanctified or else damned?"

"I don't know. But most people, especially most women, see it that way, don't they?"

"It's a simple pleasure, that's all, that's what I believe. Like wine or music. When you tire of it you change the brand, or turn off the record."

"I hope you don't tire of me too soon," he had remarked another time. They were eating fettuccine Alfredo. She had a wonderful appetite. That was another thing that made him feel good to be with her. She wasn't always whining about calories the way most women did these days, and how she'd have to starve all next week to make up for tonight. The fettuccine kept slipping off her fork and she began to laugh. Then he laughed, and it had all been so completely silly. He hadn't laughed with such foolish high spirits in—how long?

"I don't expect to tire of you," Ingrid had said frankly. "I still love Beethoven and if you don't believe I still like Château Mouton Rothschild, you can try me."

"All right, I will," he had answered and summoned the wine steward.

Then she had grown serious. "But when you tire of me, do me a favor, will you? Call me up and tell me so. Don't lie and make considerate excuses for not keeping dates. Don't try to break it to me gently. Just say, Ingrid, good-by and it's been great, but good-by. Will you do that, Theo?"

"All right, but I don't want to think about it. We've just begun," he'd said.

Still, the freedom, the freedom, like an invigorating breeze! If women only knew!

He had been able to talk to her about Liesel. For the first time he had been free to spill everything out, with no modesty, with no hesitation. Everything. And Ingrid had carefully listened. He had talked for hours while she lay on the bed, smoking cigarettes. He had talked and talked. He had told how, at first, he hadn't been able to believe in the death of Liesel or their child; how once, in a London restaurant during the war, he'd heard a woman at a table behind him speaking with a foreign accent, an accent he'd fancied Liesel *would have had* if she had known how to speak English. He had made an excuse to get up from the table and look at the woman. That was how mad he had been!

He had even recalled that young chap in London whose wife had been killed in the bombing of their house and how he, Theo, holding the fellow's hand, had sworn to himself: No, it's crazy to love and make yourself so vulnerable. I don't ever want to be so vulnerable again.

He told how, after the encounter with Franz, Liesel's face, which had faded, now returned and hung in the air before his vision, clear in every detail: the white scar where a cat had scratched her neck, the crooked tooth about which she was self-conscious, the fact that her lashes were dark and her brows blond. That face had been before him all the time, *all the time!* Sometimes he had welcomed it, aware how much he had been longing for it; sometimes he had covered his eyes and cried out, "Go away! Stay away from me! Go away!"

He had told Ingrid all of that and, in the telling and her hearing, had found relief, a softening, and ease.

He did not ever speak of Iris and Ingrid never asked him to. So much was understood between them! She quenched his thirst, appeased his hunger and was herself satisfied. They could let their minds go empty in a tide of sleep after joy and no worry about what anybody *wanted* or *needed*. Care-less woman! Woman-without-care!

Iris would never understand anyone like her.

443

Nor would my father-in-law, Theo thought grimly. He would want me stoned to death. Endless love as long as you don't transgress; no mercy if you do. The only reason he forgives me for my irreligion is that I'm a doctor. The thought amused him momentarily.

"Your work is holy. You do holy work," Joseph said often.

Well, in a sense there's truth in it, if you want to stretch the word 'holy' a bit. Theo lifted his hand from the steering wheel, flexing it inside the glove. An intricate weaving of fragile bones, and what it could do! He was proud of the work he could do, and also humble about it. Holy? Well, perhaps.

But then, all labor is holy and the body is miraculous. Labor of bent backs on mountain slopes, tension of dancers or players of the violin. What a mechanism, man! A brute at worst, and at best a self-centered, pleasure-seeking organism.

And yet, why not? As long as we don't hurt one another! (I'm not hurting anyone, am I?) Just let us flourish for our little time with our small greeds and our small sins, and die without struggle when our time is over.

"What will you do with your life?" he'd asked Ingrid one day.

"I don't know. And that's the beauty of it! To enjoy the beauty of it! I like my work. I like being healthy and young and I shall try to stay both as long as I can. Also, I like music and good food. And I like you. I like you very much, Theo."

"I'm glad," he'd said.

"But I don't want to own you. Don't be afraid. You can get away any time you want. Because I don't want to be tied either, you know."

And it was for just that reason that he had no wish to get away. Wise woman! Perversity of man!

He came now to the fork off the main road and stopped to look at the map. Right for five miles at the fork, past the general store. . . . His heart began to pound with anticipation, a nice, painless pounding. The car crept up the mountain. There were few tracks. The road hadn't been traveled much, so the place had been well chosen, after all. He drew up at the inn, which was set in a stand of spruce. There it was, her little green car. She'd got here ahead of him; she drove like a fury.

The snow was firm and deep. It wasn't too cold. With luck, there

444

would be some sunshine in the morning. Meanwhile there were food, a fire, a bed and a gay, strong, wise, sweet girl.

Weak February light fell on the rug near the window and over Iris' hands, holding a book which she wasn't reading. She was just sitting there, Anna saw, looking out at the weather. She tapped at the open door and Iris turned around.

"Hi," Anna said cheerfully. "I've got my marketing chores over with and I thought I'd take a walk. I needed some exercise."

It was the best excuse she could think of for this unusual forenoon visit. The truth was that she had detected, running through their mundane telephone conversations of the past few days, a new and alarming depression of the spirit.

"Well, sit down. Do you want some lunch?"

"Thanks, no, I'll not be staying that long." She sat down, perched rather tentatively on the chair, and wondered how to comment or what to inquire. It was always so difficult, with Iris, to find the reaching word.

"If Nellie doesn't shut off that radio in the kitchen," Iris cried suddenly, "I shall go mad, or go in and smash it."

"Too bad you're not up in Vermont with Theo. You really need a little change, Iris. It gets on a woman's nerves, being constantly with children, and no relief." Platitudes, for lack of the truth.

There was no answer. And Anna said softly, "Iris, a moment comes when we have to cut through our reserve. I've known for a long time that you're in trouble and I've been too polite, too hesitant to ask. Now I'm asking."

Iris looked up. Her face had no expression at all. It looked empty. Her voice was just as empty. "Sometimes I don't care whether I live or die. Now you know."

"What has Theo done?"

The question struck Iris like a blow. Her mouth crumpled and twisted into the grimace of tears.

"What's Theo done? Nothing, really. Just gone away, left me. We've left each other. We're in the same house, but we've left each other."

"I see." Anna spoke carefully. "Will you tell me the reasons, or don't you know them?"

"Oh, I know all right! It's because of me. I don't come up to

445

standard . . . I don't ski, I'm not a delicate blonde, I'm only mediocre at the piano. Let's face it, I'm only mediocre, period."

So that's it, Anna thought. I might have suspected it.

Iris stood and walked up and down the room. Then she sat down at the desk again, facing Anna.

"Mama . . . I know I'll be ashamed of myself for asking you this, but I have to know. Was she as beautiful as her picture?"

"I haven't seen any picture," Anna evaded.

"Please. Don't treat me like that. You saw her when you were in Vienna."

"All I remember is a pretty child. . . . Iris, darling, why are you doing this to yourself?"

"I don't know. I don't know."

A long time ago, years and years—when?—Anna had had a flash of thought: If ever I have a daughter I will not let her be vulnerable and unworldly.

"You see," Iris cried, "you see that I haven't even got self-respect anymore! I'm a mean and petty soul. To be jealous of that poor woman who went through the fire of the century and died in it! To begrudge her the only thing left: that someone who loved her should mourn for her! I'm so ashamed of myself, of this worm inside of me! Do you see what a nasty person I am?"

"You're not nasty. You never were. But you think too much about everything, yourself included." Surely there had to be some combination of words that would sound natural and wholesome and comforting. "It's normal to feel a little jealous and normal to be a little guilty about it."

"No," Iris interrupted. "You don't see what I mean. How can you? Papa adores you; there was never anybody else but you."

Anna winced, as pain cut through her, then attempted to seem casual. "Your father's a man; how do I know he tells me everything? And I don't sit around worrying about it, I assure you."

"But you do know," Iris said impatiently, "that he's not up at a country club surrounded by women or sitting alone downstairs grieving half the night. I am absolutely superfluous, don't you see? Thrown away. And I don't know how long I'll be able to live like this."

"Do you want to leave him?"

Iris stared at her. "I wish I could want to. But I don't want to, I don't think I could live through that, either."

"I wish I knew how to help you."

"Help me! You could have helped me by not giving me such a ridiculous name, for one thing! 'Iris!' Look at me, do I look like an Iris? What reason could you have had to think I would grow up and fit such a name! Unless, of course, you hoped I would look like you!"

"I'm sorry. We thought it was a lovely name, that's all."

"Oh, God," Iris said.

Her balled fists pounded the desk. Then she lowered her head to it. Such wretched suffering! Broken open. The nape of the neck was so weak, so tender, even on an adult; Anna put out her hand to touch it, then drew back, afraid to intrude.

Oh, I love her, I love her, and yet it has never been what it was with Maury. Golden Maury. Those first years on the sidewalk, the women on the camp chairs, the toddlers with pull toys, his laughter, his bright hair. An old grandmother had put out her hand and touched his head. "*Wunderkind,*" she called him. Wonder child.

But how could it have been like that for Iris? God knows I never felt joy because of her, either before or after she was born. Such misery, such despair, such guilt, must they not wear off on the child in the womb? And afterward, looking at her, searching her face for signs—crazy as it seems—that through her I would be punished. That she might be, heaven forbid, retarded, crippled, marked. So she's not retarded or crippled but without a doubt she is marked. Pallid, timid. Oh, she is valiant, poor soul, she tries for happiness and she can attain it, but then something happens; an ill wind comes and knocks her down. My fault. There must have been some way I could have taught her to be strong and sure of being loved, mustn't there? But I didn't do it. . . .

It's all vague, the past. Iris' past eludes me. She grew up, I worried. She never gave any trouble. I remember that she never was young.

Damn Theo! What has he done to her?

Perhaps if she had married that stubby, timid schoolteacher who had hung about during the war, perhaps life would be less complicated for her. He had been a humble man and Iris would have been his queen. But then every man and woman can ask how different his life would have been if he had married someone else. Surely everyone at some time or other wonders about that? A graying couple walks past my house each afternoon. They even

447

come out in their trench coats in the rain. The woman has a ruddy face; her hair is tied back with a ribbon. They take steps in unison, talking, always talking. What can they have to say to one another? "I hate chatter," Joseph says. But that man and woman lean toward each other, laughing. Would I be different if I had married a man who had so much to say to me? If I had married Paul?

Iris looked up and wiped her eyes. "Tell me, would you have wanted to die if Papa hadn't asked you to marry him?"

My God, such questions! "No. No man is worth that."

"Now I'm sure you're not like me and I'm not like you."

"I suppose not."

On a shelf above the desk stood a model of Rodin's "The Kiss." Odd that Anna had never noticed it in this room before. Fine for a museum, but, my goodness, wasn't it queer to have the naked, embracing pair exposed like that in one's house, especially with children running in and out? Iris must be far more 'free' than I about things like that. I still undress in private. Joseph is amused. I don't know why I do that. I've not been embarrassed to stand naked in front of Paul.

Anna's thoughts swirled slowly. She stood befogged, as if dazed, unsure of where to go, of what to say. How would I feel in Iris' place? I don't think I'd be as distraught as she is. Theo is the center of her life and "the centre cannot hold." Just now I told her that no man is worth dying for. Yet I've always said that if some tyrant were to demand my life or Joseph's I would say 'take mine.' Would I do that for Paul, I wonder? I wonder what Paul is doing this minute. What would he say if I could speak to him about his daughter's anguish?

But she had to deal with Iris' life, not her own. "You must speak to Theo. Speak to one another, break through the wall. You may find that he's ready, after all these months, to listen and to change." Anna's speech began to gather momentum, spilling out clichés. "Time is the great healer, you know. Especially when you've done right. The only thing it doesn't heal is the wrong you've done to somebody else."

"What do you know about that? What wrongs have you done?"

"I'm human."

After a moment Iris said, "I don't think I've done wrong to Theo."

"Perhaps not. But can you try to forget what he's done to you?"

448

"I don't even know that you can call what he's done a 'wrong.' He's simply grown tired of me. He can't help that, can he?"

"You don't know that for certain. Again I say, my dear, you analyze too deeply. You may imagine motives that aren't there. Or exaggerate them, anyway. I used to watch you doing it when you were a child."

"You were always watching me. Searching my face as though you were looking for something."

"I was? I don't remember that at all. Don't mothers always look closely at their children?"

"This was different. I always used to think you looked as if you didn't recognize me, as if you weren't quite sure who I was."

Anna was silent.

"*Do* you know who I am?"

"I don't understand!"

"An outsider. That's what I've always been."

"Aren't we all, to some extent?" Anna parried.

"Of course we're not. Look at yourself, at all the friends you have. You don't have to be alone five minutes unless you want to be."

"Friends? It depends on what you mean by friends. I know dozens of nice women, but real friends? There's Ruth, of course." Anna counted on her fingers. "And Vita Wilmot, and I'm very fond of Mary Malone. There's Molly and Jean Becker and—that's it. The rest are just good company, nice people. You expect too much from people, Iris. They won't give it and they'll always disappoint you."

"That's pretty cynical, coming from you."

"Not cynical. Just realistic. One can't expect too much, that's all."

"I don't expect anything anymore," Iris said dully.

"Come! You're a young woman! Look ahead. Think positively." (I sound like the Rotary Club. It's because I don't know what else to say.)

The doorbell rang and Iris started. "It's the children, home for lunch. Do I look as if I'd been upset?"

"You look all right. They won't notice." They were too young to see the wan face, the wrinkled skirt and blouse. Anna sighed. "I'll run along. I've a beauty parlor appointment this afternoon. Shall I make one for you?"

"You're being tactful, Mama. I know how I look and I couldn't care less."

"Then I haven't helped you at all? I did want to help you!"

"I know you did, Mama, and thanks. But as I told you when you came in, I'm beyond it. If it weren't for my children I wouldn't care whether I lived or died."

"You don't feel well today, Mrs. Friedman?" Mr. Anthony, who had been doing her hair for years, was still young enough to be Anna's grandson.

"A headache, Anthony. That's why I'm not talking."

She closed her eyes, then opened them, disturbed by brassy voices from across the room. An over-ornamented woman with a handsome, aging face was fretting. Her little fat lower lip was thrust out like a coral cocktail sausage.

"A bit further over here at the temple; tease it up, Leo, over the ear, can't you see?"

Patient Leo moved a strand of hair another fraction of an inch. Anna watched the little play. It quieted her churning thoughts to watch the woman fidget and pose, studying herself in the mirror as though she could eat herself up.

Another woman got out of the dryer and went over to sausage-lip. "How was your ski trip?"

"Very nice. We had great weather and the children loved it. We stayed at a little place in the middle of nowhere. Didn't meet a soul we knew, for a change. Oh yes, one. Dr. Stern, the plastic surgeon. And not another soul."

"Theo Stern was there? Who with? Not with his girl friend?"

"I don't know him. Jerry knows him. Why, has he got one?"

"Sure has!! It's been going on for ages. People think they can get away with things, it's really funny. The way I know is, my son Bruce has an apartment in town and it's across the hall from this tall, stunning Swedish gal. So one night, we were at Bruce's place, we go to change our clothes for theatre, we see Stern going in. He used to be at the club a lot, with his wife, mousy kind of person. Anyway, I didn't think anything of it, but when we bumped into him again a couple of weeks later, I said to Bruce, I said, 'Say, is anything going on across the hall?' And Bruce said, 'Yeah, it's his girl friend, he's there every Tuesday.'"

"Tall blond Swede?"

"Yes, I saw her once. With hair coiled to one side, you couldn't forget her."

"My God! She was *with* him! He tried to pretend he had just met her. Wait till I tell Jerry!"

Mr. Anthony put the comb down and crossed the room. When he came back to Anna the voices had been stilled.

"You told them who I was," Anna said.

"No. Not who you were. I told them to drop the subject. I'm sorry, Mrs. Friedman. Such dirty, clacking tongues."

Out on the street a wind had risen, a wind with a threat in it, fitting her fear and anger at the woman who, by disclosing what Anna didn't *want* to know, had now forced her to act. She had been presented, furiously, with a demand for action.

She fought against the bruising wind to her front door. Home was shelter in bitter weather; the blurred, stained-glass colors of books, the bowl of yellow roses on a waxed table had always shut out whatever was raging in the world outside. She came in and stood for a moment looking at these things, seeing now, perhaps for the first time, that walls are no protection, are so easily plundered, are fragile as an egg shell against the menace of the world.

I have to fight for her, she thought in terror. I have to fight for her.

A magazine setting, Theo reflected. An imitation colonial crane and iron pot hung at the hearth. On the loom in the corner someone had started a few feet of woven cloth. Cheerful fakery. But the fire was real, and so was the drink. The cold flesh tingled with heat and expectancy. Where was she, anyway? She took too long getting dressed; all women did.

"Stern! What are you doing here? I thought I was the only one who knew about this place!"

"Hello, Nelson," Theo said and rose to greet the man's wife. Bad luck! The first time he'd ever run into anybody he knew when he was with Ingrid and now it had to be Nelson from the hospital pathology department.

"Here with the family?"

"No, I took a couple of days by myself. My wife thought I needed the rest," Theo said.

"We've brought our girls with us. Join us at dinner, don't eat alone."

"Thanks, but I—on the slopes this afternoon I met a young woman, I think she's a teacher, and not wanting to eat alone, I asked her to join me. I don't know how I can get out of it now."

"Bring her along, there's room for six at the table."

"Very nice of you. Ah, there she is now." Ingrid was coming down the stairs. Her hair swept to one side in a bronze coil, fell over a yellow shirt bright as lemons. People were looking at her. She came straight to Theo.

"Well, here I am! Did you think I was never coming?"

"Dr. and Mrs. Nelson," he said, "Miss—excuse me, but I'm so bad at names, Miss Johnson, is it?"

She took the cue. "Johannes. How do you do?"

"Miss Johannes is an expert from Norway. Really an expert, you must watch her tomorrow."

"I told Stern here, let's make up a table. My wife and I are planning the North Cape cruise next summer and maybe you can give us some pointers about Norway."

"That's very nice of you, but I've already reserved a table and I don't want to upset the dining room arrangements," Ingrid said, looking at Theo.

He was flustered and annoyed with himself for being so. "I'm sorry," he began, meaning to address Nelson.

"That's all right." Ingrid's voice was pleasant and cool. "Quite all right, Doctor Stern. Of course you'll want to be with your friends."

He saw as she walked away to the corner table for two that she was furious.

Nelson leaned toward him. "Say, you move fast!" he whispered. "Get the shape of that babe!"

Theo ignored him.

Fortunately, not much conversation was required of him. Mrs. Nelson was one of those women whose monologue can fill an evening. Ordinarily he despised such trivia of restaurants, shops and travel, but tonight he was grateful. He had only to swallow his food and get rid of the Nelsons who were all going over to an inn where the girls wanted to hear a 'chantoosy' come up from a New York nightclub. Against their insistent urging Theo pleaded tiredness and got up to Ingrid's room as soon as they were out of sight.

She was sitting in bed reading. He saw at once that he was not to be invited into the bed.

"I'm sorry," he began. "But I couldn't think of any other way to

452

handle it. The man's a pest. He works in the hospital and lives not too far from me." He threw up his hands. "What else could I have done?"

She didn't answer. He felt her anger and went over to the offensive. "You could have carried it through and had dinner with us. It wouldn't have hurt you."

She laid the book down. "Not hurt me? You fool, I've never been so hurt in my life!"

He was truly astonished. "Tonight? By this?"

"Tonight. By this."

He sat down on the end of the bed. "Tell me why," he said, gently.

"It hurts more that you don't know without being told."

"I'm very puzzled. You know me well enough to know that hurting is the last thing I want to do. I've seen so many wounds; God knows I don't want to make any more."

"Very fine words," Ingrid said bitterly. "Very fine. I've heard you say them often enough. 'The only things I guess I believe in are not causing any pain.' Isn't that what you said? And, oh, yes, 'We're like insects; our lives can be wiped out in an instant.' And so you believe in laughter, and the joy of each day, and being good to one another. Oh, you can be eloquent, Theo, so eloquent!"

He was perplexed at her mockery. "You still haven't made clear what this is all about."

"What it's about is, we're finished. You and I are finished."

"You can't be serious! What have I done?"

"It's what you've not done. I've been feeling a lot of things for a good while now, though I haven't told you. And tonight just brought my feelings to a head."

"You should have told me what was going on in your mind."

"Maybe I should. But it's been vague, and I wanted to be patient, I thought maybe it would go away or something would happen in our lives. But tonight when I had to hide from those common people, I felt dirty. You were ashamed of me! I wasn't good enough for you! You couldn't dare let those people know we knew each other!"

"Ingrid! The words you use! 'Not good enough!' 'Ashamed!' When you know it was only because I have a wife and I couldn't—"

"Exactly! She doesn't have to hide, does she? But I do!"

453

Theo threw up his hands. "But you knew from the beginning that was how things were! Didn't you say you wanted to be free, that there'd be none of this heavy emotion—"

"No emotion! You *have* been damaged, haven't you? No emotion!"

"Well, of course, I didn't mean it just that way but—oh, you knew what I meant. What we both meant. The sort of thing that ties you hand and foot." He got up and stood there, looking at her. He felt totally confused.

She didn't answer.

"You knew what we both meant, didn't you?" he repeated.

"I guess," she said in a small voice, "I guess I'm not being fair to you. You did make it clear. And so did I."

"Well, then?"

"But the fact is, Theo, lately I've been thinking that I might like to be tied down. Hand and foot, as you say. I never thought I'd want that, but all of a sudden I do."

He didn't know what to say.

"I'm thirty-four. And I want someone who belongs to me. Someone on the street and in restaurants and home in bed . . . someone who belongs to *me*, not on loan from another woman."

Suddenly he began to laugh.

"What in hell are you laughing at?" she said angrily.

"Sorry. I'm not laughing at you. It's only that—you're all alike, aren't you? Why should I have thought you'd be different?"

She smiled wanly, but he saw that her eyes were wet. She reached for a cigarette, lit it and looked up. "So what do we do, Theo?"

"I don't know. I've been very happy with things as they are, and I'd be happy to go on as we are."

"You wouldn't leave Iris? Theo, if you tell me that you will, I'll go mad with joy. Otherwise, you see, this is just a dead end for me."

He walked to the window and looked out. In every crisis of his life he felt a need to get out beyond hampering walls and, if that wasn't possible, at least to look out at free space. He stood there now, watching a fresh fall of snow swirl in the circle of light at the front door below. He was hypnotized as the flakes went spiraling; they seemed, by some trick of the vision, to be rising instead of falling.

454

The day comes inevitably. Always there comes a day of reckoning and decision. Nothing lasts in its first simplicity. Not marriage, not this. He sighed. Behind him the sweet smoke puffed into the room. He turned around. Ingrid was still lying on the bed, with her ankles crossed. She looked limp and he felt terribly, terribly sad.

"I can't leave Iris," he said quietly. "I don't know what's going to happen to us eventually, but I do know I'm not ready to do that."

"Will you ever be ready?"

"I don't know."

He took her hand and it lay in his, not moving. A glossy tear rolled down her cheek as she turned her face away. He felt his own eyes fill. Why did women always make a man feel sad?

"You have a whole world to take, dear Ingrid," he said. "So take it and bless you."

Theo sat behind his desk, between a row of diplomas and the photographs of Iris with the children. Handsome devil, Anna thought; that's what they used to say when I was young. That little bit of gray, and so supple from all the skiing and tennis! Handsome devil.

He rose in surprise. "Well, Mother-in-law! What brings you here? You're much too pretty to have come for a face-lift."

"Thank you. Not this trip, anyway. You enjoyed your holiday? You came back early."

"Yes, the snow was mushy and I'd had enough."

Now that she was actually here, her bold anger ebbed and she was afraid to begin. But Theo helped her.

"You didn't come to ask me about my skiing holiday."

"No. I didn't." She sighed. "I was at the beauty parlor yesterday."

He raised his eyebrows and waited politely.

Anna looked out of the window. A pigeon was sitting on the air conditioner. She had set herself an impossible errand. But it had to be completed.

"You know, that is, you've heard that a lot of gossip goes on in beauty parlors?"

He straightened slightly in the chair and waited again.

"So it happens that I learned of something I would be happier

455

not to know. . . . You weren't alone on the trip, Theo. You have, shall we say, a 'relationship' in New York?"

"I have?"

"People, various people at various times, have seen you with a—lady. A tall, blond lady. Unless, of course, they are lying. If they are, forgive me for what I've said."

"They're not lying."

"I'm sorry. I was hoping they were."

"I could insist that they were, but you would find out the truth quite easily. And anyway, I would despise myself for the lie." He struck a match for his pipe. She saw that his hands were trembling.

"Is that all you have to say, Theo?"

"What else is there? I could say I'm not the first man and I won't be the last. I could tell you that probably two out of three men do it. But I won't. I'll just say I'm not terribly proud of it."

He pushed his chair roughly back and stood up. He walked to the window where the pigeon was preening and stood with his back to Anna.

"I admit I went a little bit crazy when all that happened last year. And Iris couldn't cope with it. I don't blame her, I guess; though I don't know, I'm not sure whether I do or not. Anyway, it began to snowball, and we just kept on downhill until we came to the bottom."

"Some snowball. Some hill," Anna said dryly.

"Then I met this girl and it happened just at a time when we—"

"I'm only concerned about Iris. I don't want to hear a word about anyone else."

"But let me just tell you. I'm sure you'll want to hear that it's all over between me and the girl—"

"When did that happen?"

"The day before yesterday. It's really over, no question about it. Finished and done with."

"I'm thankful for that . . . I think Joseph would kill you if he knew."

"You're not going to tell him?"

"Of course not. But not for your sake. For his. And for Iris'."

"And you? Don't you feel like killing me, too?"

Anna answered slowly. "I can't sit in judgment. I suppose people do what they have to do."

456

Theo turned and stared at her. "That's quite a free concept for your generation."

"Perhaps so. But all the same, I'm not going to let you crush my daughter, Theo."

"Mama! You think I want to do that? This was something entirely—all right, you don't want to hear about it. But I have to tell you: I care about Iris. I suppose you can't understand that."

"Believe it or not, I can. But the problem is, she can't."

"You've talked to her."

"Yes. Also, the day before yesterday."

"Did she tell you that we haven't been—living together? She had our bed taken down."

Anna flushed at this intimacy from him. And she said with some defiance, "Very well. That was wrong. But a woman doesn't do that without reason, even if it isn't a justifiable reason. You were going around like walking death for too long. At least, she felt it was too long. And then drowning your sorrows with the 'smart' crowd at the club! I'm not blaming you, but after all, there has to be an end to it, hasn't there? Iris is alive, she has her own life; she can't have your memories." Tears started in Anna's eyes. She pressed the lids shut. "Some women could weather all this without much damage. But she can't. I beg you to understand, Theo, she can't help herself! It's the way she's always been. She thinks she's homely and not good enough for you. She thinks you're dissatisfied, that she's been a failure. She needs rebuilding, Theo. I tried and I'll keep on trying, but I'm not the one to do it, am I? It's you."

"You make me feel like two cents," Theo said, very low. "As cheap as that."

"It wasn't my intention. I only want to throw light into a dark place, so you can see where you're going. You have three children and their home is about to fall apart. That can't happen, Theo! Do you understand me?" she cried, hearing the passion in her own voice. "The family always comes first! Always!"

"I do understand you, Mama, and I've told you, it's over. I'll go home tonight and tell Iris that it's over."

Anna looked up in horror. "Theo! She doesn't know about—the woman! If you add that to what she already thinks it will ruin her."

"But I'd like to make a new start. I'd like to bring some honesty into the situation."

"Yes, your honesty would make you feel heroic, wouldn't it? No matter what it would do to her. Theo, I swear it, you'll have a life-long enemy in me if you don't give me your word right now that you will never, never, never, in any circumstances, tell Iris about this. She's in a very bad way, Theo." Anna's voice quivered. "I'm afraid for her. I'm frightened."

"I tell you again, Mama, it's over. And Iris will never know about it, since that's your wish."

"Thank you. And remember, I was never here in this office talking to you."

He nodded. "I'll try to straighten everything out. I want to. You don't think I get any enjoyment out of living this way?"

"I don't think you do. But I have to tell you, I'm not sure you'll be able to straighten everything out. It's pretty late. And Iris isn't easy to handle. That I know."

Theo smiled ruefully. "I know it, too."

Anna rose, drawing her coat about her. "But don't get the idea that I won't fight for my daughter, stubborn and difficult or not. Because I will, if you two can't patch it up and it comes to that."

"You're deceptive, Mama. Iron underneath. You can be dented and scratched, but never pierced."

"Oh, yes, of course. Iron."

Theo walked with her through the outer rooms where patients were already waiting. She saw herself in the mirror as they passed it: tall, with bright hair lying against the dark collar of her fur; saw a man's eyes raised to stare at her. Not bad, she thought grimly, not bad for my age and the troubles I've seen.

"Mother-in-law, don't take it amiss," Theo said at the door, "but if I had been older or you had been younger when we met— Anyway, you are a remarkable woman, are you aware of that?"

She flipped her hand at him. "I wouldn't have liked your type." (But very probably I would. For you remind me, Theo, with your dash and grace, you remind me of Paul.)

Anna climbed the stairs to the sitting room where Nellie had said Iris was at her desk. She walked in boldly.

Iris looked up. "I didn't expect you."

"I know you didn't. I came to find out how you are today."

"The same as I was the last time you saw me."

The girl's voice was hollow. Strange to be still thinking of her as a girl, and she a woman of thirty-six. But there was a girlishness about the slender neck, the grieving eyes.

"I hear that Theo's home."

"He came back yesterday."

"And?"

"And nothing. He should never have married me, that's all."

"That was and is for him to judge, isn't it?" (I went about it all wrong the other day; I shall take desperate measures and win or lose.) "And suppose it were so, suppose I say, it's a little late to be thinking of that now, isn't it? A house filled with children and you talk like this? It's nuts, that's what it is!" Anna's voice rose and, remembering Nellie downstairs, she lowered it, although not the passion and intensity which mounted and filled her. "Look out there at that sky, at that world with all the sparkle! It's gorgeous, and you sit closed in here, mourning because it's not exactly what you wanted! Do you think even lucky people ever get all of what they want? Who are you that you shouldn't have a burden of some sort to carry, even one of your own making? So many of our burdens are of our own making, anyway." She stopped, thinking: Retribution? Punishment? Punishment for me, through Iris, as I once thought it might have been through Maury? Absurd. A superstitious concept. Joseph would say it wasn't. Yes, he would say, everything has to be paid for before we're through.

"You know I was happy," Iris said softly. "There wasn't a woman anywhere in the world, I swear it, who was happier than I was."

It was true, it was true. Damn Theo again! The girl was dying inside because of him. Her pain could be as clearly seen as a burn on the flesh.

This thing between a man and woman— Now, in the presence of her daughter, the ache of youth came alive again.

"How long can you go on like this?" she asked abruptly.

"I don't know. I don't know anything anymore."

"Have you talked to Theo since he got back?"

"No. He's miserable too. The holiday didn't do him any good either." Iris laughed curtly.

"Can't you feel sorry for him, then? Can you have so much feeling for the poor and oppressed of the world, and so little for him?"

Iris gasped. "You're taking Theo's part?"

"I'm not 'taking part' at all." What were Theo's words? 'A little bit crazy,' he had said. Anna went on, "It seems you've both gone

459

a little bit crazy. Not that Theo didn't have reason enough. And maybe you did, too. I can't get inside your soul. All I'm saying is, we mustn't be beaten by the pressures of life. The pressures of life," she repeated and, caught in a whirl of thoughts, heard her voice die off in a minor key.

After a moment she went on thoughtfully, "Iris, people don't like martyrs. You must learn to act, if you're to save anything, including yourself. When you don't feel joyous, pretend that you do. After a while you may actually start to feel that way."

"That advice from you? A cheap subterfuge? Is that what you've been doing all these years? Pretending?"

"What do you mean?" Anna stared at her daughter.

Iris flinched from the stare. "I don't know, if you don't."

But, Anna thought, I do know what she means. She has always had strange feelings about Paul, ever since he sent that picture years ago, perhaps even before that when Joseph and I had arguments about the Werners. No matter. I can't help what she may have thought about me, and she has enough troubles of her own just now.

Suddenly everything came together: panic, pity, impending doom, impatience and anger at having this mess dumped in her lap. Everything, but chiefly panic.

"Listen to me! Come out of your cocoon and look at the real world out there! What if you were to lose him? You, who told me two days ago that you couldn't face the thought of living without Theo! You think, if he should finally get sick of all this and walk out, that there's going to be a line of men waiting to take you and your three children? Do you? Yes," Anna said cruelly, hacking at herself as well as at Iris, "and what if he were to die? What if he were to leave one morning as usual, and a little while later some stranger rings the doorbell, the way they came to tell us about Maury, and you learn that Theo is dead? What then? Tell me!" Her breath came fast and she couldn't stop the ugly words, although she saw that Iris was horrified. "Yes, in three seconds it would be all over. For good. And you left here alone in this house with your silent dignity, your wounds, your pride and your children who have lost their father. Well, it could happen!" Iris had put her hands over her face. "And don't come to me, if it should! Don't come to me for sympathy! Because I've had enough trouble to last me a lifetime and I'm not about to take on any more."

The rotten thing was that she was taking pleasure in what she was saying, taking *pleasure* in hurting Iris! (You have no guts, Iris, that's what's the matter.) And at the same time she was so afraid. My God, if anything were to happen to you! Iris, my girl, my girl, why do things have to be so hard for you? You don't deserve it.

"I don't care if you hate me. I'm saying what's right for you to hear. I don't care if you never speak to me again. Well, of course, I do," Anna said. She was losing her breath and weakening; she gripped the frame of the door. "But if you choose not to speak to me I can't help it. Now, listen to me, go out and get your hair done! And throw away that gray—that *dustrag* you've got on. I don't want to see rags like that on you ever again. Put a smile on your face when Theo gets home. Put one on, damn it, if you have to paste it on! Now call a taxi for me. I want to go home."

Iris looked up. "That's a good idea. I was just going to ask you to leave my house."

"Well, I beat you to it."

For the first time in her life Anna went to bed without being ill with a fever. But she had never been so exhausted. It had been like pushing an enormous round load up a hill; it kept slipping back and you had to push harder to regain what you had lost.

Fortunately Joseph had gone with Eric to the city for dinner and a hockey game at the Garden. Eric always saved a day out of his vacation for his grandfather. Really, they ought to give him a great party for his twenty-first birthday, she thought, lying back against two pillows and warming her hands around the cup of tea. A beautiful party, with a little band, a group of youngsters to make live music.

We've come a long way since that day we drove home from Brewerstown with a terrified, brave little boy. Thank God for that. And pray that this trouble with Iris works out as well. But I don't know, it's so far gone. Theo's awfully independent, not easy to handle, and she's impossible.

I wonder when you can ever stop eating your heart out over a family? I hope the children haven't overheard or sensed things. Stevie especially: he's so bright, he sees everything. Sometimes I think he has a worried face, although probably that's just because he's the first child and the first child is supposedly more sensitive, more attuned to what's going on among adults. Although Maury wasn't—oh, yes, he was! You forget, you didn't find out until much, much later what had been going on under the sunny manner. Still, it's true he was never as complicated as Iris, I think.

Everybody's difficult. I, too. My God, am I difficult!

I can't agonize anymore. I want another cup of tea and haven't the strength to get up for it. I've done what I could for everyone. What counts most now, what has to count most now, is Joseph and me. I wish once more that I had his absolute faith. Still, since I know he has it, why do I guard him from all this trouble? He ought to be stronger than I. And he is, in so many ways. Only not where Iris is concerned.

The front door opened. "Anna! I'm home!" Joseph called.

"I'm upstairs, in bed."

She heard him coming up two steps at a time, like a young man. "In bed already? What's the matter?"

"Just a chill. Start of a cold. I've taken an aspirin," she fibbed.

"You're always running around with your errands and charities! Why don't you think of yourself and take it a little bit easy?" His voice was irritable and anxious.

"Don't yell at me, Joseph. Besides, look who's talking about running around. Did you have a good time?"

"Sure did. I dropped Eric off for a 'late date.' There's a crowd over at some girl's house near the Point."

"That's good. I was thinking, we ought to give him a party for his next birthday."

"Great idea! Shall I get you another blanket? Are you cold?"

"No, I'm fine. Really. I'll be perfect again in the morning," she said cheerfully.

He drew the blanket around her shoulders. "Well, I hope so. I just hope you've caught it in time before it turns into anything worse. God forbid."

"I think I have," she said. "I think perhaps I've caught it in time."

Theo came in and saw that the two narrow beds had been taken away. The old bed with the white and yellow spread was back in its place. Iris came out of the dressing room. She was wearing a robe of some sort, a hostess coat, they called it, or something like that. Anyway, it had a kind of pretty ruffled thing like daisy petals around the neck. She had been at the hairdresser's.

462

"Good evening," he said. A small laugh like a bubble rose in his throat. "I see there have been some changes in the furniture."

"Are you pleased?" she asked, without looking at him.

"Very." He waited a moment and when she looked up he moved and put her head on his shoulder. She didn't come nearer, but she didn't go away, either. They stood like that for a minute or two. He remembered the night not so long ago, when it was he who had rested his head upon her shoulder and she had tried to give comfort to him. Well, that was past.

His hands moved over her.

"Not yet," she whispered. "Not just yet."

"But soon?"

"Yes, all right. Soon. Quite soon."

40

On a day in the early fall of Eric's senior year at Dartmouth he met his cousin Chris Guthrie for lunch in New York. It was Chris's first visit home from Venezuela in three years.

"I've saved all your letters," he told Eric. "They're real nostalgia for me. I feel I'm back on the campus, snow in the air. You write extremely well. You know that, don't you?"

"They tell me I do."

"What are you planning after graduation?"

"My grandfather has a place ready for me in the firm."

Chris stirred his coffee. Then he looked up acutely. Eric reflected that all 'men of affairs' had that look. He'd been watching them at neighboring tables, in their dark suits and English shoes; they had a way of concentrating keenly, of making the moment *move*. Their eyes never *dream*, that's what it is, he thought; they never rest on anything for more than a second or two. They don't see that beyond the window the September haze is dusty amber and the city is waking to a brisker season—

"I asked you," Chris said, "I asked you whether you'd like that?"

"Excuse me. I didn't hear you. I hope to like it all right. It's an opportunity most people don't have, isn't it?"

"Starting at the top in a family business? I should think not!" Chris went on thoughtfully, "You know, when I drove you down from Brewerstown seven years ago—now I can tell it—I was as sorry for you as I think I've ever been for anyone in all my life. And now

464

that my own kids are growing up and I look at them and think of what happened to you—well, I wouldn't want them to have to face what you did."

"On the scale of world suffering I rank pretty low, in spite of everything, Chris."

"Well, if you mean hunger and want, that's something else. But there are other kinds of suffering. You had an awful lot of courage, and—"

"Chris, I'm fine. I really am."

"I can see you are. Tell me, when you think back, are things very different from when you lived with Gran and Gramp? No reason for asking, except curiosity."

"Well, the personalities are different. Very. But as to feeling wanted and all that, it's the same."

"Good. Let's see, what else can I ask you? Have you got a girl?"

Eric laughed. " 'A' girl? No."

"Good again. Don't tie yourself down too young. But to get back to the work business: tell me, have you ever considered *not* going in with your grandfather?"

"Not really. I haven't got any special ambitions. What makes you ask?"

"I'll tell you. I'm being given a tremendous job. A promotion. It'll mean four or five years in the Middle East, based in Iran."

"Gosh! Cloak and dagger! Lawrence of Arabia!"

"You can kid, but there really is a helluva lot of that stuff going on. Anyway, I was thinking: I'm supposed to get a staff together, four or five bright, young eager beavers. So I thought of you. I'd have no trouble getting you approved, that's sure." He lit a cigarette and waited a moment. "How does it sound?"

"What would I have to do?"

"Sales. Contacts. Politicking. You name it." Chris waited again, then added, "It's a fantastic part of the world. Literally. I've been there and it really got to me. When you see your first Bedouin in his *kaffiyeh*, riding a camel—"

The restaurant, the dark suits, the table with its cloth and cutlery dissolved into a bazaar of burning colors and a gaudy sky. Eric had to smile at his own extravagance.

"It's very tempting, very alluring and very sudden, Chris," he said cautiously.

"Of course. You don't think I expect a decision this minute, do

465

you? I'm coming back around Christmas and we can talk some more then. But I do want to leave one thought with you, Eric. No, two. The first is obvious: that there's a real future in a company like ours. The second ties in with your ambition to write."

"In what way?"

"Well, in order to write you have to have something to write about, don't you? You have to know people and cultures and conflict. Think of the memory bank you could establish on a job like this! Enough to draw against for the rest of your life! And I'd see that you had plenty of time for exploring."

Again, that quick look of estimation. Eric answered it slowly.

"It would be such a—a *defeat* for my grandparents."

"Yes, but they've had their lives and done what they wanted. Now it's your turn, isn't it? In time I'll have to be moving over myself, to make room for my own boys. I'm almost forty-two, you know." Chris summoned the waiter and took out his wallet. "I've got a train to make. Eric, it's been great. Every time I see you I realize how much I've missed you. Think it over; there's no rush, but I truly believe this could be the start of something great for you. I'll get in touch. And oh, yes, remember me at home."

For the last year he had been feeling that his life was sliding steadily toward the unknown. Except for the few who knew that they were fated for something definite like law or medicine or engineering, this feeling was common, Eric knew. It wasn't strong enough to be called panic; it was just *there,* a kind of scary drift into a world in which perhaps one would never be entirely at home. He tried to imagine himself sitting in the office every morning of his life, conferring with bankers and mortgage brokers, then driving out to an enormous tangle of construction out of which would emerge another grid of look-alike, boxy houses. Not that it wasn't a decent product and therefore a productive life, but as far as he was beginning to understand, it wasn't something to which he could look forward with any exhilaration. When a man has completed a thing he had wanted with all his heart to do, he sits down to rest and says, "There, that's over. I wanted to do it and I've done it!" It wasn't like that at all, at least as far as he could see.

So he kept thinking about what Chris had offered.

He certainly hadn't intended to mention it to anyone, yet one day when he was home over Thanksgiving he found himself telling Aunt Iris.

"Maybe I'm rationalizing the whole thing because I want the adventure," he concluded.

"There's nothing wrong with wanting adventure, is there?"

"I suppose not. And ever since Chris planted this seed the building business has looked duller and duller."

Iris said slowly, "Without actually thinking it over, I've sort of assumed you would write. I don't know how or in what form, but I've just thought of you that way. Perhaps because your father and I both had vague desires to do something with words . . . only, neither of us had any true gift and I believe you have."

"One doesn't just rent a room, buy a typewriter and begin to write," Eric argued and, paraphrasing Chris, "you have to live first and have something to write about."

"True. And writing isn't what you're asking about right now anyway, although it might well tie in, as your cousin says."

"You're avoiding an answer. What I want to know is, should I consider the offer?"

"Should you hurt my parents, you mean. That's what you're asking me, isn't it?"

"I'm sorry. It's not fair of me to expect you to be neutral, is it?"

"No, it isn't. Because I know what it will do to them. And still I know that you've a right to be somebody yourself, not just somebody's beloved grandson." Iris sighed. "So I guess I'll just have to throw the decision back in your lap."

Eric nodded soberly. "Only don't mention it, please? Not even to Uncle Theo. I need time to sweat this out myself."

"Not a word. I promise."

Just before Christmas he and Chris met again at the same place.

"I haven't made up my mind," Eric told him.

Chris was surprised. "What's the obstacle?"

"I keep thinking about Grandpa and Nana. He's had me down at the office telling everybody I'll be working there next year; he's even got my room set aside. *She's* bought Early American prints for the walls." And when Chris began a gesture, he went on hurriedly, "I know, you'll say it's my life and that's true, but it's a big decision and I can't make it in such a hurry."

467

"Listen," Chris said, "I want you to come in later this week. I'll get an appointment with the people here in New York for an interview. Then whatever questions you have they can answer and you won't be making the big decision just on my say-so. Only one thing—" he lowered his voice and glanced at the adjoining table, "when you give your name, spell it the way you used to, will you? Freeman? It's more American that way. I've told them that's your name."

"Why did you do that? What difference does it make?"

"It makes a difference. Take my word for it. Particularly in the Middle East, everything heating up between the Arabs and Israel."

"You mean that I shouldn't appear to be Jewish."

"Well, you aren't, are you? You were brought up an Episcopalian and you're my cousin. Who would think of asking whether you were Jewish?"

"I'm also Joseph Friedman's grandson."

"Of course, of course. But listen, Eric, it's a chilly, practical world and you've got to be practical to survive in it. I strongly advise you to play that side down for business purposes. Especially this business."

Eric grimaced. "Lousy. Dishonest. And worse than that, cruel."

"Why cruel? You aren't doing or saying anything hurtful. It's just a case of *not* saying something, a case of omission." And when Eric didn't answer, he added urgently, "Besides, aren't you forgetting the other side of yourself? Gran and Gramp and all the life you had with them?"

"Chris! You think I could forget them?"

"I certainly don't. And after all, it isn't as if you were a religious Jew. You haven't gone over to the religion, have you, Eric?" Chris asked abruptly.

"To tell the truth, I haven't any religion at all," Eric said. His voice sounded somber to his own ears.

"Well, that's the fashion these days, isn't it? So shall I make the appointment for this week or do you want to put it off till my next trip?"

"Put it off," Eric said. "As long as there's no hurry."

After leaving Chris he walked down Fifth Avenue toward Grand Central. Christmas lights in shop windows and out of doors rippled and streamed like moving water. "Adeste Fideles" clanged from a loudspeaker above the entrance to a department store. The citadel of Christmas, emporium of glitter, cathedral of twentieth-century America. The department store. He felt unusually depressed.

A bank advertised its loan service under the smiling photograph of a young couple admiring an expensive sports car. Was that the measure of contentment, the measure of a man, his ability to provide a sports car? Or a motorboat, a diamond, or any of the things for which people put themselves in hock? Worth his weight in gadgets, a man was.

Climb, forge ahead, acquire, be smart, even if you have to lie a little, even if you have to deny the truth about yourself to do it. Why not?

He began to walk faster, to breathe more deeply of the icy air. Morbid today, misanthropic. The world really isn't all that awful. Just my own personal riddle, needing to be solved. That's all it is.

If this offer had come, not from one of his mother's people, but from one of Grandpa's cronies, Mr. Duberman, let's say, or some other of the pinochle group, would it be much less of a problem?

He tried to imagine the scene, a party perhaps, everyone around a table crowded with crystal, with flowers, with silver platters and bowls of meats, half a dozen kinds of meats, half a dozen kinds of smoked fish, salads, molds and puddings, spicy condiments and pungent sauces, glossy, twisted loaves, fruit, cakes—

"Eat, here, pass the salad to Jenny, she eats like a bird—"

"If you don't taste that pudding you'll insult my wife," Grandpa would roar, and pile a ladleful of steaming noodle pudding on someone's plate.

Nana's bracelets would clash; she'd smile with pleasure and pride, diamond pinpoints flashing in her ears.

"Did you know that Eric will be going abroad next year?" Grandpa would inquire of the table at large. But everyone would be talking: on this side two of the men having a vigorous political argument; on the other side someone telling jokes, people crying with laughter. Grandpa would clink on a goblet with his knife and call above the noise.

"You've heard about our Eric? You haven't heard?"

With amusement and tenderness he constructed the scene in his mind: the sudden silence, his grandfather's announcement, the cries of congratulation; his grandmother getting up to hug him, squeezing his head against perfume and warm silk; an old man gripping his hand.

"What a smart boy! A treasure! Joseph, Anna, a treasure of a boy—"

Of course they would shed tears because he would be going away; of course his great opportunity would have to be anywhere else but in the Middle East, where now, at the end of a second millennium, people of this blood were again being threatened with slaughter. Granting all that, he knew it would still not be such unacceptable pain as this return to his mother's people, reminding them again of their losses. He wondered suddenly how it must have been for his father, making the decision which was to take him from them for good.

Pain. How do you measure it? Doctors measure it in dols: much pain, middling pain, less pain. . . .

He went back to Dartmouth the following week, with graduation only five months distant, with no decision made and sure of nothing.

Great-uncle Wendell died in early April and was buried from the home which had been in his family since the first Guthrie had come to Massachusetts three centuries before.

Eric drove down from New Hampshire, meeting as he went the first uncertain gusts of spring that blew warm whenever the sun struck through the clouds. In spite of his errand he felt exhilaration as the car rolled between stone-walled fields, down aisles of elms on old main streets, past the white, square, ample houses of his childhood. He knew exactly how these houses would look inside, the corner cupboards flanking the fireplace in the dining room, the tall clock on the landing midway between floors. The shapes and patterns of Brewerstown.

When they came back to the house from the churchyard where the Guthries lay, the faces that gathered, faces of relatives and strangers, were familiar, too. How odd that you got used to other types and faces without real awareness of the difference and the change! Now suddenly he realized that he hadn't seen faces like these in a long, long time.

Generalizations were totally unscientific. There were almost as many exceptions as the rule, and yet he could know, here in this room, that he was not among his father's people. Less tension here perhaps, less animation, color, noise? No matter; it was different.

They were an unmistakable breed, these people, shaped narrowly and of a healthy toughness that went with hardy skills like rough-weather sailing or cross-country skiing. The women, even those who weren't pretty, who had long, craggy faces, wore the marks of their kind: skirts and blouses, gold circle pins, a strong, no-nonsense manner. He would have recognized one of them if he had encountered her in Patagonia. He stood there watching the group around the coffee urn, listening to the crisp accents and gentle voices, feeling as if—as if he had just walked into his own home after a morning's absence. And quite suddenly he understood what it was that moved him so, in a way that was probably not entirely reasonable, that was just simply because—

Because they looked like Gran.

Chris was there with his wife and older boys. Chris's brothers were there also with young, pregnant wives.

Hugh came over to introduce Betsey. "I've heard you're going on an exciting venture with Chris," Betsey said. "We're all so delighted that you'll be together."

Eric flushed. "I haven't quite made up my mind," he answered.

Chris had come up behind them. "I don't know what you're waiting for," he said. For the first time he sounded impatient. "It's already April and if you want to come along you'll have to see the people in New York by the end of the month. I can't stall any longer for you, you know."

"I know."

"For the life of me I can't imagine why you don't jump at the chance!"

"I guess because it's for five years. One wants to be absolutely sure of a commitment like that."

"Well, don't think too long, that's all." Chris walked away.

Now Hugh introduced an old man who had been standing near the fireplace.

"Cousin Ted, this is Eric. You've never met, I think."

Eric took hold of a hard leathery hand, looked into a pair of concentrating eyes.

"I knew your mother when she was a baby. Never saw you, though. Never see much of my wife's family since she died. But I wanted to pay my respects today. I live over in Prides Crossing since I retired." He rambled, moving toward senility.

"I met your father once. Came to me for a job at the bank, I

471

recall. Couldn't give him one, though. Depression, you know. No jobs. You look like your mother," he said abruptly. "A fine, pretty girl, your mother was. Died too young. Look at me, I'm eighty-seven."

Someone came and led him away to the coffee urn. Eric thought, All these people know more about who I am than I do. The thought caused a bleakness and at the same time a soft wish to reach out to them.

"Remember us," Gran said.

If I turn my back now and cut myself off that'll be the end, the final end. The old people are dying or dead. Chris will go away and when he comes back we'll be strangers. At least, there's a little something between us now, a little flame that can be fanned.

Arabia. Riding with Chris of that old, first life, into a new life. . . . Someone had put pine cones in the fireplace; the sweet, sharp scent of them sifted through the warm air. Fragrance and flavor, like those of Proust's madeleine, were potent instruments always; he could smell Maine's salty coves again and Brewerstown's gilt Septembers, its fires of fall. Oh, remembered places, remembered faces! Flesh of his flesh and quiet ways; Gramp's birds and a white horse grazing, and so much more. So much.

He found Chris talking at the far end of the room. He tapped him on the shoulder.

"Chris, I'll go with you," he said.

During the week of spring recess he opened his mouth a dozen times to tell his grandparents and closed it again, feeling weak and cowardly.

"I want to buy you a good car," Grandpa said. "The jalopy was good enough for a college boy, but you ought to have a better one now. So be thinking about what you'd like and we'll take care of it after commencement."

He said, "Why don't you take a month or two off before you start putting your nose to the grindstone? Drive out to California or something? Have a ball."

Nana said, "I was thinking, would you like me to fix up your room at the office or do you want to pick out your own things? Jerry Malone just refurnished, so maybe you'd like to take a look at what he bought for some ideas—"

Grandpa said, "You haven't seen the new shopping center since we finished up, have you? How about taking a ride over with me? I have a couple of people to see there this afternoon."

Eric went along and strolled through the long expanse of malls, turns and alleys, up a level and down a level, marveling at the enormity of it all and trying to observe enough to make, later, the intelligent comments that would be expected.

But all he could feel was a pervasive sadness. So many aimless couples drifting through the afternoon with their children tugging at them, looking for amusement! Anxious men in lumber jackets, tired women with hair in curlers, wandering with their desires through mazes of stores piled with shoddy trash that they couldn't afford and didn't need! And Eric knew that if he were to express all that to his grandfather he would only stare in astonished dismay.

They got back in the car. "Well, what did you think of it?" his grandfather asked. There was a sparkle in his voice.

"It's a busy place, all right."

"Wait till you see what we're building in south Jersey. It's still only on paper but we expect to break ground in September. Maybe I'll let you work on it. I'll send you down with Matt Malone to get the feel of things. Matt's a smart boy. You can learn a lot from him."

Eric's left hand lay on the seat and suddenly his grandfather placed his own over it. He spoke very low, so that Eric could barely hear him and knew that the old man was embarrassed by his own emotion.

"For years I've envied Malone. It was wrong of me, I know. *Thou shalt not covet.* . . . But I did, all the same. All those fine sons to go into business with him! To carry on what he had built out of years of sweat, while for me it was all going down the drain. Into nothing, as if I had never existed. Until you came. I don't mind telling you, you've taken years off my shoulders. Or put years onto my life, however you want to say it. Do I make you feel uncomfortable, Eric? Forgive me this once, if I do."

"That's okay, Grandpa." My God, my God, how am I going to say it? With what words? Where? When?

On Friday evening his grandmother called him aside. "Eric, I want to ask a favor. Would you come to temple with us tonight?

473

It's the anniversary of your great-grandfather's death and Grandpa has to say Kaddish for him."

"Yes, surely, I'll go."

"Thank you, I'm glad. I know it's not your prayer, but still it will make him feel good to have you there."

He sat through the sermon not hearing it, heavy with the weight of his dilemma. He was aware from time to time of plaintive music, but only half aware. The name of Max Friedman was called in a long list of names; the sounding of its syllables made a small shock in his head and it came to him for an instant that the blood of that totally strange man—for if he were to be brought back to life what could they have to say to one another?—that strange man's blood was in him, nevertheless. The congregation rose. He felt the rustling and stood with them through the murmuring of several hundred voices all in unison. His grandmother's head was bowed, her hands were clasped, her face was serious. His grandfather's old hooded eyes were partly closed. He swayed as he held the prayer book but he was not reading it; he knew it by heart. They know I won't be saying this prayer for them, Eric thought. One of Aunt Iris' little boys will have to do that when they are dead. And yet I mean so much to them.

And now the blessing: "The Lord bless thee and keep thee; the Lord cause the light of His face to shine upon thee—"

Then "Good Sabbath," the people turning to each other in the neighboring pews, families, friends and strangers kissing or shaking hands.

"Good Sabbath." Joseph kissed Eric and kissed Anna; Anna kissed Eric and kissed Joseph.

They moved slowly in the press going down the aisle. Grandpa rested a hand on Eric's shoulder. He saw that his grandmother watched the gesture. He thought irrelevantly that her red hair was too youthful for the expression that she wore. He looked at her while she looked at her husband's hand. Something was being weighed and balanced behind her thoughtful, clever face, something of delicate complexity, spun of unspoken things. He felt, he could almost touch, an emotion so tense that a move might shatter it, whatever it was: a question held back, a plea, perhaps, for which there were no words?

He knew then, in the throb of that instant, that he couldn't go.

*   *   *

474

"You're not angry, Chris?" he asked, when he had finished his story. They had met in New York for the purpose, so Chris had expected, of taking Eric to the interview.

"I won't allow myself to be." Chris smiled but his eyes were angry. "I'll just say you're rather young for your years, completely inexperienced and far too sentimental. You're like your—" he broke off.

"Like my parents, you were going to say."

"Well, yes, I was. However, it's hardly unusual for a person to be like his parents."

"Like which of them?" Eric persisted.

"Like both. Too idealistic for their own good, each one of them."

Chris took Eric's hand. "I'm always in a hurry these days, it seems. So let's just say, 'Good luck to us both.' And if you ever need me, Eric, you'll know where I am. Keep in touch, will you? All the best," he said. His face changed; a look of gravity and softness came over it, and for an instant Eric was back in the boat, bobbing behind a curtain of willows, and Chris was saying, "Your Gran is going to die." He shook off the illusion.

"Thanks, Chris, for everything," he said, and, releasing each other's hands, they parted among the hastening crowds on Forty-third Street.

Later that week Iris told him, "I'm not sure it was the right decision for your own self-interest. But it surely was generous, Eric."

He didn't answer. Now that he had made the decision he felt that it hadn't really been generous of him at all, that actually he had been and was—would always be?—too divided to be entirely content either with staying or with going.

"I think I'd like to wander around Europe for a couple of months this summer," he said suddenly, the idea having just come. "I've never been much of anywhere."

A small inheritance from Gramp was to be given to him at commencement time. It was a legacy, literally and figuratively, from an era when a young gentleman was expected to make a tour of Europe before he 'settled down.'

"I wish I could go with you," Iris said. "But Theo says Europe smells of decay. I'm hoping someday he'll change his mind."

"This wouldn't be your summer to go anyway, would it?" For Iris was pregnant again, at thirty-seven; he wondered how pleased

475

she could be about it, and rather thought it must have been an 'accident.'

"The baby'll be here by the time you get back, I guess. It's due around the middle of October."

"I'll be back," Eric assured her.

In mid-June, after commencement, they helped him pack. His grandmother brought home a set of fine luggage, a traveling umbrella and a travel bathrobe, all highly impractical, and all a way of saying, 'have a wonderful time; we love you.' He had learned that much about them during his time in their house.

On the last night they went to Theo's and Iris' for dinner. The two boys had pooled their allowances and bought film for his camera.

"I would like some pictures of Stonehenge," Steve told Eric solemnly. "I have a book about it. Nobody seems to know who built it, do they?"

Jimmy asked Eric to find out how you play rugby and how it was different from football. Laura had helped her mother make a package of fudge, "to eat on the plane for dessert." And Eric felt the poignancy of departure.

Anna cried a little. "I don't know why I'm crying! I'm so happy that you're going to have a marvelous summer. I don't know why I'm crying."

She cried so easily. Gran would never have done that. He thought that he had been cursed with ambivalence. In some ways he was closer in feeling and expression to this woman than he had ever been able to get to Gran, and yet Gran was a part of his fibre and his life as this other grandmother could never be. She had come too late. A part of him would always be withheld from her and awkward with her.

Suddenly it occurred to him that that was what she was feeling too, and that was why she cried.

In a little town near Bath one afternoon he bought a cheap notebook at a stationer's and began to write.

I think sometimes that what is bothering me is that I no longer believe in anything. Perhaps, coming from an urban, halfway educated American in this secular age, that sounds absurd. But there it is, all the same.

Perhaps if I believed in something I would know where I belong, or where I want to belong, and among what people. You may ask, what has belief, which is so absolutely personal, got to do with belonging to this, that or the other social group? Nothing, really.

I sat half the afternoon in a Saxon church in a Thomas Hardy village. Saxon! Imagine how old! It was cold behind those thick walls, with a hot summer hush outdoors. I walked out to the churchyard. There was no one in sight except some cows chewing and drooling in the field next to the graves. Sound of bees. I read the names on the headstones where they weren't rubbed out by centuries of rain. The same names on plaques in the nave; the same on doors in the village. Thomas Brearley and Sons, Cobblers since 1743. Live here all your life; work; sing hymns on Sunday. Same work, same words, over and over. Baptized in this church, cold water on the infant's forehead, squalling at the font. Die and be buried a few steps away. Must be some truth here? If all these generations, in grieving or rejoicing, felt there was Something here, must there not certainly be Something?

In the silence, in the old, old place so small and plain and human, I could see myself on the edge of believing.

At nine or ten, going to church with Gran and Gramp, it was different then. So much awe. Used to come home to big Sunday dinner, roast and pie, wearing my best suit, feeling everything in order. Wish I could feel it again. Wish I could feel like my grandfather and Aunt Iris in the synagogue. Not so sure about Nana; I think she's trying to be like them. Naturally, she wouldn't say, or maybe doesn't even know herself. Asked Uncle Theo once about himself: had he lost faith? I never had it, he said.

Ireland. Fearful damp and chattering teeth. Fog and rain in cold stone slums. I watch old women in black shawls doing the Stations of the Cross in roadside villages. My great-great—many greats ago— came from Ireland, Gran said. Like one of these women in the shawls? But first a girl, walking the roads. So poor. Decaying teeth. Eyes like turquoise. Superstitious. Clustering, dark legends: elves, gnomes of the woods.

I go into a church. Tawdry frescoes, calendar art in candy-box colors. Effeminate figure on the cross, insipid woman holding the infant. Think of high art: the Pietà, the Mother and dead Son. The accumulated agony of the centuries: above all, human.

That's all it is: human. Need to lean on something while we stumble through life. That's all it is, isn't it? Any thinking man knows that's all it is.

Father, I believe. Help Thou mine unbelief.

Gramp always wanted to come back here and couldn't. Now I see why he wanted to. Plane trees, hill towns, old olive orchards of Provence. Snapshot of my mother, sitting in front of a vineyard. Her eyes turned to this same light. Roman faces. They've been here since then. No, before then; the Greeks came first. Marseilles was Marsallia. Ruins of a Greek city at Glanum. All these flowing rivers of life. The Rue des Israelites in a medieval town; another flowing river, but of blood. The Judengasse in Salzburg; all over Europe, locked up, chains at the two ends of the street. A unique history among peoples, myself at the tail end. Fierce beliefs. They died for them. I don't think they were worth dying for. I don't think any belief is worth dying for. Do I? Maybe I'll find one that is. Then it will be worth living for, too.

I pose myself a question, a cliché by now. Would I give my treasure, my small worldly treasure (large to me) for the lives of a thousand unknown yellow (or any other color) men on the far side of the globe? Another question: what is the value of my immortal soul (assuming that I have one) compared to the immortal soul of a squalid pimp in a New York alley? I don't know the answer to either question.

These things trouble me.

Weeks later

Juliana stands before red flowers in a window box. The house has a gable roof and a canal runs in front of it. She eats from a box of Dutch chocolates. I think I am falling in love with her.

I know I am falling in love with her. She has been working on a kibbutz in northern Galilee and is home for vacation. Why? I ask her. Why Israel? She says she wants to see the world. She says the Dutch have been good to the Jews (that I know); she says it is exciting there. Ideals in action, she tells me. A place for the young. A new country. She wants me to go back with her. Just to see what it's like, she says. I'm going. I would go anyway, even if it was to Timbuktu.

Oh, lovely Europe, your flowers and your wine, your bread, your music. We're flying southeast, over the ancient, warm and violet Mediterranean lands. I shall remember the sweetness and delight of Europe.

And I shall remember its concentration camps, Uncle Theo says.

41

So narrow is the northernmost tip of Israel that a giant of ancient legend would be able to straddle it with one foot in Lebanon and the other in Syria.

The river Jordan, mighty in the imagination of the Western world, was only a stream, Eric thought with surprise, and the falls at its source, which were held in awe by the natives, were only a faucet's trickle when compared, not with Niagara, but with any modest waterfall at home.

Nevertheless, the land was lovely.

At the crest of a low hill stood the wooden buildings of the kibbutz: dormitories, dining hall, library, school. Barns and sheds ringed the slopes; below them stretched wide orchards, and beyond these lay a flowing sea of grain.

Reapers moved through that golden sea. Young men and women climbed the trees, picked and packed the fruit. Cattle stamped in the barns. Fresh-mown grass sweetened the air. From the dining hall one heard the sound of someone practicing on the piano; from the machine shop came the clang of iron against iron. In the big kitchen from morning to night meals were in preparation. Children splashed in the swimming pool: the second generation, building on the foundation of the pioneers, had added this touch of luxury. Out of rock and the neglect of barren centuries, vision and toil had made a way of life.

And all of it lay within gunshot of the Golan Heights.

"The Syrians have crack troops up there," Juliana said, pointing eastward to bluffs that rose like a wall. "Anything that moves in the fields or on the road is a target, whenever the notion takes them. Last year, just after I got here," she said bitterly, "it was a bus going in to town. The driver was hit and of course it smashed. Eight killed, two of them children under five."

They were walking through the yards between the buildings. Juliana was very serious. "Come, I'll show you something else. On this side we're only two miles from Lebanon." They slid on slippery grass between lines of thin young pear trees. At the lower edge of the orchard she raised a screen of leafage and they looked into the ugly reptilian mouths of a row of guns.

"This is our second line of defense. The wire fences and the guards are at the border."

"It's rather sobering, to think we sleep with guns in our back yard."

"It's a safer feeling, I'll tell you that! Still, now and then they slip through anyway. You must have read about the raid on the school? It was in the next town, only twenty minutes from here. Down there through that grove, that's the border and the wire fence. If you walk straight down you'll reach it."

Eric thought, If I had gone with Chris I would have been on the other side of it. He wondered fleetingly what sort of lives were being lived on that other side, but in the short weeks he had been here he had become so much identified with these lives that he found it hard to imagine those others.

He slept in the dormitory for single men. On the wall opposite each bed hung each man's gun. Pants and shoes lay on a chair alongside the bed. You could be dressed, downstairs and out of doors in sixty seconds.

He thought of stories that Gramp had told about their ancestors who had settled the wilderness of New York State. Energy and guts. Making something out of nothing. Perhaps that was the pull of this place for him—that, and Juliana.

"Do you really like it, Eric? Do you feel anything of what I told you about when we were in Holland?" she asked.

"I'm beginning to. And I do know what you meant."

They sat down on a rock in the lowering sun. It was the Sabbath and a hush lay over everything. Work had stopped. There was deep quiet except for mild stampings and lowings from the barn.

"When I first came—I had wanted for years to come—it was

because I felt an obligation. Lots of young Europeans do, Germans, too. Now I stay because I love it. But the obligation came first."

"Tell me about it."

Juliana shuddered. "Those years of the war when I was nine, ten, eleven, we saw such things—" She was silent for a minute or two, then resumed, "A neighbor of ours, a determined woman, with convictions—"

"Like you," Eric interrupted, with a smile.

"She was a brave woman. She had a Jewish family hidden in her attic behind a camouflaged door. Just like Anne Frank. You've read the book?"

"Yes."

"Well, it was like that. Only a few people knew they were there. Whatever food we could spare, an extra apple, or some cereal at the bottom of the pot, my mother took next door. We children weren't supposed to know but I heard my mother telling my father that there were two brothers and their wives, some children and a baby. They had to hold the baby under a blanket to muffle its cries.

"So, one day the Germans came and took them away. They went straight to the hidden door. And they took our good neighbor, too, in a truck filled with people on the way to the camps, most of them to the furnaces. The husbands were separated from the wives and children from their own mothers. We heard them all the way down the street as far as the corner, crying, crying—" Juliana covered her face with her hands. "Do you think, Eric, that I shall be able to forget things like that? I don't think I will. One day the Nazis took my two uncles, my mother's younger brothers. We never heard from them again. They had been working in the underground, you see."

"And someone reported them?"

"I guess so. We were so afraid all the time for my father. I wasn't supposed to know that either, but you know how children always find out what's going on in a house. So I knew that my father was also in the underground. And at night, whenever it was late and quiet and you heard the sound of a motor or footsteps pounding toward the house, I was sure they were coming to take him away, too."

"Do any children anywhere have the kind of life children are supposed to have?" Eric burst out.

"I'm sure they do! They must or the world would be a total madhouse! Why, was your life so hard?"

481

Some other time, perhaps. Not now. "No," he murmured, "actually it was warm and beautiful." And it was true, in most ways, wasn't it? No self-pity; self-pity stinks, he thought roughly, and repeated with firmness, "it was warm and beautiful."

From the dining hall came music, a piano sonata played with fervent hands and spirit. Eric looked up questioningly.

"Shh!" Juliana motioned, and they waited in the violet dusk until the music had ended, waited even a moment longer until it had died away on the air.

She said softly, "That's Emmy Eisen. You know, the woman who helps me in the nursery sometimes? She was a piano teacher in Munich and hid there all through the war. She's so blond, they thought she was an Aryan, you see. And she had good friends, Catholic people who said she was a relative and got false papers for her. She was one of the lucky ones; she didn't get caught. But her husband did and her two sons. That's why she doesn't talk very much. I don't know whether you noticed."

"Ah, yes," Eric said.

"It's a pity she can't have a good piano for herself. The kids wreck this one. Eric, you haven't been thinking about a word I've said!"

"No," Eric said.

"Well, what have you been thinking, then?"

"I have been thinking, if you really want to know, that I love your lovely mouth and your round arms."

Farther down the hill was a hollow; tall grass and a curtain of heavy shrubbery made a small green cave, entirely hidden. Besides, it was almost dark.

"Come," he said.

She rose and followed. The soft green curtain swayed shut behind them as they passed through.

He had chosen to work in the barns. He learned to operate the milking machines; he cleaned stalls and hauled feed twice a day. This labor too reminded him of Brewerstown and of his people's past. Other than that there was little in this motley world to remind Eric of any other place.

When they were gathered at supper in the dining hall he could observe the people in all their variety. First there were the old ones, who had come here from the cities of Russian Poland and had taught themselves to work the land. Then there were their children, the sabras, blond, husky women and men: earnest people for all that they could dance and jubilate. A determined and tenacious people! Last, there were the visitors, mostly students from everywhere: a Christian girl from Australia who had come out of curiosity and for a summer's adventure; boys from Brooklyn, English Jews and German Gentiles, come for a month or two. Few intended to stay, as Juliana did.

She worked in the nursery, since in Holland she had been trained as a kindergarten teacher. Every other night she had to sleep in the nursery, which, Eric was shocked to learn, lay underground. Actually it was a bomb shelter behind a pretty blue door. He was very moved. The world had no knowledge of how these people had to live! He wondered whether even his grandparents, who cared so much, knew what it was really like. "One fears for these children living under the guns," Juliana said. "Of course, it doesn't bother the little ones. But the older ones know. They understand very well."

Many of the fifteen- and sixteen-year-olds had survived the concentration camps and wore, would always wear, the outrageous number stamped upon their arms. The boys wrestled and punched as boys did everywhere. The girls tied ribbons in their hair and practiced flirting, as girls did everywhere. But their eyes were anxious.

Juliana was good for them. She was young enough to know the current popular songs and to teach them how to use a lipstick with skill. She was just enough older to give them some of the mothering they had lost, most of them having lost it when they were still so young that they could barely remember it.

And while Eric watched her with these young people, while he walked beside her under the wind and in the sunlight, he thought: Was there ever, could there ever be, another woman like this one? With the other half of his mind he knew that every man who loves a woman thinks the same. Yet there was not and never could be another one like her.

Sweet, so sweet, with her hair bleaching and her skin turning to café au lait under this searing sun! She was healthy and sturdy, and almost as tall as he; she seemed never to be tired. He didn't ad-

483

mire 'delicate' women, nor ruffled fragility. It pleased him now to think that with a woman like Juliana a man could go anywhere in the world; nothing would be too daring or too new for her.

He hadn't followed her all this way with any thought of marriage. At twenty-one none of his friends was married and he'd had no wish to be, either. He'd had no wish to be committed to any place or any person with certitude enough to say: next year at such and such a time, in such and such a place I shall be doing this or that. Not at all. (And that, he had sometimes thought, was odd of him, because so often, talking philosophically with a friend, he'd heard himself saying that what he needed most was something that lasted.) But permanence had been for his future. He had simply wanted to follow Juliana because, of all the women he had known, she was the most enchanting.

Yet, as the summer wore on, he began to feel a sense of looming loss.

Two weddings were celebrated on the kibbutz within one day. Eric had naturally seen more than a few weddings in his time, but never so much emotion: so many tears and embraces, so much reckless dancing, so much wine. For a while he played his customary role as a wedding guest, observing with curiosity and feeling a human sympathy with their pleasure, but no kinship. And then all at once, standing among the crowd that waved the brides and grooms down the road on the way to their short seaside honeymoons—he could not have said what had been happening inside his head—but all at once the whole business seemed very, very lovely and quite inevitable. He began, in private, to think about it, and was surprised to find himself doing so. Also, he was a trifle pleased and proud. Then he began to edge toward the subject, to walk around the farthest reaches of it, testing the ground, not quite ready yet to walk straight through.

"Tell me," he asked Juliana one day, "do you plan to stay here very long?"

They were sitting on the ground, near the pool. Everyone else was in the water, but he had held her back, wanting to talk.

"Well, it does seem like home to me."

"Yes, but," Eric pressed, "do you plan to stay always?"

"That's a word I don't use. I've told you, I don't like to think that far ahead."

"I do. I want to find a place and people that are going to be right for me forever. There has to be something in the world that's forever."

"Like what?"

"Well," he said, "a house, for one thing, that you won't have to leave. Where you can plant trees and stay to see them grow old."

"Tell me what else you dream of," Juliana ordered, gently outlining his nose and cheeks with a long blade of grass.

"I dream—" he hesitated. "I dream of writing a book, one that might be remembered after I'm dead. A really great book. And I'd like to write it in a room in a house like the one I grew up in." He wanted to add, and was perhaps about to add, "And with you in the house with me," but she interrupted.

"I hope you do! Oh, I hope you get everything you ever want as long as you live!"

People usually say such things out of perfunctory kindness. So the anxious urgency in her voice startled Eric. "Do you?" he asked.

And she answered, "Yes. Because I love you, Eric. So of course I do."

Certainly this was not the first time either of them had told that to the other, but now he went further, wanting and also fearing to know. "Has there—was there ever anyone—"

Juliana looked away, beyond the noise and busy motion at the pool. "There was one, just one, but that was a long time ago and different from this."

He wasn't satisfied. "What happened?"

She looked back at him, blinking as if she were recalling herself from a distant place. "He wanted—he bothered me too much about getting married. So we quarreled and ended it. It was just as well."

Even that did not satisfy him. "And that's all?"

"All that's worth talking about."

"But tell me," he persisted, "what would have been so terrible about getting married?" And added, trying for a light touch, "I thought that's what little girls aim for, from the cradle on."

"Yes," she said, "they do. And such a pity. Poor women! Don't you feel sorry for women?"

"No," Eric said honestly. "Or rather, I never thought about it."

"Well, think about it, then! The miserable marriages they make

because they're afraid of waiting too long and being passed over!
And the miserable marriages they stay in. And the miserable
children—"

"How bleak you sound! As if there were no happy marriages.
That's not even sensible!"

She threw her hands up. "It's sensible for me, and that's all that
counts. I like my life the way it is."

His heart sank. A year or two from now would she be telling
some other man about him: "Yes, there was a young American, but
he bothered me about marriage and so we—"

"What about children?" he asked lamely. "You're so wonderful
with them. Surely you want children?"

"Right now it's wonderful enough to take care of other people's
children."

"But you can't go on doing that," he argued. "That's only a substitute for the real thing."

Juliana jumped up. "I'm boiling in this heat! Let's swim!"

"Go ahead. I'll come in a minute."

What was it? Why? She was so free in loving when they lay in
their 'green cave,' so free with her thoughts, whether glad or
sober, as long as they didn't touch on any personal future. She
baffled him. It would have been easy to understand and cope with,
if there had been another man. Once he had had a girl he liked
tremendously; then she had started to become involved with
someone else, and Eric had come straight out before the two of
them, demanding, "Who is it to be? He or I?" Funny thing! He
smiled, remembering. She had chosen Eric, and then after that he
hadn't especially wanted her.

But that had been different. That girl hadn't been Juliana. And
the rival now wasn't another man. What was it, then?

At summer's end the young foreigners left to go back to the
universities and back to jobs. Only a few would return; this had
been an adventure, but next year they would try a different place,
Nepal, perhaps, or Sweden.

"Aren't you supposed to go back to the States?" Juliana inquired
of Eric.

"I can take a while longer. I was promised a trip before I go to
work, so this can be it," he said.

Besides, he thought, the timing of all these departures was unfortunate. Everything was at the harvest, and just when more hands were needed for a few hectic weeks of twelve-hour days, suddenly there were fewer. If he were going to leave, this surely wouldn't be the right time to do it.

The truth was, he knew he couldn't leave her. Not yet.

When the harvest was finally in, holidays were taken. Eric had not seen Jerusalem. It occurred to him, since Juliana had told him how marvelous the city was, that she might like to go there with him for two or three days. So he arranged for a ride with some other people and told her, when they met at noon, what he had done.

She was indignant. "Now what gave you the right to plan my time for me?"

He thought at first that she was joking, but when he saw that she was not, he was astounded. "I should think you would thank me for having got us a lift, and saved you the trouble of scrounging for one."

"What made you so sure I wanted to go with you?"

"Have you by any chance gone out of your mind?" he demanded.

"No. I just don't like being taken for granted by a man!"

"Well, you needn't worry about that anymore," he said furiously. "I shan't take you for granted again. I shan't take you at all!" And he strode away.

He was sore with his anger all that afternoon. Women! 'Sorry for women,' she had said. Capricious, moody, childish, ungrateful, stupid— He ran out of words.

Could there perhaps be someone else? Anything was possible, yet he couldn't imagine who it might be. They'd been together so much, she hadn't had time even to talk to anyone else! Still, anything was possible.

At supper he sat purposely apart from her. But when it was over and he had to go down to the barns for the evening checkup, she followed him.

"Eric. Eric, I'm sorry." She laid her hand on his arm.

He didn't answer.

"I get that way sometimes. I know it's stupid and wrong. It wasn't decent when you were being so nice."

He melted. "Yes, but—what was it all about?"

"I just get a queer feeling sometimes about being owned. Independence is very precious to me. I get scared. I can't explain it."

"Well, all right then," he said awkwardly, far from understanding.

"And you're not going to stay angry with me? Please?"

"Well, all right," he repeated. "You want to go on Sunday?"

"I want to. Very much."

The minibus was filled. Half the passengers were children and young teen-agers. Their singing was shrill and deafening and gay. The road cut through brown fields already being plowed for winter sowing. It passed through new cement-block towns, bare, ugly and clean.

"It's all they can afford," Juliana explained when Eric made comment. "They've neither time nor money. Beauty can come later."

For beauty had been in the past, and in Jerusalem was there still. The car stopped at the crest of a hill. Below lay the pale amber city, spreading to farther hills and up their sides.

"It isn't gold," Eric remarked wonderingly, "as in the song. It's amber. Yes, that's it."

"There's an old tradition," the driver said. "One is supposed to walk into Jerusalem. Who wants to get out here?"

A few of the boys and girls got out. Juliana jumped out with them.

"I was hoping you would," Eric said.

For three days they celebrated. He followed where he was led. They needed no guidebook, for Juliana knew the city well.

"It's a great pity we can't see more," she told him. "East Jerusalem is all Arab; they don't allow us to go in. And the old Jewish quarter that had been here for two thousand years was wrecked and captured when the Arabs attacked in 1948."

Still, there was more than eyes or feet could cover in three days. Museums and archeological digs. Crowded alleys of the Old City, foul to smell and vivid to look at. Arab women in black veils and Arab men in *kaffiyehs*. Narrow shops where men hammered brass and cut leather. They followed the Way of the Cross. They heard the *muezzin*'s eerie cry in the early morning, and heard it again at noon when they went to a mosque to watch men kneel at prayer, facing toward Mecca.

In rocky fields at the city's edge goats climbed with bells jangling. A man led a string of shabby camels whose great eyes blinked patiently as they waited, tethered in the blinding sunlight. They listened to the melancholy twang of eastern music. At night they danced the hora. They wandered through dark, old shops.

"This is a street of Yemenites," Juliana explained. "Most of them are jewelers, silver crafters."

"I want to buy something for you," Eric said.

"I didn't mean that!" she protested. "I only wanted you to see because it's interesting. They've come here from Yemen—"

"Buy one of these bracelets," he commanded. "No, not that one, it's not nice enough. Pick an important one."

The shop's owner held up a handsome bracelet, its silver filigree as fine as lace.

"That's the one," Eric said firmly. "That is, if the lady likes it."

"Oh, yes," Juliana said, "the lady does!"

When they were outside she asked, "Eric, are you so rich that you can spend money this way?"

He was touched. It hadn't cost anything much at all.

"No," he said, "I'm not, although people here might think I was."

On their last day Juliana told him, "I've saved the best for now. I'm going to take you to a synagogue."

"Oh," he said, amused, "you forget! I've been in them many, many times before."

"Not like this one, you haven't. At least I don't think you have."

At the end of a long alley they stopped. "This looks like medieval Europe!" Eric exclaimed.

"Well, it is. It's been transplanted. One can find everything in this city. Didn't I tell you?"

In the box-shaped synagogue of ancient stone they separated, Juliana climbing two flights of stairs to the women's balcony where hidden women read their prayer books behind the lattices. Squinting through a minute hole she could see the men at their prayer desks below, wrapped in their shawls, and chanting. Eric must be among them but she couldn't see him.

They met again just outside the entrance.

"They all looked so old!" Eric said.

"It's only the beards and the black clothes that make them seem so."

"To think they've been praying this way for three thousand years!"

"Maybe longer."

"My grandfather went to a place like this on the lower East Side before he became 'modern.' " Eric laughed. "You know, I've an idea he would still prefer it. But my grandmother wouldn't."

"Do you realize, these people don't care about politics or wars or anything that's happening beyond their doors?"

"They're waiting for the Messiah, who'll set the world to rights."

Juliana shook her head. "They'll go on praying like this through raids and wars, and heaven forbid, even through defeat."

"That's faith. They believe. I wish I did," Eric said.

She looked at him curiously. "Don't you believe in anything?"

"Do you?" he countered.

"Yes. Freedom and individual dignity."

"Well, if that's all, why, I'll buy that."

"Maybe that's all the belief a person needs. Worth living for and dying for."

"Yes. Only, I don't want to die right now!"

"Nor I, of course not!"

"Ask me what I do want," Eric commanded.

"What do you want?"

"To live where you are. To be near you forever."

"Nothing is forever," Juliana said darkly.

"Do you really think that? I don't like to hear it."

"I know you don't."

"I want to marry you, Juliana. You must know I do."

"Ah, you're very young for your age, Eric!"

He stopped in the middle of the street. "That's a rotten thing to say!"

"Don't be annoyed with me. I only meant—I'm older than you. I'm twenty-four."

"Don't you think I figured that out? And what difference does it make, anyway?"

"None, I guess. But I also meant—you're too trusting. You scarcely know me and still you want to offer me your life on a silver platter."

"It's my life," he muttered. "I can offer it where I like."

"Ah, don't be annoyed!" she repeated. She leaned over to kiss him. "Let's buy some ice cream. My feet are tired and I'm hungry. We can sit in the park over there and eat it."

490

They sat on a bench in the park, eating ice cream out of the container. Children went chattering home from school, their bookbags slung over their shoulders. Tourist buses passed. In a yard across the street a family was decorating a succah for the Feast of Tabernacles; gourds, squash and wisps of grain were hung from or piled on the rafters. Eric followed Juliana's gaze.

"It's the harvest festival," she explained. "They take their meals outdoors in the little booth."

"A pretty custom. All people have their pretty customs."

"Of course."

Two old men passed, looking in a book together. Their beards and their hands waved in earnest discussion.

"My grandfather would love to see all this," Eric said. "I was thinking, if he had a beard and a broad black hat he'd look just like these old men. You see the same face here, over and over."

"Yes, you do."

"Is anything the matter?" Eric asked. She had laid down the ice cream spoon and was sitting with her hands in her lap.

"No. . . . Yes. . . . I have to tell you something."

He waited, but she didn't begin.

"I don't want to tell you."

He saw her agitation. "Don't, if you don't want to."

"No," she contradicted, "I do want to tell you. That is, I want to tell someone. I've always wanted to tell someone and I never have. And I can't stand it anymore! Do you know what it is to have something burning inside you, something you want to talk about and can't, that you're so sick of, so ashamed of—"

He couldn't imagine what she might have done and he was frightened.

"Do you know what that's like?" she demanded again.

"No. No. I don't."

"Do you remember that I told you about my family, how they helped those poor Jews in the attic, and how my uncles were taken by the Nazis?"

"Yes, you told me about your parents, and—"

She interrupted. "Not about my parents. About my mother." She turned her face away, addressing the air. "My mother and her brothers." She stopped and Eric waited.

A fire engine went clanging by. A police car followed with

491

screeching sirens. For a few moments it was impossible to be heard. Then quiet returned to the little park; deep quiet: crooning pigeons pecking at crumbs, a woman calling once across the street. But Juliana didn't begin again.

He waited and was about to say, "Go on," when he saw that her eyes were pressed tightly shut and her fists were clenched in her lap. He didn't know what he ought to do.

Presently she said, steadying her voice, "My father . . . when the war ended the Dutch authorities came for my father. He had been a counterspy for the Germans. One of the leaders. An important man." She opened her eyes and looked at Eric. "An important man! It was he who had turned in my uncles and the neighbors and our minister and all those others who worked in the underground. Can you believe that? My father!"

Eric drew his breath in.

"I thought my mother would lose her mind."

"Perhaps," Eric said, "it wasn't true? And the charge was false?"

Juliana shook her head slowly. "That's what we hoped. But it was true. He didn't try to deny it. He was proud of it. Proud of it, Eric! He believed in it all, the master race, the thousand-year Reich, all of it!"

Eric reached for her two hands and held them.

"Yes, I thought my mother would lose her mind. To have lived with—and, I suppose, even loved—a monster, who sent her own brothers to their death. To have lived with such a man and not known what he was."

He stroked her hair. He had no words.

"And he was kind to my sisters and me. We always had things, toys, some candy—when the country had nothing. We went out into the country together. He loved us. And he sent those other children to die."

"I'm sorry, I'm sorry," Eric said. It was all he could think of to say.

" 'Tell me,' my mother used to ask me after it happened, 'tell me, can you believe anyone, trust in anyone?' I was fourteen . . ."

"She didn't mean it that way," Eric said gently.

"I suppose not. She's doing well enough now. She has my sisters and me; she works, she lives. But still, if you could live with someone and not know what he really was, why then—" Her voice faded away.

"So that's it," Eric murmured to himself.

"What? What did you say?"

"Nothing important."

It began to grow dark and street lamps came on.

"I'm glad I told you," Juliana said. "I feel better."

"You can tell me anything," he answered, meaning it.

Yet in a way he was sorry she had told him. For he had met the rival now and seen that it was fierce and would be hard to vanquish.

"There's a child who troubles me," Juliana told Eric a few weeks later. "Do you remember, I told you about the bus that was shot at last year? There were a few children who survived but their parents were killed."

"I remember. You showed me the spot."

"Well, this one child—perhaps you know Leo, who follows me around? He's nine now, a little boy with glasses."

Eric nodded. "I shouldn't think he'd be any trouble."

"He's much too quiet. He never bothered anyone, even right after it happened. We had so much hysteria here. We were up all night with some of the children, and it went on for weeks, nightmares and crying. But never with Leo."

"Maybe you're too concerned. Have you talked to anyone about it?"

"Oh, yes! And people just say that he's very mature and very brave. And that's true, but still something bothers me."

"I'll talk to him if you like. I was a camp counselor. Maybe I still know how to talk to kids."

"I hoped you'd say that," Juliana said gratefully.

She brought Leo to him one afternoon while he was feeding the calves.

"You said you needed some help and I thought Leo might be able to help you. He's strong and tall for his age."

Leo said nothing, just stood there, neither scowling nor smiling.

"These calves," Eric explained, when Juliana had gone, "have just been weaned. And I'm trying to get them to drink their milk out of a bucket. But the problem is that they don't understand and

493

they try to knock it over and—whoa, there—see what I mean?
Now, if you could hold the bucket while I stick his head in so he
can get a taste of the milk, why, we—"

There were five calves. When they had all been fed, Eric said,
"That was kind of fun, wasn't it?"

Leo shrugged.

"Would you like to do it again another day?"

"If you need the help, I'll do it. People are supposed to help."

"Never mind that. Do you *want* to?"

"I guess so."

"I'm going down to the pasture to bring the cows in. They're far
out today." This time Eric didn't ask whether Leo wanted to go.
He simply said, "Come with me."

The boy obeyed. They picked their way down the path. The
wind made a thin whistle as it passed and moved on through the
grain fields.

"It's beautiful, isn't it?" Eric said. "You're kind of lucky to live in
such a beautiful place."

"Yes."

He tried again. All he could come up with was that trite question with which adults plague children: "What do you want to be
when you grow up?"

"Whatever the country needs. A soldier, probably."

The priggish answer puzzled Eric. "Leo, I wish you'd tell me
what you really think, not what you believe I want to hear."

The boy stopped on the path, opened his mouth as if to speak,
then closed it and went on ahead.

Pathetic shoulders! Skinny legs! Baby, boy and man! And out
of some remote corner of time and memory another question
came.

"Leo—you must think a whole lot about your father and mother,
don't you?"

A second time the child stopped. But now he looked at Eric
sharply. "You're not supposed to talk to me like that!"

"Why not? What's wrong?"

"Because I heard the doctor say and the nurse say, they have to
get our minds off what happened. And that's what I try all the time
to do, and now you come and ask me a question like that!"

"Come here," Eric said, "sit down a minute." He perched on a
large rock at the edge of the path. "You're supposed to get your

mind off it, is that what they say? But you haven't been able to do that, have you?"

"Most of the time I do," Leo persisted. "I'm not a baby, you know."

"I know you're not," Eric said gently. "But I'm not either, am I?"

Leo was puzzled. "What do you mean?"

"I mean that I lost my father and mother the same way you did, or almost the same way. In an automobile. And I still think about them, and I know I always shall."

Leo was silent, watching Eric.

Eric went on, "Yes, and often when I was younger, I cried. I thought how unfair it was that I, of all the boys I knew, had such a thing happen to me. I cried."

"It's not brave to cry," Leo said. A quiver ran over his face.

"I think it is. I think it's quite brave to be honest about the way you feel."

"Do you? Do you ever cry, now that you're old?"

"Look at me," Eric said. His eyes were filled with tears.

The child stood staring at him in wonder. And suddenly he dropped onto Eric's lap, shaking and digging his wet face into Eric's shoulder.

For a long time Eric held him. Pictures, pictures, flashing in his head . . . Gran. Chris. Nana. . . .

Then he thought, They'll be wondering why the cows are so late. But he didn't move.

At last Leo raised his head. "You won't tell anybody?"

"No."

"Not even her?"

"Who? Juliana? No, not even her. I promise."

Leo stood up and wiped his nose and eyes.

"Is there anything else you want to tell me, Leo?"

"Yes."

Eric bent down and Leo whispered, "I'd like a big toy sailboat for the pond."

"I'll make one for you. I'm pretty good at that sort of thing. Now hurry. We're late with the cows."

Arieh, who slept in the bed next to Eric's, remarked, "I notice something about you. You don't talk much lately of home. Of the country house where you grew up, or anything else."

"I guess that's so," Eric admitted.

Arieh was a sabra, born on the kibbutz. He was a country man, with a country man's slight roughness and silences.

"Everybody likes you here," he said abruptly.

"Do they?" Eric felt the flush rising on his neck. These people had few flowery social graces. You had to earn a compliment and even then, he had noticed, you often didn't get it.

"I'm glad," he answered, "because I like people here too."

"Juliana says you've done a wonderful thing with the boy."

"He's a fine child."

"Nobody else knew what to do with him. How did you know?"

"I don't think I really *knew* anything," Eric said slowly. "It was just something that came to me."

Arieh nodded. "That's good enough." He reached for the light. "Mind if I turn it out? It's been a long day."

Lying there in the quiet dark he thought about these simple days of his new life. Nourishing days they were, like mild and good bread eaten under a tree at noon, or perhaps in a kitchen on a winter's night, such a frozen country winter as he remembered from his childhood.

He labored and with each week the labor became easier, his body leaner and faster. Sometimes, passing back and forth from fields to barn, he caught a glimpse of Juliana outside with children, or on some errand alone, walking with strong rapid stride, her fine long hair lifting from her shoulders. And then the day would linger interminably while he waited for the night.

'A sound mind in a sound body.' He felt that his mind was also very strong, that there was nothing he couldn't cope with. It wasn't that he had made any stupendous decisions about himself; he was putting them off, and he knew he was. But when the time came for decisions he would be able to make them.

Then he scoffed at himself for this euphoria. "Because you're living a 'natural' life," he scoffed, "because you feel healthy, you think you can solve everything." If only she would marry him! But he knew he mustn't ask her again, knew that he would have to wait for the fear that was in her to ebb away, whenever and if ever that might be.

So the warm fall passed. Winter is sharp in Galilee; it came to Eric that shortly there would be no more evenings in their 'green cave.'

Their need for one another was so strong by now that there was seldom any preliminary talk between them. He would meet her where they had arranged, outside of her door, and walk down the hill, through the orchards.

"Come," he would say. She would spread her shawl on the tall grass and they would lie down in the shrubbery behind the great guns.

One soft night while lying there, they heard the sound of Emmy's piano carried down the hill by the wind. It rose and fell, sang and died. Music, Eric thought, drawing the word out in his mind's ear, how clearly it speaks to us! With a hundred voices it speaks: of hope and courage, of old sorrow and new joy, telling without words of how man loves the earth, of his fear of dying, and of his awe beneath the stars.

Something caught in his throat, a little gasp, and Juliana turned to him.

"When will you marry me?" he asked her, entirely forgetting his resolution.

And to his absolute, incredulous astonishment, she answered, "As soon as you like."

"Oh," he said. "Tomorrow?"

In the faint light from the sky he could see her smile. "Would you wait until my mother can get here? It shouldn't take more than a few days."

He felt, as when pain has abruptly been relieved, or as when the flesh is warmed after searing cold, a deep, deep comfort. For a little while, in complete tranquillity, they slept. When they awoke the moon was up. Hand in hand, as they so often walked, they went quietly back together, up the hill.

A burst of fire and thunder tore a hole into the sleeping night. The men were out of their beds and instantly awake, as though they had been expecting Armageddon.

"It's the gas pumps!" Arieh cried. "They've hit the pumps!"

No question who 'they' were. . . .

The tanks caught, lifting the earth in clods, raising a tower of fire. A carpet of flame fell over the roof of the cattle barn, then the garages and the stables. By then the men were into their pants and shoes, and with rifles and grenades were halfway down the stairs.

"Where to?" Eric whispered. "Follow you?"

"Yes," cried Allon. "Head down!"

There was a crack and a ping! Then another ping! and a snapping of splintered wood as bullets slammed the walls.

"Out the side door," Allon ordered. "Then around by the back way to the dining hall! Quiet, heads down, on the double!"

Eric understood. From the hall they would command the quad-rangle, nerve center of the community. Anyone who tried to cross there would be in their range.

They slid along the rear wall. From the stables came the human shrieking of the horses.

"Can't we—oh, Christ—can't we get them out?" Eric whispered.

"Are you crazy? Quiet!"

With side vision he saw the frame of the cattle barn outlined for an instant only in a square of fire. Then it collapsed: the hay had caught. The cows! Dumb creatures. Their mild eyes.

Guns were cracking and ripping all around them now as they ran. But whose guns, theirs or ours? A man ran out somewhere ahead and was struck down screaming, spinning like a top. There was unearthly howling from every building. Where were they, the attackers? The muffling darkness protected the enemy as well as themselves.

They reached the dining hall and felt for the door, which was opened from the inside, where others had already gathered. Crouching, they crept in single file: Ezra, Arieh, Allon, Eric, all of them.

And will I come through this? And will I know how to fight?

The huddled leaders whispered. The room was quiet. Outside the guns still crackled and snapped. Where? Where were the at-tackers? Was there no plan to counter them? But there had to be. . . . Eric's lungs burned. They had raced all the way uphill to the hall. His head itched; it was soaked with sweat.

"You," Allon said, "I want one of you at each window. Zack's men are holding the south dormitory, so they can't help here. There are twenty-nine of us altogether, but we don't know how many those devils have. So we've got to send to town for help. They've cut the phone wires. . . . Ezra, can you get to the truck and roll it downhill without making a sound? When you're on the road you can start the motor and then go like hell."

"I'll do it. Where's the dog? Get him out of the kitchen for me."

"He'll make noise!"

"Who, Rufus? I want him with me. He can tear a man's throat out."

Ezra and the dog slipped out through the kitchen door.

Diagonally across the quadrangle lay the nursery, with a cluster of firs beside its blue door. Juliana would be frantic in there, hearing all this without seeing or knowing—

Terror almost took Eric's voice away. "And the children? The nursery?"

"Dan's men are supposed to be there."

"I don't see them." Eric strained into the darkness, lit now to a smoky yellow by the dreadful light of the fires.

"You're not supposed to see them!" Allon spoke impatiently. "But they are there."

So there was a plan. Of course, of course there was. But suppose it hadn't worked? If Dan's men had been trapped or—?

Again there was silence in the hall, except for loud breathing. They waited. Waited.

"Where do you suppose they are?" Eric whispered to the man beside him.

"Who?"

"The Arabs."

"I don't know. How should I know? Everywhere." Avram was frightened, pretending not to be, pretending to be experienced and expert. "They'll try to rush us, thinking we're all holed up in here for defense. We'll mow them down as they come."

There was faint scratching at the door, very faint. Allon, with readied gun, pressed himself against the wall, and opened it a crack. The dog Rufus dragged himself in, whimpered and fell: a pile of bloody, ragged fur, his belly slit open.

"Oh, my God," someone said. "Then Ezra—"

They stood there, staring at each other. Someone called from a window at the front: "The south dormitory's on fire! Oh, Lord, they're jumping from the win—" The voice was cut off with a shattering blow and then a pretty tinkle of glass. Arieh—

Allon crept to him on hands and knees and turned him over. "He's dead," he said flatly, without looking around. "He shouldn't have been standing up."

"How do you know?" Eric cried, without thinking. "Maybe he—"

499

"The top of his head is shot away," Allon said. "Come and see for yourself."

Eric thought, We played chess last night. Then he thought, I'm going to vomit. But I can't be sick now.

"Listen," Allon said, "we have got to get to town. I'll go, and I need three, no, four with me. Who'll come?"

"But if they got Ezra they must be guarding the road," someone objected. "So how can you possibly—"

"Down through the orchard, and around to the road half a mile past the gates."

"It won't work, Allon! It's committing suicide! The orchard's where they must have got through in the first place!"

"Is there any other way?" Allon asked. Crouched there on his knees, wet with the blood of Arieh, he had immense authority. "Well, then, we'll have to chance it. Who goes?"

"I will," Eric said.

"No, you don't know the way well enough. Ben, Shimon, Zvi, Max, we'll go. If any one of us is hit the rest won't stop for him. One of us has to get through. Marc, you take charge here while I'm gone."

As if in reply another window was smashed out at the front; glass sprayed the floor, falling on Arieh, at whom none of them dared look.

Again they waited. Marc stood in the corner, flat against the wall, from which at an angle he could see through the farthermost window.

"They're crossing the quadrangle," he whispered suddenly.

"Who are?"

"I—it's too dark. For God's sake lower that gun!" he cried to Yigel. "They may be ours!"

They waited. Somewhere, in a history of the First World War, Eric recalled having read that the soldiers' chief complaint was the interminable waiting. With dry mouth. Wet hands. Needing to pee.

He crawled to the window and peered an inch or two above the sill at the side. Yes, there were men walking through shadow, crossing the quadrangle. They were heading toward the nursery door. Some of ours? Dan's men? Reinforcements? But then why so openly and upright? They can't be ours— His heart lurched. They must be—

At the nursery door the men stopped. There were—he counted—five of them. No, seven? It was too dim to see. They were just standing there. Why? Who?

A bullet slammed into the room, then another and another, a fusillade. Marc screamed, shot in the thigh. David fell; dead or wounded? There was no time to find out.

"They're on the roof!" Avram cried. "They've got up on the roof of the extension."

The devils! The fiends! Now they could shoot in through the windows while no one could shoot back upwards into darkness.

There were only three whole ones left: Avram, Yigel and Eric. They crawled to the back of the room, dragging Marc with them out of reach of the bullets which were coming in now like rain.

Suddenly the rain stopped. Into total silence a voice rang, speaking in accented Hebrew.

"You in there! We have a proposition to make! Can you hear?"

Avram, Yigel and Eric stood gripping each other's arms.

"Listen, we know you're there! Will Allon the boss speak up? Answer! You don't have to show yourself!"

"How do they know Allon?" Eric whispered.

"Arabs in town. Contacts across the border. Who can say?"

"Allon the boss! You'd better listen! Or we'll burn out the rest of the place! If you give us what we want we'll leave you in peace."

Avram whispered, "Shall we answer?"

"No," Yigel said fiercely.

"Yes," Eric argued, "if we can kill time talking back and forth maybe Allon will have got through to town and we'll have help."

"What do you want?" Avram called then.

"Are you the boss Allon?"

"I am. What do you want?"

"Six children. Any six. We take them back with us and hold them until your government gives back our six freedom-fighters who are in your jails."

"The freedom-fighters are the ones who attacked the schoolhouse two years ago," Yigel said to Eric. And to Avram, "Tell them to go to hell."

"You know we aren't going to do that!" Avram called back.

"You might as well! Otherwise we can kill all the children, and the rest of you, too. Look, our men are already waiting at the nursery door."

"You won't get away with that!" Avram shouted. "There are over a hundred of us on this place . . ."

"Maybe there were. But there aren't anymore."

Silence.

"When we get in that nursery there won't be one of them left alive. Allon boss! You'd do better to let us have six now. Any six."

The little ones' beds were painted with ducks and rabbits. Clowns and baby elephants danced on the walls. And Juliana slept there. My girl.

Somebody rattled the lock at the back door of the kitchen.

They jumped.

"Be careful. Don't open it."

"Who's there?" Yigel cried, pointing his revolver.

There was a loud whisper. "It's me! Shimon! Open up!"

Yigel opened the door enough to admit a young Arab, with his hands in the air and a rifle, held by Shimon, in the small of his back.

"We got this guy coming up the hill with a knife in his hand." Shimon handed the knife to Avram. "Zvi and Allon are dead. Max and Ben kept going. Maybe they'll get through to town."

"If we knew how many there were," Eric said, "maybe we could—"

"Could what?" Avram demanded scornfully.

"Ask him how many there are anyway," Eric said.

Yigel said something in Arabic and translated. "He says he doesn't know."

"Give me the knife," Eric said, and took it from Avram. He held it against the Arab's naked throat. The man pulled back in horror, gurgling, his eyes wild. "Yigel, tell him that if he doesn't answer I'll cut the way he cut the dog—and probably Ezra, too. Tell him."

Yigel spoke. The man mumbled, and Yigel translated, "He says 'four.'"

"There are at least six or seven in front of the nursery alone, and more on the roof. Tell him we want the truth," Eric commanded.

"He says five. He had forgotten to count himself."

Eric slashed the knife lightly over the Arab's shoulder. The man screamed and Eric withdrew the bloodied knife. "Answer me," he cried, "or the next time it will be your throat!"

The Arab trembled, cried out, and Yigel translated once more.

"He says there are two on the roof. He doesn't know how many at the nursery door. The rest are dead."

"All right. Tie him up," Eric said. It surprised him that Avram and Yigel obeyed without argument.

"Allon boss! What are you waiting for? Until we set fire to the nursery?"

"You won't get away with it!" Avram called back.

Christ, where were they, Max and Ben? And if they had by some miracle got through, how long would it take to reach here from town with help?

Eric crawled to the front window. A torch had been lit at the nursery door, no doubt to fire the place. In its tossing light he could count them: five, no, seven, poised at the door and waiting. He could hear their screaming laughter. The ruffians, the savages. And those piteous women on the other side of the door. Juliana— It came to him that he had never known such anger, such outrage.

He stood up yelling, not recognizing his own voice, not knowing that he was yelling. "I'm going to get them! I'm going to get them!"

"Get down!" Yigel cried. "Eric, fool, get down!"

"The dirty, rotten, murdering scum!" Eric screamed.

Yigel pulled him down. "Shut up! You can't do a thing! There are seven of them."

"I have one grenade—"

"But it's too far! They'd shoot you from the roof, those others up there! You'd never get near enough to throw it, don't waste your life—"

Spots of red and yellow rage flickered before Eric's eyes. The terrors of the world flashed through his mind as, it is said, in the instant before drowning a life flashes past. They knotted in his chest, all that were anguished, cruel and wrong: lost children, violence, corruption and early death. All of them, all of them—

His shirt ripped down the back, leaving a piece of khaki cloth in Yigel's hand as he tore out the door and down the steps with the grenade.

The survivors told it this way: He spurted across the open space toward the nursery like a football player running for a goal. He dodged and darted while bullets slashed the earth around his feet. About five yards away from the gang at the nursery door a bullet tore into his back and he fell dead, but not before he had thrown the grenade into the middle of the gang and killed them all.

It was over. The two snipers fled in terror from the roof and were captured in the orchard. By the time help arrived from town the fires were out and everything was quiet, except for the crying of the women, preparing the dead.

On the other side of the world, in America, a cablegram brought the news. It was a week now since it had come, and Joseph had aged ten years. He sat at breakfast, his first full meal in days. He finished his coffee and pushed away from the table, but didn't get up, just sat there with his mouth hanging open. Like an old man. Anna hadn't looked in the mirror at herself. God knew what she must look like! And what difference did it make?

And then (as though they hadn't had enough), Celeste came in with the mail, bringing, among the piles of bills, advertisements and letters of condolence, a letter in Eric's handwriting. It had been mailed ten days before.

Anna's hand shook, but she spoke steadily. "I have to tell you, Joseph. There's a letter from Eric."

"Read it," he answered in a flat voice.

She swallowed and obeyed. "Dear Grandpa and Nana, I have just come in from planting oats. From where I sit the dark, wet fields stretch away to the horizon; it is so beautiful." He had sat at a desk, his hand had rested on this paper only a few days ago. No, not a desk, more likely a rough, unpainted table. There were fine wrinkles around his eyes; he strained them; he would need glasses early. His eyes were so light and brilliant when his face was tanned; he would have got quite brown, working in the fields. "I don't want to seem affected or some sort of oddball, and I hope no one thinks I am, but if they do I can't help it. It's as if something were behind me, pressing me on to do something, really do something for a good cause. I hope you can truly understand."

Joseph groaned and she stopped. "Go on," he said.

"I can really feel I belong in this place. For the first time since I've been old enough to think about such things," (since he came to live with us, he means) "I feel no conflict about who I am. I'm just another pair of willing, needed hands. . . . I know you hoped so much that I would carry on your work and your name. Thousands of young men would be so grateful for a chance like

504

that, and I *am* grateful, really I am. But it's just not for me. Since I've come here, I've been sure it isn't."

"He wasn't ever going to come back," Joseph said wonderingly. "Not ever going to come back."

Anna looked at him sharply, but he was sitting quite still.

She resumed, "You two, of all people, will understand that there's something different about this country. It's not charming or graceful like Europe, not rich and strong like our own country which I love so much. But come visit me here and see for yourself what I mean and what I'm doing.

"Also, I should tell you that I have a girl. I don't know how we will resolve things between us, but I love her. She's Dutch; you'd like her at once. You know how kind the Dutch were to our people during the war—"

She finished the letter and put it down. Then she opened a thin airmail envelope, addressed in a foreign hand.

"It's from a girl, Juliana. She must be the one he meant."

"Read it."

". . . he had written to you, I think, only a day or two before it happened. But at that time he hadn't known we were going to be married. Not that it makes any difference to you now—" Anna stopped and, steadying her voice, went on, "but still you might want to know what he was doing up to the end. He was very brave, which others have told you or certainly will tell you. But more importantly, he was happy. I wanted you to know that. Also that he spoke of you often and loved you so much.

"My first thought was of running home to my mother, to my people. Then I thought no, not while this evil flourishes. But I'm going to leave here to pioneer in the Negev. I'm going to the desert, to a harder place."

There were a few more lines and good wishes.

"Poor girl," Anna said.

"Yes—poor girl."

So they sat unmoving. The morning paper and the coffee cups lay on the table between them, as on any ordinary day. Then Joseph put his head down on the table.

God, God, where are you? Anna cried silently. Why do You torment this good man? To say nothing of all the rest of humanity! The world aches and crumbles; people are eaten by cancer, they scream in madhouses, machine guns are turned on children, the

505

landlord takes half a month's earnings for the right to live in his hovel. Tell me, why do You in Your wisdom permit all this?

And why do I still believe in You in spite of it? Theo says because I need a father image. I don't know, I don't think so. I can't think at all. I don't know why I still trust You. Yet I do. I have to, or I couldn't live.

But I ask You all the same, when will You stop torturing us?

The telephone rang and she rose to answer it. She spoke a minute and came back to the table.

"That was Theo," she said quietly. "Iris has just had the baby. A boy. They're both well."

BOOK
5

"ALL THE RIVERS RUN INTO THE SEA . . ."

ECCLESIASTES

42

They told him it was a slight attack, a mild coronary. "You're better off, in a way, than a man who hasn't had a warning and goes right on doing the wrong things. Why, you'll last for years," they assured him, "as long as you exercise and eat right." But he always had done both of those things. "And don't worry," they said. Hah!

His mind wandered. Came from having nothing to do. He'd gone through the *Times* twice today and now had climbed upstairs to his round room and spread plans on the table. They were assembling the land for a shopping center in Florida. It ought to be a bonanza with all the building going on, the condominiums and retirement colonies. Now his mind sharpened, narrowed to specifics. As soon as they'd let him out of the house, by the first of the month, they said, he'd have to round up some of the chain stores. They'd want a five-and-ten, certainly; a drugstore; one of those popular shoe outfits and then a few assorted boutiques. They'd need some spectacular landscaping, an alley of royal palms down the middle, perhaps. They could call it Palm Walk.

He moved restlessly around the room. Anna had been right—it was a wonderful little place for him. He liked looking down at tree tops. He liked hearing the sounds of the household two floors below; he could hear just enough to feel he was at home, and still not be disturbed.

He felt well again, and looked well too, even had a lot of hair left without any gray in it. Anna had to dye hers: he insisted. Her face

509

was still so firm; why should her hair be old? It was dyed the burnished russet it had been naturally. She looked fifteen years younger. She was still strong, walked gracefully. You could tell a lot by the way a person walked. As for himself, he couldn't believe he was seventy-three, that it was seven years since Eric died— But better not to think of that, or of a lot of other things. Now was now. True, he had a load on his mind, a huge business with a couple of hundred men and their families dependent on him, but he could cope with it. He wanted to cope; that's how you knew you were alive. When you had one problem after the other, you solved one and moved on to the next.

Malone, now, he'd got very old. His lips trembled and his eyes watered. He won't last as long as I will, Joseph thought. Malone had been ready to retire, hadn't been up to the pressure, and fortunately had had enough sense to know it. He was better off out in Arizona. Besides, Malone had sons.

We should have had more children, he protested for the thousandth time. Iris' young boys were the only future: their own future, not their grandfather's. As it should be. But it would be good, all the same, to have one of them take over, one of them who'd care for the work and the name he had made! Land. He'd been right about its being the basis of all wealth. If you managed it correctly. But Jimmy's going to be a doctor, like his father; you can tell already. He chuckled: last week Iris found a mouse cadaver under his bed. They all say Jimmy's the apple of my eye; well, Philip's the other apple, then. Philip, my joy, my darling. Coming downstairs in his pajamas to hear Theo's quartet, and we thought he'd come for the cake! They laugh at me, but I still say, who can tell? Rubinstein and Horowitz were young once. I think he plays like an angel. We never had anyone like him before in our family. Except that niece of Anna's, that poor girl Liesel. Maybe the music comes through her, some strain way back. Not from my side, goodness knows. So Philip won't want my business either, that's for sure.

And Steve: hah! Set a bomb under it more likely, with all that socialism of his, or anarchism, whatever you want to call it! No, that's not fair. He's only a boy, not sixteen yet, and the times are radical. It's a fad. He's got a long way to go. Still, very troubling.

Thank goodness, Laura's okay. Anna all over again, with that look on her face as if the world had been made brand-new every morning!

They'll all go their ways without me. Everything will go on. These trees will get taller. People will come and go to school and the office and the supermarket; I won't be here. Kid yourself, if you want, about your energy and your ambition and not looking your age; kid yourself and let other people kid you too—as if a man can't tell when they're soft-soaping him! But the drift is there. Drifting, that's the feeling.

You just don't seem to need much anymore. Sex—forget about that! And food. You don't enjoy it, at least not the way you once did. Even sleep: how sweet it is to sleep all night through! You don't realize it until you start waking up every morning before dawn. It's still dark outside and you lie there with your eyes open, watching the light come through the blinds and hearing winter wind or else birds' first calling, like questions in the darkness, minutes apart. It's the loneliest time. Anna's still asleep. Her shoulder is fragrant; she puts perfume on before she goes to bed. We're separate after all; every human being—separate and alone. You never know that, or maybe don't admit it, until the time comes near to die.

Anna says: "Why don't you take it a little easier? You could leave more to the Malone boys. Just keep a hand in one or two days a week to see how things are going."

No. What would I do here all day? Sit around and listen to my arteries harden? Work is—it's cheerful. When I'm away for more than a couple of days I have a kind of creeping melancholy and it scares me. That's why I never liked to take trips. It's the one way I disappointed Anna, because she'd have gone hiking all over the globe and up every mountain if I'd been willing. Work and the company, Friedman-Malone; they're my *life!* Anna knows that.

He moved to the television set and switched it on. The voice came first, then a picture flaring gradually into the great blank eye of the screen. It was a replay of the Kennedy funeral the previous week: the dirge, the celebrities walking across the bridge toward Arlington and the horse with the stirrups on backwards. The horse.

Eighteen years since that other president had died. . . . He remembered the stores on Madison Avenue displaying the black-bordered portrait. Eighteen years! And this was worse: the young man with his head shot away. He turned the television off.

Death and violence. Violence and death. When your heart gives out it can't be helped, but deaths like this one! Kennedy's and Maury's, the smashed-up, bloody deaths. And Benjie Baumgarten's drowned face. What had made him think of that now? Then Eric. All unnecessary.

Oh, Maury, oh, my son, if I could have you back again I wouldn't care what you did. If I'd made it easier for you and that young girl, taken the pressure off, then maybe— Almost twenty-five years ago. And your son. I tried to make up to you through him, as if perhaps you could know I was loving and being good to your boy. But he didn't want it, not what I had to give. He didn't know what he wanted, Maury. He didn't know where he wanted to belong. Maybe in a world where everybody was the same. (Hah! When was there ever, when will there ever, be a world like that?) When he was with one kind he felt guilty about turning his back on the other. He never told us, but we knew. Your mother was the one; she figured it out, and she was right. He felt more guilty about turning his back on our side because we're the sufferers, the weak ones. Yet he was tempted toward the sunny side, the Gentile way. Who can blame him? And then he felt guilty all over again. He had no roots. That's one of the overdone words of our day but I don't know another that fits as well.

Still, Eric wasn't the only person in his position. Perhaps he made too much of it? Should just have put it in the back of his head and *lived?* But he was sensitive; he *minded* more, about everything. It seems we're a family like that, too, soft, thinking too much about ourselves and everyone around us. (Not me; I'm tough, I'm the only one not like that.)

Even my father and mother. They had nothing, they knew nothing. But my mother wanted me to be a doctor. We stood on the tenement roof. I carried the basket of clothes up for her to hang. Her eyes came straight out of history, deep eyes of Rachel and Sarah. She was younger than I am now, and she seemed so old. Their hard, hard lives. Sleeping in the dark cubby back of the store. Worried about what they'd have to put on the table: water in the child's milk again? Oh, God, to live like that!

And yet, how simple! Only one worry: money. They wouldn't believe it, if they could come back to see what people worry about now. Iris and all that child psychology, sibling rivalries, permissive schools, progressive camps. What poppycock, nothing to worry about at all.

A good thing she's gone back to teaching. I didn't think so at first, don't believe a woman should work if she doesn't have to. Seemed to me it might look as if Theo couldn't support his family. But it's really worked out all right. Iris looks as if she's doing what she wants to do. She acts more—important. Even wants to go on for a master's in special education. Guess she got restless with the usual suburban business, P.T.A., scouts, dentist, dancing classes. Always was a bright girl, Iris.

"You want me, Celeste?"

"I've brought these." Another pot of chrysanthemums. "Here's the card."

"Where're we going to put them all? There's no room for them here." Besides, the damned room looked like a funeral parlor with the flowers and potted plants, and those piles of get-well cards to be acknowledged! He'd gotten so much stuff, books and brandy and letters, even a letter from Ruth. Well over eighty now, she was. Her crabbed hand, the letters sliding downward off the page: "Dear Old Friend, We all love you."

She loves me. But I didn't help Solly. I let him die. . . .

Celeste was waiting. "I'll take it downstairs and let Mrs. Friedman put it someplace. You're feeling all right, Mr. Friedman?"

Always looked so scared, Celeste did, opening the door by inches as if she expected to find him lying dead on the floor. . . . Made you cranky, a scared face like that. And then ashamed of himself, he said heartily, "I ought to be sick more often, I get so much attention!"

"Oh, don't do that. We'll take good care of you without your being sick."

"I know you will, Celeste, I know you will."

"Would you like a cup of tea or anything?"

"Thanks, I'll take my tea when my wife comes home."

"She'll be back soon. Want the door closed?"

"You can leave it open, thanks."

Good to hear the sounds of the house, Celeste talking to the day worker downstairs. Good woman, Celeste. Member of the family. Steve ought to talk to *her*, ask *her* what she thinks! She'd tell him she had it pretty good! Beautiful room. TV set to herself. Paid vacation. The best food, all she wanted to eat. Steve ought.

Anna should be here soon. He'd made her go to the luncheon of the Hospital Guild. She hadn't wanted to leave him but she hadn't been out of the house in weeks now, since his attack. Do her good. Looked fine when she left. She dressed well, Anna did, and it

513

wasn't just the expense; you had to know what you were doing. Some of the richest men's wives looked awful. "Clothes, where are you going with the woman?" That's the way they looked, with their hair puffed out like watermelons and all the dangling bracelets. Gaudy and vulgar, they were. Anna's taste had taught him that.

She had taught him many, many things. Everything good in his life had come from her, all charm and fragrance, all gentleness and joy. Maury and Eric had come from her. And Iris—

He frowned, winced. That ugly, insane flash of thought again! He was so certain he had wiped it from his mind, but here it was back, like a stain that can't be got rid of.

That Iris may not be mine! My darling, my dear! It—it chokes me. . . . I think of how unforeseen she was: five years between births, and I'd been so troubled then, I hadn't been near Anna very much. Yes, and I think—crazy thought—I've even thought that Iris looked a little like that Werner fellow. Crazy, crazy thought that I've got to drive out! That I will drive out! I ought to be ashamed of myself.

Yet there was something between the two of them, if not that. Some thing. I don't know how far it went, but I know. Before our marriage or after?

When? Perhaps that day when I sent her to borrow the money? If it was, I have only myself to blame. I should never have made her go, never put her in a position where she— Alone in that house. All those dark stairs, dark wood banisters going up and up; a tall mirror at the end of the first flight to the room where the piano stood. Anna showed me once, and I never forgot the first time I had been inside a rich man's house.

Or perhaps a meeting on some dusky winter afternoon? In an ornate hotel, the traffic marching down Fifth Avenue ten floors below. Glasses and bottles twinkling on a table: champagne, for Anna drinks no whiskey. Yes, a table. And a bed.

He closed his eyes, pressing them shut.

As for me, there could have been women. It's so easy, especially when a man can buy things. Girls in the office. A lady lawyer at a closing once: tall, black hair coiled over a white collar. So easy. But there was never much time, I climbed so fast. Not enough time for that sort of thing. And I never really wanted it enough or I would have found the time, wouldn't I? Never really wanted it enough.

Anna.

I didn't think, when I asked her to marry me, that she would consent. There'd been nothing between us, no look, no slightest touch of the flesh to make me think I had any chance at all. Yet I asked and she said yes. In a way I knew that wasn't how it usually happens between a man and a woman. In a way I knew even then that there was *something*.

She was so young. Naïve, not of the world. And still is, to a certain extent, though she would be annoyed to be told so. Never let her guess, never let her suffer because of my darkest thoughts. Understanding. Forbearance. Whatever you want to call it. For I have had so much, that she has given me. And we have had such a life together, she and I.

Anna, my love. My love.

There was the car now. He looked at his watch. She'd come home early, not wanting to leave him so long. He heard the garage door go down, then her steps on the gravel drive. Another car came, and a door slammed. More steps. Whose?

Then Theo's and Anna's voices, coming upstairs, the voices of Jimmy and Steve below them.

"Good afternoon." Theo's mock-professor voice. "How is the patient today?" And in his normal voice, "We drew up to the stop light at the same time and the boys and I got the idea of coming along to see you."

"You're always a sight for sore eyes, you people. How's everything, Theo?"

His long-established greeting. It meant: How are you doing at the office? Busy enough but not overworked, I hope. Paying your bills with something left over after taxes. It meant: Is everything smooth at home? No troubles with the kids?

Theo's long-established answers reassured him. Yes, yes, everything was fine and there was nice news: Jimmy had made the tennis team.

"Well, congratulations!" Joseph said. "And you, Steve? You upset about something?" For Steve was frowning, with what Anna called his 'buttoned-up' expression.

"No."

"Go ahead," Theo said. "You can tell Grandpa." And, since Steve stayed silent, he went on, "Steve was at my office just now to do some papers on the copying machine. And he happened to overhear a conversation with a patient, a girl who's going to have surgery

515

because she doesn't like the shape of her nose. Steve's disgusted, not just with her, but with me! He thinks I should have booted the girl down the stairs along with her nose."

Steve spoke up. "I said, with all the wounded and suffering people in the world you should be ashamed to waste your work on a spoiled bourgeoise."

"Suffering is a matter of degree," Theo said. "If her nose makes her miserable, even though that may seem ridiculous to you, it really isn't ridiculous at all."

"I don't go for that argument. The fact is, you treat people like her because you make money doing it and that's the only reason. The profit system again."

"What's wrong with the profit system?" Joseph demanded.

"What's wrong? The profit system is wrecking the environment and destroying the human spirit. That's all."

The stance of the boy, his slight figure leaning against the wall, the proud lift of his head, angered his grandfather.

"Destroying the environment! What the devil do they teach these kids in school, anyway?"

"School!" Steve was scornful. "I do my own thinking! School doesn't teach anything, except cramming for high marks."

Joseph threw up his hands. "Bah! Socialist poppycock! It all comes down to one thing, this sort of talk. Envy. All this leveling business, pass-fail grades and that stuff; it's the people who get Cs and Ds who want it. They may give you all sorts of high-flown moral reasons, but the plain fact is they envy the people who get As."

"That doesn't apply to me," Steve said stiffly and accurately, for he had always been an A student. "I'm not envious of anybody or anything. What I am much more is guilty, and you all should be too."

Jimmy swung his tennis racket. "Aw, come on, Steve, lay off, will ya?"

But Joseph had been goaded and wanted to pursue the subject. "Guilty about what?"

"About living the way we do. You ought to be guilty about living in a house like this while millions of human beings live in shanties!"

"It took brains and hard labor to earn this house! Don't you think a man deserves some rewards for his brains and labor?"

"There's a lot of luck involved in making money." Steve spoke

quietly now, while Joseph could hear his own angry panting breath.
"Luck and a little chicanery here and there, besides."

"Steve! That's going too far!" Theo said furiously.

Joseph raised his hand. "Leave him! Chicanery, is it? I want you
to know that your grandfather has never been party to a crooked
deal! Do you hear that? Not a thing to be ashamed of. I've built
honestly. People need shelter and I build it for them. Most of them
never lived so well before. And I'm supposed to be a louse because
I make some money doing it?"

"Joseph! You're getting too excited!" Anna cried. "You're not supposed— Boys, why don't you go outside for a while and practice
serves against the garage wall?"

"Or start walking home," Theo said. "I'll catch up with you on the
way." And when they had gone downstairs, "I'm sorry. Steve is
tough to cope with. We have this all the time."

"He's angry inside," Anna said. "Maybe because Jimmy is taller?"
she questioned thoughtfully. "That can be very hard, having your
younger brother grow taller than you. And now he's breaking out
with acne besides."

"My wife, with the excuses," Joseph grumbled. "With the psychology."

"Never mind," Anna said. "There are things going on inside of a
child that we can't guess at. Iris said the guide told her Steve's IQ is
a good bit higher than Jimmy's, and still Jimmy does just as well,
and he seems so much more interested in things, his stamps and
animals and tennis and—"

"Jimmy!" Joseph interrupted. "Jimmy's always been easy on the
nerves. His own and everybody else's."

"Jimmy has always had an accepting attitude," Theo said. "He
enjoys life. No credit to him, he's very, very lucky to have been
made that way. He just seems to look at things clearly and calmly. A
couple of nights ago he asked: "If you and Mother should die what
would happen to this house?" I was taken aback for a second and
then I realized it was a perfectly reasonable question. But Steve flew
into a rage with Jimmy. He had furious tears in his eyes. I'm sure it
wasn't because of thinking that Jimmy might have hurt our feelings.
Goodness knows, Steve never takes much heed of other people's
feelings! It must have been because he's terrified of death, poor guy,
of our deaths and being left alone." Theo sighed and no one spoke

517

for a moment. Then he stood up. "Ah, well, they don't know when they're well off, do they? I suppose we didn't either, at that age. But it will all pass. I just hope Steve doesn't get involved in anything too deeply before it does. He's been talking about going south this summer on one of those marches."

Joseph intercepted Anna's distress signal. "Anna, stop protecting me. I'm not dead or dying yet."

"Of course you aren't! It's just that you get too upset. You always do!"

"Mama's right," Theo apologized. "I shouldn't have brought the subject up. Don't worry, I'll handle things."

"I know you will, Theo. But it isn't easy. What we do for our children! We spend our life's blood—"

"There was a very fine speaker at the luncheon," Anna said. "The subject was hospital costs. You would have been interested, Theo."

Joseph smiled. Transparent! Keep the conversation impersonal. Don't upset the old man. We'll just take up the time until the visit's over.

Anna and Theo forgot how clearly words carried up the stairs, even though, a few minutes later, they spoke so quietly at the front door.

Joseph could hear Theo say, "He's rather low in spirits today, isn't he? To be so upset about Steve— I don't think it can really just be Steve's nonsense."

"No, no, I know him. I should, shouldn't I? He's thinking about Maury and Eric. He gets this way sometimes, even before the attack, he did." Anna's voice lowered. "He can't bear to hear the mention of their names. I always try, when the day comes around that either of their names is called on the roll of the dead at temple, I always try to make some excuse not to go. I say I don't feel well or something."

"And does it work?"

Anna laughed. "Of course not! But I try."

You never know with Anna, what she's hiding, what planning, always to spare me. She thinks I don't know that for a time years back things weren't going well between Iris and Theo. They all covered up, but I knew. I didn't ask because I guess I was afraid to know. Anyway, they wouldn't have told me.

Thank God it's all right now; I can tell that too. He's a good man, Theo is. I like to see him come walking up from the tennis courts with the kids, talking French or German with them. And good to Iris: his voice is gentle when he speaks to her. I hear that. He'd better be.

My dear, my heart. From the day she was born, the homely, tender, appealing little thing. . . . Yet she's done well. She's turned out to be a good-looking woman in her way, not in the popular fashion, but different looking, distinguished. That's the word: distinguished. Iris.

That kid Steve had better not cause her any heartache. I'll tell him so one of these days, too. Chicanery, he said. What a word! Luck! He makes it sound so cheap, like crapshooting or slot machines. Luck! All that labor, getting up before five to reach the building sites in those early years! Scrambling for contacts and financing, sweating out the mortgage payments, that was luck?

He says we don't give value for the money. Granted, we don't give the value they gave in this house that I'm living in. How can we, with the building trades unions getting more and more every year? Squeezing the bosses dry. Still, I know a man wants his family to live decently, wants to give them things. I ought to know! So what's the answer? That I don't know. I'm sorry I don't.

I understand in a way what Steve means, even though he thinks I don't. He's a smart boy, the smartest of the lot. But I can't take to him the way I do to the others, my baby guy Philip or Jimmy. Jimmy has merry eyes. I just thought of that. Maybe because of Steve's stringy long hair? And I like immaculate fingernails, especially when I'm eating. I can't help it, I hate dirt. Damned arrogant kid! And still, you can feel something. So unhappy. Poor Steve. Wish I could get to him. Poor kid.

Anna came back with a tray, two cups of tea and a small plate of biscuits. "You're to have this and then a nap. Doctor's orders, so don't grumble."

"Who the hell needs a nap?"

"You do," she said calmly. "You want to get back to the office, so do what you're told."

She sat down, stirring the tea. Her face was placid, dignified. Firmness in the softness. Remarkable woman! Why do I always think of what my father would have said? Quality, he'd have said. He used to pick up a fine piece of cloth and smooth it between his thumb and finger. "Quality. You can always tell," he'd say.

"What are you thinking?" Anna asked.

"Of you. I didn't make a mistake when I saw you sitting on the stoop at Levinsons'."

"I'm glad."

"Are you, Anna? Sometimes I wonder. I've had too much time to think, this past month. You remember, just before I had the attack, we were at that benefit for the blind? You were talking to that fellow who publishes the art books, and I thought, 'There's the kind of man she ought to have married, the kind of man who speaks her language.'"

"You want to get rid of me?"

"Don't make a joke of it! I'm serious." He reflected: ought he to tell her the rest? Yes, yes, have it all out, all of it. "I know I promised you once never to talk about the subject again, but lately I haven't been able to put it out of my mind. About you and Werner—he was a man who spoke your language, wasn't he?"

Anna sighed deeply. "Oh, Joseph! Not again?"

"I'm sorry. I know you assured me there never was anything, but so many things don't fit: words, gestures, incidents. I needn't go over them again, because you know them and I know them. But they don't quite fit, and my sense, my instinct—"

"Senses and instincts don't prove anything," Anna interrupted. "I gave you rational answers. I can't do more than that. I feel as though I were using a sword against cobwebs when you talk about 'instincts.'"

Even in her quiet denial he heard defiance. If he were not still an invalid she would have been more vehement, he knew, more angry. He mustn't press too hard, mustn't look for trouble. He was lucky, after all, to have had her all these years, he told himself for the thousandth time. A woman like Anna could have had anyone.

"Don't torment yourself, Joseph. Don't ask me these questions. Even if you can't believe me, and I'm sorry you can't, just don't ask me anymore."

So he would never really know, never *really*. To wipe out his doubts, to know that she was totally his and always had been, that there had never, never been anyone else—what he would not give! The remaining years of his life, that's what he would give.

"I would like to be truly at peace," he said aloud.

"Then be at peace. I can't say any more than that." Anna finished her tea and stood up to stroke his forehead. Her hand was warm from the teacup, and he smelled her perfume again.

He didn't move, enjoying the sweep of her hand across his forehead, hoping she wouldn't stop. "It's beautiful here, isn't it?" he said, wanting to detain her.

"Very. It's home."

This quiet house, the view of trees, he thought suddenly, these go always to the people at the top. In Buenos Aires or Peking, no matter what the system, the quiet rooms and the view of trees belong always to the people at the top.

"If anybody thinks there can ever be a world where you can get this without effort he's crazy," he said suddenly. "I sweated to get it, Anna, I sweated."

Anna thought, I sweated for it, too. She said, "I know you did. And that's why it's time you stopped, isn't it? Look, here's George come up to see you."

The door, which had been left ajar, was pushed toward the wall and the huge black dog came lumbering in.

"It's chilly for May and he hates the cold."

"He's getting old," Joseph said glumly. This was George the Second, son of the George who had come with Eric to their house. And George the Second had a son, Albert, born just before Eric went away.

"I know. The young one wants to be outside, though. Would you like it if George took a nap with you?"

"Apparently he intends to, whether I like it or not." For George had stretched out on the couch, considerately leaving just enough room for Joseph.

"All right, lie down now. Philip will be here before you know it. And Laura said she might come too."

He lay down obediently and Anna closed the door behind her. Two or three times a week, Philip stopped in on the way home from his music lesson or religious school. What a schedule for such a little fellow, only seven! But that's the way they did it these days. And come to think of it, it hadn't been so different for Maury and Iris, either. We all push our children to excel, we want the best of all worlds for them. Only this child, this Philip, is really something special! I worry about him when they drop him off at the corner. He's got two streets to cross, and so much traffic. Of course there's a light. But he's such a little fellow.

As soon as I'm out and around again I'm going to stop in at F.A.O. Schwarz and I'm going to buy the most lavish, expensive, magnificent toy they have in the place. Anna and Iris won't approve but for once I won't care, I want to buy something for a spoiled rich kid. Something I never could have dreamed of when I was his age. I don't know what, but I'll find something.

He couldn't fall asleep. Too much rest, that was the trouble. Maybe get up and read. Anna had had a book up here the other day. She'd said something about beautiful essays by some important guy, and he'd seen she wanted to talk about it, so he'd asked her to read him a page or two. And it had been rather pretty. For a moment he had seen what she meant.

Too bad he hadn't read anything, all his life. He'd always admired scholars, but you had to be born a scholar, not made. Yet those teachers Iris was always having over at her house, nice people all of them, so genteel and with so much knowledge, poor bastards! They couldn't even afford the ten dollars it took to buy one of the books they loved so much. What sense did that make? Still, it would be a good thing to have had both worlds. There was so little he knew. Living with Anna, he was always aware of it, although she never allowed him to talk that way about himself. That time they'd been in Mexico City and her relatives had taken them to see those tremendous ruins: what a feat of construction! Anna had known all about the builders. Aztecs, were they? She had read about their palaces and priests and what the Spaniards had done to them. Yes, Anna knew so much.

Was that the book she'd been reading the other day? It had had a red cover; she'd left it on the chair. He got up. Yes, a book of essays. He'd glanced at it after she'd left the room. There had been one on growing old which she would certainly not have let him see, would have hidden from him. But he remembered it, page forty-three. Your memory is still pretty good, what do you think, hey, Joseph? The arteries can't be too hard with a memory like that.

Here it was. "On Growing Old." His eyes scanned the page. ". . . taut strings loosen, knots untie; the fingers open and drop what they have been holding to so tightly. The shoulders lighten, freed of what they have been carrying. Go, let go; where the wind sweeps and the tide takes, let go."

43

Anna walked up Fifth Avenue in shafted light, from October gilt to shadow and back again. She was youthfully exhilarated and enjoying it.

A week ago she wouldn't have believed it possible that Joseph would take a vacation! They had just broken ground for a new apartment complex in south Jersey; his little round room was awash with papers and blueprints. But then the Malones had arrived home to visit their newest grandchild and, with their descriptions of the West's great spaces, had at last caught Joseph's fancy. He had agreed to go back with them.

She could have been a wanderer. The Painted Desert, the Petrified Forest, the Navajo reservations—she had wandered through all of them in her mind. This would be a journey to known, desired places. Perhaps Joseph could be persuaded, since they would have come so far anyway, to continue on to the coast?

Eleven o'clock. She was to meet Laura at Lincoln Center at twelve-thirty for lunch and the ballet. Anna had been in the city since nine, too early for Laura; young people liked to sleep late. She had finished her shopping: just walking shoes for herself, and no new clothes, since Mary Malone was not a fashion plate. One didn't feel with her the often tiring need of looking perfect. She'd stopped at the men's department and bought some sport shirts for Joseph. He really needed them, although he would argue that his old ones

523

were good enough. How he still resisted spending on himself! She must remember to take the price tags off these so he wouldn't see and make her return them.

Thank God, he was feeling so well lately. A sudden picture out of nowhere stood in the air before her: he was reading the real estate section of the Sunday *Times*. His hands were really beautiful for a man, long-fingered, the way a pianist's or a surgeon's are supposed to be. This trip might be a start. It would be marvelous to go to Europe again, and then to Israel. Sometimes he spoke of seeing those places Eric once wrote about. True, he spoke only vaguely, yet the thought must be in his head. Her own thoughts ran faster as she strode uptown.

There's another case of gold charms. I got a better buy on them this morning for Laura's birthday, to add to her bracelet. It's hard to know what to get for her. One can't always give books. She's certainly not a child, yet not a woman either. Try to remember what I was like at fourteen. But my life was so different, living at Uncle Meyer's among strangers. Still, I must have had some of her confusions, in addition to my private ones.

I wonder, I wonder about people. There's so much I don't know. If I'd been born here and had a chance to learn, I'd have liked to study psychology. That couple now, standing on the corner quarreling. She's about to cry. He's actually walking away. What are they doing to each other? And why? Those two old women walking ahead of me; they're at least as old as I am, even older. Withered, painted faces. Legs all knotted with veins. Dressed like young girls. Fancy, pretty shoes. A young girl's innocent dancing slipper. How absurd. How—sad.

Maybe everyone is scared, scared they'll never get what they want or, if they've got it, scared that somebody will come and take it away. (If nobody does, time will.) Yes, we're all afraid of things we don't talk about.

There's a dress in the window, clouds of pink. That would be for Laura a few years from now, and was for me years ago . . . that dress Joseph bought in Paris: was there ever anything as enchanting?

Lovely, lovely day. Growing warmer, the last of Indian summer. Walk westward through the park toward Lincoln Center. Laura's never seen *Swan Lake*. She'll love it. The time I first heard *Tristan*.

Soft air now, dust on the trees. Old men playing checkers on the benches. Children roller skating. Not in school? Of course, it's Saturday. I'm forgetful lately. I've been noticing that.

Out at Seventy-second Street on Central Park West. Overshot the mark. Oh well, walk back again. Here's the street. No harm going through. Just to see. The street is filled with dark children. Puerto Ricans playing ball. They played stickball on the lower East Side, the street always loud with cries, I remember. All kinds of cries. Here's the house: is this it? Yes, it is. So small! Tall and narrow, two windows wide. A rooming house now, probably, like all the others. People sitting on the stoop. Last sun of the year. The shades are torn. Water-green velvet hung in the 'parlor.' Between the windows was a low table where the tea service was laid at four o'clock. And above that, Paul's room with the riding boots, the Yale banner and all his wonderful books.

Am I the person I was then? I don't recognize myself at all. Still, as time moves, it wasn't that long ago that I came uptown from Ruth's house and entered this one.

Blot it out. What sense is there in thinking of what might have been? Or in wondering how Paul is now? No sense, and yet I wonder. I'm still not used to thinking I may never see him again. As if he were dead.

I'm not used to the thought of Ruth's being dead! Didn't know I'd miss her as much. She'd gotten tart and envious. But she was always *there* and you could trust her. "I'll take care of you," she said that first day when I stood with my bundle and shawl, knowing nothing. I trusted her then and I wasn't wrong.

Hers was a twisted road. Sitting there that night when Solly died, and everything else was gone, not Solly only, but everything. It would have been easier if she had never had the apartment where they lived for those few years with carpets and a silk shawl on the baby grand piano. On Washington Heights when we went there last summer after her funeral, the first floor had been turned into stores. She lived above a hand laundry and a bar. Was it as depressing when we lived there? No, it's changed. And certainly I've changed. Everything has.

Dan's dead too, in Mexico. I saw him only twice in fifty-five years. I wish I could have seen him just once more.

We're going downhill.

Laura ate the bacon omelet. Her long red hair, which, Iris reported with amusement, she pressed on an ironing board, fell over the plate. She pushed it back and looked up. "I'm starved," she said.

"It smells good."

"Bacon's delicious. You've truly never tasted it?"

"Never. I remember when I came to this country, the first time I saw bacon cooking I was disgusted."

"Because you'd been taught it wasn't to be eaten. Why don't you try some?"

"Sometimes I think I might. But then your grandfather—"

"You needn't tell him. Does one have to tell a husband everything? Does one?"

"I've always thought one should." God forgive me for the lie.

"Well, then, tell him. Shouldn't a woman be free enough to do something her husband doesn't approve of?"

"I suppose you're morally right."

Laura thought a moment. "But then," she said gently, "but then, it wouldn't be worth it to you, would it? To take a *stand* on something that upset him so—you'd only be sorry afterward, wouldn't you?"

Anna smiled. "You've said it for me, better than I could have."

A perceptive child. An instrument: I play a note and she makes harmony. More of a daughter in that way than Iris ever was, although I know Iris isn't unique. I've heard enough daughters talk, and mothers, too. How would I have been toward my mother, I wonder, if she had lived? I must be careful not to be too giving to Laura, not draw her away from Iris. It's too easy for a grandparent to do that.

"Daddy played all the music from *Swan Lake* last night and we talked about the plot. You know, it's the first ballet he ever saw. His parents took him to see Pavlova dance it in Vienna. We went *thoroughly* over the music and the story. *Thoroughly.* You know how Daddy is." She laughed. "When I was young, about eight, I used to think I would become a ballerina. I really thought all you had to do was want something and you could get it."

"But now you know better."

"Mostly. At least, I believe I do. Maybe I still am childish and don't see myself. Except that sometimes I already feel grown-up."

"I know. This morning, when I saw a pink dress in a window, I forgot I was an old woman."

Laura didn't make the absurd protest that people make: *Oh, you're not old. . . .* She said instead, "It must be awful to be old. Is it really awful?"

"If you think about it too much it can be. I try not to think about how little time is left."

Laura put her chin in her hands. They were waiting for dessert, Anna's coffee and Laura's pie with double ice cream. You never knew when you took the child out to eat whether she was in one of her starving periods or on an eating binge. This week she was on a binge.

"Tell me, Nana," she asked seriously now, "have you been, are you satisfied with your life?"

"Oh, my," Anna said, "oh, my, that's much too grave a question for this nice, bright Saturday! Besides, it's impossible to answer." The questions this girl asks!

"Try."

"I can't. If you mean, am I happy in this life that I have, I should answer, yes, very. I love you all. I have friends and do interesting things, some of them a little useful, I hope. And I have pleasures, like taking my granddaughter to the ballet. But if you ask whether I might have liked another life, Pavlova's, or perhaps to be a Madame Curie— Don't you see that's what I mean, that it's impossible to answer?"

"Sometimes I'm terribly sorry for people," Laura said, with a mouthful of ice cream. "My father, for instance. I'm often sorry for him."

"Why are you?"

"He must think a lot about that other family of his, Liesel and their little boy. But he never talks about them."

Anna was silent.

"I suppose he feels that Mother wouldn't like it."

"Why do you say that?" Anna asked, making a little shrug, as if to say, I'm quite casual about this, not particularly interested.

"I don't know. I just think she wouldn't."

I wonder, wonder what they know or half know, half remember. They were all so young. No harm done, thank heaven! And anyway, who ever said a child must sail in sunny waters every day of his life?

Not even natural. Still, one speculates about what's in their heads. Delightful children, all of them. Even the boys, if you can use the word about boys. And why not? Jimmy, of course, Mr. Unflappable . . . and Steve, moody, dark and bright as quicksilver; he's the one I find most appealing. Isn't that strange? Joseph can't understand it. Steve bothers him and I can see why. He bothers me. Yet there's something I want to reach out to, something very, very warm. Philip, the dividend when we hadn't expected any more. And this girl. God keep them all. Incongruous, blessing them here in this place with the clattering of voices and dishes. God keep their soft flesh unharmed and their hearts from grief. No, that's impossible . . . well, God keep them anyway.

"It's time to go in," Laura said. "Everybody's going."

"Yes, yes," Anna said, looking at her watch. They stood up and moved through the slow crowd in the lobby. People looked at them, Anna knew, at the tall redheads, the old one and the young one.

The chandeliers, flashing ice and diamonds, rose toward the ceiling. The great hall darkened. The overture began. When the curtains drew back at last upon Prince Siegfried's forest and the enchanting waltz, Anna heard beneath the music the sigh of Laura's pleasure.

Laura hummed. "It was marvelous, marvelous! Thanks so much! I loved it!"

The taxi stopped in traffic on a seedy street of dance halls, bars and dingy movies. *Girls, Girls,* the poster read. *Miss Dawn La Rue and Miss April La Follette. Fiery Passions, Burning Loves:* that was the movie advertisement. Anna hoped Laura might look the other way but naturally she was staring at the photographs. Not burning love at all, Anna thought, just cold sex, as mechanical as pumping pistons. Not that I'm the last word on that, God knows. But still, there's no feeling in all this, no caring, and it ought to be the most alive thing in the world, oughtn't it? Wonder what makes girls do this? What makes Miss Dawn LaRue do what she does? Or what makes anybody, for that matter? For some utterly unfathomable reason, she had a vision of Miss Mary Thorne, in shirtwaist and skirt, handing to Anna a copy of *Hiawatha.*

The taxi moved away toward Grand Central. It occurred to Anna that Laura might have a question about what she had just seen, or else that she, the responsible adult, ought to have something to say to the girl about it. A dirty business! It angered her that this dirt should be foisted on a mind like Laura's. Still, you couldn't keep a girl in the dream of *Swan Lake,* either. Really, she ought to say *something.* But what? I can talk to her about anything else, but when this sort of thing comes up, so do my barriers. As they always have, all my life.

On the East Side the scene changed to clean streets and middle-class shoppers going home. Small theatres discreetly advertised foreign films.

"Oh, did you see that, Nana? I saw it last month with Joannie. It was great."

"I saw it too. It was beautiful," Anna said.

"You know what I loved about it? It was so real. French pictures always are. I mean, the girl wasn't a fabulous beauty. She had a big nose and her hair got all messy when she went swimming, the way mine does. She had the most beautiful smile, though. And the boy did too, the way he looked at her. You remember when they were going along the street, carrying one of those long loaves of bread without any paper on it, and all of a sudden he stopped and turned her face up to his as if it were a flower?"

"I remember," Anna said, although she didn't.

"When the picture ended I was crying. Then the lights came on. I hate the way they come on suddenly and simply smash your mood. My nose was running and while I was fumbling for a Kleenex this woman going out beside me looked at me and giggled. I was so furious I said, "Why don't you mind your own business?" And she looked absolutely shocked. Then I was so ashamed of myself, I could have died. Couldn't you just *die* when you do something awful like that?"

Sometimes, Anna thought, when they were in the train, they don't talk at all. They won't 'communicate,' as Iris says. And sometimes everything spills out.

"I really have to make a fresh start in school this year and do better in math, even though I don't give a damn about it. When am I ever going to use a quadratic equation, for heaven's sake?"

"I'm sure I don't know. I don't even know what it is."

"There, you see what I mean? And you're just as well off without it. Anyway, that's one of my resolutions for the year. The other is to get rid of the flab about my waist. It's disgusting."

"I don't see any flab."

529

"You can't when I'm wearing a dress. But I got new dungarees last week, and after I'd worn them in the bathtub to shrink them they fit all right, but you could really see that my waistline's awful. I've got to do something about it. You've got a good figure for your age. I don't suppose you ever had to worry about it. What kind of perfume do you use?"

"Nothing in particular. Your grandfather's always giving me presents of it so I use what he brings."

"I use Calèche. It's really marvelous. Sexy, but also refined, if you know what I mean."

She could go on prattling for hours and I'd never get tired of listening to her.

". . . I've got this enormous new blowup of D. H. Lawrence in my room. It covers half the wall."

". . . pimple cream, it actually works, but I look as if I had small-pox when it's dabbed all over my face."

". . . loved every minute of it today, although of course you can't get the same feeling after Tchaikovsky that you get, say, after Handel, can you? I mean, it's just not the same language, is it?"

If one wanted to label this fraction of time, this segment of space, it would be *eastern seaboard suburban, upper middle-class.* Grandmother treating granddaughter to the Saturday matinee. An American phenomenon. And a lovely, lovely day.

The train slowed toward their station.

"You know, Nana, I'll remember today. I'll say to my children, the first time I saw *Swan Lake* I went with my grandmother. It was a beautiful warm afternoon and we rode home together on the train."

I needn't worry about her, Anna thought. Not this child. "We'll get a taxi," she said. "I'll drop you off and then go straight on. Your grandfather will most likely be home by now."

In the taxi she gathered her packages, feeling rich with the pleasure of giving things, the charms to be hidden away for Laura's birthday and the new shirts for Joseph.

Malone's car with the Arizona license plate was parked in the driveway. Joseph must have asked them to dinner. Would the roast be big enough? She dismissed the cab and was halfway to the front door when Malone opened it.

"Hi," she began, "what a nice surprise! I wasn't expecting—" and saw his face. "What is it? What's wrong?"

"Anna, take it easy. Joseph—his heart. He fell over in the office; just fell over at the desk. We called a doctor down the hall, but—"

"Oh, God," she said. "Where is he? What hospital? Take me, hurry—"

Malone held her shoulders. His tears were running. "Oh, Anna, Anna, no hospital. It's too late."

Iris sways. Her face is gray. "I'm all right, Theo," Anna says, for he is holding her arm. "Take Iris."

The chapel is full. Noon light pours through the stained-glass windows of which Joseph was so proud. It bobs on the floor of the aisle in dots of ruby and gold. How can I think of such things? Anna wonders. But I must think of them and of the faces, mustn't look at the coffin, mustn't think of him lying in it. Look in the second row; there's Pierce, our congressman; Burgess of the Provident Bank; What's-his-name from the National Council of Christians and Jews. Faces, faces. I must remember them. Joseph would remember every one and thank them afterward. There are all those people from the hospital's board of directors. That short man coming in, he's from the building trades union; Joseph always dealt decently with workingmen and they knew it. Faces, faces. Women from the temple sisterhood. Tom and Vita Wilmot. There's Celeste's friend, Rhoda. To think she would bother to come! And Mr. Mozetti, the gardener. The Malone boys and their wives. Ruth's daughters; how fat they've all grown! And Harry; he looks shabby-sad; strange, he's still driving a taxi and Solly was always so proud of his book-learning. Strange.

Must think, must think. The rabbi is taking my arm now. I'm fragile. They're afraid I'll fall apart. But I will not. Joseph would be ashamed of me in front of all these people. The rabbi is saying that he left a good name behind him; a most priceless treasure, it can be purchased only through the labors of a good life. He means what he says, the rabbi does. He's a kind man and he knows that, this time anyway, what he's saying is true. It isn't always, but then, he has to say something good of the dead, isn't that so?

Suppose they could hear; suppose they knew what was being said about them? *De mortuis nil nisi bonum.* Maury was amused that I could remember his Latin proverbs without knowing any Latin. But I always had a good memory and a good ear.

"He lives on in the hearts of those who loved him," the rabbi says. His voice is gentle and earnest. He looks at the widow, speaking to her. "He was devoted to his faith." Yes, yes; he was. "An inspiration to his grandchildren; he gave them a sense of their identity." All along the row the grandchildren sit with scared, upturned faces. Laura is crying softly. Will they remember what he gave them? Only time will tell, a lot of time.

The beautiful, familiar words ring their stern and regal music. "Fear God and keep His commandments, for this is the whole duty of man."

Music. "O God full of compassion, Eternal Spirit of the universe, grant perfect rest under the wings of Your Presence to Joseph who has entered eternity."

We go out and get into a long black car. It looks sinister. There is a motorcycle escort: Who arranged that and why? Joseph wouldn't like it. Even in death there are status and pride. Humble people have pathetic funerals, not like this one. Now we ride through the cemetery gates. There's the Kirsch family mausoleum; it's like those royal tombs we saw in Europe. Wealth and hierarchy, even in death. Joseph would never allow anything like that . . . "Just a slab," he told me once. I'll have it put down next year, and mine next to it . . . "Anna, wife of Joseph," it will say. What a crazy person I am to be having these thoughts while they help me out of the car, holding me up by the elbows. All that green cloth draped to hide the fact that it's only a hole in the ground. All these dead, acres and acres of them. Wouldn't it be strange if they knew we were standing here? *Knew*, as they lie in the dark under the flat mown grass, under the weight of the heavy earth on their egg-shell skulls and their helpless hands. Suppose they could hear and people were saying things about them; their keen ears could hear but they would be unable to defend themselves: *Yes, but I was right! You didn't understand, I tried, I only meant—*

De mortuis nil nisi bonum.

And is that what it was all about, Joseph, that we nurtured our children and loved them and lost them, that you did nothing but work all your life, even though you said it was a pleasure to you? What was it for? That we should walk away like this and leave you in the ground? Is this what it was all about?

There is a rustle. People rise and murmur the Kaddish: "*Yit-ga-dal ve-yit-ka-dash she-mei ra-ba—*"

Iris is sobbing when Theo leads them back to the car. Why am I not crying, too? Joseph would be proud that I'm not. Still, I ought to cry.

Someone whispers, "I thought he spoke beautifully." Someone: "She's holding up well . . . she always had dignity."

The sky goes wintry. Before we reach home the rain comes, a somber, gusty, spattering rain. Lights are on all over the house. Friends and neighbors have come with pink chrysanthemums, baskets of fruit and chocolate cakes.

"Come," Celeste says, "have a cup of tea, you've had nothing all day." She leads me to the dining room, and I allow myself to be led. In spite of everything the body cherishes its comforts: the tea, the fire, the windows tight against the rain. I let them put half a chicken sandwich on my plate.

Why don't I cry?

It was the hat that brought tears. After that long day it was the sight of Joseph's crumpled rain hat, forgotten on a chair in the upstairs hall. She went into their room, holding it to her cheek—his old hat that he would never wear again—and stood there weeping, swaying in the ancient way of mourning women.

Empty, empty.

She got undressed. The bed was turned down, such a wide bed to lie in alone. She had a quick flashing picture—from what storage space in her head?—of Joseph playing at the beach and Solly with him . . . they were throwing a ball . . . "Poor Solly . . . all of his young brightness quenched," Joseph had said once, not seeing himself.

Somebody pushed open the door. It was only the old dog, George the Second, who had slept with them ever since—since Eric went away. He raised his head, turning his mild eyes toward Anna, asking where Joseph was . . . and receiving no answer he settled on the mat at Joseph's side of the bed to wait.

I wasn't good enough for him. I said that yesterday, and Iris stroked my hands. She said, "Mama, that's not true. You made him happy. You know he was happy!"

Yes, he always told me he was. It must have been hundreds of times during all our years that he told me so. And still it's true; I wasn't good enough for him.

Oh, I tried, I tried. I wanted to, and I owed it to him.

That priest who, besides Paul, is the only other being on earth who knows what I know—I wonder whether he's still alive? We never even told each other our names.

Theo knocked. "I've brought you something. May I come in?" He had a glass of water and a pill in the palm of his hand.

"I never take tranquilizers, Theo." She hadn't meant it to sound stiff-necked or proud, but it came out that way.

"Just once, tonight. You've been a good girl and you deserve a little help."

"I want to face it with my own strength."

"I know you're strong, but you're also stubborn. Now, the doctor says, take it . . ."

"All right, all right. I thought you had gone home."

"We're sitting downstairs."

"Take Iris home . . . it's been so hard for her."

"I know. Now she'll really have to finish growing up, the whole way."

"You've known that, too?"

"Of course. She was her father's little girl."

"Yes. His little girl."

After a moment Theo said, "Laura's here, sleeping in the room across the hall."

"Oh, no, why?"

"Oh, yes. She'll come back tomorrow after school and sleep here for the next few nights."

"You shouldn't burden the child with me."

"Laura's not a child. And *she's* not to be her father's baby girl, Anna. Besides, she wants to stay."

I'm overwhelmed with your love and I can't speak.

"That's what families are for," Theo said firmly. "Now, sleep."

44

With pride and pleasure Jimmy observed Janet across his parents' Thanksgiving table. It had been a wonderful vacation so far, except that he'd missed sleeping with her as they did back on the campus. She was in a bedroom just down the hall from his, but he wouldn't enter her room while they were in his family's house. Was that hypocritical? But he just couldn't have. Anyway, he didn't want his parents to have the slightest reason to find fault with Janet.

She was laughing now, flinging back her dark, curly hair. She hated that hair. No matter how strenuously it was brushed, it always fell back into a shape of its own, a round crest above a round face. Her arms, breasts and hips were round. (She would have to watch her weight in only a few more years.) Even her blue eyes were round. In all that curving softness one would expect the eyes to be naïve or vague, but they were not. They slid up from under heavy lids with sharp awareness, keen as the brain inside the curly head.

It amused him to think that she had come with the highest references, being the granddaughter of some vaguely distant relative of Nana's, that old lady, Ruth, who used to visit his grandparents before she died.

"How did you two ever meet in that huge place?" Dad inquired now. "Well," Jimmy explained, "since we're both pre-med, naturally we have a lot of the same profs. And one day after zoology lab this guy Adam Harris gave me a message. You tell the rest, Janet. I never get the relationships straight."

535

"It's the craziest thing!" Janet began. "It seems that Dr. Harris' grandfather—he's dead now—was some sort of fourth cousin to my grandmother Levinson. And that year, at some other cousin's funeral, a whole group of relatives got talking and found out that Jimmy and I were at the same university. So they decided that Adam Harris ought to introduce us. All of this in a cemetery, imagine!"

"Adam Harris thought it was very funny," Jimmy added. "Incidentally, he's the best thing that's happened in college. A gifted research man who also likes to teach. A rare bird. And human, too. A regular guy."

"I'm told that our grandfathers, yours and mine, grew up together on the lower East Side. I never knew that; did you? Well, anyway," Adam Harris had said that day, "I've delivered the message and done my duty."

"What's she like?" Jimmy had wanted to know.

"Judge for yourself, my friend. I will tell you this, though, she's damn smart. One of the best in her section. And that's all I will tell you."

It hadn't occurred to Jimmy to ignore the request, for he had a strong sense of courtesy and social obligation. So he had intended simply to call, take the girl out once for coffee and then not call again.

Janet had laughed when he'd told her. "You know, I was supposed to look you up, too. My mother'd been bugging me about it. She still exchanges New Year's cards with your grandmother since mine died, and I think that's how she learned we were both out here. My mother's impressed with your family. She thinks they're important."

Only Janet said things like that, coming right straight out with them. At first her manner had startled Jimmy, but then he grew to like it. She didn't fumble or hint; you always knew what was on her mind.

"We're fairly poor," she had told him directly. "My dad owns a shoe store. Oh, I guess I shouldn't say 'poor,' exactly. What I mean is, I can't go to med school unless I put a lot of the money away for myself. I work every summer and I've got a scholarship for college now."

"You make me feel pampered," Jimmy had admitted. "A little ashamed."

"Why? I wish I didn't have to struggle so hard. I'd be glad to have my parents give me money or get married and have a man buy things for me."

"You know I live on Washington Heights around the corner from the apartment house you used to live in," Janet was saying now to Nana. "Your husband was so good to my grandmother," she went on. "She was always talking about him. When my Uncle Harry's grandson was sick he paid for everything. She used to say they don't make people like Joseph Friedman anymore."

Nana's eyes looked wet. Ever since Grandpa died her eyes had been quick to tear at the slightest few words.

She seemed to be very interested in Adam Harris. "You admire him so much?"

"Oh, yes," Janet said. "He'll talk to you and he'll listen. He's really great."

Nana shook her head. "Strange. When I think how different the grandfather was—"

"In what way, different?"

"Well, I never knew too much about him, only that he was once a boy in your Grandpa's neighborhood and ended as one of the biggest liquor distributors in the country."

"Funny background for Dr. Harris," Jimmy remarked. "He's such a simple person. Drives a Volkswagen and wears the same suit every day."

"Interesting," Nana said, and Jimmy wondered what she was holding back. With his grandmother, you never knew. Then she inquired of Steve, "Do you know him too, this Adam Harris?"

"I don't take sciences. But I know him a little, see him around with guys at lunch. He's a sentimentalist, a phony defender of the status quo, like most of the faculty. Full of crap."

"It seems to me," Dad said, "you don't have a good opinion of anyone at college, do you, Steve?"

"Actually, no. They're all tools of the system, hirelings paid to train the young for the corporate rat race. What's there to approve of?"

"I'm sorry you find it all so miserable."

"Oh, I don't really give a damn."

Their mother, Jimmy saw, glanced at their father as she passed the cranberry sauce, and had just opened her mouth to change the subject when Steve dropped his bomb.

537

"And the reason I don't give a damn is that I intend to quit at the end of the term."

"What's that you said?" Dad asked.

"I said I intend to quit. Drop out. Leave."

"Oh, really," Dad said politely. When he talked that way, there was fire under his ice. "Oh, really? And what do you plan to do with two years of college to your credit?"

Steve shrugged. "Before I do anything else I want to stop this war."

"They'll draft you, don't you know that?"

"Not me, they won't! I won't go."

"You'll go to jail?"

"Could be," Steve said carelessly. "Or Sweden or Canada, more likely."

Their grandmother gasped and started to say something, but Mother warned her with a look. Everybody in the family knew that Dad's rare anger was not to be interfered with. Steve liked to call it the Prussian in him, although it seemed to Jimmy that he had always heard that Austrians and Prussians despised each other.

"Let's leave the war out for a moment," Dad said carefully. He laid his fork down, although the dinner wasn't half over. "Or let us assume that the war has ended, which, please God, I hope it soon will be." Dad always said 'please God,' while denying that he believed in God. "Would you still feel that an education was unnecessary?"

"This kind is. They don't teach anything you can't pick up by yourself if you want to. And I don't want to. I don't intend to train myself to spend a lifetime making money."

"You don't approve of money?"

"Not the way it's exalted in this country. Not when it's put ahead of love."

"You're very glib, but your glibness doesn't stand up under analysis. Do you think, for instance, that because a man makes money for his family he doesn't love them?"

"That's not what he said, Theo!" Mother objected, defending Steve.

Her defense of his brother was as old as Jimmy's memory. Even years before, when Laura teased him and Steve hit her, although they both were scolded, the scolding voice was different for Steve.

Did their mother hear her own anxious plaint when she spoke to him, or about him?

Steve murmured now, "If you want to get personal, I'd say it would have been better if you had cut your practice in half and given us more time."

"Cut my practice in half! I couldn't possibly have kept you in this house if I'd done that! Would that have been love?" Now his father's voice rose and although it still wasn't loud, it vibrated and seemed to shake the table. "Here you sit with good white teeth, fifteen hundred dollars at the orthodontist's—oh, I know it's vulgar to mention money, but I'm not the one who brought it up, you are. Money is part of love and don't say it isn't. Every time I wrote out a check for something you needed or something that would give you pleasure, I felt your pleasure. A piece of my love went into every dollar. Yes, and a piece of my gratitude for the country that makes it possible for me to be generous with you. Can you understand that?"

"I don't share your jingoism," Steve said.

"Jingoism! Because I speak of gratitude to this country?" Dad pushed his chair back. "Listen to me! I owe everything I am to this country that took me in. Fools like you who were lucky enough to have been born here don't know how lucky you are. I kiss this ground. I say this before all of you. I'll go out on the sidewalk in front of this house, and I'll kiss the ground! You hear me? Yes, and your grandfather felt the same way, too."

"My grandfather was a money machine," Steve said. "I'll give you this much credit: at least you do have other interests, music and tennis and reading. But he did nothing at all with his life except make money. And you know that's true."

"Oh!" their grandmother cried. "Oh, I don't understand what's happening here, never at the dinner table—"

Jimmy glanced at Janet, but she was carefully looking at her plate.

And Mother said, "Steve, I'm saddened and ashamed that, no matter what you may think, you should have so little feeling, that you should—"

"Feeling!" Dad interrupted. "Feeling! Yes, these left-wingers weep their tears for every underdog and malcontent in the four corners of the earth, but for the family that breaks its back and heart for them, no tears at all. Nothing. So you'll drop out of college;

539

never mind asking your parents what *they* think or how they feel about your throwing your life down the drain—"

A mess.

Upstairs, later, Jimmy went into Steve's room. "What the hell ever got into you? Christ, I don't care whether you want to act like a damn fool! Drop out, do what you want, but will you tell me why you had to wreck the dinner?"

"You're sore because your girl was there."

"You're damn right I am! It could have waited for a private time. There was no real reason for doing it then."

"No real reason not to, either. I didn't make the uproar, remember! I just quietly said what I was going to do and it was Dad who hit the ceiling."

"Yes, and you had a pretty good idea he would. You used to do that when Grandpa was alive too, say things that you knew were like waving a red flag in front of a bull."

"Grandpa!" Steve said scornfully.

"You didn't like Grandpa?"

Steve shrugged, loosing from his shoulders, in a gesture of total rejection, all unwanted burdens. "It's like saying I don't like Tut Ank Amen. We hadn't communicated in years. Actually he was dead years before he died, only he didn't know it."

"Sometimes you're awfully hard, Steve."

"I'm not hard. I only want the same right that everybody else in the family has to express my opinions, which seem to shock them to their foundations. They never think how I'm shocked by theirs."

"That's not so. I've heard you and Dad talk about things, politics and social justice, lots of times."

"Okay. I'll admit Dad means well. He tries to be open-minded, now and then when he's in the mood to be. He'll listen and try—or he says he tries—to understand. But basically, you know as well as I do, he's as uptight as any Wall Streeter about getting ahead and having things, cars and new carpeting and crap like that. He doesn't really care about people in places like Harlem who have to worry about food instead of carpets. And Vietnam. Sure, he thinks it's wrong, but does he do anything about it, put himself on the line? God, it stinks, the whole business, you know what I mean? Sometimes when I hear them talking about insurance and tax-free bonds and all that garbage I could puke. I could honest-to-God puke!"

"So, okay, I get what you're driving at, but all the same, it is their house and I guess they can talk about what they want in it, can't they? Hell, I don't agree with them half the time but I don't go around making waves. Let them think what they want and I can think what I want, for Pete's sake."

"What kind of relationship is it where you can't speak your mind? That's why I hate to come home, if you must know. At least on the campus I can talk freely. It's like breathing fresh air again when I get back there."

"I thought you were going to quit!"

"Yeah, and a lot of my friends are, too. I don't mean the whole campus is free. Christ, no. I meant my crowd."

Steve's crowd. Earnest, gesticulating, wrathful. He supposed they were all ultra-bright like Steve, although he didn't really know any of them except by sight, orating on the campus, gathered under the trees or in club rooms. They were names he recognized from the *Clarion Call*, flying here and there, to congressional hearings, to vigils, parades and strikes, an uneasy flock in constant flow and motion. He wondered how they ever got any work done or passed exams. After all, you had to spend *some* time cracking the books . . . even if you were brilliant like Steve. It puzzled him.

"Where there's genuine love there's understanding, isn't there? Well, isn't there?" Steve demanded now.

"Steve, you see perfectly well what I mean but you pretend you don't. I can't win an argument with you. You've got a trick way of talking and twisting things against all common sense, against what any man in the street would simply *feel* was right."

"Yeah, *feel*. Think with your blood. Like a fascist," Steve said.

He had a slow, faintly mocking habit of shutting the lids down over his eyes, dismissing you. Sometimes when he did that Jimmy wanted to hit him. Then other times, when he looked at his brother, at the blue veins that stood out on the temples under the thin, fair skin, he felt a tenderness more moving than any he ever felt for their little brother, Philip.

"I didn't want to come home for Thanksgiving, anyway," Steve said. "You forced me to come."

"I'm sorry I did," Jimmy answered quietly. "Well, okay, then, I've had enough for tonight. I'm going to bed."

"The sleep of the just," Steve mocked.

His snapping sarcasm had always been infuriating. Yet it was only a cover-up. Jimmy remembered having thought that years ago. He remembered other things, too.

There was the time when Jimmy had broken his leg and Steve had got all his assignments, brought books from the library for his project, typed his papers, fed his gerbils and tended his plants for the experiment on Mendel's Law. He remembered how, when they were very young, Steve used to get so mad about being weaker than he; never able to win a fight, he would fall into such a frenzy of out-raged despair that the fight would end with Jimmy's being sorry for him.

My brother's debtor, and his keeper. It sounded so pompous. Yet there it was.

The next afternoon, to Jimmy's relief and his parents' concern, Steve left to attend a peace rally in California.

Nana invited Jimmy and Janet to lunch. He knew that she must have been very pleased with Janet or she wouldn't have invited them. They sat in the sunny, lofty dining room, the women chatting easily, as women always seemed able to do. With half his mind he heard them discussing Janet's family, college and skirt lengths. The other half of his mind was listening to different voices.

The dinners he had eaten at this long, polished table! It seemed as if all of them had been ceremonial, although there must have been many that were not. What he remembered, though, were song and prayer, flowers, candlelight and enormous quantities of sweet-and-sour food.

"We're boring you," his grandmother said suddenly.

"No, no. I was just letting my mind wander. I was thinking of how we used to be dressed up for holiday dinners in our best suits and how everyone was so punctilious."

"Did you hate it?" Janet asked curiously.

"Oh, when I was very young I was impressed. But from about fourteen on I used to be so bored. The meals took forever. I spent the time hiding my yawns."

"People are easily bored at fourteen," Nana observed. "But you know? It was beautiful, wasn't it?"

Yes, very beautiful. Now, having been away from home and child-hood, far enough away in space and time to see it as it had been, he could think of it as a way that he would like to live over, to repeat when his turn should come.

542

"I wonder whether Mother feels the loss?" he asked. "She was so attached to Grandpa. And Dad doesn't or won't keep the holidays like that in our house."

"I imagine she misses it," Nana said quietly. "I know I do."

The silence held faint sadness.

Then Nana asked surprisingly, "Are you a religious person, Janet?"

"Yes, the tradition means a great deal to me. It always has."

His grandmother smiled. Then she said briskly, "If we're finished, why don't you show Janet through the house? She said she wants to see it."

They started in the music room. The Bach Goldberg Variations lay open on the rack of the piano.

Jimmy remarked, "I guess Philip's been here."

"Yes, he was here for supper last Sunday and he played for me."

"Do you remember how no one dared even cough when Philip was playing?"

"I do."

"With all respect, I don't think it was because Grandpa understood or even liked music."

Nana laughed. "He didn't."

"It was only because it was Philip playing."

The fierceness of that love! Jimmy wondered whether the kid had minded being displayed like that. But he guessed not. Philip was at Julliard now and, after all, what use was it to play an instrument without an audience? Thank goodness, though, he wasn't a 'different' or outlandish boy. In fact, he was a great deal better adjusted than most people were, having a sociable, almost placid nature which didn't fit with the platitudes about musicians and temperament.

They climbed the stairs to Grandpa's round room. The humidor still held the scent of rich Havanas, although it had long been empty. Blueprints lay rolled in sheaves on the shelves. A handful of fresh marigolds stood in a little cup on the desk, Nana's flowers, the same as the ones that bordered the terrace and framed the lawn on this pearl-gray day of fading fall.

Janet stood at the window. "What a lovely house!" she cried softly.

"Yes," Jimmy said. "In some ways it seems more like my childhood's house than the one I actually lived in."

Below on the one-story wing of the library, Virginia creeper climbed thickly on the walls. It took a generation for creeper to grow like that. It was so strong now you would barely be able to pull it off if you should want to. The whole house was strong.

"I remember sleeping over once when I was very little," Jimmy said. "I was terribly afraid of thunder and on that night there was an awful storm. You knew I was afraid, Nana, and you came into my room where I was lying awake. But for the first time I wasn't afraid at all, and you were so surprised. I told you that I wasn't afraid in *this* house, that nothing bad could ever hurt or scare me in *this* house. Do you remember that?"

"I don't remember it and I'm glad you told me." Nana was pleased.

Presently they kissed her good-by and rode away.

"You have a wonderful family, Jimmy," Janet said. "I love your grandmother especially. She does seem strong, like her house. She gave me—oh, I don't know exactly—a feeling of permanence. I'm the sort of person who likes things to last, Jimmy."

"I am too," he said.

In his dormitory room, Jimmy lay sprawled on the bed in a jumble of blankets, clothes and textbooks, watching Janet get dressed. He imagined that his flesh still glowed, as though the air that touched her flesh was warmed by it and brought the warmth back across the room to him. He foresaw the bleakness of the room when she would have left it, and him alone in it, until next time. In the year he had known her she had become as near to him as his pulses or his breath.

"Don't go," he said.

"Jimmy, I have to. If I stay here I won't study and I've a chemistry quiz on Thursday."

"We'll both study. I won't bother you."

"You know we won't study."

He laughed. "All right. You win."

She drew on her jacket. "Okay. I'm going. You can come to my place Friday. My roommate's going home for the weekend."

"Okay. Wait, let me get something on and I'll walk you over."

He ran around the room picking up clothes, a shirt flung over the typewriter, pants on the floor.

544

"Janet?"

"What, dear?"

"I'm sorry there was a scene at my house. A helluva thing, on your first visit! And honestly, we never have big fights like that one, only small ones now and then when Steve starts them."

"I didn't mind. I only felt bad for all of you, especially for your grandmother. I liked her so much."

"Yeah. It's been hard for her since Grandpa died. She's really great, Janet. Sometimes she can sound like somebody in a fairy tale, as if she hadn't been paying attention to the world at all. Then other times you think, She's no fool, that lady. Did I tell you she's an opera buff?"

"Do you really think Steve will drop out of college?"

"Yeah, I really do. I really do. You know," he said slowly, "Steve's kind of a genius. I mean, he could be if he wanted to. He can do languages, math, everything. Did I tell you he got in the seven-nineties on his Boards? And he never has to study the way I do. I mean, I kill myself studying. With him I think it's a question of memory; he reads a page once and the whole thing sort of prints it-self on his mind. He's fantastic."

"What is he interested in?"

"Nothing. He used to be a history buff, but then he started saying it was all crap, all slanted, the books don't tell the truth. After that he got involved with philosophy, that's his major, but I don't know whether he cares about it that much or what he plans to do with it."

"Teach is about all, isn't it?"

"He doesn't want to teach. Anyhow, the new wrinkle is that the universities are all fake, irrelevant, feeding the war machine, you know that." He thought of something and laughed. "I remember one time he told my grandfather about the philosophy major and Grandpa asked him what he was going to do with it. With Grandpa everything had to be practical. So when Steve didn't answer my grandfather said, kind of making a joke, 'Well, you could open a store: Steve Stern, Philosophy.' Everybody laughed and Steve was so mad."

"Not much humor in him."

"Not much. Especially now. It's this damned Vietnam. Seems as if that's all some people talk about."

"It's important enough, Jimmy," Janet said very seriously.

"I know. But it doesn't have to *poison* a person's whole life, does it? I plan on going ahead and being a doctor, regardless. And so do you, don't you?"

"Of course I do."

They opened the door onto an altered world. Snow, which had been sifting finely all the day, had turned into floods of sleet. It rattled like gravel as it fell. The wind slammed the door shut behind them and bent the trees, sending a shower of icicles cracking to the ground.

"The world looks angry," Janet said.

Probably you had to be born here on these midwestern plains to live easily with such savage winds, such dark gray, frozen winters. The sleet stung their cheeks. With eyes pressed half-shut against it they stumbled and slid. Janet fell. Jimmy pulled her up and they struggled on to her door. Light from the building showed her curls salted with white.

"You look sweet with the snow on your hair," he said.

She put her hand up to his cheek. "I love you, Jimmy. You're so soft, I must remember never to take advantage of you."

"I'm not worried about that."

"Don't study too late."

Walking back against the wind and sleet, he lowered his face into the woolen scarf. He felt deeply tired. It wasn't a physical fatigue. He hadn't realized how tense he'd been about the weekend at home, either because Janet might not like his family, or, more probably, that they might not like her and that she would then turn against him. But everything had worked out well enough. Now he was feeling the aftermath of tension.

He'd been especially glad that Laura and Janet had gotten on together. He thought of his sister, now that she had passed through the audacious moods of adolescence, as a kind of 'norm.' She had such a friendly attitude toward life. If he had been asked to characterize her he would have used words like 'reasonable' or 'accepting.' He supposed he might be oversimplifying but anyway, that was how he saw her. She was rather like their father.

Steve was like their mother, he mused, although whenever Jimmy had remarked it he had been contradicted. And he could see why. On the surface no two people could have been less alike, his mother being so courteous, so anxious (one read anxiety in her

eyes, in the two vertical lines between the eyebrows), so concerned to please. She had always been afraid to lose her temper.
(Because she feared that her children wouldn't love her?) She had
let them get away, very often, with far too much. Yet her same
anxiety was in Steve.

Perhaps, Jimmy thought, I am more perceptive than I think,
and shall not lack for understanding when I become a doctor.

Dad had treated him and Janet with serious respect as he took
them on a tour of the hospital on the day before Thanksgiving.
Back at his office he had had lunch sent in and they had sat with
him for an hour or more talking earnestly about doctors and medicine. After a while the conversation had drifted unexpectedly into
family, perhaps because of having seen Grandpa's name on a
bronze plaque in the lobby of the hospital.

"I miss him," Dad had said. "We were two very different people
and we disagreed about many things. Yet there has never been a
man whom I respected more or loved more." He had gone on talking and recollecting. "His family was everything to him. And, you
know, he was right. There was a time in my life when I didn't want
to be vulnerable because of family, when I wanted to put all that
away. Yet without it there's nothing. Only the black hole of the
spirit."

Jimmy had seldom heard his father so solemn. He had sounded
like Grandpa. He hadn't even been sure he understood what his
father was talking about, but he sensed that Dad had honored
them by revealing a part of himself.

Yes, Jimmy thought now, I come from decent people.

He would have liked to ask his parents specifically about Janet,
but he didn't dare. They wouldn't approve of such an early marriage. They would say that at twenty he couldn't know his own
mind or make a decision that would be permanent. But if he was
mature enough to know that he wanted to be a doctor and so to
dispose of the rest of his life, then why was he not mature enough
to make a decision about Janet? They would think otherwise, however. Most parents would.

Anyway, there was the question of money. He couldn't ask them
to support a wife for him. Dad made a fine living, but there were
four to educate and he had to work very hard to keep up. No, it
was quite impossible.

He trudged up the stairs to his room. Steve. Janet. An enormous work load. And admission to medical school. But mostly Janet.

The room was cold without her, as he had known it would be. Five years! Who knew what five years might do with their commitment to each other? A couple of hours together here and there, now and then? It could take the very life out of their relationship.

Five years. It was like saying: a century. It was like saying: never. He felt deeply tired.

"All wars," Steve repeated. "Not only the Vietnam war. All wars are fought to benefit a few who get rich or richer. The rest just die in them for nothing." The veins were prominent again in his temples. They looked bruised. One of them twitched, Jimmy observed.

It was an incongruous group at the table in the coffee shop, haphazardly come together. Jimmy and Janet had come in out of the perilous cold for a hot drink, and had been joined by Adam Harris, alone. Shortly afterward, they had seen Steve shove in, just back from the peace rally in California. He must spend all his allowance on travel, Jimmy thought. His coat was torn. It lay now, flung on the floor with a pile of paperbacks: Kafka, Fanon, Sartre.

"All wars?" Adam Harris queried. "You remind me of the student groups who vowed they wouldn't fight in any war, even though Hitler was arming under their noses. What can you say to that?"

"It was basically the same thing. If the world's financial interests hadn't fostered Hitler there would have been no need for a war. Don't you see that war and the system are reverse sides of the same coin? That the one can't exist without the other?"

Exhausted, he put his head down on his folded arms for a moment. The others stared at him and shifted restlessly. He had been with them for half an hour and the tensions he had brought had now begun to affect them, too.

Suddenly he flung his head up. "I was thinking on the plane flying back: everybody on it was dead, do you know that? Ask them about Vietnam, the schools, Latin America—you think they give a shit? No, who's going to win the next Series, can we keep the blacks out of the union, should I get out of the market, that stewardess would be a great lay. That's all they were thinking."

Adam Harris said patiently, "You're not discovering anything new or startling. People are naturally and always concerned first with themselves. Social change is slow. But it comes. Eventually, when enough people want to get out of this war in Southeast Asia, we'll get out of it. That's the way democracy works."

"Democracy! Anybody who thinks this country is a democracy needs a shrink!"

Adam Harris smiled slightly. "Do you know of a better system anywhere?"

"No, that's just the point. We have to create one from the bottom up. And we start by stopping this war. That's the first step." Steve confronted Jimmy. "Why don't you do something about it instead of just sitting on the sidelines? We've a meeting Sunday afternoon in Loomis Hall. Why don't you come and hear what it's all about?"

"I know what it's all about. I read the papers."

"Danny Congreve's going to speak. Do you know he's one of the best minds, the clearest thinkers we have? If we could have men like him running the country—"

Jimmy had thought of Congreve as a rabble-rouser. Perhaps, though, that wasn't fair? Congreve was a kind of disciple of Harold Clifford, an erstwhile Quaker and theologist who was sweeping the country from coast to coast with his antiwar fervor.

But he shook his head and with effort met Steve's blazing look. "Sunday afternoons I hit the books. You forget, I have to keep my grades up."

"An evasion," Steve objected. "You could find some time if you wanted to."

"What I want most is to be a doctor. I might just be able to do some good for the world in *my* way."

"And incidentally pull in fifty thousand a year doing it. Or will you aim for a hundred."

"Listen, since you keep badgering me, I'll tell you one reason I don't want to get involved. I've been reading too much about overturned cars and broken bank windows. I know you personally don't go in for that sort of stuff—at least I hope you don't. But I want to stay away from it altogether and, if that's your idea of cowardice, make the most of it, Steve."

"What you're afraid of is your true self," Steve said.

Adam Harris interposed. "I happen to think the war is very

wrong. But I don't think that overturning people's cars and breaking people's windows is the answer. Violence never is."

Steve stood up and wriggled into his jacket. "Violence is what we're against, don't you understand? You talk about a car or a window as if they were significant, when they're only incidents. The real violence is the shedding of blood in war, the strife in industry, the raping of nature. What we want is to bring the world back to decent values, to do away with competition and envy and anger."

He picked up his books, an abrupt, surprising shyness returning to his manner. When he wasn't passionate about his beliefs, it flashed through Jimmy's mind, all conviction went out of him. This was how he usually looked.

"Well, so long," Steve murmured. "So long." And clutching the books, with shoulders bent, he scurried out into the dimming afternoon.

The others stood up and moved toward the door. "A passionate young man, your brother," Dr. Harris remarked.

"I know," Jimmy acknowledged. "I wish—" he hesitated. "I wish he would think a little more about himself, about where he's going. We worry about him at home."

"I don't think you need worry. A great deal of this talk is only talk. People like Congreve, for instance, they sound like young wolves who want to tear the world apart, but they don't and the world goes muddling on as always."

They stood a moment on the sidewalk. "Yes," Adam Harris said, "they'll find out about violence. It's the tragic mark of our time. But eventually they'll learn that it can't accomplish anything, not in the lives of nations or individuals. It always fails in the end. Well, it's been nice talking to you two about something other than advanced vertebrate zoology."

When he had left them Janet spoke for the first time in the last half hour.

"Amazing how such a brain can be so innocent, isn't it?"

"What do you mean, innocent?"

"Well, for Pete's sake, Jimmy, all power, whether of nations or families, is founded on violence! From the oil dynasties to the British Empire, to the country's private fortunes. His own family too, I'll wager, although he may not even know it. Everything! You name it. Everything."

550

"But he did say," Jimmy countered, "that they all fail in the end."

Janet stared at him. "Yes, of course they do! When they're beaten by an adversary that's more ambitious, clever and—more violent. Don't you see?"

"At this point I don't see anything. My head's spinning."

"I don't say it's right or good, but that's the way it is."

"I'm confused. This sort of argument isn't for me. I think I'll go back to the room and tackle vertebrate zoology. It's easier."

Somebody on the floor had been using his portable television and forgotten to turn it off. From the little box with the four-cornered eye there came a tumultuous, hysterical shrieking. One thought immediately of a street accident or some other sudden horror. But it was only a quiz show. The curtain had just been drawn back to display the prizes.

Hot-eyed fools, licking their lips over a refrigerator, an electric broom, a—a *gadget!* Disgusting! he thought, switching the television off. And then: not disgusting. Pathetic. But why pathetic? Because they needed these things and it was so hard to afford them? Or because they oughtn't to want them so badly in the first place? Which? I'm getting like Steve, Jimmy thought, addling my head with impossible questions that have no answers. He sat down in the armchair by the window, suddenly tired, with a kind of drained breathlessness.

Yet so much of what Steve preached was true. The trashing of America. Litter of broken metal, rims, cans, frames of unrecognizable defunct machines. Seen from train windows: a blasted, withered landscape. Elevated highways over heaps of rusting cars among dying weeds as tall as a man; greasy puddles and smell of burning rubber, where once in the duck-filled marshes gulls had risen from the plume grass and flapped toward the sea.

Gray. Mud gray, rain gray; gray of ashes, old tires and wet cardboard boxes. And over all a stinging, mucky smog.

The trashing of America.

And a similar trashing of that small country in Southeast Asia, except that there the ruin was overlaid with blood. He felt his brother's anger, the righteous rage that sparked and shook the body of his brother.

Yet there was something wrong with that anger, too. Jimmy strained. He was not used to thinking very hard about things unre-

lated to his own difficult, demanding goal. It had never been easy
to find fluent words for his thoughts. He had heard and observed
that science majors often were like that. Perhaps that was why patients complained that doctors didn't 'relate' to them?

Yet now he knew well enough what he felt. A strong apprehen-
sion swept through him, so that he shuddered and was chilled. He
understood that those who saw what Steve saw with such searing
conviction, and what he himself half saw, could be as blind, as narrow and as ruthless as that which they fought against. He saw that
their righteous anger could be dreadfully and easily perverted,
that in its fanatic drive it might only end by tearing the world
apart, like the wolves that Adam Harris had talked about.

Although it was close to ten o'clock and the icebound campus
was deserted, with all its windows shut tight against the cold,
within minutes lights flared, telephones rang, voices called, doors
banged and the quadrangles filled. Everyone raced toward the
science building where more lights blazed from bottom to top, so
that it looked like an ocean liner on a gala night.

The stunned crowd was quiet. Voices murmured in the circle of
flashing lamps, the ominous red warnings of police cars and ambulances.

"I didn't hear anything," Jimmy said, inquiring of someone
standing next to him, "did you hear anything?"

"I thought I heard a thud or a thump, but I didn't pay any attention to it until some guys came running down my floor yelling that
there'd been an explosion in the science building. I never
thought—"

Other voices rose and faded.

". . . the building was empty!"

". . . all the ambulances?"

". . . army contracts, of course."

". . . no right to use the campus for the war machine!"

". . . aren't we part of America?"

". . . you're full of shit!"

". . . geez, there was somebody in there!"

Silence, except for small shufflings and rustlings. Among those
standing near the door an aisle was cleared, so that men coming
carefully down the slippery steps with the stretcher could pass
through.

"My God, who is it?"

"Is he dead?"

"No, not dead." Moving, with an arm flung out from under the blanket that has been put over him. The blanket slips. It is picked up and laid back, but not before it can be seen that the lower half of the body is soaked with blood and wet, mangled cloth: a mush where two legs belong.

". . . it's Dr. Harris! Oh, Christ, it's Dr. Harris!"

". . . who's he?"

". . . biology. He musta been doing papers late in his office."

". . . geez!"

"He's not dead? I mean, the face all gray and—"

". . . that's shock. Not dead. Not yet, anyway."

". . . oh, my God!"

Jimmy's knees buckled. He sat down on the steps. There was no one he knew in visible range, just a lingering crowd of strangers, watching for something else to happen. The ambulance whined down the street with its red lights revolving.

". . . the watchman saw two guys here earlier tonight. He says he can identify them."

". . . bah, rumors! I don't put stock in that stuff."

". . . I heard they found a body in there. I heard it was Dan Congreve."

". . . you're out of your cotton-pickin' head!"

". . . no, he's right, I heard two cops talking and they said so."

". . . they found two of them. You'd think they wouldn't get caught by their own explosives. They don't know the other guy's name."

". . . one body, two bodies. Soon they'll be talking about twenty."

As soon as he could control his knees Jimmy got up. His chest hurt. He wondered whether you could have a heart attack at his age. He thought of what had been under the blanket and his stomach turned over. (You'll never be much of a doctor like this!) But yesterday in the coffee shop Adam Harris had said that violence was something young people only talked about, not meaning it. The last man in the world to suffer from it! Wouldn't hurt a fly, you had only to look at him to see that. Jesus! A liquid collected in his mouth, like vomit.

He had to see his brother. Could it possibly be? No, of course not. He quailed. Ought to be ashamed of myself for harboring—funny word, 'harboring'—such a thought. Still, there was another body. Unidentified. *Steve said: One of the best minds we have, come hear him.*

Could Steve possibly—? No, of course not. Steve was no doubt still in his room, dreaming over a book, too absorbed to have heard the excitement. Besides, his room faced the other way, toward the lake. You might not even be able to see or hear anything there. Anyway, he had more likely been asleep. It was after midnight. Yes, Steve would be asleep. He always went to bed with the chickens. It was one of his traits. Of course.

Steve wasn't in his room.

He knocked and kept knocking, disturbing the people across the hall.

"What do you want?" someone called out crossly.

"I'm looking for my brother, Steve Stern."

"He's not there. He went out a couple of hours ago." The door slammed.

Now breathing was really painful. He panicked again: could a person his age really have a heart attack? There being no place else to sit, he sat down on the floor. A couple of fellows coming back to their rooms looked at him curiously, thinking, no doubt, that he was drunk.

The grandfather clock downstairs, gift of the class of 1910, went *bong!* One bong. One o'clock. He leaned his head against the door and stretched his legs. They reached almost across the width of the corridor.

Once, sitting with his father, he had watched a television play about the Nazis and the resistance in France. They had caught some woman and tortured her by pulling her toenails out. She hadn't talked, had refused to talk, just kept repeating in such an awful voice, "I have nothing more to say! I have nothing more to say!" He remembered now that he had thought: "This is a helluva thing for Dad to be looking at, bringing everything back to him. I ought to turn it off but I don't dare. Why doesn't he just get up and walk out of the room?"

But his father had just sat there. When it was over he'd been silent for a few minutes and Jimmy had been silent too. Then his father had slammed his fist into the palm of his hand so loudly that

Jimmy had imagined a fist cracking into a defenseless jaw must sound like that. He had kept sitting there, not knowing how to get up or what to say, feeling his father's anguish.

Then his father had sighed and said, "It's a great storm wind shaking the earth. It began in my youth and then a lull came, but I think the storm will rage again. I feel the grit and dust coming in the cracks."

Jimmy shuddered. He looked at his watch. It was six o'clock. He must have fallen asleep, and he ached all over. Steve hadn't come back. What he must do became entirely clear to him. He must go to his room, wash and shave, then take the seven o'clock bus downtown and go to the police headquarters. Either that other, unidentified body was Steve's, or else Steve would have to be sought somewhere. Yes, it was entirely clear.

He flexed numb legs, went downstairs and began walking toward his room. Outside the science building, where a black hole, broken glass and tumbled bricks were now visible in the daylight, was a police car with four police on guard. He walked deliberately in their direction and stopped in front of them.

"Is it true that Danny Congreve was killed in here?"

One of the policemen looked at him coldly. "You that interested?"

"Yes. Dr. Harris was a friend of mine."

"Oh. Yeah, it was Congreve. And one other in the morgue. Up to now they haven't identified him, or what's left of him."

Tears wet Jimmy's eyes. He wiped them away with his glove, but not before the others had seen them.

One of the cops said, kindly now, "They say the prof will live. He'll lose a leg, though. Maybe both."

Jimmy stood there.

"Bastard!" another cop said. "And the damndest thing—they didn't even know how to do the job properly. Killed themselves with their own dynamite."

The police radio crackled in the car and they stopped to listen. Jimmy walked away.

Lose a leg. Maybe both. He was a tennis player, Adam Harris. A good one, too. The other's in the morgue, what's left of him.

Again the pain came, a hot tightening in his chest. *My brother. A brother of mine.* My parents' son. Christ almighty!

He pushed his way up the stairs. Better get a cup of coffee before going; that way he wouldn't feel so faint. Maybe. He came around the corner of the hall, toward his door.

Steve was standing there.

They stood there looking at each other.

"You thought I was mixed up in it," Steve said.

"My God! I didn't think you— But I didn't know."

Steve's face was white. No, not white, a dreadful color, like the underside of a frog.

"Come in," Jimmy said, unlocking the door. "Come in and sit. Where were you? I've been outside your room all night."

"I was undressed, studying, when I heard all the noise and running outside my room, so I got dressed and went over. And I saw, I saw your friend." He put his hands over his face. "Jimmy, I'm sorry. So awfully sorry."

"Where were you last night?"

"I couldn't stop vomiting. So I went to the infirmary and they kept me there. One of the nurses told me this morning about Danny Congreve. Jimmy, I never thought, I could have sworn, I would have trusted him, I did trust him. I feel totally incompetent, unworthy—"

A vast relief swept through Jimmy. "Don't, don't. You're not the first person to have misjudged—"

"*This* wasn't what I wanted, what I talked about!"

"I know that, Steve."

"I've gotta get away and think."

"About what? Think about what?"

"About everything. Myself, mostly. I've got to."

"Where will you go?"

"I don't know. Some empty place. A guy I know, quiet guy, not political, just into conservation and the earth, you know, he's got a place north of San Francisco, said I could come any time I want. So I guess that's what I'll do."

"When will you go?"

"Now. Tomorrow. I want to get out of here. I've been wanting to, you know that, only now it's for different reasons. You understand?"

"I think I do." He didn't, really. He could feel pity and sadness, but he couldn't understand. Perhaps he never would.

"You'll call the folks and tell them after I've gone? I don't want to go through the hassle of talking to them right now."

"I'll call them," Jimmy said gently.

They were an hour early. They stood in the lounge at the wall of windows, looking out upon arrivals and departures, baggage carts trundling back and forth, mechanics checking, pilots boarding with their little black bags en route to Paris; Portland, Oregon; and Kuala Lumpur.

"I'll miss Philip," Steve said.

"He'll miss you, too. We all will." Do all words that are torn out of you, yes, torn and ripped, do they always sound so banal? 'Miss you': what did it mean?

"Don't crap me up, Jimmy. It'll be a lot more peaceful in the family with me gone."

Why did he feel like crying? You'd think he was seeing his brother off to certain death, when all he was seeing were things past: Steve hunching up the hill after school (why was just this such a persistent memory?); Steve and he as kids in the bathtub together, and long before that, Laura with them; three in the bathtub until they got too old, he and Steve staring at Laura, laughing about her after they had been put to bed, wondering what it feels like not to have a penis; Steve casually offering to go over his math with him, knowing he was stuck and ashamed to ask for help; Steve in the hospital with pneumonia and his mother crying in the bedroom, pretending she wasn't.

"They tried to be impartial but they always loved you more, Jimmy."

"Not more. Just differently. Because we're different, aren't we?"

Steve didn't answer. A crowd of tourists came through when their flight was called. Bound for Hawaii, with tour signs pinned on their shoulders, they were middle-aged and raucous, wearing Hawaiian print shirts under their overcoats; the men were bald or balding; the women were freshly curled and blue-rinsed. They clamored out of sight with their cameras, bags and merriment.

"I feel so sorry for people," Steve said suddenly. "For their struggles and their sicknesses, and all knowing they're going to die. I feel their pains so badly sometimes. Yet I don't like them," he mused, almost as if Jimmy weren't there. "I don't really like

557

them, do you understand what I mean? With their transistor radios and their guffawing. They're such small-minded buffoons, most of them. I don't have anything to say to them."

It seemed to Jimmy that if you tried, you could surely relate to anybody, even to a bald old guy in a Hawaiian shirt. He was human after all, like yourself, wasn't he? But probably that was too simplistic. If it were that easy Steve wouldn't be what he was.

"How's Dr. Harris? Have you heard anything?" Steve asked.

"He'll live. One leg's off at the hip, the other at the knee."

"Christ," Steve whispered. He bit his lip. "He was a gentle, decent man, Jimmy."

"Yes."

"I don't know how I can ever get over it."

"But you weren't involved! It had nothing to do with you."

"On the periphery I was, and it did."

"You didn't know what those people were going to do!"

"But I should have known, that's the point. You see what I mean about myself? I don't understand people. They never say what they mean or mean what they say."

"Do you feel that way about me?"

"No, it's funny, you're probably the only one I can read clearly."

"I must be pretty empty, then!"

"Don't joke. I know you're trying to make the moment easier. I think if I get away, just get out where it's warm enough to be out-doors all year and plant things, work in the earth, use my hands, I think maybe that will help. Maybe I'll straighten out in my mind what I want to do."

"Yes, yes, it ought to be a good thing," Jimmy said awkwardly.

"The land needs healing, too," Steve said. "Maybe I can help heal it?"

The question, rhetorical, hung in the air.

Mother said once of Steve that there are people to whom living comes hard. They see the world as it ought—or so they think—it ought to be. But they are never at home in it as it is, for what reason neither they nor anyone else can say. Well, that was a neat enough summing up. But what was to be done about it?

The flight to San Francisco was called and Steve picked up his bag.

"Well, Jimmy?"

Jimmy put his arms out. They hugged each other. Steve felt so light, so light and frail in his arms. Then Steve turned and walked abruptly away. It seemed to Jimmy that, of all the crowd pushing toward the plane, Steve was the only one traveling alone, although that was probably not so. He only looked that way, hurrying with his rapid walk, his shoulders forward and, although Jimmy could not see his face, the expression of anxiety that he so often wore.

The loaded plane slid down the field to the takeoff point, where it went out of sight behind a wing of the terminal building. Jimmy watched until it came in sight again, taxiing to the far end of the field where it waited for takeoff. Even from this distance he imagined he could see it trembling, an insect with two rows of seats in its thorax, and a roaring heart too big for its skin. He thought he could even hear its mighty whir as, gathering all its strength, it tensed itself and leaped, rose into the lurid air and headed west.

Back in his room he waited for Janet. The hour moved so slowly. He ought to be using the time. The pile of books, the assignment notebook on the desk, were urging him to use it. But a lethargy had come over him, lying on him like heavy, pressing hands.

He ought to call his parents. They would take the news with an assumption of calm, not wanting him, Jimmy, to know the force of the blow. (Would they always, all their lives, shield and protect him, or would a time come when it would be their children who would shield them?) They would go into the dining room at the next dinner hour and tell Laura and Philip, keeping their manner light, that Steve had gone but would surely be back, that while they thought it was a grave mistake, people had to make their own mistakes and were sometimes the better for having learned from them. (That would be Mother talking.)

Afterward, upstairs in their bedroom, she would cry, and come to breakfast the next morning with slightly swollen eyes and claim a head cold. (Was this a harbinger of years to come that, already while they were still only in late middle age, not really old at all, already he could feel this way for them? And feel the end that was inevitable? A tooth parting from its socket, a wrenching of bone out of bone, that's how it would be.)

The telephone rang. He got up to answer it, hoping it wasn't his parents, because he hadn't yet framed what he was going to say.

559

It was his grandmother. She had never telephoned him at college and a fear of some disaster shot through him.

"It's all right, everything's all right," she said, as though she could read his fear. "Except that we've heard what happened on your campus."

"Yes. It was awful." Inadequate word, so far from the unspeakable truth.

"Has Steve gone yet?"

"Well, yes. As a matter of fact, I just came back from the airport. What made you ask, Nana?"

"I just had a feeling. I felt he might go in a hurry because of all this."

"That's just how it happened."

"You haven't told your parents yet?"

"No. I'll do it tomorrow. I sort of wanted to get myself together first."

"I know. I won't say anything. Besides, that's not why I called. I wanted to talk about you."

"About me?"

"About you and Janet. You know, Jimmy, she's a marvelous girl."

"You think so?" Jubilance in his voice, and a little cracking sob. Exhausted. Too much of everything, this whole long week.

"Yes, I do. When are you going to marry her?"

Jubilance faded. "We've another year of college and four years of medical school, Nana."

"Five years are too long to wait. It's waste and a sin to put off living while you're young and when you have the capacity to live. So many people haven't got it."

He threw his free hand helplessly into the air. "What can we do?"

"You can let me give you the money to marry her."

Years before she had come into his room during a thunderstorm, sensing his fear. Now again, across more than a thousand miles, she had sensed his need. Tears burned and he blinked them back, as though she were able to see them.

"It's too much to take from you," he said quietly.

"I'm the best judge of that, don't you think?"

His parents wouldn't like it. They liked—his father especially liked—to be self-sufficient. They wouldn't even let him take it from Nana, he was sure. They were always saying she did too much as it was. And they were right.

Hope sank.

"Jimmy? Are you there? Well, what do you say?"

He thought of something. "Would you, do you suppose we could borrow it from you? We could start to pay you back as soon as we go into our internships." Hope rose. "Interns get pretty good pay. Would you consider that?"

"Listen, I called you, didn't I? I want you to get married. I want to give, I mean lend you, enough so you'll be able to."

"With interest, it would have to be," he said proudly.

"Of course, with interest, what else? A business deal is a business deal. Right?"

She was playing a game, humoring his pride. He was quite aware of what she was doing, and yet this was the only way he would have it.

"How much interest?" he asked.

"Well, five and a half, six percent. The same as I get from tax exempts."

"The ordinary rate's much higher."

"I know. But a grandmother and a grandson, after all! I don't want to get rich on you. So, five and a half, all right? And you figure out what you'll need for light housekeeping, two rooms and your monthly expenses, above your allowances. You do that and mail it to me this week. Hear?"

"I hear. Nana, Janet's coming any minute and when I tell her, she won't believe it! I'm so grateful, I can't start to tell you, I—"

"Then don't. Listen, this call's getting expensive. My telephone bill is a disgrace this month. Write me a letter, Jimmy." The receiver clicked.

He stood there wiping his wet eyes and shaking his head. A dollar more on the telephone bill, and thousands to support them for the next five years!

There was such a great churning, such a twisting in his knotted chest. Steve, Adam Harris, Nana and Janet, all of life past and to come, churning and twisting. He wished he could sit down and weep with it as a woman might, without shame.

Before the knock came he knew by the footsteps in the hall that it was Janet.

"I'm so sorry," she cried. "Oh, I'm so sorry about Steve!"

Through all the thicknesses of cloth, through her quilted jacket, he felt heartbeats. At least, he felt his own. Wave after wave of comfort rolled over him, just standing there like that. The knot in his chest untwisted itself in a wash of sedative and healing warmth. He held to her as though she were a tower, and he almost a foot taller than she!

It came to his mind that he could give her the news now, but he didn't want to speak just yet. He unbuttoned her jacket and then her blouse, loosened her skirt and led her willingly to the bed.

He thought he heard her whisper into his shoulder, "Don't worry, don't be sad about anything, not about your brother, not about anything, I'm here, I'll always be here." And then he heard nothing, saw nothing, just sank into a bliss like summer night, as warm and throbbing, and lay there in that night until at last he raised his head into what might have been the dawn of morning, into a gold so luminous that it flickered into silver and a silence so vibrant that it trembled into music.

45

W ill you please make iced tea?" Anna asked, coming into the kitchen. "And bring out the walnut cake? I'm having a guest this afternoon."

Celeste turned from the stove. "My, that's a nice dress! I was saying to Miss Laura just last week, your grandmother looks like herself again."

During these few years since Joseph's death she hadn't paid much attention to appearances. At the beginning she had worn mourning for a year, although her friends had insisted that people didn't anymore, and that Joseph wouldn't have wanted her to. But she had known better. He, who had cared so much about old conventions, would have wanted her to.

Now she adjusted the dress where her narrow gold bracelet had caught in the sleeve. It was fine, cream-colored linen, a dress for summer, that brief, beloved season, and she took pleasure in it.

"The gentleman and I will have our tea outside," she added. "It's much too nice to be indoors."

"Gentleman!" Celeste repeated. "Gentleman!"

Anna smiled, "Yes, an old friend," and went out, leaving Celeste to wonder.

She had not long to wait. The car paused at the entrance to the drive—he would be looking for the number to make certain of the house—then started up, crackling over the gravel, and came to a stop not far from where Anna stood. It was a small foreign sports car, a young man's car. The door slammed and Paul Werner came up the steps.

Anna didn't move, forgetting to offer him her hand. He stood there, looking at her.

"You don't change at all," he said.

"You haven't that much, either."

He had gone gray, but his hair, still thick and smooth, shone silver against tanned skin. The eyes—the family eyes—were brilliant, like the young eyes of a child.

Suddenly Anna felt a dreadful awkwardness. What had she done? Why ever had she allowed him to come here? Leading him to the terrace, she murmured, "Sun or shade?" and when he had chosen shade, sat down and could think of nothing more to say.

But Paul spoke easily. "What a lovely place! It suits you. Old house, old trees, and so quiet."

"Yes, we've been very happy here."

"I'm glad you answered my note. I was afraid you might not."

"Why shouldn't I have? There's no reason anymore why I shouldn't."

"I was sorry to learn of Joseph's death. He was a fine man."

"Yes." 'Fine man.' A banal expression, gone meaningless through thoughtless overuse. All dead men became fine men. Yet in Paul's mouth, at this moment, the words had impact, the flavor of truth. Yes, he had been, Joseph had.

"You knew that I also lost my wife?" Paul asked.

"No! I'm sorry. When?"

"Almost three years ago."

"As long as that! I'm sorry," Anna repeated.

"Yes. Well." He crossed his legs, his foot swaying into a path of sunlight. His shoe was new and polished. She remembered—such an absurd thing to remember—that he had always worn fine shoes and had narrow feet.

She stood up. "I'll just remind Celeste. You'd like iced tea? Or something else?"

"Tea will be fine, thank you."

She was grateful, returning with the tray, for the small fuss of the tea ritual, serving the lemon and sugar, slicing the cake. It gave one something to talk about.

"A long time, Anna."

She looked up. Paul was smiling at her, and she smiled back.

"For people who—knew each other rather well, we're both pretty tongue-tied," he said.

She shook her head wonderingly. "Where does one begin?"

"Suppose we begin with Iris. How is she?"

"She's a middle-aged woman, Paul. That's hard to believe, isn't it?"

"Our two lives are hard to believe. But go on."

"She's grown so strong and competent! And a great help to me! Joseph left a good deal of property, and Iris is the only one of us who seems to know how to talk to lawyers and accountants. She's got a marvelous head for business. I think she surprises herself. Goodness knows, she doesn't get it from me!"

Paul smiled again, without comment.

"And the children are grown. Jimmy is going to be a doctor and—"

He interrupted. "The husband? It's still a good marriage?"

Anna nodded. She could have told him volumes, couldn't she? But the thought of putting into words the myriad complexities of all those lives was exhausting. There wasn't enough time and anyway, the effort would be futile. It wasn't possible to make them real to him: Iris, Theo, Steve and all the rest. People he didn't know at all.

"Nothing to tell me?"

She threw up her hands.

"I understand I'm asking you to give flesh and life to phantoms. To sum up years in a few minutes."

"I know you would like to see them, Paul. I know that."

"And I know I never can. Unless—" he stopped.

"Would you like to see some pictures, at least? I've just fixed up an album of new ones. I'll bring it out," Anna offered.

He bent over the album. He had a graceful back, his body unthickened and unslowed by age. He would live to be very old, quite likely, remaining supple to the end. She had a flash of memory: the day she had first seen him, still almost a boy, dashing up the steps of his house, with arms full of gifts from abroad.

"The girl looks like you, Anna. She's lovely."

"She's a lovely person, Laura. Kind and sensitive and gay."

"Fine-looking boys, too. Who's the young one?"

"That's our Philip." (Joseph's little genius, she thought wistfully. Oh, he's good, but he's not that good!) "I'd forgotten, he wasn't even born when I saw you last." The words rang mournfully. She wanted to defy the mournfulness. "Iris has a happy household," she said. "All growing up well." Why mention Steve's crisis or the worries over Jimmy's acceptance at medical school or the worries about Laura's boy friends? These were all normal nowadays, anyhow, more's the pity.

"It seems like madness when I realize that these are all partly my people," Paul said.

"I know." She felt a darting pain in her chest. Or had she only imagined it? They said one could. Psychosomatic.

He put the album aside. It occurred to Anna that it was rude to keep him sitting outdoors. "Would you like to see the house?" she asked.

He nodded and they went into the coolness, through the dining room where Joseph in his dark suit looked soberly from the wall, and finally into Anna's favorite sitting room at the back of the house. Here the light was caught and held in every season. It was the room where she lived now; magazines lay on the tables, and a ski sweater that she was knitting for Laura lay on the white and yellow sofa.

"This room looks familiar," Paul said.

She didn't understand. "Familiar?"

"You don't remember? My mother's sitting room was always yellow and white. They were her favorite colors," he said quietly.

That room! Oh, yes! She felt a prickling flush from her neck to her forehead. She had forgotten.

Paul was examining the watercolors that covered one wall. "These are very fine. Did you select them yourself?"

"Yes, years ago. Joseph always left things like that to me. He wasn't interested in art."

"Very good taste, Anna. You could get triple what you paid for them. Not, I suppose, that you care about that."

"No, I bought them because they make me feel contented. That's the only reason."

They were simple works, spare of line: pond lilies and water weeds; a long vertical painting of a dead tree raising its arms into a thunderous sky; a small square picture of lichen on a wet, black rock.

"Charming," Paul said. He walked to the window again and stood looking out at the shimmering afternoon, just stood silently looking.

When she followed his gaze she saw only the tea things on the garden table and the tops of the phlox, their towered flowerets showing mauve and cerise above the wall. A breath of their pungent fragrance came through the open window.

Anna sat down and waited. How strange it was that he should be standing here in her house! How briefly he had entered her life, only a few weeks' worth of hours at most, if you were to add them all together! And he had done as much to change her life as anyone could. She recalled now what had not crossed her mind in years, for she had buried the memory, locked it away in a top drawer and hidden the key: those nights in his parents' house, so long ago, and her own dry sobbing, the swallowed tears, the fist in the mouth. Youth, its pains more piercing than any of the deeper griefs that come later!

"You've had some good in life, when all's said and done." Paul spoke into the stillness. "In spite of the trouble I gave you, haven't you, Anna?"

"It wasn't only trouble," she said gently.

"Wasn't it, Anna?"

"There were moments of great, great joy."

"Moments!" he exclaimed. "Moments! Out of a lifetime! That's all I was able to give you."

"Are you forgetting? You gave me my daughter as well."

"And how are things between you?"

"She is a real daughter to me. I couldn't want more."

"I'm glad."

He sat down facing her. She began to feel tense, and, picking up her knitting, twisted the yarn mechanically around the needle.

"I'm glad I could do something besides make life hard for you, Anna."

"I never thought that. But you know, I have just thought of something else."

"What is it?"

"I've never had a chance to tell you and thank you. After that time at the opera, when Joseph was so terribly angry and I told you I couldn't see or hear from you again, you never betrayed my trust, or subjected me to the smallest risk. And you could have. Another man might have."

Paul looked at her steadily. "I would have cut my right arm off first. You know that, Anna."

She put her hand to her cheek. "Oh, God!" she cried.

There was a silence. After a moment he spoke again.

"So that's how it's been for us. I wish it had been otherwise."

A locust rattled like a rivet and cut itself off in mid-rattle. From the tall wild grass beyond the lawn came the steady chirp of grasshoppers. Sounds of summer past the halfway mark: full bloom of summer moving toward its close, while late roses curled at the edges, scorched in the heat.

"The sad end of summer," Paul said as if he had been reading Anna's mind. "When the locusts make all that noise you can be sure it's almost over."

"Until next year," she said.

"You always were an optimist, weren't you. You find the cup half full."

"And you find it half empty."

"Often I do."

She smiled at him. "Then you must rush to fill it, mustn't you?"

"As a matter of fact, that's what I plan to do. I came to tell you about it. I'm going to go abroad to live."

"Abroad? For good?"

"Yes. I've been, as I needn't tell you, the most loyal American. Yet a part of me has always been in love with antiquity. I have a longing for one of those old villages in southern France where the ruins go back to the Greeks. Or else perhaps someplace in Italy. The lake country—Lugano, Como. Have you been there?"

"No, I missed those."

"Ah, you'd love Lugano, Anna. It's not tropical, but golden warm, with great, great peace. Yes, I'd like to buy a place there. Would you come with me? Would you?"

"Why," she said, astonished. "I really—"

"I know I've dropped a bombshell. And it's late, I know that too. But that's all the more reason why one ought to salvage something."

Why was it that the distant past was so much clearer than things which had happened only a few years ago? She was able now to feel herself, yes, actually to feel herself, back in the posture of the adoring greenhorn girl when he, a young god descended, stood so high above her. Yet here he sat, supplicating, and she could have wept for him, wept for them both.

"It could be very lovely for us to be married, Anna, even now."

Lugano. Stony, narrow streets and blossoming trees. The two of them walking the streets, under the trees. A table on a terrace in the sun and a bottle of wine and the two of them. A room in an old house, with the night breeze coming through the windows as they fell asleep together and the morning breeze flowing when they awoke together. She couldn't speak for longing and delight.

And yet she already knew the only possible answer.

"You know," Paul said, "that something sprang to life between you and me at the very beginning. And it's still alive. It's lived through every kind of disappointment and mistake, through time and distance. Nothing's killed it. Can't we give it a chance to flourish at last? Can't we let it go free?"

"If we were alone in the world—" she began. "But we never are. There are always others."

"Tell me what you mean."

She met his anxious eyes and spoke with utmost tenderness. "There are those who came before and are gone. There are those who came after. It's just not possible. Not possible."

"But why?"

"Because this is Joseph's family, Paul. Don't you see?"

He shook his head. "No, Anna. No."

She rose and came to stand before him, putting her hands on his shoulders. "Look at me. Listen, my dear, my very dear. Can you imagine yourself at Theo's and Iris' table, facing them and me and their children? Can you see how I could possibly bring you into this family, in which your daughter doesn't know she is your daughter and your grandchildren don't know who you are?"

He didn't answer.

"Iris has always had vague, uneasy thoughts about you and me, I know she has. And if they were to be sharply awakened again—can you imagine that?"

Still, he didn't answer.

"It would be madness. Don't you know that it would be? And that I couldn't bear it?"

"You couldn't bear it," he repeated, very low.

"And you couldn't, either."

She broke away and walked to the end of the room. Tears came and, with her back to him, she rubbed them roughly away on her arm.

I mustn't touch him again, mustn't let him touch me.

"Again the family," Paul said. "Always the family, coming ahead of everything else."

"But you do understand why, don't you?"

"Yes. Still, if I could change your mind, I would. And to hell with them all."

"You don't mean that."

"No, of course I don't." And then, abruptly, he said, "You know, I envy Joseph."

"Envy him? He's dead!"

"Yes, but while he lived he—lived."

The mantel clock chimed in the next room, marking the hour— that indifferent, cheerful little clock which his parents had given—as it marked all the hours, whether of pleasure or pain, of coming or going. All the same, no matter.

"Is this truly final, Anna?" Paul asked.

She turned to look at him. This was the last time, really the last. Oh, the eyes, the marvelous blue eyes, the laughter, the strength, the gentleness; the wonderful mouth, the hands—

"Is this your final answer?"

"Paul, Paul—it has to be."

No tears, Anna. You've said good-by to people you love so many times and in so many ways, all your life long. This is another good-by. That's all it is. No tears, Anna.

"Well, then. I shan't see you again. I shall be in Europe before the end of the year."

"I'll think of you. I'll always think of you."

She gave him her hand and he held it for a long moment between both of his own. Then he dropped it.

"No, don't see me out. Good-by, Anna," and he left through the tall door to the terrace, stepped over the low wall onto the grass and out of sight.

The engine started up; the gravel spurted. When she knew he was gone, she went out to the terrace. The glass from which he had drunk was on the table; his fork lay on the plate. She looked at the chair where he had sat.

All, all a mystery. Our contradictory loves and loyalties. What we want to do. What we ought to do.

The clock chimed through the open window, chimed the half hour and the hour. Shadows laid long blue-gray streamers on the lawn and the sun had gone far west before Anna finally stood up again and went back into the house.

46

S ome call it the Sea of Galilee. The Israelis call it Kinneret,
the harp-shaped lake. The hotel is crowded with people come from
all over the world to see it: Americans; Japanese with their cameras,
two or three apiece slung over their shoulders; a party of French
nuns whom Anna and Laura have encountered three or four times
by now, from Eilat northward through Jerusalem.

Laura is already asleep. Light comes through the windows; light
of the moon or stars? Anna gets up to look out where the lake lies
below and trees droop like dark blue fountains. There is a diamond
glitter on the water, the scattered radiance of phosphorescence. She
thinks she hears the splash of fish.

Sleep comes quickly to her but so lightly that it doesn't last. She
remembers how Joseph used to complain about that and about early
waking. For a long time she lies now, hearing Laura's soft breathing
from the other bed, thinking of the morning. As soon as she falls
asleep again she dreams.

Some are old, troubling dreams. There is the dream in which two
people are one and one is two: Maury and Eric are each other.
There is the dream in which Joseph comes driving up in his car, and
she runs to him with impulsive joy, but he turns his head coldly
away. He will not speak to her; she knows it is because she has
wounded him and there can be no balm for the wound.

She dreams a new dream about Laura and Robby McAllister. He
is a nice boy, intelligent and friendly, with freckles and thick blond

571

eyelashes. Laura has been living with him in college. He is of the wrong religion. Besides, he won't marry her, anyway. Men don't marry women who are had so easily. Or is that no longer true? Life has been changing so fast that she is often not quite sure whether a thing is still true or not.

She stirs and wakes again.

And if he should want her, his parents won't. They will surely reject her. Fear dries Anna's mouth. In the first morning light she sees Laura's shirt and jeans on the chair: childish clothing for a child. Careless, foolish little thing!

Iris knows about it. "Does your mother know?" she asked Laura. "Oh, yes, she knows, she's a little afraid I'll be hurt. She hopes I know what I'm doing." Is that all? Nothing about right and wrong, nothing at all of the truths we've been living with, or trying to live with, for all these thousands of years? What can be the matter with Iris? What kind of mother is she, anyway?

I sound like Joseph.

Laura said in Paris, "Mother told me not to tell you, that you'd be shocked."

"Then why have you told me?"

"I like to be honest about everything."

Honest about everything! The byword of this generation. It doesn't matter what you do as long as you come out in the open with it.

"Does your father know?" Anna asked her.

"No, he'd be too upset. He believes in the double standard, you see. It's natural for men, but nice girls mustn't."

"I quite agree with him."

"Nana, I don't *understand* you! Why? What's the difference between men and women. I mean—"

"Women get pregnant," Anna said scornfully. "That's the difference."

"Not these days, they don't."

Can you believe it? Can you believe it? Anna thinks now. She moves quietly around the room, getting dressed. Throwing themselves cheaply away, cooking and washing for and sleeping with a man who owes you nothing in return, no loyalty, no responsibility; who can walk out between now and an hour from now! Good God!

Loud voices go down the corridor. People have no manners

anymore, no consideration, making a racket at seven o'clock in the morning.

Her foot hurts where the new shoe has raised a blister. Outrageous, at the price you have to pay for shoes. Nobody gives honest value anymore. Everything is, as the kids say, a "rip-off." Yes, it is, and they're the worst of the lot, ripping off their elders.

She knows she is tired, irritable and cross. In two more days she'll be home. She'll take a book out into the yard, a book about any century except this crazy one in which she lives, and sit there. Just sit and let the world stew.

She oughtn't to have put off traveling for so long. Five years ago she would have been steadier on her feet. She had resisted cruises, because of all the old widows she knew whose families put them on ships to pass time in luxury and to get rid of them safely. (There are doctors on cruise ships and Mama will be well taken care of in case anything happens.) Then this summer the desire came to go abroad. She wanted to see France again, having never forgotten its allure. And she wanted to see Israel.

"But Mama, why this summer?" Iris objected. "You know I'm finishing the dissertation for my doctorate. I couldn't possibly take time off."

"I'm not asking you to. I'm quite capable of going alone."

"Mama! You're seventy-seven!"

"I might die, you mean. So they'll send the body back."

"Mama, it's disgraceful to talk like that! Can't you wait till next summer? I promise I'll go with you then."

"As you said, I'm seventy-seven. I can't take the chance of waiting till next summer."

She wore them down. So it was arranged that Iris would 'put her on the plane' and Laura, who was hosteling through Europe with a group of girls, would meet her in Paris and go on with her to Israel.

She was more excited than she admitted to herself, so that the reality turned out to be anticlimax. Flying to Europe! It sounds dramatic but it is really almost like sitting in an inter-city bus and doesn't take as long as some bus trips. That trip to Europe in 1929—ah, that was something else! You bought a diary and a steamer coat and dinner dresses; the orchestra played while you danced with the thrilling tremble of the engines underneath you, as

573

the ship pressed on, pushed on across the ocean, the tumbling sea, the world. The very sound of it! Long, mournful vowels: across the world. Now that is all gone.

Still, Paris was what it was the first time. It pleased her that the room had the same view and that there were tall gladioli in the lobby. With delight she heard again the sound of the language, crisp sound of taffeta, ripple of water plunging into water. She watched the people going in and out: businessmen walking briskly, carrying their briefcases; women with poodles in rhinestone collars, patient little animals yawning under the tea tables.

Laura arrived. Darling Laura! Thoughtful enough to have worn a dress, for which Anna was grateful. Although, to tell the truth, if she had appeared in that handsome lobby in her dungarees with the backpack, Anna would have been so overjoyed to see her that she would have forgiven her.

She wanted a bath. Like a waif, she exclaimed over the enormous tub in the enormous bathroom. She came out of it all fresh and fragrant with Anna's bath oil.

"Nana, is it all right if I invite a friend to dinner?"

"Is it all right! I've been expecting you to. Several friends, if you want."

"Just one. We've been traveling together all summer."

"Fine. Do I know her?"

"Not her. Him."

And that was how Anna learned about Robby McAllister.

Laura opens her eyes and blinks into glorious light. Her skin is moist and pink with sleep, like a baby's when he wakes from his nap. And that boy, Anna thinks, that boy sees her like this every morning, takes it as his right, as if he owned her! Anna is outraged at the boldness of him and outraged at Laura.

Fool! Fool! Wrecking your life when you have everything and are too stupid to know you have it!

I sound like Joseph.

"Did you sleep well, Nana? I'm starved," Laura says.

"Well, don't take too long stuffing yourself. The driver will be here for us at eight-thirty," Anna orders, hearing the sharpness of her own voice.

Laura gives her a strange look and says nothing. She dresses and eats a quick breakfast in silence.

The cemetery is on top of a hill. Having been guided through the kibbutz—nurseries, library and dining hall (here he walked, ate, worked)—past the cattle barns, the great, clumsy, gentle animals staring solemnly as they go by, they begin the climb.

It seems that everything you want to see in foreign countries must be reached by a mountain of steps. Still, she's doing well enough, trying not to hold too hard to Laura's arm.

"Careful, Nana," Laura says. She has been told to watch out, that old women fall and break their hips and get pneumonia. Anna almost hears Theo's warnings and cautions to watch for failing heart, exhaustion, stroke. The young must take care of the old.

But unbeknownst to the young, the old also take care of them. Anna has been watching Laura, never leaving her alone with the room waiter at breakfast or with male guides; guarding her against bold eyes and impertinences (there's an old-fashioned word that you never hear nowadays: impertinence). Although to guard a girl who has tramped all through Europe with a boy she's not married to does seem rather absurd, doesn't it?

The graves lie in a level square of grass cut out of an evergreen grove. Laura finds the marker.

"What does it say?" Anna asks.

"Just the name and the dates of birth and death according to the Hebrew calendar."

The guide says in English, "You know Hebrew, and your grandmother doesn't?"

"In my time," Anna replies, "the sacred tongue was for boys to learn."

She tries to sort out what she feels. This is, after all, the true reason she has come so far. She remembers how she and Joseph spoke of coming here, how they dreaded the moment when they would stand where she is standing now.

"Did you by any chance know him?" she asks the guide.

"No, I wasn't here then. But I heard about him." His hands move in a gesture both rueful and fatalistic. "Our history is ongoing, you see. We need to remember our brave ones. And so on this place we all know about the American boy and what he did that night. Although it was a long time ago."

It was almost noon. A voice calls in the barnyard and another briefly answers. Birds, which have been flurrying and whistling

575

through the morning fall still. Heat pours on the scrap of earth where Eric lies, and all over this hard-held land between Syria and Lebanon, whose very tree tops can be seen from where they stand.

"So terrible." Laura speaks into the stillness. "So terrible, when he had finally found the place where he was happy."

"He wouldn't have stayed," Anna says, with sudden knowledge. "He would have become disillusioned with this, too."

"You surprise me, Nana. I should think you would have thought this was the right place for him."

"No. He was looking for something. He would have spent the rest of his life looking for a place to belong, a perfect place, and never finding it."

"Does anyone?"

"Find it? Oh, yes, some people never even have to look. Your grandfather was one. He was blessed that way."

Laura's mouth opens, as if to ask, "And you?" But she doesn't ask it.

Anna stretches her hand out into the burning air. Blue veins and brown spots disfigure the hand, as with some disease. But it is only age. My flesh, she thinks, mine lying here. Joseph's and that of his old mother whom, for no reason at all, I never liked. And Agatha's. Delicate Agatha and her people with their cool, Gentile austerity. Out of that poor young pair, their love and their anguish, came this boy.

"I don't understand very much," she says out loud and clearly.

Laura and the guide turn to her in surprise. Then the guide says, "Your driver's waving. It's time to go if you've a plane to catch."

"Wait a minute, wait a minute. I'm coming."

The others walk to the gate. With consideration and respect they leave her alone. Memorize it before you go: loose sweep of evergreen branches over the wall; two half-grown laurels at the right and a row of geraniums along the path.

Peace, Eric, son of my son, wherever you are and if you are. Shalom.

"It's always sad to leave a place that's so beautiful," Laura remarks, "even when you've only been in it a few days."

They are coming down out of the hills in late afternoon. Below lie the Mediterranean and orange groves cleft by a highway, along which traffic is speeding toward the airport.

"So it's meant something to you, being here?"

"Oh, yes! You feel, you can't help but feel, there's something here. After thousands of years! It's lasted so long, it gets to you. I didn't think it would," and Laura touches her heart.

"Yes," Anna says. "Yes."

"Nana, tell me something. I've been feeling that you haven't said anything because you wanted harmony on this trip, but that you've been very angry at me all the same. Have you been?"

Anna turns to her. "I was. But I'm not anymore."

"Why not?"

"It just all went away, the anger, hurt, or whatever you want to call it."

"I'm glad," Laura says simply.

As always, Anna sees both sides of the question. (Joseph used to complain that she never kept firm opinions.) She knows one thing, though, that you can't live by slogans. What's honest for one is a lie to another.

The main thing is to live. Foster life. Cherish it. Plant flowers and if you can't pull the weeds up, hide them.

"L'chaim," she says, speaking aloud for the second time that day.

The driver smiles through the rear-view window. "You're right, Mrs.," he says. "I'd drink to that if I had anything to drink. L'chaim. To life."

47

It was not what anyone could call a 'proper' wedding. Joseph would have been horrified for more reasons than one. Still, Anna thought, it's very moving. Laura had wanted to be married in Anna's garden and she hoped Iris' and Theo's feelings weren't hurt, although they didn't seem to be. But Iris had never bothered about a garden and Anna's was lovely, the pears heavy on her famous espaliered trees, the phlox full-crowned in mauve and violet, and on the air a sweetness like cinnamon or vanilla, the bouquet of summer.

The judge was a woman, mother of one of Robby's college friends. The two young people stood before her, hand in hand, he wearing slacks and an open-necked shirt, she in a long white cotton shift, with her red braids hanging over a white shawl. Like me as a greenhorn, Anna thought. Laura's face turned up to Robby in simple worship. Just yesterday Iris had stood like that, her solemn gaze framed in lace. Robby began to speak the poem which they had chosen for their wedding service, while Philip played very softly on the portable organ.

> "Oh the earth was made for lovers, for damsel and hopeless swain
> For sighing, and gentle whispering, and unity made of twain.
> All things do go a courting, in earth, or sea, or air,
> God hath made nothing single but thee in His world so fair!"

578

"Emily Dickinson's one of our favorites, Nana," Laura had said. "You've read her poems, I'm sure?"

Flattering that her granddaughter had been sure! It just happened that she had read some, Emily Dickinson having been one of Maury's favorites, too, along with Millay, Robinson and Frost.

Now Laura answered.

> "Approach that tree with caution, then up it boldly climb,
> And seize the one thou lovest, nor care for space, or time!
> Then bear her to the greenwood, and build for her a bower,
> And give her what she asketh, jewel, or bird, or flower—
> And bring the fife, and trumpet, and beat upon the drum—
> And bid the world Goodmorrow, and go to glory home!"

No one stirred. The judge began to speak. One wondered what the assorted guests might be thinking of all this. Iris had been terribly troubled, Theo not as much so, yet more than one would have expected from a man who claimed to have no beliefs and no allegiances.

"There'll be none of us left at the rate things are going," Iris kept saying. "And when I think of Papa I could cry."

It was true. Joseph, watching his darling Laura married in such fashion, Laura for whom he had no doubt already imagined a stately wedding of the ancient tradition in the chapel he had built!

But Robby was a remarkable young man, and Joseph was dead. There was no fighting the times; it would be like fighting the tides to try. This was the way it always had been, in greater or lesser degree. Waxing and waning. Some stayed, some went.

For Robby's people, conservative small-town folk standing quietly in their print dresses and white gloves, for them too this surely was not a first choice. But this was a different time and generation. People didn't fight to the death for their first choices anymore.

Anna's eyes roamed over the group, over the young New York girls with flat shoes, and long, straight hair. Their faces were as unmade-up as in Anna's own youth and as different from their fashionable mothers' as it is possible to be. Full circle.

Ah, there were the Malones, come all the way from Arizona! He must be—let's see, Joseph would be eighty-two, so Malone must be eighty-five. And Joseph always worried so about his health, always said Malone wouldn't last.

Too bad that one had to wait for a funeral or a wedding to see people whom one didn't see for years, or never had seen. She had seen the twins—twins again after two generations!—when they had visited Mexico in 1954, but Rainaldo and Raimundo had only been a little more than one year old.

Anna had had a letter a month before, enclosing, as always, snapshots of the increasing family. So many of them, generation after generation! Prospering, too, to judge by the façade of a house which looked more lavish than the ones they had visited, and those had been very handsome houses, indeed. Dena looked very old. The paper was splotched; her sight was failing. But she had wanted Anna to know that her granddaughter's twin sons were going to be in New York on their way to Europe, and wouldn't Anna like to see them?

So here they were, one of them speaking no English at all, the other just able to understand and be understood. They also spoke a little Yiddish, learned from their grandparents, but only a little, and Anna's Yiddish was rusty enough. In their fine, dark suits with black velvet yarmulkes on their curly hair, they stood courteously and correctly. From where she was Anna could watch their dignified, skeptical expressions. She was ruefully amused. They were strictly Orthodox: what could they be thinking? Thinking it wasn't a real wedding at all, no doubt.

"And so, by the authority vested in me by the State of New York—"

Man and wife. They kissed, as if nobody else were there. Oh, my! And then the congratulations and laughter, more kissing, and it was over. Darling Laura.

She'd wanted bare feet, said she liked the natural look of it in a garden. There had been such a fuss over that, Theo being the most scandalized. "How far out can you get?" Iris had wailed, Iris who was always the first to excuse the innovations of the young. Fortunately, a pair of sandals had come as a present from Steve, handmade white sandals, with a bag and belt to match. He was 'into'— loathsome expression—leather handwork on the commune. And because Steve had made the sandals, Laura wore them, which had settled the matter, thank goodness.

Theo walked beside Anna into the house. "It was very lovely after all, Theo," Anna said.

"It was cockeyed, and you know it."

"I don't. It was honest and poetic. Not my style or yours, but theirs."

"These kids today! These kids!"

"At least your daughter is married, and that's more than a lot of parents can say these days."

"Steve could have come to his sister's wedding," Theo remarked darkly.

"He'll come home one day. Maybe sooner than we expect."

"I don't know that I can forgive him for not being here today."

"He wanted to come, can't you see? That's why he sent all those things. They're so carefully made, it must have taken him weeks of work. But he just couldn't face everyone. That's the reason."

"Messed up his life," Theo muttered stubbornly. "An unforgivable mess."

Suddenly Anna felt Joseph's presence, felt in her mouth the words of authority that he would have used if he had been convinced he was right.

"People get into situations they never wanted to get into. And it's hard getting out. You know that, Theo." It was the first and only time she had reminded him. It hurt her to do it. But she knew by his silence that Steve would have no trouble from his father when he did come home.

"Look at your Philip!" she cried gaily. "He's become a man overnight! He seems much older than sixteen, don't you think? And I thought he played beautifully."

Laura and Robby hadn't wanted a reception line, so people simply clustered around them, wandered about the garden and drifted into the house where the champagne had already been opened.

Anna took a glass and handed another to Theo. "Come, drink! Every man's upset at his daughter's wedding. There's nothing wrong with you, in case you're thinking it's odd to be feeling depressed."

Theo grinned. "As a matter of fact, I was."

She patted his arm. "You've an awful lot to be happy about, Theo," she said, not meaning to lecture him.

She saw that he understood. They were both looking over at Iris, who was standing at the fireplace talking to Janet's parents and some others. She could have been photographed for one of those 'social' magazines in which gracious ladies stand before fireplaces or under

581

the curve of a stairway. How Iris would have been amused at that!

"What are you laughing at now?" Theo inquired.

"I was thinking about that woman who asked you one time why Iris didn't have her nose fixed, since you were 'in the business.' "

"I wouldn't have done it even if Iris had wanted it."

Yes, Ruth had been right, all those years ago. Now in middle age an authentic beauty *had* come upon Iris. It was at this moment almost astonishing and she understood that Theo was seeing it, too. Iris' dark hair, which had gone only a little gray, was parted in the center. She had worn it that way for so long that Anna couldn't remember when it had been different. . . . Her face was all pure curves: the high strong arch of the nose, the eyebrows, the fine mouth. When you looked away you wanted to look back again at her face.

Now people were crowding in from the garden, thrusting out hands to shake and cheeks to kiss, giving greetings and compliments.

Someone, some friend of Theo's?—(Too old.) Friend of Joseph's? (Too young. My memory certainly isn't what it used to be.)—paused for conversation.

"What a marvelous house! And the grounds! One doesn't expect to see grounds like these so near New York these days."

"Ah, but it's changed! When we first moved here, it was so quiet you could sit outside at night and all you'd hear was katydids. Now you hear the traffic on the highway."

The man sighed. "I know. They're building a development in what used to be an apple orchard across the road from me. It's very sad," he said, and moved on.

For a moment she was left alone. When I die, she thought, they'll sell this property. No one wants these big houses anymore. They'll tear it down and build garden apartments or else turn it into some sort of business. There's an insurance company at the corner already.

It had been tactfully suggested that perhaps Anna might want to sell the house and take an apartment. It was the suggestion she had herself urged upon Joseph when he had the first heart attack. He had resisted as strongly as she did in her turn. No, the house was home; she was able to afford it and she wanted to stay in it. She had planted trees: birches, locust and firethorn. There were all those books in the library, and the things in Joseph's round room that mustn't be disturbed, his collection of pipes that would go to the grandsons. And what would she do with Albert? Such a big dog, in an apartment! No, it was unthinkable.

Iris was still talking at the far end of the room. She must have been saying something amusing, because people were laughing. Then she laughed too, clapping her palms together in a pretty gesture. How far she had come! Truly, truly, prayers are answered, Anna thought. Well, sometimes they are, at any rate.

But to think that Iris would be the one to manage things! No one else in the family had any idea of business. Dear Theo never knew whether he had a nickel or a dollar in his pocket. So it was Iris who had learned how to deal with property and investments for the estate. No doubt she would know what to do with this old house when the time came.

I hope it won't be torn down, Anna thought. Perhaps there will be someone who can use it. And there will be a child's swing under the ash tree again. They'll keep the feeders filled for the winter birds.

"Nana," Laura said, "have you met Robby's aunt? This is Aunt Margaret, his favorite. He talks about her so much, and I talk about you, so it's only right for you to meet and know each other."

"Margaret Taylor." A stout, friendly woman, with the dignity that large women can have, took Anna's hand. "Your little bride is darling. We all love her already."

"I'm glad. Sending them so far away when they get married, one can only hope they'll be loved."

"They're going to New Mexico, I understand. They'll adore it. The most marvelous colors, and all that space."

"I've heard. I've never been farther west than Pennsylvania." Strange. In all these years. And we could have afforded it. Why didn't we?

"You grew up in New York, Mrs. Friedman?"

"I came to this country when I was seventeen and I've lived in New York or near it ever since."

"Such an exciting city! I wish we could manage to come more often, but somehow one never finds the time. When I was young I used to visit; my older brother, fifteen years older than I, had a friend from Yale who was just wonderful to us all. For years, at Christmas, when we'd come for a week of shopping and opera, they'd insist that Mother and my sister and I stay at their house.

583

Paul Werner, his name was, and they lived in the most sumptuous apartment on Fifth Avenue, near the museum. I've never seen such a place. Perhaps you knew the family?"

"I know who you mean," Anna said, and the woman sped on. "They had quite marvelous art. I was an art major at college and I was so impressed! It was all Hudson River School; it went out of favor for a while, but I needn't tell you how it's prized today. He had so much charm, Paul Werner. Young as I was, I sensed it. Too much charm for the woman he married. She was a fine person, but awfully dull, I thought."

"You haven't seen him since she died?"

"Oh, no, not since I was in my twenties. But my sister's kept in touch; she saw him just a couple of years ago, in Italy. He had a villa on Lake Maggiore, you know, an old house filled with Renaissance furniture and modern art. That's the style these days, to mix incongruous things, isn't it? Oh, Donald, come meet Laura's grandmother; this is my husband."

"And whom are you ladies talking about? Paul Werner? I couldn't help but overhear."

"I was telling Mrs. Friedman about him. I don't know how the subject came up; we just drifted into it."

"My wife never got over him. Her closest brush with royalty."

"Oh, Donald, you're the worst tease! You know you were just as impressed as I was! One felt so *alive* with Paul, and he did have a touch of the regal, in a very nice way."

She turned to Anna. "But you said you knew him?"

"I was a maid in his parents' house," Anna said. *Now, that's a shocker, isn't it?*

They did look, for an instant, shocked; but they pulled their faces together and said pleasantly, almost simultaneously, "Well, it's a real American success story, isn't it, your life?"

"I guess you might call it that," Anna replied.

Her reaction was a slight one, not piercing-sharp as she might once have expected it to be, but a small painful twinge, and quite controlled.

Yet, without being noticed, she went upstairs to her room. The heavy earrings had begun to hurt. Iris had made her get all her jewelry out of the vault for the wedding. It was proper to be adorned for the wedding of one's granddaughter, and yet in a way it was silly to dress up such old hands and such a wrinkled neck.

584

Sighing, she removed the earrings, easing the pressure, and leaned forward to look at herself in the mirror.

Funny, when you get old your nose droops. My nose was never this large. Theo says it has something to do with cartilage. But I don't look too awful. I've held up well enough. I look calm. I always did. Faces deceive. Even after that conversation just now, I still manage to look calm. Only my head aches. She put her hands to her temples; there was a stronger beat there than usual.

The great diamond, Joseph's marvelous ring, lay like an oval teardrop on her finger. It had the pink fire of sunlight and rainbows. Strange to think that it had been torn out of the deepest, darkest earth with all that light in it. When I'm put into the earth it will go on living in the light, its pink fire blazing on some other, living hand: whose? Not Iris', nor Laura's . . . neither of them would wear a thing like this or want it any more than I did. Joseph's marvelous ring.

She got up slowly and went back downstairs. People were moving through the lovely rooms in their bright dresses and white summer suits. It was the last time the house would glow like this. Philip was sixteen. She could give a wedding party for him too, but it would be amazing if she were still here when he was old enough to be married. And as for Steve, who knew?

From where Anna stood at the foot of the stairs she could see directly into the living room where her portrait hung. So young in the pink dress, with that faint look of surprise which she was certain she saw and which no one else had ever admitted to seeing! Wouldn't she really have been surprised if she could have foreseen the things that would happen! Yet how could she have foreseen what it was like to be seventy-eight years old? One never imagines oneself that old.

"Nana!" Jimmy cried. "Janet and I have been looking for you. Everyone's going in to eat."

"I've been admiring the house," Janet said. "Every time I come here I see more gorgeous things, your china, and all the silver— Well, someday."

"Someday what?" Jimmy asked.

"Someday we'll have it, too. With both of us working we'll be able to have a nice home," she said confidently, and quickly added, "I don't mean like this, of course, but nice."

Joseph would have approved of this girl. The work ethic, he

always said. You worked and you were rewarded. A bright, practical girl, not lazy, not ashamed to say what she wanted. Two more years and she'd be a doctor. All that and a brand-new baby asleep upstairs. *She* would love the diamond! She would wear it with joy. So she's the one who shall have it. Time to divest yourself, the lawyers said tactfully, which was a way of saying that you can't last much longer and you ought to be thinking about inheritance taxes.

"I'm going to leave you all the silver," Anna said suddenly.

Janet flushed. "Nana! I didn't mean—"

"Don't be silly, I know you didn't mean anything. But things like these should be enjoyed. Iris calls them dust collectors and Laura's going to be digging on a Navajo reservation, so she won't want them. That's why I want you to have them."

"You'd better keep some for Laura just in case," Janet said, adding mischievously, "they may get tired of archeology in a trailer and decide they really do want some of the things they've been scoffing at."

Anna smiled. "You may be right. Anyway, I'll start making my list tomorrow."

"What morbid talk at a wedding!" Jimmy protested.

"Not morbid at all. Just practical."

Jimmy took her arm. "Well, practical or not, we're going in where the food is."

At once her obligation as a hostess came to Anna's mind: the special menu for the Mexican twins, who were as strict in observance of the dietary laws as any of their ancestors had been. She summoned Celeste to check. The young men had been seated with Anna, all other guests being free to sit where they chose, which was yet another of Robby's and Laura's innovations.

It pleased her to see that so many of the young, including the bride and groom, had already settled themselves at her table. All these beautiful young people in their astonishing variety! Robby, pink-cheeked, frank and not too unlike Jimmy. Raimundo and Rainaldo, looking positively Spanish, and just three generations out of the Polish village; how to explain that? The reserve, that was it; that Latin formality which made them seem so much older than these American boys, although they were the same age.

What irony! Vain, good-hearted, ambitious, clever Eli; all his had been eradicated, while Dan the schlemiel, the humble, lived on in these handsome boys and many more. Landed in Mexico with nothing, in an unknown country which these his descendants take for granted, no doubt, as though it had always been theirs. And those who come from me take this America for granted, too, instead of seeing the miracle it is. My mind wanders. Strange, timeless people, I think, so contradictory, so tenacious.

Fragments of conversation float like balloons above the table. Young people are so earnest these days. In my time you danced at a wedding. How they love to talk! Well, fashions change, round and round. That much I can see from my vantage point; it's one of the rewards, the very few rewards, of being old. Everything passes. The revolution of only a few years ago, the dirt, the fury, even the beards all gone or going. So something else will take its place to worry and confuse us!

Jimmy was saying, explaining to one of Robby's friends, "Janet and I don't observe all that." (They are talking about Rainaldo and Raimundo.) "But we do think the religious tradition should be selectively maintained. One doesn't step out and away from such a long, gallant history. Besides, it's important for children to have a sense of identity."

High talk, fine talk. They have to analyze everything, give reasons for everything. It's the disease of the times. But never mind their reasons, as long as some of them stay with the tradition.

Robby said, "I've been learning a lot from Laura about the immigrant generation. It's fascinating to think that when they came here at the start of this century they were really skipping two or three hundred years in one stop. Out of the late middle ages, actually. Some hadn't even seen a railroad!"

Quite true. I was ten years old before I saw one, nice boy. Nice boy with bright green eyes, so serious and interested in everything! Only I do hope you decide to buy a suit sometime. You can't apply for a job wearing slacks and a shirt. Or maybe you can these days?

A very pretty girl spoke from the far end of the table. "There'll have to be changes. We can't just go on exploiting people and destroying the environment. It's simply too late for 'every man for himself.' Otherwise there'll never be any peace on earth."

As if there ever could be, anyway! But no, I shouldn't say that. What do I know of the future? One has to try. Maybe the vision

587

and energy of these young will do what we didn't do, didn't even try to do or concern ourselves with. For us it was enough to take care of ourselves!

So I don't know. It's all for them to solve if they can.

Rainaldo—it must be he, because he spoke a little English—caught Anna's eye. How rude of her. She'd been neglecting them. She smiled. He smiled back and, by way of making conversation, pointed to the candlesticks.

"Very beautiful silver, Aunt. Very old. Two hundred years, I think."

"You're right. They belonged to my great-grandmother. That's your—let's see, great, great, how many greats, four, no, five?"

Rainaldo threw up his hands. "Fantastic! It does something—" he pointed to his heart—"to think about it."

"Yes," Anna said, "it does."

"In Mexico we also have very fine silver. I am used to see it. That picture—portrait, painting? That is Uncle Joseph, I think? My grandfather told me about him."

The portrait hung behind her. From his end of the table Joseph had always faced himself. She turned.

"Yes, it's a good likeness. I mean, he really did look like that."

Not when he was young. In youth he had had an anxious look. But here in this portrait he was confident, a little stern perhaps. A patriarch presiding at the family table.

"Laura talks about him so much," Robby said. "I wish I could have known him."

"He was a simple man," Anna explained, as if she had been asked to sum him up. "All he wanted, really, was to keep the family together. I think that everything else was just a means to that end."

There was a little flurry of voices and laughter. A group stood up and came over to Anna's table. Theo called out. "I want to ask everyone to drink to my mother-in-law. May she live a hundred and twenty years!" The glasses touched and he added, "It isn't every man who can wish his mother-in-law long life and mean it." His ·es met Anna's and stayed in a long look.

And I would like to drink to the memory of Papa," Iris said "On a day like this especially we remember him."

·s inevitable, at any and every gathering, that the resem-
·me be played.

"Do you look like him, Iris?" Doris Berg inquired. "Standing there beneath his picture it seems to me perhaps you do look a little like your father."

Iris asked, "Do you think I do, Mama?"

She wants to be told she looks like him. "I'm never very good at seeing resemblances. I always think everyone looks like himself."

Doris Berg persisted. "Oh, I don't think so! Some people are carbon copies of each other. Jimmy looks just like Theo, and Philip looks like Iris. Iris does have a high forehead, something like her father's, but still," doubtfully, head on one side, "still it's hard to say . . . maybe you don't look like him. You *are* a mystery, Iris."

And Mary Malone said, "But our bride is her grandmother all over again! The red hair and the eyes, you couldn't mistake those! What curious, wide eyes you had, Anna! I remember when I first met you, you looked as if you couldn't see or know enough, as if you were just in love with the world."

It was over. The bride and groom had driven away on a camping trip. Celeste had appeared at the front door with boxes of rice. That was another tradition which Laura and Robby had wanted to dispense with, but Celeste had had other ideas and they had run down the driveway to their car through a rain of rice. Theo and Iris stood next to Anna until the car was out of sight. Their hands were joined.

Anna touched Theo's arm. "She isn't gone, Theo. You haven't lost her."

"How do you know?"

"Because. They go their separate ways, but there's a chain that holds them to you all the same." She almost, but not quite, believed it herself.

When the guests and the caterers were gone and only the family was left, Anna went upstairs.

"I've got to get this rig off," she complained.

"I'll help you," Iris offered. "It was a lovely wedding after all, wasn't it? I thought it was going to be so hippie. . . . Oh, that darn dog again!" For Albert had pushed the door open and greeted Anna with wet nose and dripping whiskers.

"Look at your dress!"

"It can be cleaned, I don't mind. I'm worried about Albert. He's apt to outlive me, and you don't like dogs."

589

"Mother, you're so morbid!"

It was the second time that day that she'd been told that, and she didn't feel morbid at all. Didn't people ever want to face facts?

"Still, I do believe Laura and Robby would take him. They'll have plenty of space. . . . I must write and ask them."

"Do please allow them to have their honeymoon first before you start talking to them about death. Let me put your corsage in water."

Hideous things, orchids. I always liked cheerful flowers, like dahlias and asters, almost anything but orchids. Joseph always bought them for occasions; he seemed so pleased when he gave them to me. I never told him they remind me of snakes.

"Here, give me the necklace. I'll just put it in this box overnight and take it to the vault for you in the morning. What's this?"

"That's not my jewelry box." Anna was embarrassed. It was a fancy tin box that once, long ago, had held candy. In it she had hidden the last cutting of her own long red hair.

Iris lifted it out, a shining spiral that fell almost to her knees. "Mama, what hair! It's beautiful! I'd forgotten how beautiful . . ."

"A long time ago."

"It doesn't seem so long. I remember at my wedding, you wore a pink dress. You used to wear a lot of pink, so clever with your hair. You were the most striking woman there. Nobody looked at me; they all looked at you."

"Iris, I hate to tell you, but you do say the most idiotic things. You were a lovely bride, as lovely as any," Anna argued firmly.

Iris' eyes filled. My daughter looks at me and I can tell what she is thinking as clearly as though the bones of her forehead were transparent. She is remembering childhood and mothering and she's guilty because she always loved Joseph more than she loved me. I put out my hand; she lays hers in it, but she doesn't feel comfortable with my touch. She never has, though I don't know why. But it's something she can't help, any more than she can help loving Theo.

Janet knocked on the open door. "May I come in? I thought I'd bring the baby to visit."

She laid the baby in Anna's lap. Anna put her finger out and the tiny hand wound around it. The baby's eyelids were shut like two fragile shells. Oh, to be young again, to produce a thing like this!

She felt a sudden panic. Something had gone absolutely blank in her head. She couldn't remember: was it a boy or a girl, this child of Jimmy's? I can't remember, she thought in horror . . . I can't shame myself by asking. They'll think I'm senile and I'm not that at all, not yet, although God knows and I know that my arteries are hardening. A pity, because otherwise I can see things in a clearer light than ever.

"The baby's not too thin?" She drew the blanket slyly away. A pink sweater. Ah, a girl. Of course. My great-granddaughter.

"The doctors don't want them to be fat, Mama. You know that."

Rebecca, that was the name. Rebecca Ruth, after Janet's two grandmothers. Too bad Ruth couldn't have lived to see her. Isn't it funny that we should be great-grandmothers to the same child? A good name. Thank heavens, they hadn't given her one of those phony names that people used these days, like Judy with an 'i' on the end or Gloria with a 'y' stuck in it for no good reason. Rebecca Ruth, you've just arrived and I'm about to leave. We'll overlap by a few years at most. I'd like to live till you're old enough to keep some memory of me. What vanity!

But I'm the link, the only one in this house tonight who ties them all together, Rainaldo and Raimundo, Philip and Steve. . . . I hold up my hand. Is it true that some of the cells in me are the same as in this baby? I wish I knew more about biology. I wish I knew more about everything. Think of the things Rebecca Ruth will see and know! Things I can't even conceive of. And my mother stood at the door of our house, talking of a marvelous time when every woman might learn to read.

But one thing was true then that's still true now. I told Theo there's a tie that holds us all together, and I said it to comfort him, but I meant it. It's there, or nothing has any value at all. And I know *that's* not true. It's the lifeline of the family, and if we can hold to it then we can make good children and the world will be better. Maybe that's putting it all too simply in these tangled times, but then, the truest things are always simple, aren't they?

Oh, I'd like to stay a little longer to see what Philip does with his talent, to watch over Iris (though I'm certain she doesn't need it anymore). How can I die and leave them all? I worry so! You silly fool, you think they can't manage without you? Anna, the indispensable!

The baby stirred and puckered her peach face. "I'll take her," Janet said, "it's feeding time again."

591

Anna thought of something. "I should like to have my picture taken with her. It will be a fine thing for her to have. Not many people can know what their great-grandmothers looked like. Why, I've been curious all my life about the people who came before me! And there was never any way to find out. Certainly no pictures."

"We'll have a photographer come in the morning," Iris declared. "We'll take the boys from Mexico—I never remember those names! We'll take the whole family. Here's Philip. You played wonderfully, darling."

"Nana," Philip said, "I've come with the tape recorder. I hope you haven't forgotten. Nana and I," he explained to Janet, "are doing the story of her life for posterity. It was my idea. Because of what Nana always says about families and people knowing their ancestors. All that stuff."

Anna clasped her hands. "I don't know what to say! It's not as if I'd had a heroic life or anything."

"Nana! You're not backing out?"

She was suddenly quite, quite tired. But he looked so disappointed! He has my father's pale eyes, set far apart, and he moves like him, clumsily. How can he understand what life was like for his great-grandfather, maker of boots and harness? For him it's a story, picturesque and touching. For him my father is truly dead, as we all are when the last person who knew our faces and heard our voices is gone. The most we do is to save a little part of the life that was.

"No," she said, "I'm not backing out."

"Great!" He straightened up from the machine. "Just sit back comfortably, Nana, and begin at the beginning."

The beginning? Sometimes it was so cloudy and far away that she thought it had never been like that at all. Then again, it was like the morning of today, so that you could reach out and touch it, could feel it and smell the air. Soft, foggy, fragrant air of Europe. Keen American air. Beautiful America, more wonderful, painful, generous, difficult and kind than she could have dreamed when she had been a child and longed so much to see it.

"Just say whatever comes into your head, as far back as you can remember. It doesn't matter what. Only don't leave anything out."

She wanted to laugh, but the boy-face was so earnest, so eager.

"Relax, Nana. I'll tell you when I'm about to start."

She closed her eyes. The lamp light shone through her lids, making a tracery of red. Veins, like a design in lace. Yes, think. All a brilliant muddle, a heap of flowers, or colored paper blown in the wind. Eric, coming bravely toward them over the grass. Maury in the Yale processional and Maury on the kitchen floor, eating an apple. Iris, frail child, holding Joseph's hand. Birdsong over Eric's grave. And Joseph's whisper: *How lovely you are.*

A jumble and a flickering, far, far back. Do I really remember that my mother wore a dark blue shawl with a small white pattern? Can it be possible that I remember her voice at prayer, that it was low for a woman? *Blessed be Thou oh Lord, King of the universe,* she said, in that childhood room for whose warmth and safety we search all the rest of our lives and never find again.

"Are you ready, Nana? I'm starting the tape."

"There was a town. Yes, that's a good beginning." The words were rapid and clear. "It was on the other side of the world and not much of a town, just one wide, muddy street running to the river. It may be there still, for all I know, although my people are long gone. There was a board fence around my father's house, and in the kitchen a black iron stove. There were red flowers on the wallpaper, and my mother sang."